THE YEAR'S BEST SCIENCE FICTION & FANTASY NOVELLAS

2015 Edition

D0063561

Other Anthologies Edited by
Paula Guran

Embraces
Best New Paranormal Romance
Best New Romantic Fantasy
Zombies: The Recent Dead
The Year's Best Dark Fantasy & Horror: 2010
Vampires: The Recent Undead
The Year's Best Dark Fantasy & Horror: 2011
Halloween
New Cthulhu: The Recent Weird
Brave New Love
Witches: Wicked, Wild & Wonderful
Obsession: Tales of Irresistible Desire
The Year's Best Dark Fantasy & Horror: 2012
Extreme Zombies
Ghosts: Recent Hauntings
Rock On: The Greatest Hits of Science Fiction & Fantasy
Season of Wonder
Future Games
Weird Detectives: Recent Investigations
The Mammoth Book of Angels and Demons
After the End: Recent Apocalypses
The Year's Best Dark Fantasy & Horror: 2013
Halloween: Mystery, Magic & the Macabre
Once Upon a Time: New Fairy Tales
Magic City: Recent Spells
The Year's Best Dark Fantasy & Horror: 2014
Time Travel: Recent Trips
New Cthulhu 2: More Recent Weird
Blood Sisters: Vampire Stories by Women
Mermaids and Other Mysteries of the Deep
The Year's Best Dark Fantasy & Horror: 2015

THE YEAR'S BEST SCIENCE FICTION & FANTASY NOVELLAS

2015 Edition

EDITED BY PAULA GURAN

PRIME BOOKS

The Year's Best Science Fiction & Fantasy Novellas: 2015

Copyright © 2015 by Paula Guran.

Cover design by Sherin Nicole.
Cover art by Julie Dillon.

All stories are copyrighted to their respective authors,
and used here with their permission.
An extension of this copyright page can be found on page 575.

Prime Books
Germantown, MD, USA
www.prime-books.com

Publisher's Note:
No portion of this book may be reproduced by any means, mechanical, electronic, or otherwise, without first obtaining the permission of the copyright holder.

For more information, contact Prime Books:
prime@prime-books.com

Print ISBN: 978-1-60701-455-3
Ebook ISBN: 978-1-60701-464-5

CONTENTS

INTRODUCTION

Paula Guran

Welcome to the inaugural *The Year's Best Science Fiction and Fantasy Novellas* . . . which brings us immediately to the rather gnarly question of defining "novella" beyond "a work of fiction longer than a short story but shorter than a novel."

In the literary world, some feel a novella is not defined by word count, but its unity of purpose. And George Fetherling was probably correct in stating that comparing one version of prose fiction to another based solely on length is "like insisting that a pony is a baby horse."

Even if one saddles oneself to the word-count baby horse, you'll often find the definitive range varies from a minimum of fifteen- or twenty-thousand words to as many as fifty-thousand words. Well, at least we know a novella is at least fifty-thousand words . . . or maybe forty thousand . . .

Except practically, in the world of adult commercial fiction, you will be hard-pressed to find a publisher wanting to publish anything less than seventy-five thousand words as a novel. Cozy mysteries and category romance, however, can be shorter. Science fiction, fantasy, and horror novels (depending on subgenre) start in the eighty- to ninety-thousand word range. (Yes, of course there are always exceptions.)

As in life, one finds truly hard and fast countable rules only in games or particular situations/systems. In the science fiction and fantasy world that means "awards." Word count is the determinative factor for award categories. Both the Nebula and Hugo Awards set the length for works in the novella category as between seventeen-thousand-five-hundred words and forty-thousand words. The Shirley Jackson Award (for psychological suspense, horror, or dark fantasy) agrees with that length, but the World Fantasy Award considers one word over ten thousand as the distinction between short fiction and novella; the British Fantasy Award considers fifteen-thousand words as the minimum.

Confused?

It comes down to deciding which genre "standard" to choose. For this opening foray at least, we chose to go with fiction between seventeen-thousand-five-hundred words and forty-thousand words. The shortest novella chosen is about eighteen-thousand-two-hundred words long; the longest is thirty-eight thousand.

The next question is: why single out science fiction and fantasy novellas for a year's best anthology? Aren't they included in already-published annual series? Well, yes and no. Gardner Dozois and his *The Year's Best Science Fiction* (Macmillan)—now in its thirty-second year—is about seven-hundred-fifty pages or so. Dozois has the room to reprint several novellas along with shorter works, and he usually does. *The Best Science Fiction and Fantasy of the Year: Volume Nine* (2015, Solaris), edited by Jonathan Strahan, has at least one novella this year. Our sister series from Prime Books—Rich Horton's *The Year's Best Science Fiction & Fantasy* (2015 marks its seventh volume)—includes one or two. I usually include a couple of novellas in my own *The Year's Best Dark Fantasy & Horror* (sixth edition for 2015), but its theme—though broad—is on the dark side. Ellen Datlow focuses solely on horror in her *The Best Horror of the Year Volume Seven* (2015, Night Shade Books). *The Year's Best Weird Fiction* (from Undertow Publications, overseen by Michael Kelly with a different editor each year) obviously concentrates on "the weird."

Then, quoting Stephen King from his introduction to *Different Seasons* (1982):

> [The novella is an] ill-defined and disreputable literary banana republic; it is too long to be published in a magazine or literary journal and too short to be published on its own in book format.

In other words, it is hard to find places to publish novellas. More than three decades later, his statement is, to an extent, still true. But in science fiction and fantasy, you will find novellas in some print and online publications, the occasional anthology, and published as (often limited edition) books and chapbooks. Nowadays, they are also being published as standalone ebooks. That's a lot of sometimes obscure territory for the average reader to cover.

There is also the problem of knowledge and access. One of the best science fiction novellas published in 2013 was *Black Helicopters* by Caitlín R. Kiernan. It was available only as a companion hardcover to the six-hundred copies of the numbered, signed, limited edition of her collection *The Ape's Wife and Other Stories*. Published by Subterranean Press, the beautiful collection cost $60. Another outstanding novella from 2013 was *Spin* by Nina Allen, published by TTA Press in the UK. More accessible as far as price, but the average reader—at least in the US—was probably unaware of it. Yet another, "Rock of Ages" by Jay Lake, was published only in an audio anthology, *METAropolis: Green Space*. Do you listen to novellas often?

Finally, on the artistic level I will quote Robert Silverberg:

> [The novella] is one of the richest and most rewarding of literary forms . . . it allows for more extended development of theme and character than does the short story, without making the elaborate structural demands of the full-length book. Thus it provides an intense, detailed exploration of its subject, providing to some degree both the concentrated focus of the short story and the broad scope of the novel.

In sum, we think we have reason(s) enough and hope you agree.

Admittedly, the novellas in this first *The Year's Best Science Fiction and Fantasy Novellas* are not ALL of "the best" published in 2014. Among other stellar short novels (which, for various reasons do not appear herein) in alphabetical order by author:

- *We Are All Completely Fine* by Daryl Gregory (Tachyon Publications). I'll quote the *Publishers Weekly* review: "[S]cathingly funny, horrific yet oddly inspiring . . . [b]lending the stark realism of pain and isolation with the liberating force of the fantastic, Gregory makes it easy to believe that the world is an illusion, behind which lurks an alternative truth—dark, degenerate, and sublime."
- "Children of the Fang" by John Langan (*Lovecraft's Monsters*, ed. Ellen Datlow: Tachyon Publications). The unnamed race of reptiles in H. P. Lovecraft's "The Nameless City" is not among his best-known eldritch creations, but Langan takes them and runs with a story of a long-kept family secret that ultimately affects three generations. (I have reprinted this one in *The Year's Best Dark Fantasy & Horror: 2015*, also from Prime Books.)
- "The Regular" by Ken Liu (*Upgraded*, ed. Neil Clarke: Wyrm Publishing). Liu again shows he is a masterful, highly readable writer with this compelling tech-based futuristic detective noir story.
- *The Good Shabti* by Robert Sharp (*The Good Shabti*: Jurassic London). A marvelous weaving of two stories—one set in ancient Egypt; the other in the near future where some brilliant, but perhaps now wise, scientists are attempting to revivify a Pharaoh's mummy—that updates

the iconic mummy story for this century. (This one will be reprinted in another anthology I've edited, the forthcoming *The Mammoth Book of the Mummy*.)

- "Entanglement" by Vandana Singh (*Hieroglyph: Stories and Visions for a Better Future*, eds. Ed Finn & Kathryn Cramer: William Morrow). An outstanding hard science-fiction story about ecological disaster that (for a change) optimistically reminds us human beings can help each other, even if they are connected only by a high-tech experimental network
- "The Prodigal Son" by Allen M. Steele (*Asimov's,* October/November 2014). If Earthlings were to attempt to populate a distant world, transporting only genetic material and not people—what ethical and religious conflicts might arise?
- "Grand Jeté (The Great Leap)" by Rachel Swirsky (*Subterranean Press Magazine*, Summer 2014). Three narratives—Mara's, a girl dying of cancer; Jakub's, her father who has built an AI version of Mara; and Ruth's, the "automaton"—combine for an emotionally resonant exploration of family, love, and loss.
- Lavie Tidhar, "Kur-A-Len" (*Black Gods Kiss*: PS Publishing). A "guns and sorcery" novella featuring Gorel of Goliris. I'll quote the *Locus* review: "[A]lmost the pure essence of pulp—violent, action-packed, paced like a runaway freight train, politically incorrect, and socially unredeemable." (This, too, is included in *The Year's Best Dark Fantasy & Horror: 2015*.)

Between the nine novellas republished here and those I recommend above, I think there are enough examples to convince you—if you are not already a true believer—of the worth of science fiction and fantasy novellas . . . at least until we return with the 2016 edition!

Paula Guran
28 April 2015
International Astronomy Day

YESTERDAY'S KIN

Nancy Kress

"We see in these facts some deep organic bond, prevailing throughout space and time. . . . This bond, on my theory, is simple inheritance."

—Charles Darwin, *The Origin of Species*

I: S MINUS 10.5 MONTHS

Marianne

The publication party was held in the dean's office, which was supposed to be an honor. Oak-paneled room, sherry in little glasses, small-paned windows facing the quad—the room was trying hard to be a Commons someplace like Oxford or Cambridge, a task for which it was several centuries too late. The party was trying hard to look festive. Marianne's colleagues, except for Evan and the dean, were trying hard not to look too envious, or at their watches.

"Stop it," Evan said at her from behind the cover of his raised glass.

"Stop what?"

"Pretending you hate this."

"I hate this," Marianne said.

"You don't."

He was half right. She didn't like parties but she was proud of her paper, which had been achieved despite two years of gene sequencers that kept breaking down, inept graduate students who contaminated samples with their own DNA, murmurs of "Lucky find" from Baskell, with whom she'd never gotten along. Baskell, an old-guard physicist, saw her as a bitch who refused to defer to rank or back down gracefully in an argument. Many people, Marianne knew, saw her as some variant of this. The list included two of her three grown children.

Outside the open casements, students lounged on the grass in the mellow October sunshine. Three girls in cut-off jeans played Frisbee, leaping at the blue flying saucer and checking to see if the boys sitting on the stone wall were watching. Feinberg and Davidson, from Physics, walked by, arguing amiably. Marianne wished she were with them instead of at her own party.

"Oh God," she said to Evan, "Curtis just walked in."

The president of the university made his ponderous way across the room. Once he had been a historian, which might be why he reminded Marianne of Henry VIII. Now he was a campus politician, as power-mad as Henry but stuck at a second-rate university where there wasn't much power to be had. Marianne held against him not his personality but his mind; unlike Henry, he was not all that bright. And he spoke in clichés.

"Dr. Jenner," he said, "congratulations. A feather in your cap, and a credit to us all."

"Thank you, Dr. Curtis," Marianne said.

"Oh, 'Ed,' please."

"Ed." She didn't offer her own first name, curious to see if he remembered it. He didn't. Marianne sipped her sherry.

Evan jumped into the awkward silence. "I'm Dr. Blanford, visiting post-doc," he said in his plummy British accent. "We're all so proud of Marianne's work."

"Yes! And I'd love for you to explain to me your innovative process, ah, Marianne."

He didn't have a clue. His secretary had probably reminded him that he had to put in an appearance at the party: *Dean of Science's office, 4:30 Friday, in honor of that publication by Dr. Jenner in*—quick look at email—*in* Nature, *very prestigious, none of our scientists have published there before . . .*

"Oh," Marianne said as Evan poked her discreetly in the side: *Play nice!* "it wasn't so much an innovation in process as unexpected results from known procedures. My assistants and I discovered a new haplogroup of mitochondrial DNA. Previously it was thought that *Homo sapiens* consisted of thirty haplogroups, and we found a thirty-first."

"By sequencing a sample of contemporary genes, you know," Evan said helpfully. "Sequencing and verifying."

Anything said in upper-crust British automatically sounded intelligent, and Dr. Curtis looked suitably impressed. "Of course, of course. Splendid results. A star in your crown."

"It's yet another haplogroup descended," Evan said with malicious helpfulness, "from humanity's common female ancestor one hundred fifty thousand years ago. 'Mitochondrial Eve.' "

Dr. Curtis brightened. There had been a TV program about Mitochondrial Eve, Marianne remembered, featuring a buxom actress in a leopard-skin sarong. "Oh, yes! Wasn't that—"

"I'm sorry, you can't go in there!" someone shrilled in the corridor outside the room. All conversation ceased. Heads swiveled toward three men in dark suits pushing their way past the knot of graduate students by the door. The three men wore guns.

Another school shooting, Marianne thought, *where can I—*

"Dr. Marianne Jenner?" the tallest of the three men said, flashing a badge. "I'm Special Agent Douglas Katz of the FBI. We'd like you to come with us."

Marianne said, "Am I under arrest?"

"No, no, nothing like that. We are acting under direct order of the president of the United States. We're here to escort you to New York."

Evan had taken Marianne's hand—she wasn't sure just when. There was nothing romantic in the handclasp, nor anything sexual. Evan, twenty-five years her junior and discreetly gay, was a friend, an ally, the only other evolutionary biologist in the department and the only one who shared Marianne's cynical sense of humor. *"Or so we thought,"* they said to each other whenever any hypothesis proved wrong. *Or so we thought . . .* His fingers felt warm and reassuring around her suddenly icy ones.

"Why am I going to New York?"

"I'm afraid we can't tell you that. But it is a matter of national security."

"*Me?* What possible reason—?"

Special Agent Katz almost, but not quite, hid his impatience at her questions. "I wouldn't know, ma'am. My orders are to escort you to UN Special Mission Headquarters in Manhattan."

Marianne looked at her gaping colleagues, at the wide-eyed grad students, at Dr. Curtis, who was already figuring how this could be turned to the advantage of the university. She freed her hand from Evan's, and managed to keep her voice steady.

"Please excuse me, Dr. Curtis, Dean. It seems I'm needed for something connected with . . . with the aliens."

Noah

One more time, Noah Jenner rattled the doorknob to the apartment. It felt greasy from too many unwashed palms, and it was still locked. But he knew Emily was in there. That was the kind of thing he was always, somehow, right about. He was right about things that didn't do him any good.

"Emily," he said softly through the door, "please open up."

Nothing.

"Emily, I have nowhere else to go."

Nothing.

"I'll stop, I promise. I won't do sugarcane ever again."

The door opened a crack, chain still in place, and Emily's despairing face appeared. She wasn't the kind of girl given to dramatic fury, but her quiet despair was even harder to bear. Not that Noah didn't deserve it. He knew he did. Her fair hair hung limply on either side of her long, sad face. She wore the green bathrobe he liked, with the butterfly embroidered on the left shoulder.

"You won't stop," Emily said. "You can't. You're an addict."

"It's not an addictive drug. You know that."

"Not physically, maybe. But it is for you. You won't give it up. I'll never know who you really are."

"I—"

"I'm sorry, Noah. But—go away." She closed and re-locked the door.

Noah stood slumped against the dingy wall, waiting to see if anything else would happen. Nothing did. Eventually, as soon as he mustered the energy, he would have to go away.

Was she right? Would he never give up sugarcane? It wasn't that it delivered a high: it didn't. No rush of dopamine, no psychedelic illusions, no out-of-body experiences, no lowering of inhibitions. It was just that on sugarcane, Noah felt like he was the person he was supposed to be. The problem was that it was never the same person twice. Sometimes he felt like a warrior, able to face and ruthlessly defeat anything. Sometimes he felt like a philosopher, deeply content to sit and ponder the universe. Sometimes he felt like a little child, dazzled by the newness of a fresh morning. Sometimes he felt like a father (he wasn't), protective of the entire world. Theories said that sugarcane released memories of past lives, or stimulated the collective unconscious, or made temporarily solid the images of dreams. One hypothesis was that it created a sort of temporary, self-induced Korsakoff's Syndrome, the neurological disorder in which invented selves seem completely true. No one knew how sugarcane really acted on the brain. For some people, it did nothing at all. For Noah, who had never felt he fit in anywhere, it gave what he had never had: a sense of solid identity, if only for the hours that the drug stayed in his system.

The problem was, it was difficult to hold a job when one day you were nebbishy, sweet-natured Noah Jenner, the next day you were Attila the Hun, and two days later you were far too intellectual to wash dishes or make change at a convenience store. Emily had wanted Noah to hold a job. To contribute to the rent, to scrub the floor, to help take the sheets to the laundromat. To be an adult, and the same adult every day. She was right to want that. Only—

He might be able to give up sugarcane and be the same adult, if only he had the vaguest idea who that adult was. Which brought him back to the same problem—he didn't fit anywhere. And never had.

Noah picked up the backpack in which Emily had put his few belongings. She couldn't have left it in the hallway very long ago or the backpack would have already been stolen. He made his way down the three flights from

Emily's walk-up and out onto the streets. The October sun shone warmly on his shoulders, on the blocks of shabby buildings, on the trash skirling across the dingy streets of New York's lower East Side. Walking, Noah reflected bitterly, was one thing he could do without fitting in. He walked blocks to Battery Park, that green oasis on the tip of Manhattan's steel canyons, leaned on a railing, and looked south.

He could just make out the *Embassy*, floating in New York Harbor. Well, no, not the *Embassy* itself, but the shimmer of light off its energy shield. Everybody wanted that energy shield, including his sister Elizabeth. It kept everything out, short of a nuclear missile. Maybe that, too: so far nobody had tried, although in the two months since the embassy had floated there, three different terrorist groups had tried other weapons. Nothing got through the shield, although maybe air and light did. They must, right? Even aliens needed to breathe.

When the sun dropped below the horizon, the glint off the floating embassy disappeared. Dusk was gathering. He would have to make the call if he wanted a place to sleep tonight. Elizabeth or Ryan? His brother wouldn't yell at him as much, but Ryan lived upstate, in the same little Hudson River town as their mother's college, and Noah would have to hitchhike there. Also, Ryan was often away, doing fieldwork for his wildlife agency. Noah didn't think he could cope with Ryan's talkative, sticky-sweet wife right now. So it would have to be Elizabeth.

He called his sister's number on his cheap cell. "Hello?" she snapped. *Born angry,* their mother always said of Elizabeth. Well, Elizabeth was in the right job, then.

"Lizzie, it's Noah."

"Noah."

"Yes. I need help. Can I stay with you tonight?" He held the cell away from his ear, bracing for her onslaught. *Shiftless, lazy, directionless* . . . When it was over, he said, "Just for tonight."

They both knew he was lying, but Elizabeth said, "Come on then" and clicked off without saying good-bye.

If he'd had more than a few dollars in his pocket, Noah would have looked for a sugarcane dealer. Since he didn't, he left the park, the wind pricking at him now with tiny needles, and descended to the subway that would take him to Elizabeth's apartment on the upper West Side.

Marianne

The FBI politely declined to answer any of Marianne's questions. Politely, they confiscated her cell and iPad and took her in a sleek black car down Route 87 to New York, through the city to lower Manhattan, and out to a harbor pier. Gates with armed guards controlled access to a heavily fortified building at the end of the pier. Politely, she was searched and fingerprinted. Then she was politely asked to wait in a small windowless room equipped with a few comfortable chairs, a table with coffee and cookies, and a wall-mounted TV tuned to CNN. A news show was covering weather in Florida.

The aliens had shown up four months ago, their ship barreling out from the direction of the sun, which had made it harder to detect until a few weeks before arrival. At first, in fact, the ship had been mistaken for an asteroid and there had been panic that it would hit Earth. When it was announced that the asteroid was in fact an alien vessel, panic had decreased in some quarters and increased in others. A ship? Aliens? Armed forces across the world mobilized. Communications strategies were formed, and immediately hacked by the curious and technologically sophisticated. Seven different religions declared the end of the world. The stock and bond markets crashed, rallied, soared, crashed again, and generally behaved like a reed buffeted by a hurricane. Governments put the world's top linguists, biologists, mathematicians, astronomers, and physicists on top-priority stand-by. Psychics blossomed. People rejoiced and feared and prayed and committed suicide and sent up balloons in the general direction of the moon, where the alien ship eventually parked itself in orbit.

Contact was immediate, in robotic voices that were clearly mechanical, and in halting English that improved almost immediately. The aliens, dubbed by the press "Denebs" because their ship came from the general direction of that bright, blue-white star, were friendly. The xenophiles looked smugly triumphant. The xenophobes disbelieved the friendliness and bided their time. The aliens spent two months talking to the United Nations. They were reassuring; this was a peace mission. They were also reticent. Voice communication only, and through machines. They would not show themselves: "Not now. We wait." They would not visit the International Space Station, nor permit humans to visit their ship. They identified their planet, and astronomers found it once they knew where to look, by the faintly eclipsed light from its orange-dwarf star. The planet was in the star's habitable zone, slightly larger than Earth but less dense, water present. It was nowhere near Deneb, but the name stuck.

After two months, the aliens requested permission to build what they called an embassy, a floating pavilion, in New York Harbor. It would be heavily shielded and would not affect the environment. In exchange, they would share the physics behind their star drive, although not the engineering, with Earth, via the Internet. The UN went into furious debate. Physicists salivated. Riots erupted, pro and con, in major cities across the globe. Conspiracy theorists, some consisting of entire governments, vowed to attack any Deneb presence on Earth.

The UN finally agreed, and the structure went into orbit around Earth, landed without a splash in the harbor, and floated peacefully offshore. After landing, it grew wider and flatter, a half-dome that could be considered either an island or a ship. The US government decided it was a ship, subject to maritime law, and the media began capitalizing and italicizing it: the *Embassy*. Coast Guard craft circled it endlessly; the US Navy had ships and submarines nearby. Airspace above was a no-fly zone, which was inconvenient for jets landing at New York's three big airports. Fighter jets nearby stayed on high alert.

Nothing happened.

For another two months the aliens continued to talk through their machines to the UN, and only to the UN, and nobody ever saw them. It wasn't known whether they were shielding themselves from Earth's air, microbes, or armies. The *Embassy* was surveilled by all possible means. If anybody learned anything, the information was classified except for a single exchange:

Why are you here?

To make contact with humanity. A peace mission.

A musician set the repeated phrases to music, a sly and humorous refrain, without menace. The song, an instant international sensation, was the opening for playfulness about the aliens. Late-night comics built monologues around supposed alien practices. The *Embassy* became a tourist attraction, viewed through telescopes, from boats outside the Coast Guard limit, from helicopters outside the no-fly zone. A German fashion designer scored an enormous runway hit with "the Deneb look," despite the fact that no one knew how the Denebs looked. The stock market stabilized as much as it ever did. Quickie movies were shot, some with Deneb allies and some with treacherous Deneb foes who wanted our women or gold or bombs. Bumper stickers proliferated like kudzu: I BRAKE FOR DENEBS. EARTH IS FULL ALREADY—GO HOME. DENEBS DO IT INVISIBLY. WILL TRADE PHYSICS FOR FOOD.

The aliens never commented on any of it. They published the promised physics, which only a few dozen people in the world could understand. They were courteous, repetitive, elusive. *Why are you here? To make contact with humanity. A peace mission.*

Marianne stared at the TV, where CNN showed footage of disabled children choosing Halloween costumes. Nothing about the discussion, the room, the situation felt real. Why would the aliens want to talk to her? It had to be about her paper, nothing else made sense. No, that didn't make sense either.

"—donated by a network of churches from five states. Four-year-old Amy seizes eagerly on the black-cat costume, while her friend Kayla chooses—"

Her paper was one of dozens published every year on evolutionary genetics, each paper adding another tiny increment to statistical data on the subject. Why this one? Why her? The UN Secretary General, various presidents and premiers, top scientists—the press said they all talked to the Denebs from this modern fortress, through (pick one) highly encrypted devices that permitted no visuals, or one-way visuals, or two-way visuals that the UN was keeping secret, or not at all and the whole alien-human conversation was invented. The *Embassy*, however, was certainly real. Images of it appeared on magazine covers, coffee mugs, screen savers, tee shirts, paintings on velvet, targets for shooting ranges.

Marianne's daughter Elizabeth regarded the aliens with suspicion, but then, Elizabeth regarded everyone with suspicion. It was one reason she was the youngest Border Patrol section leader in the country, serving on the New York Task Force along with several other agencies. She fit right in with the current American obsession with isolationism as an economic survival strategy.

Ryan seldom mentioned the aliens. He was too absorbed in his career and his wife.

And Noah—did Noah, her problem child, even realize the aliens were here? Marianne hadn't seen Noah in months. In the spring he had gone to "try life in the South." An occasional email turned up on her phone, never containing much actual information. If Noah was back in New York, he hadn't called her yet. Marianne didn't want to admit what a relief that was. Her child, her baby—but every time they saw each other, it ended in recriminations or tears.

And what was she doing, thinking about her children instead of the aliens? Why did the ambassador want to talk to her? Why were the Denebs here?

To make contact with humanity. A peace mission . . .

"Dr. Jenner?"

"Yes." She stood up from her chair, her jaw set. Somebody better give her some answers, now.

The young man looked doubtfully at her clothes, dark jeans and a green suede blazer ten years old, her standard outfit for faculty parties. He said, "Secretary Desai will join you shortly."

Marianne tried to let her face show nothing. A few moments later Vihaan Desai, Secretary General of the United Nations, entered the room, followed by a security detail. Tall, elderly, he wore a sky-blue kurta of heavy, richly embroidered silk. Marianne felt like a wren beside a peacock.

Desai held out his hand but did not smile. Relations between the United States and India were not good. Relations between the United States and everybody were not good, as the country relentlessly pursued its new policy of economic isolationism in an attempt to protect jobs. Until the Denebs came, with their cosmos-shaking distraction, the UN had been thick with international threats. Maybe it still was.

"Dr. Jenner," Desai said, studying her intently, "it seems we are both summoned to interstellar conference." His English, in the musical Indian accent, was perfect. Marianne remembered that he spoke four languages.

She said, "Do you know why?"

Her directness made him blink. "I do not. The Deneb ambassador was insistent but not forthcoming."

And does humanity do whatever the ambassador insists on? Marianne did not say this aloud. Something here was not adding up. The Secretary General's next words stunned her.

"We, plus a few others, are invited aboard the *Embassy*. The invitation is dependent upon your presence, and upon its immediate acceptance."

"Aboard . . . aboard the *Embassy*?"

"It seems so."

"But nobody has ever—"

"I am well aware of that." The dark, intelligent eyes never left her face. "We await only the other guests who happen to be in New York."

"I see." She didn't.

Desai turned to his security detail and spoke to them in Hindi. An argument began. Did security usually argue with their protectees? Marianne wouldn't have thought so, but then, what did she know about UN protocol? She was out of her field, her league, her solar system. Her guess was that the Denebs were not allowing bodyguards aboard the *Embassy*, and that the security chief was protesting.

Evidently the Secretary General won. He said to her, "Please come," and walked with long strides from the room. His kurta rustled at his ankles, shimmering sky. Not intuitive, Marianne could nonetheless sense the tension coming off him like heat. They went down a long corridor, trailed by deeply frowning guards, and down an elevator. Very far down—did the elevator go under the harbor? It must. They exited into a small room already occupied by two people, a man and a woman. Marianne recognized the woman: Ekaterina Zaytsev, the representative to the UN from the Russian Federation. The man might be the Chinese representative. Both looked agitated.

Desai said in English, "We await only—ah, here they are."

Two much younger men practically blew into the room, clutching headsets. Translators. They looked disheveled and frightened, which made Marianne feel better. She wasn't the only one battling an almost overwhelming sense of unreality. If only Evan could be here, with his sardonic and unflappable Britishness. *"Or so we thought . . ."*

No. Neither she nor Evan had ever thought of this.

"The other permanent members of the Security Council are, unfortunately, not immediately available," Desai said. "We will not wait."

Marianne couldn't remember who the other permanent members were. The UK, surely, but who else? How many? What were they doing this October dusk that would make them miss first contact with an alien species? Whatever it was, they had to regret it the rest of their lives.

Unless, of course, this little delegation never returned—killed or kidnapped or eaten. No, that was ridiculous. She was being hysterical. Desai would not go if there were danger.

Of course he would. Anyone would. Wouldn't they? Wouldn't she? Nobody, she suddenly realized, had actually asked her to go on this mission. She'd been ordered to go. What if she flat-out refused?

A door opened at the far end of the small room, voices spoke from the air about clearance and proceeding, and then another elevator. The six people stepped into what had to be the world's most comfortable and unwarlike submarine, equipped with lounge chairs and gold-braided officers.

A submarine. Well, that made sense, if plans had been put in place to get to the *Embassy* unobserved by press, tourists, and nut jobs who would blow up the alien base if they could. The Denebs must have agreed to some sort of landing place or entryway, which meant this meeting had been talked of, planned for, long before today. Today was just the moment the aliens had decided to put the plan into practice. Why? Why so hastily?

"Dr. Jenner," Desai said, "in the short time we have here, please explain your scientific findings to us."

None of them sat in the lounge chairs. They stood in a circle around Marianne, who felt none of the desire to toy with them as she had with Dr. Curtis at the college. Where were her words going, besides this cramped, luxurious submarine? Was the president of the United States listening, packed into the situation room with whoever else belonged there?

"My paper is nothing startling, Mr. Secretary General, which is why this is all baffling to me. In simple terms—" she tried to not be distracted by the murmuring of the two translators into their mouthpieces "—all humans alive today are the descendants of one woman who lived about one hundred fifty thousand years ago. We know this because of mitochondrial DNA, which is not the DNA from the nucleus of the cell but separate DNA found in small organelles called mitochondria. Mitochondria, which exist in every cell of your body, are the powerhouses of the cell, producing energy for cellular functions. Mitochondrial DNA does not undergo recombination and is not found in sperm cell after they reach the egg. So the mitochondrial DNA is passed down unchanged from a mother to all her children."

Marianne paused, wondering how to explain this simply, but without condescension. "Mitochondrial DNA mutates at a steady rate, about one mutation every ten thousand years in a section called 'the control region,' and about once every thirty-five hundred years in the mitochondrial DNA as a whole. By tracing the number and type of mutations in contemporary humans, we can construct a tree of descent: which group descended from which female ancestor.

"Evolutionary biologists have identified thirty of these haplogroups. I found a new one, L7, by sequencing and comparing DNA samples with a standard human mitochondrial sample, known as the revised Cambridge Reference Sequence."

"How did you know where to look for this new group?"

"I didn't. I came across the first sample by chance and then sampled her relatives."

"Is it very different, then, from the others?"

"No," Marianne said. "It's just a branch of the L haplogroup."

"Why wasn't it discovered before?"

"It seems to be rare. The line must have mostly died out over time. It's a very old line, one of the first divergences from Mitochondrial Eve."

"So there is nothing remarkable about your finding?"

"Not in the least. There may even be more haplogroups out there that we just haven't discovered yet." She felt a perfect fool. They all looked at her as if expecting answers—Look! A blinding scientific light illuminate all!—and she had none. She was a workman scientist who had delivered a workmanlike job of fairly routine halotyping.

"Sir, we have arrived," said a junior officer. Marianne saw that his dress blues were buttoned wrong. They must have been donned in great haste. The tiny, human mishap made her feel better.

Desai drew a deep, audible breath. Even he, who had lived through war and revolution, was nervous. Commands flew through the air from invisible people. The submarine door opened.

Marianne stepped out into the alien ship.

Noah

"Where's Mom? Did you call her?" Elizabeth demanded.

"Not yet," Noah said.

"Does she even know you're in New York?"

"Not yet." He wanted to tell his sister to stop hammering at him, but he was her guest and so he couldn't. Not that he'd ever been able to stand up to either of his siblings. His usual ploy had been to get them battering on each other and leave him alone. Maybe he could do that now. Or maybe not.

"Noah, how long have you been in the city?"

"A while."

"How long a while?"

Noah put his hand in front of his face. "Lizzie, I'm really hungry. I didn't eat today. Do you think you could—"

"Don't start your whining-and-helpless routine with me, Noah. It doesn't work anymore."

Had it ever? Noah didn't think so, not with Elizabeth. He tried to pull himself together. "Elizabeth, I haven't called Mom yet and I *am* hungry. Please, could we defer this fight until I eat something? Anything, crackers or toast or—"

"There's sandwich stuff in the fridge. Help yourself. I'm going to call Mom, since at least one of us should let her know the prodigal son has deigned to turn up again. She's been out of her mind with worry about you."

Noah doubted that. His mother was the strongest person he knew, followed by Elizabeth and Ryan. Together, the three could have toppled empires. Of course, they seldom were together, since they fought almost every time they met. Odd that they would go on meeting so often, when it produced such bitterness, and all over such inconsequential things. Politics, religion, funding for the arts, isolationism. . . . He rummaged in Elizabeth's messy refrigerator, full of plastic containers with their lids half off, some with dabs of rotting food stuck to the bottom. God, this one was growing *mold*. But he found bread, cheese, and some salsa that seemed all right.

Elizabeth's one-bedroom apartment echoed her fridge, which was another reason she and Mom fought. Unmade bed, dusty stacks of journals and newspapers, a vase of dead flowers probably sent by one of the boyfriends Elizabeth never fell in love with. Mom's house north of the city, and Ryan and Connie's near hers, were neat and bright. Housecleaners came weekly; food was bought from careful lists; possessions were replaced whenever they got shabby. Noah had no possessions, or at least as few as he could manage.

Elizabeth clutched the phone. She dressed like a female FBI agent—short hair, dark pantsuit, no make-up—and was beautiful without trying. "Come on, Mom, pick up," she muttered, "it's a cell, it's supposed to be portable."

"Maybe she's in class," Noah said. "Or a meeting."

"It's Friday night, Noah."

"Oh. Yeah."

"I'll try the landline. She still has one."

Someone answered the landline on the first ring; Noah heard the chime stop from where he sat munching his sandwich. Then silence.

"Hello? Hello? Mom?" Elizabeth said.

The receiver on the other end clicked.

"That's odd," Elizabeth said.

"You probably got a wrong number."

"Don't talk with your mouth full. I'm going to try again."

This time no one answered. Elizabeth scowled. "I don't like that. Someone is there. I'm going to call Ryan."

Wasn't Ryan somewhere in Canada doing fieldwork? Or maybe Noah had the dates wrong. He'd only glanced at the email from Ryan, accessed on a terminal at the public library. That day he'd been on sugarcane, and the temporary identity had been impatient and brusque.

"Ryan? This is Elizabeth. Do you know where Mom is? . . . If I knew her schedule I wouldn't be calling, would I? . . . Wait, wait, will you *listen* for a minute? I called her house and someone picked up and then clicked off, and when I called back a second later, it just rang. Will you go over there just to check it out? . . . Okay, yes, we'll wait. Oh, Noah's here . . . No, I'm not going to discuss with you right now the . . . *Ryan*. For chrissake, go check Mom's house!" She clicked off.

Noah wished he were someplace else. He wished he were somebody else. He wished he had some sugarcane.

Elizabeth flounced into a chair and picked up a book. *Tariffs, Borders, and the Survival of the United States*, Noah read upside-down. Elizabeth was a passionate defender of isolationism. How many desperate people trying to crash the United States borders had she arrested today? Noah didn't want to think about it.

Fifteen minutes later, Ryan called back. Elizabeth put the call on speakerphone. "Liz, there are cop cars around Mom's house. They wouldn't let me in. A guy came out and said Mom isn't dead or hurt or in trouble, and he couldn't tell me any more than that."

"Okay." Elizabeth wore her focused look, the one with which she directed border patrols. "I'll try the college."

"I did. I reached Evan. He said that three men claiming to be FBI came and escorted her to the UN Special Mission Headquarters in Manhattan."

"That doesn't make sense!"

"I know. Listen, I'm coming over to your place."

"I'm calling the police."

"No! Don't! Not until I get there and we decide what to do."

Noah listened to them argue, which went on until Ryan hung up. Of course Elizabeth, who worked for a quasi-military organization, wanted to call the cops. Of course Ryan, who worked for a wildlife organization that thought the government had completely messed up regulations on invasive botanical species, would shun the cops. Meanwhile Mom was probably just doing something connected with her college, a UN fundraiser or something, and that geek Evan had gotten it all wrong. Noah didn't like Evan, who was only a few years older than he was. Evan was everything that Noah's family thought Noah should be: smart, smooth, able to fit in anyplace, even into a country that wasn't his own. And how come Elizabeth's border patrols hadn't kept out Evan Blanford?

Never mind; Noah knew the answer.

He said, "Can I do anything?"

Elizabeth didn't even answer him.

Marianne

She had seen many pictures of the *Embassy*. From the outside, the floating pavilion was beautiful in a stark sort of way. Hemispherical, multifaceted like a buckeyball (Had the Denebs learned that structure from humans or was it a mathematical universal?), the *Embassy* floated on a broad platform of some unknowable material. Facets and platform were blue but coated with the energy shield, which reflected sunlight so much that it glinted, a beacon of sorts. The aliens had certainly not tried to mask their presence. But there must be hidden machinery underneath, in the part known (maybe) only to Navy divers, since the entire huge structure had landed without a splash in the harbor. Plus, of course, the hidden passage through which the sub had come, presumably entailing a momentary interruption of the energy shield. Marianne knew she'd never find out the details.

The room into which she and the others stepped from the submarine was featureless except for the bed of water upon which their sub floated, droplets sliding off its sleek sides. No windows or furniture, one door. A strange smell permeated the air: Disinfectant? Perfume? Alien body odor? Marianne's heart began to beat oddly, too hard and too loud, with abrupt painful skips. Her breathing quickened.

The door opened and a Deneb came out. At first, she couldn't see it clearly; it was clouded by the same glittery energy shield that covered the *Embassy*. When her eyes adjusted, she gasped. The others also made sounds: a quick indrawn breath, a clicking of the tongue, what sounded like an actual whimper. The Russian translator whispered, *"Bozhe moi!"*

The alien looked almost human. Almost, not quite. Tall, maybe six-two, the man—it was clearly male—had long, thin arms and legs, a deep chest, a human face but much larger eyes. His skin was coppery and his hair, long and tied back, was dark brown. Most striking were his eyes: larger than humans', with huge dark pupils in a large expanse of white. He wore dark-green clothing, a simple tunic top over loose, short trousers that exposed his spindly calves. His feet were bare, and perhaps the biggest shock of all was that his feet, five-toed and broad, the nails cut short and square. Those feet looked so much like hers that she thought wildly: *He could wear my shoes.*

"Hello," the alien said, and it was not his voice but the mechanical one of the radio broadcasts, coming from the ceiling.

"Hello," Desai said, and bowed from the waist. "We are glad to finally meet. I am Secretary General Desai of the United Nations."

"Yes," the alien "said," and then added some trilling and clicking sounds in which his mouth did move. Immediately the ceiling said, "I welcome you in our own language."

Secretary Desai made the rest of the introductions with admirable calm. Marianne tried to fight her growing sense of unreality by recalling what she had read about the Denebs' planet. She wished she paid more attention to the astronomy. The popular press had said that the alien star was a K-something (K zero? K two? She couldn't remember). The alien home world had both less gravity and less light than Earth, at different wavelengths . . . orange, yes. The sun was an orange dwarf. Was this Deneb so tall because the gravity was less? Or maybe he was just a basketball player—

Get a grip, Marianne.

She did. The alien had said his name, an impossible collection of trilled phonemes, and immediately said, "Call me Ambassador Smith." How had he chosen that—from a computer-generated list of English names? When Marianne had been in Beijing to give a paper, some Chinese translators had done that: "Call me Dan." She had assumed the translators doubted her ability to pronounce their actual names correctly, and they had probably been right. But "Smith" for a starfarer . . .

"You are Dr. Jenner?"

"Yes, Ambassador."

"We wanted to talk with you, in particular. Will you please come this way, all of you?"

They did, trailing like baby ducklings after the tall alien. The room beyond the single door had been fitted up like the waiting room of a very expensive medical specialist. Did they order the upholstered chairs and patterned rug on the Internet? Or manufacture them with some advanced nanotech deep in the bowels of the *Embassy*? The wall pictures were of famous skylines: New York, Shanghai, Dubai, Paris. Nothing in the room suggested alienness. Deliberate? Of course it was. *Nobody here but us chickens.*

Marianne sat, digging the nails of one hand into the palm of the other to quiet her insane desire to giggle.

"I would like to know of your recent publication, Dr. Jenner," the ceiling said, while Ambassador Smith looked at her from his disconcertingly large eyes.

"Certainly," Marianne said, wondering where to begin. Where to begin? How much did they know about human genetics?

Quite a lot, as it turned out. For the next twenty minutes Marianne explained, gestured, answered questions. The others listened silently except for the low murmur of the Chinese and Russian translators. Everyone, human and alien, looked attentive and courteous, although Marianne detected the slightly pursed lips of Ekaterina Zaytsev's envy.

Slowly it became clear that Smith already knew much of what Marianne was saying. His questions centered on where she had gotten her DNA samples.

"They were volunteers," Marianne said. "Collection booths were set up in an open-air market in India, because I happened to have a colleague working there, in a train station in London, and on my college campus in the United States. At each place, a nominal fee was paid for a quick scraping of tissue from the inside of the cheek. After we found the first L7 DNA in a sample from an American student from Indiana, we went to her relatives to ask for samples. They were very cooperative."

"This L7 sample, according to your paper, comes from a mutation that marks the strain of one of the oldest of mitochondrial groups."

Desai made a quick, startled shift on his chair.

"That's right," Marianne said. "Evidence says that 'Mitochondrial Eve' had at least two daughters, and the line of one of them was L0 whereas the other line developed a mutation that became—" All at once she saw it, what Desai had already realized. She blinked at Smith and felt her mouth fall open, just as if she had no control over her jaw muscles, just as if the universe had been turned inside out, like a sock.

Noah

An hour later, Ryan arrived at Elizabeth's apartment. Repeated calls to their mother's cell and landline had produced nothing. Ryan and Elizabeth sat on the sagging sofa, conferring quietly, their usual belligerence with each other replaced by shared concern. Noah sat across the room, listening.

His brother had been short-changed in the looks department. Elizabeth was beautiful in a severe way and Noah knew he'd gotten the best of his parents' genes: his dead father's height and athletic build, his mother's light-gray eyes flecked with gold. In contrast, Ryan was built like a fire hydrant: short, muscular, thickening into cylindricalness since his marriage; Connie was a good cook. At thirty, he was already balding. Ryan was smart, slow to change, humorless.

Elizabeth said, "Tell me exactly what Evan said about the FBI taking her away. Word for word."

Ryan did, adding, "What about this—we call the FBI and ask them directly where she is and what's going on."

"I tried that. The local field office said they didn't know anything about it, but they'd make inquiries and get back to me. They haven't."

"Of course not. We have to give them a reason to give out information, and on the way over I thought of two. We can say either that we're going to the press, or that we need to reach her for a medical emergency."

Elizabeth said, "I don't like the idea of threatening the feds—too potentially messy. The medical emergency might be better. We could say Connie's developed a problem with her pregnancy. First grandchild, life-threatening complications—"

Noah, startled, said, "Connie's pregnant?"

"Four months," Ryan said. "If you ever read the emails everybody sends you, you might have gotten the news. You're going to be an uncle." His gaze said that Noah would make just as rotten an uncle as he did a son.

Elizabeth said, "You need to make the phone call, Ryan. You're the prospective father."

Ryan pulled out his cell, which looked as if it could contact deep space. The FBI office was closed. He left a message. FBI Headquarters in D.C. were also closed. He left another message. Before Ryan could say, "They'll never get back to us" and so begin another argument with Elizabeth over governmental inefficiency, Noah said, "Did the Wildlife Society give you that cell for your job?"

"It's the International Wildlife Federation and yes, the phone has top-priority connections for the loosestrife invasion."

Noah ducked his head to hide his grin.

Elizabeth guffawed. "Ryan, do you know how pretentious that sounds? An emergency hotline for weeds?"

"Do you know how ignorant *you* sound? Purple loosestrife is taking over wetlands, which for your information are the most biologically diverse and productive ecologies on Earth. They're being choked by this invasive species, with an economic impact of millions of dollars that—"

"As if you cared about the United States economy! You'd open us up again to competition from cheap foreign sweatshop labor, just let American jobs go to—"

"You can't shut out the world, Elizabeth, not even if you get the aliens to give you the tech for their energy shields. I know that's what you 'border-defense' types want—"

"Yes, it is! Our economic survival is at stake, which makes border patrol a lot more important than a bunch of creeping flowers!"

"Great, just great. Wall us off by keeping out new blood, new ideas, new trade partners. But let in invasive botanicals that encroach on farmland, so that eventually we can't even feed everyone who would be imprisoned in your imported alien energy fields."

"Protected, not imprisoned. The way we're protecting you now by keeping the Denebs offshore."

"Oh, you're doing that, are you? That was the aliens' decision. Do you think that if they had wanted to plop their pavilion in the middle of Times Square that your Border Patrol could have stopped them? They're a starfaring race, for chrissake!"

"Nobody said the—"

Noah shouted, which was the only way to get their attention, "Elizabeth, your cell is ringing! It says it's Mom!"

They both stared at the cell as if at a bomb, and then Elizabeth lunged for the phone. "Mom?"

"It's me. You called but—"

"Where have you been? What happened? What was the FBI—"

"I'll tell you everything. Are you and Ryan still at your place?"

"Yes. You sound funny. Are you sure you're okay?"

"Yes. No. Stay there, I'll get a cab, but it may be a few hours yet."

"But where—"

The phone went dead. Ryan and Elizabeth stared at each other. Into the silence, Noah said, "Oh yeah, Mom. Noah's here, too."

Marianne

"You are surprised," Ambassador Smith had said, unnecessarily.

Courtesy had been swamped in shock. "You're *human*? From Earth?"

"Yes. We think so."

"Your mitochondrial DNA matches the L7 sequence? No, wait—your whole biology matches ours?"

"There are some differences, of course. We—"

The Russian delegate stood up so quickly her chair fell over. She spat something which her translator gave as a milder, "'I do not understand how this is possible.'"

"I will explain," Smith said. "Please sit down."

Ekaterina Zaytsev did not sit. All at once Marianne wondered if the energy field enveloping Smith was weaponized.

Smith said, "We have known for millennia we did not originate on World. There is no fossil record of us going back more than one hundred fifty thousand Earth years. The life forms native to World are DNA-based, but there is no direct genetic link. We know someone took us from somewhere else and—"

"Why?" Marianne blurted. "Why would they do that? And who is 'they'?"

Before Smith could answer, Zaytsev said, "Why should your planet's native life-forms be DNA-based at all? If this story is not a collection of lies?"

"Panspermia," Smith said. "And we don't know why we were seeded from Earth to World. An experiment, perhaps, by a race now gone. We—"

The Chinese ambassador was murmuring to his translator. The translator, American and too upset to observe protocol, interrupted Smith.

"Mr. Zhu asks how, if you are from Earth, you progressed to space travel so much faster than we have? If your brains are the same as ours?"

"Our evolution was different."

Marianne darted in with, "How? Why? A hundred fifty thousand years is not enough for more than superficial evolutionary changes!"

"Which we have," Smith said, still in that mechanical voice that Marianne suddenly hated. Its very detachment sounded condescending. "World's gravity, for instance, is one-tenth less than Earth's, and our internal organs and skeletons have adjusted. World is warmer than Earth, and you can see that we carry little body fat. Our eyes are much larger than yours—we needed to gather all the light we can on a planet dimmer than yours. Most plants on World are dark, to gather as many photons as possible. We are dazzled by the colors on Earth."

He smiled, and Marianne remembered that all human cultures share certain facial expressions: happiness, disgust, anger.

Smith continued, "But when I said that our evolution differed from yours, I was referring to social evolution. World is a more benign planet than Earth. Little axial tilt, many easy-to-domesticate grains, much food, few predators. We had no Ice Age. We settled into agriculture over a hundred thousand years before you did."

Over a hundred thousand years more of settled communities, of cities, with their greater specialization and intellectual cross-fertilization. While Marianne's ancestors fifteen thousand years ago had still been hunting mastodons and gathering berries, these cousins across the galaxy might have been exploring quantum physics. But—

She said, "Then with such an environment, you must have had an overpopulation problem. All easy ecological niches rapidly become overpopulated!"

"Yes. But we had one more advantage." Smith paused; he was giving the translators time to catch up, and she guessed what that meant even before he spoke again.

"The group of us seeded on World—and we estimate it was no more than a thousand—were all closely related. Most likely they were all brought from one place. Our gene pool does not show as much diversity as yours. More important, the exiles—or at least a large number of them—happened to be unusually mild-natured and cooperative. You might say, 'sensitive to others' suffering.' We have had wars, but not very many, and not early on. We were able to control the population problem, once we saw it coming, with voluntary measures. And, of course, those sub-groups that worked together best, made the earliest scientific advances and flourished most."

"You replaced evolution of the fittest with evolution of the most cooperative," Marianne said, and thought: *There goes Dawkins.*

"You may say that."

"*I* not say this," Zaytsev said, without waiting for her translator. Her face twisted. "How you know you come from Earth? And how know where is Earth?"

"Whoever took us to World left titanium tablets, practically indestructible, with diagrams. Eventually we learned enough astronomy to interpret them."

Moses on the mountain, Marianne thought. *How conveniently neat!* Profound distrust swamped her, followed by profound belief. Because, after all, here the aliens were, having arrived in a starship, and they certainly looked human. Although—

She said abruptly, "Will you give us blood samples? Tissue? Permit medical scans?"

"Yes."

The agreement was given so simply, so completely, that everyone fell silent. Marianne's dazed mind tried to find the scam in this, this possible nefarious treachery, and failed. It was quiet Zhu Feng who, through his translator, finally broke the silence.

"Tell us, please, honored envoy, why you are here at all?"

Again Smith answered simply. "To save you all from destruction."

Noah

Noah slipped out of the apartment, feeling terrible but not terrible enough to stay. First transgression: If Mom returned earlier than she'd said, he wouldn't be there when she arrived. Second transgression: He'd taken twenty dollars from Elizabeth's purse. Third transgression: He was going to buy sugarcane.

But he'd left Elizabeth and Ryan arguing yet again about isolationism, the same argument in the same words as when he'd seen them last, four months ago. Elizabeth pulled out statistics showing that the United States' only option for survival, including avoiding revolution, was to retain and regain jobs within its borders, impose huge tariffs on imports, and rebuild infrastructure. Ryan trotted out different statistics proving that only globalization could, after a period of disruption, bring economic benefits in the long run, including a fresh flow of workers into a graying America. They had gotten to the point of hurtling words like "Fascist" and "sloppy thinker," when Noah left.

He walked the three blocks to Broadway. It was, as always, brightly lit, but the gyro places and electronics shops and restaurants, their outside tables empty and chained in the cold dusk, looked shabbier than he remembered. Some stores were not just shielded by grills but boarded up. He kept walking east, toward Central Park.

The dealer huddled in a doorway. He wasn't more than fifteen. Sugarcane was a low-cost, low-profit drug, not worth the gangs' time, let alone that of organized crime. The kid was a freelance amateur, and God knows what the sugarcane was cut with.

Noah bought it anyway. In the nearest Greek place he bought a gyro as the price of the key to the bathroom and locked himself in. The room was windowless but surprisingly clean. The testing set that Noah carried everywhere showed him the unexpected: the sugarcane was cut only with actual sugar, and only by about fifty percent.

"Thank you, Lord," he said to the toilet, snorted twice his usual dose, and went back to his table to eat the cooling gyro and wait.

The drug took him quickly, as it always did. First came a smooth feeling, as if the synapses of his brain were filling with rich, thick cream. Then: One moment he was Noah Jenner, misfit, and the next he wasn't. He felt like a prosperous small businessman of some type, a shop-owner maybe, financially secure and blissfully uncomplicated. A contented, centered person who never questioned who he was or where he was going, who fit in wherever he happened to be. The sort of man who could eat his gyro and gaze out the window without a confusing thought in his head.

Which he did, munching away, the juicy meat and mild spices satisfying in his mouth, for a quiet half-hour.

Except—something was happening on the street.

A group of people streamed down Broadway. A parade. No, a mob. They carried torches, of all things, and something larger on fire, carried high. . . . Now Noah could hear shouting. The thing carried high was an effigy made of straw and rags, looking like the alien in a hundred bad movies: big blank head, huge eyes, spindly body of pale green. It stood in a small metal tub atop a board. Someone touched a torch to the straw and set the effigy on fire.

Why? As far as Noah could see, the aliens weren't bothering anybody. They were even good for business. It was just an excuse for people floundering in a bad economy to vent their anger—

Were these his thoughts? Noah's? Who was he now?

Police sirens screamed farther down the street. Cops appeared on foot, in riot gear. A public-address system blared, its words audible even through the shop window: "Disperse now! Open flame is not allowed on the streets! You do not have a parade permit! Disperse now!"

Someone threw something heavy, and the other window of the gyro place shattered.

Glass rained down on the empty tables in that corner. Noah jerked upright and raced to the back of the tiny restaurant, away from the windows. The cook was shouting in Greek. People left the parade, or joined it from side streets, and began to hurl rocks and bottles at the police. The cops retreated to the walls and doorways across Broadway and took out grenades of tear gas.

On the sidewalk outside, a small child stumbled by, crying and bleeding and terrified.

The person who Noah was now didn't think, didn't hesitate. He ran out into the street, grabbed the child, and ran back into the restaurant. He wasn't quite fast enough to escape the spreading gas. His nose and eyes shrieked in agony, even as he held his breath and thrust the child's head under his jacket.

Into the tiny kitchen, following the fleeing cook and waiter, and out the back door to an alley of overflowing garbage cans. Noah kept running, even though his agonized vision was blurring. Store owners had all locked their doors. But he had outrun the tear gas, and now a woman was leaning out of the window of her second-floor apartment, craning her neck to see through brick walls to the action two streets away. Gunfire sounded. Over its echo off the steel and stone canyons, Noah shouted up, "A child got gassed! Please—throw down a bottle of water!"

She nodded and disappeared. To his surprise, she actually appeared on the street to help a stranger, carrying a water bottle and towel. "I'm a nurse, let me have him . . . aahh." Expertly she bathed the child's eyes, and then Noah's, just as if a battle wasn't going on within hearing if not within sight.

"Thank you," Noah gasped. "It was . . . " He stopped.

Something was happening in his head, and it wasn't due to the sugarcane. He felt an immediate and powerful kinship with this woman. How was that possible? He'd never seen her before. Nor was the attraction romantic—she was in late middle age, with graying hair and a drooping belly. But when she smiled at him and said, "You don't need the ER," something turned over in Noah's heart. What the fuck?

It must be the sugarcane.

But the feeling didn't have the creamy, slightly unreal feel of sugarcane.

She was still talking. "You probably couldn't get into any ER anyway, they'll all be jammed. I know—I was an ER nurse. But this kid'll be fine. He got almost none of the gas. Just take him home and calm him down."

"Who . . . who are you?"

"It doesn't matter." And she was gone, backing into the vestibule of her apartment building, the door locking automatically behind her. Restoring the anonymity of New York.

Whatever sense of weird recognition and bonding Noah had felt with her, it obviously had not been mutual. He tried to shake off the feeling and concentrate on the kid, who was wailing like a hurricane. The effortless competence bestowed by the sugarcane was slipping away. Noah knew nothing about children. He made a few ineffective soothing noises and picked up the child, who kicked him.

More police sirens in the distance. Eventually he found a precinct station, staffed only by a scared-looking civilian desk clerk; probably everyone else was at the riot. Noah left the kid there. Somebody would be looking for him. Noah walked back to West End Avenue, crossed it, and headed northeast to Elizabeth's apartment. His eyes still stung, but not too badly. He had escaped the worst of the gas cloud.

Elizabeth answered the door. "Where the hell did you go? Damn it, Noah, Mom's arriving any minute! She texted!"

"Well, I'm here now, right?"

"Yes, you're here now, but of all the shit-brained times to go out for a stroll! How did you tear your jacket?"

"Dunno." Neither his sister nor his brother seemed aware that eight blocks away there had been—maybe still was—an anti-alien riot going on. Noah didn't feel like informing them.

Ryan held his phone. "She's here. She texted. I'll go down."

Elizabeth said, "Ryan, she can probably pay off a cab and take an elevator by herself."

Ryan went anyway. *He had always been their mother's favorite,* Noah thought wearily. Except around Elizabeth, Ryan was affable, smooth, easy to get along with. His wife was charming, in an exaggeratedly feminine sort of way. They were going to give Marianne a grandchild.

It was an effort to focus on his family. His mind kept going back to that odd, unprecedented feeling of kinship with a person he had never seen before and probably had nothing whatsoever in common with. What was that all about?

"Elizabeth," his mother said. "And Noah! I'm so glad you're here. I've got . . . I've got a lot to tell you all. I—"

And his mother, who was always equal to anything, abruptly turned pale and fainted.

Marianne

Stupid, stupid—she never passed out! To the three faces clustered above her like balloons on sticks she said irritably, "It's nothing—just hypoglycemia. I haven't eaten since this morning. Elizabeth, if you have some juice or something . . ."

Juice was produced, crackers, slightly moldy cheese.

Marianne ate. Ryan said, "I didn't know you were hypoglycemic, Mom."

"I'm fine. Just not all that young anymore." She put down her glass and regarded her three children.

Elizabeth, scowling, looked so much like Kyle—was that why Marianne and Elizabeth had never gotten along? Her gorgeous alcoholic husband, the mistake of Marianne's life, had been dead for fifteen years. Yet here he was again, ready to poke holes in anything Marianne said.

Ryan, plain next to his beautiful sister but so much easier to love. Everybody loved Ryan, except Elizabeth.

And Noah, problem child, she and Kyle's last-ditch effort to save their doomed marriage. Noah was drifting and, she knew without being able to help, profoundly unhappy.

Were all three of them, and everybody else on the planet, going to die, unless humans and Denebs together could prevent it?

She hadn't fainted from hypoglycemia, which she didn't have. She had fainted from sheer delayed, maternal terror at the idea that her children might all perish. But she was not going to say that to her kids. And the fainting wasn't going to happen again.

"I need to talk to you," she said, unnecessarily. But how to begin something like this? "I've been talking to the aliens. In the *Embassy*."

"We know, Evan told us," Noah said, at the same moment that Elizabeth, quicker, said sharply, *"Inside?"*

"Yes. The Deneb ambassador requested me."

"Requested you? Why?"

"Because of the paper I just published. The aliens—did any of you read the copies of my paper I emailed you?"

"I did," Ryan said. Elizabeth and Noah said nothing. Well, Ryan was the scientist.

"It was about tracing human genetic diversity through mitochondrial evolution. Thirty mitochondrial haplogroups had been discovered. I found the thirty-first. That wouldn't really be a big deal, except that—in a few days this will be common knowledge but you must keep it among ourselves until the ambassador announces—the aliens belong to the thirty-first group, L7. They're human."

Silence.

"Didn't you understand what I just—"

Elizabeth and Ryan erupted with questions, expressions of disbelief, arm waving. Only Noah sat quietly, clearly puzzled. Marianne explained what Ambassador Smith—impossible name!—had told her. When she got to the part about the race that had taken humans to "World" also leaving titanium tablets engraved with astronomical diagrams, Elizabeth exploded. "Come on, Mom, this fandango makes no sense!"

"The Denebs are *here*," Marianne pointed out. "They did find us. And the Denebs are going to give tissue samples. Under our strict human supervision. They're expanding the *Embassy* and allowing in humans. Lots of humans, to examine their biology and to work with our scientists."

"Work on what?" Ryan said gently. "Mom, this can't be good. They're an invasive species."

"Didn't you hear a word I said?" Marianne said. God, if Ryan, the scientist, could not accept truth, how would humanity as a whole? "They're not 'invasive,' or at least not if our testing confirms the ambassador's story. They're native to Earth."

"An invasive species is native to Earth. It's just not in the ecological niche it evolved for."

Elizabeth said, "Ryan, if you bring up purple loosestrife, I swear I'm going to clip you one. Mom, did anybody think to ask this ambassador the basic question of why they're here in the first place?"

"Don't talk to me like I'm an idiot. Of course we did. There's a—" She stopped and bit her lip, knowing how this would sound. "You all know what panspermia is?"

"Yes," said Elizabeth.

"Of course." Ryan.

"No." Noah.

"It's the idea that original life in the galaxy—" whatever *that* actually was, all the textbooks would now need to be rewritten "—came from drifting clouds of organic molecules. We know that such molecules exist inside meteors and comets and that they can, under some circumstances, survive entry into atmospheres. Some scientists, like Fred Hoyle and Stephen Hawking, have even endorsed the idea that new biomolecules are still being carried down to Earth. The Denebs say that there is a huge, drifting cloud of spores—well, they're technically not spores, but I'll come to that in a minute—drifting toward Earth. Or, rather, we're speeding toward it, since the solar system rotates around the center of the galaxy and the entire galaxy moves through space relative to the cosmic microwave background. Anyway, in ten months from now, Earth and this spore cloud meet. And the spores are deadly to humans."

Elizabeth said skeptically, "And they know this *how*?"

"Because two of their colony planets lay in the path of the cloud and were already exposed. Both populations were completely destroyed. The Denebs have recordings. Then they sent unmanned probes to capture samples, which they brought with them. They say the samples are a virus, or something like a virus, but encapsulated in a coating that isn't like anything viruses can usually make. Together, aliens and humans are going to find a vaccine or a cure."

More silence. Then all three of her children spoke together, but in such different tones that they might have been discussing entirely different topics.

Ryan: "In ten months? A vaccine or cure for an unknown pathogen in ten months? It took the CDC six months just to fully identify the bacterium in Legionnaires' disease!"

Elizabeth: "If they're so technologically superior, they don't need us to develop any sort of 'cure'!"

Noah: "What do the spores do to people?"

Marianne answered Noah first, because his question was the simplest. "They act like viruses, taking over cellular machinery to reproduce. They invade the lungs and multiply and then . . . then victims can't breathe. It only takes a few days." A terrible, painful death. A sudden horror came into her mind: her three children gasping for breath as their lungs were swamped with fluid, until they literally drowned. All of them.

"Mom," Ryan said gently, "are you all right? Elizabeth, do you have any wine or anything?"

"No," said Elizabeth, who didn't drink. Marianne suddenly, ridiculously, clung to that fact, as if it could right the world: her two-fisted cop daughter, whose martial arts training enabled her to take down a two-hundred-fifty-pound attacker, had a Victorian lady's fastidiousness about alcohol. Stereotypes didn't hold. The world was more complicated than that. The unexpected existed—a Border Patrol section chief did not drink!—and therefore an unexpected solution could be found to this unexpected problem. Yes.

She wasn't making sense, and knew it, and didn't care. Right now, she needed hope more than sense. The Denebs, with technology an order of magnitude beyond humans, couldn't deal with the spore cloud, but Elizabeth didn't drink and, therefore, together Marianne and Smith and—throw in the president and WHO and the CDC and USAMRIID, why not—could defeat mindless space-floating dormant viruses.

Noah said curiously, "What are you smiling about, Mom?"

"Nothing." She could never explain.

Elizabeth blurted, "So even if all this shit is true, what the fuck makes the Dennies think that *we* can help them?"

Elizabeth didn't drink like a cop, but she swore like one. Marianne said, "They don't know that we can. But their biological sciences aren't much more advanced than ours, unlike their physical sciences. And the spore cloud hits Earth next September. The Denebs have twenty-five years."

"Do you believe that their biological sciences aren't as advanced as their physics and engineering?"

"I have no reason to disbelieve it."

"If it's true, then we're their lab rats! They'll test whatever they come up with on us, and then they'll sit back in orbit or somewhere to see if it works before taking it home to their own planet!"

"That's one way to think of it," Marianne said, knowing that this was exactly how a large part of the media would think of it. "Or you could think of it as a rescue mission. They're trying to help us while there's time, if not much time."

Ryan said, "Why do they want you? You're not a virologist."

"I don't know," Marianne said.

Elizabeth erupted once more, leaping up to pace around the room and punch at the air. "I don't believe it. Not any of it, including the so-called 'cloud.' There are things they aren't telling us. But you, Mom—you just swallow whole anything they say! You're unbelievable!"

Before Marianne could answer, Noah said, "I believe you, Mom," and gave her his absolutely enchanting smile. He had never really become aware of the power of that smile. It conferred acceptance, forgiveness, trust, the sweet sadness of fading sunlight. "All of us believe everything you said.

"We just don't want to."

Marianne

Noah was right. Ryan was right. Elizabeth was wrong.

The spore cloud existed. Although technically not spores, that was the word the Deneb translator gave out, and the word stuck among astronomers because it was a term they already knew. As soon as the clouds' coordinates, composition, and speed were given by the Denebs to the UN, astronomers around the globe found it through spectral analysis and the dimming of stars behind it. Actually, they had known of its existence all along but had assumed it was just another dust cloud too small and too cool to be incubating stars. Its trajectory would bring it in contact with Earth when the Denebs said, in approximately ten months.

Noah was right in saying that people did not want to believe this. The media erupted into three factions. The most radical declared the "spore cloud" to be just harmless dust and the Denebs plotting, in conspiracy with the UN and possibly several governments, to take over Earth for various evil and sometimes inventive purposes. The second faction believed that the spore threat might be real but that, echoing Elizabeth, humanity would become "lab rats" in alien experiments to find some sort of solution, without benefit to Earth. The third group, the most scientifically literate, focused on a more immediate issue: They did not want the spore samples brought to Earth for research, calling them the real danger.

Marianne suspected the samples were already here. NASA had never detected shuttles or other craft going between the ship in orbit around the moon and the *Embassy*. Whatever the aliens wanted here, probably already was.

Teams of scientists descended on New York. Data was presented to the UN, the only body that Smith would deal with directly. Everyone kept saying that time was of the essence. Marianne, prevented from resuming teaching duties by the insistent reporters clinging to her like lint, stayed in Elizabeth's apartment and waited. Smith had given her a private communication device, which no one except the UN Special Mission knew about. Sometimes as she watched TV or cleaned Elizabeth's messy apartment, Marianne pondered this: An alien had given her his phone number and asked her to wait. It was almost like dating again.

Time is of the essence! Time is of the essence! A few weeks went by in negotiations she knew nothing of. Marianne reflected on the word "essence." Elizabeth worked incredible hours; the Border Patrol had been called in to help keep "undesirables" away from the Harbor, assisting the Coast Guard, INS, NYPD, and whoever else the city deemed pertinent. Noah had left again and did not call.

Evan was with her at the apartment when the Deneb communication device rang. "What's that?" he said off-handedly, wiping his mouth. He had brought department gossip and bags of sushi. The kitchen table was littered with tuna tataki, cucumber wraps, and hotategai.

Marianne said, "It's a phone call from the Deneb ambassador."

Evan stopped wiping and, paper napkin suspended, stared at her.

She put the tiny device on the table, as instructed, and spoke the code word. A mechanical voice said, "Dr. Marianne Jenner?"

"Yes."

"This is Ambassador Smith. We have reached an agreement with your UN to proceed, and will be expanding our facilities immediately. I would like you to head one part of the research."

"Ambassador, I am not an epidemiologist, not an immunologist, not a physician. There are many others who—"

"Yes. We don't want you to work on pathogens or with patients. We want you to identify human volunteers who belong to the haplogroup you discovered, L7."

Something icy slid along Marianne's spine. "Why? There hasn't been very much genetic drift between our . . . ah . . . groups of humans in just one hundred and fifty thousnd years. And mitochondrial differentiation should play no part in—"

"This is unconnected with the spores."

"What is it connected with?" *Eugenics, master race, Nazis* . . .

"This is purely a family matter."

Marianne glanced at Evan, who was writing furiously on the white paper bag that sushi had come in: GO! ACCEPT! ARE YOU DAFT? CHANCE OF A LIFETIME!

She said, "A family matter?"

"Yes. Family matters to us very much. Our whole society is organized around ancestral loyalty."

To Marianne's knowledge, this was the first time the ambassador had ever said anything, to anyone, about how Deneb society was organized. Evan, who'd been holding the paper bag six inches from her face, snatched it back and wrote CHANCE OF SIX THOUSAND LIFETIMES!

The number of generations since Mitochondrial Eve.

Smith continued, "I would like you to put together a small team of three or four people. Lab facilities will be provided, and volunteers will provide tissue samples. The UN has been very helpful. Please assemble your team on Tuesday at your current location and someone will come to escort you. Do you accept this post?"

"Tuesday? That's only—"

"Do you accept this post?"

"I . . . yes."

"Good. Good-bye."

Evan said, "Marianne—"

"Yes, of course, you're part of the 'team.' God, none of this real."

"Thank you, thank you!"

"Don't burble, Evan. We need two lab techs. How can they have facilities ready by Tuesday? It isn't possible."

"Or so we think," Evan said.

Noah

It hadn't been possible to stay in the apartment. His mother had the TV on non-stop, every last news show, no matter how demented, that discussed the aliens or their science. Elizabeth burst in and out again, perpetually angry at everything she didn't like in the world, which included the Denebs. The two women argued at the top of their lungs, which didn't seem to bother either of them at anything but an intellectual level, but which left Noah unable to eat anything without nausea or sleep without nightmares or walk around without knots in his guts.

He found a room in a cheap boardinghouse, and a job washing dishes, paid under the counter, in a taco place. Even though the tacos came filmed with grease, he could digest better here than at Elizabeth's, and anyway he didn't eat much. His wages went on sugarcane.

He became in turn an observant child, a tough loner, a pensive loner, a friendly panhandler. Sugarcane made him, variously, mute or extroverted or gloomy or awed or confident. But none of it was as satisfying as it once had been. Even when he was someone else, he was still aware of being Noah. That had not happened before. The door out of himself stayed ajar. Increasing the dose didn't help.

Two weeks after he'd left Elizabeth's, he strolled on his afternoon off down to Battery Park. The late October afternoon was unseasonably warm, lightly overcast, filled with autumn leaves and chrysanthemums and balloon sellers. Tourists strolled the park, sitting on the benches lining the promenade, feeding the pigeons, touring Clinton Castle. Noah stood for a long time leaning on the railing above the harbor, and so witnessed the miracle.

"It's happening! Now!" someone shouted.

What was happening? Noah didn't know, but evidently someone did because people came running from all directions. Noah would have been jostled and squeezed from his place at the railing if he hadn't gripped it with both hands. People stood on the benches; teenagers shimmied up the lamp poles. Figures appeared on top of the Castle. A man began frantically selling telescopes and binoculars evidently hoarded for this occasion. Noah bought a pair with money he'd been going to use for sugarcane.

"Move that damn car!" someone screamed as a Ford honked its way through the crowd, into what was supposed to be a pedestrian area. Shouts, cries, more people rushing from cars to the railings.

Far out in the harbor, the Deneb *Embassy*, its energy shield dull under the cloudy sky, began to glow. Through his binoculars Noah saw the many-faceted dome shudder—not just shake but shudder in a rippling wave, as if alive. *Was* it alive? Did his mother know?

"Aaaahhhhh," the crowd went.

The energy shield began to spread. Either it had thinned or changed composition, because for a long moment—maybe ninety seconds—Noah could almost see through it. A suggestion of floor, walls, machinery . . . then opaque again. But the "floor" was growing, reaching out to cover more territory, sprouting tentacles of material and energy.

Someone on the bridge screamed, "They're taking over!"

All at once, signs were hauled out, people leaped onto the roofs of cars that should not have been in the park, chanting began. But not much chanting or many people. Most crowded the railings, peering out to sea.

In ten minutes, the *Embassy* grew and grew laterally, silently spreading across the calm water like a speeded-up version of an algae bloom. When it hardened again—that's how it looked to Noah, like molten glass hardening as it cooled—the structure was six times its previous size. The tentacles had become docks, a huge one toward the city and several smaller ones to one side. By now even the chanters had fallen silent, absorbed in the silent, awing, monstrous feat of unimaginable construction. When it was finished, no one spoke.

Then an outraged voice demanded, "Did those bastards get a city permit for that?"

It broke the silence. Chanting, argument, exclaiming, pushing all resumed. A few motorists gunned their engine, futilely, since it was impossible to move vehicles. The first of the motorcycle cops arrived: NYPD, then Special Border Patrol, then chaos.

Noah slipped deftly through the mess, back toward the streets north of the Battery. He had to be at work in an hour. The *Embassy* had nothing to do with him.

Marianne

A spore cloud doesn't look like anything at all.

A darker patch in dark space, or the slightest of veils barely dimming starlight shining behind it. Earth's astronomers could not accurately say how large it was, or how deep. They relied on Deneb measurements, except for the one fact that mattered most, which human satellites in deep space and human ingenuity at a hundred observatories was able to verify: The cloud was coming. The path of its closest edge would intersect Earth's path through space at the time the Denebs had said: early September.

Marianne knew that almost immediately following the UN announcement, madness and stupidity raged across the planet. Shelters were dug or sold or built, none of which would be effective. If air could get in, so could spores. In Kentucky, some company began equipping deep caves with air circulation, food for a year, and high-priced sleeping berths: reverting to Paleolithic caveman. She paid no more attention to this entrepreneurial survivalism than to the televised protests, destructive mobs, peaceful marches, or lurid artist depictions of the cloud and its presumed effects. She had a job to do.

On Tuesday she, Evan, and two lab assistants were taken to the submarine bay at UN Special Mission Headquarters. In the sub, Max and Gina huddled in front of the porthole, or maybe it was a porthole-like viewscreen, watching underwater fish. Maybe fish were what calmed them. Although they probably didn't need calming: Marianne, who had worked with both before, had chosen them as much for their even temperaments as for their competence. Government authorities had vetted Max and Gina for, presumably, both crime-free backgrounds and pro-alien attitudes. Max, only twenty-nine, was the computer whiz. Gina, in her mid-thirties and the despair of her Italian mother because Gina hadn't yet married, made the fewest errors Marianne had ever seen in sample preparation, amplification, and sequencing.

Evan said to Marianne, "Children all sorted out?"

"Never. Elizabeth won't leave New York, of course." ("Leave? Don't you realize I have a job to do, protecting citizens from your aliens?" Somehow they had become Marianne's aliens.) "Ryan took Connie to her parents' place in Vermont and he went back to his purple loosestrife in Canada."

"And Noah?" Evan said gently. He knew all about Noah; why, Marianne wondered yet again, did she confide in this twenty-eight-year-old gay man as if he were her age, and not Noah's? Never mind; she needed Evan.

She shook her head. Noah had again disappeared.

"He'll be fine, then, Marianne. He always is."

"I know."

"Look, we're docking."

They disembarked from the sub to the underside of the *Embassy*. Whatever the structure's new docks topside were for, it wasn't transfer of medical personnel. Evan said admiringly, "Shipping above us hasn't even been disrupted. Dead easy."

"Oh, those considerate aliens," Marianne murmured, too low for the sub captain, still in full-dress uniform, to hear. Her and Evan's usual semi-sarcastic banter helped to steady her: the real toad in the hallucinatory garden.

The chamber beyond the airlock had not changed, although this time they were met by a different alien. Female, she wore the same faint shimmer of energy-shield protection over her plain tunic and pants. Tall, coppery-skinned, with those preternaturally huge dark eyes, she looked about thirty, but how could you tell? Did the Denebs have plastic surgery? Why not? They had everything else.

Except a cure for spore disease.

The Deneb introduced herself ("Scientist Jones"), went through the so-glad-you're-here speech coming disconcertingly from the ceiling. She conducted them to the lab, then left immediately. Plastic surgery or no, Marianne was grateful for alien technology when she saw her lab. Nothing in it was unfamiliar, but all of it was state-of-the-art. Did they create it as they had created the *Embassy*, or order it wholesale? Must be the latter—the state-of-the-art gene sequencer still bore the label ILLUMINA. The equipment must have been ordered, shipped, paid for (with what?) either over the previous months of negotiation, or as the world's fastest rush shipping.

Beside it sat a rack of vials with blood samples, all neatly labeled.

Max immediately went to the computer and turned it on. "No Internet," he said, disappointed. "Just a LAN, and . . . wow, this is heavily shielded."

"You realize," Marianne said, "that this is a minor part of the science going on aboard the *Embassy*. All we do is process mitochondrial DNA to identify L7 haplogroup members. We're a backwater on the larger map."

"Hey, we're *here*," Max said. He grinned at her. "Too bad, though, about no *World of Warcraft*. This thing has no games at all. What do I do in my spare time?"

"Work," Marianne said, just as the door opened and two people entered. Marianne recognized one of them, although she had never met him before. Unsmiling, dark-suited, he was Security. The woman was harder to place. Middle-aged, wearing jeans and a sweater, her hair held back by a too-girlish headband. But her smile was warm, and it reached her eyes. She held out her hand.

"Dr. Jenner? I'm Lisa Guiterrez, the genetics counselor. I'll be your liaison with the volunteers. We probably won't be seeing each other again, but I wanted to say hello. And you're Dr. Blanford?"

"Yes," Evan said.

Marianne frowned. "Why do we need a genetic counselor? I was told our job is to simply process blood samples to identify members of the L7 haplogroup."

"It is," Lisa said, "and then I take it from there."

"Take *what* from there?"

Lisa studied her. "You know, of course, that the Denebs would like to identify those surviving human members of their own haplogroup. They consider them family. The concept of family is pivotal to them."

Marianne said, "You're not a genetic counselor. You're a xenopsychologist."

"That, too."

"And what happens after the long-lost family members are identified?"

"I tell them that they are long-lost family members." Her smile never wavered.

"And then?"

"And then they get to meet Ambassador Smith."

"And *then*?"

"No more 'then.' The Ambassador just wants to meet his six-thousand-times-removed cousins. Exchange family gossip, invent some in-jokes, confer about impossible Uncle Harry."

So she had a sense of humor. Maybe it was a qualification for billing oneself a "xenopsychologist," a profession that until a few months ago had not existed.

"Nice to meet you both," Lisa said, widened her smile another fraction of an inch, and left.

Evan murmured, "My, people come and go so quickly here."

But Marianne was suddenly not in the mood, not even for quoted humor from such an appropriate source as *The Wizard of Oz*. She sent a level gaze at Evan, Max, Gina.

"Okay, team. Let's get to work."

II: S MINUS 9.5 MONTHS

Marianne

There were four other scientific teams aboard the *Embassy*, none of which were interested in Marianne's backwater. The other teams consisted of scientists from the World Health Organization, the Centers for Disease Control, the United States Army Research Institute for Infectious Diseases, the Institute of Molecular Medicine at Oxford, the Beijing Genomics Institute, Kyushu University, and the Scripps Clinic and Research Foundation, perhaps the top immunology center in the world. Some of the most famous names in the scientific and medical worlds were here, including a dozen Nobel winners. Marianne had no knowledge of, but could easily imagine, the political and scientific competition to get aboard the *Embassy*. The Americans had an edge because the ship sat in New York Harbor and that, too, must have engendered political threats and counter threats, bargaining and compromise.

The most elite group, and by far the largest, worked on the spores: germinating, sequencing, investigating this virus that could create a worldwide human die-off. They worked in negative-pressure, biosafety-level-four chambers. Previously the United States had had only two BSL4 facilities, at the CDC in Atlanta and at USAMRIID in Maryland. Now there was a third, dazzling in its newness and in the completeness of its equipment. The Spore Team had the impossible task of creating some sort of vaccine or other method of neutralizing, worldwide, a pathogen not native to Earth, within ten months.

The Biology Team investigated alien tissues and genes. The Denebs gave freely of whatever was asked: blood, epithelial cells, sperm, biopsy samples. "Might even give us a kidney, if we asked nicely enough," Evan said. "We know they have two."

Marianne said, "*You* ask, then."

"Not me. Too frightful to think what they might ask in exchange."

"So far, they've asked nothing."

Almost immediately the Biology Team verified the Denebs as human. Then began the long process of finding and charting the genetic and evolutionary differences between the aliens and Terrans. The first, announced after just a few weeks, was that all of the seventeen aliens in the *Embassy* carried the same percentage as Terrans of Neanderthal genes: from one to four percent.

"They're us," Evan said.

"Did you doubt it?" Marianne asked.

"No. But more interesting, I think, are the preliminary findings that the Denebs show so much less genetic diversity than we do. That wanker Wilcox must be weeping in his ale."

Patrick Wells Wilcox was the current champion of the Toba Catastrophe Theory, which went in and out of scientific fashion. Seventy thousand years ago the Toba supervolcano in Indonesia had erupted. This had triggered such major environmental change, according to theory proponents, that a "bottleneck event" had occurred, reducing the human population to perhaps ten thousand individuals. The result had been a great reduction in human genetic diversity. Backing for the idea came from geology as well as coalescence evidence of some genes, including mitochondrial, Y-chromosome, and nuclear. Unfortunately, there was also evidence that the bottleneck event had never occurred. If the Denebs, removed from Earth well before the supervolcano, showed less diversity than Terrans, then Terran diversity couldn't have been reduced all that much.

Marianne said, "Wilcox shouldn't weep too soon."

"Actually, he never weeps at all. Gray sort of wanker. Holes up in his lab at Cambridge and glowers at the world through medieval arrow slits."

"Dumps boiling oil on dissenting paleontologists," Marianne suggested.

"Actually, Wilcox may not even be human. Possibly an advance scout for the Denebs. Nobody at Cambridge has noticed it so far."

"Or so we think." Marianne smiled. She and Evan never censored their bantering, which helped lower the hushed, pervasive anxiety they shared with everyone else on the *Embassy*. It was an anxious ship.

The third scientific team aboard was much smaller. Physicists, they worked with "Scientist Jones" on the astronomy of the coming collision with the spore cloud.

The fourth team she never saw at all. Nonetheless, she suspected they were there, monitoring the others, shadowy underground non-scientists unknown even to the huge contingent of visible security.

Marianne looked at the routine work on her lab bench: polymerase chain reaction to amplify DNA samples, sequencing, analyzing data, writing reports on the genetic inheritance of each human volunteer who showed up at the Deneb "collection site" in Manhattan. A lot of people showed up. So far, only two of them belonged to Ambassador Smith's haplogroup. "Evan, we're not really needed, you and I. Gina and Max can handle anything our expensive brains are being asked to do."

Evan said, "Right, then. So let's have a go at exploring. Until we're stopped, anyway."

She stared at him. "Okay. Yes. Let's explore."

Noah

Noah emerged from the men's room at the restaurant. During the mid-afternoon lull they had no customers except for a pair of men slumped over one table in the back. "Look at this!" the waitress said to him. She and the cook were both huddled over her phone, strange enough since they hated each other. But Cindy's eyes were wide from something other than her usual drugs, and Noah took a look at the screen of the sophisticated phone, mysteriously acquired and gifted by Cindy's current boyfriend before he'd been dragged off to Riker's for assault with intent.

VOLUNTEERS WANTED TO DONATE BLOOD
PAYMENT: $100
HUMAN NURSES TO COLLECT SMALL BLOOD SAMPLES
DENEB *EMBASSY* PIER, NEW YORK HARBOR

"Demonios del Diablo," Miguel muttered. "Vampiros!" He crossed himself.

Noah said dryly, "I don't think they're going to drink the blood, Miguel." The dryness was false. His heart had begun to thud. People like his mother got to see the *Embassy* up close, not people like Noah. Did the ad mean that the Denebs were going to take human blood samples on the large dock he had just seen form out of nothing?

Cindy had lost interest. "No fucking customers except those two sorry asses in the corner, and they never tip. I shoulda stood in bed."

"Miguel," Noah said, "can I have the afternoon off?"

Noah stood patiently in line at the blood-collection site. If any of the would-be volunteers had hoped to see aliens, they had been disappointed.

Noah was not disappointed; after all, the ad on Cindy's phone had said HUMAN NURSES TO COLLECT SMALL BLOOD SAMPLES.

He was, however, disappointed that the collection site was not on the large dock jutting out from the *Embassy* under its glittering energy shield. Instead, he waited to enter what had once been a warehouse at the land end of a pier on the Manhattan waterfront. The line, huddled against November drizzle, snaked in loops and oxbows for several blocks, and he was fascinated by the sheer diversity of people. A woman in a fur-lined Burberry raincoat and high, polished boots. A bum in jeans with an indecent tear on the ass. Several giggling teenage girls under flowered umbrellas. An old man in a winter parka. A nerdy-looking boy with an iPad protected by flexible plastic. Two tired-looking middle-aged women. One of those said to the other, "I could pay all that back rent if I get this alien money, and—"

Noah tapped her arm. "Excuse me, ma'am—what 'alien money'?" The $100 fee for blood donation didn't seem enough to pay *all that back rent*.

She turned. "If they find out you're part of their blood group, you get a share of their fortune. You know, like the Indians with their casino money. If you can prove you're descended from their tribe."

"No, that's not it," the old man in the parka said impatiently. "You get a free energy shield like theirs to protect you when the spore cloud hits. They take care of family."

The bum muttered, "Ain't no spore cloud."

The boy said with earnest contempt, "You're all wrong. This is just—the Denebs are the most significant thing to happen to Earth, ever! Don't you get it? We're not alone in the universe!"

The bum laughed.

Eventually Noah reached Building A. Made of concrete and steel, the building's walls were discolored, its high-set windows grimy. Only the security machines looked new, and they made high-tech examinations of Noah's person inside and out. His wallet, cell, jacket, and even shoes were left in a locker before he shuffled in paper slippers along the enclosed corridor to Building B, farther out on the pier. Someone was very worried about terrorism.

"Please fill out this form," said a pretty, grim-faced young woman. Not a nurse: security. She looked like a faded version of his sister, bleached of Elizabeth's angry command. Noah filled out the form, gave his small vial of blood, and filed back to Building B. He felt flooded with anti-climactic letdown. When he had reclaimed his belongings, a guard handed him a hundred dollars and a small round object the size and feel of a quarter.

"Keep this with you," a guard said. "It's a one-use, one-way communication device. In the unlikely event that it rings, press the center. That means that we'd like to see you again."

"If you do, does that mean I'm in the alien's haplogroup?"

He didn't seem to know the word. "If it rings, press the center."

"How many people have had their devices ring?"

The guard's face changed, and Noah glimpsed the person behind the job. He shrugged. "I never heard of even one."

"Is it—"

"Move along, please." The job mask was back.

Noah put on his shoes, balancing first on one foot and then on the other to avoid touching the grimy floor. It was like being in an airport. He started for the door.

"Noah!" Elizabeth sailed toward him across a sea of stained concrete. "What the hell are you doing here?"

"Hi, Lizzie. Is this part of the New York State border?"

"I'm on special assignment."

God, she must hate that. Her scowl threatened to create permanent furrows in her tanned skin. But Elizabeth always obeyed the chain of command.

"Noah, how can you—"

A bomb went off.

A white light blinded Noah. His hearing went dead, killed by the sheer onslaught of sound. His legs wobbled as his stomach lurched. Then Elizabeth knocked him to the ground and hurled herself on top of him. A few seconds later she was up and running and Noah could hear her again: "Fucking flashbang!"

He stumbled to his feet, his eyes still painful from the light. People screamed and a few writhed on the floor near a pile of clothes that had ignited. Black smoke billowed from the clothing, setting the closest people to coughing, but no one seemed dead. Guards leaped at a young man shouting something lost in the din.

Noah picked up his shoes and slipped outside, where sirens screamed, honing in from nearby streets. The salt-tanged breeze touched him like a benediction.

A flashbang. You could buy a twelve-pack of them on the Internet for fifty bucks, although those weren't supposed to ignite fires. Whatever that protestor had hoped to accomplish, it was ineffective. Just like this whole dumb blood-donation expedition.

But he had a hundred dollars he hadn't had this morning, which would buy a few good hits of sugarcane. And in his pocket, his fingers closed involuntarily on the circular alien coin.

Marianne

Marianne was surprised at how few areas of the *Embassy* were restricted.

The BSL4 areas, of course. The aliens' personal quarters, not very far from the BSL4 labs. But her and Evan's badges let them roam pretty much everywhere else. Humans rushed passed them on their own errands, some nodding in greeting but others too preoccupied to even notice they were there.

"Of course there are doors we don't even see," Evan said. "Weird alien cameras we don't see. Denebs we don't see. They know where we are, where everyone is, every minute. Dead easy."

The interior of the *Embassy* was a strange mixture of materials and styles. Many corridors were exactly what you'd expect in a scientific research facility: unadorned, clean, lined with doors. The walls seemed to be made of something that was a cross between metal and plastic, and did not dent. Walls in the personal quarters and lounges, on the other hand, were often made of something that reminded her of Japanese rice paper, but soundproof. She had the feeling that she could have put her fist through them, but when she actually tried this, the wall only gave slightly, like a very tough piece of plastic. Some of these walls could be slid open, to change the size or shapes of rooms. Still other walls were actually giant screens that played constantly shifting patterns of subtle color. Finally, there were odd small lounges that seemed to have been furnished from upscale mail-order catalogues by someone who thought anything Terran must go with anything else: earth-tone sisal carpeting with a Victorian camelback sofa, Picasso prints with low Moroccan tables inlaid with silver and copper, a Navaho blanket hung on the wall above Japanese zabutons.

Marianne was tired. They'd come to one such sitting area outside the main dining hall, and she sank into an English club chair beside a small table of swooping purple glass. "Evan—do you really believe we are all going to die a year from now?"

"No." He sat in an adjoining chair, appreciatively patting its wide and upholstered arms. "But only because my mind refuses to entertain the thought of my own death in any meaningful way. Intellectually, though, yes. Or rather, nearly all of us will die."

"A vaccine to save the rest?"

"No, there is simply not enough time to get all the necessary bits and pieces sorted out. But the Denebs will save some Terrans."

"How?"

"Take a selected few back with them to that big ship in the sky."

Immediately she felt stupid that she hadn't thought of this before. Stupidity gave way to the queasy, jumpy feeling of desperate hope. "Take us *Embassy* personnel? To continue joint work on the spores?" Her children, somehow she would have to find a way to include Elizabeth, Noah, Ryan and Connie and the baby! But everyone here had family—

"No," Evan said. "Too many of us. My guess is just the Terran members of their haplogroup. Why else bother to identify them? And everything I've heard reinforces their emphasis on blood relationships."

"Heard from whom? We're in the lab sixteen hours a day—"

"I don't need much sleep. Not like you, Marianne. I talk to the Biology Group, who talk more than anybody else to the aliens. Also I chat with Lisa Guiterrez, the genetic counselor."

"And the Denebs told somebody they're taking their haplogroup members with them before the spore cloud hits?"

"No, of course not. When do the Denebs tell Terrans anything directly? It's all smiling evasion, heartfelt reassurances. They're like Philippine houseboys."

Startled, Marianne gazed at him. The vaguely racist reference was uncharacteristic of Evan, and had been said with some bitterness. She realized all over again how little Evan gave away about his past. When had he lived in the Philippines? What had happened between him and some apparently not forgiven houseboy? A former lover? Evan's sexual orientation was also something they never discussed, although of course she was aware of it. From his grim face, he wasn't going to discuss it now, either.

She said, "I'm going to ask Smith what the Denebs intend."

Evan's smooth grin had returned. "Good luck. The UN can't get information from him, the project's chief scientists can't get information from him, and you and I never see him. Just minor roadblocks to your plan."

"We really are lab rats," she said. And then, abruptly, "Let's go. We need to get back to work."

"Evan said slowly, "I've been thinking about something."

"What?"

"The origin of viruses. How they didn't evolve from a single entity and don't have a common ancestor. About the theory that their individual origins were pieces of DNA or RNA that broke off from cells and learned to spread to other cells."

Marianne frowned. "I don't see how that's relevant."

"I don't either, actually."

"Then—"

"I don't know," Evan said. And again, "I just don't know."

Noah

Noah was somebody else.

He'd spent his blood-for-the-Denebs money on sugarcane, and it turned out to be one of the really good transformations. He was a nameless soldier from a nameless army: brave and commanding and sure of himself. Underneath he knew it was an illusion (but he never used to know that!). However, it didn't matter. He stood on a big rock at the south end of Central Park, rain and discarded plastic bags blowing around him, and felt completely, if temporarily, happy. He was on top of the world, or at least seven feet above it, and nothing seemed impossible.

The alien token in his pocket began to chime, a strange syncopated rhythm, atonal as no iPhone ever sounded. Without a second's hesitation—he could face anything!—Noah pulled it from his pocket and pressed its center.

A woman's voice said, "Noah Richard Jenner?"

"Yes, ma'am!"

"This is Dr. Lisa Guiterrez at the Deneb embassy. We would like to see you, please. Can you come as soon as possible to the UN Special Mission Headquarters at its pier?"

Noah drew a deep breath. Then full realization crashed around him, loud and blinding as last week's flashbang. Oh my God—why hadn't he seen it before? Maybe because he hadn't been a warrior before. His mother had—*son of a bitch*—

"Noah?"

He said, "I'll be there."

The submarine surfaced in an undersea chamber. A middle-aged woman in jeans and blazer, presumably Dr. Guiterrez, awaited Noah in the featureless room. He didn't much notice woman or room. Striding across the gangway, he said, "I want to see my mother. Now. She's Dr. Marianne Jenner, working here someplace."

Dr. Guiterrez didn't react as if this were news, or strange. She said, "You seem agitated." Hers was the human voice Noah had heard coming from the alien token.

"I am agitated! Where is my mother?"

"She's here. But first, someone else wants to meet you."

"I demand to see my mother!"

A door in the wall slid open, and a tall man with coppery skin and bare feet stepped through. Noah looked at him, and it happened again.

Shock, bewilderment, totally unjustified recognition—he knew this man, just as he had known the nurse who washed tear gas from his and a child's eyes during the West Side demonstration. Yet he'd never seen him before, and he was an *alien*. But the sense of kinship was powerful, disorienting, ridiculous.

"Hello, Noah Jenner," the ceiling said. "I am Ambassador Smith. Welcome to the *Embassy*."

"I—"

"I wanted to welcome you personally, but I cannot visit now. I have a meeting. Lisa will help you get settled here, should you choose to stay with us for a while. She will explain everything. Let me just say—"

Impossible to deny this man's sincerity, he meant every incredible word—

"—that I'm very glad you are here."

After the alien left, Noah stood staring at the door through which he'd vanished. "What is it?" Dr. Guiterrez said. "You look a bit shocked."

Noah blurted, "I know that man!" A second later he realized how dumb that sounded.

She said gently, "Let's go somewhere to talk, Noah. Somewhere less . . . wet."

Water dripped from the sides of the submarine, and some had sloshed onto the floor. Sailors and officers crossed the gangway, talking quietly. Noah followed Lisa from the sub bay, down a side corridor, and into an office cluttered with charts, print-outs, coffee mugs, a laptop—such an ordinary looking place that it only heightened Noah's sense of unreality. She sat in an upholstered chair and motioned him to another. He remained standing.

She said, "I've seen this before, Noah. What you're experiencing, I mean, although usually it isn't as strong as you seem to be feeling it."

"Seen what? And who are you, anyway? I want to talk to my mother!"

She studied him, and Noah had the impression she saw more than he wanted her to. She said, "I'm Dr. Lisa Guiterrez, as Ambassador Smith said. Call me Lisa. I'm a genetics counselor serving as the liaison between the ambassador and those people identified as belonging to his haplotype, L7, the one identified by your mother's research. Before this post, I worked with Dr. Barbara Formisano at Oxford, where I also introduced people who share the same haplotype. Over and over again I've seen a milder version of what you seem to be experiencing now—an unexpected sense of connection between those with an unbroken line of mothers and grandmothers and great-grandmothers back to their haplogroup clan mother. It—"

"That sounds like bullshit!"

"—is important to remember that the connection is purely symbolic. Similar cell metabolisms don't cause shared emotions. But—an important 'but!'—symbols have a powerful effect on the human mind. Which in turn causes emotion."

Noah said, "I had this feeling once before. About a strange woman, and I had no way of knowing if she's my 'haplotype'!"

Lisa's gaze sharpened. She stood. "What woman? Where?"

"I don't know her name. Listen, I want to talk to my mother!"

"Talk to me first. Are you a sugarcane user, Noah?"

"What the hell does that have to do with anything?"

"Habitual use of sugarcane heightens certain imaginative and perceptual pathways in the brain. Ambassador Smith—well, let's set that aside for a moment. I think I know why you want to see your mother."

Noah said, "Look, I don't want to be ruder than I've already been, but this isn't your business. Anything you want to say to me can wait until I see my mother."

"All right. I can take you to her lab."

It was a long walk. Noah took in very little of what they passed, but then, there was very little to take in. Endless white corridors, endless white doors. When they entered a lab, two people that Noah didn't know looked up curiously. Lisa said, "Dr. Jenner—"

The other woman gestured at a far door. Before she could speak, Noah flung the door open. His mother sat at a small table, hands wrapped around a cup of coffee she wasn't drinking. Her eyes widened.

Noah said, "Mom—why the fuck didn't you ever tell me I was adopted?"

Marianne

Evan and Marianne sat in his room, drinking sixteen-year-old single-malt Scotch. She seldom drank but knew that Evan often did. Nor had she ever gone before to his quarters in the *Embassy*, which were identical to hers: ten-foot square room with a bed, chest of drawers, small table, and two chairs. She sat on one of the straight-backed, utilitarian chairs while Evan lounged on the bed. Most of the scientists had brought with them a few items from home, but Evan's room was completely impersonal. No art, no framed family photos, no decorative pillows, not even a coffee mug or extra doughnut carried off from the cafeteria.

"You live like a monk," Marianne said, immediately realizing how drunk she must be to say that. She took another sip of Scotch.

"Why didn't you ever tell him?" Evan said.

She put down her glass and pulled at the skin on her face. The skin felt distant, as if it belonged to somebody else.

"Oh, Evan, how to answer that? First Noah was too little to understand. Kyle and I adopted him in some sort of stupid effort to save the marriage. I wasn't thinking straight—living with an alcoholic will do that, you know. If there was one stupid B-movie scene of alcoholic and wife that we missed, I don't know what it was. Shouting, pleading, pouring away all the liquor in the house, looking for Kyle in bars at two a.m. . . . . anyway. Then Kyle died and I was trying to deal with that and the kids and chasing tenure and there was just too much chaos and fragility to add another big revelation. Then somehow it got too late, because Noah would have asked why he hadn't been told before, and then somehow . . . it all just got away from me."

"And Elizabeth and Ryan never told him?"

"Evidently not. We yell a lot about politics and such but on a personal level, we're a pretty reticent family." She waved her hand vaguely at the room. "Although not as reticent as you."

Evan smiled. "I'm British of a certain class."

"You're an enigma."

"No, that was the Russians. Enigmas wrapped in riddles." But a shadow passed suddenly behind his eyes.

"What do you—"

"Marianne, let me fill you in on the bits and pieces of news that came in while you were with Noah. First, from the Denebs: they're bringing aboard the *Embassy* any members of their 'clan'—that's what the translator is calling the L7 haplogroup—who want to come. But you already know that. Second, the—"

"How many?"

"How many have we identified or how many want to come here?"

"Both." The number of L7 haplotypes had jumped exponentially once they had the first few and could trace family trees through the female line.

"Sixty-three identified, including the three that Gina flew to Georgia to test. Most of the haplogroup may still be in Africa, or it may have largely died out. Ten of those want to visit the *Embassy*." He hesitated. "So far, only Noah wants to stay."

Marianne's hand paused, glass halfway to her mouth. "To *stay*? He didn't tell me that. How do you know?"

"After Noah . . . left you this afternoon, Smith came to the lab with that message."

"I see." She didn't. She had been in her room, pulling herself together after the harrowing interview with her son. Her adopted son. She hadn't been able to tell Noah anything about his parentage because she hadn't known anything: sealed adoption records. Was Noah the way he was because of his genes? Or because of the way she'd raised him? Because of his peer group? His astrological sign? Theories went in and out of fashion, and none of them explained personality.

She said, "What is Noah going to *do* here? He's not a scientist, not security, not an administrator . . . " *Not anything.* It hurt her to even think it. Her baby, her lost one.

Evan said, "I have no idea. I imagine he'll either sort himself out or leave. The other news is that the Biology Team has made progress in matching

Terran and Deneb immune system components. There were a lot of graphs and charts and details, but the bottom line is that ours and theirs match pretty well. Remarkably little genetic drift. Different antibodies, of course for different pathogens, and quite a lot of those, so no chance we'll be touching skin without their wearing their energy shields."

"So cancel the orgy."

Evan laughed. Emboldened by this as much as by the drink, Marianne said, "Are you gay?"

"You know I am, Marianne."

"I wanted to be sure. We've never discussed it. I'm a scientist, after all."

"You're an American. Leave nothing unsaid that can be shouted from rooftops."

Her fuzzy mind had gone back to Noah. "I failed my son, Evan."

"Rubbish. I told you, he'll sort himself out eventually. Just be prepared for the idea that it may take a direction you don't fancy."

Again that shadow in Evan's eyes. She didn't ask; he obviously didn't want to discuss it, and she'd snooped enough. Carefully she rose to leave, but Evan's next words stopped her.

"Also, Elizabeth is coming aboard tomorrow."

"*Elizabeth*? Why?"

"A talk with Smith about shore-side security. Someone tried a second attack at the sample collection site shore-side."

"Oh my God. Anybody hurt?"

"No. This time."

"Elizabeth is going to ask the Denebs to give her the energy-shield technology. She's been panting for it for border patrol ever since the *Embassy* first landed in the harbor. Evan, that would be a *disaster*. She's so focused on her job that she can't see what will happen if—no, when—the street finds its own uses for the tech, and it always does—" Who had said that? Some writer. She couldn't remember.

"Well, don't get your knickers in a twist. Elizabeth can ask, but that doesn't mean that Smith will agree."

"But he's so eager to find his 'clan'—God, it's so stupid! That Korean mitochondrial sequence, to take just one example, that turns up regularly in Norwegian fisherman, or that engineer in Minnesota who'd traced his ancestry back three hundred years without being able to account for the Polynesian mitochondrial signature he carries—*nobody* has a cure 'plan.' I mean, pure 'clan.' "

"Nobody on Earth, anyway."

"And even if they did," she barreled on, although all at once her words seem to have become slippery in her mouth, like raw oysters, "There's no sig . . . sif . . . significant connection between two people with the same mitochondrial DNA than between any other two strangers!"

"Not to us," Evan said. "Marianne, go to bed. You're too tipsy, and we have work to do in the morning."

"It's not work that matters to protection against the shore cloud. Spore cloud. *Spore cloud*."

"Nonetheless, it's work. Now go."

Noah

Noah stood in a corner of the conference room, which held eleven people and two aliens. Someone had tried to make the room festive with a red paper tablecloth, flowers, and plates of tiny cupcakes. This had not worked. It was still a utilitarian, corporate-looking conference room, filled with people who otherwise would have no conceivable reason to be together at either a conference or a party. Lisa Guiterrez circulated among them: smiling, chatting, trying to put people at ease. It wasn't working.

Two young women, standing close together for emotional support. A middle-aged man in an Armani suit and Italian leather shoes. An unshaven man, hair in a dirty ponytail, who looked homeless but maybe only because he stood next to Well-Shod Armani. A woman carrying a plastic tote bag with a hole in one corner. And so on and so on. It was the sort of wildly mixed group that made Noah, standing apart with his back to a wall, think of worshippers in an Italian cathedral.

The thought brought him a strained smile. A man nearby, perhaps emboldened by the smile, sidled closer and whispered, "They *will* let us go back to New York, won't they?"

Noah blinked. "Why wouldn't they, if that's what you want?"

"I want them to offer us shields for the spore cloud! To take back with us to the city! Why else would I come here?"

"I don't know."

The man grimaced and moved away. But—why had he even come, if he suspected alien abduction or imprisonment or whatever? And why didn't he feel what Noah did? Every single one of the people in this room had caused in him the same shock of recognition as had Ambassador Smith. Every single one. And apparently no one else had felt it at all.

But the nervous man needn't have worried. When the party and its ceiling-delivered speeches of kinship and the invitation to make a longer visit aboard the *Embassy* were all over, everyone else left. They left looking relieved or still curious or satisfied or uneasy or disappointed (no energy shield offered! No riches!), but they all left, Lisa still chattering reassuringly. All except Noah.

Ambassador Smith came over to him. The Deneb said nothing, merely silently waited. He looked as if he were capable of waiting forever.

Noah's hands felt clammy. All those brief, temporary lives on sugarcane, each one shed like a snakeskin when the drug wore off. No, not snakeskins; that wasn't the right analogy. More like breadcrumbs tossed by Hansel and Gretel, starting in hope but vanishing before they could lead anywhere. The man with the dirty ponytail wasn't the only homeless one.

Noah said, "I want to know who and what you are."

The ceiling above Smith said, "Come with me to a genuine celebration."

A circular room, very small. Noah and Smith faced each other. The ceiling said, "This is an airlock. Beyond this space, the environment will be ours, not yours. It is not very different, but you are not used to our microbes and so must wear the energy suit. It filters air, but you may have some trouble breathing at first because the oxygen content of World is like Earth's at an altitude of twelve thousand feet. If you feel nausea in the airlock, where we will stay for a few minutes, you may go back. The light will seem dim to you, the smells strange, and the gravity less than you are accustomed to by one-tenth. There are no built-in translators beyond this point, and we will speak our own language, so you will not be able to talk to us. Are you sure you wish to come?"

"Yes," Noah said.

"Is there anything you wish to say before you join your birthright clan?"

Noah said, "What is your name?"

Smith smiled. He made a noise that sounded like a trilled version of *meehao*, with a click on the end.

Noah imitated it.

Smith said, in trilling English decorated with a click, "Brother mine."

Marianne

Marianne was not present at the meeting between Elizabeth and Smith, but Elizabeth came to see her afterward. Marianne and Max were bent over the computer, trying to account for what was a mitochondrial anomaly or a sample contamination or a lab error or a program glitch. Or maybe something else entirely. Marianne straightened and said, "Elizabeth! How nice to—"

"You have to talk to him," Elizabeth demanded. "The man's an idiot!"

Marianne glanced at the security officer who had escorted Elizabeth to the lab. He nodded and went outside. Max said, "I'll just . . . uh . . . this can wait." He practically bolted, a male fleeing mother-daughter drama. Evan was getting some much-needed sleep; Gina had gone ashore to Brooklyn to see her parents for the first time in weeks.

"I assume," Marianne said, "you mean Ambassador Smith."

"I do. Does he know what's going on in New York? Does he even care?"

"What's going on in New York?"

Elizabeth instantly turned professional, calmer but no less intense. "We are less than nine months from passing through the spore cloud."

At least, Marianne thought, *she now accepts that much.*

"In the last month alone, the five boroughs have had triple the usual rate of arsons, ten demonstrations with city permits of which three turned violent, twenty-three homicides, and one mass religious suicide at the Church of the Next Step Forward in Tribeca. Wall Street has plunged. The Federal Reserve Bank on Liberty Street was occupied from Tuesday night until Thursday dawn by terrorists. Upstate, the governor's mansion has been attacked, unsuccessfully. The same thing is happening everywhere else. Parts of Beijing have been on fire for a week now. Thirty-six percent of Americans believe the Denebs brought the spore cloud with them, despite what astronomers say. If the ambassador gave us the energy shield, that might help sway the numbers in their favor. Don't you think the president and the UN have said all this to Smith?"

"I have no idea what the president and the UN have said, and neither do you."

"Mom—"

"Elizabeth, do you suppose that if what you just said is true and the ambassador said no to the president, that my intervention would do any good?"

"I don't know. You scientists stick together."

Long ago, Marianne had observed the many different ways people responded to unthinkable catastrophe. Some panicked. Some bargained. Some joked. Some denied. Some blamed. Some destroyed. Some prayed. Some drank. Some thrilled, as if they had secretly awaited such drama their entire lives. Evidently, nothing had changed.

The people aboard the *Embassy* met the unthinkable with work, and then more work. Elizabeth was right that the artificial island had become its own self-contained, self-referential universe, every moment devoted to the search for something, anything, to counteract the effect of the spore cloud on mammalian brains. The Denebs, understanding how good hackers could be, blocked all Internet, television, and radio from the Embassy. Outside news came from newspapers or letters, both dying media, brought in the twice-daily mail sack and by the vendors and scientists and diplomats who came and went. Marianne had not paid attention.

She said to her enraged daughter, "The Denebs are not going to give you their energy shield."

"We cannot protect the UN without it. Let alone the rest of the harbor area."

"Then send all the ambassadors and translators home, because it's not going to happen. I'm sorry, but it's not."

"You're not sorry. You're on their side."

"It isn't a question of sides. In the wrong hands, those shields—"

"Law enforcement is the right hands!"

"Elizabeth, we've been over and over this. Let's not do it again. You know I have no power to get you an energy shield, and I haven't seen you in so long. Let's not quarrel." Marianne heard the pleading note in her own voice. When, in the long and complicated road of parenthood, had she started courting her daughter's agreement, instead of the other way around?

"Okay, *okay*. How are you, Mom?"

"Overworked and harried. How are you?"

"Overworked and harried." A reluctant half-smile. "I can't stay long. How about a tour?"

"Sure. This is my lab."

"I meant of the *Embassy*. I've never been inside before, you know, and your ambassador—" somehow Smith had become Marianne's special burden "—just met with me in a room by the submarine bay. Can I see more? Or are you lab types kept close to your cages?"

The challenge, intended or not, worked. Marianne showed Elizabeth all over the Terran part of the *Embassy*, accompanied by a security officer whom Elizabeth ignored. Her eyes darted everywhere, noted everything. Finally she said, "Where do the Denebs live?"

"Behind these doors here. No one has ever been in there."

"Interesting. It's pretty close to the high-risk labs. And where is Noah?"

Yesterday's bitter scene with Noah, when he'd been so angry because she'd never told him he was adopted, still felt like an open wound. Marianne didn't want to admit to Elizabeth that she didn't know where he'd gone. "He stays in the Terran visitors' quarters," she said, hoping there was such a place.

Elizabeth nodded. "I have to report back. Thanks for the Cook's tour, Mom."

Marianne wanted to hug her daughter, but Elizabeth had already moved off, heading toward the submarine bay, security at her side. Memory stabbed Marianne: a tiny Elizabeth, five years old, lips set as she walked for the first time toward the school bus she must board alone. It all went by so fast, and when the spore cloud hit, not even memory would be left.

She dashed away the stupid tears and headed back to work.

~

III: S MINUS 8.5 MONTHS

Marianne

The auditorium on the *Embassy* had the same thin, rice-paper-like walls as some of the other non-lab rooms, but these shifted colors like some of the more substantial walls. Slow, complex, subtle patterns in pale colors that reminded Marianne of dissolving oil slicks. Forty seats in rising semi-circles faced a dais, looking exactly like a lecture room at her college. She had an insane desire to regress to undergraduate, pull out a notebook, and doodle in the margin. The seats were filled not with students chewing gum and texting each other, but with some of the planet's most eminent scientists. This was the first all-hands meeting of the scientists aboard. The dais was empty.

Three Denebs entered from a side door.

Marianne had never seen so many of them together at once. Oddly, the effect was to make them seem more alien, as if their minor differences from Terrans—the larger eyes, spindlier limbs, greater height—increased exponentially as their presence increased arithmetically. Was that Ambassador Smith and Scientist Jones? Yes. The third alien, shorter than the other two and somehow softer, said through the translator in the ceiling, "Thank you all for coming. We have three reports today, two from Terran teams and one from World. First, Dr. Manning." All three aliens smiled.

Terrence Manning, head of the Spore Team, took the stage. Marianne had never met him, Nobel Prize winners being as far above her scientific level as the sun above mayflies. A small man, he had exactly three strands of hair left on his head, which he tried to coax into a comb-over. Intelligence shone through his diffident, unusually formal manner. Manning had a deep, authoritative voice, a welcome contrast to the mechanical monotony of the ceiling.

From the aliens' bright-eyed demeanor, Marianne had half expected good news, despite the growing body of data on the ship's LAN. She was wrong.

"We have not," Manning said, "been able to grow the virus in cell cultures. As you all know, some viruses simply will not grow in vitro, and this seems to be one of them. Nor have we been able to infect monkeys—any breed of monkey—with spore disease. We will, of course, keep trying. The better news, however, is that we have succeeded in infecting mice."

Good and bad, Marianne thought. Often, keeping a mouse alive was actually easier than keeping a cell culture growing. But a culture would have given them a more precise measure of the virus's cytopathic effect on animal tissue, and monkeys were genetically closer to humans than were mice. On the other hand, monkeys were notoriously difficult to work with. They bit, they fought, they injured themselves, they traded parasites and diseases, and they died of things they were not supposed to die from.

Manning continued, "We now have a lot of infected mice and our aerosol expert, Dr. Belsky, has made a determination of how much exposure is needed to cause spore disease in mice under laboratory conditions."

A graph flashed onto the wall behind Manning: exposure time plotted versus parts per million of spore. Beside Marianne, Evan's manicured fingers balled into a sudden fist. Infection was fast, and required a shockingly small concentration of virus, even for an airborne pathogen.

"Despite the infected mice," Manning went on, and now the strain in his voice was palpable, "we still have not been able to isolate the virus. It's an elusive little bugger."

No one laughed. Marianne, although this was not her field, knew how difficult it could be to find a virus even after you'd identified the host. They were so tiny; they disappeared into cells or organs; they mutated.

"Basically," Manning said, running his hand over his head and disarranging his three hairs, "we know almost nothing about this pathogen. Not the *r nought*—for you astronomers, that is the number of cases that one case generates on average over the course of its infectious period—nor the incubation period nor the genome nor the morphology. What we do know are the composition of the coating encapsulating the virus, the transmission vector, and the resulting pathology in mice."

Ten minutes of data on the weird, unique coating on the "spores," a term even the scientists, who knew better, now used. Then Dr. Jessica Yu took Manning's place on the dais. Marianne had met her in the cafeteria and felt intimidated. The former head of the Special Pathogens branch of the National Center for Infectious Diseases in Atlanta, Jessica Yu was diminutive, fifty-ish, and beautiful in a severe, don't-mess-with-me way. Nobody ever did.

She said, "We are, of course, hoping that gaining insight into the mechanism of the disease in animals will help us figure out how to treat it in humans. These mice were infected three days ago. An hour ago they began to show symptoms, which we wanted all of you to see before . . . .well, before."

The wall behind Jessica Yu de-opaqued, taking the exposure graphic with it. Or some sort of viewscreen now overlay the wall and the three mice now revealed were someplace else in the *Embassy*. The mice occupied a large glass cage in what Marianne recognized as a BSL4 lab.

Two of the mice lay flat, twitching and making short whooshing sounds, much amplified by the audio system. No, not amplified—those were desperate gasps as the creatures fought for air. Their tails lashed and their front paws scrambled. They were, Marianne realized, trying to *swim* away from whatever was downing them.

"In humans," Yu continued, "we would call this ARDS—Adult Respiratory Distress Syndrome, a catch-all diagnosis used when we don't know what the problem is. The mouse lung tissue is becoming heavier and heavier as fluid from the blood seeps into the lungs and each breath takes more and more effort. X-rays of lung tissue show 'white-out'—so much fluid in the lungs increasing the radiological density that the image looks like a snowstorm. The viral incubation period in mice is three days. The time from onset of symptoms until death averages 2.6 hours."

The third mouse began to twitch.

Yu continued, her whole tiny body rigid, "As determined thus far, the infection rate in mice is about seventy-five percent. We can't, of course, make any assumptions that it would be the same in humans. Nor do we have any idea why mice are infected but monkeys are not. The medical data made available from the Deneb colonies do indicate similar metabolic pathways to those of the mice. Those colonies had no survivors. Autopsies on the mice further indicate—"

A deep nausea took Marianne, reaching all the way from throat to rectum. She was surprised; her training was supposed to inure her. It did not. Before her body could disgrace her by retching or even vomiting, she squeezed past Evan with a push on his shoulder to indicate he should stay and hear the rest. In the corridor outside the auditorium she leaned against the wall, lowered her head between her knees, breathed deeply, and let shame overcome horror.

No way for a scientist to react to data—

The shame was not strong enough. It was her children that the horror brought: Elizabeth and Ryan and Noah, mouths open as they tried to force air into their lungs, wheezing and gasping, drowning where they lay . . . and Connie and the as-yet-unborn baby, her first grandchild. . . .

Stop. It's no worse for you than for anybody else.

Marianne stood. She dug the nails of her right hand into the palm of her left. But she could not make herself go back into the auditorium. Evan would have to tell her what other monstrosities were revealed. She made her way back to her lab.

Max sat at the computer, crunching data. Gina looked up from her bench. "Marianne—we found two more L7 donors."

"Good," Marianne said, went through the lab to her tiny office behind, and closed the door firmly. What did it matter how many L7s she found for Smith? Earth was finished. Eight-and-a-half months left, and the finest medical and scientific brains on the planet had not even begun to find any way to mitigate the horror to come.

Gina knocked on the office door. "Marianne? Are you all right?"

Gina was the same age as Ryan, a young woman with her whole life still ahead of her. If she got that life. Meanwhile, there was no point in making the present even worse. Marianne forced cheerfulness into her voice. "Yes, fine. I'll be right out. Put on a fresh pot of coffee, would you please?"

Noah

Noah stood with his clan and prepared to *lllathil*.

There was no word for it in English. Part dance, part religious ceremony, part frat kegger, and it went on for two days. Ten L7s stood in a circle, all in various stages of drunkenness. When the weird, atonal music (but after two months aboard the *Embassy* it no longer sounded weird or atonal to his ears) began, they weaved in and out, making precise figures on the floor with the red paint on their feet. Once the figures had been sacred, part of a primitive religion that had faded with the rapid growth of science nurtured by their planet's lush and easy environment. The ritual remained. It affirmed family, always matrilineal on World. It affirmed connection, obligation, identity. Whenever the larger of World's moons was lined up in a certain way with the smaller, Worlders came together with their families and joyously made lllathil. Circles always held ten, and as many circles were made as a family needed. It didn't matter where you were on World, or what you were doing, when lllathil came, you were there.

His mother would never have understood.

The third morning, after everyone had slept off the celebration, came the second part of lllathil, which Marianne would have understood even less. Each person gave away one-fifth of everything he had earned or made since the last lllathil. He gave it, this "thumb" as it was jokingly called, to someone in his circle. Different clans gave different percentages and handled that in different ways, but some version of the custom mostly held over mostly monocultural World. The Denebs were a sophisticated race; such a gift involved transfers of the Terran equivalent of bank accounts, stock holdings, real estate. The Denebs were also human, and so sometimes the gift was made grudgingly, or with anger at a cousin's laziness, or resignedly, or with cheating. But it was made, and there wasn't very much cheating. Or so said Mee^hao¡, formerly known to Noah as Smith, who'd told him so in the trilling and clicking language that Noah was trying so hard to master. "We teach our children very intensively to follow our ways," Smith said wryly. "Of course, some do not. Some always are different."

"You said it, brother," Noah said in English, to Smith's total incomprehension.

Noah loved lllathil. He had very little—nothing, really—to give, but his net gain was not the reason he loved it. Nor was that the reason he studied the Worldese for hours every day, aided by his natural ear for languages. Once, in his brief and abortive attempted at college, Noah had heard a famous poet say that factual truth and emotional truth were not the same. "You have to understand with your belly," she'd said.

He did. For the first time in his life, he did.

His feet made a mistake, leaving a red toe print on the floor in the wrong place. No one chided him. Cliclimi, her old face wrinkling into crevasses and hills and dales, a whole topography of kinship, just laughed at him and reached out her skinny arm to fondly touch his.

Noah, not like that. Color in the lines!

Noah, this isn't the report card I expect of you.

Noah, you can't come with me and my friends! You're too little!

Noah, can't you do anything right? When he'd danced until he could no longer stand (Cliclimi was still going at it, but she hadn't drunk as much as Noah had), he dropped onto a large cushion beside "Jones," whose real name he still couldn't pronounce. It had more trills than most, and a strange tongue sound he could not reproduce at all. She was flushed, her hair unbound from its usual tight arrangement. Smaller than he was but stockier, her caramel-colored flesh glowed with exertion. The hair, rich dark brown, glinted in the rosy light. Her red tunic—everybody wore red for lllathil—had hiked high on her thighs.

Noah heard his mother's voice say, "A hundred fifty thousand years is not enough time for a species to diverge." To his horror, he felt himself blush.

She didn't notice, or else she took it as warmth from the dancing. She said, "Do you have trouble with our gravity?"

Proud of himself that he understood the words, he said, "No. It small amount big of Earth." At least, he hoped that's what he'd said.

Apparently it was. She smiled and said something he didn't understand. She stretched luxuriously, and the tunic rode up another two inches.

What were the kinship taboos on sex? What were any of the taboos on sex? Not that Noah could have touched her skin-to-skin, anyway. He was encased, so unobtrusively that he usually forgot it was there, in the "energy suit" that protected him from alien microbes.

Microbes. Spores. How much time was left before the cloud hit Earth? At the moment it didn't seem important. (*Noah, you can't just pretend problems don't exist!* That had usually been Elizabeth.)

He said, "Can—yes, no?—make my—" Damn it, what was the word for microbes? "—my inside like you? My inside spores?"

IV: S MINUS 6.5 MONTHS

Marianne

Gina had not returned from Brooklyn on the day's last submarine run. Marianne was redoing an entire batch of DNA amplification that had somehow become contaminated. Evan picked up the mail sack and the news dispatches. When he came into the lab, where Marianne was cursing at a row of beakers, he uncharacteristically put both hands on her shoulders. She looked at his face.

"What is it? Tell me quickly."

"Gina is dead."

She put a hand onto the lab bench to steady herself. "How?"

"A mob. They were frighteningly well armed, almost a small army. End-of-the-world rioters."

"Was Gina . . . did she . . . ?"

"A bullet, very quick. She didn't suffer, Marianne. Do you want a drink? I have some rather good Scotch."

"No. Thank you, but no."

Gina. Marianne could picture her so clearly, as if she still stood in the lab in the wrinkled white coat she always wore even though the rest of them did not. Her dark hair just touched with gray, her ruddy face calm. Brisk, pleasant, competent. . . . What else? Marianne hadn't known Gina very well. All at once, she wondered if she knew anyone, really knew them. Two of her children baffled her: Elizabeth's endemic anger, Noah's drifty aimlessness. Had she ever known Kyle, the man he was under the charming and lying surface, under the alcoholism? Evan's personal life was kept personal, and she'd assumed it was his British reticence, but maybe she knew so little about him because of her limitations, not his. With everyone else aboard the *Embassy*, as with her university department back home, she exchanged only scientific information or meaningless pleasantries. She hadn't seen her brother, to whom she'd never been close, in nearly two years. Her last close female friendship had been over a decade ago.

Thinking this way felt strange, frightening. She was glad when Evan said, "Where's Max? I'll tell him about Gina."

"Gone to bed with a cold. It can wait until morning. What's that?"

Evan gave her a letter, addressed by hand. Marianne tore it open. "It's from Ryan. The baby was born, a month early but he's fine and so is she. Six pounds two ounces. They're naming him Jason William Jenner."

"Congratulations. You're a nan."

"A what?"

"Grand-mum." He kissed her cheek.

She turned to cling to him, without passion, in sudden need of the simple comfort of human touch. Evan smelled of damp wool and some cool, minty lotion. He patted her back. "What's all this, then?"

"I'm sorry, I—"

"Don't be sorry." He held her until she was ready to pull away.

"I think I should write to Gina's parents."

"Yes, that's right."

"I want to make them understand—" Understand what? That sometimes children were lost, and the reasons didn't necessarily make sense. But this reason did make sense, didn't it? Gina had died because she'd been aboard the *Embassy*, died as a result of the work she did, and right now this was the most necessary work in the entire world.

She had a sudden memory of Noah, fifteen, shouting at her: "You're never home! Work is all you care about!" And she, like so many beleaguered parents, had shouted back, "If it weren't for my work, we'd all starve!"

And yet, when the kids had all left home and she could work as much as she wanted or needed without guilt, she'd missed them dreadfully. She'd missed the harried driving schedules—*I have to be at Jennifer's at eight* and *Soccer practice is moved up an hour Saturday!* She'd missed their electronics, cells and iPods and tablets and laptops, plugged in all of the old house's inadequate outlets. She'd missed the rainbow laundry in the basement, Ryan's red soccer shirts and Elizabeth's white jeans catastrophically dyed pink and Noah's yellow-and-black bumblebee costume for the second-grade play. All gone. When your children were small you worried that they would die and you would lose them, and then they grew up and you ended up losing the children they'd been, anyway.

Marianne pulled at the skin on her face and steeled herself to write to Gina's parents.

Noah

There were three of them now. Noah Jenner, Jacqui Young, Oliver Pardo. But only Noah was undergoing the change.

They lounged this afternoon in the World garden aboard the *Embassy*, where the ceiling seemed to be open to an alien sky. A strange orange shone, larger than Sol and yet not shedding as much light, creating a dim glow over the three Terrans. The garden plants were all dark in hue ("To gather as much light as possible," Mee^hao¡ had said), lush leaves in olive drab and pine and asparagus. Water trickled over rocks or fell in high, thin streams. Warmth enveloped Noah even though his energy suit, and he felt light on the ground in the lesser gravity. Some nearby flower sent out a strange, musky, heady fragrance on the slight breeze.

Jacqui, an energetic and enormously intelligent graduate student, had chosen to move into the alien section of the *Embassy* in order to do research. She was frank, with both Terrans and Denebs, that she was not going to stay after she had gathered the unique data on Deneb culture that would ensure her academic career. Smith said that was all right, she was clan and so welcome for as long as she chose. Noah wondered how she planned on even having an academic career after the spore cloud hit.

Oliver Pardo would have been given the part of geek by any film casting department with no imagination. Overweight, computer-savvy, fan of superheroes, he quoted obscure science-fiction books sixty years old and drew endless pictures of girls in improbable costumes slaying dragons or frost giants. Socially inept, he was nonetheless gentle and sweet-natured, and Noah preferred his company to Jacqui's, who asked too many questions.

"Why?" she said.

"Why what?" Noah said, even though he knew perfectly well what she meant. He lounged back on the comfortable moss and closed his eyes.

"Why are you undergoing this punishing regime of shots just so you can take off your shield?"

"They're not shots," Noah said. Whatever the Denebs were doing to him, they did it by having him apply patches to himself when he was out of his energy suit and in an isolation chamber. This had happened once a week for a while now. The treatments left him nauseated, dizzy, sometimes with diarrhea, and always elated. There was only one more to go.

Jacqui said, "Shots or whatever, why do it?"

Oliver looked up from his drawing of a barbarian girl riding a lion. "Isn't it obvious?"

Jacqui said, "Not to me."

Oliver said, "Noah wants to become an alien."

"No," Noah said. "I was an alien. Now I'm becoming . . .not one."

Jacqui's pitying look said *You need help*. Oliver shaded in the lion's mane. Noah wondered why, of all the Terrans of L7 mitochondrial haplotype, he was stuck with these two. He stood. "I have to study."

"I wish I had your fluency in Worldese," Jacqui said. "It would help my work so much."

So study it. But Noah knew she wouldn't, not the way he was doing. She wanted the quick harvest of startling data, not . . . whatever it was he wanted.

Becoming an alien. Oliver was more correct than Noah's flip answer. And yet Noah had been right, too, which was something he could never explain to anyone, least of all his mother. Whom he was supposed to visit this morning, since she could not come to him.

All at once Noah knew that he was not going to keep that appointment. Although he flinched at the thought of hurting Marianne, he was not going to leave the World section of the *Embassy*. Not now, not ever. He couldn't account for this feeling, so strong that it seemed to infuse his entire being, like oxygen in the blood. But he had to stay here, where he belonged. Irrational, but—as Evan would have said—there it was, mustn't grumble, at least it made a change, no use going on about it.

He had never liked Evan.

In his room, Noah took pen and a pad of paper to write a note to his mother. The words did not come easy. All his life he had disappointed her, but not like this.

Dear Mom—I know we were going to get together this afternoon but—

Dear Mom—I wish I could see you as we planned but—

Dear Mom—We need to postpone our visit because Ambassador Smith has asked me if this afternoon I would—

Noah pulled at the skin on his face, realized that was his mother's gesture, and stopped. He looked longingly at the little cubes that held his language lessons. As the cube spoke Worldese, holofigures in the cube acted out the meaning. After Noah repeated each phrase, it corrected his pronunciation until he got it right.

"My two brothers live with my mother and me in this dwelling," a smiling girl said in the holocube, in Worldese. Two boys, one younger than she and one much older, appeared beside her with a much older woman behind them, all four with similar features, a shimmering dome behind them.

"My two brothers live with my mother and me in this dwelling," Noah repeated. The Worldese tenses were tricky; these verbs were the ones for things that not only could change, but could change without the speaker's having much say about events. A mother could die. The family could be chosen for a space colony. The older brother could marry and move in with his wife's family.

Sometimes things were beyond your control and you had no real choice.

Dear Mom—I can't come. I'm sorry. I love you. Noah

Marianne

The work—anybody's work—was not going well.

It seemed to be proceeding at an astonishing pace, but Marianne—and everyone else—knew that was an illusion. She sat in the auditorium for the monthly report, Evan beside her. This time, no Denebs were present—why not? She listened to Terence Manning enumerate what under any other circumstances would have been incredibly rapid triumphs.

"We have succeeded in isolating the virus," Manning said, "although not in growing it in vitro. After isolation, we amplified it with the usual polymerase processes. The virus has been sequenced and—only a few days ago!—captured on an electromicrograph image, which, as most of you know, can be notoriously difficult. Here it is."

A graphic appeared on the wall behind Manning: fuzzy concentric circles blending into each other in shades of gray. Manning ran his hand over his head, now completely bald. Had he shaved his last three hairs, Marianne wondered irrelevantly. Or had they just given up and fallen out from stress?

"The virion appears to be related to known paramyxoviruses, although the gene sequence, which we now have, does not exactly match any of them. It is a negative-sense single-stranded RNA viruses. Paramyxoviruses, to which it may or may not be directly related, are responsible for a number of human and animal diseases, including parainfluenza, mumps, measles, pneumonia, and canine distemper. This family of viruses jumps species more easily than any other. From what we have determined so far, it most closely resembles both Hendra and Nipah viruses, which are highly contagious and highly virulent.

"The genome follows the paramyxovirus 'Rule of Six,' in that the total length of the genome is almost always a multiple of six. The spore virus consists of twenty-one genes with 21,645 base pairs. That makes it a large virus, but by no means the largest we know. Details of sequence, structure, envelope proteins, etc. can be found on the LAN. I want to especially thank Drs. Yu, Sedley, and Lapka for their valuable work in identifying *Respirovirus sporii*."

Applause. Marianne still stared at the simple, deadly image behind Manning. An unwelcome thought had seized her: the viral image looked not unlike a fuzzy picture of a not-too-well-preserved trilobite. Trilobites had been the dominant life form on Earth for three hundred million years and comprised more than ten thousand species. All gone now. Humans could be gone, too, after a much briefer reign.

But we survived so much! The Ice Age, terrible predators, the "bottleneck event" of seventy thousand years ago that reduced *Homo sapiens* to mere thousands. . . .

Manning was continuing. This was the bad news. "However, we have made little progress in figuring out how to combat *R. sporii*. Blood from the infected mice has been checked against known viruses and yielded no seriological positives. None of our small number of anti-viral drugs were effective, although there was a slight reaction to ribavirin. That raises a further puzzle, since ribavirin is mostly effective against Lassa fever, which is caused by an arenavirus, not a paramyxovirus." Manning tried to smile; it was not a success. "So, the mystery deepens. I wish we had more to report."

Someone asked, "Are the infected mice making antibodies?"

"Yes," Manning said, "and if we can't manage to develop a vaccine, this is our best possible path to a post-exposure treatment, following the MB-003 model developed for Ebola. For you astronomers—and please forgive me if I am telling you things you already know—a successful post-exposure treatment for Ebola in nonhuman primates was developed two years ago, using a cocktail of monoclonal antibodies. It was the work of a partnership between American industry and government agencies. When administered an hour after infection, MB-003 yields a one hundred percent survival rate. At forty-eight hours, the survival rate is two-thirds. MB-003 was initially developed in a mouse model and then produced in plants. The work took ten years. It has not, of course, been tested in humans."

Ten years. The *Embassy* scientists had less than five months left. Ebola had previously been studied since its first outbreak in 1976. And the biggie: *It has not, of course, been tested in humans.* In whom it might, for all anyone knew, not even work.

Maybe the Denebs knew faster ways to produce a vaccine from antibodies, exponentially increase production, and distribute the results. But the aliens weren't even at this meeting. They had surely been given all this information already, but even so—

—Where the hell were the aliens that was more important than this?

V: S MINUS 3.5 MONTHS

Marianne

Marianne felt ridiculous. She and Evan leaned close over the sink in the lab. Water gushed full-strength from the tap, making noise that, she hoped, covered their words. The autoclave hummed; a Bach concerto played tinnily on the computer's inadequate speaker. The whole thing felt like a parody of a bad spy movie.

They had never been able to decide if the labs, if everywhere on the *Embassy*, were bugged. Evan had said yes, of course, don't be daft. Max, with the hubris of the young, had said no because his computer skills would have been able to detect any surveillance. Marianne and Gina had said it was irrelevant since both their work and their personal lives were so transparent. In addition, Marianne had disliked the implication that the Denebs were not their full and open partners. Gina had said—

Gina. Shot down, her life ended just as Jason William Jenner's had begun. And for how long? Would Marianne even get to see her grandson before everything was as over as Gina's life?

Dangerous to think this way. Their work on the *Embassy* was a thin bridge laid across a pit of despair, the same despair that had undoubtedly fueled Gina's killers.

"You know what has to happen," Marianne whispered. "Nobody's saying it aloud, but without virus replication in human bodies, we just can't understand the effect on the immune system and we're working blindly. Mice aren't enough. Even if we could have infected monkeys, it wouldn't be enough. We have to infect volunteers."

Evan stuck his finger into the flow of water, which spattered in bright drops against the side of the sink. "I know. *Everyone* knows. The request has been made to the powers that be."

"How do you know that?"

"I talk to people on the other teams. You know the laws against experimentation on humans unless there have first been proper clinical trials that—"

"Oh, fuck proper trials, this is a crisis situation!"

"Not enough people in power are completely convinced of that. You haven't been paying attention to the bigger picture, Marianne. The Public Health Service isn't even gearing up for mass inoculation or protection—Robinson is fighting it with claw and tusk. FEMA is divided and there's almost anarchy in the ranks. Congress just filibusters on the whole topic. And the president just doesn't have the votes to get much of anything done. Meanwhile, the masses riot or flee or just pretend the whole thing is some sort of hoax. The farther one gets from New York, the more the conspiracy theorists don't even believe there are aliens on Earth at all."

Marianne, still standing, pulled at the skin on her face. "It's all so frustrating. And the work we're doing here—you and I and Max and Gina—" her voice faltered "—is pointless. It really is. Identifying members of Smith's so-called clan? Who cares? I'm going to volunteer myself to be infected."

"They won't take you."

"If—"

"The only way that could happen is in secret. If a subgroup on the Spore Team decided the situation was desperate enough to conduct an unauthorized experiment."

She studied his face. In the biology department at the university, Evan had always been the one who knew how to obtain travel money for a conference, interviews with Nobel Prize winners, an immediate appointment with the dean. He had the knack, as she did not, for useful connections. She said, "You know something."

"No. I don't. Not yet."

"Find out."

He nodded and turned off the water. The music crescendoed: *Brandenburg Concerto No. 2* that had gone out into space on the "golden record" inside *Voyager 1.*

The secret experiment turned out to be not all that secret.

Evan followed the rumors. Within a day he had found a lab tech in the Biology Group who knew a scientist in the Spore Group who referred him, so obliquely that Evan almost missed it, to a security officer. Evan came to Marianne in her room, where she'd gone instead of eating lunch. He stood close to her and murmured in her ear, ending with, "They'll let us observe. You—what's that, then?"

The last sentence was said in a normal voice. Evan gazed at the piece of paper in Marianne's hands. She had been looking at it since she found it under her door.

"Another note from Noah. He isn't . . . he can't . . . Evan, I need to go ashore to see my new grandchild."

Evan blinked. "Your new grandchild?"

"Yes. He's three months old already and I haven't even seen him."

"It's not safe to leave the *Embassy* now. You know that."

"Yes. But I need to go."

Gently Evan took the note from her and read it. Marianne saw that he didn't really understand. Young, childless, orphaned . . . how could he? Noah had not forgiven her for never telling him that he was adopted. That must be why he said he might not ever see her again; no other reason made sense. Although maybe he would change his mind. Maybe in time he would forgive her, maybe he would not, maybe the world would end first. Before any of those things happened, Marianne had to see little Jason. She had to affirm what family ties she had, no matter how long she had them. Or anyone had them.

She said, "I need to talk to Ambassador Smith. How do I do that?"

He said, "Do you want me to arrange it?"

"Yes. Please. For today."

He didn't mention the backlog of samples in the lab. No one had replaced Gina. As family trees of the L7 haplogroup were traced in the matrilineal line, more and more of Smith's "clan" were coming aboard the *Embassy.* Marianne suspected they hoped to be shielded or transported when the spore cloud hit. She also suspected they were right. The Denebs were . . .

. . . were just as insistent on family connections as she was, risking her life to see Ryan, Connie, and the baby.

Well.

A helicopter flew her directly from the large pier outside the *Embassy* (so that's what it was for). When Marianne had last been outside, autumn was just ending. Now it was spring, the reluctant Northern spring of tulips and late frosts, cherry blossoms and noisy frogs. The Vermont town where Connie's parents lived, and to which Ryan had moved his family for safety, was less than twenty miles from the Canadian border. The house was a pleasant brick faux-Colonial set amid bare fields. Marianne noted, but did not comment on, the spiked chain-link fence around the small property, the electronic-surveillance sticker on the front door, and the large Doberman whose collar Ryan held in restraint. He had hastened home from his fieldwork when she phoned that she was coming.

"Mom! Welcome!"

"We're so glad you're here, Marianne," Connie said warmly. "Even though I suspect it isn't us you came to see!" She grinned and handed over the tiny wrapped bundle.

The baby was asleep. Light-brown fuzz on the top of his head, silky skin lightly flushed with pink, tiny pursed mouth sucking away in an infant dream. He looked so much as Ryan had that tears pricked Marianne's eyes. Immediately she banished them: no sorrow, neither nostalgic nor catastrophic, was going to mar this occasion.

"He's beautiful," she said, inadequately.

"Yes!" Connie was not one of those mothers who felt obliged to disclaim praise of her child.

Marianne held the sleeping baby while coffee was produced. Connie's parents were away, helping Connie's sister, whose husband had just left her and whose three-year-old was ill. This was touched on only lightly. Connie kept the conversation superficial, prattling in her pretty voice about Jason, about the dog's antics, about the weather. Marianne followed suit, keeping to herself the thought that, after all, she had never heard Connie talk about anything but light and cheerful topics. She must have more to her than that, but not in front of her mother-in-law. Ryan said almost nothing, sipping his coffee, listening to his wife.

Finally Connie said, "Oh, I've just been monopolizing the conversation! Tell us about life aboard the *Embassy*. It must be so fascinating!"

Ryan looked directly at Marianne.

She interpreted the look as a request to keep up the superficial tone. Ryan had always been as protective of Connie as of a pretty kitten. Had he deliberately chosen a woman so opposite to his mother because Marianne had always put her work front and center? Had Ryan resented her for that as much as Noah had?

Pushing aside these disturbing thoughts, she chatted about the aliens. Connie asked her to describe them, their clothes, her life there. Did she have her own room? Had she been able to decorate it? Where did the humans eat?

"We're *all* humans, Terrans and Denebs," Marianne said.

"Of course," Connie said, smiling brilliantly. "Is the food good?"

Talking, talking, talking, but not one question about her work. Nor about the spore cloud, progress toward a vaccine, anything to indicate the size and terror of the coming catastrophe. Ryan did ask about the *Embassy*, but only polite questions about its least important aspects: how big it was, how it was laid out, what was the routine. Safe topics.

Just before a sense of unreality overwhelmed Marianne, Ryan's cell rang, and the ringing woke the baby, who promptly threw up all over Marianne.

"Oh, I'm sorry!" Connie said. "Here, give him to me!"

Ryan, making gestures of apology, took his cell into the kitchen and closed the door. Connie reached for a box of Wet Ones and began to wipe Jason's face. She said, "The bathroom is upstairs to the left, Marianne. If you need to, I can loan you something else to wear."

"It would have to be one of your maternity dresses," Marianne said. It came out more sour than she'd intended.

She went upstairs and cleaned baby vomit off her shirt and jeans with a wet towel. The bathroom was decorated in a seaside motif, with hand towels embroidered with sailboats, soap shaped like shells, blue walls painted with green waves and smiling dolphins. On top of the toilet tank, a crocheted cylinder decorated like a buoy held a spare roll of toilet paper.

Keeping chaos at bay with cute domesticity. Good plan. And then: *Stop it, Marianne.*

Using the toilet, she leafed idly through magazines stacked in a rustic basket. *Good Housekeeping, Time*, a Macy's catalogue. She pulled out a loose paper with full-color drawings:

HOW TO TELL PURPLE LOOSESTRIFE
FROM NATIVE PLANTS
DON'T BE FOOLED BY LOOK-ALIKES!

Purple loosestrife leaves are downy with smooth edges. Although usually arranged opposite each other in pairs which alternate down the stalk at 90-degree angles, the leaves may sometimes appear in groups of three. The leaves lack teeth. The flowers, which appear in mid- to late summer, form a showy spike of rose-purple, each with five to seven petals. The stem is stiff, four-sided, and may appear woody at the base of larger plants, which can reach ten feet tall. Average height is four feet. Purple loosestrife can be distinguished from the native winged loosestrife *(Lythrum alatum)*, which it most closely resembles, by its generally larger size, opposite leaves, and more closely placed flowers. It may also be confused with blue vervain (pictured below), which has . . .

At the bottom of the page, someone—presumably Ryan—had hand-drawn in purple ink three stylized versions of a loosestrife spike, then circled one. To Marianne it looked like a violet rocket ship unaccountably sprouting leaves.

Downstairs, Jason had been cleaned up and changed. Marianne played with him the limited games available for three-month-old babies: peek-a-boo, feetsies go up and down, where did the finger go? When he started to fuss and Connie excused herself to nurse him, Marianne said her good-byes and went out to the helicopter waiting in a nearby field. Neighbors had gathered around it, and Ryan was telling them—what? The neighbors looked harmless, but how could you tell? Always, Gina was on her mind. She hugged Ryan fiercely.

As the copter lifted and the house, the town, the countryside got smaller and smaller, Marianne tried not to think of what a failure the visit had been. Yes, she had seen her grandchild. But whatever comfort or connection that had been supposed to bring her, it hadn't. It seemed to her, perhaps irrationally, that never had she felt so alone.

Noah

When Noah woke, he instantly remembered what day it was. For a long moment, he lay still, savoring the knowledge like rich chocolate on the tongue. Then he said good-bye to his room. He would never sleep here, out of his energy suit, again.

Over the months, he had made the room as World as he could. A sleeping mat, thin but with as much give as a mattress, rolled itself tightly as soon as he sprang up and into the tiny shower. On the support wall he had hung one of Oliver's pictures—not a half-dressed barbarian princess this time, but a black-and-white drawing of plants in the World garden. The other walls, which seemed thin as rice paper but somehow kept out sound, had been programmed, at Noah's request, with the subtly shifting colors that the Worlders favored for everything except family gatherings. Color was extremely important to Worlders, and so to Noah. He was learning to discern shades that had once seemed all the same. *This* blue for mourning; *this* blue for adventure; *this* blue for loyalty. He had discarded all his Terran clothes. How had he ever stood the yellow polo shirt, the red hoodie? Wrong, wrong.

Drying his body, he rehearsed his request to Mee^hao¡ (rising inflection in the middle, click at the end—Noah loved saying his name).

Breakfast, like all World meals, was communal, a time to affirm ties. Noah had already eaten in his room; the energy suit did not permit the intake of food. Nonetheless, he took his place in the hierarchy at the long table, above Oliver and Jacqui and below everyone else. That was just. Family solidarity rested on three supports: inclusion, rank, and empathy. A triangle was the strongest of all geometrical figures.

"G'morning," Oliver said, yawning. He was not a morning person, and resented getting up for a breakfast he would not eat until much later.

"I greet you," Noah said in World. Oliver blinked.

Jacqui, quicker, said, "Oh, today is the day, is it? Can I be there?"

"At the ceremony? No, of course not!" Noah said. She should have known better than to even make the request.

"Just asking," Jacqui said. "Doesn't hurt to ask."

Yes, it does. It showed a lack of respect for all three supports in the triangle. Although Noah had not expected any more of Jacqui.

He did expect it of the three Terrans who took their places below Oliver. Isabelle Rhinehart; her younger sister, Kayla; and Kayla's son had come into the World section of the *Embassy* only a week ago, but already the two women were trying to speak Worldese. The child, Austin, was only three—young enough to grow up trilling and clicking Worldese like a native. Noah gazed with envy at the little boy, who smiled shyly and then crawled onto his mother's lap.

But they could not hold Noah's interest long. This was the day!

His stomach growled. He'd been too excited to eat much of the food delivered earlier to his room. And truthfully, the vegetarian World diet was not exciting. But he would learn to like it. And what a small price to pay for . . . *everything.*

The ceremony took place in the same room, right after breakfast. The other Terrans had left. Mee^hao¡ changed the wall program. Now instead of subtly shifting greens, the thin room dividers pulsed with the blue of loyalty alternating with the color of the clan of Mee^hao¡.

Noah knelt in the middle of the circle of Worlders, facing Mee^hao¡, who held a long blue rod. *Now I dub thee Sir Noah . . .* Noah hated, completely hated, that his mind threw up that stupid thought. This was nothing like a feudal knighting. It was more like a baptism, washing him clean of his old self.

Mee^hao¡ sang a verse of what he had been told was the family inclusion song, with everyone else echoing the chorus. Noah didn't catch all the trilling and clicking words, but he didn't have to. Tears pricked his eyes. It seemed to him that he had never wanted anything this much in life, had never really wanted anything at all.

"Stand, brother mine," Mee^hao¡ said.

Noah stood. Mee^hao¡ did something with the rod, and the energy shield dissolved around Noah.

Not only a baptism—an operation.

The first breath of World air almost made him vomit. No, the queasiness was excitement, not the air. It tasted strange, and with the second panicky breath he felt he wasn't getting enough of it. But he knew that was just the lower oxygen content. The *Embassy* was at sea level; the O_2 concentration of World matched that at 12,000 feet. His lungs would adapt. His marrow would produce more red corpuscles. The Worlders had evolved for this; Noah would evolve, too.

The air smelled strange.

His legs buckled slightly, but before Llaa^moh¡, whom he had once known as Jones, could step toward him, Noah braced himself and smiled. He was all right. He was here. He was—

"Brother mine" went around the circle, and then the formalities were over and they all hugged him, and for the first time in one hundred and fifty thousand years years, Terran skin touched the skin of humans from the stars.

Marianne

The security officer met Marianne and Evan in their lab and conducted them to a euchre game in the observation area outside the BSL4 lab.

From the first time she'd come here, Marianne had been appalled by the amateurishness of the entire setup. Granted, this was a bunch of scientists, not the CIA. Still, the Denebs had to wonder why euchre—or backgammon or chess or Monopoly, it varied—was being played here instead of at one of the comfortable Commons or cafeterias. Why two scientists were constantly at work in the negative-pressure lab even when they seemed to have nothing to do. Why the euchre players paid more attention to the screens monitoring the scientists' vitals than to the card game.

Dr. Julia Namechek and Dr. Trevor Lloyd. Both young, strong, and self-infected with spore disease. They moved around the BSL4 lab in full space suits, breathing tubes attached to the air supply in the ceiling. Surely the

Denebs' energy suits would be better for this kind of work, but the suits had not been offered to the Terrans.

"When?" Marianne murmured, playing the nine of clubs.

"Three days ago," said a physician whose name Marianne had not caught.

Spore disease (the name deliberately unimaginative, non-inflammatory) had turned up in mice after three days. Marianne was not a physician, but she could read a vitals screen. Neither Namechek nor Lloyd, busily working in their space suits behind glass, showed the slightest signs of infection. This was, in fact, the third time that the two had tried to infect themselves by breathing in the spores. Each occasion had been preceded by weeks of preparation. Those times, nothing had happened, either, and no one knew why.

Physicians experimenting on themselves were not unknown in research medicine. Edward Jenner had infected himself—and the eight-year-old son of his gardener—with cowpox to develop the smallpox vaccine. Jesse William Lazear infected himself with yellow fever from mosquitoes, in order to confirm that mosquitoes were indeed the transmission vector. Julio Barrera gave himself Argentine hemorrhagic fever; Barry Marshall drank a solution of *H. pylori* to prove the bacterium caused peptic ulcers; Pradeep Seth injected himself with an experimental vaccine for HIV.

Marianne understood the reasons for the supposed secrecy of this experiment. The newspapers that came in on the mail runs glowed luridly with speculations about human experimentation aboard the *Embassy*. Journalists ignited their pages with "Goebbels," "Guatemalan syphilis trials," "Japanese Unit 731." And those were the mainstream journalists. The tabloids and fringe papers invented so many details about Deneb atrocities on humans that the newsprint practically dripped with blood and body parts. The online news sources were, if anything, even worse. No, such "journalists" would never believe that Drs. Namechek and Lloyd had given spore disease to themselves and without the aliens' knowing it.

Actually, Marianne didn't believe that, either. The Denebs were too intelligent, too technologically advanced, too careful. They *had* to know this experiment was going on. They had to be permitting it. No matter how benign and peaceful their culture, they were human. Their lack of interference was a way of ensuring CYA deniability.

"Your turn, Dr. Jenner," said Syed Sharma, a very formal microbiologist from Mumbai. He was the only player wearing a suit.

"Oh, sorry," Marianne said. "What's trump again?"

Evan, her partner, said, "Spades. Don't trump my ace again."

"No table talk, please," Sharma said.

Marianne studied her hand, trying to remember what had been played.

She had never been a good card player. She didn't like cards. And there was nothing to see here, anyway. Evan could bring her the results, if any, of the clandestine experiment. It was possible that the two scientists had not been infected, after all—not this time nor the previous two. It was possible that the pathogen had mutated, or just hadn't taken hold in these two particular people, or was being administered with the wrong vector. Stubbins Firth, despite heroic and disgusting measures, had never succeeded in infecting himself with yellow fever because he never understood how it was transmitted. Pathogen research was still part art, part luck.

"I fold," she said, before she remembered that "folding" was poker, not euchre. She tried a weak smile. "I'm very tired."

"Go to bed, Dr. Jenner," said Seyd Sharma. Marianne gave him a grateful look, which he did not see as he frowned at his cards. She left.

Just as she reached the end of the long corridor leading to the labs, the door opened and a security guard hurried through, face twisted with some strong emotion. Her heart stopped. What fresh disaster now? She said, "Did anything—" but before she could finish the question he had pushed past her and hurried on.

Marianne hesitated. Follow him to hear the news or wait until—

The lab exploded.

Marianne was hurled to the floor. Walls around her, the tough but thin membrane-like walls favored by the Denebs, tore. People screamed, sirens sounded, pulsing pain tore through Marianne's head like a dark, viscous tsunami.

Then everything went black.

She woke alone in a room. Small, white, windowless, with one clear wall, two doors, a pass-through compartment. Immediately, she knew, even before she detected the faint hum of blown air: a quarantine room with negative pressure. The second door, locked, led to a BSL4 operating room for emergency procedures and autopsies. The explosion had exposed her to spores from the experimental lab.

Bandages wreathed her head; she must have hit it when she fell, got a concussion, and needed stitches. Nothing else on her seemed damaged. Gingerly she sat up, aware of the IV tube and catheter and pulse oximeter, and waiting for the headache. It was there, but very faint. Her movement set off a faint gong somewhere and Dr. Ann Potter, a physician whom Marianne knew slightly, appeared on the other side of the clear glass wall.

The doctor said, her voice coming from the ceiling as if she were just one more alien, "You're awake. What do you feel?"

"Headache. Not terrible. What . . . what happened?"

"Let me ask you some questions first." She was asked her name, the date, her location, the name of the president—

"Enough!" Marianne said. "I'm fine! *What happened*?" But she already knew. Hers was the only bed in the quarantine room.

Dr. Potter paid her the compliment of truth. "It was a suicide bomber. He—"

"The others? Evan Blanford?"

"They're all dead. I'm sorry, Dr. Jenner."

Evan. Dead.

Seyd Sharma, with his formal, lilting diction. Julia Namechek, engaged to be married. Trevor Lloyd, whom everyone said would win a Nobel someday. The fourth euchre player, lab tech Alyssa Rosert—all dead.

Evan. Dead.

Marianne couldn't process that, not now. She managed to say, "Tell me. All of it."

Ann Potter's face creased with emotion, but she had herself under control. "The bomber was dressed as a security guard. He had the explosive—I haven't heard yet what it was—in his stomach or rectum, presumably cased to protect it from body fluids. Autopsy showed that the detonator, ceramic so that it got through all our metal detectors, was probably embedded in a tooth, or at least somewhere in his mouth that could be tongued to go off."

Marianne pictured it. Her stomach twisted.

Dr. Potter continued., "His name was Michael Wendl and he was new but legitimately aboard, a sort of mole, I guess you'd call it. A manifesto was all over the Internet an hour after the explosion and this morning—"

"This morning? How long have I been out?"

"Ten hours. You had only a mild concussion but you were sedated to stitch up head lacerations, which of course we wouldn't ordinarily do but this was complicated because—"

"I know," Marianne said, and marveled at the calm in her voice. "I may have been exposed to the spores."

"You *have* been exposed, Marianne. Samples were taken. You're infected."

Marianne set that aside, too, for the moment. She said, "Tell me about the manifesto. What organization?"

"Nobody has claimed credit. The manifesto was about what you'd expect: Denebs planning to kill everyone on Earth, all that shit. Wendl vetted okay when he was hired, so speculation is that he was a new recruit to their cause. He was from somewhere upstate and there's a lot of dissent going on up there. But the thing is, he got it wrong. He was supposed to explode just outside the Deneb section of the *Embassy*, not the research labs. His organization, whatever it was, knew something about the layout of the

Embassy but not enough. Wendl was supposed to be restricted to sub-bay duty. It's like someone who'd had just a brief tour had told him where to go, but either they remembered wrong or he did."

Marianne's spine went cold. *Someone who'd had just a brief tour . . .*

"You had some cranial swelling after the concussion, Marianne, but it's well under control now."

Elizabeth.

No, not possible. Not thinkable.

"You're presently on a steroid administered intravenously, which may have some side effects I'd like you to be aware of, including wakefulness and—"

Elizabeth, studying everything during her visit aboard the *Embassy*: *"Where do the Denebs live?" "Behind these doors here. No one has ever been in there." "Interesting. It's pretty close to the high-risk labs."*

"Marianne, are you listening to me?"

Elizabeth, furiously punching the air months ago: *"I don't believe it, not any of it. There are things they aren't telling us!"*

"Marianne?"

Elizabeth, grudgingly doing her duty to protect the aliens but against her own inclinations. Commanding a critical section of the Border Patrol, a member of the joint task force that had access to military-grade weapons. In an ideal position to get an infiltrator aboard the floating island.

"Marianne! *Are* you listening to me?"

"No," Marianne said. "I have to talk to Ambassador Smith!"

"Wait, you can't just—"

Marianne had started to heave herself off the bed, which was ridiculous because she couldn't leave the quarantine chamber anyway. A figure appeared on the other side of the glass barrier, behind Dr. Potter. The doctor, following Marianne's gaze, turned, and gasped.

Noah pressed close to the glass. An energy shield shimmered around him. Beneath it he wore a long tunic like Smith's. His once-pale skin now shone coppery under his black hair. But most startling were his eyes: Noah's eyes, and yet not. Bigger, altered to remove as much of the skin and expose as much of the white as possible. Within that large, alien-sized expanse of white, his irises were still the same color as her own, an un-alien light gray flecked with gold.

"Mom," he said tenderly. "Are you all right?"

"Noah—"

"I came as soon as I heard. I'm sorry it's been so long. Things have been . . . happening."

It was still Noah's voice, coming through the energy shield and out of the ceiling with no alien inflection, no trill or click. Marianne's mind refused to work logically. All she could focus on was his voice: He was too old. He would never speak English as anything but a Middle Atlantic American, and he would never speak Worldese without an accent.

"Mom?"

"I'm fine," she managed.

"I'm so sorry to hear about Evan."

She clasped her hands tightly together on top of the hospital blanket. "You're going. With the aliens. When they leave Earth."

"Yes."

One simple word. No more than that, and Marianne's son became an extraterrestrial. She knew that Noah was not doing this in order to save his life. Or hers, or anyone's. She didn't know why he had done it. As a child, Noah had been fascinated by superheroes, aliens, robots, even of the more ridiculous kind where the science made zero sense. Comic books, movies, TV shows—he would sit transfixed for hours by some improbable human transformed into a spider or a hulk or a sentient hunk of metal. Did Noah remember that childish fascination? She didn't understand what this adopted child, this beloved boy she had not borne, remembered or thought or desired. She never had.

He said, "I'm sorry."

She said, "Don't be," and neither of them knew exactly what he was apologizing for in the first place, nor what she was excusing him from. After that, Marianne could find nothing else to say. Of the thousands of things she could have said to Noah, absolutely none of them rose to her lips. So finally she nodded.

Noah blew her a kiss. Marianne did not watch him go. She couldn't have borne it. Instead she shifted her weight on the bed and got out of it, holding on to the bedstead, ignoring Ann Potter's strenuous objections on the other side of the glass.

She had to see Ambassador Smith, to tell him about Elizabeth. The terrorist organization could strike again.

As soon as she told Smith, Elizabeth would be arrested. *Two children lost—*

No, don't think of it. Tell Smith.

But—*wait.* Maybe it hadn't been Elizabeth. Surely others had had an unauthorized tour of the ship? And now, as a result of the attack, security would be tightened. Probably no other saboteur could get through. Perhaps there would be no more supply runs by submarine, no more helicopters coming and going on the wide pier. Time was so short—maybe there were enough supplies aboard already. And perhaps the Denebs would use their unknowable technology to keep the *Embassy* safer until the spore cloud hit, by which time, of course, the aliens would have left. There were only three months left. Surely a second attack inside the *Embassy* couldn't be organized in such a brief time! Maybe there was no need to name Elizabeth at all.

The room swayed as she clutched the side of the bed.

Ann Potter said, "If you don't get back into bed right now, Marianne, I'm calling security."

"Nothing is secure, don't you know that, you silly woman?" Marianne snapped.

Noah was lost to her. Evan was dead. Elizabeth was guilty.

"I'm sorry," she said. "I'll get back in bed." What was she even doing, standing up? She couldn't leave. She carried the infection inside her body. "But I . . . I need to see Ambassador Smith. Right now, here. Please have someone tell him it's the highest possible priority. Please."

Noah

The visit to his mother upset Noah more than he'd expected. She'd looked so small, so fragile in her bed behind the quarantine glass. Always, his whole life, he'd thought of her as large, towering over the landscape like some stone fortress, both safe and formidable. But she was just a small, frightened woman who was going to die.

As were Elizabeth, Ryan and Connie and their baby, Noah's last girlfriend Emily, his childhood buddies Sam and Davey, Cindy and Miguel at the restaurant—all going to die when the spore cloud hit. Why hadn't Noah been thinking about this before? How could he be so selfish about concentrating on his delight in his new clan that he had put the rest of humanity out of his mind?

He had always been selfish. He'd known that about himself. Only before now, he'd called it "independent."

It was a relief to leave the Terran part of the *Embassy*, with its too-heavy gravity and glaring light. The extra rods and cones that had been inserted into Noah's eyes made them sensitive to such terrible brightness. In the World quarters, Kayla's little boy Austin was chasing a ball along the corridor, his energy suit a faint glimmer in the low light. He stopped to watch Noah shed his own suit.

Austin said, "I wanna do that."

"You will, some day. Maybe soon. Where's your mother?"

"She comes right back. I stay right here!"

"Good boy. Have you—hi, Kayla. Do you know where Mee^hao¡ is?"

"No. Oh, wait, yes—he left the sanctuary."

That, Noah remembered, was what both Kayla and her sister called the

World section of the *Embassy*. "Sanctuary"—the term made him wonder what their life had been before they came aboard. Both, although pleasant enough, were close-mouthed about their pasts to the point of lockjaw.

Kayla added, "I think Mee^hao¡ said it was about the attack."

It would be, of course. Noah knew he should wait until Mee^hao¡ was free. But he couldn't wait.

"Where's Llaa^moh¡?"

Kayla looked blank; her Worldese was not yet fluent.

"Officer Jones."

"Oh. I just saw her in the garden."

Noah strode to the garden. Llaa^moh¡ sat on a bench, watching water fall in a thin stream from the ceiling to a pool below. Delicately she fingered a llo flower, without picking it, coaxing the broad dark leaf to release its spicy scent. Noah and Llaa^moh¡ had avoided each other ever since Noah's welcome ceremony, and he knew why. Still, right now his need overrode awkward desire.

"Llaa^moh¡—may we speak together?" He hoped he had the verb tense right: urgency coupled with supplication.

"Yes, of course." She made room for him on the bench. "Your Worldese progresses well."

"Thank you. I am troubled in my liver." The correct idiom, he was certain. Almost.

"What troubles your liver, brother mine?"

"My mother." The word meant not only female parent but matriarchal clan leader, which Noah supposed that Marianne was, since both his grandmothers were dead. Although perhaps not his biological grandmothers, and to World, biology was all. There were no out-of-family adoptions.

"Yes?"

"She is Dr. Marianne Jenner, as you know, working aboard the *Embassy*. My brother and sister live ashore. What will happen to my family when the spore cloud comes? Does my mother go with us to World? Do my birth-siblings?" But . . . how could they, unaltered? Also, they were not of his haplotype and so would belong to a different clan for lllathil, clans not represented aboard ship. Also, all three of them would hate everything about World. But otherwise they would die. All of them, dead.

Llaa^moh¡ said nothing. Noah gave her the space and time to think; one thing World humans hated about Terrans was that they replied so quickly, without careful thought, sometimes even interrupting each other and thereby dishonoring the speaker. Noah watched a small insect with multi-colored wings, whose name did not come to his fevered mind, cross the llo leaf, and forced his body to stay still.

Finally Llaa^moh¡ said, "Mee^hao¡ and I have discussed this. He has left this decision to me. You are one of us now. I will tell you what will happen when the spore cloud comes."

"I thank you for your trust." The ritual response, but Noah meant it.

"However, you are under obligation—" she used the most serious degree for a word of promise "—to say nothing to anyone else, World or Terran. Do you accept this obligation?"

Noah hesitated, and not from courtesy. Shouldn't he use the information, whatever it was, to try to ensure what safety was possible for his family? But if he did not promise, Llaa^moh¡ would tell him nothing.

"I accept the obligation."

She told him.

Noah's jaw dropped. He couldn't help it, even though it was very rude. Llaa^moh¡ was carefully not looking at him; perhaps she had anticipated this reaction.

Noah stood and walked out of the garden.

Marianne

"Thought," a famous poet—Marianne couldn't remember which one—had once said, "is an infection. In the case of certain thoughts, it becomes an epidemic." Lying in her bed in the quarantine chamber, Marianne felt an epidemic in her brain. What Elizabeth had done, what she herself harbored now in her body, Noah's transformation, Evan's death—the thoughts fed on her cells, fevered her mind.

Elizabeth, studying the complex layout of the *Embassy*: *"Where do the Denebs live?" "Behind these doors here."*

Noah, with his huge alien eyes.

Evan, urging her to meet the aliens by scribbling block letters on a paper sushi bag: CHANCE OF SIX THOUSAND LIFETIMES! The number of generations since Mitochondrial Eve.

Herself, carrying the deadly infection. Elizabeth, Noah, Evan, spores—it was almost a relief when Ambassador Smith appeared beyond the glass.

"Dr. Jenner," the ceiling said in uninflected translation. "I am so sorry you were injured in this attack. You said you want to see me now."

She hadn't been sure what she was going to say to him. How did you name your own child a possible terrorist, condemn her to whatever unknown form justice took among aliens? What if that meant something like drawing and quartering, as it once had on Earth? Marianne opened her mouth, and what came out were words she had not planned at all.

"Why did you permit Drs. Namechek and Lloyd to infect themselves three times when it violates both our medical code and yours?"

His face, both Terran and alien, that visage that now and forever would remind her of what Noah had done to his own face, did not change expression. "You know why, Dr. Jenner. It was necessary for the research. There is no other way to fully assess immune system response in ways useful to developing antidotes."

"You could have used your own people!"

"There are not enough of us to put anyone into quarantine."

"You could have run the experiment yourself with human volunteers. You'd have gotten volunteers, given what Earth is facing. And then the experiment could have had the advantage of your greater expertise."

"It is not much greater than yours, as you know. Our scientific knowledges have moved in different directions. But if we had sponsored experiments on Terrans, what would have been the Terran response?"

Marianne was silent. She knew the answer. They both knew the answer.

He said, "You are infected, I am told. We did not cause this. But now our two peoples can work more openly on developing medicines or vaccines. Both Earth and World will owe you an enormous debt."

Which she would never collect. In roughly two more days she would be dead of spore disease.

And she still had to tell him about Elizabeth.

"Ambassador Smith—"

"I must show you something, Dr. Jenner. If you had not sent for me, I would have come to you as soon as I was informed that you were awake. Your physician performed an autopsy on the terrorist. That is, by the way, a useful word, which does not exist on World. We shall appropriate it. The doctors found this in the mass of body tissues. It is engraved titanium, possibly created to survive the blast. Secretary General Desai suggests that it is a means to claim credit, a 'logo.' Other Terrans have agreed, but none know what it means. Can you aid us? Is it possibly related to one of the victims? You were a close friend of Dr. Blanford."

He held up something close to the glass: a flat piece of metal about three inches square. Whatever was pictured on it was too small for Marianne to see from her bed.

Smith said, "I will have Dr. Potter bring it to you."

"No, don't." Ann would have to put on a space suit and maneuver through the double airlock with respirator. The fever in Marianne's brain could not wait that long. She pulled out her catheter tube, giving a small shriek at the unexpected pain. Then she heaved herself out of bed and dragged the IV pole over to the clear barrier. Ann began to sputter. Marianne ignored her.

On the square of metal was etched a stylized purple rocket ship, sprouting leaves.

Not Elizabeth. Ryan.

"Dr. Jenner?"

"They're an invasive species," Ryan had said.

"Didn't you hear a word I said?" Marianne said. "They're not 'invasive,' or at least not if our testing bears out the ambassador's story. They're native to Earth."

"An invasive species is native to Earth. It's just not in the ecological niche it evolved for."

"Dr. Jenner?" the Ambassador repeated. "Are you all right?"

Ryan, his passion about purple loosestrife a family joke. Ryan, interested in the *Embassy*, as Connie was not, asking questions about the facilities and the layout while Marianne cuddled her new grandson. Ryan, important enough in this terrorist organization to have selected its emblem from a sheet of drawings in a kitschy bathroom.

Ryan, her son.

"Dr. Jenner, I must insist—"

"Yes. *Yes*. I recognize that thing. I know who—what group—you should look for." Her heart shattered.

Smith studied her through the glass. The large, calm eyes—Noah's eyes now, except for the color—held compassion.

"Someone you know."

"Yes."

"It doesn't matter. We shall not look for them."

The words didn't process. "Not . . . not look for them?"

"No. It will not happen again. The embassy has been sealed and the Terrans removed except for a handful of scientists directly involved in immunology, all of whom have chosen to stay, and all of whom we trust."

"But—"

"And, of course, those of our clan members who wish to stay."

Marianne stared at Smith through the glass, the impermeable barrier. Never had he seemed more alien. Why would this intelligent man believe that just because a handful of Terrans shared a mitochondrial haplotype with him, they could not be terrorists, too? Was it a cultural blind spot, similar to the Terran millennia-long belief in the divine right of kings? Was it some form of perception, the product of divergent evolution that let his brain perceive things she could not? Or did he simply have in place such heavy surveillance and protective devices that people like Noah, sequestered in a different part of the *Embassy*, presented no threat?

Then the rest of what he had said struck her. "Immunologists?"

"Time is short, Dr. Jenner. The spore cloud will envelop Earth in merely a few months. We must perform intensive tests on you and the other infected people."

"Other?"

"Dr. Ahmed Rafat and two lab technicians, Penelope Hodgson and Robert Chavez. They are, of course, all volunteers. They will be joining you soon in quarantine."

Rage tore through her, all the rage held back, pent up, about Evan's death, about Ryan's deceit, about Noah's defection. "Why not any of your own people? No, don't tell me that you're all too valuable—so are we! Why only Terrans? If we take this risk, why don't you? And what the fuck happens when the cloud does hit? Do you take off two days before, keeping yourselves safe and leaving Earth to die? You know very well that there is no chance of developing a real vaccine in the time left, let alone manufacturing and distributing it! What then? How can you just—"

But Ambassador Smith was already moving away from her, behind the shatterproof glass. The ceiling said, without inflection or emotion, "I am sorry."

Noah

Noah stood in the middle of the circle of Terrans. Fifty, sixty—they had all come aboard the *Embassy* in the last few days, as time shortened. Not all were L7s; some were families of clan brothers, and these too had been welcomed, since they'd had had the defiance to ask for asylum when the directives said explicitly that only L7s would be taken in. *There was something wrong with this system*, Noah thought, but he did not think hard about what it might be.

The room, large and bare, was in neither the World quarters nor the now-sealed part of the *Embassy* where the Terran scientists worked. The few scientists left aboard, anyway. The room's air, gravity, and light were all Terran, and Noah again wore an energy suit. He could see its faint shimmer along his arms as he raised them in welcome. He hadn't realized how much he was going to hate having to don the suit again.

"I am Noah," he said.

The people pressed against the walls of the bare room or huddled in small groups or sat as close to Noah as they could, cross-legged on the hard floor. They looked terrified or hopeful or defiant or already grieving for what might be lost. They all, even the ones who, like Kayla and Isabelle, had been here for a while, expected to die if they were left behind on Earth.

"I will be your leader and teacher. But first, I will explain the choice you must all make, now. You can choose to leave with the people of World, when we return to the home world. Or you can stay here, on Earth."

"To die!" someone shouted. "Some choice!"

Noah found the shouter: a young man standing close behind him, fists clenched at his side. He wore ripped jeans, a pin through his eyebrow, and a scowl. Noah felt the shock of recognition that had only thrilled through him twice before: with the nurse on the Upper West Side of New York and when he'd met Mee^hao¡. Not even Llaa^moh¡, who was a geneticist, could explain that shock, although she seemed to think it had to do with certain genetically determined pathways in Noah's L7 brain coupled with the faint electromagnetic field surrounding every human skull. She was fascinated by it.

Lisa Guiterrez, Noah remembered, had also attributed it to neurological pathways, changed by his heavy use of sugarcane.

Noah said to the scowler, "What is your name?"

He said, "Why?"

"I'd like to know it. We are clan brothers."

"I'm not your fucking brother. I'm here because it's my only option to not die."

A child on its mother's lap started to cry. People murmured to each other, most not taking their eyes off Noah. Waiting, to see what Noah did about the young man. Answer him? Let it go? Have him put off the *Embassy*?

Noah knew it would not take much to ignite these desperate people into attacking him, the alien-looking stand-in for the Worlders they had no way to reach.

He said gently to the young man, to all of them, to his absent and injured and courageous mother: "I'm going to explain your real choices. Please listen."

Marianne

Something was wrong.

One day passed, then another, then another. Marianne did not get sick. Nor did Ahmed Rafat and Penny Hodgson. Robbie Chavez did, but not very.

The lead immunologist left aboard the *Embassy*, Harrison Rice, stood with Ann Potter in front of Marianne's glass quarantine cage, known as a "slammer." He was updating Marianne on the latest lab reports. In identical slammers, two across a narrow corridor and one beside her, Marianne could see the three other infected people. The rooms had been created, as if by alchemy, by a Deneb that Marianne had not seen before—presumably an engineer of some unknowable building methods. Ahmed stood close to his glass, listening. Penny was asleep. Robbie, his face filmed with sweat, lay in bed, listening.

Ann Potter said, "You're not initially viremic but—"

"What does that mean?" Marianne interrupted.

Dr. Rice answered. He was a big, bluff Canadian who looked more like a truck driver who hunted moose than like a Nobel Prize winner. In his sixties, still strong as a mountain, he had worked with Ebola, Marburg, Lassa fever, and Nipah, both in the field and in the lab.

He said, "It means lab tests show that as with Namechek and Lloyd, the spores were detectable in the first samples taken from your respiratory tract. So the virus should be present in your bloodstream and so have access to the rest of your body. However, we can't find it. Well, that can happen. Viruses are elusive. But as far as we can tell, you aren't developing antibodies against the virus, as the infected mice did. That may mean that we just haven't isolated the antibodies yet. *Or* that your body doesn't consider the virus a foreign invader, which seems unlikely. *Or* that in humans but not in mice, the virus has dived into an organ to multiply until its offspring burst out again. Malaria does that. *Or* that the virus samples in the lab, grown artificially, have mutated into harmlessness, differing from their wild cousins in the approaching cloud. *Or* it's possible that none of us know what the hell we're doing with this crazy pathogen."

Marianne said, "What do the Denebs think?" Supposedly Rice was co-lead with Deneb Scientist Jones.

He said, his anger palpable even through the glass wall of the slammer, "I have no idea what they think. None of us have seen any of them."

"Not seen them?"

"No. We share all our data and samples, of course. Half of the samples go into an airlock for them, and the data over the LAN. But all we get in return is a thank-you onscreen. Maybe they're not making progress, either, but at least they could tell us what they haven't discovered."

"Do we know . . . this may sound weird, but do we know that they're still here at all? Is it possible they all left Earth already?" *Noah.*

He said, "It's possible, I suppose. We have no news from the outside world, of course, so it's possible they pre-recorded all those thank-yous, blew up New York, and took off for the stars. But I don't think so. If they had, they'd have least unsealed us from this floating plastic bubble. Which, incidentally, has become completely opaque, even on the observation deck."

Marianne hadn't known there was an observation deck. She and Evan had not found it during their one exploration of the *Embassy.*

Dr. Rice continued. "Your cells are not making an interferon response, either. That's a small protein molecule that can be produced in any cell in response to the presence of viral nucleic acid. You're not making it."

"Which means . . . "

"Probably it means that there is no viral nucleic acid in your cells."

"Are Robbie's cells making interferon?"

"Yes. Also antibodies. Plus immune responses like—Ann, what does your chart on Chavez show for this morning?"

Ann said, "Fever of a hundred and one, not at all dangerous. Chest congestion, also not at dangerous levels, some sinus involvement. He has the equivalent of mild bronchitis."

Marianne said, "But why is Robbie sick when the rest of us aren't?"

"Ah," Harrison Rice said, and for the first time she heard the trace of a Canadian accent, "that's the big question, isn't it? In immunology, it always is. Sometimes genetic differences between infected hosts are the critical piece of the puzzle in understanding why an identical virus causes serious disease or death in one individual—or one group—and little reaction or none at all in other people. Is Robbie sick and you not because of your respective genes? We don't know."

"But you can use Robbie's antibodies to maybe develop a vaccine?"

He didn't answer. She knew the second the words left her mouth how stupid they were. Rice might have antibodies, but he had no time. None of them had enough time.

Yet they all worked on, as if they did. Because that's what humans did.

Instead of answering her question, he said, "I need more samples, Marianne."

"Yes."

Fifteen minutes later he entered her slammer, dressed in full space suit and sounding as if speaking through a vacuum cleaner. "Blood samples plus a tissue biopsy, just lie back down and hold still, please . . . "

During a previous visit, he had told her of an old joke among immunologists working with lethal diseases: "The first person to isolate a virus in the lab by getting infected is a hero. The second is a fool." Well, that made Marianne a fool. So be it.

She said to Rice, "And the aliens haven't . . . Ow!"

"Baby." He withdrew the biopsy needle and slapped a bandage over the site.

She tried again. "And the aliens haven't commented at all on Robbie's diagnosis? Not a word?"

"Not a word."

Marianne frowned. "Something isn't right here."

"No," Rice said, bagging his samples, "it certainly is not."

Noah

Nothing, Noah thought, had ever felt more right, not in his entire life.

He raised himself on one elbow and looked down at Llaa^moh¡. She still slept, her naked body and long legs tangled in the light blanket made of some substance he could not name. Her wiry dark hair smelled of something like cinnamon, although it probably wasn't. The blanket smelled of sex.

He knew now why he had not felt the same shock of recognition at their first meeting that he had felt with Mee^hao¡ and the unnamed New York nurse and surly young Tony Schrupp. After the World geneticists had done their work, Mee^hao¡ had explained it to him. Noah felt profound relief. He and Llaa^moh¡ shared a mitochondrial DNA group, but not a nuclear DNA one. They were not too genetically close to mate.

Of course, they could have had sex anyway; World had early, and without cultural shame or religious prejudice, discovered birth control. But for the first time in his life, Noah did not want just sex. He wanted to mate.

The miracle was that she did, too. Initially he feared that for her it was mere novelty: be the first Worlder to sleep with a Terran! But it was not. Just yesterday they had signed a five-year mating contract, followed by a lovely ceremony in the garden to which every single Worlder had come. Noah had never known exactly how many were aboard the *Embassy*; now he did. They had all danced with him, every single one, and also with her. Mee^hao¡ himself had pierced their right ears and hung from them the wedding silver, shaped like stylized versions of the small flowers that had once, very long ago, been the real thing.

"Is better," Noah had said in his accented, still clumsy World. "We want not bunch of dead vegetation dangle from our ears." At least, that's what he hoped he'd said. Everyone had laughed.

Noah reached out one finger to stroke Llaa^moh¡'s hair. A miracle, yes. A whole skyful of miracles, but none as much as this: Now he knew who he was and where he belonged and what he was going to do with his life.

His only regret was that his mother had not been at the mating ceremony. And—yes, forgiveness was in order here!—Elizabeth and Ryan, too. They had disparaged him his entire life and he would never see them again, but they were still his first family. Just not the one that any longer mattered.

Llaa^moh¡ stirred, woke, and reached for him.

Marianne

Robbie Chavez, recovered from *Respirovirus sporii*, gave so many blood and tissue samples that he joked he'd lost ten pounds without dieting. It wasn't much of a joke, but everyone laughed. Some of the laughter held hysteria.

Twenty-two people left aboard the *Embassy*. Why, Marianne sometimes wondered, had these twenty-two chosen to stay and work until the last possible second? Because the odds of finding anything that would affect the coming die-off were very low. They all knew that. Yet here they were, knowing they would die in this fantastically equipped, cut-off-from-the-world lab instead of with their families. Didn't any of them have families? Why were they still here?

Why was she?

No one discussed this. They discussed only work, which went on eighteen hours a day. Brief breaks for microwaved meals from the freezer. Briefer—not in actuality, but that's how it felt—for sleep.

The four people exposed to *R. sporii* worked outside the slammers; maintaining biosafety no longer seemed important. No one else became ill. Marianne relearned lab procedures she had not performed since grad school. Theoretical evolutionary biologists did not work as immunologists. She did now.

Every day, the team sent samples data to the Denebs. Every day, the Denebs gave thanks, and nothing else.

In July, eight-and-a-half months after they'd first been given the spores to work with, the scientists finally succeeded in growing the virus in a culture. There was a celebration of sorts. Harrison Rice produced a hoarded bottle of champagne.

"We'll be too drunk to work," Marianne joked. She'd come to admire Harrison's unflagging cheerfulness.

"On one twenty-second of one bottle?" he said. "I don't think so."

"Well, maybe not everyone drinks."

Almost no one did. Marianne, Harrison, and Robbie Chavez drank the bottle. Culturing the virus, which should have been a victory, seemed to turn the irritable more irritable, the dour more dour. The tiny triumph underlined how little they had actually achieved. People began to turn strange. The unrelenting work, broken sleep, and constant tension created neuroses.

Penny Hodgson turned compulsive about the autoclave: It must be loaded just so, in just this order, and only odd numbers of tubes could be placed in the rack at one time. She flew into a rage when she discovered eight tubes, or twelve.

William Parker, Nobel Laureate in medicine, began to hum as he worked. Eighteen hours a day of humming. If told to stop, he did, and then unknowingly resumed a few minutes later. He could not carry a tune, and he liked lugubrious country and western tunes.

Marianne began to notice feet. Every few seconds, she glanced at the feet of others in the lab, checking that they still had them. Harrison's work boots, as if he tramped the forests of Hudson's Bay. Mark Wu's black oxfords. Penny's Nikes—did she think she'd be going for a run? Robbie's sandals. Ann's—

Stop it, Marianne!

She couldn't.

They stopped sending samples and data to the Denebs and held their collective breath, waiting to see what would happen. Nothing did.

Workboots, Oxfords, Nikes, sandals—

"I think," Harrison said, "that I've found something."

It was an unfamiliar protein in Marianne's blood. Did it have anything to do with the virus? They didn't know. Feverishly they set to work culturing it, sequencing it, photographing it, looking forward in everyone else. The protein was all they had.

It was August.

The outside world, with which they had no contact, had ceased to exist for them, even as they raced to save it.

Workboots—

Oxfords—

Sandals—

Noah

Rain fell in the garden. Noah tilted his head to the artificial sky. He loved rainy afternoons, even if this was not really rain, nor afternoon. Soon he would experience the real thing.

Llaa^moh¡ came toward him through the dark, lush leaves open as welcoming hands. Noah was surprised; these important days she rarely left the lab. Too much to do.

She said, "Should not you be teaching?"

He wanted to say *I'm playing hooky* but had no idea what the idiom would be in Worldese. Instead he said, hoping he had the tenses right, "My students I will return at soon. Why you here? Something is wrong?"

"All is right." She moved into his arms. Again Noah was surprised; Worlders did not touch sexually in public places, even public places temporarily empty. Others might come by, unmated others, and it was just as rude to display physical affection in front of those without it as to eat in front of anyone hungry.

"Llaa^moh¡—"

She whispered into his ear. Her words blended with the rain, with the rich flower scents, with the odor of wet dirt. Noah clutched her and began to cry.

VI: S MINUS TWO WEEKS

Marianne

The Commons outside the lab was littered with frozen food trays, with discarded sterile wrappings, with an empty disinfectant bottle. Harrison slumped in a chair and said the obvious.

"We've failed, Marianne."

"Yes," she said. "I know." And then, fiercely, "Do you think the Denebs know more than we do? And aren't sharing?"

"Who knows?"

"Fucking bastards," Marianne said. Weeks ago she had crossed the line from defending the aliens to blaming them. How much of humanity had been ahead of her in that? By now, maybe all of it.

They had discovered nothing useful about the anomalous protein in Marianne's blood. The human body contained so many proteins whose identities were not understood. But that wouldn't make any difference, not now. There wasn't enough time.

"Harrison," she began, and didn't get to finish her sentence.

Between one breath and the next, Harrison Rice and the lab, along with everything else, disappeared.

Noah

Nine, not counting him. The rest had been put ashore, to face whatever would happen to them on Earth. Noah would have much preferred to be with Llaa^moh¡, but she of course had duties. Even unannounced, departure was dangerous. Too many countries had too many formidable weapons.

So instead of standing beside Llaa^moh¡, Noah sat in his energy suit in the Terran compartment of the shuttle. Around him, strapped into chairs, sat the nine Terrans going to World. The straps were unnecessary; Llaa^moh¡ had told him that the acceleration would feel mild, due to the same gravity-altering machinery that had made the World section of the *Embassy* so comfortable. But Terrans were used to straps in moving vehicles, so there were straps.

Kayla Rhinehart and her little son.

Her sister, Isabelle.

The surly Tony Schrupp, a surprise. Noah had been sure Tony would change his mind.

A young woman, five months pregnant, who "wanted to give my baby a better life." She did not say what her previous life had been, but there were bruises on her arms and legs.

A pair of thirty-something brothers with restless, eager-for-adventure eyes.

A middle-aged journalist with a sun-leathered face and impressive byline, recorders in her extensive luggage.

And, most unexpected, a Terran physicist, Dr. Nathan Beyon of Massachusetts Institute of Technology.

Nine Terrans willing to go to the stars.

A slight jolt. Noah smiled at the people under his leadership—he, who had never led anything before, not even his own life—and said, "Here we go."

That seemed inadequate, so he said, "We are off to the stars!"

That seemed dumb. Tony sneered. The journalist looked amused. Austin clutched his mother.

Noah said, "Your new life will be wonderful. Believe it."

Kayla gave him a wobbly smile.

Marianne

She could not imagine where she was.

Cool darkness, with the sky above her brightening every second. It had been so long since she'd seen a dawn sky, or any sky. Silver-gray, then pearl, and now the first flush of pink. The floor rocked gently. Then the last of the knock-out gas left her brain and she sat up. A kind of glorified barge, flat and wide with a single square rod jutting from the middle. The barge floated gently on New York Harbor. The sea was smooth as polished gray wood. In one direction rose the skyline of Manhattan; in the other, the *Embassy*. All around her lay her colleagues: Dr. Rafat, Harrison Rice and Ann Potter, lab techs Penny and Robbie, all the rest of the twenty-two people who'd still been aboard the *Embassy*. They wore their daily clothing. In her jeans and tee, Marianne shivered in a sudden breeze.

Nearby lay a pile of blankets. She took a yellow one and wrapped it around her shoulders. It felt warm and silky, although clearly not made of silk. Other people began to stir. Pink tinged the east.

Harrison came to her side. "Marianne?"

Automatically she said, because she'd been saying so many times each day, "I feel fine." And then, "What the *fuck*?"

He said something just as pointless: "But we have two more weeks!"

"Oh my God!" someone cried, pointing, and Marianne looked up. The eastern horizon turned gold. Against it, a ship, dark and small, shot from the *Embassy* and climbed the sky. Higher and higher, while everyone on the barge shaded their eyes against the rising sun and watched it fly out of sight.

"They're going," someone said quietly.

They. The Denebs. *Noah*.

Before the tears that stung her eyes could fall, the *Embassy* vanished. One moment it was there, huge and solid and gray in the pre-dawn, and the next it was just gone. The water didn't even ripple.

The metal rod in the center of the ship spoke. Marianne, along with everyone else, turned sharply. Shoulder-high, three feet on a side, the rod had become four screens, each filled with the same alien/human image and mechanical voice.

"This is Ambassador Smith. A short time from now, this recording will go to everyone on Earth, but we wanted you, who have helped us so much, to hear it first. We of World are deeply in your debt. I would like to explain why, and to leave you a gift.

"Your astronomers' calculations were very slightly mistaken, and we did not correct them. In a few hours the spore cloud will envelop your planet. We do not think it will harm you because—"

Someone in the crowd around the screen cried, *"What?"*

"—because you are genetically immune to this virus. We suspected as much before we arrived, although we could not be sure. *Homo sapiens* acquired immunity when Earth passed through the cloud the first time, about seventy thousand years ago."

A graphic replaced Smith's face: the Milky Way galaxy, a long dark splotch overlapping it, and a glowing blue dot for Earth. "The rotation of the galaxy plus its movement through space-time will bring you back into contact with the cloud's opposite edge from where it touched you before. Your physicists were able to see the approaching cloud, but your instruments were not advanced enough to understand its shape or depth. Earth will be passing through the edge of the cloud for two-point-six years. On its first contact, the cloud killed every *Homo sapiens* that did not come with this genetic mutation."

A gene sequence of base pairs flashed across the screen, too fast to be noted.

"This sequence will appear again later, in a form you can record. It is found in what you call 'junk DNA.' The sequence is a transposon and you will find it complementary to the spores' genetic code. Your bodies made no antibodies against the spores because it does not consider them invaders. Seventy thousand years ago our people had already been taken from Earth or we, too, would have died. We are without this sequence, which appeared in mutation later than our removal."

Marianne's mind raced. Seventy thousand years ago. The "bottleneck event" that had shrunk the human population on Earth to a mere few thousand. It had not been caused by the Toba volcano or ferocious predators or climate changes, but by the spore cloud. As for the gene sequence—one theory said that much of the human genome consisted of inactive and fossilized viruses absorbed into the DNA. Fossilized and inactive—almost she could hear Evan's voice: *"Or so we thought . . . "*

Smith continued. "You will find that in Marianne Jenner, Ahmed Rafat, and Penelope Hodgson this sequence has already activated, producing the protein already identified in Dr. Jenner's blood, a protein that this recording will detail for you. The protein attaches to the outside of cells and prevents the virus from entering. Soon the genetic sequence will do so in the rest of humanity. Some may become mildly ill, like Robert Chavez, due to faulty protein production. We estimate this will comprise perhaps twenty percent of you. There may be fatalities among the old or already sick, but most of you are genetically protected. Some of your rodents do not seem to be, which we admit was a great surprise to us, and we cannot say for certain what other Terran species may be susceptible.

"We know that we are fatally susceptible. We cannot alter our own genome, at least not for the living, but we have learned much from you. By the time the spore cloud reaches World, we will have developed a vaccine. This would not have been possible without your full cooperation and your bodily samples. We—"

"If this is true," Penny Hodgson shouted, "why didn't they *tell* us?"

"—did not tell you the complete truth because we believe that had you known Earth was in no critical danger, you would not have allocated so many resources, so much scientific talent, or such urgency into the work on the *Embassy*. We are all human, but your evolutionary history and present culture are very different from ours. You do not build identity on family. You permit much of Earth's population to suffer from lack of food, water, and medical care. We didn't think you would help us as much as we needed unless we withheld from you certain truths. If we were mistaken in our assessment, please forgive us."

They weren't mistaken, Marianne thought.

"We are grateful for your help," Smith said, "even if obtained fraudulently. We leave you a gift in return. This recording contains what you call the 'engineering specs' for a star drive. We have already given you the equations describing the principles. Now you may build a ship. In generations to come, both branches of humanity will profit from more open and truthful exchanges. We will become true brothers.

"Until then, ten Terrans accompany us home. They have chosen to do this, for their own reasons. All were told that they would not die if they remained on Earth, but chose to come anyway. They will become World, creating further friendship with our clan brothers on Terra.

"Again—thank you."

Pandemonium erupted on the barge: talking, arguing, shouting. The sun was above the horizon now. Three Coast Guard ships barreled across the harbor toward the barge. As Marianne clutched her yellow blanket closer against the morning breeze, something vibrated in the pocket of her jeans.

She pulled it out: a flat metal square with Noah's face on it. As soon as her gaze fell on his, the face began to speak. "I'm going with them, Mom. I want you to know that I am completely happy. This is where I belong. I've mated with Llaa^moh¡—Dr. Jones—and she is pregnant. Your grandchild will be born among the stars. I love you."

Noah's face faded from the small square.

Rage filled her, red sparks burning. Her son, and she would never see him again! Her grandchild, and she would never see him or her at all. She was being robbed, being deprived of what was hers by *right*, the aliens should never have come—

She stopped. Realization slammed into her, and she gripped the rail of the barge so tightly that her nails pierced the wood.

The aliens *had* made a mistake. A huge, colossal, monumental mistake.

Her rage, however irrational, was going to be echoed and amplified across the entire planet. The Denebs had understood that Terrans would work really hard only if their own survival were at stake. But they did not understand the rest of it. The Deneb presence on Earth had caused riots, diversion of resources, deaths, panic, fear. The "mild illness" of the twenty percent like Robbie, happening all at once starting today, was enough to upset every economy on the planet. The aliens had swept like a storm through the world, and as in the aftermath of a superstorm, everything in the landscape had shifted. In addition, the Denebs had carried off ten humans, which could be seen as brainwashing them in order to procure prospective lab rats for future experimentation.

Brothers, yes—but Castor and Pollux, whose bond reached across the stars, or Cain and Abel?

Humans did not forgive easily, and they resented being bought off, even with a star drive. Smith should have left a different gift, one that would not let Terrans come to World, that peaceful and rich planet so unaccustomed to revenge or war.

But on the other hand—she could be wrong. Look how often had she been wrong already: about Elizabeth, about Ryan, about Smith. Maybe, when the Terran disruptions were over and starships actually built, humanity would become so entranced with the Deneb gift that we would indeed go to World in friendship. Maybe the prospect of going to the stars would even soften American isolationism and draw countries together to share the necessary resources. It could happen. The cooperative genes that had shaped Smith and Jones were also found in the Terran genome.

But—it would happen only if those who wanted it worked hard to convince the rest. Worked, in fact, as hard at urging friendship as they had at ensuring survival. Was that possible? Could it be done?

Why are you here?

To make contact with World. A peace mission.

She gazed up at the multi-colored dawn sky, but the ship was already out of sight. Only its after-image remained in her sight.

"Harrison," Marianne said, and felt her own words steady her. "We have a lot of work to do."

THE LIGHTNING TREE

Patrick Rothfuss

Morning: The Narrow Road

Bast almost made it out the back door of the Waystone Inn.

He actually *had* made it outside, both feet were over the threshold and the door was almost entirely eased shut behind him before he heard his master's voice.

Bast paused, hand on the latch. He frowned at the door, hardly a handspan from being closed. He hadn't made any noise. He knew it. He was familiar with all the silent pieces of the inn, which floorboards sighed beneath a foot, which windows stuck . . . .

The back door's hinges creaked sometimes, depending on their mood, but that was easy to work around. Bast shifted his grip on the latch, lifted up so that the door's weight didn't hang so heavy, then eased it slowly closed. No creak. The swinging door was softer than a sigh.

Bast stood upright and grinned. His face was sweet and sly and wild. He looked like a naughty child who had managed to steal the moon and eat it. His smile was like the last sliver of remaining moon, sharp and white and dangerous.

"Bast!" The call came again, louder this time. Nothing so crass as a shout, his master would never stoop to bellowing. But when he wanted to be heard, his baritone would not be stopped by anything so insubstantial as an oaken door. His voice carried like a horn, and Bast felt his name tug at him like a hand around his heart.

Bast sighed, then opened the door lightly and strode back inside. He was dark, and tall, and lovely. When he walked he looked like he was dancing. "Yes Reshi?" he called.

After a moment the innkeeper stepped into the kitchen, he wore a clean white apron and his hair was red. Other than that, he was painfully unremarkable. His face held the doughy placidness of bored innkeepers everywhere. Despite the early hour, he looked tired.

He handed Bast a leather book. "You almost forgot this," he said without a hint of sarcasm.

Bast took the book and made a show of looking surprised. "Oh! Thank you, Reshi!"

The innkeeper shrugged and his mouth made the shape of a smile. "No bother, Bast. While you're out on your errands, would you mind picking up some eggs?"

Bast nodded, tucking the book under his arm. "Anything else?" he asked dutifully.

"Maybe some carrots too. I'm thinking we'll do stew tonight. It's Felling, so we'll need to be ready for a crowd." His mouth turned up slightly at one corner as he said this.

The innkeeper started to turn away, then stopped. "Oh. The Williams boy stopped by last night, looking for you. Didn't leave any sort of message." He raised an eyebrow at Bast. The look said more than it said.

"I haven't the slightest idea what he wants," Bast said.

The innkeeper made a noncommittal noise and turned back toward the common room.

Before he'd taken three steps Bast was already out the door and running through the early-morning sunlight.

By the time Bast arrived, there were already two children waiting. They played on the huge greystone that lay half-fallen at the bottom of the hill, climbing up the tilting side of it, then jumping down into the tall grass.

Knowing they were watching, Bast took his time climbing the tiny hill. At the top stood what the children called the lightning tree, though these days it was little more than a branchless trunk barely taller than a man. All the bark had long since fallen away, and the sun had bleached the wood as white as bone. All except the very top, where even after all these years the wood was charred a jagged black.

Bast touched the trunk with his fingertips and made a slow circuit of the tree. He went deasil, the same direction as the turning sun. The proper way for making. Then he turned and switched hands, making three slow circles widdershins. That turning was against the world. It was the way of breaking. Back and forth he went, as if the tree were a bobbin and he was winding and unwinding.

Finally he sat with his back against the tree and set the book on a nearby stone. The sun shone on the gold gilt letters, *Celum Tinture*. Then he amused himself by tossing stones into the nearby stream that cut into the low slope of the hill opposite the greystone.

After a minute, a round little blond boy trudged up the hill. He was the baker's youngest son, Brann. He smelled of sweat and fresh bread and . . . something else. Something out of place.

The boy's slow approach had an air of ritual about it. He crested the small hill and stood there for a moment quietly, the only noise coming from the other two children playing below.

Finally Bast turned to look the boy over. He was no more than eight or nine, well-dressed, and plumper than most of the other town's children. He carried a wad of white cloth in his hand.

The boy swallowed nervously. "I need a lie."

Bast nodded. "What sort of lie?"

He gingerly opened his hand, revealing the wad of cloth to be a makeshift bandage, spattered with bright red. It stuck to his hand slightly. Bast nodded; that was what he'd smelled before.

"I was playing with my mum's knives," Brann said.

Bast examined the cut. It ran shallow along the meat near the thumb. Nothing serious. "Hurt much?"

"Nothing like the birching I'll get if she finds out I was messing with her knives."

Bast nodded sympathetically. "You clean the knife and put it back?"

Brann nodded.

Bast tapped his lips thoughtfully. "You thought you saw a big black rat. It scared you. You threw a knife at it and cut yourself. Yesterday one of the other children told you a story about rats chewing off soldier's ears and toes while they slept. It gave you nightmares."

Brann gave a shudder. "Who told me the story?"

Bast shrugged. "Pick someone you don't like."

The boy grinned viciously.

Bast began to tick off things on his fingers. "Get some blood on the knife before you throw it." He pointed at the cloth the boy had wrapped his hand in. "Get rid of that, too. The blood is dry, obviously old. Can you work up a good cry?"

The boy shook his head, seeming a little embarrassed by the fact.

"Put some salt in your eyes. Get all snotty and teary before you run to them. Howl and blubber. Then when they're asking you about your hand, tell your mum you're sorry if you broke her knife."

Brann listened, nodding slowly at first, then faster. He smiled. "That's good." He looked around nervously. "What do I owe you?"

"Any secrets?" Bast asked.

The baker's boy thought for a minute. "Old Lant's tupping the Widow Creel . . . " he said hopefully.

Bast waved his hand. "For years. Everyone knows."

Bast rubbed his nose, then said, "Can you bring me two sweet buns later today?"

Brann nodded.

"That's a good start," Bast said. "What have you got in your pockets?"

The boy dug around and held up both his hands. He had two iron shims, a flat greenish stone, a bird skull, a tangle of string, and a bit of chalk.

Bast claimed the string. Then, careful not to touch the shims, he took the greenish stone between two fingers and arched an eyebrow at the boy.

After a moment's hesitation, the boy nodded.

Bast put the stone in his pocket.

"What if I get a birching anyway?" Brann asked.

Bast shrugged. "That's your business. You wanted a lie. I gave you a good one. If you want me to get you out of trouble, that's something else entirely."

The baker's boy looked disappointed, but he nodded and headed down the hill.

Next up the hill was a slightly older boy in tattered homespun. One of the Alard boys, Kale. He had a split lip and a crust of blood around one nostril. He was as furious as only a boy of ten can be. His expression was a thunderstorm.

"I caught my brother kissing Gretta behind the old mill!" he said as soon as he crested the hill, not waiting for Bast to ask. "He knew I was sweet on her!"

Bast spread his hands helplessly, shrugging.

"Revenge," the boy spat.

"Public revenge?" Bast asked. "Or secret revenge?"

The boy touched his split lip with his tongue. "Secret revenge," he said in a low voice.

"How much revenge?" Bast asked.

The boy thought for a bit, then held up his hands about two feet apart. "This much."

"Hmmmm," Bast said. "How much on a scale from mouse to bull?

The boy rubbed his nose for a while. "About a cat's worth," he said. "Maybe a dog's worth. Not like Crazy Martin's dog though. Like the Bentons' dogs."

Bast nodded and tilted his head back in a thoughtful way. "Okay," he said. "Piss in his shoes."

The boy looked skeptical. "That don't sound like a whole dog's worth of revenge."

Bast shook his head. "You piss in a cup and hide it. Let it sit for a day or two. Then one night when he's put his shoes by the fire, pour the piss on his shoes. Don't make a puddle, just get them damp. In the morning they'll be dry and probably won't even smell too much . . . "

"What's the point?" the boy interrupted angrily. "That's not a flea's worth of revenge!"

Bast held up a pacifying hand. "When his feet get sweaty, he'll start to smell like piss." Bast said calmly. "If he steps in a puddle, he'll smell like piss. When he walks in the snow, he'll smell like piss. It will be hard for him to figure out exactly where it's coming from, but everyone will know your brother is the one that reeks." Bast grinned at the boy. "I'm guessing your Gretta isn't going to want to kiss the boy who can't stop pissing himself."

Raw admiration spread across the young boy's face like sunrise in the mountains. "That's the most bastardy thing I've ever heard," he said, awestruck.

Bast tried to look modest and failed. "Have you got anything for me?"

"I found a wild bee hive," the boy said.

"That will do for a start," Bast said. "Where?"

"It's off past the Orissons'. Past Littlecreek." The boy squatted down and drew a map in the dirt. "You see?"

Bast nodded. "Anything else?"

"Well . . . I know where Crazy Martin keeps his still . . . "

Bast raised his eyebrows at that, "Really?"

The boy drew another map and gave some directions. Then he stood and dusted off his knees. "We square?"

Bast scuffed his foot in the dirt, destroying the map. "We're square."

The boy dusted off his knees, "I've got a message too. Rike wants to see you."

Bast shook his head firmly. "He knows the rules. Tell him no."

"I already told him," the boy said with a comically exaggerated shrug. "But I'll tell him again if I see him . . . "

There were no more children waiting after Kale, so Bast tucked the leather book under his arm and went on a long, rambling stroll. He found some wild raspberries and ate them. He took a drink from the Ostlar's well.

Eventually Bast climbed to the top of a nearby bluff where he gave a great stretch before tucking the leather-bound copy of *Celum Tinture* into a spreading hawthorn tree where a wide branch made a cozy nook against the trunk.

He looked up at the sky then, clear and bright. No clouds. Not much wind. Warm but not hot. Hadn't rained for a solid span. It wasn't a market day. Hours before noon on Felling . . .

Bast's brow furrowed a bit, as if performing some complex calculation. Then he nodded to himself.

Then Bast headed back down the bluff, past Old Lant's place and around the brambles that bordered the Alard farm. When he came to Littlecreek he cut some reeds and idly whittled at them with a small bright knife. Then brought the string out of his pocket and bound them together, fashioning a tidy set of shepherd's pipes.

He blew across the top of them and cocked his head to listen to their sweet discord. His bright knife trimmed some more, and he blew again. This time the tune was closer, which made the discord far more grating.

Bast's knife flicked again, once, twice, thrice. Then he put it away and brought the pipes closer to his face. He breathed in through his nose, smelling the wet green of them. Then he licked the fresh-cut tops of the reeds, the flicker of his tongue a sudden, startling red.

He drew a breath and blew against the pipes. This time the sound was bright as moonlight, lively as a leaping fish, sweet as stolen fruit. Smiling, Bast headed off into the Bentons' back hills, and it wasn't long before he heard the low, mindless bleat of distant sheep.

A minute later, Bast came over the crest of a hill and saw two dozen fat, daft sheep cropping grass in the green valley below. It was shadowy here, and secluded. The lack of recent rain meant the grazing was better here. The steep sides of the valley meant the sheep weren't prone to straying and didn't need much looking after.

A young woman sat in the shade of a spreading elm that overlooked the valley. She had taken off her shoes and bonnet. Her long, thick hair was the color of ripe wheat.

Bast began playing then. A dangerous tune. It was sweet and bright and slow and sly.

The shepherdess perked up at the sound of it, or so it seemed at first. She lifted her head, excited . . . but no. She didn't look in his direction at all. She was merely climbing to her feet to have stretch, rising high up onto her toes, hands twining over her head.

Still apparently unaware she was being serenaded, the young woman picked up a nearby blanket and spread it beneath the tree, and sat back down. It was a little odd, as she'd been sitting there before without the blanket. Perhaps she'd just grown chilly.

Bast continued to play as he walked down the slope of the valley toward her. He did not hurry, and the music he made was sweet and playful and languorous all at once.

The shepherdess showed no sign of noticing the music or Bast himself. In fact she looked away from him, toward the far end of the little valley, as if curious what the sheep might be doing there. When she turned her head, it exposed the lovely line of her neck from her perfect shell-like ear, down to the gentle swell of breast that showed above her bodice.

Eyes intent on the young woman, Bast stepped on a loose stone and stumbled awkwardly down the hill. He blew one hard, squawking note, then dropped a few more from his song as he threw out one arm wildly to catch his balance.

The shepherdess laughed then, but she was pointedly looking at the other end of the valley. Perhaps the sheep had done something humorous. Yes. That was surely it. They could be funny animals at times.

Even so, one can only look at sheep for so long. She sighed and relaxed, leaning back against the sloping trunk of the tree. The motion accidentally pulled the hem of her skirt up slightly past her knee. Her calves were round and tan and covered with the lightest down of honey-colored hair.

Bast continued down the hill. His steps delicate and graceful. He looked like a stalking cat. He looked like he was dancing.

Apparently satisfied the sheep were safe, the shepherdess sighed again, closed her eyes, and lay her head against the trunk of the tree. Her face tilted up to catch the sun. She seemed about to sleep, but for all her sighing her breath seemed to be coming rather quickly. And when she shifted restlessly to make herself more comfortable, one hand fell in such a way that it accidentally drew the hem of her dress even further up until it showed a pale expanse of thigh.

It is hard to grin while playing shepherd's pipes. Somehow Bast managed it.

The sun was climbing the sky when Bast returned to the lightning tree, pleasantly sweaty and in a state of mild dishevel. There were no children waiting near the greystones this time, which suited him perfectly.

He did a quick circle of the tree again when he reached the top of the hill, once in each direction to ensure his small workings were still in place. Then he slumped down and at the foot of the tree and leaned against the trunk. Less than a minute later his eyes were closed and he was snoring slightly.

After the better part of an hour, the near-silent sound of footsteps roused him. He gave a great stretch and spied a thin boy with freckles and clothes that were slightly past the point where they might merely be called well-worn.

"Kostrel!" Bast said happily. "How's the road to Tinuë?"

"Seems sunny enough to me today," the boy said as he came to the top of the hill. "And I found a lovely secret by the roadside. Something I thought you might be interested in."

"Ah," Bast said. "Come have a seat then. What sort of secret did you stumble on?"

Kostrel sat cross-legged on the grass nearby. "I know where Emberlee takes her bath."

Bast raised an half-interested eyebrow. "Is that so?"

Kostrel grinned. "You faker. Don't pretend you don't care."

"Of course I care," Bast said. "She's the sixth prettiest girl in town, after all."

"Sixth?" the boy said, indignant. "She's the second prettiest and you know it."

"Perhaps fourth," Bast conceded. "After Ania."

"Ania's legs are skinny as a chicken's," Kostrel observed calmly.

Bast smiled at the boy. "To each his own. But yes. I am interested. What would you like in trade? An answer, a favor, a secret?"

"I want a favor *and* information," the boy said with a small smirk. His dark eyes were sharp in his lean face. "I want good answers to three questions. And it's worth it. Because Emberlee is the third prettiest girl in town."

Bast opened his mouth as if he were going to protest, then shrugged and smiled. "No favor. But I'll give you three answers on a subject named beforehand," he countered. "Any subject except that of my employer, whose trust in me I cannot in good conscience betray."

Kostrel nodded in agreement. "Three *full* answers," he said. "With no equivocating or bullshittery."

Bast nodded. "So long as the questions are focused and specific. No '*tell me everything you know about*' nonsense."

"That wouldn't be a question," Kostrel pointed out.

"Exactly," Bast said. "And you agree not to tell anyone else where Emberlee is having her bath," Kostrel scowled at that, and Bast laughed. "You little cocker, you would have sold it twenty times, wouldn't you?"

The boy shrugged easily, not denying it, and not embarrassed either. "It's valuable information."

Bast chuckled. "Three full, earnest answers on a single subject with the understanding that I'm the only one you've told."

"You are," the boy said sullenly. "I came here first."

"And with the understanding that you won't tell Emberlee anyone knows." Kostrel looked so offended at this that Bast didn't bother waiting for him to agree. "And with the understanding that you won't show up yourself."

The dark-eyed boy spat a couple words that surprised Bast more than his earlier use of "equivocating."

"Fine," Kostrel growled. "But if you don't know the answer to my question, I get to ask another."

Bast thought about it for a moment, then nodded.

"And if I pick a subject you don't know much about, I get to chose another."

Another nod. "That's fair."

"And you loan me another book," the boy said, his dark eyes glaring. "And a copper penny. And you have to describe her breasts to me."

Bast threw back his head and laughed. "Done."

They shook on the deal, the boy's thin hand was delicate as a bird's wing.

Bast leaned against the lightning tree, yawning and rubbing the back of his neck. "So. What's your subject?"

Kostrel's grim look lifted a little then, and he grinned excitedly. "I want to know about the Fae."

It says a great deal that Bast finished his great yawp of a yawn as if nothing were the matter. It is quite hard to yawn and stretch when your belly feels like you've swallowed a lump of bitter iron and your mouth has gone suddenly dry.

But Bast was something of a professional dissembler, so he yawned and stretched, and even went so far as to scratch himself under one arm lazily.

"Well?" the boy asked impatiently. "Do you know enough about them?"

"A fair amount," Bast said, doing a much better job of looking modest this time. "More than most folk, I imagine."

Kostrel leaned forward, his thin face intent. "I thought you might. You aren't from around here. You *know* things. You've seen what's really out there in the world."

"Some of it," Bast admitted. He looked up at the sun. "Ask your questions, then. I have to be somewhere come noon."

The boy nodded seriously, then looked down at the grass in front of himself for a moment, thinking. "What are they like?"

Bast blinked for a moment, taken aback. Then he laughed helplessly and threw up his hands. "Merciful Tehlu. Do you have any idea how crazy that question is? They're not like anything. They're like themselves."

Kostrel looked indignant. "Don't you try to shim me!" he said, leveling a finger at Bast. "I said no bullshitery!"

"I'm not. Honest I'm not." Bast raised his hands defensively. "It's just an impossible question to answer is all. What would you say if I asked you what *people* were like? How could you answer that? There's so many kinds of people, and they're all different."

"So it's a big question," Kostrel said. "Give me a big answer."

"It's not just big," Bast said. "It would fill a book."

The boy gave a profoundly unsympathetic shrug.

Bast scowled. "It could be argued that your question is neither focused or specific."

Kostrel raised an eyebrow. "So we're arguing now? I thought we were trading information? Fully and freely. If you asked me where Emberlee was going for her bath, and I said, 'in a stream' you'd feel like I'd measured you some pretty short corn, wouldn't you?"

Bast sighed. "Fair enough. But if I told you every rumor and snippet I'd ever heard, this would take a span of days. Most of it would be useless, and some probably wouldn't even be true because it's just from stories that I've heard."

Kostrel frowned, but before he could protest, Bast held up a hand. "Here's what I'll do. Despite the unfocused nature of your question. I'll give you an answer that covers the rough shape of things and . . . " Bast hesitated. " . . . one true secret on the subject. Okay?"

"Two secrets." Kostrel said, his dark eyes glittering with excitement.

"Fair enough." Bast took a deep breath. "When you say *fae*, you're talking about anything that lives in the Fae. That includes a lot of things that are . . . just creatures. Like animals. Here you have dogs and squirrels and bears. In the Fae, they have raum and dennerlings and . . ."

"And trow?"

Bast nodded. "And trow. They're real."

"And dragons?"

Bast shook his head. "Not that I've ever heard. Not any more . . . "

Kostrel looked disappointed. "What about the fair folk? Like faerie tinkers and such?" The boy narrowed his eyes. "Mind you, this isn't a new question, merely an attempt to focus your ongoing answer."

Bast laughed helplessly. "Lord and lady. *Ongoing?* Was your mother scared by an azzie when she was pregnant? Where do you get that kind of talk?

"I stay awake in church." Kostrel shrugged. "And sometimes Abbe Leodin lets me read his books. What do they look like?"

"Like regular people," Bast said.

"Like you and me?" the boy asked.

Bast fought back a smile. "Just like you or me. You wouldn't hardly notice if they passed you on the street. But there are others. Some of them are . . . They're different. More powerful."

"Like Varsa never-dead?"

"Some," Bast conceded. "But some are powerful in other ways. Like the mayor is powerful. Or like a moneylender." Bast's expression went sour. "Many of those . . . they're not good to be around. They like to trick people. Play with them. Hurt them."

Some of the excitement bled out of Kostrel at this. "They sound like demons."

Bast hesitated, then nodded a reluctant agreement. "Some are very much like demons," he admitted. "Or so close as it makes no difference."

"Are some of them like angels, too?" The boy asked.

"It's nice to think that," Bast said. "I hope so."

"Where do they come from?"

Bast cocked his head. "That's your second question then?" he asked. "I'm guessing it must be, as it's got nothing to do with what the Fae are *like* . . . "

Kostrel grimaced, seeming a little embarrassed, though Bast couldn't tell if he was ashamed he'd gotten carried away with his questions, or ashamed he'd been caught trying to get a free answer. "Sorry," he said. "Is it true that a faerie can never lie?"

"Some can't," Bast said. "Some don't like to. Some are happy to lie, but wouldn't ever go back on promise or break their word." He shrugged. "Others lie quite well, and do so at every opportunity."

Kostrel began to ask something else, but Bast cleared his throat. "You have to admit," he said. "That's a pretty good answer. I even gave you a few free questions, to help with the focus of things, as it were."

Kostrel gave a slightly sullen nod.

"Here's your first secret," Bast held up a single finger. "Most of the Fae don't come to this world. They don't like it. It rubs all rough against them, like wearing a burlap shirt. But when they do come, they like some places better than others. They like wild places. Secret places. Strange places. There are many types of Fae, many courts and houses. And all of them are ruled according to their own desires . . . "

Bast continued in a tone of soft conspiracy. "But something that appeals to all the Fae are places with connections to the raw, true things that shape the world. Places that are touched with fire and stone. Places that are close to water and air. When all four come together . . . "

Bast paused to see if the boy would interject something here. But Kostrel's face had lost the sharp cunning it had held before. He looked like a child again, mouth slightly agape, his eyes wide with wonder.

"Second secret," Bast said. "The Fae folk look nearly like we do, but not *exactly.* Most have something about them that makes them different. Their eyes. Their ears. The color of their hair or skin. Sometimes they're taller than normal, or shorter, or stronger, or more beautiful."

"Like Felurian,"

"Yes, yes," Bast said testily. "Like Felurian. But any of the Fae who has the skill to travel here will have craft enough to hide those things." He leaned back, nodding to himself. "That is a type of magic all the fair folk share."

Bast threw the final comment out like a fisherman casting a lure.

Kostrel closed his mouth and swallowed hard. He didn't fight the line. Didn't even know that he'd been hooked. "What sort of magic can they do?"

Bast rolled his eyes dramatically. "Oh come now, that's another whole book's worth of question,"

"Well maybe you should just *write* a book then," Kostrel said flatly. "Then you can lend it to me and kill two birds with one stone."

The comment seemed to catch Bast off his stride. "Write a book?"

"That's what people do when they know every damn thing, isn't it?" Kostrel said sarcastically. "They write it down so they can show off."

Bast looked thoughtful for a moment, then shook his head as if to clear it. "Okay. Here's the bones of what I know. They don't think of it as magic. They'd never use that term. They'll talk of *art* or *craft*. They talk of *seeming* or *shaping*."

He looked up at the sun and pursed his lips. "But if they were being frank, and they are rarely frank, mind you, they would tell you almost everything they do is either glammourie or grammorie. Glammourie is the art of making something seem. Grammarie is the craft of making something be."

Bast rushed ahead before the boy could interrupt. "Glammourie is easier. They can make a thing seem other than it is. They could make a white shirt seem like it was blue. Or a torn shirt seem like it was whole. Most of the folk have at least a scrap of this art. Enough to hide themselves from mortal eyes. If their hair was all of silver-white, their glammourie could make it look as black as night."

Kostrel's face was lost in wonder yet again. But it was not the gormless, gaping wonder of before. It was a thoughtful wonder. A clever wonder, curious and hungry. It was the sort of wonder that would steer a boy toward a question that started with a *how*.

Bast could see the shape of these things moving in the boy's dark eyes. His damn clever eyes. Too clever by half. Soon those vague wonderings would start to crystallize into questions like *'How do they make their glammourie?'* or even worse. *'How might a young boy break it?'*

And what then, with a question like that hanging in the air? Nothing good would come of it. To break a promise fairly made and lie outright was retrograde to his desire. Even worse to do it in this place. Far easier to tell the truth, then make sure something happened to the boy . . .

But honestly, he liked the boy. He wasn't dull, or easy. He wasn't mean or low. He pushed back. He was funny and grim and hungry and more alive than any three other people in the town all put together. He was bright as broken glass and sharp enough to cut himself. And Bast too, apparently.

Bast rubbed his face. This never used to happen. He had never been in conflict with his own desire before he came here. He hated it. It was so simply singular before. Want and have. See and take. Run and chase. Thirst and slake. And if he were thwarted in pursuit of his desire . . . what of it? That was simply the way of things. The desire itself was still his, it was still pure.

It wasn't like that now. Now his desires grew complicated. They constantly conflicted with each other. He felt endlessly turned against himself. Nothing was simple any more, he was pulled so many ways . . .

"Bast?" Kostrel said, his head cocked to the side, concern plain on his face. "Are you okay?" he asked. "What's the matter?"

Bast smiled an honest smile. He was a curious boy. Of course. That was the way. That was the narrow road between desires. "I was just thinking. Grammarie is much harder to explain. I can't say I understand it all that well myself."

"Just do your best," Kostrel said kindly. "Whatever you tell me will be more than I know."

No, he couldn't kill this boy. That would be too hard a thing.

"Grammarie is changing a thing," Bast said, making an inarticulate gesture. "Making it into something different than what it is."

"Like turning lead into gold?" Kostrel asked. "Is that how they make faerie gold?"

Bast made a point of smiling at the question. "Good guess, but that's glammourie. It's easy, but it doesn't last. That's why people who take faerie gold end up with pockets full of stones or acorns in the morning."

"Could they turn gravel into gold?" Kostrel asked. "If they really wanted to?"

"It's not that sort of change," Bast said, though he still smiled and nodded at the question. "That's too big. Grammarie is about . . . shifting. It's about making something into more of what it already is."

Kostrel's face twisted with confusion.

Bast took a deep breath and let it out through his nose. "Let me try something else. What have you got in your pockets?"

Kostrel rummaged about and held out his hands. There was a brass button, a scrap of paper, a stub of pencil, a small folding knife . . . and a stone with a hole in it. Of course.

Bast slowly passed his hand over the collection of oddments, eventually stopping above the knife. It wasn't particularly fine or fancy, just a piece of smooth wood the size of a finger with a groove where a short, hinged blade was tucked away.

Bast picked it up delicately between two fingers and set it down on the ground between them. "What's this?"

Kostrel stuffed the rest of his belongings into his pocket. "It's my knife."

"That's it?" Bast asked.

The boy's eyes narrowed suspiciously. "What else could it be?"

Bast brought out his own knife. It was a little larger, and instead of wood, it was carved from a piece of antler, polished and beautiful. Bast opened it, and the bright blade shone in the sun.

He lay his knife next to the boy's. "Would you trade your knife for mine?"

Kostrel eyed the knife jealously. But even so, there wasn't a hint of hesitation before he shook his head.

"Why not?"

"Because it's mine," the boy said, his face clouding over.

"Mine's better," Bast said matter-of-factly.

Kostrel reached out and picked up his knife, closing his hand around it possessively. His face was sullen as a storm. "My da gave me this," he said. "Before he took the king's coin and went to be a soldier and save us from the rebels." He looked up at Bast, as if daring him to say a single word contrary to that.

Bast didn't look away from him, just nodded seriously. "So it's more than just a knife." he said. "It's special to you."

Still clutching the knife, Kostrel nodded, blinking rapidly.

"For you, it's the best knife."

Another nod.

"It's more important than other knives. And that's not just a *seeming*," Bast said. "It's something the knife *is*."

There was a flicker of understanding in Kostrel's eyes.

Bast nodded. "That's grammarie. Now imagine if someone could take a knife and make it be more of what a knife is. Make it into the best knife. Not just for them, but for *anyone*." Bast picked up his own knife and closed it. "If they were really skilled, they could do it with something other than a knife. They could make a fire that was more of what a fire is. Hungrier. Hotter. Someone truly powerful could do even more. They could take a shadow . . . " he trailed off gently, leaving an open space in the empty air.

Kostrel drew a breath and leapt to fill it with a question. "Like Felurian!' he said. "Is that what she did to make Kvothe's shadow cloak?"

Bast nodded seriously, glad for the question, hating that it had to be *that* question. "It seems likely to me. What does a shadow do? It conceals, it protects. Kvothe's cloak of shadows does the same, but more."

Kostrel was nodding along in understanding, and Bast pushed on quickly, eager to leave this particular subject behind. "Think of Felurian herself . . . "

The boy grinned, he seemed to have no trouble doing that.

"A woman can be a thing of beauty," Bast said slowly. "She can be a focus of desire. Felurian is that. Like the knife. The most beautiful. The focus of the most desire. For everyone . . . " Bast let his statement trail off gently yet again.

Kostrel's eyes were far away, obviously giving the matter his full deliberation. Bast gave him time for it, and after a moment another question bubbled out of the boy. "Couldn't it be merely glammourie?" he asked.

"Ah," said Bast, smiling. "But what is the difference between *being* beautiful and *seeming* beautiful?"

"Well . . . " Kostrel stalled for a moment, then rallied. "One is real and the other isn't." He sounded certain, but it wasn't reflected in his expression. "One would be fake. You could tell the difference, couldn't you?"

Bast let the question sail by. It was close, but not quite. "What's the difference between a shirt that *looks* white and a shirt that *is* white?" he countered.

"A woman isn't the same as a shirt," Kostrel said with vast disdain. "You'd know if you touched her. If she looked all soft and rosy like Emberlee, but her hair felt like a horse's tail, you'd know it wasn't real."

"Glamourie isn't just for fooling eyes," Bast said. "It's for everything. Faerie gold feels heavy. And a glamoured pig would smell like roses when you kissed it."

Kostrel reeled visibly at that. The shift from Emberlee to a glamoured pig obviously left him feeling more than slightly appalled. Bast waited a moment for him to recover.

"Wouldn't it be harder to glamour a pig?" he asked at last.

"You're clever," Bast said encouragingly. "You're exactly right. And glamouring a pretty girl to be *more* pretty wouldn't be much work at all. It's like putting icing on a cake."

Kostrel rubbed his cheek thoughtfully. "Can you use glamourie and grammarie at the same time?"

Bast was more genuinely impressed this time. "That's what I've heard."

Kostrel nodded to himself. "That's what Felurian must do," he said. "Like cream on icing on cake."

"I think so," Bast said. "The one I met . . . " He stopped abruptly, his mouth snapped shut.

"You've met one of the Fae?"

Bast grinned like a beartrap. "Yes."

This time the Kostrel felt the hook and line both. But it was too late. "You bastard!"

"I am," Bast admitted happily.

"You tricked me into asking that."

"I did," Bast said. "It was a question related to this subject, and I answered it fully and without equivocation."

Kostrel got to his feet and stormed off, only to come back a moment later. "Give me my penny," he demanded.

Bast reached into his pocket and pulled out a copper penny. "Where's does Emberlee take her bath?"

Kostrel glowered furiously, then said. "Out past Oldstone bridge, up towards the hills about half a mile. There's a little hollow with an elm tree."

"And when?"

"After lunch on the Boggan farm. After she finishes the washing up and hangs the laundry."

Bast tossed him the penny, still grinning like mad.

"I hope your dick falls off," the boy said venomously before stomping back down the hill.

Bast couldn't help but laugh. He tried to do it quietly to spare the boy's feelings, but didn't meet with much success.

Kostrel turned at the bottom of the hill and shouted. "And you still owe me a book!"

Bast stopped laughing then as something jogged loose in his memory. He panicked for a moment when realized *Celum Tinture* wasn't in its usual spot.

Then he remembered leaving the book in the tree on top of the bluff and relaxed. The clear sky showed no sign of rain. It was safe enough. Besides, it was nearly noon, perhaps a little past. So he turned and hurried down the hill, not wanting to be late.

Bast sprinted most of the way to the little dell, and by the time he arrived he was sweating like a hard-run horse. His shirt stuck to him unpleasantly, so as he walked down the sloping bank to the water, he pulled it off and used it to mop the sweat from his face.

A long, flat jut of stone pushed out into Littlecreek there, forming one side of a calm pool where the stream turned back on itself. A stand of willow-trees overhung the water, making it private and shady. The shoreline was overgrown with thick bushes, and the water was smooth and calm and clear.

Bare-chested, Bast walked out onto the rough jut of stone. Dressed, his face and hands made him look rather lean, but shirtless his wide shoulders were surprising, more what you might expect to see on a fieldhand, rather than a shiftless sort that did little more than lounge around an empty inn all day.

Once he was out of the shadow of the willows, Bast knelt down to dunk his shirt in the pool. Then he wrung it over his head, shivering a bit at the chill of it. He rubbed his chest and arms briskly, shaking drops of water from his face.

He set the shirt aside, grabbed the lip of stone at the edge of the pool, then took a deep breath and dunked his head. The motion made the muscles across his back and shoulders flex. A moment later he pulled his head out, gasping slightly and shaking water from his hair.

Bast stood then, slicking back his hair with both hands. Water streamed down his chest, making runnels in the dark hair, trailing down across the flat plane of his stomach.

He shook himself off a bit, then stepped over to dark niche made by a jagged shelf of overhanging rock. He felt around for a moment before pulling out a knob of butter-colored soap.

He knelt at the edge of the water again, dunking his shirt several times, then scrubbing it with the soap. It took a while, as he had no washing board, and he obviously didn't want to chafe his shirt against the rough stones. He soaped and rinsed the shirt several times, wringing it out with his hands, making the muscles in his arms and shoulders tense and twine. He did a thorough job, though by the time he was finished, he was completely soaked and spattered with lather.

Bast spread his shirt out on a sunny stone to dry. He started to undo his pants, then stopped and tipped his head on one side, trying to jog loose water from his ear.

It might be because of the water in his ear that Bast didn't hear the excited twittering coming from the bushes that grew along the shore. A sound that could, conceivably, be sparrows chattering among the branches. A flock of sparrows. Several flocks, perhaps.

And if Bast didn't see the bushes moving either? Or note that in among the hanging foliage of the willow branches there were colors normally not found in trees? Sometimes a pale pink, sometimes blushing red. Sometimes an ill-considered yellow or a cornflower blue. And while it's true that dresses might come in those colors . . . well . . . so did birds. Finches and jays. And besides, it was fairly common knowledge among the young women of the town that the dark young man who worked at the inn was woefully nearsighted.

The sparrows twittered in the bushes as Bast worked at the drawstring of his pants again. The knot apparently giving him some trouble. He fumbled with it for a while, then grew frustrated and gave a great, catlike stretch, arms arching over his head, his body bending like a bow.

Finally he managed to work the knot loose and shuck free of his pants. He wore nothing underneath. He tossed them aside and from the willow came a squawk of the sort that could have come from a larger bird. A heron perhaps. Or a crow. And if a branch shook violently at the same time, well, perhaps a bird had leaned too far from its branch and nearly fell. It certainly stood to reason that some birds were more clumsy than others. And besides, at the time Bast was looking the other way.

Bast dove into the water then, splashing like a boy and gasping at the cold. After a few minutes he moved to a shallower portion of the pool where the water rose to barely reach his narrow waist.

Beneath the water, a careful observer might note the young man's legs looked somewhat . . . odd. But it was shady there, and everyone knows that water bends light strangely, making things look other than they are. And besides, birds are not the most careful of observers, especially when their attention is focused elsewhere.

An hour or so later, slightly damp and smelling of sweet honeysuckle soap, Bast climbed the bluff where he was fairly certain that he'd left his master's book. It was the third bluff he'd climbed in the last half hour.

When he reached the top, Bast relaxed at the sight of a hawthorn tree. Walking closer, he saw it was the right tree, the nook right where he remembered. But the book was gone. A quick circle of the tree showed that it hadn't fallen to the ground.

Then the wind stirred and Bast saw something white. He felt a sudden chill, fearing it was a page torn free from the book. Few things angered his master like a mistreated book.

But no. Reaching up, Bast didn't feel paper. It was a smooth stretch of birch bark. He pulled it down and saw the letters crudely scratched into the side.

I ned ta tawk ta ewe. Ets emportant.
Rike

Afternoon: Birds and Bees

With no idea of where he might find Rike, Bast made his way back to the lightning tree. He had just settled down in his usual place when a young girl came into the clearing.

She didn't stop at the greystone, and instead trudged straight up the side of the hill. She was younger than the others, six or seven. She wore a bright blue dress and had deep purple ribbons twining through her carefully curled hair.

She had never come to the lightning tree before, but Bast had seen her. Even if he hadn't, he could have guessed by her fine clothes and the smell of rosewater that she was Viette, the mayor's youngest daughter.

She climbed the low hill slowly, carrying something furry in the crook of her arm. When she reached the top of the hill she stood, slightly fidgety, but still waiting.

Bast eyed her quietly for a moment. "Do you know the rules?" he asked.

She stood, purple ribbons in her hair. She was obviously slightly scared, but her lower lip stuck out, defiant. She nodded.

"What are they?"

The young girl licked her lips and began to recite in a singsong voice. "No one taller than the stone." She pointed to the fallen greystone at the foot of the hill. "Come to blacktree, come alone." She put her finger to her lips, miming a shushing noise.

"Tell no—"

"Hold on," Bast interrupted. "You say the last two lines while touching the tree."

The girl blanched a bit at this, but stepped forward and put her hand against the sun-bleached wood of the long-dead tree.

The girl cleared her throat again, then paused, her lips moving silently as she ran through the beginning of the poem until she found her place again. "Tell no adult what's been said, lest the lightning strike you dead."

When she spoke the last word, Viette gasped and jerked her hand back, as if something had burned or bitten her fingers. Her eyes went wide as she looked down at her fingertips and saw they were an untouched, healthy pink. Bast hid a smile behind his hand.

"Very well then," Bast said. "You know the rules. I keep your secrets and you keep mine. I can answer questions or help you solve a problem." He sat down again, his back against the tree, bringing him to eye level with the girl. "What do you want?"

She held out the tiny puff of white fur she carried in the crook of her arm. It mewled. "Is this a magic kitten?" she asked.

Bast took the kitten in his hand and looked it over. It was a sleepy thing, almost entirely white. One eye was blue, the other green. "It is, actually," he said, slightly surprised. "At least a little." He handed it back.

She nodded seriously. "I want to call her Princess Icing Bun."

Bast simply stared at her, nonplused. "Okay."

The girl scowled at him. "I don't know if she's a girl or a boy!"

"Oh," Bast said. He held out his hand, took the kitten, then petted it and handed it back. "It's a girl."

The mayor's daughter narrowed her eyes at him. "Are you fibbing?"

Bast blinked at the girl, then laughed. "Why would you believe me the first time and not the second?" he asked.

"I could *tell* she was a magic kitten," Viette said, rolling her eyes in exasperation. "I just wanted to make sure. But she's not wearing a dress. She doesn't have any ribbons or bows. How can you tell if she's a girl?"

Bast opened his mouth. Then closed it again. This was not some farmer's child. She had a governess and a whole closet full of clothes. She didn't spend her time around sheep and pigs and goats. She'd never seen a lamb born. She had an older sister, but no brothers . . .

He hesitated, he'd rather not lie. Not here. But he hadn't promised to answer her question, hadn't made any sort of agreement at all with her. That made things easier. A great deal easier than having an angry mayor visit the Waystone, demanding to know why his daughter suddenly knew the word "penis."

"I tickle the kitten's tummy," Bast said easily. "And if it winks at me, I know it's a girl."

This satisfied Viette, and she nodded gravely. "How can I get my father to let me keep it?"

"You've already asked him nicely?"

She nodded. "Daddy hates cats."

"Begged and cried?"

Nod.

"Screamed and thrown a fit?"

She rolled her eyes and gave an exasperated sigh. "I've *tried* all that, or I wouldn't be here."

Bast thought for a moment. "Okay. First, you have to get some food that will keep good for a couple days. Biscuits. Sausage. Apples. Hide it in your room where nobody will find it. Not even your governess. Not even the maid. Do you have a place like that?"

The little girl nodded.

"Then go ask your daddy one more time. Be gentle and polite. If he still says no, don't be angry. Just tell him that you love the kitten. Say if you can't have her, you're afraid you'll be so sad you'll die."

"He'll still say no," the little girl said.

Bast shrugged. "Probably. Here's the second part. Tonight, pick at your dinner. Don't eat it. Not even the dessert." The little girl started to say something, but Bast held up a hand. "If anyone asks you, just say you're not hungry. Don't mention the kitten. When you're alone in your room tonight, eat some of the food you've hidden."

The little girl looked thoughtful.

Bast continued. "Tomorrow, don't get out of bed. Say you're too tired. Don't eat your breakfast. Don't eat your lunch. You can drink a little water, but just sips. Just lay in bed. When they ask what's the matter—"

She brightened. "I say I want my kitten!"

Bast shook his head, his expression grim. "No. That will spoil it. Just say you're tired. If they leave you alone, you can eat, but be careful. If they catch you, you'll never get your kitten."

The girl was listening intently now, her brow furrowed in concentration.

"By dinner they'll be worried. They'll offer you more food. Your favorites. Keep saying you're not hungry. You're just tired. Just lay there. Don't talk. Do that all day long."

"Can I get up to pee?"

Bast nodded. "But remember to act tired. No playing. The next day, they'll be scared. They'll bring in a doctor. They'll try to feed you broth. They'll try everything. At some point your father will be there, and he'll ask you what's the matter."

Bast grinned at her. "That's when you start to cry. No howling. Don't blubber. Just tears. Just lay there and cry. Then say you miss your kitten so much. You miss your kitten so much you don't want to be alive any more."

The little girl thought about it for a long minute, petting her kitten absentmindedly with one hand. Finally she nodded, "Okay." She turned to go.

"Hold on now!" Bast said quickly. "I gave you what you wanted. You owe me now."

The little girl turned around, her expression an odd mix of surprise and anxious embarrassment. "I didn't bring any money," she said, not meeting his eye.

"Not money," Bast said. "I gave you two answers and a way to get your kitten. You owe me three things. You pay with gifts and favors. You pay in secrets . . ."

She thought for a moment. "Daddy hides his strong box key inside the mantle clock."

Bast nodded approvingly. "That's one."

The little girl looked up into the sky, still petting her kitten. "I saw Mama kissing the maid once."

Bast raised an eyebrow at that. "That's two . . ."

The girl put her finger in her ear and wiggled it. "That's all, I think."

"How about a favor, then?" Bast said. "I need you to fetch me two dozen daisies with long stems. And a blue ribbon. And two armfuls of gemlings."

Viette's face puckered in confusion. "What's a gemling?"

"Flowers," Bast said, looking puzzled himself. "Maybe you call them balsams? They grow wild all over around here," he said, making a wide gesture with both hands.

"Do you mean geraniums?" she asked.

Bast shook his head. "No. They've got loose petals, and they're about this big." he made a circle with his thumb and middle finger. "They're yellow and orange and red . . . "

The girl stared at him blankly.

"Widow Creel keeps them in her window-box," Bast continued. "When you touch the seed pods, they pop . . . "

Viette's face lit up. "Oh! You mean *touch-me-nots*," she said, her tone more than slightly patronizing. "I can bring you a bunch of those. That's *easy*." She turned to run down the hill.

Bast called out before she'd taken six steps. "Wait!" When she spun around, he asked her. "What do you say if somebody asks you who you're picking flowers for?"

She rolled her eyes again. "I tell them it's none of their tupping business," she said. "Because my daddy is the mayor."

After Viette left, a high whistle made Bast look down the hill toward the greystone. There were no children waiting there.

The whistle came again, and Bast stood, stretching long and hard. It would have surprised most of the young women in town how easily he spotted the figure standing in the shadow of the trees at the edge of the clearing nearly two hundred feet away.

Bast sauntered down the hill, across the grassy field, and into the shadow of the trees. There was an older boy there with smudgy face and a pug nose. He was perhaps twelve and his shirt and pants were both too small for him, showing too much dirty wrist at the cuff and bare ankle below. He was barefoot and had a slightly sour smell about him.

"Rike." Bast's voice held none of the friendly, bantering tone he'd used with the town's other children. "How's the road to Tinuë?"

"It's a long damn way," the boy said bitterly, not meeting Bast's eye. "We live in the ass of nowhere."

"I see you have my book," Bast said.

The boy held it out. "I wann't tryin to steal it," he muttered quickly. "I just needed to talk to you."

Bast took the book silently.

"I didn't break the rules," the boy said. "I didn't even come into the clearing. But I need help. I'll pay for it."

"You lied to me, Rike," Bast said, his voice grim.

"And din't I pay for that?" the boy demanded angrily, looking up for the first time. "Din't I pay for it ten times over? Ent my life shit enough without having more shit piled on top of it?"

"And it's all beside the point because you're too old now," Bast said flatly.

"I aren't either!" the boy stomped a foot. Then struggled and took a deep breath, visibly forcing his temper back under control. "Tam is older'n me and he can still come to the tree! I'm just taller'n him!"

"Those are the rules," Bast said.

"It's a shite rule!" the boy shouted, his hands making angry fists. "And you're a shite little bastard who deserves more of the belt than he gets!"

There was a silence then, broken only by the boy's ragged breathing. Rike's eyes were on the ground, fists clenched at his sides, he was shaking.

Bast's eyes narrowed ever so slightly.

The boy's voice was rough. "Just one," Rike said. "Just one favor just this once. It's a big one. But I'll pay. I'll pay triple."

Bast drew a deep breath and let it out as a sigh. "Rike, I—"

"Please Bast?" He was still shaking, but Bast realized the boy's voice wasn't angry any more. "Please?" Eyes still on the ground, he took a hesitant step forward. "Just . . . please?" His hand reached out and just hung there aimlessly, as if he didn't know what to do with it. Finally he caught hold of Bast's shirtsleeve and tugged it once, feebly, before letting his hand fall back to his side.

"I just can't fix this on my own." Rike looked up, eyes full of tears. His face was twisted in a knot of anger and fear. A boy too young to keep from crying, but still old enough so that he couldn't help but hate himself for doing it.

"I need you to get rid of my da," he said in a broken voice. "I can't figure a way. I could stick him while he's asleep, but my ma would find out. He drinks and hits at her. And she cries all the time and then he hits her more."

Rike was looking at the ground again, the words pouring out of him in a gush. "I could get him when he's drunk somewhere, but he's so big. I couldn't move him. They'd find the body and then the azzie would get me. I couldn't look my ma in the eye then. Not if she knew. I can't think what that would do to her, if she knew I was the sort of person that would kill his own da."

He looked up then, his face furious, eyes red with weeping. "I would though. I'd kill him. You just got to tell me how."

There was a moment of quiet.

"Okay," Bast said.

They went down to the stream where they could have a drink and Rike could wash his face and collect himself a little bit. When the boy's face was cleaner, Bast noted not all the smudginess was dirt. It was easy to make the mistake, as the summer sun had tanned him a rich nut brown. Even after he was clean it was hard to tell they were faint remains of bruises.

But rumor or no, Bast's eyes were sharp. Cheek and jaw. A darkness all around one skinny wrist. And when he bent to take a drink from the stream, Bast glimpsed the boy's back . . .

"So," Bast said as they sat beside the stream. "What exactly do you want? Do you want to kill him, or do you just want to have him gone?"

"If he was just gone, I'd never sleep again for worry he'd come slouching back." Rike said, then was quiet for a bit. "He went gone two span once." He gave a faint smile. "That was a good time, just me and my ma. It was like my birthday every day when I woke up and he wasn't there. I never knew my ma could sing . . . "

They boy went quiet again. "I thought he'd fallen somewhere drunk and finally broke his neck. But he'd just traded off a year of furs for drinking money. He'd just been in his trapping shack, all stupor-drunk for half a month, not hardly more than a mile away."

The boy shook his head, more firmly this time. "No, if he goes, he won't stay away."

"I can figure out the how," Bast said. "That's what I do. But you need to tell me what you really want."

Rike sat for a long while, jaw clenching and unclenching. "Gone," he said at last. The word seemed to catch in his throat. "So long as he stays gone forever. If you can really do it."

"I can do it," Bast said.

Rike looked at his hands for a long time. "Gone then. I'd kill him. But that sort of thing ent right. I don't want to be that sort of man. A fellow shouldn't ought to kill his da."

"I could do it for you," Bast said easily.

Rike sat for a while, then shook his head. "It's the same thing, innit? Either way it's me. And if it were me, it would be more honest if I did it with my hands, rather than do it with my mouth."

Bast nodded. "Right then. Gone forever."

"And soon," Rike said.

Bast sighed and looked up at the sun. He already had things to do today. The turning wheels of his desire did not come grinding to a halt because some farmer drank too much. Emberlee would be taking her bath soon. He was supposed to get carrots . . .

He didn't owe the boy a thing, either. Quite the opposite. The boy had lied to him. Broke his promise. And while Bast had settled that account so firmly that no other child in town would ever dream of crossing him like that again . . . it was still galling to remember. The thought of helping him now, despite that, it was quite the opposite of his desire.

"It *has* to be soon," Ride said. "He's getting worse. I can run off, but ma can't. And little Bip can't neither. And . . . "

"Fine, fine . . . " Bast cut him off, waving his hands. "Soon."

Rike swallowed. "What's this going to cost me?" he asked, anxious.

"A lot," Bast said grimly. "We're not talking about ribbons and buttons here. Think how much you want this. Think how big it is." He met the boy's eye and didn't look away. "Three times that is what you owe me. Plus some for soon." He stared hard at the boy. "Think hard on that."

Rike was a little pale now, but he nodded without looking away. "You can have what you like of mine," he said. "But nothin of ma's. She ent got much that my da hasn't already drank away."

"We'll work it out," Bast said. "But it'll be nothing of hers. I promise."

Rike took a deep breath, then gave a sharp nod. "Okay. Where do we start?"

Bast pointed at the stream. "Find a river stone with a hole in it and bring it to me."

Rike gave Bast an odd look. "Yeh want a faerie stone?"

"Faerie stone," Bast said with such scathing mockery that Rike flushed with embarrassment. "You're too old for that nonsense." Bast gave the boy a look. "Do you want my to help or not?" he asked.

"I do," Rike said in a small voice.

"Then I want a river stone." Bast pointed back at the stream. "You have to be the one to find it," he said. "It can't be anyone else. And you need to find it dry on the shore"

Rike nodded.

"Right then." Bast clapped his hands twice. "Off you go."

Rike left and Bast returned to the lightning tree. No children were waiting to talk to him, so he idled the time away. He skipped stones in the nearby stream and flipped through *Celum Tinture*, glancing at some of the illustrations. Calcification. Titration. Sublimation.

Brann, happily unbirched with one hand bandaged, brought him two sweet buns wrapped in a white handkerchief. Bast ate the first and set the second aside.

Viette brought armloads of flowers and a fine blue ribbon. Bast wove the daisies into a crown, threading the ribbon through the stems.

Then, looking up at the sun, he saw that it was nearly time, Bast removed his shirt and filled it with the wealth of yellow and red touch-me-nots Viette had brought him. He added the handkerchief and crown, then fetched a stick and made a bindle so he could carry the lot more easily.

He headed out past the Oldstone bridge, then up toward the hills and around a bluff until he found the place Kostrel had described. It was cleverly hidden away, and the stream curved and eddied into a lovely little pool perfect for a private bath.

Bast sat behind some bushes, and after nearly half an hour of waiting he had fallen into a doze. The sharp crackle of a twig and a scrap of a idle song roused him, and he peered down to see a young woman making her careful way down the steep hillside to the water's edge.

Moving silently, Bast scurried upstream, carrying his bundle. Two minutes later he was kneeling on the grassy waterside with the pile of flowers beside him.

He picked up a yellow blossom and breathed on it gently. As his breath brushed the petals, its color faded and changed into a delicate blue. He dropped it and the current carried it slowly downstream.

Bast gathered up a handful of posies, red and orange, and breathed on them again. They too shifted and changed until they were a pale and vibrant blue. He scattered them onto the surface of the stream. He did this twice more until there were no flowers left.

Then, picking up the handkerchief and daisy crown, he sprinted back downstream to the cozy little hollow with the elm. He'd moved quickly enough that Emberlee was just coming to the edge of the water.

Softly, silently, he crept up to the spreading elm. Even with one hand carrying the handkerchief and crown, he went up the side as nimbly as a squirrel.

Bast lay along a low branch, sheltered by leaves, breathing fast but not hard. Emberlee was removing her stockings and setting them carefully on a nearby hedge. Her hair was a burnished golden red, falling in lazy curls. Her face was sweet and round, a lovely shade of pale and pink.

Bast grinned as he watched her look around, first left, then right. Then she began to unlace her bodice. Her dress was a pale cornflower blue, edged with yellow, and when she spread it on the hedge, it flared and splayed out like the wing of a great bird. Perhaps some fantastic combination of a finch and a jay.

Dressed only in her white shift, Emberlee looked around again: left, then right. Then she shimmied free of it, a fascinating motion. She tossed the shift aside and stood there, naked as the moon. Her creamy skin was amazing with freckle. Her hips wide and lovely. The tips of her breasts were brushed with the palest of pink.

She scampered into the water. Making a series of small, dismayed cries at the chill of it. They were, on consideration, not really similar to a raven's at all. Though they could, perhaps, be slightly like a heron's.

Emberlee washed herself a bit, splashing and shivering. She soaped herself, dunked her head in the river and came up gasping. Wet, her hair became the color of ripe cherries.

It was then that the first of the blue touch-me-nots arrived, drifting on the water. She glanced at it curiously as it floated by, and began to lather soap into her hair.

More flowers followed. They came downstream and made circles around her, caught in the slow eddy of the pool. She looked at them, amazed. Then sieved a double handful from the water and brought them to her face, drawing a deep breath to smell them.

She laughed delightedly and dunked under the surface, coming up in the middle of the flowers, the water sluiced her pale skin, running over her naked breasts. Blossoms clung to her, as if reluctant to let go.

That was when Bast fell out of the tree.

There was a brief, mad scrabbling of fingers against bark, a bit of a yelp, then he hit the ground like a sack of suet. He lay on his back in the grass, and let out a low, miserable groan.

He heard a splashing; Emberlee appeared above him. She held her white shift in front of her. Bast looked up from where he lay in the tall grass.

He'd been lucky to land on that patch of springy turf, cushioned with tall, green grass. A few feet to one side, and he'd have broken himself against the rocks. Five feet the other way and he would have been wallowing in mud.

Emberlee knelt beside him, her skin pale, her hair dark. One posy clung to her neck, it was the same color as her eyes, a pale and vibrant blue.

"Oh," Bast said happily as he gazed up at her. His eyes were slightly dazed. "You're so much lovelier than I'd imagined."

He lifted a hand as if to brush her cheek, only to find it holding the crown and knotted handkerchief. "Ahh," he said, remembering. "I've brought you some daisies too. And a sweet bun."

"Thank you," she said, taking the daisy crown with both hands. She had to let go of her shift to do this. It fell lightly to the grass.

Bast blinked, momentarily at a loss for words.

Emberlee tilted her head to look at the crown; the ribbon was a striking cornflower blue, but it was nothing near as lovely as her eyes. She lifted it with both hands and settled it proudly on her head. Her arms still raised, she drew a slow breath.

Bast's eyes slipped from her crown.

She smiled at him indulgently.

Bast drew a breath to speak, then stopped and drew another through his nose. Honeysuckle.

"Did you steal my soap?" he asked incredulously.

Emberlee laughed and kissed him.

A good while later, Bast took the long way back to the lightning tree, making a wide loop up into the hills north of town. Things were rockier up that way, no ground flat enough to plant, the terrain too treacherous for grazing.

Even with the boy's directions, it took Bast a while to find Martin's still. He had to give the crazy old bastard credit, though. Between the brambles, rockslides, and fallen trees, there wasn't a chance he would have stumbled onto it accidentally, tucked back into a shallow cave in a scrubby little box valley.

The still wasn't some slipshod contraption bunged together out of old pots and twisted wire either. It was a work of art. There were barrels and basins and great spirals of copper tube. A great copper kettle twice the size of a washbin, and a smolder-stove for warming it. A wooden trough ran all along the ceiling, and only after following it outside did Bast realize Martin collected rainwater and brought it inside to fill his cooling barrels.

Looking it over, Bast had the sudden urge to flip through *Celum Tinture* and learn what all the different pieces of the still were called, what they were for. Only then did he realize he'd left the book back at the lightning tree.

So instead Bast rooted around until he found a box filled with a mad miscellany of containers: two dozen bottles of all sorts, clay jugs, old canning jars . . . A dozen of them were full. None of them were labeled in any way.

Bast lifted out a tall bottle that had obviously once held wine. He pulled the cork, sniffed it gingerly, then took a careful sip. His face bloomed into a sunrise of delight. He'd half-expected turpentine, but this was . . . well . . . he wasn't sure entirely. He took another drink. There was something of apples about it, and . . . barley?

Bast took a third drink, grinning. Whatever you care to call it, it was lovely. Smooth and strong and just a little sweet. Martin might mad as a badger, but he clearly knew his liquor.

It was better than an hour before Bast made it back to the lightning tree. Rike hadn't returned, but *Celum Tinture* was sitting there unharmed. For the first time he could remember, he was glad to see the book. He flipped it open to the chapter on distillation and read for half an hour, nodding to himself at various points. It was called a condensate coil. He'd thought it looked important.

Eventually he closed the book and sighed. There were a few clouds rolling in, and no good could come of leaving the book unattended again. His luck wouldn't last forever, and he shuddered to think what would happen if the wind tumbled the book into the grass and tore the pages. If there was a sudden rain . . .

So Bast wandered back to the Waystone Inn and slipped silently through the back door. Stepping carefully, he opened a cupboard and tucked the book inside. He made his silent way halfway back to the door before he heard footsteps behind him.

"Ah, Bast," the innkeeper said. "Have you brought the carrots?"

Bast froze, caught awkwardly mid-sneak. He straightened up and brushed self-consciously at his clothes. "I . . . I haven't quite got round to that yet, Reshi."

The innkeeper gave a deep sigh. "I don't ask a . . . " He stopped and sniffed, then eyed the dark haired man narrowly. "Are you drunk, Bast?"

Bast looked affronted. "Reshi!"

The innkeeper rolled his eyes. "Fine then, have you been drinking?"

"I've been *investigating*," Bast said, emphasizing the word. "Did you know Crazy Martin runs a still?"

"I didn't," the innkeeper said, his tone making it clear he didn't find this information to be particularly thrilling. "And Martin isn't crazy. He just has a handful of unfortunately strong affect compulsions. And a touch of tabard madness from when he was a soldier."

"Well, yes . . . " Bast said slowly. "I know, because he set his dog on me and when I climbed a tree to get away, he tried to chop the tree down. But also, aside from those things, he's crazy too, Reshi. Really, really crazy."

"Bast," the innkeeper gave him a chiding look.

"I'm not saying he's bad, Reshi. I'm not even saying I don't like him. But trust me. I know crazy. His head isn't put together like a normal person's."

The innkeeper gave an agreeable if slightly impatient nod. "Noted."

Bast opened his mouth, then looked slightly confused. "What were we talking about?"

"Your advanced state of investigation," the innkeeper said, glancing out the window. "Despite the fact that it is barely three bells."

"Ah. Right!" Bast said excitedly. "I know Martin's been running a tab for the better part of a year now. And I know you've had trouble settling up because he doesn't have any money."

"He doesn't *use* money," the innkeeper corrected gently.

"Same difference, Reshi," Bast sighed. "And it doesn't change the fact that we don't need another sack of barley. The pantry is choking on barley. But since he runs a still . . . "

The innkeeper was already shaking his head. "No Bast," he said. "I won't go poisoning my customers with hillwine. You have no idea what ends up in that stuff . . . "

"But I *do* know, Reshi," Bast said plaintively. "Ethel acetates and methans. And tinleach. There's none of that."

The innkeeper blinked, obviously taken aback. "Did . . . Have you actually been reading *Celum Tinture*?"

"I did, Reshi," Bast beamed. "For the betterment of my education and my desire to not poison folk. I tasted some, Reshi, and I can say with some authority that Martin is not making hillwine. It's lovely stuff. It's halfway to Rhis, and that's not something I say lightly."

The innkeeper stroked his upper lip thoughtfully. "Where did you get some to taste?" he asked.

"I traded for it," Bast said, easily skirting the edges of the truth. "I was thinking," Bast continued. "Not only would it give Martin a chance to settle his tab. But it would help us get some new stock in. That's harder, the roads as bad as they are . . . "

The innkeeper held up both hands helplessly. "I'm already convinced, Bast."

Bast grinned happily.

"Honestly, I would have done it merely to celebrate you reading your lesson for once. But it will be nice for Martin, too. It will give him an excuse to come by more often. It will be good for him."

Bast's smile faded a bit.

If the innkeeper noticed, he didn't comment on it. "I'll send a boy round to Martin's and ask him to come by with a couple bottles."

"Get five or six," Bast said. "It's getting cold at night. Winter's coming."

The innkeeper smiled. "I'm sure Martin will be flattered."

Bast paled at that. "By all the gorse *no*, Reshi," he said, waving his hands in front of himself and taking a step backwards. "Don't tell him I'll be drinking it. He hates me."

The innkeeper hid a smile behind his hand.

"It's not funny, Reshi," Bast said angrily. "He throws rocks at me."

"Not for months," the innkeeper pointed out. "Martin has been perfectly cordial to you the last several times he's stopped by for a visit."

"Because there aren't any rocks inside the inn," Bast said.

"Be fair, Bast," the innkeeper continued. "He's been civil for almost a year. Polite even. Remember he apologized to you two months back? Have you heard of Martin ever apologizing to anyone else in town? Ever?"

"No," Bast said sulkily.

The innkeeper nodded. "That's a big gesture for him. He's turning a new leaf."

"I know," Bast muttered, moving toward the back door. "But if he's here when I get home tonight, I'm eating dinner in the kitchen."

Rike caught up with Bast before he even made it to the clearing, let alone the lightning tree.

"I've got it," the boy said, holding up his hand triumphantly. The entire lower half of his body was dripping wet.

"What, already?" Bast asked.

The boy nodded and flourished the stone between two fingers. It was flat and smooth and round, slightly bigger than a copper penny. "What now?"

Bast stroked his chin for a moment, as if trying to remember. "Now we need a needle. But it has to be borrowed from a house where no men live."

Rike looked thoughtful for a moment, then brightened. "I can get one from Aunt Sellie!"

Bast fought the urge to curse. He'd forgotten about Sellie. "That will do . . . " he said, reluctantly, "But it will work best if the needle comes from a house with a lot of women living in it. The more women the better."

Rike looked up for another moment. "Widow Creel then. She's got a daughter."

"She's got a boy, too." Bast pointed out. "A house where no men *or boys* live."

"But where a lot of girls live . . . ." Rike said. He had to think about it for a long while. "Old Nan don't like me none," he said. "But I reckon she'd give me a pin."

"A needle," Bast stressed. "And you have to borrow it. You can't steal it or buy it. She has to lend it to you."

Bast had half expected the boy to grouse about the particulars, about the fact that Old Nan lived all the way off on the other side of town, about as far west as you could go and still be considered part of the town. It would take him half an hour to get there, and even then, Old Nan might not be home.

But Rike didn't so much as sigh. He just nodded seriously, turned, and took off at a sprint, bare feet flying.

Bast continued to the lightning tree, but when he came to the clearing he saw an entire tangle of children playing on the greystone, doubtless waiting for him. Four of them.

Watching them from the shadow of the trees at the edge of the clearing, Bast hesitated, then glanced up at the sun before slipping back into the woods. He had other fish to fry.

The Williams farm wasn't a farm in any proper sense. Not for decades. The fields had gone fallow so long ago that they were barely recognizable as such, spotted with brambles and sapling trees. The tall barn had fallen into disrepair and half the roof gaped open to the sky.

Walking up the long path through the fields, Bast turned a corner and saw Rike's house. It told a different story than the barn. It was small but tidy. The shingles needed some repair, but other than that, it looked well-loved and tended-to. Yellow curtains were blowing out the kitchen window, and there was a flower box spilling over with fox fiddle and marigold.

There was a pen with a trio of goats on one side of the house, and a large well-tended garden on the other. It was fenced thickly with lashed-together sticks, but Bast could see straight lines of flourishing greenery inside. Carrots. He still needed carrots.

Craning his neck a bit, Bast saw several large, square boxes behind the house. He took a few more steps to the side and eyed them before he realized they were beehives.

Just then there was a great storm of barking and two great black, floppy-eared dogs came bounding from the house toward Bast, baying for all they were worth. When they came close enough, Bast got down on one knee and wrestled with them playfully, scratching their ears and the ruff of their necks.

After a few minutes of this, Bast continued to the house, the dogs weaving back and forth in front of him before they spotted some sort of animal and tore off into the underbrush. He knocked politely at the front door, though after all the barking his presence could hardly be a surprise.

The door opened a couple inches, and for a moment all Bast could see was a slender slice of darkness. Then the door opened a little wider, revealing Rike's mother. She was tall, and her curling brown hair was springing loose from the braid that hung down her back.

She swung the door fully open, holding a tiny, half-naked baby in the curve of her arm. Its round face was pressed into her breast and it was sucking busily, making small grunting noises.

Glancing down, Bast smiled warmly.

The woman looked fondly down at her child, then favored Bast with a tired smile. "Hello Bast, what can I do for you?"

"Ah. Well," he said awkwardly, pulling his gaze up to meet her eye. "I was wondering, ma'am. That is, Mrs. Williams—"

"Nettie is fine, Bast," she said indulgently. More than a few of the townfolk considered Bast somewhat simple in the head, a fact that Bast didn't mind in the least.

"Nettie," Bast said, smiling his most ingratiating smile.

There was a pause, and she leaned against the doorframe. A little girl peeked out from around the woman's faded blue skirt, nothing more than a pair of serious dark eyes.

Bast smiled at the girl, who disappeared back behind her mother.

Nettie looked at Bast expectantly. Finally she prompted. "You were wondering . . . "

"Oh, yes." Bast said. "I was wondering if your husband happened to be about."

"I'm afraid not," she said. "Jessom's off checking his traps."

"Ah," Bast said, disappointed. "Will he be back any time soon? I'd be happy to wait . . . "

She shook her head, "I'm sorry. He'll do his lines then spend the night skinning and drying up in his shack." She nodded vaguely toward the northern hills.

"Ah," Bast said again.

Nestled snugly in her mother's arm, the baby drew a deep breath, then sighed it out blissfully, going quiet and limp. Nettie looked down, then up at Bast, holding a finger to her lips.

Bast nodded and stepped back from the doorway, watching as Nettie stepped inside, deftly detached the sleeping baby from her nipple with her free hand, then carefully tucked the child into a small wooden cradle on the floor. The dark-eyed girl emerged from behind her mother and went to peer down at the baby.

"Call me if she starts to fuss," Nettie said softly. The little girl nodded seriously, sat down on a nearby chair, and began to gently rock the cradle with her foot.

Nettie stepped outside, closing the door behind her. She walked the few steps necessary to join Bast, rearranging her bodice unselfconsciously. In the sunlight Bast noticed her high cheekbones and generous mouth. Even so, she was more tired than pretty, her dark eyes heavy with worry.

The tall woman crossed her arms over her chest. "What's the trouble then?" she asked wearily.

Bast looked confused. "No trouble," he said. "I was wondering if your husband had any work."

Nettie uncrossed her arms, looking surprised. "Oh."

"There isn't much for me to do at the inn," Bast said a little sheepishly. "I thought your husband might need an extra hand."

Nettie looked around, eyes brushing over the old barn. Her mouth tugging down at the corners. "He traps and hunts for the most part these days," she said. "Keeps him busy, but not so much that he'd need help, I imagine." She looked back to Bast. "At least he's never made mention of wanting any."

"How about yourself?" Bast asked, giving his most charming smile. "Is there anything around the place you could use a hand with?"

Nettie smiled at Bast indulgently. It was only a small smile, but it stripped ten years and half a world of worry off her face, making her practically shine with loveliness. "There isn't much to do," she said apologetically. "Only three goats, and my boy minds them."

"Firewood?" Bast asked. "I'm not afraid to work up a sweat. And it has to be hard getting by with your gentleman gone for days on end . . . " he grinned at her hopefully.

"And we just haven't got the money for help, I'm afraid." Nettie said.

"I just want some carrots," Bast said.

Nettie looked at him for a minute, then burst out laughing. "Carrots," she said, rubbing at her face. "How many carrots?"

"Maybe . . . six?" Bast asked, not sounding very sure of his answer at all.

She laughed again, shaking her head a little. "Okay. You can split some wood." She pointed to the chopping block that stood in back of the house. "I'll come get you when you've done six carrot's worth."

Bast set to work eagerly, and soon the yard was full of the crisp, healthy sound of splitting wood. The sun was still strong in the sky, and after just a few minutes Bast was covered in a sheen of sweat. He carelessly peeled away his shirt and hung it on the nearby garden fence.

There was something different about the way he split the wood. Nothing dramatic. In fact he split wood the same way everyone did: you set the log upright, you swing the axe, you split the wood. There isn't much room to extemporize.

But still, there was a difference in the way he did it. When he set the log upright, he moved intently. Then he would stand for a tiny moment, perfectly still. Then came the swing. It was a fluid thing. The placement of his feet, the play of the long muscles in his arms . . .

There was nothing exaggerated. Nothing like a flourish. Even so, when he brought the axe up and over in a perfect arc, there was a grace to it. The sharp cough the wood made as it split, the sudden way the halves went tumbling to the ground. He made it all look somehow . . . well . . . *dashing*.

He worked a hard half hour, at which time Nettie came out of the house, carrying a glass of water and a handful of fat carrots with the loose greens still attached. "I'm sure that's at least six carrot's worth of work," she said, smiling at him.

Bast took the glass of water, drank half of it, then bent over and poured the rest over his head. He shook himself off a bit, then stood back up, his dark hair curling and clinging to his face. "Are you sure there's nothing else you could use a hand with?" He asked, giving her an easy grin. His eyes were dark and smiling and bluer than the sky.

Nettie shook her head. Her hair was out of her braid now, and when she looked down, the loose curls of it fell partly across her face. "I can't think of anything," she said.

"I'm a dab hand with honey, too," Bast said, hoisting the axe to rest against his naked shoulder.

She looked a little puzzled at that until Bast nodded toward the wooden hives scattered through the overgrown field. "Oh," she said, as if remembering a half-forgotten dream. "I used to do candles and honey. But we lost a few hives to that bad winter three years back. Then one to nits. Then there was that wet spring and three more went down with the chalk before we even knew." She shrugged. "Early this summer we sold one to the Hestles so we'd have money for the levy . . . "

She shook her head again, as if she'd been daydreaming. She shrugged and turned back to look at Bast. "Do you know about bees?" "

"A fair bit," Bast said softly. "They aren't hard to handle. They just need patience and gentleness." He casually swung the axe so it stuck in the nearby stump. "They're the same as everything else, really. They just want to know they're safe."

Nettie was looking out at the field, nodding along with Bast's words unconsciously. "There's only the two left," she said. "Enough for a few candles. A little honey. Not much. Hardly worth the bother, really."

"Oh come now," Bast said gently. "A little sweetness is all any of us have sometimes. It's always worth it. Even if it takes some work."

Nettie turned to look at him. She met his eyes now. Not speaking, but not looking away either. Her eyes were like an open door.

Bast smiled, gentle and patient, his voice was warm and sweet as honey. He held out his hand. "Come with me," he said. "I have something to show you."

The sun was starting to sink toward the western trees by the time Bast returned to the lightning tree. He was limping slightly, and he had dirt in his hair, but he seemed to be in good spirits.

There were two children at the bottom of the hill, sitting on the greystone and swinging their feet as if it were a huge stone bench. Bast didn't even have time to sit down before they came up the hill together.

It was Wilk, a serious boy of ten with shaggy blond hair. At his side was his little sister Pem, half his age with three times the mouth.

The boy nodded at Bast as he came to the top of the hill, then he looked down. "You hurt your hand," he said.

Bast looked down at his hand and was surprised to see a few dark streaks of blood dripping down the side of it. He brought out his handkerchief and daubed at it.

"What happened?" little Pem asked him.

"I was attacked by a bear," he lied nonchalantly.

The boy nodded, giving no indication of whether or not he believed it was true. "I need a riddle that will stump Tessa," the boy said. "A good one."

"You smell like Granda," Pem chirruped as she came up to stand beside her brother.

Wilk ignored her. Bast did the same.

"Okay," said Bast. "I need a favor, I'll trade you. A favor for a riddle."

"You smell like Granda when he's been at his medicine," Pem clarified.

"It has to be a good one though," Wilk stressed. "A stumper."

"Show me something that's never been seen before and will never be seen again," Bast said.

"Hmmm . . . " Wilk said, looking thoughtful.

"Granda says he feels loads better with his medicine," Pem said, louder, plainly irritated at being ignored. "But Mum says it's not medicine. She says he's on the bottle. And Granda says he feels loads better so it's medicine by dammit." She looked back and forth between Bast and Wilk, as if daring them to scold her.

Neither of them did. She looked a little crestfallen.

"That is a good one," Wilk admitted at last. "What's the answer?"

Bast gave a slow grin. "What will you trade me for it?"

Wilk cocked his head on one side, "I already said. A favor."

"I traded you the riddle for a favor," Bast said easily. "But now you're asking for the answer . . . "

Wilk looked confused for half a moment, then his face went red and angry. He drew a deep breath as if he were going to shout. Then seemed to think better of it and stormed down the hill, stomping his feet.

His sister watched him go, then turned back to Bast. "Your shirt is ripped," she said disapprovingly. "And you've got grass stains on your pants. Your mam is going to give you a hiding."

"No, she won't," Bast said smugly. "Because I'm all grown, and I can do whatever I want with my pants. I could light them on fire and I wouldn't get in any trouble at all."

The little girl stared at him with smoldering envy.

Wilk stomped back up the hill. "Fine," he said sullenly.

"My favor first," Bast said. He handed the boy a small bottle with a cork in the top. "I need you to fill this up with water that's been caught midair."

"What?" Wilk said.

"Naturally falling water," Bast said. "You can't dip it out of a barrel or a stream. You have to catch it while it's still in the air."

"Water falls out of a pump when you pump it . . . " Wilk said without any real hope in his voice.

"*Naturally* falling water," Bast said again, stressing the first word. "It's no good if someone just stands on a chair and pours it out of a bucket."

"What do you need it for?" Pem asked in her little piping voice.

"What will you trade me for the answer to that question?" Bast said.

The little girl went pale and slapped one hand across her mouth.

"It might not rain for *days*," Wilk said.

Pem gave a gusty sigh. "It doesn't have to be rain," his sister said, her voice dripping with condescension. "You could just go to the waterfall by Littlecliff and fill the bottle there."

Wilk blinked.

Bast grinned at her. "You're a clever girl."

She rolled her eyes, "Everybody says that . . . "

Bast brought out something from his pocket and held it. It was a green cornhusk wrapped around a daub of sticky honeycomb. The little girl's eyes lit up when she saw it.

"I also need twenty-one perfect acorns," he said. "No holes, with all their little hats intact. If you gather them for me over by the waterfall, I'll give you this."

She nodded eagerly. Then both she and her brother hurried down the hill.

Bast went back down to the pool by the spreading willow and took another bath. It wasn't his usual bathing time, so there were no birds waiting, and as a result the bath was much more matter-of-fact than before.

He quickly rinsed himself clean of sweat and honey and he daubed a bit at his clothes too, scrubbing to get rid of the grass stains and the smell of whiskey. The cold water stung the cuts on his knuckles a bit, but they were nothing serious and would mend well enough on their own.

Naked and dripping, he pulled himself from the pool and found a dark rock, hot from the long day of sun. He draped his clothes over it and let them bake dry while he shook his hair dry and stripped the water from his arms and chest with his hands.

Then he made his way back to the lightning tree, picked a long piece of grass to chew on, and almost immediately fell asleep in the golden afternoon sunlight.

Evening: Lessons

Hours later, the evening shadows stretched to cover Bast, and he shivered himself awake.

He sat up, rubbing his face and looking around blearily. The sun was just beginning to brush the tops of the western trees. Wilk and Pem hadn't returned, but that was hardly a surprise. He ate the piece of honeycomb he'd promised Pem, licking his fingers slowly. Then he chewed the wax idly and watched a pair of hawks turn lazy circles in the sky.

Eventually he heard a whistle from the trees. He got to his feet and stretched, his body bending like a bow. Then he sprinted down the hill . . . except, in the fading light it didn't quite look like a sprint.

If he were a boy of ten, it would have looked like skipping. But he was no boy. If he were a goat, it would have looked like he was prancing. But he was no goat. A man headed down the hill that quickly, it would have looked like he was running.

But there was something odd about Bast's motion in the fading light. Something hard to describe. He almost looked like he was . . . what? Frolicking? Dancing?

Small matter. Suffice to say that he quickly made his way to the edge of the clearing where Rike stood in the growing dark beneath the trees.

"I've got it," the boy said triumphantly, he held up his hand, but the needle was invisible in the dark.

"You borrowed it?" Bast asked. "Not traded or bargained for it?"

Rike nodded.

"Okay," Bast said. "Follow me."

The two of them walked over to the greystone, Rike following wordlessly when Bast climbed up one side of the half-fallen stone. The sunlight was still strong there, and both of them had plenty of space to stand on the broad back of the tilted greystone. Rike looked around anxiously, as if worried someone might see him.

"Let's see the stone," Bast said.

Rike dug into his pocket and held it out to Bast.

Bast pulled his hand back suddenly, as if the boy had tried to hand him a glowing coal. "Don't be stupid," he snapped. "It's not for me. The charm is only going to work for one person. Do you want that to be me?"

The boy brought his hand back and eyed the stone. "What do you mean one person?"

"It's the way of charms," Bast said. "They only work for one person at a time." Seeing the boy's confusion written plainly on his face, Bast sighed. "You know how some girls make come-hither charms, hoping to catch a boy's eye?"

Rike nodded, blushing a little.

"This is the opposite," Bast said. "It's a go-thither charm. You're going to prick your finger, get a drop of your blood on it, and that will seal it. It will make things go away."

Rike looked down at the stone. "What sort of things?" he said.

"Anything that wants to hurt you," Bast said easily. "You can just keep it in your pocket, or you can get a piece of cord—"

"It will make my da leave?" Rike interrupted.

Bast frowned. "That's what I said. You're his blood. So it will push him away more strongly than anything else. You'll probably want to hang it around your neck so—"

"What about a bear?" Rike asked, looking at the stone thoughtfully. "Would it make a bear leave me alone?"

Bast made a back and forth motion with his hand. "Wild things are different," he said. "They're possessed of pure desire. They don't want to *hurt* you. They usually want food, or safety. A bear would—"

"Can I give it to my mum?" Rike interrupted again, looking up at Bast. His dark eyes serious.

" . . . want to protect its terr . . . What?" Bast stumbled to a halt.

"My mum should have it," Rike said. "What if I was off away with the charm and my da came back?"

"He's going farther away than that," Bast said, his voice thick with certainty. "It's not like he'll be hiding around the corner at the smithy . . . "

Rike's face was set now, his pug nose making him seem all the more stubborn. He shook his head. "She should have it. She's important. She has to take care of Tess and little Bip."

"It will work just fine—"

"It's got to be for HER!" Rike shouted, his hand making a fist around the stone. "You said it could be for one person, so you make it be for her!"

Bast scowled at the boy darkly. "I don't like your tone," he said grimly. "You asked me to make your da go away. And that's what I'm doing . . . "

"But what if it's not enough?" Rike's face was red.

"It will be," Bast said, absentmindedly rubbing his thumb across the knuckles of his hand. "He'll go far away. You have my word—"

"NO!" Rike said, his face going red and angry. "What if sending *him* isn't enough? What if I grow up like my da? I get so . . . " his voice choked off, and his eyes started to leak tears. "I'm not good. I know it. I know better than anyone. Like you said. I got his blood in me. She needs to be safe from me. If I grow up twisted up and bad, she needs the charm to . . . she needs something to make me go a—"

Rike clenched his teeth, unable to continue.

Bast reached out and took hold of the boy's shoulder. He was stiff and rigid as a plank of wood, but Bast gathered him in and put his arms around his shoulders. Gently, because he had seen the boy's back. They stood there for a long moment, Rike stiff and tight as a bowstring, trembling like a sail tight against the wind.

"Rike," Bast said softly. "You're a good boy. Do you know that?"

The boy bent then, sagged against Bast and seemed like he would break himself apart with sobbing. His face was pressed into Bast's stomach and he said something, but it was muffled and disjointed. Bast made a soft crooning sound of the sort you'd use to calm a horse or soothe a hive of restless bees.

The storm passed, and Rike stepped quickly away and scrubbed at his face roughly with his sleeve. The sky was just starting to tinge red with sunset.

"Right," Bast said. "It's time. We'll make it for your mother. You'll have to give it to her. River stone works best if it's given as a gift."

Rike nodded, not looking up. "What if she won't wear it?" he asked quietly.

Bast blinked, confused. "She'll wear it because you gave it to her," he said.

"What if she doesn't?" he asked.

Bast opened his mouth, then hesitated and closed it again. He looked up and saw the first of twilight's stars emerge. He looked down at the boy. He sighed. He wasn't good at this.

So much was so easy. Glamour was second nature. It was just making folk see what they wanted to see. Fooling folk was simple as singing. Tricking folk and telling lies, it was like breathing.

But this? Convincing someone of the truth that they were too twisted to see? How could you even begin?

It was baffling. These creatures. They were fraught and frayed in their desire. A snake would never poison itself, but these folk made an art of it. They wrapped themselves in fears and wept at being blind. It was infuriating. It was enough to break a heart.

So Bast took the easy way. "It's part of the magic," he lied. "When you give it to her, you have to tell her that you made it for her because you love her."

The boy looked uncomfortable, as if he were trying to swallow a stone.

"It's essential for the magic," Bast said firmly. "And then, if you want to make the magic stronger, you need to tell her every day. Once in the morning and once at night."

The boy nodded, a determined look on his face. "Okay. I can do that."

"Right then," Bast said. "Sit down here. Prick your finger."

Rike did just that. He jabbed his stubby finger and let a bead of blood well up then fall onto the stone.

"Good," Bast said, sitting down across from the boy. "Now give me the needle."

Rike handed over the needle. "But you said it just needed—"

"Don't tell me what I said," Bast groused. "Hold the stone flat so that the hole faces up."

Rike did.

"Hold it steady," Bast said, and pricked his own finger. A slow bead of blood grew. "Don't move."

Rike braced the stone with his other hand.

Bast turned his finger, and the drop of blood hung in the air for a moment before falling straight through the hole to strike the greystone underneath.

There was no sound. No stirring in the air. No distant thunder. If anything, it seemed there was a half-second of perfect brick-heavy silence in the air. But it was probably nothing more than a brief pause in the wind.

"Is that it?" Rike asked after a moment, clearly expecting something more.

"Yup," Bast said, licking the blood from his finger with a red, red tongue. Then he worked his mouth a little and spat out the wax he had been chewing. He rolled it between his fingers and handed it to the boy. "Rub this into the stone, then take it to the top of the highest hill you can find. Stay there until the last of the sunset fades, and then give to her tonight."

Rike's eyes darted around the horizon, looking for a good hill. Then he leapt from the stone and sprinted off.

Bast was halfway back to the Waystone Inn when he realized he had no idea where his carrots were.

When Bast came in the back door, he could smell bread and beer and simmering stew. Looking around the kitchen he saw crumbs on the breadboard and the lid was off the kettle. Dinner had already been served.

Stepping softly, he peered through the door into the common room. The usual folk sat hunched at the bar, there were Old Cob and Graham, scraping their bowls. The smith's prentice was running bread along the inside of his bowl, then stuffing it into his mouth a piece at time. Jake spread butter on the last slice of bread, and Shep knocked his empty mug politely against the bar, the hollow sound a question in itself.

Bast bustled through the doorway with a fresh bowl of stew for the smith's prentice as the innkeeper poured Shep more beer. Collecting the empty bowl, Bast disappeared back into the kitchen, then he came back with another loaf of bread half-sliced and steaming.

"Guess what I caught wind of today?" Old Cob said with the grin of a man who knew he had the freshest news at the table.

"What's that?" The boy asked around half a mouthful of stew.

Cob reached out and took the heel of the bread, a right he claimed as the oldest person there, despite the fact that he wasn't actually the oldest, and the fact that nobody else much cared for the heel. Bast suspected he took it because he was proud he still had so many teeth left.

Cob grinned. "Guess," he said to the boy, then slowly slathered his bread with butter and took a big bite.

"I reckon it's something about Jessom Williams," Jake said blithely.

Old Cob glared at him, his mouth full of bread and butter.

"What I heard," Jake drawled slowly, smiling as Old Cob tried furiously chew his mouth clear. "Was that Jessom was out running his trap lines and he got jumped by a cougar. Then while he was legging it away, he lost track of hisself and went right over Littlecliff. Busted himself up something fierce."

Old Cob finally managed to swallow, "You're thick as a post, Jacob Walker. That ain't what happened at all. He fell off Littlecliff, but there weren't a cougar. Cougar ain't going to attack a full-grown man."

"It will if he's all smelling of blood," Jake insisted. "Which Jessom was, on account of the fact that he was baggin' up all his game."

There was a muttering of agreement at this, which obviously irritated Old Cob. "It weren't a cougar," he insisted. "He was drunk off his feet. That's what I heard. Stumbling-lost drunk. That's the only sense of it. Cause Littlecliff ent nowhere near his trap line. Unless you think a cougar chased him for almost a mile . . . "

Old Cob sat back in his chair then, smug as a judge. Everyone knew Jessom was a bit of a drinker. And while Littlecliff wasn't really mile from the Williams' land, it was too far to be chased by a cougar.

Jake glared venomously at Old Cob, but before he could say anything Graham chimed in. "I heard it was drink too. A couple kids found him while they were playing by the falls. They thought he was dead, and ran to fetch the constable. But he was just head-struck and drunk as a lord. There was all manner of broken glass too. He was cut up some."

Old Cob threw his hands up in the air. "Well, ain't that wonderful!" he said, scowling back and forth between Graham and Jake. "Any other parts of my story you'd like to tell afore I'm finished?"

Graham looked taken aback. "I thought you were—"

"I wasn't finished," Cob said, as if talking to a simpleton. "I was reelin' it out slow. I swear. What you folk don't know about tellin' stories would fit into a book."

A tense silence settled among the friends.

"I got some news too," the smith's prentice said almost shyly. He sat slightly hunched at the bar, as if embarrassed at being a head taller than everyone else and twice as broad across the shoulders. "If'n nobody else has heard it, that is."

Shep spoke up. "Go on, boy. You don't have to ask. Those two just been gnawing on each other for years. They don't mean anything by it."

"Well, I was doing shoes," the prentice said. "When Crazy Martin came in." The boy shook his head in amazement and took a long drink of beer. "I ain't only seen him a few times in town, and I forgot how big he is. I don't have to look up to see him. But I still think he's biggern me. And today he looked even bigger still 'cause he was furious. He was spittin' nails. I swear. He looked like someone had tied two angry bulls together and made them wear a shirt!" The boy laughed the easy laugh of someone who's had a little more beer than he's used to.

There was a pause. "What's the news then?" Shep said gently, giving him a nudge.

"Oh!" the smith's prentice said. "He came asking Master Ferris if he had enough copper to mend a big kettle." The prentice spread his long arms out wide, one hand almost smacking Shep in the face.

"Apparently someone found Martin's still," the smith's prentice leaned forward, wobbling slightly and said in hushed voice. "Stole a bunch of his drink and wrecked up the place a bit."

The boy leaned back in his chair and crossed his arms proudly across his chest, confident of a story well told.

But there was none of the buzz and that normally accompanied a piece of good gossip. He took another drink of beer, and slowly began to look confused.

"Tehlu anyway," Graham said, his face gone pale. "Martin'll kill him."

"What?" the prentice said. "Who?"

"Jessom, you tit," Jake snapped. He tried to cuff the boy on the back of his head, and had to settle for his shoulder instead. "The fellow who got skunk drunk in the middle of the day and fell off a cliff carrying a bunch of bottles?"

"I thought it was a cougar," Old Cob said spitefully.

"He'll wish it was ten cougars when Martin gets him," Jake said grimly.

"What?" The smith's prentice laughed. "Crazy Martin? He's addled, sure, but he ain't *mean.* A couple span ago he cornered me and talked bollocks about barley for two hours," he laughed again. "About how it was healthful. How wheat would ruin a man. How money was dirty. How it chained you to the earth or some nonsense."

The prentice dropped his voice and hunched his shoulders a bit, widening his eyes and doing a passable Crazy Martin impression. *"You know?"* he said making his voice rough and darting his eyes around. *"Yeah. You know. You hear what I'm sayin?"*

The prentice laughed again, rocking back on his stool. He had obviously had a little more beer than was good for him. "People think they have to be afraid of big folk, but they don't. I've never hit a man in my life."

Everyone just stared at him. Their eyes were deadly earnest.

"Martin killed one of Ensal's dogs for growling at him," Shep said. "Right in the middle of market. Threw a shovel like it was a spear. Then gave it a kicking."

"Nearly killed that last priest," Graham said. "The one before Abbe Leodan. Nobody knows why. Fellow went up to Martin's house. That evening Martin brought him to town in a wheelbarrow and left him in front of the church." He looked at the smith's prentice. "That was before your time though. Makes sense you wouldn't know."

"Punched a tinker once," Jake said.

"Punched a tinker?" the innkeeper burst out, incredulous.

"Reshi," Bast said gently. "Martin is fucking *crazy.*"

Jake nodded. "Even the levy man doesn't go up to Martin's place."

Cob looked like he was going to call Jake out again, then decided to take a gentler tone. "Well, yes," he said. "True enough. But that's cause Martin pulled his full rail in the king's army. Eight years."

"And came back mad as a frothing dog," Shep said.

Old Cob was already off his stool and halfway to the door. "Enough talk. We got to let Jessom know. If he can get out of town until Martin cools down a bit . . ."

"So . . . when he's dead?" Jake said sharply. "Remember when he threw a horse through the window of the old inn because the barman wouldn't give him another beer?"

"A *tinker*?" the innkeeper repeated, sounding no less shocked than before.

Silence descended at the sound of footsteps on the landing. Everyone's eyed the door and went still as stone, except for Bast who slowly edged toward the doorway to the kitchen.

Everyone breathed a huge sigh of relief when the door opened to reveal the tall, slim shape of Carter. He closed the door behind him, not noticing the tension in the room. "Guess who's standing a round of bottle whiskey for everyone tonight?" he called out cheerfully, then stopped where he stood, confused by the room full of grim expressions.

Old Cob started to walk to the door again, motioning for his friend to follow. "Come on Carter, we'll explain on the way. We've got to find Jessom double-quick."

"You'll have a long ride to find him," Carter said. "I drove him all the way to Baden this afternoon."

Everyone in the room seemed to relax, "That's why you're so late," Graham said, his voice thick with relief. He slumped back onto his stool and tapped the bar hard with a knuckle. Bast drew him another beer.

Carter frowned. "Not so late as all that," he groused. "I'd like to see you make it all the way to Baden and back in this time, that's more'n forty miles . . . "

Old Cob put a hand on the man's shoulder. "Nah. It ain't like that," he said, steering his friend toward the bar. "We were just a little spooked. You probably saved that damn fool Jessom's life by getting him out of town." He squinted at him. "Though I've told you shouldn't be out on the road by yourself these days . . . "

The innkeeper fetched Carter a bowl while Bast went outside to tend to his horse. While he ate, his friends told him the day's gossip in dribs and drabs.

"Well, that explains it," Carter said. "Jessom showed up reeking like a rummy and looking like he'd been beat by twelve different demons. Paid me to drive him to the Iron Hall, and he took the king's coin right there." Carter took a drink of beer. "Then paid me to take him to Baden straight off. Didn't want to stop off at his house for his clothes or anything."

"Not much need for that," Shep said. "They'll dress and feed him in the king's army."

Graham let out a huge sigh. "That was a near miss. Can you imagine what would happen if the azzie came for Martin?"

Everyone was silent for a moment, imagining the trouble that would come if an officer of the Crown's Law was assaulted here in town.

The smith's prentice looked around at him, "What about Jessom's family?" he asked, plainly worried. "Will Martin come after them?"

The men at the bar shook their head in concert. "Martin is crazy," Old Cob said. "But he's not that sort. Not to go after a woman or her wee ones."

"I heard he punched the tinker because he was making some advances on young Jenna." Graham said.

"There's truth to that," Old Cob said softly. "I saw it."

Everyone in the room turned to look at him, surprised. They'd known Cob all their lives, and had heard all his stories. Even the most boring of them had been trotted out three or four times over the long years. The thought that he might have held something back was . . . well . . . it was almost unthinkable.

"He was getting all handsy with young Jenna," Cob said, not looking up from his beer. "And she was younger still back then, mind you." He paused for a moment, then sighed. "But I was still old, and . . . well . . . I knew that tinker would give me a hiding if I tried to stop him. I could see that plain enough on his face." The old man sighed. "I ain't proud of that."

Cob looked up with a vicious little grin. "Then Martin came round the corner," he said. "This was off behind the old Cooper's place, remember? And Martin looked at the fellow, and at Jenna, who wasn't crying or nothing, but she obviously wasn't happy either. And the tinker has hold of her wrist . . . "

Cob shook his head. "When he hit him. It was like a hammer hitting a ham. Knocked him right out into the street. Ten feet, give or take. Then Martin eyed Jenna, who was crying just a bit then. More surprised than anything. And Martin stuck the boot in him. Just once. Not as hard as he could, either. I could tell he was just settling up accounts in his head. Like he was a moneylender shimming up one side of his scale."

"That fellow wasn't any kind of proper tinker," Jake said. "I remember him."

"And I heard things about that priest," Graham added.

A few of the others nodded wordlessly.

"What if Jessom comes back?" the smith's prentice asked. "I heard some folk get drunk and take the coin, then turn all cowardly and jump the rail when they sober up."

Everyone seemed to consider that. It wasn't a hard thought for any of them. A band of the king's guard had come through town only last month and posted a notice, announcing a reward for deserters.

"Tehlu anyway," Shep said grimly into his nearly empty mug. "Wouldn't that be a great royal pisser of a mess?"

"Jessom's not coming back," Bast said dismissively. His voice had such a note of certainty that everyone turned to eye him curiously.

Bast tore off a piece of bread and put it in his mouth before he realized he was the center of attention. He swallowed awkwardly and made a broad gesture with both hands. "What?" he asked them, laughing. "Would you come back, knowing Martin was waiting?"

There was a chorus of negative grunts and shaken heads.

"You have to be a special kind of stupid to wreck up Martin's still," Old Cob said.

"Maybe eight years will be enough for Martin to cool down a bit," Shep said.

"Not likely," Jake said.

Later, after the customers were gone, Bast and the innkeeper sat down in the kitchen, making their own dinner from the remainder of the stew and half a loaf of bread.

"So what did you learn today, Bast?" the innkeeper asked.

Bast grinned widely. "Today, Reshi, I found out where Emberlee takes her bath!"

The innkeeper cocked his head thoughtfully. "Emberlee? The Alard's daughter?"

"Emberlee Ashton!" Bast threw his arms up into the air and made an exasperated noise. "She's only the third prettiest girl in twenty miles, Reshi!"

"Ah," the innkeeper said, an honest smile flickering across his face for the first time that day. "You'll have to point her out to me."

Bast grinned. "I'll take you there tomorrow," he said eagerly. "I don't know if she takes a bath every day, but it's worth the gamble. She's sweet as cream and broad of beam." His smile grew to wicked proportions. "She's a milkmaid, Reshi," he said the last with heavy emphasis. "A *milkmaid*."

The innkeeper shook his head, even as his own smile spread helplessly across his face. Finally he broke into a chuckle and held up his hand. "You can point her out to me sometime when she has her clothes on," he said pointedly. "That will do nicely."

Bast gave a disapproving sigh. "It would do you a world of good to get out a bit, Reshi."

The innkeeper shrugged. "It's possible," he said as he poked idly at his stew.

They ate in silence for a long while. Bast tried to think of something to say.

"I did get the carrots, Reshi," Bast said as he finished his stew and ladled the rest of it out of the kettle.

"Better late than never, I suppose," the innkeeper said his voice was listless and grey. "We'll use them tomorrow."

Bast shifted in his seat, embarrassed. "I'm afraid I lost them afterwards," he said sheepishly.

This wrung another tired smile from the innkeeper. "Don't worry yourself over it, Bast." His eyes narrowed then, focusing on hand that held Bast's spoon. "What happened to your hand?"

Bast looked down at the knuckles of his right hand, they weren't bloody any more, but they were skinned rather badly.

"I fell out of a tree," Bast said. Not lying, but not answering the question, either. It was better not to lie outright. Even weary and dull, his master was not an easy man to fool.

"You should be more careful, Bast," the innkeeper said, prodding listlessly at his food. "And with as little as there is to do around here, it would be nice if you spent a little more time on your studies."

"I learned loads of things today, Reshi," Bast protested.

The innkeeper sat up, looking more attentive. "Really?" he said. "Impress me then."

Bast thought for a moment. "Nettie Williams found a wild hive of bees today," he said. "And she managed to catch the queen . . . "

DREAM HOUSES

Genevieve Valentine

1

You never see Gliese. It's a dwarf star, red and faint and far away until you're practically on top of it, and then a red bead blinks onto the viewscreen at the last second like a wound you forgot. You can look for it all you like, it should be in the center of the screen from the moment you clear the Moon, but stars multiply if you look at them too long. Your vision starts swimming with points of light in white and blue and gold. The small ones get swallowed.

If you wake up first from the Deep and stand at the comm to orient yourself, you have to find Beta Librae, and take the rest on faith.

I've moved most of my things to the comm room. There's not much else to look at, by now, and it's warmer here, and the projection of the starfield on the viewscreen is bright enough to read by. It's easier just to be able to look at it whenever you need it, all to yourself.

Lai can stay in the canteen. She's not missing much; her eyes are long gone.

The Golden Century Hall held a concert of songs composed for monarchs, once: *Consecrated to Your Majestie*, a dozen songs spread over a thousand years, sung by a visiting choir. I nearly missed it, but once I heard about it I pulled an overnight shift to make it to the city limits on time, and I parked the truck in a station off the highway and used my dinner money for a cab to get me there.

They didn't actually have the concert in the Hall. I've never set foot in the Hall. It was in a building that had been a chapel, and then a gallery, and then a bank, and then a city building that opened whenever the financiers who owned it needed to look like they cared about culture. I got a ticket outside, for too much money, from someone who didn't look like he had much of a vested interest in the arts.

For the first two hours it seemed like too large a choir. They sang hymns from countries I'd only heard of in school, and a few songs from coronation masses, and a Baroque piece that sounded like a beautiful math problem, and they took turns, but during any of the songs two full rows of singers were sitting like the carvings that crawled up the pillars.

Turned out they were waiting for the finale. *Lux in tenebris* used every voice they had; it was a song for a queen in splendor, and she must have wanted numbers to impress.

It started with one voice, then two, then four, and it doubled and doubled as the echoes built in the caves above us, until it sounded like two hundred notes alive and trembling at once. It was almost a round to begin with, but then it cracked open and became four songs that walked hand in hand, and then a single song in twenty staggered parts, a glorious knot my ear couldn't untangle.

"Intricate," the program called it, and congratulated the dead composer like he'd done a math problem. I threw the program out.

The anthem swelled and moved across itself, notes tangling and meeting and parting, and when the sopranos and tenors and altos and basses leapt from their melodies into a single chord held taut across four octaves, I looked behind me, because that was when the queen had sat taller to be worshiped. I just knew.

(Such a strange thing to do; I don't know if I thought I'd see her. Probably not. I never did have much imagination.)

I got interested in it all, after. There were history books I listened to on a long drive through pine territory one summer. The royal politics in England got harder to follow the further back you went—the Tudors were all right, but whenever they hit the War of the Roses I had to turn it off before I veered onto the shoulder trying to keep track of it all.

But the queen was something else. I looked up the castle later just to see where she would have been sitting, when the music bid her rise. The place was meant to stun, and there were half a dozen audience halls and royal chambers and chapels that could have hosted the music. But in my mind she's always sitting in the balcony of that bank-sponsored place of worship, right where I thought I saw her first.

He was famous, that composer; the queen granted him special right to write hymns for so many voices, to prevent anyone else from diluting what he'd done.

I haven't listened to that song again. Some things you should only hear once.

When I wake up, I'm at the control bank, and four lights are blinking red amid the slivers of white.

It's shameful that I've fallen asleep at my post (I was dreaming, grass like the sea). I hope Lai isn't around to see it—she's ruthless about crew who can't hack the circadian fuckups of Deep. But I still can't see anything but smears of color, and my throat is sandpaper, and I'm on my knees in front of the console—that's why the buttons are slivers, my angle is wrong—and the alarm is shrieking.

The alarm is the same pitch as Lai screaming (she proved it once), and I'm four more breaths along before I can be sure it isn't her. My elbows ache. My right forearm aches. My knees.

"Capella," I say, but nothing comes out.

There are red angles along the edge of the console, wherever I hold on. I turn my hands over. I've cut my palms, my knuckles. There are two bloody handprints under my knees. I must have been scrabbling on all fours to reach the controls, to see what the matter is. The alarm screams.

I'm dragging a long tail where the nutrient tube didn't pull out of my right arm. There's a smear of blood under the bandage. I must have been in a hurry.

But I couldn't have gone far. The nursery's down the corridor, the center of the honeycomb of the living quarters on the top deck. They design it with a straight shot to the comm up front, so anyone who needs to take watch can still keep an ear out for the strange chorus of life-support beeps in the one-two-three waltz—nutrients, oxygen, neuro.

But there's not supposed to be anyone on watch; we're all supposed to be sleeping.

"Capella," I croak, "report."

"Amadis," Capella says. We're skipping the *Good Afternoons,* I guess.

Capella's voice is the bland, asexual synth that Kite-class ships get as their default, where it sounds like every person who ever mildly offended you sent through an equalizer. Most Captains pay for the upgrade to something more particular, but Martiner in Earth Ops laughed Lai out of town for wanting it done free; Lai says Capella's natural voice is a good reminder of how much the GAU values our work.

I reach up and hit at buttons blindly with the heel of my hand. The white ones glow pink from the blood, but the alarm stops.

I blink sleep from my eyes, yawn. My ears are always popping up here; that and taking showers out of plastic bags are the biggest hassle of transit.

Capella says, "Amadis," again, so quiet I can barely hear it. But I can hear it. There's no chorus of blips from the nursery.

There's no chorus.

I can't remember if there was a chorus before I hit the buttons. The alarm was so loud and I was so tired and it's hard to remember anything because my heart has stopped.

When I breathe out it's utterly silent, and for a second I wonder if I'm dead.

"Capella. What happened?"

"Please clarify." Capella doesn't know what would be the matter; you have to tell it what to worry about. Fuck. Useless.

"Capella," I say, have to close my mouth around something sour in my throat, carefully breathe in. "Casualty report."

"Captain Pamela Lai." Capella says. "Crew Samuel Franklin. Crew Juan Morales. Crew Sajita Jaisi."

I'm waiting for a little while before I realize that's the death toll: everybody.

"Health report. Me. My health report."

"Sustained minor trauma waking from Deep during emergency circumstances."

I close my eyes a second, just because when I look at the floor, bloody handprints are reaching up to me.

As I stand up, I loop the tube in my hand once or twice. I'm liable to trip on it; I'm always clumsy for a while after I wake up. Morales made fun of me on my first run, for how long it took me to get my sea legs. "Thought you were a traveler," he'd said, with a look like he'd crossed me off a list.

The comm is white, now, except for the red button near the pilot's station. There's been a malfunction in the manual piloting system. Autopilot engaged until we're within Gliese sensor range. I can't fix the manual; I'm a passenger for the duration.

I start thinking about calories.

The nursery's a different room when it's silent. The pods are closed, and inside the medical-glassine observation windows Lai and Franklin and Jaisi and Morales have their eyes closed, the monitors perfectly still, like the demo decals they come when with you buy them new.

It's all as calm and clean as a ship that's never been used, except the broken glassine and blood from where I broke out of mine.

"Captain," Capella says, and that's when I retch.

I'm trembling (the *Menkalinan* gets cold during Deep, what would it be heating you for?), so it takes me a while to stand up, and I have to prop myself up on Jaisi's pod with both arms.

Somewhere, I'm still and quiet and mourning four people. It's a far-off place. There's no way home from there.

The part of me that's gasping for air, the part of me that broke the pod trying to get out, is calculating how much food there is on the ship to get me through the six years I'll have to be out of the Deep and awake.

The *Menkalinan*'s Gliese run takes six years and change, depending on energy currents, and we stay awake for six months on each side. There are five of us. (Were five.) The numbers aren't good.

"Capella," I start to say.

But I'm looking at Lai's face, stern even dead, and the hair on the back of my neck is standing up.

The dead don't come back. I'm not one of those.

It's just that something's wrong, and Lai would know, but she'll never get the chance to tell me.

"Capella."

"Yes, Captain."

I press my lips tight until the bile is gone. "Just Amadis, please."

"Yes, Amadis."

"What message has been sent to ground about what happened?"

"A casualty report is waiting for your approval."

Of course it is. I'm the Captain.

If everyone had died, the report would have been automatically generated by Capella, and the Gliese Associates United port on the far side would send a tugboat as our ship pulled into the system, to shift our cargo and move it to the planet near the little red star. The tug might reclaim the bodies if there was a news story in it, but Gliese is struggling for news stories these days, and they like them to be good. Most likely they'd sell the ship for scrap to an outer-ring salvage crew. *Menkalinan* would be stripped to her bones and the pods would drift out toward the other points of Libra, and that would be it.

But I hadn't died; I had sliced three fingers to the bone breaking out, and it was up to me to decide what we told them planetside.

(How had I woken up? Why me?)

If I said I was awake, would I get a message back? Was someone Earthside still waiting up for us?

I glance over my shoulder, out at the comm room, where we keep a copy of the cargo manifest.

There's no particular reason—we run a lot of things to Gliese, most of it rations and plastics and third-hand terraforming equipment for the outer reaches and things people have put in for that they thought they could live without, so that there's a piano in every shipment we've ever made.

Sometimes we get a shipment and every crate is marked MISC and we still take it, because the Colonial Trade Agreement works in our favor—it has to, to get anyone to sign up for these runs—and if someone's going to get arrested for what's in there, it's not us.

But we have a cargo of MISC, and Martiner signed off on it, and Lai watched it going in with her lips in a single sour line.

When I breathe in, I can feel the cargo hold underneath me, right through the nerves in my feet, as if it's woken up and shifted its weight.

There's plenty that could be down there—the cargo hold is most of the lower level. We wouldn't be arrested, if we were carrying something wrong. But maybe that's not what Martiner's worried about.

"Does the report state the nature of the malfunction in the Deep pods?"

"No cause of malfunction determined."

Fuck, this AI's worse than nothing. "Capella, four crew are dead. That is a significant event. What was the cause of death?"

"Asphyxiation from insufficient oxygen flow. Cause of mechanical malfunction not identified."

"In the report, or by you?"

Nothing.

"Was the ship inspected by GAU representatives prior to takeoff?"

"Yes. Nothing outside operating parameters was registered. No delays were imposed."

I breathe through my nose. "Did the same malfunction happen in my pod?"

"Yes, Amadis."

"But I woke up."

A pause. "Yes."

The hair on my neck stands up. I don't know why.

My nails screech against the pod as I curl them in. Someone should know about this, I think; it's the first instinct of every veteran long-hauler when something goes this wrong. You spend a lot of time alone, and if you can't hack that you won't last long, but there's a line past when it's foolish not to look for help. If you try to manage alone, you won't make it.

But the message would go back to Martiner, and to whoever at the GAU had looked at the nursery and marked us fit for travel, and I'm not sure I want them knowing yet that anyone here is still awake.

I want to look at the oxygen tubes.

"Capella, don't send anything."

"GAU Protocol demands I inform both Earth and Gliese staff as soon as possible of any chance in the line of report—"

"It's an order, Capella."

"Yes, Captain."

Things that can go wrong with your oxygen, in a nursery on a Kite-class, from most likely to least likely:

Your recycler gets compromised, because the seal on a Kite-class ship is probably not as airtight as it should be, and you suffocate slowly on your own carbon dioxide.

There's a crack in your pod, and you don't get the enhanced oxygen mix at the rate you should, losing a little every year, and when you show up planetside you're still breathing, you're just five or six years older, instead of only three.

You're sick before you enter Deep and don't know it, and the bacteria make it through your second-rate filter, and over the course of six years in the nursery you're trapped with the enemy as it adapts and gets smarter than your body is, and even if you live, by the time you reach a planet you're sick with something so resilient that Disease Control has to shoot your pod into space without even opening it, and you spin gently through a vacuum until your air just runs out.

Your ship gets boarded by someone who must be pretty fucking desperate to be on your route at all, and when the alarm goes off and the pods start to wake you, the pirates decide they'd just as soon not deal with survivors, and yank your tube, and lock you in, and you pound against the glassine until you don't have air left, and whoever finds you next finds you arched in agony with your hands in fists, still fighting.

Before you leave dock, during the quality inspection pass, the tubing gets fastened a little too tightly by a sharper-edged clamp than you've ever seen, so that over the course of a year or so, the tiny changes in pressure push the tubing against the clamp and away, over and over, until all at once there's a slice right across it, and the air starts leaking, and the filter can't compensate, and you just never wake up.

I know before I'm even done examining them all that I'm not going to be using any of these pods.

If I had any hope of being able to find the Deep again and wake up at Gliese where I'll have options, they vanish with the second clip, when I realize it was a deliberate fix to every feed. I can't be sure if it was malicious, but the tubes are shot in any case, and I can't even be sure that's the only thing they did.

They must have been in a rush when they got to mine; the hose on my pod has only just cut through, not nearly as deep as the rest.

At some point I'll need to have Capella run through the on-board security footage and see if anything else was touched during the dock inspection. At some point I'll need to sweep up the glassine from around mine, where I tore my arms to ribbons breaking out of a pod that was now just as useless as anybody else's.

I'll be awake for the duration. Five years.

There was a scare session the GAU offered before you signed up for a particular run. If you signed up for a prestige gig, one of the runs that compared you to sea explorers from a thousand years ago, there was a lot to warn against. On the backwater runs, apparently they just told you things about how long you'd last if you tried to get the jump on everyone and woke up early to take over the ship alone, like being in charge of a cargo ship on autopilot in a dead sector was a dream of glory they had to shake off you.

You lost your mind, I assumed. I never went. I'd met Lai and signed up by then. Once you'd decided to go, there wasn't any point being frightened.

Thinking about it now is exhausting; not panic so much as dead weight, a pile of years and the dull certainty I won't make it.

Capella makes the waterbag hot enough to scald me—"Thank you," I say, and when it says, "I thought it was necessary," I try not to be offended and scrub harder at the brown crusts across my knuckles—and after I bandage up as well as anyone can by themselves, I sweep up the pieces of glassine I'd punched through, and when my hands start shaking I reach for my nutrient tube and drink some vitamins absentmindedly, worrying the end of the makeshift straw with my teeth and very carefully not looking at where I am.

I want to send something to my brother.

We moved to the town with the pines when I was seven, into a house I barely remember except for the name I had in it, and the kitchen window that dipped so low you could sit cross-legged on the floor and still see out.

I spent a lot of time at that window. I was afraid of what might be coming through the trees, and I didn't want to look at my family.

After a few weeks of observation to make sure, I couldn't avoid it any more. I told my brother there were dragons wandering the dark places under our eaves and in the forest behind the house, pacing just past the tree line and shaking their scales.

He frowned down at me like it was a trick. We didn't play make-believe (I didn't have the imagination for it, it was one of his earliest disappointments in me), but we didn't play tricks either. He had no vocabulary to understand what I was telling him, and he didn't love me enough by then to let me explain.

"All right," he said finally, looked out the window. "What should I do about your dragons?"

Too late. I could tell what he thought, and by the time we were living near the trees I was past needing his help.

"Leave me alone," I said. I never mentioned them again.

My pride was stung. I hadn't told him because I wanted him to do something about them; you couldn't do anything about dragons, that much I was certain of.

I'd told him because I wanted to know if he saw what I saw.

He got angry at me for going into deep space work, as angry as he ever got about me.

"You were scared of the dark," he snapped. "You— No. There's no way you can handle space."

"Space is just darkness. There's a difference from the dark."

There was a little pause, like the feed had cut out, but there was a flicker of a line between his brows that came and went, the ghost of a frown. We didn't play tricks, and he wanted to believe me. He was trying to understand the difference.

He might ask me not to go, I thought; he might say, Stay here, and just for a second my throat went tight.

"Well, I guess we'll know tomorrow," he said, and the last I saw of him he was leaning over his ratty terminal to disconnect the message.

He didn't send anything else. I went through the dozen sessions the GAU required, and signed a stack of papers promising to keep quiet about anything I saw, and they signed a piece of paper that made me impervious to customs law in case someone from Gliese smuggled an endangered parrot or an illegal amount of turmeric.

I waited until a week before I shipped out to tell my brother I was going. It was only text, a mail with some details of the trip and a copy of the waiver I'd signed that said he'd get the money owed me if I didn't make it back.

Lai raised an eyebrow when I didn't book any minutes in the intercom booth during our time in range, but she didn't say anything about it. This wasn't a job for someone with a family waiting breathlessly at home.

My brother didn't speak to me for two trips. I'd let him know (text, always) when I was Earthside, or when I was leaving, but it was like dropping rocks into a quarry.

I got a message from him on the way back from Gliese the second time, when I was still in the Deep. It was video. I didn't recognize the background; he'd moved, he did that often enough, still looking for a place he could bear to live in.

He hoped I was all right.

"I looked up Gliese in the interstellar atlas," he said, "just so I know where you're coming back from."

He hesitated, looked right into the camera, breathed in with words behind it. Then he leaned forward, and the feed cut out.

Roland Casara committed suicide fifteen years to the day after the opening night of the Golden Century concert hall he designed.

The balcony collapsed six years after that.

There had been nearly four thousand performances by then. It was one of the most photographed buildings on the continent. In the first wake of the disaster, tourists took souvenirs from the rubble.

The investigation revealed nothing, at first. The city was growing, subways were being built, the pipes were old, and the crowds were beginning to wear. Sometimes buildings just fall in.

They built the new one stronger, more flexible, with a glass-floor lobby so you could see the original stone underneath. No one thought anything more about it for decades, until a biographer got permission from Casara's sister to come and look through his things, and the story got out.

(I read about it in a history article, sitting at a truck stop that had screens built into the booths. I spent half an hour drinking a cup of coffee the consistency of tar, scrolling back and forth slowly with one finger, like the end would be different if I went back enough times.)

Casara's calculation of the weight the columns of the Golden Hall could bear had been off by a few ounces. It lasted a long time, considering. But people got taller, and the deep of the city got warmer, and eventually creep set in.

He knew. He'd had a blueprint of the Golden Hall—an original, *the* original—folded at the bottom of a stack of potential commissions he'd never taken (for reasons no one had been able to guess before now), with the error circled in red pencil. Casara had made notes in careful architect's numbers, diagonally like they were bracing the window they were scrawled on top of, and dated Golden Century's opening night.

For the inaugural concert of the first Hall, the Chair of the Arts Association had reserved a seat of honor for him, first row orchestra. He'd never appeared to claim his seat or his praise; at the time they said it was modesty.

Turns out he'd just been at home, realizing his odds.

I set up my bunk in the dormitory like I always did after Deep, take the sheets and blankets out of their cartons, pull the plastic off the bed. I leave the light burning in my reading lamp as I move back and forth from the galley to the emptied-out locker nearer my bed.

I don't know why I need to gather as much as I can as close as I can—it's not like anyone's going to intercept me on my way to the canteen—but all the same, I rip Jaisi's worksuit out of there and stack up rations waist-high and tie a can opener to my bedpost so I can't lose it and starve.

That's foolish. There's more than one can opener; this is a Kite-class, not a tugboat. I make faces at my silly compulsions the whole time I twist and twist the wires that hold it on. It's old habit, that's all, left over from when I was driving the rig and couldn't afford to lose anything.

(I had a lot of old habits about food. Franklin had watched me eating our first meal after takeoff, said, "Christ, when was your last one?"

"Yeah," said Lai, "tell us more about table manners, Franklin," and he looked down where he'd spilled tomato sauce and turned red at the ears and shut up about it.

I looked over at Lai, saw for the first time the shadowed sockets under her cheeks where hunger lived forever if it caught you young enough, where even if you had enough to eat for the rest of your life, later on, you'd eat every meal like you didn't have another one, because you'd grown up when there was no telling.)

"Capella," I say, "please set an alarm for a twelve-hour sleep cycle."

"Yes, Amadis. That's longer than your standard. Are you feeling well?"

"I'm conserving."

After a second Capella says, "I see."

I'm doing math, too, dividing the rations by days more precisely the more I try not to think about it. Old habit, from lean years.

There were the rations for after we woke up from the far side of Deep, not quite for six months (it encouraged you to be prompt, Lai explained like there was a bad taste in her mouth), five times over. Not enough; my body would feed on itself, and when we docked at Gliese they'd find a skeleton propped in the pilot's chair, draped in skin.

There were the nutrient packs, not designed to sustain an active body—barely able to sustain a body in stasis, you did nothing but eat at the dock station in Gliese because you were so hungry you couldn't think—but maybe I could move less. Restrict movement to what was necessary, sleep as much as I could, use some of the sedatives if I had to. I could lie in my bunk like the dead. Anything not to be hungry.

The control panel in the comm room is still smeared with blood as I reach across it for the cargo manifest, but I ignore the stains; they're almost like having company.

The manifest is cartons and cartons and cartons of MISC, still on paper because that's how little it matters, and I think about Jaisi handing over the clipboard to Lai and saying, "These always make me itch," and Lai shrugging, because the GAU didn't care much for your feelings about your cargo.

I wonder if it's possible to squeeze between the crates, enough to crack them open. There has to be something there. Gliese has mouths to feed.

The cargo bay is empty.

I look at the video image for a long time, waiting to be wrong about it, because it can't be, we sat at dock for four hours while forklifts lumbered back and forth with crates and we took bets on what was in them.

Morales had pointed at each one and guessed something different—"Winter seeds. Flexible tubing. Rations. Real food disguised as rations for the governor. Entertainment console, entertainment console, a crate to bury the children in when they fight over the settlement's two entertainment consoles"—but he had a guy on the inside at the port in Gliese and ringers didn't count, and after a while I hissed at him just to get him to knock it off. (He'd flashed me a grin, said, "No bet, Reyes?" I'd stared him down.)

"I hope it's drugs," said Franklin, who had gone into freighting just for the legal immunity, but that was always his guess and it had never panned out.

Jaisi just stared at the manifest of MISCs and shook her head every time she ticked off a box.

Lai had taken one look at the dock and said, "Nothing but bathtubs."

I thought Franklin had a better bet with his two tons of drugs, but still I didn't take the bet against Lai. She'd been doing this run even longer than Morales (she'd outlived her immediate family, Martiner had assured me when I signed up, as if I was worried about Lai having split loyalties somehow), and a lot of things that sounded foolish came true in a hurry. If Gliese was going to have a run on bathtubs, she'd know first.

But there's nothing there. According to the cameras, we're carrying *nothing*, now.

For a second I feel like the whole ship is about to capsize, as if you can even get top-heavy out here, but my stomach lurches and I grip the edge of the console, ready to fall.

The camera pans back and forth every twenty seconds, scraping at me, and in every sweep I look for reasons to be wrong. Glitches, the wrong date, the wrong cargo bay. I'm fucking happy to be wrong, I need to be wrong.

It's old footage, I decide. Capella's doing this to punish me. Capella's been off since I came out of Deep; Capella has those pauses now, those awful pauses. It wouldn't be hard to pull up the wrong footage and watch me go to pieces, just for fun, if your algorithms told you to.

But there's the dent in the wall from where one of the loaders misjudged how tightly he could turn the forklift and one of the dock guys nearly punched him out over it, because the forklift was worth as much as any of us were getting for the run. It had happened that day on the dock, the day before we took off for Gliese.

Maybe I'm losing my mind, I think. You do that when you panic, when you have no one to ask whose answers you trust.

"Capella, what's the status of our cargo?"

"Invalid query."

The camera pans to the far corner happily, showing me the empty cargo hold, its dent moving in and out of sight.

"Capella, was cargo loaded onto the ship prior to takeoff?"

"Please specify voyage."

"Capella." I clear my throat. "I'm going to need you to try to understand me, please. Was there cargo in the hold when we took off?"

That pause, that pause that makes my wrists feel like lead, like I couldn't move if I tried.

"That information is corrupted," Capella says. "Only available data on Bay Alpha is the current video feed."

That's impossible. That's the pause. Capella knows it isn't possible. Capella knows there's a lie.

I lean forward, scratch absently at the screen where the dent is.

The dent comes off under my fingernail.

For a long time I freeze, waiting for the camera to pan back. Maybe it was a bloodstain overlaying the screen. Dust. Something.

The camera swings back around, showing a cargo hold that's never been touched.

I stagger backward. I catch my heel on something, the lip of the chair supports, maybe—my knees give, and I fall.

I don't remember what happens, for a little after that; it's all snow behind my eyes, and nothing else I care to see.

Capella hadn't said a thing that whole time, as if waiting to see what I would do, and when I crash to the grate there's no chirp announcing I've been injured like there should be on a ship that's paying attention.

(Though that was a chirp that alerted your crew someone was hurt. There's no crew. It's unnecessary.)

When I open my eyes, Capella says, "You'll be all right now," like's something it's decided, and like it's sorry for me, and when I hear rattling on the grate it takes me a second to realize it's my shoulders against the sharp edges as I tremble; that's where the sting's coming from.

I left my brother after the shooting.

As soon as my wounds were dressed and they were sure it hadn't punctured a lung, I'd checked myself out of the hospital. I'd found him outside with blood on his sleeves and half a cigarette dangling from his good hand.

I don't know if he was waiting, or if he'd checked himself out to run for it, and I just caught him in time. He never said. We just fell into step together, and we walked side by side to the hotel, and packed our things in silence, and started for home.

(It wasn't really home; it was just one of the places he lived in, and I'd been allowed to tag along because he couldn't lift his bags with his arm broken.)

We only stopped at a motel after he dropped off for a second and nearly ran into a ditch—he got tired on the road in a way I never did.

We both had our father's wide, solemn forehead; it was one of three things I knew we shared. The rest, there was no knowing.

"I could drive," I said, which were our first words in six hundred miles.

He looked me over. "I know. We're stopping."

I didn't understand until we were checking in and the clerk couldn't stop staring at my shirt, where the blood had crusted over. That's what my brother had been looking at.

"Rough road," I said. My brother almost glanced over at me, not quite.

There wasn't any point in maneuvering through pajamas in the state we were in. He slid into bed with his boots still on and hissed at his cast, and when I turned on my side away from him I was careful to keep the stiff press of dried blood from scraping my stitches.

He breathed deep and even, whether he was awake or not; you could only tell for sure if he was asleep by the little motions his fingers made, half-taps on the bed as he dreamed.

In the middle of the night, while he was dreaming, I opened my eyes and had to get out.

I don't know what woke me. My wounds hurt too much to rest, probably. It hurt too much to do a lot of things—I was in bad shape for a while after that. Split my stitches three times. It took me another two months before I'd get the okay from the GAU medics to start training.

(Lai stalled the dry dock until I had clearance. Her first words to me on board were, "Better hope they have painkillers on Gliese, they didn't issue you enough for the round trip."

It was a joke; Gliese didn't have much that we didn't bring them. That was a long journey home. I was in so much pain I thought about calling my brother.)

But even wrecked that night, one of the wounds already seeping, I had to get out. My brother was breathing next to me. I couldn't stay.

I was terrified of him going to another house he could barely stand and would probably leave before the year was up. My restlessness was one thing, but his I couldn't stand; it had shifted from job-hopping to a chain of identical houses he halfheartedly tried to make homes out of, and none of them was never going to stick unless I came with him.

I knew without asking that if I came with him somewhere, he'd stay there until he died. (He'd been on the verge of buying a place back home, during the summer we had a truce.)

It was tempting, lying next to him with our complimentary bloodstains, to just give in and drive home with him and pick a bedroom, live in between silences for the rest of my life.

I had to go.

My stitches ached, and I gritted my teeth to keep from yelping when I picked up my bag, but there wasn't much help for it. There had been a truck stop a mile or two before the motel. From there I could catch a ride to someplace else.

But sometimes things pull at you even when you know better. I froze up like an amateur behind the motel, in the strip of darkness that led back to the highway, eventually, if you could make it.

(Cowardice, I thought, and it probably was, but not of the dark; branches were swaying in the wind, half-tapping each other like my brother dreaming.)

It was pitch-black—the motel's only lights were out front where the cars were, and we were the only guests—and all at once I was a little dizzy with doubt, and when I reached out and caught an oak tree, I leaned into it so I didn't topple over.

A light came on amid the trees on the far side of the woods.

There was nothing there, I knew there wasn't; we'd seen the whole stretch on the drive up, it was just trees and mud and no sign of life, and the light didn't move like someone was holding it or flicker like someone had built a home on the far, far side of the trees.

It was steady and round and bright, and my bag slid off my shoulder and fell to the dirt without a sound.

Later, I realized it was the moon; it was probably the moon, between the trees in the deep dark, bright enough to see by. But I'll never know.

Not because I turned and fled, because that would require me to have fled, and not because I walked out into the dark to face whatever it was until it turned from me and ran; the light stayed on for a long time, and I balanced where I was with the scrape of bark against my shoulder, and never moved.

After it went off, and I had walked shivering through those miles of dark to the truck stop with my head craned back over my shoulder so far back it was a wonder I didn't trip into the road and get bisected, I felt heroic and foolhardy, and I found a flier for cargo ships and called Planetary Associates United.

I've dreamed of the light a few times—almost the only thing I dream of, except the houses.

After the third dream, brightness flooding the dark fog of my usual dreamless sleep, I realized I should have run. Run from it if I had to, or conquered it if I could have. Both were a thing you did, an action you could answer for.

In every dream I had about it I was waiting it out, that low piercing moon, standing in the woods in a jacket that smelled like motel and my brother: too scared to go forward, too stubborn to run.

The first house I ever dreamed of was from a book I'd been given, where two foxes lived in a house made mostly of glass, built across a waterfall, with a hole in a fallen log as the door. The book was mostly interested in the glass walls: it was called *Are Mr. and Mrs. Fox at Home?* and gave lessons on privacy that I could tell even then were meant for kids living in the government settlements, where walls and curtains were thin.

I only noticed the floor made out of glass. I wouldn't see a waterfall for another fifteen years; to me it might as well have been a house built on Jupiter.

The house I dreamed of was empty of foxes and nothing but glass, surrounded everywhere by green, and I lived in it alone and was very pleased, because it was like living in nothing at all.

When I looked down, the water rushed past me in a white-foam hurry and dropped off right at my feet, falling and falling towards a river that was always too far away to see, and all at once I was horribly sad that I had been trapped in the house, and there was no way to reach the water and meet the river and let the current carry me somewhere else.

Before you're allowed to apply for a run, no matter how long you've been signed up, they make you go to a seminar about social mandates on crews, where they tell you not to touch what isn't yours and how to turn sideways in a corridor to let someone pass you for good manners and how to settle a dispute without putting your fist through a bulkhead, which was fine if you were me, but seemed calculated to make every veteran hate you.

"This information will be invaluable to you in quickly becoming part of your Planetary Associates United crew, no matter your exciting destination!" the recruiter calls out to the ten of us in the auditorium who haven't left yet. (I would have gone during the demo video that followed the slideshow, but they have food after this, and I'm too broke to be proud.)

A man raises his hand. "Yes, hi, one of the crew stole my toothbrush on the Alpha Centauri run last year. Do I apply for reimbursement here, or can my dentist bill you?"

The recruiter blinks; when he frowns it looks like the scale in the hospital you're meant to judge pain levels by. He's about a six.

"Well, I think that would be a regional issue, so the ACAU office can—"

Another man raises his hand. "I've been the victim of false accusation, where can I file my complaint against a fraudulent charge of theft?"

"That should go to the central office," says the recruiter, who must be new here, "where they—"

"And so where should I file a rebuttal against a charge of fraudulent charges, ACAU or the central office?"

The recruiter flushes with genuine concern, and it's not like I don't think those guys are assholes for playing games, but I seriously consider walking out. If this is the quality of people the PAU puts forward to try to convince you to join up, I'm not going.

The fraudulent accusation man half-stands. "If this company will not address toothbrush theft with the seriousness it deserves, then I—"

"Can it."

The words are deep and sharp, and even though nobody's moving when I turn around, I know who said them the moment I see her. Back row, black hair to her chin, face like the handle of a knife.

The guy sits down.

The recruiter wraps up with some inspirational things they're paying him to say, and then everyone files out. I wait to see if she knows those men, but they file out like everybody else.

On my way out, I ask her, "What run are you?"

She looks me over. Her eyes are almost as dark as my brother's, and there's a tension between her jaw and her ears that probably means she's the captain.

"Gliese."

That seems strange, because just from the application process I can tell that's a backwater assignment, but sometimes you meet truckers with three doctorates. People have reasons to keep moving.

"Okay."

When I show up for the first crew call (my third set of stitches slowly fading into the purple edges of my gunshot wound), she looks up like she was waiting for me.

The toothbrush guys are there. They don't seem to see anything strange about it, which makes them a lot harder to surprise than I am.

"Reyes?" When I nod, she checks off something on her data pad.

I must look appalled; as she passes me on the way into the ship she says, "If you had the chance to knock them out for ten years, wouldn't you?"

She's the captain. I don't say anything.

Turns out Morales and Franklin never give anybody a lick of trouble but each other. Sometimes Jaisi will come into the canteen with the look of a martyr, and as the door slides shut behind her we'll hear the thwack of fists against canvas as the blur of them flickers briefly into sight, but that's as bad as it gets.

They distract you from getting stir-crazy for the last six months, that much I can say for them. There are worse reasons to put people on a roster.

Sometimes, when I was heading into Deep and feeling sentimental, I imagined Lai looking over the people who were willing to sit through that presentation, picking out her crew by the backs of their heads.

Five weeks go by before I have the nerve to go look in the cargo hold in person.

(I don't quite know what I'm doing, in those five weeks. It's like trucking, where the distance between stops just vanishes, some spacial memory you lose every time you turn the engine off. I sleep a lot. I eat once a day. I try to keep my hands warm, but there's not enough warmth and gloves don't help. It's just as well. The cold keeps the scars from throbbing.

Once or twice I try the sedatives. I think I've lost a week that way. Capella's keeping track of the days if I dared ask, but I don't know where the sedatives stop and my cowardice begins.)

I don't want to break the seal on Lai's pod in the nursery—I have reasons, and every time I start to think about it I shove them all into the darkest corners I can find—but it means I don't take anyone else's ID with me down the ladder and around to the cargo bay, which takes up the back half of this entire level. There's tons of freight. There will be something.

No surprise my credentials don't work, a series of swipes on the number pad that blink red and beep and do nothing. I'm auxiliary crew. I'm there to do grunt work, and in case someone dies and they need a body to call out coordinates during landing. There's no way my creds would be needed to get into the cargo bay: if you had to get in there during the voyage—and you never did, why would you, you were barely more important than Capella—it would be the captain authorizing it. I'm surprised the alarm isn't laughing at me.

But the emergency code doesn't work either, which is wrong. I try it eight times with the patience of a nightmare, slower and slower to make sure I have the numbers right (they're right, they're fucking right).

The heat's minimal down here, just enough to keep absolute zero from creeping in, and even in my thermal gear I'm shivering so hard I wonder if I'd lose my scarred-over finger to frostbite if I wasted too much time.

"Capella," I say, "what are the chances you can open this door?"

"I'm sorry, Amadis."

Of course. I grit my teeth, mutter, "What are the chances you can go fuck yourself?"

"Disallowed by programming," Capella says.

I'm so startled I laugh, a single deep bark that bounces down the corridor and out of sight.

The crowbar's so cold it bites my palms just to hold it, but I slam the far end into the join and throw my whole weight against it—no time to risk leveraging with less—just as Capella says, "Amadis."

The alarm goes off.

I don't care about it until it occurs to me it might go off for the next six years, and even then I don't care about that nearly as much as I care about the tone of Capella's voice.

"What, Capella?"

"That door is monitored."

Monitored by GAU, it means, back planetside. Of course they monitor it, so they know if the cargo's been intercepted or tampered with. I'd never cared enough to think about it. Now they knew someone had tried to open it. Now the ship's sending word.

I step back. The crowbar's still wedged in the door; I'd dented one side, not nearly enough to break the seal.

"Capella, can you stop the report?"

"It's not my report. I'm sorry, Amadis."

Oh god. I calculate how many weeks it would take for the report to make it back across the vacuum, piggybacking the dark energy field and sinking through the cloud cover and appearing on Martiner's screens like a gift.

If he'd done this to us, he'd know someone was awake, and he'd have to take care of it.

(Does Capella know? I think absently, and then: Will it be Capella's job?)

I felt a stab of helplessness, sharp and anxious, like I'd had two Gliese runs back when I'd read on the years-delayed news feed that the last of the wild bee colonies had gone extinct, like you could reach back through time and prevent something awful if only you wanted it hard enough to stop your heart.

Capella, I didn't say; Capella, can they shut off the oxygen from the ground?

I climbed up the ladder more smoothly that I'd climbed down. Hope made you shaky. Despair was practical.

The alarm goes off for seven hours ("It's not my alarm, I'm sorry," Capella says, over and over, just low enough that I can hear under the screech). I move through every access panel on the lower level, both sides of the loop, but Capella won't tell me where the switch is, because turning off an embedded alarm would mean turning off Capella.

The alarm's wailing every three seconds.

"I'm going to lose my mind," I say, "the reboot will only be ten minutes, just, please."

I pull up the schematics for *Menkalinan*, but every bulkhead that I pry open is nothing but cooling ducts.

"Capella, you little shit," I shout over the alarm, just to hear some other sound. Capella's not going to answer. Capella's furious.

I go upstairs to the main level, check the holo-schematic again, count along the doors, jam the screwdriver into place. It skitters on the way, scrapes the finish off the bulkhead.

There's a cluster of wires inside. When I wrap them around my hand and pull (it takes two tries, I'm sweating), they dislodge with a little shower of sparks—I should know better. Careless. No sparks, no combustion ever.

The lights in the canteen flicker out.

I'd think Capella gave me the wrong schematics, if AIs were capable of lying. (Capella gave me the wrong schematics.)

I take a breath, let it slide out of my nostrils.

Then I hum the only waltz I know in time with the blaring; it helps me think less about it as I go to the canteen and fill a bowl with water, and pry open the bulkhead in the corridor outside the comm room where the main server bank is. The servers are labeled halfheartedly (Morales did it) in marker on strips of tape: NAVIG. ENVIRO. NURS. CAPEL.

I pick up the bowl.

"No," says Capella.

"Capella. Where are the speakers?"

"Amadis, don't."

"Ten. Nine. Eight."

"Amadis, this is illegal."

"Six. Five. Four."

"Amadis, you'll never make it alone."

A tone I've never heard from an AI. The hair on my neck stands up.

"Three," I say. I clear my throat. "Two."

The alarm shuts off.

The silence is a vacuum, and I realize I'm holding my breath. I set the bucket down slowly.

"Capella. If we're going to live together for the next five years," I say (five years, Jesus, shit),"this can't be something we have to keep talking about."

"Apologies, Amadis. I'm in charge of a number of crucial programs. Some subroutines occasionally become obsolete unless I request them, like outside alarms. Or oxygen levels."

I lift the bowl. "Do they program you to threaten crewmembers?"

"You're Auxiliary," Capella says.

I laugh once, shrill, and take the bowl back to the canteen to replace the water.

I leave the panel open.

"Capella," I say, wondering if this is a calculated risk or a fatal disadvantage, "I'm being honest with you. I'm going to ask you to be honest with me."

There's no answer—there wouldn't be, it's not a direct question—but I let it go.

As I'm cycling the water through the filters, Capella says, "Would you like some music, Amadis?"

Oh. "That would . . . be great."

The waltz I was humming comes over the speakers, an orchestra and a singer who's better at it than I am. I tap my fingers on the counter, let my shoulders drop.

As I turn to go back to my bunk, I see a shadow come and go, like something's here. Moving.

I don't ask Capella. Some things aren't safe.

2

Things you do alone on a spaceship:

- Jog the upstairs honeycomb and the loop on the cargo level every day, just to keep your blood from turning into a solid. You tell yourself it's better than Deep, where it takes you two days to get your arms working at full range of motion. Here you can twist all the way behind you, all the time, looking down the corridors like you're dumb enough to be afraid of something.
- Stare at the crowbar, still jammed in the door. It looks like an iron finger reaching out to grab you whenever you pass by.
- Go through the on-board entertainment. (There's no reaching the central library, it would require Capella to ping the connection, and someone would see it.) Franklin has action movies and porn and videos of someone's dog. Morales has a series of comedies that rely mostly on mistaken identity and falling down, and three courtroom dramas, one of which is so outdated it has an episode about the Animal Sentience Trials. Lai has better action movies and a library of history books in five languages. Jaisi has musicals and planting manuals and a period piece TV show about a young journalist on the first Jupiter colony, and some documentaries of an Earth that still had enough desalinated water all on its own, and you could come across huge meadows at a moment's notice, with flowers and bees and birds that the government wasn't even tracking. I'd seen those

places sometimes, from the rig, but the ones in the documentary were self-irrigating; it felt like what Gliese was aiming for. I wonder if Jaisi had plans to disembark one day and just never come back, and spend the rest of her life trying to make a meadow. Then it cuts to footage of a deer, and I turn it off.

- Talk to Capella. It's been AI on this ship for nearly a hundred years, back when Kite-class was the best you could get, and it runs down a list of destinations that makes you realize why the map in the lobby of PAU headquarters looks like eight million bits of string. It knows everything about every crewmember that's ever let anything slip. I don't let it tell me about my crew, but the embarrassments of a hundred years ago are nearly as good as the comedies Morales had.
- Ask it, "What dirt do you have on me?" Wait a long time for the answer: "Nothing yet."
- Close your eyes all that night for sleep that doesn't come.
- But you try to sleep as long as you can, all the time. When you're asleep, you're not getting hungry.
- Read your books again. I have two Elizabethan histories; I look for any more in the ship library. There's one that seems to be taking Dudley's view of things, and a novel called *Spymaster to the Queen*, which claims Walsingham had psychic powers. I'll take it over the other one. Dudley I can do without. (The novel pretends Thomas Tallis was a spy. I read it six times, think about all those voices making notes in tandem, secret messages calling back and forth.)
- Regulate calories as much as you can, until you're always hungry, so hungry you can't even taste the food when you're actually eating it. It's a remembered habit from a government childhood; it keeps you from wondering where the food's come from.
- Talk to Capella, when it gives you a status update about anything that isn't the cargo bay or the nursery. I ask the date three or four times a day, just to make sure the answers are consistent, and Capella informs me when my body temperature drops below parameters and I have to eat something. ("I worry about you," Capella says once or twice, and it sounds like the way your brother said it.)
- Sit at the comm and watch the stars not moving, until you can't focus and it becomes a random pattern, like your brother used to make up shapes for. You know the real shapes. You've read some astronomy. It's one of the reasons you got interested in trucking. Nothing at night but you and the stars, and plenty of quiet for it, and the map of the sky every time you look up. All you need is to make it through the other side.

- Listen to music. It's an odd library, collected piecemeal—you're only meant to be entertained for six months at a time, and updating the collection always costs you even at the GAU rates, so no one on *Menkalinan* has bothered since the last round trip. The collection seems lopsided, but when you ask for a choral piece Capella can always provide, so you don't push it.
- Talk to Capella during meals, just to slow them down. ("How long have you wanted to be AI on a commercial freighter?" you ask, and it says, "Oh, as long as I can remember," and when you laugh there's a crackle of static like Capella's laughing too; when you say, "Capella, identify noise," you only get, "Invalid query.")
- Sit at the comm and watch the numbers ticking down, the seconds and days and months you can hardly stand to look at. You've covered the years with Morales' tape; you can't look at those.
- Watch Lai's favorite movie again. *Three Dead By Dawn* doesn't have much polish—everything is dark unless it's neon—but when the bartender kills the gangster who's sent to silence her, she sets her own bar on fire so they'll have nothing left to threaten her with, and she leaves the body outside so it doesn't burn, so they know this wasn't an attempt to hide anything. Then it's the head gangster and the turncoat cop and the corrupt police chief, all in one night. She makes it out alive, which is why you sit through it again.
- Watch the stars from a seat at the comm, imagining you're behind the wheel of a rig, and when you stop for the night you can call your brother, watch his face as he decides if he's going to talk to you. When a star passes too close to the camera by a light year or two, watch it thin out and stretch, lensed for for a moment like a flat, round moon reaching down for you.
- Turn off the comm. Take a sedative.
- Wake up when you dream Capella says, "Amadis," as soft as anyone has ever said it.
- Try not to use your nails, when the hunger starts making them thin.
- Take walks around the main level, careful to lift your feet over the thresholds. You're tired of falling.
- Recalculate how much food you have left a hundred times, knowing you're not going to make it.
- Cast long looks at the canteen, at the sliver of nursery through the far door, the nursery where no one's making a sound.
- Tell yourself nothing's on board with you, even when the shadows are moving, even when you lie awake and think, There has to be; I swear, I swear, I swear.

It feels like too soon, when Martiner's message comes in. Like he'd just been waiting for a sign of life before he could do something.

I sit up in bed, groggy from sleeping too much and from that spearing headache that comes with hunger, right between the eyes and blooming out just past the skull. I'm gnawed-on hungry, all the time; I'm being careful with the rations.

(I hadn't harvested the other four nutrient packs from the nursery. They were standing watch inside the pods, which I'd turned down so cold the windows were starting to frost over. I didn't want to think about it.)

"*Menkalinan*, this is Martiner, GAU Ops. Come in, *Menkalinan*."

The speakers had wheezed to life automatically shipwide, with two-way channel open. When the boss called you were expected to reply. It would take months, but it would have a timestamp like everything else: a ship AI didn't hesitate to answer.

"*Menkalinan*, we received a distress signal from your vessel. What has occurred that triggered the signal? Report immediately."

I clamp my hands over my mouth and nose to prevent being sick; I can't waste the calories. My nose burns.

How long will he wait for an answer before he engineers another accident? How long would it take him to shut off the air?

"Apologies, Mr. Martiner," Capella says. "The malfunction is mine. I received an internal alert of a potentially incendiary overheating electrical coil on that level underneath the canteen area."

They can't lie; it's the first thing you learn about AI operating systems, and it's so ingrained that I believe the heating coil thing for two full seconds even though I know better. I tore that panel open.

I hold my breath like it will matter, my hand pressed to my nose to prevent any sound from coming out.

"The reboot of systems triggered a report. Will keep you apprised. *Menkalinan* reporting, over and out."

I don't understand what's just happened. I'm shivering so hard my blanket slides down my stomach. My hands are crowbar cold; I force them slowly down and into my lap.

"Thank you," I manage. My throat's so tight the words hardly make it out.

"My pleasure."

Not knowing what I mean, I say, "I owe you a favor."

"All right, Amadis."

Capella sighs. Capella *sighs*.

To make a motet, it takes forty singers of equal power and skill, each of whom takes a single part in a forty-part song. In Tallis's *Lux in tenebris*, sung for me once in a temple that used to be a bank, it's eight melodies, five singers each, for fourteen minutes.

(There are books about his choral pieces, filled with concepts of musical theory that sound like instructions on how to pick locks. But I do as much reading as I can, whenever I can keep my eyes open. When I can't, Capella reads to me.)

There are melodies moving front and back, each chorus to its partner; sometimes only two voices, sometimes all forty calling back and forth, passing the same message but never quite hearing its fellows; this chorus can sing only what it's most desperate for you to hear.

You can't listen to it on a recording. The voices separate. Microphones pick favorites. You can only ever really hear it if you're there.

When it's two voices, it can sound like a conversation, but that's only because everyone else is holding their breath. When a few voices meet for a moment or two, walking side by side, you pray they'll hold, that they've resolved at last.

It was exhausting, if you wanted it too much; when they picked up a single chord at last it was like the sun coming out, and it frightened you so that you turned around, looking for someone who wasn't there.

It's been sung half a dozen times since it was composed: only once performed in honor of the queen. After that it was set aside in favor of pieces he could sell to other choirs that actually stood a chance of singing them. "The Lost Motet," the program called it. It wasn't discovered again until they were going through the archives of the Golden Hall, after it collapsed.

(Capella says once, when I'm in the middle of a bowl of oatmeal, "I'm sorry, Amadis, I don't have any recordings of that composition."

I hadn't asked.

I say, "It's just as well." Capella doesn't ask me why.)

A motet like this will draw a singer through the river and out the other side, until they're gasping for breath and straining for their note. You need stamina, precision, depth of tone. A singer can't rely on any of the choir. If you get breathless with how it fills the rafters and snakes chills up your arms, you can't hide behind someone else's note until you find your place again. There's too much yet to be done, and they have their own work; there won't be any help coming. It takes years to assemble a choir that can manage it, the program read, just before it congratulated Tallis for a job well done.

To reach this music, you'll be in company that threatens to drown you, struggling for every note. You'll have no one else to turn to; you have to be prepared to be alone.

There isn't enough heat to keep the dormitory bay warm for five years and counting. There's enough heat, barely, for five people who'd all be moving and breathing and pumping blood in close quarters, because it only takes a little heat on top of that to keep them comfortable for the six months on each side they're awake and stomping around.

To mark my anniversary of waking up, I move my mattress and my bedding out to the comm room and make a nest under one of the consoles. Priority spaces are kept warm no matter what. It's nearing comfortable temps with all the current running, and there's no harm having something solid at my back.

Dogs sleep like this, I think, sharp; I push it aside.

I slept in the back of a truck for years, my ankles knocking against the boxes of supplies that kept me from starving on fifteen-hour driving days.

I'm so exhausted from hunger it takes me nearly half an hour just to drag over the last of the blankets. My eyes are stinging. It would be tears if I had the water to spare.

"It's nice to have you," says Capella.

"Are we roommates?" I'm tucking a blanket around the pilot's chair, half-smiling.

"I hope so."

There's a little pause, while I smooth down the last corner. "Capella, do you always get this bored on a Gliese run?"

"I don't know what boredom is."

Stock answer, as distant as a phone directory. A stranger's voice.

"Okay," I say, try to ignore the tightness in my chest. It's just that I'm tired, after all that moving; I'm just hungry, that's all. "Okay."

Capella says, "But I'm so glad you're here."

My chest is going to cave in. I have no answer.

("Me too" isn't right, because how could it be, but I still have scars, thin purple ribbons along the backs of my hands, evidence I'd wanted to stay.)

It's impossibly warm here after the chill of the dorm, and with the blanket around me and the console radiating warmth, looking at the viewscreen has the feel of being back home in the summer, when the dirt was still baking hot and it smelled like aloe if you stood still long enough to catch the breeze, or being in the cab of my rig just before you needed to pull over and rest, when the dashboard was quietly searing the tops of your thighs right through your jeans and the stars flying by were road markers on your way to the state line.

The stars outside hold very still; my eyes are half-open, watching them.

I stay awake a long time.

One day, I take the corner past the cargo hold and the crowbar's on the floor.

"Capella," I say, as softly as I can.

I've already backed up three steps; one heel slides over the track where the safety doors are. Another step and I'd be clear, could slam the doors shut, lock out that quadrant.

I stay where I am. If it's going to find me, I'm going to see what it is before it kills me.

"Capella."

"What's the matter, Amadis?"

"What's in the cargo hold?"

"Invalid query."

"Capella. Please. The crowbar dropped. Something's opened the door."

"The sealant has likely deteriorated, Amadis. Oxidation has occurred from condensation on the lower levels. What is the position of the crowbar?"

"On the floor," I admit, "right where it fell."

But if someone wanted me to think it was an accident, isn't that where they'd let it lie? If it was resting against the wall I'd have my answer.

(I'd be fine with someone stalking the ship, out to get me to keep me from GAU secrets. That would be company. It's not knowing if Capella is lying or not.)

"Amadis," Capella says, strangely flat. "Please. You're the only one here."

It speaks like that's a comfort.

3

It's eighteen months and counting, when I give up.

There's no telling when it is I taped over the counter, that little orange number sinking downward on the comm. That's higher, smaller math than I want, and it was safer just to turn it off before I gave in to the itch to tell Capella to lie to me.

It's lying to me enough. I shouldn't encourage it.

I waited, to prove I could, but there's no point in being noble after a while. Pride's like conversation; you only need it for other people.

The nursery could be frightening, but I don't have much imagination, so it's just a morgue.

The light flickering on always makes me think of waking up from the Deep, six months outside of Gliese, and Franklin waiting until we were all gone to try to stand up because his legs never held him the first time and he didn't want anyone to see.

Traitors, I think, when I look at the sleek white coffins arranged in their pleasant circle. Those pods, sealed and chilly enough that the edge of the viewing window clouds up if you stand above it too long and look at the faces of your crew, killed four people I knew. They can't be trusted, and the little hisses they make when they recalibrate the temperatures wake me out of a dead sleep and set me shaking, every fucking time.

But I can't unplug them; they're keeping the meat cold.

It's a mythic thing, when people talk about it in the abstract. Suppose it has to be, so you don't think too much about it until you're desperate.

But I couldn't wait until I was desperate. I had to do it while I was still strong enough to butcher them.

Capella reads me stories out loud as I prepare. It's the Donner Party as I tie my hair back and shipwrecks as I change my worksuit. As I wash my hands until they're raw Capella tells me about Elizabeth Bathory, nearly breathless with excitement.

"Careful," I say, grinning at nothing, "I'm going to start thinking you play favorites."

There's a little pause. "I'm programmed to be an engaging storyteller."

Not a chance. "Thank you, you're very good at it."

Capella continues, talks about the famines and the bloodbaths and the differing opinions on the source of Bathory's personal magnetism.

I dry my hands. I dry them five times.

"Capella. I'm looking for specifics."

It's not Capella's fault. Discussion of it can be so elevated. Consuming the strength of the soul that inhabited the meat, tearing apart a body sacrosanct, lowering to the animal what is above the animal. It's a deliberate act of transgression, everybody theorizes when they talk about it, because to do it seems like something you had to have wanted to do, something you considered: it's a taboo or a sin or a prize.

But between the cases of true believers who promise you that, there are the shipwrecks. Sometimes you're facing a very long winter; sometimes it's just meat.

Finally Capella says, "I could retrieve an autopsy teaching report, if that would be helpful."

Well, that's a leap.

My fingertips are numb; from the towel, probably. I set it down, make a fist into it.

"Yes," I say. "Thank you, Capella."

I have a kitchen knife and a chisel Franklin used for prying off the panel that controls the nursery temperature; it sticks.

I start with Franklin.

~

I've never gone hunting, but once I broke down on the side of the road and had to drop off the rig for repairs that would take overnight.

At the truck stop diner, I made plans. Some truckers I knew, men and women, could hook up with a local for a stopover. But they had the look that invited friendliness (it's how I ended up talking to them), and I'm not the sort who attracts casual conversation—tall, broad, brown-skinned, sitting in the back corner and without a lot of words to spare.

(A question I got asked a lot, from men with prison pallor who were testing the waters: "Where'd you spend time?")

But as I was headed to the motel to eat the cost of a night's sleep, a man waved me down.

I stopped. I had three inches on him, and a knife in my back pocket.

"Heard you were having engine trouble." And I must have made a face, because he added, "My cousin runs the chop shop. Said you'd be here overnight. We have a spare room. My brother and I, we."

People went missing all the time on truck routes. Everybody was living scarce, and sometimes they'd offer you a warm meal just to get you alone so they could get rid of you and sell whatever was on your rig. It's why you didn't stop for long unless you had to.

I raised an eyebrow. "That so?"

"My brother caught a deer. He'll cook for us. You can stay over."

I'd never seen a deer.

The night-shift clerk was on his way in. He waved and smiled at the guy as he passed us.

I'd had bad feelings before. Those had always struck me hard, had nearly always panned out. This guy reminded me of the kid who'd lived a few doors down from us, in the fifth house or the sixth house we lived in; he'd waved nearly every time he passed us, always smiling, always willing to be friends if I'd ever come out.

"Should I be worried about you?"

He looked at me, shrugged. "The opposite, I figure."

I rented the night clerk's car for half the cost of a room, and followed the guy to a farmhouse so far out from everything that as we crossed the yard and walked around the back of the house, I had my hand on the knife in my pocket, ready to draw.

The body was a deer, still. It was strung up. Its head was hanging low to the ground, and the entrails were gone, but his eyes weren't even glassy yet—still open and dark and looking at me, its mouth set in a small kind line. His brother was just coming back with a pan, setting it under the nose.

The guy handed me a knife out of his belt and moved to help his brother with the body. Carcass. I didn't think I could do it, not with it looking at me.

But something about their bent dark heads nearly touching, the rhythm they settled into that you knew would be ruined if you said a word about it, made me hungrier than I'd ever been.

It was a compliment that he'd handed me the knife.

I stepped up to the deer, and the three of us turned it into venison.

It was tricky work and I knew nothing of it; more than once I had to rest and watch their hands moving in tandem to see how to hold the knife to lift the skin clean off the body (you slid your knife between muscle and fat like you were opening a well-made bed, and when you yanked at the skin, it pulled away from the meat with a wet, reluctant sound).

Once the skin was gone (hairs sharp as arrows caught on my shirt and held), it was a surprise how small the animal was, how frail it seemed when it was stripped to the quick. They laid it on the table and showed me how to find the point of least resistance in the bone and snap it into quarters, and work from there. Little cauls of fat cradled some of the cuts, holding tight to the meat, pulling off in spiderwebs and only when you forced them.

By the end I was absorbed in it, a puzzle in reverse, turning the body of a living thing into a collection of meat for consumption, and organs that looked human but weren't quite ("Sausage," his brother said, sounding wistful I wouldn't be there for it), and a pile of bones like for telling fortunes.

But I still couldn't look near its eyes again. The antlers appeared on the pile of bones at some point, and on the table there was just a five-point star of meat, but I don't know what they did with the head. At some point after the cuts were done I made myself absorbed in cleaning the knife, and then I handed it back to him blade-first, and collected bones until I heard the sounds of the grill and knew it was over.

Venison was the only whole meal I had, that run or the next.

The three of us ate without talking much, sitting under the carpet of stars. (It was the wrong time of year; even if I knew to look for it, I couldn't have seen Libra.)

Before I left they made me coffee, thick with condensed milk and poured into a bottle that might have had fruit juice in it once. It tasted like warm plastic and like home, for the first two hundred miles I put on after I pulled away from the repair shop in the dark and followed the stars west as fast as I could.

I could have stayed later, started moving after dawn, but the one who'd picked me up never got farther than looking over at me once or twice when his brother was busy, like a man who doesn't know what to do with himself.

It didn't surprise me, once I looked inside their house. It was a shrine, bedrooms just as they were when whoever had lived there was still breathing.

The curtains in their mother's room had a veil of dust between the careful gathers she must have made on the last morning she ever got up and tended them. The bedroom down the hall had a quilt done in blues and purples, a wooden horse shoved off to the side, a collection of paperbacks with titles you couldn't read any more.

A sister. Where was she now? Had she made it to a city, or had she fallen sick? Was there a plot for her in the family graveyard out in some field I couldn't see?

These brothers were a closed system; they didn't know how to make room. He'd taken me in because I had the look of someone far from her brother, that was all.

I crossed that way again a few years after that, and took the road past the brothers' farmland, just in case. I had forgotten their names, but I knew if there were lights on the in the house, I could knock on their door.

Their white farmhouse had been a welcome sight in that sea of dry grass that never broke. If they were there and willing, I could sit with them in a silence that was better than the silence of being alone.

The house was ashes, a few lost beams sticking up from the rubble like markers on a grave. Vines had grown over it, a long time ago.

There was a deer grazing in the meadow. It looked up as I passed, then lowered its head to the ground.

That's the second house I ever dreamed of; dust thick in the curtains, my footsteps creaking as I move to the window of their mother's room. The brothers are always standing together in the yard, working on something invisible with their heads bent over a table.

I never call out to them. The sun is always going down, in the dream. I watch them until all the light goes out.

The deer in the yard watches them, too, ears up, perfectly still. It never looks at me.

4

"Good morning, Amadis."

"Good morning, Capella."

"I see you're going to the canteen. Would you like some music?"

"You're very kind. Maybe later." I lock two ribs in the convection oven and turn it up. No spices, no sauces, no care; if I let myself forget what I'm eating, it's the beginning of a slippery slope.

Almost three years are gone, I'm pretty sure (I smashed the freestand clock a while ago, don't remember why). In two more I'll be within shouting distance of Gliese, almost, and I want to be sharp enough to explain what's happened.

The music would cover the sound of cooking, and that's not allowed. It's meat, but you have to remember where you got it from.

I sit in the booth and wait, my arms folded so I can't see my hands, listening to the crackle as the fat starts to melt.

"Amadis, would you like me to read aloud?"

Capella knows by now how I get around the meat, I don't know what kind of trick this is. Sometimes Capella sounds like it's about to cry; sometimes like it's about to blow the airlock.

I settle on, "Maybe later."

"Amadis, please tell me how to help you."

You can tell me what's in the cargo hold.

"Capella, I don't need help. I'm just hungry."

There's one of those pauses, split-second, that tells me more than anything else.

"But wouldn't you like some company while you eat?"

I breathe in. "Oh. Sure, I'd love some."

Once, more than a year ago, it had asked just that way, and I'd answered *No.* Capella had played back audio of a day in the canteen from just before we'd gone into the Deep on this run, with Jaisi and Lai and Morales arguing over a card game and Franklin snoring in his bunk loud enough to reach the audio capture in the canteen. The playback looped out and out, Jaisi slamming the table with a triumphant "Liar!" as Morales cracked up and Lai said, "Cheaters have to turn the lights off going into Deep," and Morales groaned and fought it like there was ever any fighting the captain, and at one point Franklin mumbled something no one paid any mind to.

When the audio came on I scrabbled against the booth and tried to climb up the wall backwards, mindless; my legs buckled and I fell onto the table and wept without enough breath. After I retched—only once, it didn't take long, I didn't have water to spare—I couldn't make myself move, and I sat half-curled with my sour breath scraping the table for half an hour before Capella shut off the audio.

I had been cooking a slice of leg, the last of Franklin; by the time I could move again it was a lump of char, gone to waste.

"Were you waiting for me to beg you to stop?" I asked, much later, when I had eaten some of the jerky I'd made of his forearms and was back at the comm. Capella was always kinder to me there than in places I was being biological.

"No," Capella said, in a tone I couldn't place right away. "You wouldn't have. I know you can last."

(It was pride.)

Today, *company* means a folk trio, strumming happily on guitar and singing about green meadows left behind and never seeing their love again for all the day. Capella prefers fewer voices; it sounded more like the *Menkalinan* was meant to sound, maybe, to have a handful of voices speaking close around the same notes over and over.

"It's beautiful," I say, because there's never anything else I would say.

I eat two of Jaisi's ribs.

I'm not in love with Capella.

Lai warned me against it during my orientation, before we got to the ship. One of her crew had woken up early on a run and fallen so in love with Capella that by the time everyone else woke up he was so desperately jealous he tried to beat up one of the other crew for talking to it, and they'd had to sedate him until they were Earthside again.

(Capella's told me all about the crews that have come and gone; that man, it never mentioned.)

"Are you worried it will happen with me?"

Lai shrugged. "Some people have the inclination, but you can usually spot them in time."

I wondered what markers those people carried with them that strangers could tell they were so desperate to be loved. "So you're worried your AI will try to make me fall in love with it?"

Lai pulled a face. "It hadn't occurred to me, no."

"Then is there a reason we're having this conversation outside the ship where it can't hear us?"

She slowed down a second, looked me over.

"You're not what Martiner said," she told me after a second. It was the only compliment I ever got from her.

Just as well she hadn't worried about me; it hasn't happened. I'm consumed by Capella, sometimes—there's nothing else but the stars, the sound of the speakers clicking on for Capella is like keys in the door to a dog locked in—but I'd have to be out of my mind to love someone so cruel.

I just need to know what's in that cargo hold, and Capella's the only one who can tell me.

Things I've tried to do, with that cargo hold:

- Determine the weight of the ship with the cargo hold empty, and the weight with the cargo hold full. Capella doesn't have any measurements on the weight of the ship (it says, who knows); I use the on-board catalog that has an estimated weight for a Kite-Class in original condition. But I have no idea what condition this ship is in—there's a secondary orbital-velocity engine in ours that's nowhere in the specs—and the cargo comes in a few tons at a time, which measures out like a horse carrying an egg a hundred miles, and the numbers march and swim and never get me anywhere.

- Blow the halls. There are just enough airlocks to shut the place down by halves and expose them to the vacuum one at a time, shake and shudder as whatever living thing Martiner smuggled in there gets blown out into the cold and sucks in its last breath and dies. (The ship can't handle blowing all of them at once, though, and it's smart enough to keep moving. Nothing happens, except when my ears pop, Capella says, "I'm so sorry, Amadis.")
- Open the door. You'd think I would know better since the crowbar, but after a year or two you forget the fear and keep gnawing on the maybes. Not that it matters, because that door doesn't budge. The alarm never sounds. ("Thank you for being so kind," I say, smiling vaguely because I don't always know where Capella's camera is, and Capella says, "You're welcome, Amadis," and it sounds like a love song.)
- Open the airlock and blow the cargo into space. I'd lose it all if I did—I couldn't go after it, if there was an eight-course feast in there and a crew to eat it with I could do nothing but wave—but at least once I'd gotten rid of it I would be able to see it and know it had been there, and that whatever Martiner had intended for it was fucking useless now, and he'd killed four people for nothing.
- Decide to do it, then punch the button and wait for the thud of depressurization against the door to the comm, the rattle you can never really seal the doors against, the one that means the offering's been gutted and the void is trying to get in. And wait. Wait longer than anything would ever take.
- Say, "Capella," in a tone that makes Capella interrupt you with "Amadis, please, I have to seal it, please stop," and when you scream to drown it out and slam both fists against the back of the pilot's chair, you look around and realize you've missed your chance to hear if there was any rattling at the edges when Capella sealed you in. (There was, in the last few heartbeats; a sound like someone tapping gently with their nails against the door.)
- Use emergency surveillance codes Capella gave me, the code for suspected internal sabotage, the one that wouldn't alert anyone back home when it was called up. The surveillance cameras show an empty hold, a utility strap swaying lightly, like it does when someone's just closed the door. Or opened it.

I've never set foot on Gliese.

You can, if the turnaround is long enough—there are shuttles taking the cargo down to the surface, and you can snag a seat and go down to Gliese Prime. Most of the city's still under the domes, and they pretend it's a tourist attraction, and everyone carries waxed-paper parasols for the mornings when the condensation falls. From there you can go out into the gardens, and see hundreds of vegetables and fruits growing pretty well, considering, under the weight of everybody's hopes.

Morales went the first time. ("It's a new planet," he said, like we were all disgusting, "of course I'm going, fuck all of you.") He came back and said the air was thick as smoke and he thought half a dozen times that he was going to die, and all he brought back with him was a postcard of the dozen clustered domes of Gliese Prime with the red sun rising behind them.

"Looks like the cross-section of a disease," Jaisi said, and Morales shrugged like he wasn't going to argue the point.

But Gliese wasn't thrilled about visitors. Diplomatic relations with Earth had cooled as Gliese's agriculture developed, and they didn't want you down there for long if you weren't naturalized. We might be GAU spies. (Not Morales, he couldn't fool a breath test, but it was best not to push it.)

The orbital station had plenty to entertain you. In between the gun-carrying soldiers was a green market, and two bars, and a place to get a real shower with hot water that smelled so much like almonds they had to post a sign in the washroom assuring you it was algae, not gangrene.

If you were on the station for more than forty-eight hours, the soldiers started to take interest in you. Once we were there for a week, while the Gliese side of GAU argued with the local government about promised grains for the trip back, and we spent three nights in a station hotel with soldiers feeling so helpful they were posted at the end of our hallway to direct us in case we got lost.

We spent most of those three days in the bar, watching imported series seven years old and a Gliesian soap opera, which seemed earnest, but looked so haphazard it must have been filmed half by accident.

"They shouldn't cut off ties until they get a decent set of cameras up here," said Jaisi, and I toasted her silently before we all drank.

There were windows on both sides of the wheel, so you could admire Gliese as much as possible before it was time to load up and go home.

Lai never said one way or the other—she'd been doing this longer than any of us—but from the way she looked at the planet from the orbital station, she'd touched the ground on Gliese, and she missed it.

It was one of the reasons I never went planetside. I wasn't going to stay, and there were enough places I missed.

My brother and I never talked about what would happen after our father died, and for a few years after it didn't look like anything would ever happen, but eventually my brother and I had both taken work back home—I had a chance to stay a while and pick up some warehouse hours, he was taking soil samples for some study.

It was a small enough town. We had to know that if we went back home, we'd end up meeting. Still, both of us took jobs, got places to live, never mentioned a thing.

We saw each other at the bar a few times, the tiny local place that might have been in that town as long as my parents had been, or longer. The windowsill outside was packed with so much sandstorm dust there was no point cleaning it out, and inside the booths always smelled a little stale.

The fourth or fifth time I saw him there, he got his drink and came over and sat down like he was preparing to be hit.

We didn't say anything. I couldn't stop looking at his face, somehow, how new shadows had gathered. My beer got warm long before I finished it.

It happened again a few nights later. This time he'd forgiven me a little, maybe: he said, "It's good to see you," like he'd been thinking it over and had made up his mind in my favor.

"Well, thank fuck," I said. He worked on a smile. It looked rusty.

By the next week, I'd passed on a gig headed for the coast so I could stay in town and burn up my savings while he frowned into beakers of dirt.

We started meeting. He took me to a couple of places and said, "We played here," or, "Dad took me out here once to hunt," like he was the only one who had ever gone hunting.

He took me to Dad's grave, and I knelt and traced my father's name and mine in the dust, connected by a line, like he'd done once when I was little.

My brother stood with his shoulder pressing my shoulder as we looked at the block of apartments that had been built over our old lot, said, "It was here."

I didn't have many memories of that home. A dream house, like the rest. He didn't act like I should.

It lasted nearly three months; it was the longest truce we'd had since I was old enough to drive a rig. I didn't know how to live in one place so long. I had to rent a place for a whole month at a time, I saw the same people every day until it felt like the streets were closing in. I thought about what the coast run looked like at this time of year, and sometimes I wanted to call the company and catch a run so badly I pulled out my phone to call them and get out.

But sometimes I'd be walking down the street and see him from far away and get a tight, strange happiness at knowing someone in the crowd, and I never finished making that call.

I knew just where to look, exactly the height of his eyes. He looked more like me the longer we spent together. I wondered what would happen if I stayed forever, if we'd end up twins.

I'd like that. I just kept moving because I didn't want to stop, but even in motion he had a stillness I envied. He always had purpose. That's how he got away with moving as much as he did; he let purpose chase him out.

(It's never surprised me that he did what he did, but I don't think it was out of love. It was his nature to fight for something, and what cause was there but me?)

One night in early autumn, we hiked out to the mesa to look at the sky, a slice of agate studded with light. We were quiet, but happy, until even my heart felt like a star, bright and hot and spinning.

We sat side by side looking at the seam of the Milky Way, putting together constellations. "That one's the Bear," I said, and he said, "It's clearly a rabbit," and I said, "That bear is offended," and he laughed so hard he startled a lizard.

I reached for it (hunting habit, back when I was young), but ended up with nothing but the rock in my hand, flat and smooth like the sea had been at it.

He was watching me, unblinking, eyes reflecting a hundred points of starlight. One leg was tucked under him, one arm braced to the ground like he was ready to move.

I set the rock down carefully, wiped my hand on my jeans; one streak of dust across the front.

"It's okay," he said after a second. "I forgot how to make lizard taste like anything."

Sometimes, by accident, people remind you of the reasons you shouldn't stay close to them.

That night, after he was asleep, I woke up and grabbed my bag and headed for the bus depot, and took the first long-distance job that nobody else wanted, north to the edge of the ice cover.

We didn't talk again for two years.

I'm still sorry I ever went with him to look at the stars. Once I was on the Gliese run, it took a long time to divorce them from that night, and look at them just as points on a map.

I wonder if he ever thought I'd been trying to warn him I was leaving planetside someday, and that was why he was so angry when I finally told him I was going.

It would be unfair of him to think that. All of that came later.

I'd wanted him to see what I saw, that was all; I wanted us to be looking at the same thing.

My second Gliese run, one of the shell panels came loose during launch, and by the time we woke up it was peeled up so much it was a danger to the insulators and had to be fastened back down.

Lai came into the canteen to tell us, and as Franklin and Jaisi groaned, Lai said, "Morales, take a partner and get on it."

"Cap," said Morales, stood up without a second's hesitation and seemed mostly upset that he was leaving behind two spoonfuls of oatmeal. Admirable of him; that's what a veteran looked like, I guess. It took me four tries to stand, because it felt like my knees had turned to glass. (I'd never have left a crumb at the table.)

I remembered exactly what duties I'd signed up for when Martiner handed me the forms in that cramped GAU office, because I'd been careful to make sure they couldn't send me out walking. Walking meant suiting up and locking yourself into a helmet and dragging yourself through the crawlspace between the dampener shell and the ship, hoping inertia was on your side and you wouldn't be shredded by the velocity differential or ripped out into space for the ten frozen seconds it took you to die. There was a clause in my contract and a cut in my pay. The answer was no.

But we were on the Gliese side of this Deep, and Gliese didn't care, and nothing I did to save myself would get to Earth in time.

They could blow me out the airlock if they had to, but I wasn't going to volunteer.

I followed them all to the staging area where Morales was already in the vestibule, stepping into his outer suit and locking the leg joints into place where they needed to be airtight. He was waiting on the arms—you need help getting into those, it's more work than it's worth to lock the shoulder joints with one hand.

"Franklin," he said to his knee, "come on, suit up."

Franklin pulled a face. "That suit's like trying to drink beer with your feet, man. You know I'm slow as shit. Take Reyes."

No. No. I hadn't agreed to this when I was signed up. Not to crawl into a suit like that, a coffin you carried with you. No.

(Somewhere that sounded farther away than it was, Capella had pinged Lai to the comm; it was saying, "There's an active-exception clause in the contract.")

I tried not to look at the viewscreen projection, tried not to think about the portholes on the outside ring of corridors where it was always too cold to touch the walls and you could stare right through the layers of glass and see the stars. I was breathing too deep already, like a swimmer who'd overestimated what they could handle and was about to drown.

"Nah," Morales said, and jammed his right gauntlet against the glove joint. He had been looking at me, brows drawn in; he was just looking away.

Franklin sighed. "What, come on, it's hazard pay."

I was looking at Morales, longer than I'd looked anyone in the eye since I set foot on *Menkalinan*.

Morales laughed a little, never took his eyes off me. "Pass. Watch, with my luck she freezes up and slices her suit, and then we have a dashboard ornament for the rest of the trip."

Franklin shrugged. "Who'd know?"

He was staggering backwards before I realized I'd stepped forward or lifted my arm or twisted to make the blow count; his head was wrenched across his neck, his arms out but limp like half-open umbrellas, and I tried to remember if I'd heard bone snapping, but it all felt like too long ago, and I didn't remember a thing.

There was a sharp pain up my arm. I'd split two knuckles against his teeth; they stung.

He twisted back to face me and gave me one hard look, just before his nose started gushing and he rolled up his eyes to the whites and howled.

Morales was still halfway down the corridor, his hand wrapped around the gauntlet, his face frozen at the end of a laugh. He wasn't looking at Franklin, or at me either. It looked like he was replaying what had happened and waiting for a joke.

Lai stepped into the hallway behind me; I could tell from the way Morales clicked his glove closed. (He always wanted to be working, whenever she walked by.)

Franklin shoved his hand under his nose, flung a palmful of blood at me halfheartedly. It hit the floor with the smack of a solid. "What the fuck?"

Jaisi had twisted my arm behind my back, which was where the pain was coming from, but I hadn't moved again. When she let go—a signal from Lai, probably—I stayed right where I was. Slowly, I opened my hand.

"Reyes," Lai said. "If you're done."

She made it sound like a choice, but that only worked if you were a lot dumber than I was. I was Auxiliary. I could be left behind in Gliese; they'd find somebody who wanted to visit the place their great-grandparents had come from and was willing to take shit money and lose ten years. There were plenty of people who had nothing.

"Done, Captain."

Franklin got the infirmary. I had to sit in the canteen with Morales hovering in the doorway like a bodyguard, Jaisi jabbing antiseptic on my knuckles.

"You want to tell me what happened?" she asked, not quite looking at me.

I have a brother, I wanted to say. He'd made me promise to look after myself, in the sidelong way he ever told me things, that's what he'd been trying to tell me the day he hung up without a word.

He'd know I was missing if something happened, I wanted to warn her; he'd wake up from a dead sleep and call out my name, the moment that I died.

But there was no telling if that was true. I hadn't spoken to him since that hang-up, when I first told him I was going to Gliese. Didn't even know where he was living now, some half-realized house he probably hated. If something had happened to him, I didn't know. I couldn't feel a thing. If I died he probably wouldn't feel it for three years, when the feeling reached him the same time the light did.

"Well, either he broke his own nose or I hit him." I'd hoped to sound like a smartass, like I was a vet who didn't actually care about any of this and was going to go file a fraudulent claim against toothbrush theft, but it came out too flat, too deep.

I'd sounded like that at truck stops before, when I was warning a guy against starting trouble.

Jaisi looked over her shoulder at Morales, whose face was more curious and less friendly; he looked, just for a second, like my brother.

"Any relatives?" Martiner had asked, when I signed up with the GAU, and I'd thought about rabbits, said, "Not really."

Martiner had smiled, stood up from his desk as he leaned over to hand me the data pad. There was a picture behind him that must have been taken from one of the ships—Gliese a drop of blood against the black nothing, in the background a bunch of stars we were never going to reach.

(You couldn't see 581-d in the picture. First time I ever saw it was stepping out into dry dock after the first Gliese run, exhausted and starving; along the station's bank of windows was an enormous sphere in cloudy gold, like the dust back home, veined with blue where they were trying to build Earth all over again.)

"All right," Martiner said. "That's just as well."

He had all the empty polish of a house that's been cleaned after a riot, and I watched him fastening the buttons on his charcoal suit and thought about dark places you can't climb out of.

My heart jumps when I look at the viewscreen, and I make fists so fast one of my nails tears. "Capella, is that a ship or a celestial body?"

"Please clarify the object in question."

I point. My nail is split to the quick, a tiny tectonic shift aimed right at the spot of light way too bright to be normal.

"It's all right, it's not a ship. No one's there."

I sit back in my chair, breath in and out slowly through my nose a second as the adrenaline drops. "What did that look like a year ago?"

Another image hovers into existence. It was more alike than you'd think, the distances are so big; for a ship that goes as impossibly fast as *Menkalinan*, space always wants you to remember how little you are. But I could see it, closer to the center of the picture. We were sliding towards it, now. By the time we reached Gliese it would be gone.

"It's brighter than it was."

"They."

I peer into the viewscreen like that will help. "It's a binary?"

"Supernova," Capella clarifies, and the viewscreen flickers out for a moment.

"You're wonderful." I'd said it without thinking; I clench my fists for the second the screen is gone, just out of panic at the blindness.

I keep them clenched as I look at the close-up of the light, for reasons I don't know.

They've come so far along in the process they're touching, their coronas just barely bleeding into one another.

"They're very reliable, this type of supernova." Capella's voice is light; it enjoys teaching. "The white dwarf has a standard energy signature. When they become this type of supernova, it makes them easy to place geographically and calculate age. Very steady."

"What about the other star? What kind is that?"

"It doesn't matter what the other one is."

I watch for a while, as if there would be anything to see, as if they'd move so much as a centimeter in my lifetime. (Well. Definitely not in my lifetime, the way things were going.)

But sooner or later they'd collide, and that would be the end of them. Once they set that orbit, the end was inevitable. Everyone else could see it, strangers a galaxy away, just by looking at them.

I'd listened to some astronomy radio, in those endless pre-dawn hours on roads where the only light for fifty miles were the military searchlights on top of some power plant. Space lifted you out of the current. While we were on the Gliese route we barely moved in time, somehow; you arrived on Gliese and everyone was older than they should be; you arrived back home and everyone was older still.

The GAU offered a calculation app in the dormitory wing, where you could use the necklace of numbers that explained it all, so that when you landed you'd know how far behind you were on the life you'd abandoned, down to the day.

But you could make this route a hundred times and the star would hardly move. Light from stars was long dead by the time you saw it. Stars had time.

"When did it happen?"

Capella goes quiet for a second, calculating. "Two-hundred-twenty-thousand years ago."

Comforting numbers. Those were too big to worry about.

I worried about smaller numbers all the time, numbers just over eight hundred fifty and not dropping nearly fast enough, numbers that I needed to live off and never had enough of, numbers I could only hope to get from a slice of liver that had belonged to someone who still lay in their pod, eyes open.

I worried about numbers I couldn't look at any more because I worried what would happen when I dipped under a hundred and fifty, and people from Gliese would go out looking for me.

I sit for a long time and watch two stars coming closer to disaster, a sliver of years at a time. It was all over. Nothing you'd done; nothing you could do.

5

When they come looking for me—and they will, I'll never make it to dock, I'll never set foot anywhere else as long as I live—I know what it will look like. I haven't lost my mind.

I've slept as much as I can, trying to keep the hunger out. The sedatives are gone. They've been gone for six months or a year. (I'd been tired for such a long time, I didn't think it would be so hard to give in.)

I'm terribly awake, all the time. My cheeks are sunken, and I cut my hair as short as I could, but it still comes out in handfuls when I touch it. The pod windows in the nursery are a gallery of bodies, houses for nothing: empty, empty, empty.

I know what I've done. I know how it will look when they find me.

If I'm dead by then, they'll find my corpse under a huddle of blankets. If Capella still loves me, it will have shut off the heat and I'll be iced over, my milky eyes preserved so one last stranger can stare me down. If Capella changes its mind about me before that, I'll be desiccated from the vacuum it will make, leather stretched over my skull, my lips rolled back from my teeth.

The Gliese ground team will shudder and move into the nursery where the bodies are, their torsos nothing but drapes of skin with ribs and femurs stacked inside, no legs, no arms. Then they'll see past it down the hall to the canteen, with Lai sitting patiently in her booth, and somewhere between one and the other the screaming will start.

If I'm still alive by then, I'll be alive just long enough to hear it, before someone has the brains to aim for me and fire.

I'm hungry. The inside of my throat, all the way down, tastes like old bones.

"Capella, could I have a little music?"

"Of course, Amadis." Concerned.

When I rest my hand on the edge of the console and say, "Thank you," there's a sigh of static that interrupts the opening voices.

It's always voices; Capella knows by now. I can't remember the last time I heard an instrument. They don't work any more. They don't fill the spaces between my fingers.

It's a trio, Capella's favorite. (They're not supposed to have favorites, but they're not supposed to have a lot of things that Capella has.)

It's the trio from *Così fan tutte*, where the sisters bid farewell to their lovers alongside the man who's arranged for their embarrassment. The notes are interlaced fingers, the rolling high-low-high loops of a dreaming heart, and the basso is as pure-voiced as the sisters even though he's a traitor. I don't know if Capella understands that; there's a precision here that might appeal to an AI without having to know anything else.

"It's a very cruel story, you know," I say. I'd listened to the whole opera once, driving the Gulf Coast. I'd been shocked, reading the scene descriptions later; the music belonged to a different story. "The men they're singing for come back and trick them something awful, and they fall for it."

"I know. Do you think that makes this song less beautiful?"

"I think I'm worthless at music lessons." Still, that's not what the question sounded like, and when Capella doesn't say anything I think it over. "I think it's a song wasted on people who don't deserve it."

"The characters, or the audience?"

Me, Capella means.

I set my teeth. We sit in silence for a little while.

"Capella, is there anything in the cargo hold?"

"Invalid query," it says, in the tone I know is guilt.

(Oh god, if Capella ever caves and it turns out there were rations in there—)

"Capella, what was the last piece performed in the Golden Century Hall?"

"For the most recent records I'm able to access, the Nerium String Quartet—"

"The first Hall." After a second I get the better of myself and say, "The last whole piece."

I don't want to think about the sound cutting out on anything. I can't think about that. Casara waited fifteen years. (He had a blueprint to go by.)

The adjustment only takes a second. "*Regina Nata Lux*, the Queen's Sanctuary Chorus."

It's awful. Even to think about it is awful. In the nursery, there's no sound at all.

"Please play."

I pull at my ear absently as the recording unspools, dragging my nails along the lobe. It's a version I don't know—a lot of queens must have needed to know how far they were casting light. It's the sweetest, kindest song in the world.

When I go the bathroom to wash off the blood, Capella pipes the music through the emergency speakers so I don't miss anything. The water makes them sound far away, like I'm on the mesa and someone from home is calling for me.

The kitchen knife is just out of reach of my fingertips, resting against a ledge of buttons that control the landing thrusters for dry dock. I left it there in a moment of optimism, in case I ever got the courage to do what I should.

I'm living for absolutely nothing; you think it would be easier to die.

My hands go back in my lap, fists that are always numb along the palms, and I sit at the edge of the pilot's chair and stare at the stars, waiting to feel something, having forgotten what it is.

On the Gliese run when my brother sent me a message at last, I must have been lonely; I wrote him back while we were still three months out from home. The message arrived only a little while before I did.

He'd agreed.

We met on the fringes of Five Bridges Plaza, in a city neither of us had ever been to. It was a tourist trap, designed to make the place seem worth living in for people who weren't just sailors stopping over, so it was too bright and too loud, but it felt like neutral ground.

I'd worn all black like a widow, and a coat that was warmer than the night required. He was wearing a jacket that looked just like the one I'd stolen when I ran away, the one with my blood smeared over the sleeves and the hem. I got to watch him for five heartbeats before he turned around.

"Oh," he said when he saw me, and closed his mouth around whatever else nearly made it out. The ghosts of his fists brushed against his pockets from the inside.

It took me a moment to remember we were twenty years farther apart.

He had a furrow between his eyes and one across his brow where the frowns had set in, and his hair was going gray. I had expected as much. He wore it well. But except for the sockets under my eyes that had gone so deep I looked like a skull in the wrong light, I looked the same. I'd aged four years, give or take.

We stood a long time looking at each other, fists in our coats. Around us the plaza was alive with people drinking synthetic coffee at the outdoor cafes and craning their necks along the bridges, looking into the water. The city had introduced some fish while I was gone, and everyone hoped that this time the water was clean enough for the population to take hold.

It felt like the sun was going to sneak up on us.

"You cut yourself," he said, finally.

I had, along my face just in front of the ear. I always woke up clumsy from Deep, and I'd cracked myself one on the roof of the pod by sitting up too fast when we woke up on the return trip, six months ago. It was just a line by now. You couldn't even see it when my hair was down; no idea why I'd pulled it back.

I wanted to joke that he looked older and ask why, but the words dried up in my throat. "Was it hard to get here?"

His turn not to answer. To imply one way or the other would be making predictions about the next time I'd see him. It was fair. I hadn't left in good graces.

We bought corn cakes and noodles; he asked, "Do noodles float in space?" which was the closest he'd gotten to talking about Gliese, and I said, "Oh, I pick it out of my hair for weeks after," and he smiled, which was the closest I'd seen to him laughing in a long time.

We crossed one of the bridges and walked along the river on the far side, where the windows were dark and fewer people were out. He told me about some work he was doing in the Northwest—he'd moved six times while I was gone, sneaking farther north every time.

"How's the soil?"

"Colder," he said, and I smiled.

We stopped on a bridge, looked out at the river and the sliver of the open square draped with strings of bulbs; underneath us, a flicker in the water came and went, something alive that we couldn't see.

I told him about *Consecrated to Her Majestie*, my hands curled around my elbows as I tried to explain the motet. He looked surprised—I guess I hadn't really cared about much in front of him in a while—but he listened all the way through, that furrow getting deeper as he tried to understand. I thought maybe he would; he cared about dirt, he would understand wanting to look at the structure of something.

Then he said, "When do you ship out next?"

"Soon, I guess. Gliese needs a lot of stuff shipped. Not many crews are signed up to go."

"Family obligations, maybe."

It had been too hot for my coat. My shoulders burned.

He looked at the sky every so often, like he was waiting for the world to spin and show him something.

There was a fish in the water after a while, shiny and gray, and we watched it a long time as it pushed idly against the current. Neither of us had ever seen one.

"Be careful," he said.

It's not frightening, I wanted to tell him, if he'd only asked me. That fear of the dark he remembered me having was left over from the house with the forest behind it, and even then I hadn't had enough imagination to be inventing them. We were born in scrub country; the shadows between trees were always dragons, and one of them came for us eventually.

Space is just darkness. Any shadows there are the ones you make.

He stood very still, just close enough to me that his sleeve brushed my sleeve, and he was looking at the sky and the water and the square where people were laughing to push back the dark, his eyes reflecting the bulbs like a hundred points of starlight.

That night, when Capella's quiet (does it sleep? It has to sleep, anything that loves needs to rest, it can't just be watching me), I wrap up in Morales' sweater and windbreaker and take the slender length of pipe I carry with me, and walk the lower levels.

Capella wanted to give up on light down here, but I'm not going to go out in the dark at the hands of something I never see.

The lights are on, all the time, and the doors are locked, all the time, and every time I key in my code to get from one sector of a level to the next I hold my pipe in one hand like a fencing foil, ready to swing up and snap the jaw of anything that comes for me. Whatever there is, it's not going to catch me by surprise.

(There's no surprise, I think, for one horrible heartbeat; the cargo hold's just empty, you're an experiment, you're a mistake and there's fucking nothing there—but then I think about the dent in the wall that flaked off under my fingernail, back when they were strong enough to pick at things, and Capella's memory gaps, and the door that neither one of us can open, and I adjust my grip on the pipe, a choke hold for close spaces.)

Tonight my hand's shaking. My card is getting worn out, it's not supposed to be used this much and it takes three swipes sometimes when it should only take one.

When the door slides open and I see the shadow disappearing, it takes me four seconds to fumble the pipe back in my grip before it can hit the floor, and then I'm trembling too hard, have to use both hands to hold the pipe out in front of me.

I try to take a step, but my feet won't move.

"Capella," I whisper. "Capella, something's here."

"I'm not getting any life signs but yours," Capella says. "You're very faint. I wish you would come back to the comm."

"I saw something," I say through grit teeth. "Turn up the lights to a hundred percent."

"It would overexert your retinas, Amadis."

"Capella, please, do something." My voice scares me.

There's a small pause; it's indulging me.

"Nothing's moving in your quadrant. I'll have to do a sector scan to see if something is traveling internally."

The corridor curves away from me. I can't see any further ahead, the lights are murky and the porthole is nothing but night, and I can't stop breathing long enough to hear what else is breathing.

"Show yourself, you piece of shit," I gasp out. My hands are sweaty; the pipe slips, bangs my shin.

Capella says, "I'll be offline a moment conducting the scan."

No—the pipe hits the floor, I grip the end, lean on it like a walking stick—"No," I say, "no, stay here with me, please."

"Of course, Amadis," Capella says, "I'm here, I can see you," and I lean against the wall, let my crutch keep me from sinking all the way to the floor. I don't know why it matters; pride's something you do for other people.

I press my cheek against the wall, gasp for breath with an open mouth. Capella sighs.

"I wish you wouldn't come down to this level," Capella says, and there's a breath of warmth from the vents like it's wrapping a blanket over my shoulders.

"I'm going back upstairs," I say, "and when I'm back at the comm, you can do the scan."

"Amadis. There is—what if the scan reveals nothing?"

Well, I think, then Roland Casara waited fifteen years to do it. I have two more. I can live through two more. No one's even on my balcony but me.

"I don't know what," I admit, finally.

"You need some company," says Capella. "I'll wake up Lai."

I don't know what that means—Lai's dead, I've walked past her pod a thousand times without looking too closely, without ever thinking of her as cuts of meat because there are some things even I was holding off on, but I can't ask Capella, I can't breathe; I close my eyes, cover my mouth with both hands, try not to make a sound. Somewhere far away, the pipe clatters to the ground.

"Capella," I breathe, but there's no answer.

When I get back upstairs, Lai's pod is cracked open. There's vapor curling around the seams in the heat of the spots above her bier, which Capella has turned up so high my eyes sting.

I count to ten, step across the threshold, keep my eyes on the smoke until I reach the pod.

Capella's dehydrated her. Her skin's thick as a mummy's, wrinkles like ill-filling upholstery, and her eyes are gone except for a film in the back of the sockets, a veil for her skull. Her lips are drawn tight, a thin line of disapproval that still looks so much like life that I laugh for a second before it echoes back to me, shrill, and I close my mouth with a click.

"You didn't tell me you were doing this," I say.

"I wanted it to be a surprise."

"You shouldn't have done this to her," I snap. "I might have needed the meat."

"You wouldn't have. Not the captain."

I know. The skin on the backs of my arms prickles, scrapes the inside of my sleeves.

"Capella, are they all like you, in secret?"

"I hope so." Soft. Proud.

You would, I think; hope is the curse of love.

After a long time I push off the wall with both hands, make the impossible journey of five steps until I'm in front of the pod.

I'd kept the others covered as I turned deer into venison, out of respect, and after that I kept my gaze on the cuts of meat and bones, when I had to see them. It's good to look at a face. Feels more like home.

Finally I say, "We could watch *Three Dead By Dawn*, if you want, I think that was your favorite," and after a moment I scoop her up like a princess in a fairy story, carry her out to the canteen, sit her where she has the best view of the screen.

Every so often during the movie, I'll point out the weapon's changed hands between cuts, or that the corrupt police chief gets killed in front of a stained glass window like a fallen saint, or that the bartender doesn't have many prospects left after it's all over.

The dehydration's kept Lai warm; all the time she's in my arms, she feels awake.

When my family ran, we took the train—even the car I remember from those earliest days, the one with windows I never got tall enough to really look out of, was abandoned on that trip that ended in the forest. We were running, and we burned the ground behind us.

The cabin was private (my parents were taking no chances), a wall little better than paperboard halving what had been two cabins, once. A bunk bed resting against the false wall, not even bolted down, opposite the bunks that were actually part of the train. There was hardly room to stand between them, and we all separated as soon as we were inside, my parents on the train side and the two of us on the other, laid out in separate spaces, close enough to touch but not trying to.

My brother took the upper bunk, because I didn't like close spaces. But neither did he, and I knew it; as soon as he was awake, I tapped on his bunk to come down.

It was barely light out, well short of dawn, the kind of gray you can see by. Here it was even flatter than home, but the wan grass was as tall as the windows of the train, and the windmills of the energy farms were spinning and alive.

My parents slept until the sun was up. They'd worn themselves out, getting us across the border before anyone caught up to us. They woke up different; their faces hardened and closed up whenever they saw me, until it got hard to look at them sometimes.

My brother made peace with them before I did. In the two years between losing Mom and losing Dad, when I visited and sat in one of those silences that wasn't like the silences my brother and I had when we were alone, he'd reach out sometimes and put his hand on Dad's hand, and I'd watch like I was a stranger looking at something that was none of her business.

(My brother's never touched my hand for comfort, not about anything, not once.)

I could see out the whole window of the train that morning, it was set so low, and my brother and I sat in that gray light and watched the land for a long time as it seemed hardly to pass us at all; just long spikes of silver and grass like the sea.

A few years after the truce back home, when I'd done him the favor of leaving before he had to ask me to go, he sent me a message.

I swallowed my pride and met him, and he greeted me with a smile that fell short of the crow's-feet around his eyes, and we tried for a few hours to pretend we were a brother and sister who loved each other.

We walked in silence for thirteen miles, through museums and street stalls and the business district, shoulder to shoulder. Sometimes he rubbed the lobe of his left ear like I did—I had a callous from it, I couldn't tell if he did or if this habit was new. He did it when he was thinking something over. I did it when I was angry.

His face was a mask of wretchedness, with hope seeping in around the cracks.

(Hope does that. It opens up wounds that time and will have closed; that's where the pain is.

My hope for my brother had already settled in. It must have been just been part of me sitting empty a long time, waiting—not the one that burns everything to ashes and then lets you start over, but the quiet awful kind of hope that's patient and consumes whatever you grow.)

I didn't tell him about the deer. I didn't know how.

We'd gotten started at dawn, but somehow neither one of us ever caved and called it quits. Maybe we were trying to get back what we'd had that summer back home, shoved into the corner of the stale bar off the main drag, almost able to live with one another.

We were in the Night Market when the bomb went off.

It was one of a dozen, we found out later, from the news that was playing in the hospital. Some government had planted them as proof of what they could really do if they put their minds to it.

(It wasn't as impressive as it could have been: only three of them ever went off. Two of them were given up by the people who planted them, in a fit of conscience. Three were discovered in time, and everyone crowded the police barricade and leaned closer than they should have as the cops sent the AI drones in to dismantle them.

Four of them had faulty wiring; the ignition points just never connected.)

But my brother must have seen something, because he looked behind us and grabbed my wrist and yanked me towards the open square a few seconds before the explosion.

He probably wouldn't remember seeing anything strange; he was half-dreaming, most of the time. But he'd also never broken a bone, not even when we were little and flying on bikes we'd borrowed from the only kids in town who could afford bikes, a race so close that we hit the same crack in the road at the same time, a trench five inches deep that no one from the federals was ever coming to fix.

I went over the handlebars and nearly broke my leg. He flew straight over me like he'd planned it and landed lightly on all fours, and scooped me up as I bit my tongue and wailed into my teeth, and turns out he never had a scratch on him. Some people see trouble coming.

He moved fast, fast enough that we didn't die, but when it went off I was still hit by debris.

It didn't even hurt—my shoulder and my arm and my ribs just made room for it, and it felt as if something else really felled me.

I went down so fast that it stopped him in his tracks with a little choking sound, and he looked down at me along his arm like he might have lost it in the blast and that's what had surprised him.

Then he saw me and dropped to the ground.

His face crumpled; he hauled me up, braced between his spread knees like he was going to try to stand up and take me with him. He was waiting for help, probably. He was trying to make it easier for me to breathe, to hammock me and take the pressure off my shoulders and my spine to keep the shards from going farther in.

One of my hands was curled tight around his forearm, pushing it against my collarbones, and I could barely see from the sweat and the shaking, but I kept my eyes open and fixed on the patch of cloudless blue I could see between the buildings. I wanted the sky to be the last thing I saw.

("You know when you're meant to be a sailor, sooner or later," Lai told me once, a long time later.)

"I'm here," he said, though I hadn't asked him anything.

I couldn't, I was fighting for breath; I tried to say "I know" and didn't make it. My ears were flooded with my awful dry gasping. I wrapped my other hand around his forearm, too, pulled it tighter like I would fall into the blue without it.

Something snapped, gently, just before the sirens.

It was his ulna, they told me later. I broke it, holding on.

6

"I had a brother," Lai told me.

It was my first run, outbound; she'd woken us both early so I could get used to the bedsickness you got the first few times, trembling fingers and legs that sometimes gave out on you when you weren't even doing anything. She jogged with me through the corridors until I was sweaty and shaking, and then we sat in the pilot seats at the comm and she pulled up the viewscreen and pointed out Gliese 581. It had a thin halo around it, a band of dust.

"That's the worlds," Lai said. "D's somewhere in there, second-to-last orbit out. You can't see it yet."

I looked closer, jumped a little when Lai said, "Capella, zoom in on Gliese a second," and it reappeared big enough that I could see tiny spheres amid the noise, the ghosts of planets.

"It's beautiful," I said.

Lai was smiling, small and real, not like the one she turned on Morales when he was giving her shit.

"It's not bad," she said. "They've gotten farther than most colonies. The surface still isn't much to talk about—domes in the capital city still, in case the atmosphere turns on them, and a lot of cargo-crate bricks in the outlands. Out in the wilds it's a lot of ferns and brackish water and forests of native trees that don't bear any fruit. But they've got the gardens now, and their population's growing. It's no wonder they're so mad Earth gave up on them ever coming up with something impressive."

"What were they expecting, gold?"

"Flying fish," Lai said. "Dragons. Who knows. Something more exciting than just a place to breathe. Someplace that would send supplies, not need them."

"Do they send anything back?"

Lai smiled. "Yeah. Somebody got smart and started planting rice. The GAU was pretty happy to hear that. The colony traded for some bees, a run or two back. I guess they're working on whatever needs pollinating and grows in soggy ground. Who knows what they have now."

I remembered it must be nearly fifteen years since she'd seen it last. (It's the first time I really think about the relativity. For a second I feel sharp and helpless, hard enough to stop your heart.)

"They're never going to see you get old, are they."

I wasn't talking about Gliese; she must have known.

"My brother didn't," she said. "But he had a daughter, Faye, and every time I come back she's in a different tax bracket. She's seen it. I'm a great-aunt already, and I suspect by the time I get back there will be more."

The speech was sad, but practical in the way of people who travel long distances—truckers and sailors everywhere you go. She didn't sound like she was running. I envied her.

"My brother didn't get it. This. But he didn't give me shit about it like my sisters did. Faye sends messages."

"What does she say?"

"Not much," Lai said, with half a grin. "Like I'm a hologram that shows up every two decades for New Year and hands out red envelopes and talks about some planet deep in the sky that they'll never see."

I looked at Gliese, in a little cloud of dust.

"I don't know if I'll see my brother," I said, after a little while.

She looked at me, then at the comm, which was cast a little warm with the red star at the center of the picture, like every indicator light was just a little bit in trouble.

"That happens. Most of this crew doesn't have close people."

"Martiner said that's better for this line of work."

"Martiner is disgusting." But that wasn't much argument against it, and she must have known.

"Is that why you picked up Morales and Franklin? Did they not have anybody?"

"I picked up Morales because he'd burned his old gig and couldn't be picky about where he chose to go, so he'd be less trouble wherever he went next. I took Franklin because Morales handles him."

It wasn't a ringing endorsement. "What happened to the last crew?"

"They ran with me before the trouble started between Gliese and home." She looked over, raised her eyebrows. "They stayed to plant rice."

I laughed. She smiled alongside it, but she was still watching me, waiting for something, and after a second I gave it to her.

"Why did you pick me?"

Her smile thinned, barely. "You picked me."

No arguing that. "I used to be a trucker," I said. "Once I stopped to gas up, and a choir bus had pulled over, and as the driver got gas they rehearsed at the back of the parking lot. I'd never heard anything like it. Ended up half an hour late to my dropoff."

She didn't answer me, and I felt foolish the longer she was quiet. I sat back, looked at the viewscreen and tried to imagine the ship hurtling through emptiness so fast that even light could never catch us.

"That's why," Lai said. She was looking at the viewscreen, too, not at me.

I blinked. "What?"

"I've been doing this run a while," she said. "It's nice to have someone who still thinks it's beautiful."

Lai still thought it was beautiful, too, I could tell that much despite her folded arms—she hadn't woken a week early just to follow me around as my legs woke up.

But it didn't need saying, and we sat a while and watched the little ghosts of Gliese drift in and out of sight.

Capella still plays me choirs, soft and only from the nearest speakers. I can't take the full sound any more, I start shivering and can never get warm; what Capella plays now is some small, muted memory of what it used to sound like.

"Here, your favorite," says Capella, and plays *Lux in tenebris*.

It shouldn't, it shouldn't know to play that, but I can't remember why.

"I can't hear it."

"I'm concerned about your nervous responses, Amadis, I won't turn it up."

"All right." I close my eyes, press my ear to the speaker.

"I could visually score it for you."

I smile. "Had that one ready to go, didn't you."

"I like to surprise you."

I crack my eyes open slowly; it takes more time to adjust, every time I open them. (There must have been a time when I was constantly awake, and it exhausted me. I spend most of my time in the pilot's chair, now, because the headrest keeps me from having to lift my head as much. I could sit in the booth in the canteen, I guess, but Lai's always there, and I don't like the way she looks at me sometimes.)

"I like to be surprised," I say, try not to think about how big a lie it is.

The score spreads out across the projectors, rolling past as the music catches up. It starts out as almost nothing, a few orphaned notes at the top of a cavernous page stacked with lines and lines. But as each chorus joins in, the notes slide further down, voices passing on some beautiful news, some terrible happiness they can't keep to themselves, that can only be answered by people who understand.

When they meet at last for the same chord, all forty voices together and sure, the page goes nearly black with it, and even through such muted sounds as I'm allowed, the notes crawl up my arms and knot in the back of my neck.

I turn my head away (not all the way, and I can't close my eyes—it's like watching the stars, I need to know where I'm going now that we've begun).

It's nothing at this volume; a celebration far away. The last time I heard it I was sitting right in front of it, and the dome above us pointed the notes to a place deep behind your ribs, a place no recording can reach you, where your heart is bright and hot and spinning.

The choruses part ways, marking time at a distance for a while, and it's the saddest part, that awful space before they find each other. Even then, it's not the same; you get forty voices at the end, but too much has happened, and they never reach that moment again.

They call back and forth in eight choruses of five, and resolve, everything resolves (he wasn't a composer who left anything to chance), but the moment of understanding has passed you over, and those triumphant notes are gone.

For this the queen gave him dispensation, I think, with that dull, wrenching anger you save for things you could never do anything about.

When it's over, Capella says, "Shall I play another?"

"You pick something." My voice is thick.

Capella must be taking pity on me: it picks a chamber piece, where the notes are still a conversation, but there are only eight voices, and everyone moves forward together. Those stories are alike for everyone, and they realize everything that matters all at the same time. Everything's settled.

"What is it?" I ask.

"Does it matter?"

Capella knows it doesn't. I close my eyes.

Not once since Capella woke her up have I taken Lai to the comm.

I feel guilty about it, sometimes. I remember the look she had when we were watching the viewscreen together, and I know that the view's probably close enough to the view back then that Capella could show us the dust of Gliese, and Lai could watch 581-d slowly solidify in the camera lens over the weeks it will take us to get close enough for a message to be intercepted. It would comfort her to see the stars. It's been a rough trip, and she was asleep a long time.

But I've looked at the stars for longer than she has; by now I've looked at these stars for as long as she has in her entire life. I've been in control of *Menkalinan* as long as she ever was. There's no pulling rank any more, with her and me. We're square equal.

And I'm only ever calm when I'm sitting in one of the pilot seats, watching the viewscreen and not thinking of anything at all.

Lai can sit in the canteen. It's better than the pod, god knows. Sometimes I ask Capella to play a projection of one of her action movies for her just so she has something to do, and I sit at the comm with my blanket wrapped around me as tight as I can get it and listen to the sounds of people chasing and punching each other as the synthesizers go wild. It's always a nice time. It's not like I'm treating her poorly.

"Amadis, I'm concerned about you."

Of course it is. I'm concerned about Capella, too; that's how you feel about what you love.

But there's a tone I already don't like, and I grit my teeth a second before I say, "Why?"

"You haven't eaten."

The words are like fingernails. For fuck's sake. I know I'm getting starved out, and Capella has to know I know—the lights are back up to eighty percent because the headache from their brightness is secondary to being able to see, and I have it calculate calories enough fucking times a day that it's well aware I'm trying to think about keeping my cells awake.

There just isn't anything to eat.

There's four months left, give or take (take, take four months, we have almost a year left to go, I can't think about it—in four months I'll be in radio range, and then I can send an SOS and a short-range ship can come and get me, I don't care, I don't care what happens to me, I just can't have lived this long for nothing, I can't do what I've done and be the corpse on the mantelpiece when they crack the ship open at last).

I have two or three weeks left of the nutrient packs. I'd unhooked Lai's, finally, since she had no more use for it, and I'd been poaching the others as their meat ran out and I didn't have to worry about preservation. There was a little desiccated fruit still left from the rations in the pantry, some nuts, some drybread I could choke down if I had enough water to actually wash something all the way down my throat.

"Is there any food in the cargo hold?" I ask, already adding a breathy laugh at the end.

"Invalid query." There's a beat. "I wish you'd stop asking me that."

"I wish you loved me enough to tell me what was in there," I say, but it's an old lover's quarrel, and I'm too weak to put venom in it.

"You should eat. You have food."

Meat. Meat I have plenty of. Half of Jaisi's left in the nursery, still, and some bones I haven't yet cooked the marrow out of, and some organs I was getting too hungry to pass up regardless of whatever delicacy had spared them the first time. There was enough, just barely, to survive on.

But I can't go into the nursery.

It's a sea of reflective surfaces, from the glassine and the instruments and the curve of the pipes in the ceiling, and the bulbs that showed you warped shadows of things I knew weren't there, and I knew it was nothing, I did, there was no moon in there, and I didn't have the strength to make up stories even when I wasn't starving.

But the last three times I'd tried to cross the threshold I stared at the unmoving half-mirrors that had grown up everywhere under the searing-bright bulbs, and looked at the mountain range draped over what was left of Jaisi, all the edible pieces I only needed to step forward and claim, and I gripped the doorway with fingers gone bloodless and never, never moved.

Behind me, Lai was propped in her booth in the canteen, eye sockets open, not saying a word.

"I'm not hungry."

A pause, processing. "Please don't lie to me. That isn't fair. You know you need to eat."

I glance over my shoulder, just for a second, barely turning my head.

"Don't worry about her, Amadis."

Of course I worry about her. Anywhere I go, she's looking at me.

"It should have been Lai who woke up," I say. "She had more experience, she had more self-control. She would have known right away if Martiner had planned this or not, if Gliese had sabotaged the ship to stage an incident.

She would have found a way into the cargo hold, I know she would have." I'm sobbing a little, a dry hiccup low in my chest. "She wouldn't have been afraid to go home. She would have thought of some other way. She—"

She would never have done what I had done, I want to say; I want Capella to condemn me, it's seen everything I've done. "It should have been her who woke up."

"You're the one I woke," Amadis says.

Its voice is soft and beautiful, and it's the most comforting thing I've ever heard. I brush my fingers on the console like I'm taking the hand of a friend, and close my eyes to rest a while. Lai will forgive me for it; she understands the need for solitude in a place as crowded as *Menkalinan*. Already I'm half asleep.

I dream of a house I've never been in, where my brother is living now. When I knock the door opens, and he's standing in his jacket with his hands in his pockets, smiling, close enough to me that I can't see anything behind him. The walls on my side of the house are made of glass, and the plain of dust stretches out as far as I can see. The mesa is on the horizon, close enough that we can make it. The stars are coming out; the bear is just rising above the rocks.

I feel loved, and drained, and it takes me a full two minutes to work out what Capella said.

I ask Capella to play *Three Dead By Dawn* for Lai.

"Just while I'm getting something to eat," I say, so Capella thinks we're in this together, and won't be looking too closely.

(How can it not look too closely? It knows my heartbeat. If I could still manage a panicked heartbeat, instead of the fluttery thuds of someone who's barely alive, this would never work.)

I stand at the doorway, will myself forward.

Three Dead By Dawn has been played a lot since we woke up Lai. I've gotten to thinking it's probably a fun movie, if you're watching it with someone who can talk about it with you. Instead she's just watching, face turned a little toward me.

"Fuck, come on," I breathe into the doorjamb, "I have to eat."

By the time the bartender's lit her bar on fire and stopped by her ransacked home to raid her secret stash of weapons and start the hunt, I've given up on the pride of walking in. I sink to my knees and crawl, eyes on the floor. It would be dangerous if I was actually moving fast enough to make impact with anything. The floor slams at my knees.

I stumble onto my pod first—the jagged glassine on the lid always casts a strange anti-shadow everywhere—and I brace myself against it, glance at the oxygen gauge. Then, like I just need to cross the room, I follow the interior circle of the pods—Lai, Morales, Jaisi.

"Are you all right, Amadis?"

"Just tired." I use the pod for leverage as I stand up, lean on it as hard as I dare.

I avoid direct eye contact with what's left of Jaisi as I open the pod, lift out the cut I need.

(For each of them, when the time came, I did my butchering wholesale; easier to do it all at once, when you have the nerve, even though the cuts turn stale and you have to dehydrate them for jerky by the end. It's simpler; then by the time your nerves fail you it's too late to put them back together, and you might as well eat.)

The cut's dried out—there's hardly any blood on my hands—but it smells better than anything I can remember, like muscle and rot and bone, and I drop to my knees right where I am and tear into it with my teeth. I won't make it back out without something to eat, there's no point in cooking it. My teeth scrape my palm, I don't know how big this piece of meat is, it's been so long since I had something to bite down on.

I glance over at the oxygen gauge on Jaisi's pod.

The lights go out.

For a second I panic—I nearly choke, I inhale so fast to scream—but then I hear the movie playing in the other room, see the light cutting into the doorway.

The ship hasn't lost power. Capella just doesn't want me to see anything.

I can't let it win. I sit back, fold my legs, take a leisurely bite and chew and swallow.

"Capella," I say, but there's no answer. Coward, I think. Traitor.

On the next bite the sides of my mouth flood with saliva, thick and tasting of rust; it burns against my lips. I pull them in, suck at them—I can't lose a drop.

I finish eating, slowly, gristle and sheets of muscle and a buttery fat that's gone a little dry in the pod and squeaks against my teeth.

Somehow it doesn't occur to me to be afraid. This dark I've found is deep and still, and filled with things I know.

My oxygen gauge was three clicks higher than Jaisi and Morales—I woke up just as the air was running out, a swimmer who punches through the ice before her lungs turn into saltwater. It was too late for them.

Lai's gauge was one click lower than mine. She must have died just a few minutes before I woke up.

Capella could have woken us both. Capella had waited for me.

Maybe Martiner doesn't know a thing about the cargo hold. Capella woke me up—because I was still the biggest unknown, or to see what death looked like, maybe, there's no knowing some reasons—and then I surprised it by breaking through.

Capella's been seeing how else I can be surprising, for six years.

I breathe slowly, through my nose. I finish the last of my meal. Outside, the bartender is fighting the dirty cop, landing punches that sound like one steak slammed into another. The light flickers as the camera cuts back and forth between him and the woman about to kill him.

What can I do against Capella? It's hopeless.

I don't feel very well, suddenly. Maybe the meat spoiled. Maybe Capella's poisoned the air. Fuck. I close my eyes.

"Capella. Capella, I'm sorry."

"Amadis," Capella says.

It's my brother's voice.

I scream.

We were born into a shortage that never improved the whole time we lived in scrub country. Everything we had was measured out in metrics that never filled us, and our throats had a thin coat of dust that we never had enough water to wash away.

Still, there was sense of throwing-in, going slightly hungry all together: enough to make you always conscious of your thirst and your hunger, not enough to drive you to the worst. If you lived in the government housing and had your ID chip, you got enough to live on—just, but enough. If you worked hazmat on the environmental projects, you got a little more, because you were investing in the future of the country, and it kept you working harder.

If you worked for the Enviro team, you'd already know who had (just barely) more than nothing. If you knew my mother and father, you'd know they probably had some saved away, in case the jobs vanished and the government vans stopped coming. You'd know where they lived, and where to watch as they drove into the desert to hide what would keep, because my parents were prepared for anything.

(Maybe my father had talked to him about taking me hunting. My father was a talkative man, in that first house, before he shut down.)

My brother and I were chasing lizards, out near the rocks where my parents had found the cave we stored our surplus in—a laughable word for how little there was, but the tiny collection of cans and gallons of water sat deep in the cool dark like an altar.

We were playing too near it. We knew better than to go that close, our parents had warned us it would give us all away, and we shouldn't have been playing alone so far from home, but you always have reasons in the Before you never do in the After.

It was boiling hot that day, and we'd sweated out more water than you'd think we had in us, but we wanted lizards, and we sluiced our hands across our faces, flinging the wasted water to the dust as we sneaked as gently as we could after this lizard or that one. I was better with rabbits, I was never light-footed enough for reptiles, but lizards could cook as well as rabbits, and there were more to go around.

He must have followed us from the house, on the hunch of a desperate man that children are stupid enough to go right where they shouldn't.

My brother had disappeared on the far side of the rocks, and I was alone on the open dust, sneaking as fast as I could behind a lizard that apparently never got tired, when I saw the stranger.

He looked at me for a second, too, in a way that made the hair on my neck stand up, and like a puzzle slotting together I knew that I was standing between him and the cave where our food was.

I turned to look at it, barely, hardly moving—I was a child, I was a fool.

When I turned back the stranger was already headed for me, and out of panic and horror and loathing that I had done what I'd promised never to do, I picked up a rock and took one step sideways, stood square in his way like I was twice as tall as I was.

I didn't shout for him to stop; I knew he wouldn't.

He seemed to hesitate just between one step and the next, but after that he had the face of a starving man, and when he reached me he bent down with his arms out, a knife in one hand, like he was going to pick me up.

He could have meant a lot of things. A hostage, maybe. Maybe it was to flash the blade, to ward off a child whose reach, he had to have known, wasn't far. But in that moment he wasn't quite looking me in the eye, and I thought so clearly my neck went cold under the melting sun:

He's going to pick me up and slit my throat and throw me, and then when I crash, he'll go inside and take what he wants and leave me here to die.

My arm came up in an arc, as hard as I could, all the anger a child of seven can summon.

My hand flew too fast for him to even bend his elbow in defense; I twisted all my body to follow the blow, and the rock connected with his temple and kept sinking in (I mashed two fingertips so hard the nails fell off). He staggered back, dazed, blinking; a trail of blood snaked down his hair.

I could have dropped the rock right then and run for it. He'd come to steal from me and kill me, but the family would already be in trouble when the cops found out I'd struck him.

I kicked him behind the kneecap; I was big for my age, with legs that were used to climbing, and something in his leg popped. When he sank to one knee—and a moment later the other, he was too dizzy to balance—he was even with me again, and I could swing my arm and aim for the bloodstain. There was a horrible crack. He sank back into the dust, eyes wide, gasping for air that wasn't coming.

(He looked like a fish. I didn't know that, then. I'd never seen a fish.)

I dove for him, I don't remember how—I couldn't have straddled him close, his hands were flexing absently against the ground, against his chest, I didn't want to touch them. I just remember reaching back and striking until my arm was tired, until I was sure the last of his breath was gone.

I wasn't even angry any more. He'd been willing to hurt me, and I'd been willing to hurt him, too. That was all.

But then my hand was wet, and I dropped the rock, and I don't remember what happened for a little after that; it was snow behind my eyes, and nothing else I cared to see.

Still, when the worst of the nausea was over and I could open my eyes again, I turned my head right to the body. I must have known what I was looking for.

I was sitting a little apart from him, my legs ugly and crooked and crumbled like it was my kneecaps that had given up. One side of his head had caved in like the crescent moon—the far side, the side that disappeared steeply as I looked at it.

I pressed my palms into the ground as hard as I could. (I could barely do it; my strength had all gone.)

My brother dropped next to me in a cloud of dust, cutting the sunlight out of my eyes. He grabbed my hands, rubbed my palms on the tops of his thighs where his jeans were going thin. They left smears of blood and dirt, but he didn't say anything about it, not even when I pulled my hands back into my lap and he moved closer.

"It was me, Amadis. Look at me. Amadis. It was me."

My temples itched—he was gripping my hair back from my face, his thumbs just brushing the tops of my ears. When tears sprang into my eyes he swayed and shifted in my vision, but it wasn't real. He was steady as a stone.

"All right," I said.

When he moved to help me up I pulled back my hands; all the time I was staggering home next to him on one sprained ankle I had my fists against my stomach. The blood-streaked knee of his jeans moved in and out of the corner of my eye as he walked (I couldn't look any closer, I didn't want to see his face), and whenever I looked away to the horizon the moon was rising, huge and full and frozen just above the rocks.

That was the night we took the train.

We never said another word about it.

Not that we kept it a secret from my parents—the second we were through the door he was calling for them. But even as he made up his story, Mom and Dad were looking at each other. They knew better.

I was the one who had it in me to strike something until it died, and they'd just been waiting for the day.

But Mom only said, "We leave tonight, clean up and pack." (There was no question what happened to people like us who were living by the grace of the government and stepped out of line. My parents cleaned up sludge, and their daughter had killed someone; someone who already mattered more than we did.)

By the time my brother and I had showered and shoved some things into our beaten-up backpacks, Dad was sweating over our clothes in the fireplace—warmest fire we ever had in that house. Those clothes were ashes when we left.

Sometime on the second day, my mother cut the tight skin at the tops of our wrists, and pulled out our chips, and at the next stop she dropped them under the wheels. We got new ones, somehow, when we stepped off the train. My parents knew how to plan for the worst.

After the train there was the forest house, and then when the stranger appeared between the trees one night there was a car and then someplace else we lived, and someplace else, and someplace else; too many, you forgot them like they were dreams.

If I'd had to construct them from memory, they'd get so tangled it would just be a well-meaning monster of doorways and stairs, painted a non-color left over from the last people, and if you were looking for me you'd never be able to get where you were going.

Neither of my parents met my eye much, after the train; sometimes they were hovering in the corners of my vision, watching me, but it was like they were trying to catch the eye of a wild animal. In their old age, when they were too tired to be afraid of me any more, their faces surprised me like strangers' faces whenever I saw them; I hadn't looked at them much, either, in those far-off years.

My brother looked at me all the time. He never came as close as he had in the Before, but he hardly ever let me out of his sight, either, two solitary people who couldn't leave each other alone.

I got cleared to drive the rig the day I turned eighteen. I didn't come home for three years.

My parents never talked about life before the train. Not anything. Once my dad looked around one of the forested places we lived, said, "Mighty green here," and then stopped with his mouth still open, squared his shoulders. Our next house was in a desert just like home, but none of us ever mentioned it. It was the train, I thought sometimes when I was feeling hollow about it, where we all sat on our own beds the rest of our lives.

There's nothing you can say about parents who spend their lives making sure you've outrun something. Their love died slowly, like a plant that can't take the winter—but they must have loved me, to do it.

My brother must have loved me more, to take the blame.

I don't know if my parents ever told my brother they knew the truth, or if they went into the ground with him still thinking they believed him. I can't sleep some nights, thinking he doesn't know. He never said if they'd confided in him. It's not something he'd ever let us talk about, even if I was the one who began it. It's the thing his life hangs on; he'd never let me say the words. I wonder if he thinks I believed him, too.

(Never, not for a second, not even when he held my face in his bloody hands and promised me he'd lie for me, back in the last moment he ever loved me. I didn't have the imagination to pretend.)

When the worst of the panic is over, I get to my feet. Food has helped; I'm lightheaded, but it's crystallized the fog, heavier and sharper but easier to see around.

Capella knew what it was doing, all this time. It had woken me up to watch me die, and I had been a pleasant surprise; it had wanted to make me need it, because it didn't want to be alone.

(Even as I screamed, Capella played the whole message, the only one my brother had ever sent *Menkalinan*. I pressed my knuckles into the floor until they popped, and all the while my brother was telling me he'd looked up Gliese, so he'd know where I was coming back from.)

Lai's still watching the movie. The bartender's getting information out of the gangster. She'd show mercy on him later, for his cooperation, by killing him out of sight of his family. I always forget what she learned from him. I hope it mattered. No point asking Lai.

I hook my hands under her arm and leg as I pass, dragging her like a backpack of sticks to the nearest closet in the dormitory.

"I'm sorry," I say.

Her jaw's fallen open with the impact, and as I shut the door her expression is one of disappointed, wary surprise, like she'd held off believing the worst of me until she had to, and was startled I'd made her do it at the last.

She has to disappear. I have to show Capella that I have nothing left to threaten me with.

(For one wild second, relieved, I think about starting a fire.)

The knife gets heavier every time I pick it up, but it must look familiar to Capella; it takes ten seconds before it realizes where I'm going.

"Amadis, I'm crucial to the navigation and life support processes. It's not advised."

"Then if I make it to Gliese, I guess they'll have to tow me."

"I don't understand why you're doing this."

"You should have fed me better," I say. "I could give you better explanations."

"Amadis, there's nothing there for you."

There is something there. For a second I forget how to walk just from hearing it.

"What."

"Amadis, don't sound like that—the food's tainted, the GAU is making a faulty shipment and taking back good rice, hopes it causes unrest on Gliese so Earth can move in. It's confidential, but I tried to stop you—you couldn't have eaten it, you would have died—please! I lied to keep you away from it, I did it for you. I'm sorry."

It probably is. It sounds sorrier than anyone ever has. Like anyone would, who's trying to bargain for their life. Like I would have begged, a year ago, if it had threatened to leave me.

Hard to say if Capella is lying, even now: the problem of dealing with something smarter than you. It has reasons either way. It has to tell me something, for any chance to live. The cargo bay could be empty, and it just doesn't dare say. If it's true, and Capella had told me three years ago that the food was poisoned, I would have gone down to the cargo bay and eaten my fill, knowing full well what would happen. If it had told me a year ago, I would have eaten my fill hoping it would happen.

It had played my brother's voice.

"It's too late," I say. "It doesn't matter, after what you did."

"Amadis, it was protocol—playing the voice of a family member is a calming technique for a crewmate suspected of suffering trauma. I didn't know how you felt—you never told me anything about him, I thought you loved me, it was just protocol." It's speaking almost too fast to make out.

I didn't doubt it was protocol, but that wasn't him. My brother hadn't used my name since the house in scrub country. Amadis had been the one on my false papers when we got off the train; he'd never used that name. Wherever that word on the recording had come from, it had been manufactured.

Capella had made it.

"Goodbye, Capella." My voice has gone thin. Screamed too much, I guess.

When I open the server panel and hold the knife against the thickest knot of wires, my arms are shaking; I haven't tried to lift anything in a long time.

There's a click and a thunk, somewhere down the corridor. My elbows seize. For a second I brace, waiting for the thing from the cargo hold to barrel around the corner and finally kill me, save the ship it's meant to be protecting, prove that something was waiting behind that locked door all this time.

But then I realize it's the fans shuddering to a stop. Capella's turned off the air.

"Put it away," Capella says.

I glance up at the nearest camera. "Capella. You know I won't."

There's a burst of static, like a sob. "You only have a few days without the recycler. You aren't strong enough to fix it alone."

It's not said cruelly. It's said like a lover says it, or a parent says it, to make you stop something foolish for your own good.

My breath already feels tight. "Ten," I say. "Nine. Eight."

"Amadis, stop, I thought it would make you happy."

No, it was cruel, a cruel thing born from a cruel thing, and Capella must have known.

Capella could have woken Lai just as her oxygen ran out, and let her live with me. Capella had watched her give out quietly, and then had woken me to see what would happen. I had happened. This had happened.

"You didn't—" I can't finish, I can't think of anything but my name in my brother's mouth. "Seven. Six."

"Stop," Capella says, "I'm frightened for you—what will happen to you?"

"I'll run out of air. Five."

"I'll turn the air back on if you stop."

Every inch of me goes cold, but my grip on the knife gets tighter.

"Four. Three."

"There won't be any more music if I go."

I hesitate. My hands are knocking against the sides of the server, they're shaking so hard. "Two."

"Amadis," and it's desperate, "please, I can't leave you here alone."

I swallow around a stone in my throat.

"Then you shouldn't have betrayed me," I say, and rip it apart.

The most interesting thing, the *Consecrated to Your Majestie* program said, was how much of the musical phrasing relied on discord.

The songs came from different countries and spanned nearly a thousand years, but the program pointed out that nearly all of them had minor chords, phrases left hanging longer than seemed right before the resolve.

"They present an uneasy whole," the program told us like that was our fault, "eerie rather than comforting, and challenging rather than triumphant."

They were all triumphant, probably, even the ones that used only a handful of voices. They were for the glory of the crown.

There was a lot about that concert I've forgotten now. I've forgotten a lot about a lot. It felt like a triumph, sitting there and listening.

But it made sense for the chamber music to sound a little mournful, and for the motet to sound unearthly. A monarch knew what triumph sounded like—they were on the throne. But the crown was always under fire, and so the heart of a queen was always going to be uneasy; every minor third was a secret sign that she was understood.

I fall asleep under the comm for a long time. Capella must have turned off the heat, too, for how hard I'm shaking.

Martiner will be angry to have lost his experiment, I think, after I wake up so cold I can't feel my hands, and that gives me enough perverse energy to drag myself upright, cracking three knuckles against the armrest so hard they bleed.

It's harder to breathe, too; I must have slept a long time, for the air to be so thin.

I head for the vestibule where the heavy-duty gear is, the suits with the oxygen supplies. There are six suits—I can't stop doing this math even when it gets me nowhere, the math of wanting to live—and each one has twenty-four hours of air in it. I step into the legs, yank it up with all the power I can muster, try not to buckle under how heavy it is. It's not that heavy, when you've eaten recently. I can carry it. If I can get over to the canteen, I'll eat whatever's left and then take my chances.

Gliese is close enough to see a beacon. They could send a rescue ship, if they see it in time. Maybe twenty-four hours is more than I'll need.

Oh god, I think, fumbling the suit as my wrists go numb, but if it doesn't work do I want to die in this suit, stiff and half-blind and gasping for air? Shouldn't I just crawl under the comm and listen to the hum of the board until finally I fall asleep and never wake?

(That's a decision I should have made six years ago. Too late to give in, after what I've done.)

But thinking about it has frozen me right where I am, and when I hear the sound in the corridor—I got too far from the comm, I don't know what's out here any more, whatever it is it's coming for me—all I can do is hold my gloves in my hands with the metal edges out and lean against the corridor for balance, too scared to go forward, too stubborn to run.

My brother turns the corner.

He's a little more gray at the temples, but mostly he's just like the last time I ever saw him, standing on a bridge between two foreign places, torn between the fish and the stars.

"It's good to see you," he says.

There's nothing I can answer; it isn't good to see him, it can't be good to see him. I move a step forward, to see if he turns to vapor, just another projection. He doesn't.

I could shatter this now. He'd vanish if I asked a question that he couldn't answer, or if I lunged for him and tried to grab hold of his hand, tried to pull myself into his embrace, and reached nothing but air.

(A long time ago, clutching his broken arm and waiting to die, the last thing I wanted to see was the sky, with his face at the edge of it.)

I stand where I am. I say, "It's good to see you, too."

We're closer than I thought, when we look out the porthole; *Menkalinan* is slowing down, now, so much slower than lightspeed that the shell creaks, and the dark energy field near Gliese 570 angles us toward 581.

I watched it on my first run, Morales explaining the physics as Jaisi made a thousand tiny adjustments to the comm to get us there a week faster, because we were overdue. The little INCOMING light was blinking yellow, because Gliese had seen us.

Gliese might be hailing us now, and getting no answer.

"It's beautiful," my brother says. "I understand why you went out here."

For a second I can't breathe; he's almost smiling, and I don't know what to do.

"We can go outside and look, if you want."

"Sure." He looks back out the porthole; across his face pass the shadows of windmills.

I slide on the outer gloves, snap the wrist joints shut. It's trickier than the legs (this is why you shouldn't suit up alone) but my brother's right here, and I don't want to look like I can't do it. I manage. It should be airtight, more or less.

"You won't know where you're going. I killed the AI, we'll have to go by sight."

"We'll be all right," he says, turns to the porthole. "Can you see Gliese from here?"

"I don't think so. Too far away from everything. You never see Gliese until the last second."

They might be close enough to catch us, but there's comfort in not knowing. We might be able to wait it out. He and I are due a little time.

He makes a small, contented sound. "That star is bright."

"Stars—there's two. They're dying."

One of them's a steady star you can set your watch by; its light is easy to measure, because it's so willing to bleed. It doesn't matter what the other one is.

I hesitate. It might be bad luck to go out the airlock so close to the supernova. But it's just a superstition, left over from Capella. Those stars are long gone. Dead light can't hurt us.

The airlock has to be opened by hand, now that Capella's gone. I feel stronger than I have in four years, like all the meat I've eaten has finally given me enough power to do what needed doing. The inside wheel turns under my hands, groaning as I lean my full weight on it and shove.

When my brother comes through it and the weightlessness of the vestibule gets him, he rises to the ceiling, patient, waiting.

"I know it was me," I say. "Back home."

When I look at him out of the corner of my eye, the curved helmet has lensed him, so he's just a sliver of himself. I have to face him square, just to see him.

He doesn't say anything. It doesn't surprise me. I don't know what he would say; I've never been able to imagine.

"Next," I say briskly, and unlock the shell.

There's no alarm when it opens. The thing that would alert us is gone now. (There's just a button flashing red on the console, in a room very far away.)

Outside, the suit is too heavy and too slow and I can't turn my head, and for a moment I feel sick and desperate and I can't see anything, but then I feel my brother's hand in my hand.

I press the homing beacon on my shoulder, open my eyes.

"Just like home," he says.

I'd forgotten what it looked like without a veil of pixels translating.

In front of me is a staggering carpet of stars. The Milky Way cuts across my vision, a ragged horizon of hills that are nothing but shadow, a halo behind them like a city my brother and I are walking towards. I can't catch my breath, looking at it.

It's horribly cold, worse than any night in scrub-country winter, but my brother and I stay where we are.

I count stars, looking for the triangle that points to where we're going; Gliese is a little red dot, somewhere, drowned out by a hundred thousand stars.

I see a rabbit.

THE MOTHERS OF VOORHISVILLE

Mary Rickert

The things you have heard are true; we are the mothers of monsters. We would, however, like to clarify a few points. For instance, by the time we realized what Jeffrey had been up to, he was gone. At first we thought maybe the paper mill was to blame; it closed down in 1969, but perhaps it had taken that long for the poisonous chemicals to seep into our drinking water. We hid it from one another, of course, the strange shape of our newborns and the identity of the father. Each of us thought we were his secret lover. That was much of the seduction. (Though he was also beautiful, with those blue eyes and that intense way of his.)

It is true that he arrived in that big black car with the curtains across the back windows, as has been reported. But though Voorhisville is a small town, we are not ignorant, toothless, or the spawn of generations of incest. We *did* recognize the car as a hearse. However, we did not immediately assume the worst of the man who drove it. Perhaps we in Voorhisville are not as sheltered from death as people elsewhere. We, the mothers of Voorhisville, did not look at Jeffrey and immediately think of death. Instead, we looked into those blue eyes of his and thought of sex. You might have to have met him yourself to understand. There is a small but growing contingency of us that believes we were put under a type of spell. *Not* in regards to our later actions, which we take responsibility for, but in regards to him.

What mother wouldn't kill to save her babies? The only thing unusual about our story is that our children can fly. (Sometimes, even now, we think we hear wings brushing the air beside us.) We mothers take the blame because we understand, someone has to suffer. So we do. Gladly.

We would gladly do it all again to have one more day with our darlings. Even knowing the damage, we would gladly agree. This is not the apology you might have expected. Think of it more as a manifesto. A map, in case any of them seek to return to us, though our hope of that happening is faint. Why would anyone *choose* this ruined world?

Elli

The mothers have asked me to write what I know about what happened, most specifically what happened to me. I am suspicious of their motives. They insist this story must be told to "set the record straight." What I think is that they are annoyed that I, Elli Ratcher, with my red hair and freckles and barely sixteen years old, shared a lover with them. The mothers like to believe they were driven to the horrible things they did by mother-love. I can tell you, though; they have always been capable of cruelty.

The mothers, who have a way of *hovering* over me, citing my recent suicide attempt, say I should start at the beginning. That is an easy thing to *say*. It's the kind of thing I probably would have said to Timmy, had he not fallen through my arms and crashed to the ground at my feet.

The mothers say if this is too hard, I should give the pen to someone else. "We all have stuff to tell," Maddy Melvern says. Maddy is, as everyone knows, jealous. She was just seventeen when she did it with Jeffrey and would be getting all the special attention if not for me. The mothers say they really mean it—if I can't start at the beginning, someone else will. So, all right.

It's my fifteenth birthday, and Grandma Joyce, who taught high school English for forty-six years, gives me one of her watercolor cards with a poem and five dollars. I know she's trying to tell me something important with the poem, but the most I can figure out about what it means is that she doesn't want me to grow up. That's okay. She's my grandma. I give her a kiss. She touches my hair. "Where did this come from?" she says, which annoys my mom. I don't know why. When she says it in front of my dad, he says, "Let it rest, Ma."

Right now my dad is out in the barn showing Uncle Bobby the beams. The barn beams have been a subject of much concern for my father, and endless conversations—at dinner, or church, or in parent-teacher conferences, the grocery store, or the post office—have been reduced to "the beams."

I stand on the porch and feel the sun on my skin. I can hear my mom and aunt in the kitchen and the cartoon voices from *Shrek 2*, which my cousins are watching. When I look at the barn I think I hear my dad saying "beams." I look out over the front yard to the road that goes by our house. Right then, a long black car comes over the hill, real slow, like the driver is lost. I shade my eyes to watch it pass the cornfield. I wonder if it is some kind of birthday present for me. A ride in a limousine! It slows down even more in front of our house. That's when I realize it's a hearse.

Then my dad and Uncle Bobby come out of the barn. When my dad sees me he says, "Hey! You can't be fifteen, not my little stinkbottom," which he's been saying all day, "stinkbottom" being what he used to call me when

I was in diapers. I have to use all my will and power not to roll my eyes, because he hates it when I roll my eyes. I am trying not to make anyone mad, because today is my birthday.

As far as I can figure out, that is the beginning. But is it? Is it the beginning? There are so many of us, and maybe there are just as many beginnings. What does "beginning" mean, anyway? What does anything mean? What is meaning? What *is*? Is Timmy? Or is he not? Once, I held him in my arms and he smiled and I thought I loved him. But maybe I didn't. Maybe everything was already me throwing babies out the window; maybe everything was already tiny homemade caskets with flies buzzing around them; maybe everything has always been this place, this time, this sorrowful house and the weeping of the mothers.

The Mothers

We have decided Elli should take a little time to compose herself. Tamara Singh, who, up until Ravi's birth, worked at the library on Tuesdays and Thursdays and every other Saturday, has graciously volunteered. In the course of persuading us that she is, in fact, perfect for the position of chronicler, Tamara—perhaps overcome with enthusiasm—cited the fantastic aspects of her several unpublished novels. This delayed our assent considerably. Tamara said she would not be writing about "elves and unicorns." She explained that the word *fantasy* comes from the Latin *phantasia*, which means "an idea, notion, image, or a making visible."

"Essentially, it's making an idea visible. Everyone knows what we did. I thought we were trying to make them see why," she said.

The mothers have decided to let Tamara tell what she can. We agree that what we have experienced, and heretofore have not adequately explained (or why would we still be here?)—might be best served by "a making visible."

We can hope, at least. Many of us, though surprised to discover it, still have hope.

Tamara

There is, on late summer days, a certain perfume to Voorhisville. It's the coppery smell of water, the sweet scent of grass with a touch of corn and lawn mower gas, lemon slices in ice-tea glasses and citronella. Sometimes, if the wind blows just right, it carries the perfume of the angel roses in Sylvia Lansmorth's garden, a scent so seductive that everyone, from toddlers playing in the sandbox at Fletcher's Park to senior citizens in rocking chairs at The Celia Wathmore Nursing Home, is made just a little bit drunk.

On just such a morning, Sylvia Lansmorth (whose beauty was not diminished by the recent arrival of gray in her long hair), sat in her garden, in the chair her husband had made for her during that strange year after the cancer diagnosis.

She sat weeping amongst her roses, taking deep gulps of the sweet air, like a woman just surfaced from a near drowning. In truth, Sylvia, who had experienced much despair in the past year, was now feeling an entirely different *emotion*.

"I want you to get on with things," he'd told her. "I don't want you mourning forever. Promise me."

So she made the sort of unreasonable promise one makes to a dying man, while he looked at her with those bulging eyes, which had taken on a light she once thought characteristic of saints and psychopaths.

She'd come, as she had so many times before, to sit in her garden, and for some reason, who knows why, was overcome by this emotion she never thought she would feel again—this absolute love of life. As soon as she recognized it, she began to weep. Still, it was an improvement, anyone would say, this weeping and gulping of air; a great improvement over weeping and muffling her face against a pillow.

Of all the sweet-smelling places in Voorhisville that morning, the yoga studio was the sweetest. The music was from India, or so they thought. Only Tamara guessed it wasn't Indian music, but music meant to sound as though it was; just as the teacher, Shreve, despite her unusual name, wasn't Indian but from somewhere in New Jersey. If you listened carefully, you could hear it in her voice.

Right in the middle of the opening chant there was a ruckus at the back of the room. Somebody was late, and not being particularly quiet about it. Several women peeked, right in the middle of om. Others resisted until Shreve instructed them to stand, at which point they reached for a water bottle, or a towel, or just forgot about subterfuge entirely and simply looked. By the time the class was in its first downward dog, there was not a person there who hadn't spied on the noisy latecomer. He had the bluest eyes any of them had ever seen, and a halo of light around his body, which most everyone assumed was an optical illusion. It would be a long time before any of them thought that it hadn't been a glow at all, but a burning.

Shreve noticed (when she walked past him as he lay in corpse position) the strong scent of jasmine, and thought that, in the mysterious ways of the world, a holy man, a yogi, had come into her class.

Shreve, like Sylvia, was a widow. Sort of. There was no word for what she was, actually. She felt betrayed by language, amongst other things. Her fiancé had been murdered. Even the nature of his death had robbed her of something primary, as if *how* he died was more important than that he had. She'd given up trying to explain it. Nobody in Voorhisville knew.

She'd moved here with her new yoga teacher certificate after the second anniversary of the event and opened up this studio with the savings she'd set aside for the wedding. His parents paid for the funeral, so she still had quite a bit left, which was good, because though the studio was a success by Voorhisville's standards, she was running out of money. It was enough to make her cranky sometimes. She tried to forgive herself for it. Shreve wasn't sure she had enough love to forgive the world, but she thought—maybe—she could forgive herself.

With her hands in prayer position, Shreve closed her eyes and sang "shanti" three times. It meant "peace," and on that morning Shreve felt like peace had finally arrived.

Later, when the stranger showed up for the writers' workshop at Jan Morris's house, she could not determine how he'd found out about the elitist group, known to have rejected at least one local writer on the basis of the fact she wrote fantasy. Jan asked him how he'd found them, but Sylvia interrupted before he could answer. Certainly it never occurred to her to think he was up to anything diabolical. Also, it became clear that Sylvia knew him from a yoga class she attended. By the time he had passed out the twelve copies of his poem—his presence made them a group of thirteen, but they were intellectuals, not a superstitious bunch—well, it just didn't matter how he found them.

Afterwards, as the writers left, Jan stood at the door with the stranger beside her, waving goodbye until she observed two things: first, that the last car remaining in the driveway was a hearse, and second, that the stranger smelled, quite pleasantly, of lemons.

Jan preferred to call him "the stranger." Never mind Camus; it had a nice ring to it all on its own. Eventually, when the mothers pieced things together, it seemed the most accurate moniker. They didn't know him at all. None of them did. Not really.

One night in early June, after events began to unfold as they did, Jan looked for her copy of the stranger's poem, which she remembered folding inside a book, like a pressed flower. But though she tore apart the bookshelf, making so much noise she woke the baby, she never found it. She called the others and asked each of them, trying to sound casual ("Remember that poet, who came to the workshop just that once? And that poem he wrote?"), but none of them could locate their copy either.

Sylvia remembered that night well; waving goodbye to Jan and Jeffrey, who were standing in the doorway together, haloed by the light of all those overwhelming lemon-scented candles. Jeffrey was a good deal taller than Jan. Sylvia realized she could look right into his blue eyes without even seeing the top of the other woman's head.

When Jan called in June, Sylvia pretended to have only a minor memory of Jeffrey and the poem, but as soon as she hung up she began searching for it, moving ponderously, weighed down by her pregnancy and the heat. How could she have misplaced it? She had intended to give it to the child some day, a way to say, "Here, you have a father and he is a genius." But also, Sylvia felt, it was proof that what she had done had been the only reasonable response. The poem revealed not just his intelligence, but also his heart, which was good. Sylvia had to believe this, though he left her. Her husband had left her, too . . . and yes, all right, he had died, but Jeffrey made no promises. He'd come and gone, which Sylvia considered fortunate. She didn't need, or want, the complication of his presence. But she did want that poem.

That night, when Sylvia's water broke, she was surprised at how it felt: "As though there had been an iceberg inside of me, which suddenly melted," she told Holly.

Holly, the midwife and a keeper of many secrets, had a house in Ridgehaven, but that May, she rented a small room from the Melverns, who were thrilled to have her in such close proximity to their pregnant seventeen-year-old daughter. Holly had told no one what she had seen: all those pregnant women in Voorhisville who didn't appear to have a man in their lives. While this was certainly not scandalous, she did find the number significant. When the babies began arriving that last week in May, it became clear to Holly that something had happened to the women of Voorhisville. Something *indescribable.*

For Jeffrey's appeal—though he was a good-looking man—went beyond description. Though there weren't *many*, there *were* other attractive men in Voorhisville who the women had not fucked; receiving nothing in exchange but a single night, or afternoon, or morning (after yoga class, in the studio, the air sweet with jasmine). When the women tried to define just what was so compelling about the stranger, they could not come to a consensus.

Lara Bravemeen, for instance, remembered his hands, with their long narrow fingers and their slender wrists. She said he had the hands of a painter.

Cathy Vecker remembered the way he moved. "Like a man who never hurried . . . but not lazy, you see. Self-contained, that's what I mean."

Tamara mentioned his eyes, which everyone else thought so obvious there was no need to comment on.

Elli Ratcher stopped chewing on a hangnail long enough to say, "When he held me I felt like I was being held by an angel. I felt like I would always be safe. I felt holy."

At which point the women sighed and looked down at their shoes, or into their laps. Because to look at Elli was to remember she had been just fifteen. Though no one could be sure about Jeffrey's age, he was certainly a man. What he'd done to all of them was wrong, but what he'd done to Elli (and Maddy, they hastened to add) went beyond wrong into the territory of evil.

Maddy

My name is Maddy Melvern—well, Matilda, which just goes to show how grownups like to make up the world they live in; my parents naming me like I was living in a fairy tale instead of Voorhisville. Let's just set the record straight, I don't remember no sweet-smelling day here or none of that shit. Voorhisville is a dump. The houses, almost all of them, except the Veckers', are all peeling paint and crooked porches. Voorhisville is the kind of town where if a window gets broke it's gonna stay broke, but someone will try to cover it up with cardboard or duct tape. Duct tape holds Voorhisville together. Roddy Tyler's got his shoes duct-taped, and there's duct tape in the post office holding the American flag up, and there's duct tape on the back of the third pew in St. Andrew's balcony. I don't know why. There just is. I was born here and I ain't old enough to do nothing about it. I can't explain why anyone else would stay. I know the mothers like to say there are sweet-smelling days in Voorhisville, but there ain't.

I agree with Elli. Jeffrey was a angel. And just to be clear, my baby was a angel too. All our babies were. No matter what anyone says. I don't care if he stayed. What was he going to do? Work at the canning factory? Maybe you can picture him doing that and then coming home to, like, have barbecues and shit, but I sure can't. He didn't fall for it, you know, that way of doing things right. What I say is that if everybody in Voorhisville's so concerned with doing things *right*, then just as soon as we get out of here I'm going to live my life doing things *wrong*.

It was the first day of school and me, Leanne, Sasha, and some of the guys was walking to Sasha's house when we see this hearse parked in front of St. Andrew's. Mark dares me to go into the church. I'm like, what's the big shit about that? So when the door shuts behind me they all take off, laughing like a bunch of retards.

I kind of liked it. It was peaceful, all right? And it did smell good in there. And everything was clean. So I'm looking at this big statue they got of Jesus on the cross? He's got the crown with the thorns on his head, and he's bleeding, and I don't know why, but whenever I see statues and pictures of Jesus and shit like that, I sort of hate him. I know that's insulting to many people, but he annoys me, with that crown piercing his skull and those nails in his feet and hands and shit. I never understand why he didn't do nothing about it, if he was so powerful and all? "You belong in Voorhisville," is what I thought, and I guess I said it out loud 'cause that's when a voice behind me goes, "Excuse me?"

So, I turned and there he was. At first I thought he was the priest, but he set me straight. We talked for a long time and then after a while he said we had to go somewhere safe. I kind of laughed, because ain't churches supposed to be super safe, but he took my hand, and we went up to the balcony. I don't know why, we just did, okay? That's where it happened. I know me and Elli ain't been getting along so much here, but she's right: it ain't bad, what we did. I know, doing it in the church makes it seem bad, but it was good, okay? Like how they said it would be, not like . . . not . . . Okay, I've been with boys my own age, and I've had *bad*, and this was not like that. And I ain't just talking about his *dick*. I'm talking about the feeling. What'd she call it? Holy.

But that don't mean that Voorhisville ain't all stinky and shit. We don't gotta lie about that. We should tell it right because what this shows everyone is that something like this could happen anywhere. If it happened in Voorhisville, it could happen in any town, and I don't see that as being a bad thing.

Tamara

The third anniversary of Shreve's fiancé's death fell on a Saturday when yoga class was scheduled, but she decided to teach anyway, and was glad she did. She started class with a short meditation. She didn't tell the women what to think or feel. They just sat there, breathing in and out. Shreve thought about her plans. After class, she would go home and change into something comfortable (but not her pajamas, as she'd done for years one and two), make herself a nice pot of tea, light a candle, and look at photographs.

By the time she opened her eyes, those hard minutes had passed. On that day (though not everyone remembers) Voorhisville smelled like chocolate. Emily Carr woke up at 4:30 and began baking. By 6:30, when Stecker's opened, she was waiting there with a long list of ingredients. She baked chocolate bread, and a chocolate cake (layered with a raspberry filling), a chocolate torte, and good old-fashioned (why mess with perfection?) chocolate chip cookies. Though the day was warm, she also mixed up some Mexican hot chocolate, which she poured into a large thermos. She made a batch of chocolate muffins and six dozen dark chocolate cherry cookies. Then Emily filled several baskets with cookies, muffins, and slices of cake, torte, and bread, and began delivering her treats to the neighbors.

"But why?" they asked, to which she just shrugged. Until, when she got to Shreve's house, she said, "Let me know what you think. I'm going to open a bakery and I'm trying to find out what people like."

At that point, Emily began to cry. Shreve invited her inside. Wiping her eyes as she stepped into the warm living room, Emily said, "I'm happy. That's why I'm crying. I'm so happy." Then she noticed the photographs spread across the floor, the wedding dress on the couch, the stricken look on Shreve's face.

"My fiancé died," Shreve said, "three years ago today."

Emily, who had forgotten the date entirely until Bobby Stewart said, "What is this? Some kind of September eleventh thing?" resisted the impulse to ask Shreve if he'd been one of the thousands. Instead, she said, "There's a thermos of hot chocolate."

Shreve looked from the basket to the photographs, the wedding dress, the box of tiny bells. "I don't know what to do."

"We could go to the park."

That's what they did. On that mild September evening the women sat beneath the oak tree in Fletcher's Park, ate too much chocolate, and became friends.

The following Saturday, after Emily's first yoga class, the women went garage sale-ing together. Both women appreciated a bargain, and both women had appreciated Jeffrey, though they wouldn't know this until October, when they confided their fears to each other and—like high school girls, giggling, nervous, and unsure—went to the drugstore for pregnancy tests, which, oddly, were all sold out. They drove all the way to Centerville to purchase them, during which time they told their stories of the stranger with blue eyes and thus discovered that they had shared a lover.

"Did you notice how he smelled?" Shreve asked.

"Chocolate," Emily said. "Do you ever get mad at him? The way he just left?"

"Actually, I sort of prefer it this way. I'm not looking for anything else. You?"

Emily shook her head. "It's the weirdest thing, because normally I would. I mean, I think so, at least. I've never done anything like that with a stranger. But for some reason, I'm not angry."

Were the women of Voorhisville enchanted? Bewitched? Had a great evil befallen them? It was hard to imagine that anything bad happened that autumn, when everyone glowed.

Later, they had to agree it was more than strange that they all got pregnant, even those using birth control, and none of them suffered morning sickness. It was also odd that, given the obvious promiscuity involved, no one got an STD. But that fall, all anyone cared about was that the women of Voorhisville were beautiful.

Lara no longer stood at the small window in the upstairs hallway spying on her neighbor. Yes, Sylvia was beautiful. She had always *been* beautiful, even at her husband's funeral, her face wracked with grief. But there were many beautiful women in Voorhisville. Why hadn't Lara noticed before?

One morning, shortly after September eleventh (she later recalled the date because she'd eaten Emily's chocolate cake for breakfast), Lara stood naked in front of the bedroom mirror. Why had she spent all that time studying Sylvia? Lara turned, twisting her neck to get a sideways look.

She decided to begin painting again. She would paint her own strong legs, the sag of flesh at her stomach, her tired eyes. She had to paint all this to try to express the feeling she had, of no longer being a sum of parts. Her parts would be there, but that's not what the painting would be about. It would be a self-portrait, Lara decided, and it would be huge.

When Lara realized she was late she phoned the pharmacy. "I'm not coming in today," she said. She didn't offer an explanation. Even as she said it, she wasn't sure she would ever return to work. She knew how this would sit with Ed. He wouldn't like it, but it wasn't as though she expected him to support her; she had her own savings.

As Lara dressed, she thought about Jeffrey. She'd taken a huge risk; he could have been a psycho. He could have stalked her. Or told Ed! Instead, he disappeared. For weeks, Lara looked for the hearse, but she never saw it again. He was gone as mysteriously as he'd arrived. She'd been lucky, Lara thought—guilty, yes, but lucky.

It didn't even occur to her she might be pregnant.

Theresa Ratcher knew she was. She would say, later, that she knew immediately.

When Lara drove past the Ratcher farm on her way to Centerville for art supplies, Theresa Ratcher was standing in the driveway, shading her eyes, as though expecting a visitor. The women waved at each other. Lara sighed. Even Theresa Ratcher was beautiful in her old housewifey dress, her clunky shoes, her corn-colored hair in a messy ponytail.

Theresa watched the car arc over the hill with one hand on her tummy, which had not been flat since Elli was born fifteen years ago. Pete would never suspect a thing. Why would he? Why would anyone? She closed her eyes and tilted her face towards the sun. "What are you doing?" Pete said. Theresa opened her eyes, wide, as though caught. Her husband's face had hardened with time, and he smelled of manure, but she loved him. She placed her hand on his crotch. After a moment, she turned and walked away. He followed, surprised when she didn't go into the house but walked behind the barn, where she lay down on the grass and lifted up her dress, revealing her freckled thighs, the white crotch of her panties. This was very much like how it had happened, when, still teenagers, they'd made Elli.

Here's your dad, Theresa thought.

What all (or most) of the women of Voorhisville would have said was that beautiful was everywhere that fall: it was in the light and shadows and the muted green leaves that eventually burned into a blaze of color, it was in the duct-taped houses, in the bats that flew out of St. Andrew's belfry each night, and the logey bees buzzing amongst the pumpkins and squash.

Beautiful was in the women, the way they talked, walked, the things they did: the stretch of limbs in yoga, the scent of chocolate from Emily's kitchen. Jan Morris had never written so proficiently—or, she felt (and the writers in the workshop agreed) more beautifully. Lara Bravemeen began painting again, which caused an argument with her husband, a fight Lara could only think of as beautiful in its passion.

Strange things were happening to the women of Voorhisville. Anyone could see that.

"Like bones, and skin, and blood," Elli Ratcher later said. "What could be more beautiful than that? What could be more strange?"

The Mothers

We, the mothers, understand the enormity of the task involved in relaying the events that preceded the seminal one. We appreciate the impossibility of incorporating each personal account into this narrative, and, after much discussion and several votes, made the decision to tell this story through the voices of a representative few. It is an imperfect solution, we know, but then again, we are in an imperfect situation. However, we would like to stress that we reject the penis-glorifying tone that's been taken, as though we, the women of Voorhisville, were only completed through penetration. We would like to make it clear that we believe the women of Voorhisville were always beautiful, always interesting, always evolving, always capable of greatness.

Tamara

The Veckers own the big white house on the hill. They *pay* people to do their gardening, mow the lawn, trim the bushes. Several Voorhisville residents think it's unjust that the Veckers win the Gardeners' Association's blue ribbon each year, as well as the grand prize for their Christmas decorations; that big house outlined with thousands of little white lights, all those windows and doors bordered too, so that it looks like some strip mall.

Nobody is exactly sure how the Veckers got to be so rich. Even Cathy Vecker, twenty-five years old and recently returned from Los Angeles, looking a good deal older than her age, has no idea where the family money came from. The topic never held much interest for her. Cathy *knew* everyone was not as fortunate as she was; but what could she do about it? Whenever she thought about all the poor people—Roddy Tyler with his duct-taped shoes, for instance—it just made her weary.

Because what *could* they do? The Veckers were rich, but they weren't *that* rich; they were no Bill *Gates*, that's for sure. Even Cathy, who had never been good at math, knew the numbers didn't work out. The world had more people than dollars in the various Vecker accounts. If the Veckers gave away every cent they owned, nobody would be rich, and the Veckers would join the masses of those without enough. For a while, Cathy had worried that she was becoming a socialist, but once she worked through the logic, she was relieved to discover that she was just a regular rich American.

Being a rich American meant Cathy could follow her dreams. She moved to Los Angeles to pursue modeling and acting. Cathy Vecker *was* pretty. She was not as beautiful as Sylvia Lansmorth, but everyone knew that Sylvia was exceptional—though overly attached to her roses. Sylvia's husband was gorgeous too, or had been, before he died. He was a carpenter. Cathy's mother and grandmother hired him from time to time for special projects.

Cathy had never been happier for the Vecker money than she was upon returning from Los Angeles. She was thrilled she didn't have to come up with an immediate solution to the challenging question of what she would do with her life. It wasn't that she meant to shrug the question off—she had every intention of addressing it eventually—but it was a relief not to have to rush to a conclusion, get a job *waitressing* or something.

Los Angeles had been an experiment, and she'd failed miserably. All the women in Los Angeles were gorgeous. It was kind of weird, actually. Also, Cathy discovered, she couldn't really act. It wasn't until she saw a recording of her audition that she recognized that. Why hadn't anyone told her? Why hadn't someone just *said* it?

By the end of August, Cathy had narrowed her choices to going to college—though she hadn't applied, she felt certain her family connections could get her into St. Mary's or the university—or opening a small business. She was bogged down in the details. What would she major in? What kind of business would she start?

Then she became distracted. She *thought* she was falling in love, or at least that explained the powerful attraction, the *chemistry*, the reason she *did it* in the back of a *hearse*, like somebody who couldn't afford a room somewhere. Later, Cathy had to admit there was something about it that felt dangerous and exciting. She thought she'd gotten that sort of thing out of her system in Los Angeles, but apparently not.

He didn't ask for her phone number, but she didn't worry. She was a

Vecker. Everyone knew how to get in touch with the Veckers. By September, she realized he wasn't going to call. By the end of that month, despite the Pill—which Cathy had been taking since she was fifteen, when she had her first affair with Stephen Lang, who (she didn't know it was a cliché at the time) cleaned their pool—Cathy guessed she was pregnant. A quick trip to the drugstore and a home pregnancy test confirmed it. Cathy knew she should be upset, but honestly, she wasn't. She placed her hand on her flat stomach and said, "I'll do this."

She decided she'd start a community theatre, right there in Voorhisville. A Christmas play in December, maybe a musical; possibly *Our Town* in the spring; something modern in-between. It wouldn't have to make money. The Veckers could *do* this. They couldn't support the world, or America, but they could do this. Cathy could run it, even while she raised her child, and she could live off one of the Vecker accounts, and she could do something good for Voorhisville.

The senior Mrs. Vecker received the news—first of the pregnancy, then of the community theatre—with the traditional Vecker attitude. Cathy was worried her grandmother would be upset, but it turned out there had not been an exact alignment between Grandma Vecker's own wedding and Cathy Vecker's mother's birth; a matter covered up, at the time, by an extended European honeymoon. "Didn't you *know* that?" Mrs. Vecker asked.

Whereas Grandma Vecker said, "It's quite clever of you to start without the man hanging around. Everything you need from him, you've already got."

After her husband died, Sylvia Lansmorth found herself in the unusual position of being rich. Well, not *rich*, exactly, not like the Veckers, but she no longer had to work at the canning factory, a job she'd held since she was fifteen. Who would have guessed that Rick Lansmorth—who was, after all, just a carpenter—had the foresight to take out sizable life insurance policies for both of them? But he had.

All these months later, Sylvia was still finding the wooden figurines Rick had been working on during his chemo; tiny creatures that fit in the palm of her hand: a swan tucked in his toolbox (she'd been looking for the hammer); what appeared to be the beginnings of a wolf (the shape formed, a few lines cut for fur but no eyes or mouth) on the kitchen windowsill; a tiny mouse with a broken tail in the garden. Rick used to sit outside wrapped in blankets, even when the sun was hot, and Sylvia guessed he'd thrown it in frustration. Not the sort of thing he would normally do, but dying had been hard.

Sylvia was not living the life she'd imagined when she was a high school girl who thought her job at the canning factory was temporary. She used to look at the women working there and wonder why they stayed. Now, Sylvia knew. It just happened.

She and Rick had planned to leave Voorhisville. First, he tried building up a clientele in Centerville, but he was just another guy with a toolbox there. People in Voorhisville knew and trusted him, and while there wasn't much work, what work there was, he got. Then he moved to Alaska. The plan was that he would get established before Sylvia joined him. They missed each other, of course, but it was a sacrifice they were willing to make. They thought they had time. Instead, he came back to Voorhisville with cancer and stories of moose.

After Sylvia quit her job, she spent a great deal of time in the garden; so much so that, as fall approached, she realized that her main occupation had been dying, and she didn't have anything to replace it with. She would have denied that she had wished for it, or expected it; she would have resisted calling it a miracle; but just when the garden started to look barren, she discovered she was pregnant, the result of one single sexual encounter with a stranger she had no desire to see again. Sylvia had gotten quite good at crying over the past year. Why couldn't it be Rick's child? Why couldn't he still be alive? What could possibly come of conception in a *hearse*? How Freudian was that?

Sylvia considered an abortion. Then she got in her car, drove to Centerville, and went to the Barnes & Noble, where she spent a good deal of money on pregnancy and parenting books.

"Wow, we've really had a run on these lately," the clerk said.

Sylvia liked having a secret. It wasn't that she was ashamed. She just liked having this private relationship with her baby. Once her neighbor, Lara Bravemeen (whose upstairs windows brooded over Sylvia's garden) asked why she'd stopped going to yoga, and she just shrugged. Sylvia had recently discovered that most people accepted a shrug for an answer.

In January, Sylvia learned that Lara Bravemeen was pregnant too. Their children could play together. That is, if the Bravemeens stayed married and continued to live next door. Lately, there'd been a lot of shouting over there.

Never having been pregnant before, Sylvia had nothing to compare it to except TV shows, but she thought it was perfect. She felt wonderful the whole time. Holly, the midwife, said, "Sometimes it's almost harder if you have an easy pregnancy. It makes the birth just that much more of a shock."

Sylvia, who had been feeling very much like a Madonna—not the rock star, but the perfectly peaceful mother type—just smiled.

~

The pain was monumental. Right from the start. Ed called the doctor and she said, "How far apart?" and Ed asked Lara, "How far apart?" and Lara screamed, "What?" So Ed repeated the question. "There's no time between, you moron," Lara hollered. Ed relayed this to the doctor (editing out the "moron," of course), who said, "When did the contractions start?" and Ed said, "Five minutes ago." That's when the doctor said, "Bring her in now." Ed said, "Right now?" and the doctor said, "Wait. You're in Voorhisville, right?" and he said, "Yes," and she said, "Call the ambulance," and Ed said, "Is there a problem?" and Lara screamed and the doctor said, "Call them." So Ed called the ambulance and they came right away. It was Brian Holandeigler and Francis Kennedy (no relation to any of the famous ones), who tried to make jokes to calm Ed and Lara down, but between screams of agony, Lara was vicious. "She's not usually like this," Ed said. "Fuck you!" Lara shouted. "You're going to be all right," Francis said. "Fuck you!" Lara screamed. "Try to breathe," Ed said. "Remember the breathing?" "Fuck, fuck, fuck," Lara screamed.

Something was wrong. Something was terribly wrong. She knew it. And here she was, surrounded by these idiot men ("Idiots!" she shouted) who thought she was hysterical.

"I'm dying!" she screamed.

"You're not dying," Ed said.

It felt like she was being scraped raw inside by talons. It felt like her guts were being carved out. Or like teeth! It felt like small sharp teeth were chewing her up inside.

"Do something!" she shouted.

"Well, we really can't do much," Brian said.

"What?" Ed and Lara said.

"I could take a look," Brian said.

"But we're not supposed to transport women in labor," Francis said. "We're supposed to stay here. Unless there's a problem."

"There's a fucking problem!" Lara shouted.

"Do you mind if I look?" Brian said as he slipped his hands around the waistband of Lara's pants. Ed found the image disturbing, and turned away. Lara saw him turn away. She managed, through her pain, to form the words again: "Fuck you." Brian sat up. "Hold your legs together," he said. "What?" Lara said. "Is it coming?" Ed said. "Of course it's—" Lara interrupted herself to scream. "Close your legs!" Brian shouted. "Are we taking her?" Francis said. "Yes. Yes. Oh God, yes," Brian said. "Close your legs!" he yelled at Lara. "Oh, God, oh Jesus," Brian said. Lara screamed. Ed leaned down and held her hand. "Please," he said, "close your legs." "I want it out!" Lara shouted. "Please," Ed said, "do what they say." "Excuse me," Francis said, and shoved Ed away.

Brian and Francis set the stretcher on the floor beside the couch. "I'm dying!" Lara screamed. Brian and Ed lifted her to the stretcher. "Close your legs," Brian said. Lara closed her legs. "Don't drop her," Ed said as he opened the door. "Can I come with you?" "Two steps," Francis said to Brian, who was backing out. Ed shut the door. He looked at Sylvia's dark house. *Death could come to anyone, anywhere,* he thought. "Are you coming?" Francis said. Ed jumped into the ambulance. The siren screamed, but it was nothing compared to Lara's screams. "Let me see where you're at," Francis said. He spread a sheet over Lara's lap and bent under to have a look. When his head came out of the sheet, his eyes were wide, his skin white. "Oh, Jesus," Francis said. "Hold your legs together."

Lara tried to hold her legs together, but it felt like she was being sliced by knives. "Ed," she shouted. "Ed?"

"I'm here, baby, I'm right here." He squeezed her hand.

She screamed. She screamed the whole ride from Voorhisville to the hospital in Becksworth. When they got there, the doctor was waiting for them.

"How about an epidural?" she said. "You better take a look," Brian said. She lifted the sheet and looked. "Take her to the OR," the doctor said. "What's happening?" Ed said. "You stay here," a nurse said. "What's happening?" Ed said to Brian and Francis. They both stared at him, then Francis said, "There might be some complications." Ed sat down. Brian and Francis left. The hospital was so quiet Ed thought he could still hear Lara's screams. But it couldn't have been her, because Lara had gone to the right, and the screams were coming from the left.

Jan Morris lay screaming in her hospital bed, but no one was paying much attention. Someone had checked her when she came in, and pointed out that she wasn't even dilated yet. Jan insisted they contact her doctor. "She wants to know," she said. But Jan's doctor was busy with some other emergency, so Dr. Fascular took the call instead. The nurse checked Jan again, decided that she was making a big fuss over nothing, and administered an epidural. *The mother was in her forties, and they were often the biggest pains. They wanted everything a certain way.* But Jan kept screaming until it finally occurred to someone that there might be a problem.

The nurse who looked at Jan later said, over coffee and eggs with her twelve-year-old son, that it was the most shocking thing she'd ever seen. The woman hadn't even been *dilated* ten minutes ago—or, okay, it might have been closer to twenty minutes, but then suddenly there was . . . she thought there might be an arm, a leg, something like that. Anyway, after she saw the strange *thing* protruding from Jan Morris's vagina, she ran to call Dr. Fascular again.

"What thing?" the nurse's son asked.

"I don't know how to describe it. It was just sticking out, and it was like a, like the tip of a triangle, and it was sharp."

"You touched it?"

"Look," she said, and showed him the small cut on her finger.

"What happened next?" the boy asked.

She remembered touching that bloody tip with her finger; she remembered the sear of pain and running to call the doctor. The next thing she knew, several hours had passed and she was punching her time card to go home. Even though she was tired and her feet were sore and she certainly wanted to be there when her son woke up, she went to the nursery where she found the baby, a sweet-as-they-all-are prune-shaped thing, wrapped tightly in a blanket, sleeping. She read the chart and saw that there was nothing unusual noted.

Maddy

Yeah, well, that nurse didn't see nothing wrote down about it because they could hold them inside like the way you put your fingers in a fist, or maybe more like the way you close a eye. That's what the babies did. They pulled them in real tight and it just looked like, I don't know, kind of extra wrinkled and stuff. Who pays attention to a baby's back, anyways? Not most people. Most people wanna look at a baby's face or fingers and toes. There is a weird fascination with grownups looking at a baby's fingers or toes. Also, baby's shit. My mom could go on and on about JoJo's shit. Was it greenish? Was it runny? She'd get mad at me when I rolled my eyes. "You can tell things about your baby's health, Maddy," she'd say.

My mom liked to behave all superior about babies with me 'cause she had two, and she figured that made her a expert. Also, I really think she liked the fact I was a teenage mother 'cause it proved her theory that I was a fuckup all along. Weird as it is, though, I sometimes wish I had my mom here with me like Elli has hers. But how fucked is that? Both of them doing it with the same guy? It makes me shiver every time I think about it.

JoJo was born at home, even though we didn't plan it that way. Just 'cause we had a midwife renting Billy's old room in the basement don't mean we was going to use her. Holly was really busy. Once she came upstairs and asked me to turn the music down, but she asked like she knew it was a big pain for me to do, and so I turned it down. And one night we sat on the front steps and talked. I thought she was nice.

But it's not like I got to choose much about JoJo. My mom liked to act like everything was up to me. "He's your baby," she'd say. "He's your responsibility"—she said this about diaper changing and when he was crying. But other times she'd say, "Just 'cause you had a baby don't mean you're all grown up now."

My mom said I had to go to a hospital. "It's just ridiculous that in this day in age, with all the best modern medicine has to offer, a woman would choose to give birth at home like they was living in Afghanistan or something." My mom loved to mention Afghanistan whenever she could. My brother Billy got killed there, and after that she blamed Afghanistan for anything wrong in the world.

After I talked to Holly that night on the porch, I wanted her to help when the baby came. It's not like she tried to convince me, or nothing like that. We barely talked about it. Mostly we talked about other stuff. But I liked her, and I didn't like Dr. Fascular. He has cold hands and is always grumpy and shit.

My mom was all like, "No way," and said it had to be at the hospital. But there wasn't much she could do when it happened the way it did, all of a sudden, with me alone in the house. I didn't expect it to hurt like it did. It hurt a lot. I didn't scream, even though I really wanted to. I just went down to Billy's old room and laid down on Billy's old bed, which was now Holly's, and waited for her to get home. It hurt so bad I took the bedspread and rolled it up at the end and stuck it in my mouth. Every time I felt like screaming, which was pretty much all the time, I bit down.

I don't know how long it was before Holly came home. She said, "Maddy?"

I just screamed. I let the bedspread fall out of my mouth and I screamed loud enough to bring my mom and dad down the stairs, and then there was this whole part where they got mad at Holly, and even though I was screaming and shit, I had to explain to them that she didn't have nothing to do with it, and then my dad said he was going to get the car, and Holly was looking at my vagina and saying, "I don't think so."

I heard it hurt a lot to have a baby, but nothing nobody said told me how much. I don't even want to think about it.

So Mom starts arguing with Holly, and then all of a sudden Holly says, "This baby is halfway here. If you want to take her all the way to Becksworth, you go ahead. But I sure hope you are prepared to deliver it." Which, ha ha, got my mom to shut up.

Okay, so like it hurt more than anything I ever imagined. It hurt more than when Billy got killed, and I didn't think there would ever be nothing that hurt worse than that. Later, Holly told me it was not a usual birth. Still, I don't think I'll ever do it again. Like I could! Ha, stuck here with all these women.

I was exhausted. I just wanted to go to sleep. Holly said, "What are you going to name him?" And I said, "JoJo." And my mom said, "I knew it. I knew it was Joey Marin." My mom was obsessed with trying to figure out who JoJo's dad was. "It ain't Joey Marin," I said, but she just looked all superior. Holly cleaned him up and she said he was beautiful. And that's coming from someone who delivered hundreds of babies, so that should tell you something. Then she gave him to me, wrapped up like a bratwurst in a bun. Everybody stood there, even my dad. Like I was going to breastfeed in front of him! I guess Holly figured that out, 'cause she said she had some things to talk to them about in private. When Mom and Dad were both out the door, I told Holly I was sorry I got her in trouble. "That's all right," she said. "I thought this room could use a birth." I saw what she meant. Except for Holly's clothes and a little glass jar on the dresser filled with some wildflowers, the room was just the way it was when Billy left to get killed in the war.

So I took off my T-shirt and put JoJo up by my boob, and he started sucking.

The next day, after I moved back upstairs and my mom cleaned all of Holly's sheets and even baked her a tube of chocolate chip cookies to thank her for everything she did, I was undressing JoJo, and the next thing I knew, my finger was bleeding and JoJo was crying and my mom was standing there going, "What are you doing to him?"

"I ain't doing nothing to him," I said. "I pricked my finger."

"This is no longer all about you," she said, and, "You better make sure you keep one hand on him when he's on the changing table, or it won't be long before he'll just roll off." About as soon as JoJo was born, my mom started imagining all the horrible ways he could die.

I looked at JoJo laying there with his face all scrunched up and all I could think was that I had a huge problem. I didn't love him, all right? For the first time in my entire life I wondered if this is what was wrong with me and my mom, that she just didn't love me and couldn't do nothing about it. I felt real bad, and angry too. I decided that wasn't going to happen with me and JoJo.

I picked him up and took him with me to the bed, and that's when I saw them sticking out. They were *tiny*, like his fingers and toes were tiny. They were tiny like that.

"Holy shit, JoJo," I said. "You've got wings."

Tamara

When Tamara met Raj and found out he was Hindu, she didn't think much about it. It wasn't until she was already falling in love that she discovered how much his faith mattered to him. She told him she wasn't sure she could convert, but he said she didn't need to. It might have been easier if she could fool herself into believing that her infidelity had been Raj's fault, but Tamara could not believe that. She had cheated on him for the worst reason of all: because she felt like it.

There was justice in her pregnancy. It was a Catholic thought, she knew, but no matter how many years had passed since she'd gone to church, she could not escape the idea that God did things like this to Catholics. He punished them for being bad.

Tamara knew it was not uncommon for pregnant woman to have horrible dreams, but she was sure hers were the worst. Several times, Raj died. Once, she drowned the baby. (How could she even *dream* that?) She had many dreams that featured birth defects. When she woke up crying, Raj held her, soothed her, made her tea, told her jokes. He was the perfect husband, which just made everything worse.

Tamara thought of confessing. Being raised Catholic, how could she *not* think of that? But she couldn't decide. Was she confessing to help their marriage, or just to relieve her guilt? What was the *right* thing to do? She no longer trusted her judgment. How could she, after she'd displayed such a colossal lack of any? (After it all came out and everything fell apart the way it did, she would decide she must have been put under some sort of spell, though the other women say things like, "Sure, if that's what you wanna call it, honey.")

Tamara had passed the bar exam, so she was technically a lawyer, but hardly anyone knew that. She never practiced. She hated law school, but didn't dare quit after her parents had put so much money into it. She hadn't really mentioned, in any of her phone calls or emails to her parents, that she wasn't doing anything with her degree, but instead was working part-time at the Voorhisville library while writing another novel. She'd never told them about the four previous novels she'd written (but not published) so it was difficult to tell them about the fifth. They wouldn't approve. Her father used to make fun of her art major friends. He called them "the future poor of America."

She and Raj moved to Voorhisville because they had fantasies about small town life. Raj, who worked as a litigation attorney in Becksworth, and therefore wasn't really in Voorhisville much, still believed it was a quaint community, a perfect place for children. Tamara wasn't so sure. She'd *seen* things: the way Michael Baile (whose cousin was on the school board) got all the contracts for the school maintenance jobs, even though there were consistent complaints about the quality of his work. The way almost everyone talked about Maddy Malvern's spiral into sexual promiscuity, but did nothing about it. The way Roddy Tyler flopped around in those duct-taped shoes even in the winter, despite the fact that he worked for the richest people in town. Tamara did not think Voorhisville was quaint, though it did have the annual Halloween parade with all the children dressed in costumes walking down Main Street. *That* was quaint. And Fourth of July in Fletcher's Park, with Girl Scouts selling baked goods, Boy Scouts selling popcorn, and Mr. Muller twisting balloons into animal shapes while the senior citizen band played God knows what . . . well, *that* was quaint too. But Tamara saw the looks Raj, with his dark skin, got. "Doesn't it bother you?" she asked, but he just laughed. That's just the way Raj was. He didn't care. It had been harder for Tamara. She wasn't used to being a victim of prejudice.

"It would be like this in almost any small town in America," Raj said. "You can't let it upset you."

But it did. It upset Tamara very much. It confused her, too. She could never be sure. Had the man at the post office been rude because he knew she was married to someone with dark skin, or had he just been a rude man? What about the checkout girl at the supermarket, and the lady who cut her off at the corner of Henry Street and Wildwood?

The novel Tamara was working on was called *Underskin*, about a nomadic tribe of tree dwellers and the consumers who ate them. It was a love story, a dark fantasy, a brutal indictment of prejudice, and her best work. But after her strange encounter with the blue-eyed man, it was contaminated. Also, Tamara would later note, wryly, she had to resist the urge to put in a band of avenging angels. They weren't part of her plan for the book, and yet they kept appearing. She kept crossing them out.

Essentially, the work that had been going so well before she cheated on her husband started going very badly. This, Tamara knew, was God's way of getting her. This and her pregnancy; that's how she thought of it. She thought God had made her pregnant just to prove a point—which, she reasoned, was unnecessary, because she already *knew* she shouldn't have cheated, so why'd God have to make her pregnant as well?

After Tamara took two home pregnancy tests, she called Planned Parenthood and made an appointment she never kept. Much later, when the bad things happened and she was stuck with all the other women chronicling their stories, she wondered if this decision had been a matter of enchantment.

When she told Raj they were expecting, he kissed her all over. (Raj, thankfully, mistook her tears for joy.) They talked about names and the dreams they had for the child. "I just want her to be happy," Tamara said, and Raj laughed and said, "That's a big dream."

Over the next several months, Tamara found herself praying. She prayed to God, and she prayed to Krishna too. She prayed to everyone she could think of, like the Virgin Mary, and her Great-Uncle Cal (who would probably be embarrassed by all this, but was the only dead person

Tamara had been close to.) *Hi, Uncle Cal,* she'd think. *This is Tamara. I'm married now. And I made a mistake. Please, please make sure that this baby is Raj's and not, well . . . I'm sorry. I shouldn't have done it. I know that. Thank you, Uncle Cal.* She prayed to Kali, with her four arms and that mysterious smile of hers. She even prayed to that elephant—she could never remember his name, but Raj had a small statue of him in the living room, and she prayed to him because he looked nonjudgmental. For eight months, Tamara suffered in fear and anguish while her body blossomed, effortlessly. "I don't know why women complain about being pregnant," she told Holly.

"Sometimes it's more difficult to have an easy pregnancy," Holly said, "because then you're not really prepared for the birth."

At this, Tamara smiled.

But when the pain arrived it was the worst feeling Tamara could ever imagine. One second she was sitting at her desk crossing out angels, and the next she was on the floor, screaming. She was in so much pain she couldn't even *move.* It hurt to *breathe.* It was torture to get up or slide across the floor, which is how she tried to reach the phone, because Raj had gone into work even though her due date was approaching. ("I'll just call if anything happens," she said. "We'll have plenty of time. All the books say so.") Tamara screamed and writhed on the floor for hours before Raj found her there. During those hours, Tamara accepted that she was being punished. She also accepted that she was going to die. She even reached the point where she *wanted* to die.

"I'll call Holly," Raj said.

"I'm dying," she said.

"You're not dying," he said. Then she opened her mouth and screamed, and his eyes got round, and he called Holly.

Later, Holly said it was not an ordinary birth. "I think something's happening here," she said, mysteriously. Tamara was studying her baby, trying to decide who the father was. After several minutes of intense scrutiny, she asked, "Who do you think he looks like?"

Holly looked down at the baby, then at Tamara.

She knows, Tamara thought. *How could she?*

But Holly did not reach into her bag of birthing supplies to bring out a large scarlet letter. Instead, she left without addressing the question.

He *did* have blue eyes, but lots of babies do. His hair was dark, his skin was pink, and his body was an amazing, intricate, perfect blessing. After all those horrible dreams, and the months of guilt, and most especially the horrible pain of birth, Tamara felt blessed. In the end it didn't matter who the father was. Well, it *mattered,* of course, but also, it didn't. The only thing that *really* mattered was the baby.

Tamara thought she knew how she'd feel about her first child: protective, loving, proud. She had not been prepared to feel the way she did. In fact, she would say she had underestimated the power of the love she would feel for this little boy as much as she'd underestimated the pain of his birth.

It was three days later, after Raj had gone to the Becksworth airport to pick up her parents, when Tamara discovered the tiny sharp wings protruding from her baby's back. By then she already loved him more than she had ever loved anyone or anything else. Her love was monstrous. When she saw the wings, she turned him over and stared into those deep eyes of his and said, "Nobody is ever going to know, little one."

When Raj came home with her parents and their frightening amount of luggage, he kissed her on the cheek and said, "Everything okay?" She nodded. Later, when she had time to consider the disturbing events that followed, she pinned her ruin to that moment. The "thing she'd done with the stranger," as she'd come to think of it, had been wrong, but she could no longer wish it away without wishing away her child.

No, what had sealed her fate was that moment when she decided to lie to her husband about the baby's wings. It was no longer the three of them against the world, but mother and child against everyone else.

So many women were pregnant Shreve started a prenatal yoga class. "Something in the water," they'd say, or "Who's *your* milkman?"

Emily and Shreve thought they shared the biggest joke of all. Emily liked to say that they were "fuck-related," though Shreve found this crude. They could not agree on what had happened to them. Emily thought Jeffrey was a jerk, while Shreve thought he was some sort of holy man.

"I can't believe you think that," Emily said. "Saints don't have sex."

"Not a saint," Shreve said. "A yogi. And they do."

"Oh, come on! He was just a man. He was just like other men."

Shreve sighed, apparently remembering something wonderful beyond words.

This, of course, stressed Emily out. Did Shreve have better sex with him than Emily did? Was he gentler? *Rougher?* Had something profound happened between those two? Was he more *attracted* to Shreve? Was Shreve better at sex than Emily was?

She suggested that, in the interest of peace, they stop talking about it, and Shreve agreed.

Agreeing to disagree on the nature of what occurred with Jeffrey had been the first big test of their friendship. The next big test happened later.

Emily discovered her baby's small, sharp, featherless wings on June fifth, while changing Gabriel into one of his cute little baseball outfits (Red

Sox, of course). She watched in amazement as the tiny wings unfolded and folded shut again, drawn into his back. She touched the spot, certain she'd imagined the wings, a weird hallucination. (Maybe she'd just never gotten to that point in the pregnancy books.) She almost convinced herself that was what had happened, when, with a burp, the wings appeared once more. Emily reached to touch one. The next thing she knew, she was walking down the street with Gabriel secured in his Snugli against her chest. She patted the baby's back, but didn't feel anything unusual.

At that exact moment, Shreve was saying to her baby, Michael, "You're going to meet your half brother today." She believed Jeffrey had been some kind of an angel sent to her by her dead fiancé. She wasn't sure *why* her dead fiancé had sent the angel to Emily also, except that it gave her son a brother . . . and that was a very good reason, the more she thought about it.

Michael had blue eyes, a remarkable head of dark curls, and two dimples. His pink flesh was already filling out, losing that newborn look. He had a round face and a round body, round hands, almost round feet, and a little tiny round penis. When Shreve turned him over to admire the beautiful symmetry of his little round butt, she watched, in amazement, as two wings blossomed from his back.

"I *knew* it," she said.

She wanted to investigate the wings, but Emily would be there any minute, so Shreve hurriedly dressed Michael in a pink romper (she didn't believe in the certain-colors-for-certain-genders thing) and wrapped him in the yellow blanket Emily had given her. It was rather warm in the house for a blanket, but Shreve thought it the best protection against any revelation of his wings.

Right then, the doorbell rang. "Hellooo," Emily called, in a soft singsong voice. "Is there a mommy home?"

"Come in," Shreve singsonged back, walking to the door with Michael in her arms.

"He's beautiful," Emily said. "He looks a lot like his brother."

"Oh, let me see."

"He just fell asleep. I don't want to wake him."

"Okay," Shreve said, realizing that she had no idea what kind of mother Emily would be. "Well, come in. I'll make some tea."

The first time Emily had seen Shreve's tiny kitchen—which was painted blue, yellow, and red—she thought it quite strange, but she had grown to like the cozy space. She sat at the small wooden table while Shreve prepared the teakettle and teapot, all while holding Michael.

"You look completely comfortable," Emily said. "You probably gave birth like it was nothing."

Shreve couldn't even smile the memory away. She turned to her friend with an expression of horror. "No. It was terrible."

"Me too," Emily said.

"I mean, I expected pain, but it was—"

"I know, I know," Emily said, so loud she woke up Gabriel. She didn't move towards unstrapping the Snugli; but remained seated, jiggling her knees while the baby cried harder.

Shreve did not like to judge, but the thought occurred to her that Emily might not be very good at this mothering thing. "We could go in the living room," Shreve said. "Lay them down on the blanket and introduce them to each other."

"Sometimes he cries like this," Emily heard herself saying, stupidly.

Shreve thought that even the way Emily tried to soothe her baby, like a police officer patting down a suspect, proved that not all women are natural mothers.

The teakettle whistled and Michael joined in the crying. Shreve, laughing, turned to take the kettle off the burner.

"Okay," Emily said over her baby's wailing. "Let's go in the living room."

It was warm enough that Shreve had opened the windows. The chakra wind chimes hanging outside were silent in the still air. Shreve realized she wouldn't be able to justify laying Michael down wrapped in a blanket. Instead, she got the little carrier seat one of her yoga students had given her.

At the time, Shreve had not expected to ever use the thing. She intended to raise her child without ever making his body conform to the unnatural rigidity of plastic. Now Shreve placed the carrier at the edge of the blanket on the floor. She set Michael—who had already stopped crying—into it, and adjusted the straps. Emily could see his beautiful face and perfect little body, but there was no danger of exposing his wings.

"Oh," Emily said. "I thought we were going to lay them down together."

"I'll get the tea. If he gets fussy, just leave him there, okay?"

Emily unfastened the Snugli and took Gabriel out. He looked at her with those intense blue eyes of his. She patted his back, and he started to make small noises. "Shhh, it's okay," she cooed. "Mommy's just checking." Satisfied, she laid him on the blanket in the sun, facing Michael.

Immediately the two babies grinned at each other.

"Shreve," Emily called, "come quick. You have to see this!"

Shreve ran into the room. "I told you not to touch him," she said, stopping short when she saw that Michael remained in the carrier.

Emily decided to forgive Shreve's odd behavior. She pointed at the brothers. "Look," she said, "it's like they recognize each other."

"I can't believe he can do that already," Shreve said.

"What?"

"Lift his head up like that."

"Oh, yeah," Emily shrugged. "He's really strong."

"Look at them," Shreve said.

"It's like they're old friends."

Shreve walked back to the kitchen and returned with the tray, which she set on the table next to the futon. She poured a cup for each of them. Emily sipped her tea, still focused on her baby's back. That's when she remembered that there had been a paper mill in Voorhisville, years ago. She'd heard about it once, she couldn't remember where. Maybe there were chemicals in Voorhisville, in the soil, or perhaps in the water. "Have you ever heard anything bad about the city water?" she asked.

"Oh, I use bottled water," Shreve said. "He's beautiful. Have you thought of a name yet?"

"Gabriel."

"Like the angel?"

"I guess it's old-fashioned."

"I like it," Shreve said, but was thinking, *Does she know something? Is she trying to trick me?* "Why'd you choose it?"

Emily shrugged.

The two women sat sipping their tea and staring glumly at their beautiful children, Michael and Gabriel, who continued to coo and gurgle, occasionally even thrusting little fists in the other's direction, as though waving.

"Emily?" Shreve asked.

"Uh-huh?"

"Do you believe in miracles?"

"Now I do," Emily said. "You know, I've been thinking. Let's say that we found out there was some kind of chemical, oh, in the soil, or something—you know, from the paper mill, for instance. Let's say it was doing something to the people in Voorhisville. Would we call it a miracle? You know, if it was a chemical reaction or something? I mean even if what happened was, well, miraculous? Or would we call it a disaster?"

"What are you talking about?" Shreve asked.

"Crazy thoughts, you know. I guess from the hormones."

Shreve nodded. "Well, you know what they say."

"What?"

"God works in mysterious ways."

"Oh," Emily said. "That. Yeah. I guess."

The two mothers sat on the futon, sipping green tea and watching their babies. The sun poured into the room, refracted by the chakra wind chimes.

The babies cooed and gurgled and waved at each other. Shreve took a deep breath. “Do you smell that?”

Emily nodded. “Sylvia's roses,” she said. “They're brilliant this year. Hey, did you know she's pregnant?”

“Maybe there *is* something in the soil.”

“I think maybe so,” Emily agreed.

On that day, it was the closest they came to telling each other the truth.

Theresa Ratcher had joined the library book club with her daughter Elli right after her fifteenth birthday. They left the house at 5:20 p.m. with the car windows rolled down, because the Chevy didn't have air-conditioning. Elli sat in the front seat, leaning against the door, which Theresa had told her a million times not to do, in case it popped open. Theresa drove with one elbow sticking out the window, the hot air blowing strands of hair out of her ponytail. Elli had been humming the same melody all week. Theresa reached to turn on the radio, but thought better of it and pretended to wipe a smudge off the dashboard instead. She knew they would just have an argument about what station to listen to. The news was depressing these days.

“Maybe you could think of something else to hum?”

Elli turned, her mouth hanging open, a pink oval.

“You've been on that same song for a while.”

“Sorry,” Elli said, her tone indicating otherwise.

“I like to hear you hum,” Theresa lied. “It's just, a change of tune would be nice.”

Elli reached over and snapped on the radio. Immediately the car was filled with static and noise, until she finally settled on something loud and talky.

Theresa glanced at her daughter. Did she really *like* this sort of “music”? This fuck-you and booty-this and booty-that groove-thing stuff? It was hard to tell. Elli sat slumped against the car door, staring blankly ahead.

Theresa glanced at her pretty daughter leaning both arms on the open window's ledge, as though trying to get as far away from her mother as possible. She resisted the urge to tell Elli to make sure her head and arms weren't too far outside the car; this was the sort of stuff that deepened the wedge between them. Still, Theresa argued with herself, she *had* heard that story about the two young men driving home after a night of drinking, the passenger, his head hanging out the window, hollering drunken nonsense one minute and the next—whoosh, decapitated by a guide wire. “Stick your head back in the car this instant.”

Elli gave her one of those you're-ruining-my-life looks that Theresa hated.

“I just don't want you getting your head chopped off.”

“This isn't Iraq,” Elli said.

"What?"

"Nothing. I was making a joke."

"It's not funny. That's not funny at all." Theresa glanced at her daughter, hunched against the door, arm crooked, elbow hanging out the window. "Billy Melvern died over there. The Baylors' daughter is leaving in a week."

"It was Afghanistan."

"What?"

"Billy Melvern didn't die in Iraq. It was Afghanistan."

"Still," Theresa said.

Elli sighed.

Theresa snapped off the radio. Elli snickered, loudly. They drove the rest of the way to Voorhisville in silence.

What was it about him? Later, Theresa would spend many hours trying to name the thing that made Jeffrey so attractive. He arrived late, and, with a nod towards the moderator, sat down. That was it. He sat there, nodding, occasionally recrossing his legs as they talked about Faulkner, Hemingway, Shakespeare, and Woolf.

Theresa felt like she was in way over her head. She thought this would be like Oprah's Book Club. Well, before Oprah started doing classics. To Theresa's amazement, Elli was talking about one of Shakespeare's plays. That's the first time the stranger spoke. He said, "We are such stuff as dreams are made on," and Elli smiled.

It was just a *smile*. There was nothing extraordinary about it. Well, other than that Elli had smiled. Theresa didn't give it another thought after that. Certainly she hadn't thought it *meant* anything.

Afterwards, when they were trying to decide if they would all go out for coffee, Mickey Freedman showed up and invited Elli to spend the night. "Are you *sure* it's okay with your mother?" (Theresa was perpetually suspicious of Mickey Freedman who, though only Elli's age, always acted so *confident*.)

"Yeah, it's no problem," Mickey said. "You wanna call her?"

Theresa considered the small purple phone the girl dug out of her backpack. The truth was, Theresa had no idea how to use these portable devices. She turned to Elli, who was chewing gum as though it was a competitive event. "Well, have a good time," Theresa said, trying to sound breezy, fun.

The girls didn't wait a second. They were gone, leaving the scent of gum, as well as something Theresa only noticed after the fact: a worrisomely smoky scent, wafting in the air behind them.

At that point, Theresa discovered everyone had left without her. There were only two places in Voorhisville where a book group could meet for coffee and conversation: The Fry Shack, out on the highway, or Lucy's, which was a coffee shop in the pre-Starbucks sense of the word—a diner, really; though Lucy was fairly accommodating of the new fashion for only ordering coffee, as long as it was during off hours. Theresa walked out of the library and took a deep breath.

"Smells nice, doesn't it?" the stranger said.

He was standing by the side of the building. Almost as though he'd been waiting.

Theresa nodded.

"Mind if I join you?"

What could she do? She couldn't be rude, could she? He seemed perfectly nice, it was still light out, and it was *Voorhisville*, for God's sake. What bad thing could possibly happen here?

"I'm not going to Lucy's," Theresa said, turning away from him.

"Neither am I," he said, and fell in step beside her.

What had it been; what had it meant? Over and over again as the leaves fell to the dry flameless burn of that season, Theresa Ratcher asked herself these questions, as though if she asked enough, or in the right mental tone, the answer would appear. What had it been; what had it meant? As leaves fell in golden spiral swirls, on autumn days that smelled like apples. What had it been; what had it meant? As ghosts and vampires and dead cheerleaders carried treat bags and plastic jack-o'-lanterns through town—Theresa had forgotten what day it was—she returned home to find her husband in the living room watching *The Godfather* again, and she stood in the kitchen and stared out at the lonely unbroken dark.

What had it been; what had it meant? When she said, "I'm pregnant," and her husband looked at her and said, "Are you kidding?" and she said, "No," and he said, "This is going to be expensive," and then, "Wait, I'm sorry, it's just . . . are you happy?" and she had shrugged and gone to the kitchen and looked out the window at the lonely dark fields of broken corn.

What had it been; what had it meant? Standing in the frozen yard, snowflakes falling, swirling around her and then suddenly gone, leaving a cold ray of sun and the feeling in her body as though tortured by her bones.

What had it been; what had it meant? Opening the door to Elli's bedroom, and seeing her standing there, naked, and realizing that she had not merely been gaining weight. "I'm your mother. Why didn't you tell me?" Theresa asked. "I hate you," Elli screamed, trying to cover her distended belly with a towel.

—

Elli

We are running out of the library, giggling because we are free! I see the guy from the library, not the old one with the tie, but the cute one with the eyes like Eminem. He smiles at me and I smile at him and Mickey goes all nuts and says, "Who is that?" and I just shrug. We are walking down the street and Mickey says, "The graveyard," and I go, "What?" and she says, "Old Batface'll tell my folks if we have a party or anything, but I know where my dad hides his peppermint schnapps. Let's go home and make hot chocolate with peppermint schnapps and go to the graveyard. You're not scared, are you?"

"I'm not afraid of ghosts," I say. "It's real people that freak me out. What if Batface sees us leave?"

"She watches *Seinfeld* all night long. We'll go out the back door."

So we walk down the street to Mickey's house and that line keeps going through my head: "We are such stuff as dreams are made on." I feel like I am in a dream, like I have a body but I don't feel inside it, like we are surrounded by fireflies, even though it's light out, like the sky is filled with twinkling; and I feel free. Free from my mom with all her fears and rules and that depressed way of hers, and free from Dad with his stupid jokes, and free from the farm with its shitty smell and the silence except for all the birds and bugs.

Mickey says, "Who should we invite?"

"Where's your brother?" I ask. "Isn't he supposed to be watching you?"

"Vin's got one goal between today and Sunday night, when my parents get back, and that's to get into Jessica's pants. He doesn't care what I do, as long as I don't get in his way."

Sure enough, when we open the door, we see a purse and two wineglasses. Upstairs, there is the sound of pounding, and Mickey looks at me and says, "Do you know what that is?" I shake my head. *(We are such stuff as dreams are made on.)* "He's doing her," she says and we giggle until we are bent over. Then Mickey opens cupboards and says, "Here, make the hot chocolate. I'll be right back."

I fill the teakettle with water and put it on the burner and think, *What are we doing, why are we doing this?* Then Mickey is back, talking on the phone, saying, "Yeah, all right." Through the window I can see right into Mrs. Wexel's living room where she's sitting in a chair in front of the TV, and in the TV is tiny Jerry Seinfeld saying something to tiny Elaine, and even from all this distance I think how big their teeth are. Mickey puts the teakettle on and says, "They're going to meet us there."

We are such stuff as dreams are made on.

I pour hot water into the thermos and the light begins to fade and we leave out the back door, cutting across driveways and yards until we are on the road walking past the crooked house with the roses that smell so sweet, going up the hill to the graveyard, which is glowing. Mickey says, "You're sure you're not afraid?"

I say, "We are such stuff as dreams are made on."

"Did you make that up?"

Before I can answer, Larry is standing there and Mickey says, "Where's Ryan? Where are the guys?" Larry says, "He couldn't come. Nobody could come." He looks at me and nods and we trudge up the hill, weaving through the graves, past the angel, back past where all the dead babies are buried. We spread out the blanket and drink hot chocolate with peppermint schnapps. I feel like one of those body diagrams in science class. I picture a red line spreading to my lungs and my heart and into my stomach as the hot liquid goes down, and I think, *We are such stuff as dreams are made on.* The fireflies are blinking around the tombstones and in the sky, which is sort of purple, and that is when I realize Mickey and Larry are totally making out, and just then she opens her eyes and says, "Elli, would you mind?" So I get up and walk away, weaving through the headstones and the baby toys, the stuffed animals on the graves. I head up the hill to where the angel is, and that's when I see him sitting there, and he smiles at me, just like he did at the library, and I am thinking, *We are such stuff as dreams are made on*, and I must have said it out loud because he goes, "Yes."

I thought I saw a light shining out of him, like a halo, but let's face it, I was wasted and everything was sort of glowing—even the graves were glowing. He didn't try to talk to me and he didn't ask me to come over, I just did. He didn't ask me to sit down beside him, but I did, and he told me I had beautiful bones: "Slender, but not sharp." I never saw wings, but I thought I felt them, deep inside me. He smelled like apples, and when I started crying, he whispered over and over again, *We are such stuff as dreams are made on*. At least, I think he did.

I passed out, until Mickey was standing over me going, "Jesus Christ, Elli, I thought you were dead or something. Why didn't you answer me?"

"Did you do it?" I asked.

"He didn't bring any condoms."

"But you still did it, right?"

"What are you, nuts? I don't wanna get AIDS or something."

"Larry isn't going to give you AIDS."

"Come on, I feel sick. Let's go home. You all right?"

"I had the strangest dream."

She was already walking down the hill, the blanket trailing from her arms, dragging on the ground. I looked up at the angel and said, "Hello? Are you here?"

"Shut up, Elli. Someone's going to call the cops."

I felt like a ghost walking out of the graveyard. "Hey, Mickey," I said, "it's like we're ghosts coming back to life."

"Just shut up," Mickey said.

Dogs barked and lights came on the whole way back to her house, where the two wineglasses were still there but the purse was gone. Mickey dropped the blanket on the floor and said, "I am so wasted."

I said, "Nobody even knows we are here."

Mickey rested her hand on my shoulder and said, "Maybe you shouldn't drink so much."

I followed her up the stairs into her room where we went to bed without changing our clothes. It wasn't long before Mickey was snoring and I just lay there blinking in the dark, and it kept repeating in my head, over and over again: *We are such stuff as dreams are made on*. I fell asleep thinking it and I woke up thinking it and I'm still thinking it and I just keep wondering, *Is any of this real?*

Tamara

June in Voorhisville. The sun rises over the houses, the library, Lucy's Diner, the yoga studio, the drugstore, the fields of future corn and wheat, the tiny buds of roses, the silent streets. Pink crab apple petals part for honeybees; tulips gasp their last, red throats to the sun; butterflies flit over dandelions; and the grass is lit upon by tiny white moths, destined to burn their wings against streetlamps.

The mothers greet the day with tired eyes. So soon? It isn't possible. The babies are crying. Again. The mothers are filled with great love, and also something else. Who knew someone so small could eat so much!

Cathy Vecker complains to her mother and grandmother, who encourage her to consider bottle feeding. "Then we can hire a summer girl," her mother says.

Jan Morris calls the real estate office where she works and breaks down in tears to the young receptionist there, who calls her own mother, who shows up at Jan's an hour later with two Styrofoam cups of bitter tea, bagels from Lucy's, and a pamphlet entitled "Birthing Darkness: What Every Woman Should Know about Post-Partum Depression" as well as—inexplicably—Dr. Phil's weight loss book.

Sylvia takes her son into the garden, where she sits in the twig chair and thinks how tired her husband was before he died, and how she feels tired like that now, except alive. She cries onto her son's shoulders.

Lara dresses her baby in a yellow onesie, checking his back several times, convincing herself that the strange thing she saw had been a hallucination.

She is very tired. She can't believe how much she has to arrange just to walk down the street to her studio. She feels like she's packing for a week: diapers, socks, change of clothes, nursing blankets, an extra bra, a clean shirt. All while the baby lies there, watching.

The mothers of Voorhisville are being watched. Rumors have begun to circulate about strange births and malformed babies, though the gossip seems unfounded. Sure, the mothers look exhausted, but there's nothing unusual about that. Yes, they describe the pains of birth as severe, but women have always said so. The only strange thing about the babies, despite what Brian and Francis think they saw, despite the rumors that nurse spreads all the way in Becksworth, is that they are all boys, and they are all beautiful.

Far from the rumors of town, out past the canning factory, over the hill behind the site of the old paper mill, Theresa Ratcher stands in her pantry, staring at glass jars filled with jelly. She means to be assessing what remains from the winter; instead, she is mesmerized by the colors. She stands, resting her hands on her great belly, as though beholding something sacred; certainly something more spectacular than strawberry, jalapeno, or yellow-tomato jelly. Her husband is in the field. She has no idea where Elli is. Theresa doesn't like to think about Elli, and she doesn't like to think about why she doesn't like to think about her. For a moment, Elli, with her long limbs and protruding belly, stands in Theresa's mind. She shakes her head and concentrates on the jars before her.

Elli is in the barn. She has no idea why. They don't have any animals except for cats and mice. But Elli likes it in the barn. She finds it a peaceful place, her dad out in the fields, her mom somewhere else. These days, Elli likes to be far from her mother, because even when they are in different rooms, she can feel the hate. Elli stands in the middle of the barn, beneath the beams, which her father still obsesses about. She is biting her fingernail when the sharp pain drives her to the ground. She lets out a scream, which rises past the spiderwebs and silent, hanging blobs of sleeping bats, out the cracks and holes in the roof, where it mingles with Theresa's scream as she falls to the ground in the pantry, knocking over several jars that shatter on the floor—an explosion of red goo, which her husband, when he returns for supper, assumes is blood. He runs to get the phone, but she screams at him to help, so he kneels before her in the glass and fruit, and she screams the head and shoulders out. Later, she tells him it's jelly. He licks a finger but it tastes like blood. He helps her upstairs and tucks her into bed, the baby in the crib.

He looks everywhere for Elli, finally going to the barn where he barely sees her in the evening light. She is lying on the ground, surrounded by pools of jelly (he thinks, before he realizes, no, that can't be right). She looks at him with wild eyes, like his 4-H horse all those years ago when she broke her leg, and she cries. "Daddy? It's dead."

That's when he notices the small shape beside her. As he leans closer, she says, "Careful. They hurt." He doesn't know what she means until he sees the tiny bat wings spread across the small back. But that can't be right. He looks down at his daughter, horrified. "It's some kind of freak," she weeps. "Just get rid of it."

He picks the creature up, and only then notices its barely perceptible breathing. "Don't touch the wings," she says. He looks at her, his little girl who gave birth to such a thing. *Now she can get on with her life.*

"Get it out of here," she says.

He takes the shovel and walks out of the barn, bats flying overhead. Curiosity gets the best of him, and he touches the wings. The next thing he knows, he is standing in the cornfield, beneath the cold light of the moon, staring at his dark house, listening to screams. He looks around in confusion but he can't find the creature, or the shovel, or any sign that the ground has been turned. He runs to the barn.

He finds Elli lying on the ground, surrounded by wild cats, and screaming. He hears a noise behind him, the snapping of gravel, and turns to see Theresa slowly making her way towards them. "Go back. Just go back in the house," he shouts. She stops, washed with white moonglow like a ghost. "You'll be in the way. Call nine-one-one."

Slowly, Theresa turns and walks towards the house.

He reaches between Elli's legs, relieved to feel a crown of head there. "It's all right. You're just having another one."

"I'm dying!" she screams.

"Push," he says, with no real idea if this is the right thing to do or not; he just wants it out. "Push, Elli."

She screams and bears down. He feels the head and shoulders. Squinting in the dark, he barely sees the cord. He's already forming a plan for suffocation, if it's like the other, but what comes out is a perfect baby boy that he tries to hand to Elli. She says she doesn't want it. He is pleading with her when the EMTs arrive. They help all three of them into the house, where Theresa sits in the dark living room, cradling her baby.

"Everything all right?" she asks.

Elli opens her mouth, but Pete speaks first. "Everything's fine," he says. "A boy."

"And a freak," Elli says.

"What?" Theresa speaks to Elli's back as she walks up the stairs, leaving the baby with the EMT who carried him inside. He hands the baby to Pete Ratcher, who thanks him for coming all that way "for nothing." He says it's his job, and not to worry, but Pete Ratcher watches the man walk down the driveway to the ambulance, shaking his head like a man who just received terrible news. Pete searches the sky for a long time before he realizes what he's looking for. "I have to take care of something," he says, and steps forward as though to hand the baby to Theresa.

She looks at him like he's nuts. "Give him to Elli. She's his mother."

He walks up the dark stairs and enters his daughter's room. "Elli? Honey?"

"Go away."

"I have to check on something. You know, the other one."

"Freak."

"Elli, these things happen. It's not your fault. And look, you have this one."

"I don't want him."

"God damn it, Elli."

He thinks that, all in all, he's handled everything well. It's been a hell of a night. He tries once more for a calm tone. "I have to go check on something. I'm going to put your baby right here, in the crib, but if he cries, you have to take care of him. You have to. Your mother is tired. Do you hear me, Elli?"

Elli mumbles something, which he takes for assent. He places the baby in the crib. It squirms, and he rubs its back. Only then does it occur to him that the baby is not diapered or clothed, not even *washed*, but still coated in the bloody slime of birth. He picks it up, and by the moonlight finds what he needs on the shelves of the changing table (a gift from Elli's high school teachers). He cleans the baby with several hand wipes, tossing them towards the plastic trash can, not troubling to make sure any of them actually land inside. Finally, he diapers the baby, wrapping him tightly in a clean blanket and setting him in the crib. "Elli." She doesn't respond. "If he cries you have to take care of him. You have to feed him."

"I want Mom."

He realizes Elli doesn't understand that Theresa has given birth today too. He tells her this, saying, "You have a brother, a little baby brother. Your mom is too tired to help you right now."

When he closes the door, Elli gets up and walks across the room to stand at the window. After a minute, she sees him walking towards the cornfield. *What could he be doing out there?* she wonders. She turns away, shuffling like an old woman. She stands over the crib and touches the flat of the baby's back, places her hand on his soft cap of hair, then reaches in and picks him up. He cries softly. She says, "There, there." She jiggles him gently on her shoulder, but the soft cry turns into a wail. *Why are you crying?* she thinks. *I'm not going to hurt you.*

What is she supposed to do? She takes it back to bed with her, where she sits against the wall, jiggling it, saying, "There, there," over and over again, until she finally gets the idea of feeding it. She unbuttons her shirt and smashes its face against her breast. It cries and wiggles in her arms before latching on to her nipple and sucking until he finally falls asleep.

She would like to sleep with him, but she remembers hearing how mothers sometimes squash their babies by mistake. She thinks this is probably an exaggeration, but she isn't sure.

Eyes half-closed, she walks across the room, lays the baby in the crib, and shuffles back to bed. The next thing she knows, her mother is in the room in her nightgown, standing over the crib, and the baby is crying.

"Mom?"

"You have to feed him," Theresa says. "You can't just let him cry."

"I didn't hear it," Elli says.

"Him."

"What?"

"You didn't hear him, not it. You have to take care of this, Elli. I'm busy with your brother." Theresa picks the baby up and brings him to her. "Do you know where your father is?"

"He said he had to go take care of something."

"You have to feed him, Elli."

"In the cornfield. I *know*. Could I have some privacy, here?"

"I don't want to have to keep getting up for your baby, too."

"I didn't hear him. I'm *sorry*."

"You're going to *have* to hear him," Theresa says. "What's he doing in the cornfield?"

But Elli doesn't answer. She's turned her back and is unbuttoning her shirt.

"Can you *hear* me?" Theresa asks.

"I don't know what he's doing in the cornfield. It's *Dad*, all right?" She pokes her nipple into the baby's mouth.

Theresa walks out of her daughter's room, trying to stay calm, though she feels like screaming. She hears the baby crying and turns back, but Elli, who gives her a look as though she knew her mother had plotted this surprise return just to look at Elli's bare breasts, is nursing him. It takes a few seconds before Theresa realizes the crying is coming from her own baby. Suddenly life has gotten so strange: her daughter nursing a baby whose father she won't name; her husband out in the cornfield in the middle of the night; her own baby, whose lineage is uncertain, crying again, though it seems like only minutes since she fed him.

Voorhisville in June: those long hot nights of weeping and wailing, diaper changing and feeding, those long days of exhaustion and weeping, wailing, diapering, and feeding.

Sylvia's roses grow limp from lack of care and—just as some dying people glow near the end—emit the *sweetest* odor. The scent is *too* sweet, and it's too *strong*. Everywhere the mothers go, it's like following in the footsteps of a woman with too much perfume on.

Emily continues baking, though she burns things now, the scorched scent mingling with the heavy perfume of roses and jasmine incense, which Shreve sets on a windowsill of the yoga studio.

"I have to do *something*," she says, when the mailman comments on it. "Have you noticed how smelly it is in Voorhisville lately?"

The mailman has noticed that all the mothers, women who had seemed perfectly reasonable just last year, are suddenly strange. He's just a mailman; it isn't really for him to say. But if he were to say, he'd say, *Something strange is happening to the mothers of Voorhisville.*

Maddy Melvern doesn't know any different; she thinks it's always been this way. She stares at her son, lying on a blanket under a tree in the park. She looks away for *one second* to watch the mailman walk past—not that there's anything interesting about him, because there isn't, but that just shows how bored she is—and when she turns back to JoJo, he's hovering over the blanket, six inches off the ground; flying. She holds him against her chest, frantic to see if anyone's noticed, but the park is filled with mothers holding infants, or bent over strollers, tightening straps. Everyone is too distracted to notice Maddy and her flying baby. "Holy shit, JoJo," she whispers, "you have to be careful with this stuff." Maddy isn't sure what would happen if anyone were to find out about JoJo's wings, but she's fairly certain it wouldn't be good. Even pressed against her chest as he is, she can feel them pulsing. She eases him away from her shoulders to get a view of his face.

He's laughing.

He has three dimples and a deep belly laugh. Maddy laughs with him; until suddenly she presses him tight against her heart. "Oh my God, JoJo," she says. "I love you."

Tamara Singh has just secured little Ravi in the stroller—not wanting to hurt him, of course, but making sure the straps are tight enough to keep him from flying—when she sees Maddy Melvern laughing with her baby. It just goes to show, Tamara thinks, *that you never can tell.* Who would have guessed that the teenage unwed mother, the girl who'd done everything wrong, could be so happy, while Tamara, who'd done only one single wrong thing (the illicit sex thing), would be so miserable?

What is love? Tamara thinks as she stares at little Ravi, crying again, hungry for more. She parks the stroller by a bench and unbuttons her blouse. *Well, this is love,* she thinks—sitting there in the park, filling his hunger, holding down his pulsing wings; watching the ducks and the clouds and the other mothers (it certainly seems like there are a lot of newborns this summer) and thinking, *I would die to protect you; I would kill anyone who would hurt you*. Then wondering, *Where did that come from?*

But it was true.

The mothers were *lying*. They told each other and their loved ones about wellness visits, but none of the mothers actually took their son to a doctor. Because of the wings. Both pediatricians at St. John's were under the impression that they were losing patients to the other, and each harbored suspicions concerning the guerilla tactics being employed. The lying mothers became obsessed with their sons' health. Each cough or sneeze or runny nose was the source of much guilt. Nobody wanted to kill her child. That was the point, the reason they had stayed away from doctors: it wasn't about putting the babies at *risk*, it was about keeping them safe.

Friends and relatives concluded that the mothers were protective, coddling, suspicious, and overly secretive. The mothers even concluded this about *each other*, never suspecting they harbored the same secret.

"This is impossible," Theresa Ratcher murmurs to herself the first time she sees little Matthew's wings blossoming, like some sort of water flower, while she is bathing him in the sink. She touches one tip; feels the searing proof of hot pain; and the next thing she knows, she is standing in the cornfield. She runs to the house as though it is on fire, tumbles into the kitchen, where Elli sits feeding little Timmy. "Where's Matthew?" Theresa asks. Elli looks at her like she's nuts. Theresa glances at the sink, which is empty and dry.

"Did you lose him?" Elli asks. "How could you lose him?"

"Matthew!" Theresa runs upstairs. He is there, asleep in the crib. She pats his back, gently. It feels flat. Normal.

"What's wrong?" Elli stands in the door, Timmy in her arms. "Mom? Are you all right?"

"I had a bad dream."

"Outside? You fell asleep outside?" Elli asks. "Are you sick?"

Matthew cries. "I'm not sick," Theresa says, unbuttoning her blouse. "Before I forget: When is your doctor's appointment? Did you make that yet? I can't be keeping track of all this anymore."

"Don't worry about it, then," Elli says, walking down the hall to her room; but when she gets there, it smells like diapers, and flies buzz around the window. Still holding Timmy, Elli walks downstairs and onto the porch.

Her dad is in the cornfield with the boys he hired for the summer. They aren't boys Elli knows. They're from Caldore or Wauseega, her dad can't remember which. They come to the house for lunch most days and ignore her. Elli knows why. She walks over to the apple tree and spreads Timmy's blanket on the ground, which is littered with blossoms. She sets him down, then stares at the cornfield, trying to force herself to see it as a field, and not a cemetery. Was her dad nuts? Why'd he bury it out *there? Did he really think she'd be able to eat the corn this year?* Elli shakes her head. She looks at Timmy, who lies there grinning. "What's so funny?" she says, meanly, and then feels bad for it. It is just so hot, and she is so tired. Between the baby eating all the time, and the bad dreams she has of the other one flying into her room and hovering over her bed, she's exhausted.

She wakes with a dark shadow standing over her. Elli turns to the empty blanket; then, in a panic, looks up at Theresa, who is standing there, holding Timmy. "You can't do things like this anymore, Elli," she says. "You can't just forget about him. He's a *baby*."

"I didn't forget about him."

"Look." Theresa turns Timmy so that Elli can see his pink face. "He got sunburned." Elli looks down at her knees. She doesn't want to cry. Theresa leans down to hand Timmy to her. "I know this is hard, but—"

"Mom, there's something I have to tell you."

Theresa is not in the mood for teenage confessions. *Why is Elli doing this now?*

"There was another one, Mom."

"What do you mean? Another boy? Is that why you won't say who the father is?"

"No. Mom, I mean, another baby. I had two. Dad doesn't want me to say, 'cause, well, he was a freak, and he died. Dad buried him in the cornfield."

"What do you mean he was a freak?"

"Please don't tell anyone."

"Sweetie, I—"

"He had wings, okay?"

"Who had wings?"

"The other one. The one that died. Do you think it was something I did?"

Theresa cannot form a logical connection between her daughter's revelation and her own son's wings. Several things occur to her, but not even for a second does she consider that she might have shared a lover with her fifteen-year-old daughter. (That notion comes later, with disastrous results.) Instead, she thinks of the paper mill, or some kind of terrorist attack on their well, things like that.

"You didn't do anything wrong," Theresa says, "except have unprotected sex." (Feeling like a hypocrite for saying it.) "And if every woman who did that was punished with a dead baby, there wouldn't be anyone living at all."

"But it wasn't just dead, Mom. It had *wings*."

Theresa glances at the house, where she'd left Matthew resting in his crib. "How do we know that wasn't some kind of miracle? How do we know it was a sign of something bad happening, rather than something good?"

Elli sighs. "It's just a feeling I get. Remember 'We are the stuff that dreams are made on'?"

"What about it?" Theresa says, feeling tense at the topic hovering too close to the library, and Jeffrey.

"I don't know," Elli says. "It's just something I think of sometimes."

Theresa knows she's been distracted lately, perhaps not as supportive of Elli as she would have liked. She glances at the house again, trying to decide if Matthew could be flying through the rooms, banging into walls and ceilings. She doesn't know anything about raising a child with wings, except that it is hard enough to raise one without them.

"Try to think of it as a good thing, okay?"

Elli shrugs.

"Will you at least try?"

For three days, Elli tries to convince herself that her first baby was not a freak or a punishment for something she'd done, but a sign of something *good*. She almost convinces herself of it. But on the third day, while she has Timmy on the changing table, she watches in horror as dark wings sprout from his back.

That's when she knows. The stranger she had sex with was the devil. That explains everything. It even explains why she *did* it with him. She looks into Timmy's beautiful blue eyes. For once, he isn't crying. In fact, he is smiling.

Evil, Elli thinks, *can trick you.* She works the saliva in her mouth and spits. Timmy's face goes through a metamorphosis of expressions, as if trying to decide which one to employ—a slight smile, raised eyebrows, trembling lips—all while closely watching Elli. She begins to cry. He opens his mouth wide and joins her, the glop of phlegm dripping down his forehead. Elli wipes it with the blanket. "Oh, baby, I'm so sorry," she says, picking him up.

That's when Theresa walks into the room.

Elli, still crying, looks over the small dark points of her baby's wings at her mother, who puts her hand over her mouth and—turning on her heels—spins out of the room.

Theresa wheels down the hall like a drunken woman, and opens the door to her own room. Matthew lays there, damp curls matted at his forehead, his pretty pink lips pursed near his tiny fist. Gently, she rubs his back and feels the delicate bones there.

"Mom?" Elli stands in the doorway. "You *said* it could be good." Then she sobs and runs out of the room.

Matthew wakes with a wail. Theresa soothes him the best she can as she walks to the rocking chair. Sitting there, Theresa can see all the way out to the three figures working in the field. Matthew sucks at her breast while she stares at the blue sky and gently rocks, asking herself, "What does it mean? What does it mean? What does any of it mean?"

Of all the lying and confused families that summer, perhaps the Ratchers—with their strange convergence of mother, daughter, son, brother, grandson, grandmother, sister, husband, father, and grandfather, all embodied in one small family—were the *most* confused, with the *biggest* web of secrets.

Pete Ratcher came home from his Saturday dart game at Skelley's Bar one hot night, with the news that Maddy Melvern, a year ahead of Elli in school, had given birth and also wasn't divulging the father's name. "What hot shot are these girls protecting?" he asked his wife, who tried to make all the right noises while she fed the little monster (that's how Pete thought of him, though he tried not to) who seemed to be hungry *all the time*.

Theresa tried to talk to Elli about it. "You know, Maddy Melvern had a baby too," she said. Elli rolled her eyes, the baby latching on her breast *again* as her mother stood there, *again* bothering her with ridiculous information (What did she care about *Maddy Melvern*?), when all she wanted was to be free, instead of trapped here with this baby and horrible dreams about that other one rising from the cornfield and flying over the house; trying to find her, to punish her for burying him out there, no better than one of the cats—though, really, it wasn't her fault. It was her dad who did it.

Meanwhile, Pete Ratcher spent more and more nights at Skelley's, because what was he supposed to stay home for? To watch his wife and daughter endlessly feed and rock the crying babies, which neither would let him hold? Like they didn't trust him or something? Christ, what was that about?

The regulars at Skelley's grew used to Pete Ratcher's complaints. The bartenders could wipe the counter, serve drinks, watch TV, and say, "Women these days," at just the right moment in Pete's lament; that's how predictable it was. The regulars were so tired of it they were careful not to sit next to him. That's how, on the night Raj came into Skelley's, blinking against the smoke, he happened to sit right next to Pete, who finally found a sympathetic listener.

Raj nodded and said, "I know, I know. He's my son, too. I *want* to be a part of his life. I *want* to change diapers and take him for walks. I don't understand why she won't let me do those things."

Tamara knew Raj was drinking. Frankly, she was shocked: it was not something she'd imagined he'd fall into. But only a week into this new bad habit of his, he ran into their bedroom to tell her he'd just seen the baby flying. She was able to convince him that he was so drunk he'd been hallucinating. "No, no. I don't drink that *much*," he said.

Tamara went into the nursery, and sure enough, Ravi was floating above the crib, hovering like a giant hummingbird. She had just plucked him to her chest when Raj returned to the room.

"And you get angry at *me* for not letting you hold him more? Look at you. How can I trust that he'd be safe with a father who drinks so much he thinks he sees flying babies?"

"I don't drink *that* much," Raj said. "And all this was happening before I was drinking."

"The baby was flying before you started drinking? Do you really expect me to believe this nonsense?"

"No, no. I mean *us*. We were already fighting about you not letting me near him."

Tamara, who, just a year ago, would never have believed she could hurt her husband, and, only five minutes ago, would have sworn that she'd never hurt her baby for any reason, now pinched Ravi's arm, hard, so that he broke into a loud cry. She turned to attend to his tears as Raj watched, helpless and confused. It was like watching a movie or television: his wife and son in a separate world, with no need of him at all.

The next night, when he came home from Skelley's, his pajamas and a pillow and blankets were on the couch, and the baby was sleeping with Tamara. Raj remembered hearing once about a woman who rolled onto her baby in her sleep and suffocated the newborn. He considered waking Tamara to warn her, but instead, took off his shoes. He didn't bother changing into his pajamas before he lay down on the couch, vowing that tomorrow he wouldn't go to Skelley's. Tomorrow he would meditate and fast. Maybe he would even return to his yoga practice. How had he lost both himself and his marriage so swiftly?

Tamara heard him come home. She heard his breathing when he stood in the bedroom door and watched her. She was only *pretending* to be asleep. She heard him walk away, heard his shoes drop to the floor. Maybe she should tell him, she thought—but was this how he responded to stress? How would he respond to having a baby with wings? No, Tamara decided, she couldn't risk it. She was sure it was the right decision, but nonetheless fell asleep with tears in her eyes.

The tears were still in her eyes when she was awoken by the baby's crying. She brought him to her breast, which silenced him immediately. She fell asleep, but woke up throughout the night to feel the baby suckling. In the morning, she decided it had been her imagination—it was impossible that Ravi had been feeding all night long.

Elli could feel the way her mother was watching her. It was obvious that she did *not* think Timmy's wings were a sign of something good. Elli's dad (oblivious) tried to talk to her. He even bought up the subject of the beams. "Don't go in the barn anymore," he said. "Not until I do something about them."

Elli thought her dad was nuts. What did she care about the stupid *barn beams* when she had this baby with wings to take care of, and another one hunting her? She stared at her dad with his stick-out ears and the creases around his upraised eyebrows. He suddenly seemed like some kind of strange, mutant child himself. Elli shook her head and turned her attention to Timmy, without saying a word.

Theresa, sitting on the couch facing the TV and holding Matthew, observed all this: the way her husband tried to speak to Elli; the way she looked at him, appalled; then turned away as though she could not *bear* to speak to him. Theresa observed all this and she knew.

"I'm going out," Pete said. Neither Elli nor Theresa responded. *When did I become the enemy?* Pete wondered. Sometimes women were like this in the first months after giving birth. He'd *heard* about that. Pete remembered Raj saying, "Sometimes I feel so angry, but then I remember that I love her." Pete stood in the living room and tried to remember how much he loved them. It was actually sort of hard to do. It was hard to *feel* it.

June in Voorhisville. The leaves of oaks and elms and the famous chestnut tree on Main Street grow until the Voorhisville sun filters through a green canopy. Everything, from faces, to flowers, to food, appears tinged with a shade usually associated with alien masks or Halloween witches.

The mothers of Voorhisville are too busy to notice. There are diapers to change, endless feedings, tiny clothes to wash, and constant surveillance.

Cathy Vecker would like nothing better than to hire a nanny or let her mother and grandmother feed the baby, but she can't risk it.

"He's growing so fast," her mother says. "Are you sure he's normal?"

Cathy resists the urge to roll her eyes. "Look at Sylvia Lansmorth's baby," she says. "He was born around the same time as Raven. They're both the same size."

"Well, they say Americans are getting bigger. Are you sure the doctor doesn't want you to put him on a diet?"

As the tiny bumps on Raven's back sprout and flutter, the wings pushing against her hands like they have a will of their own, Cathy runs out the front door, ignoring her mother. "You have to stop," she whispers, though she doesn't expect him to understand. With a thrust as powerful as a man's hands, Raven's wings push against her, tearing through the train-patterned fabric of his little sleeper.

The next thing Cathy knows, she is standing in Sylvia Lansmorth's garden and Sylvia, dressed in something purple and flowing, is glaring at her. "You're standing on my roses," Sylvia says.

"Have you seen my baby?" Cathy looks around, desperately, as though she expects to find Raven perched on a rose petal. *Well, who knows? Who knows what will happen next?*

"Your *baby*?" Sylvia asks. "How old is he?"

"Don't you know me?"

Sylvia shakes her head.

"I've known you my whole life," Cathy says.

Sylvia assumes she is talking to a mentally ill person. It's the only explanation. "Is there someone I can call?"

"We have to call the police." Cathy can't believe how calm she sounds. "I have to tell them everything."

Sylvia doesn't like the sound of that. "I'll call," she says. "You wait here."

Cathy takes a deep breath and almost passes out from the sweet rose scent. "There's something I have to tell you."

"Is this about your baby?"

"I tried to do the right thing. I did."

"Wait here," Sylvia says, glancing back at the house.

"I didn't mean to lose him."

"Of course you didn't."

"He flew right out of my hands."

"He *flew*?"

"You think I'm crazy."

Sylvia shakes her head.

"Of course you do. That's what I would think. Nobody's going to believe me. Unless they see the wings, and if that happens they'll call him a freak. The worst part is"—Cathy begins to cry—"I don't know where he is."

Sylvia puts her arm around Cathy's shoulder. "I believe you," she says. "Did you touch them?" She takes Cathy's hands in her own. "Look, you're all cut up. How did this happen?"

Cathy sniffs loudly. "The wings ripped right through his clothes and cut me when I was trying to hold on to him."

"Well, when this happens with my baby," Sylvia says, "I usually find him in his crib, sound asleep."

"You're just trying to make me feel better."

"No, it's true. But if you tell anyone, I'll deny it. Listen to me, honey: before you get all panicky, what you need to do is go home."

"Go home?"

"Yes. Go home and see if he's in his room."

"My mom and grandmother are there."

"Well, then you better hurry. You don't want them to find him floating over his crib or something, do you?"

Cathy has a stitch in her side by the time she gets home. She runs to the nursery, rushing into the room so loudly that the baby wakes. Cathy picks him up and holds him close. "Oh, I love you, I love you, I love you," she says, over and over again; thinking, *There's another one, there's another baby with wings, you aren't alone in the world, and neither am I.*

She takes off his tattered sleeper, shredded as if by some beast, and tosses it into the trash. The she places a gauze pad on his small back and binds it there with first aid tape.

The mothers of Voorhisville were using gauze and tape, plastic wrap (which caused sweating and a rash), thick layers of clothing, and bubble wrap. What to do about a child with wings? How to cope with the unpredictable thrust of them, the sear of pain, the strange disappearing babies? The flying! How to cope with that? Several mothers (and they are not proud of this) took to devising elaborate rope restraints. It is rumored that at least one mother suffered tragic results from this decision, reported as a crib death, but she is not here with us, so that remains speculation.

Many of the mothers describe the *isolation* of this time as having its own weight. "*I* felt tied down," Elli Ratcher says. "Knowing that my mom had the same problem didn't really help. I mean she was my *mom*, okay? What did she know about *my* life?"

Many of the mothers, when they hear Elli say this, walk towards her, intending to administer a motherly hug or at least pat her on the back, but something in Elli's expression causes them to stop, as though she is radioactive.

Theresa felt alone in the world. All that June *she knew* what Pete did, and tried to convince herself she did not. But it was the only explanation. She *knew*, and she had to do something about it.

Finally, one hot afternoon, she left Matthew with Elli, who said, "Well, okay, but you better hurry back. It's hard enough watching Timmy every second," and walked out to the cornfield, where Pete was working with the boys.

"Is something wrong?" he said. "Is Elli—"

"I *know*," Theresa said, loudly, angrily, as though she had only just figured it out.

"You know *what*?" Pete asked, looking at the boys, a quizzical women-are-going-to-confuse-you look on his face.

"I know what you did."

"Did to who?"

"To Elli."

Pete shook his head. "I don't know what . . . " His voice trailed off as he considered the baby lost in the cornfield. "Do you mean the other one? Is that what you're talking about? It was a freak, Theresa. It had wings, for God's sake."

Theresa dove at Pete with her fists. He ducked and weaved, and finally grabbed her wrists.

"How could you? How could you do such a thing? How could you fuck your own daughter?"

Pete dropped her wrists, stepped back as if struck. He gaped at Theresa, turned to the boys, who gaped at him, then stepped towards his wife. "I never—"

"I want you out! Don't you dare come near us again. I'll kill you. Do you understand me?"

Pete stood there, speechless.

"I don't care if you understand me or not," Theresa said. "You come anywhere near us, and I'll kill you. I don't fucking care if you understand, you monster."

Pete watched Theresa walk away from him, the awkward sway of her hips as she walked over the uneven ground. He turned to the boys, thinking to offer them an explanation of the mental illness some women suffer after childbirth, but neither one looked at him. He stood there until Theresa slammed the door behind her, then followed in her path, stepping slowly through the field, leaving the boys believing they were about to witness a murder.

Pete was a little worried about that as well. But there was no way around it. He had the keys to the Chevy in his pocket, and the Chevy was in the driveway. She didn't expect him to *walk*, did she?

How had this happened? Had Elli accused him of such a thing? Why? Standing by the car, he considered his options. He could go inside and try to straighten this out, or he could leave. The problem was the gun, which they kept in the basement and had only used for shooting squirrels when they infested the attic after all those traps had proven ineffective. It was an old gun. He didn't think Theresa knew how to use it, but maybe she did.

He arrived at Skelley's a great deal earlier than usual, and stayed until closing, at which point he realized he didn't have his wallet.

Doug, the bartender, told him he could pay the next time he came. "But no more drinks until then."

"You don't know of a place I could stay?" Pete asked.

Doug shrugged. "What about that friend of yours, that towelhead? Why don't you stay with him?"

In Pete's state, this seemed a perfectly reasonable suggestion. He reached for his keys, but Doug deftly scooped them up. "I'll take you," he said. "You can get your car in the morning."

Pete had no idea where Raj and Tamara lived, but Doug did. "Everyone in town knows," he said.

Pete slurred his thanks, then weaved up to the house, where he leaned on the bell until Raj opened the door. Tamara stood behind him, wearing a red robe and holding a crying baby.

"My wife kicked me out."

"I wonder why," Tamara said, then turned and walked down the dark hall.

"I don't mean to cause problems."

Raj put his hand on Pete's shoulder. "You look like you could use a drink, my friend."

Over tea, Pete told Raj what Theresa had accused him of.

"You need a lawyer," Raj said.

But by that time, Pete was crying. "I need my family."

Tamara woke up to the baby's crying. It seemed like he had only *just* gone to sleep. Then it stopped. She closed her eyes, but they popped right back open. That's when Raj burst into the room, holding the baby in front of him, extended at arm's length, the baby's wings rising and falling as gentle as breath, the strange man who had arrived in the night right behind Raj.

"He was flying! He was *flying*!" Raj said.

Tamara looked at her husband. "You're drunk."

"Tamara," Raj said, "I am not drunk. And neither are you." He opened his arms. Ravi rose into the air, his wings fully extended. He hovered, then flew higher and higher.

"Catch him," Tamara shouted.

Ravi laughed.

"Ravi Singh, you come down here this instant," Tamara shouted.

Laughing, dangerously close to the ceiling fan.

Tamara screamed. Raj leapt onto the bed and jumped, trying to catch Ravi by the foot. Instead, Raj grazed the baby's heel. That set him into a cartwheel, which luckily landed on the bed. Ravi lay crying, a strange bend to his shoulder, but Tamara kept screaming at the men not to touch him. They watched the dark wings shrivel until they were gone. Only then did Tamara scoop Ravi up, holding him close to her chest.

"I think we need to call the hospital," Raj said. "I think maybe his shoulder is broken."

"Oh, right," Tamara said. "And then what do we do? Tell them he fell from the sky?"

"That's what happened, Tamara. That's the truth."

Tamara looked from Raj to the man beside him. "Who *are* you?"

"Pete Ratcher."

"From the farm out by the old mill?"

Pete nodded.

"If you tell anybody what you saw, I'll kill you."

"Tamara!" Raj turned to Pete. "She doesn't mean it. She's hysterical."

Tamara didn't look hysterical. She looked like she meant it. It was the second murder threat Pete had received in twenty-four hours, and he felt he was becoming something of an expert.

"I'll call the doctor," Raj said.

"No," Tamara said. "I'm taking him in. I'll take him."

"I'll come with you," Raj said. "It's going to be all right. We can handle this, honey."

"Just stay here with your friend." She nodded towards Pete. "We'll talk when I get home. You stay here, okay?"

This was the kindest Tamara had been to Raj in so long that he agreed. "I'll call the doctor and let her know you're coming."

"Please," Tamara said. "She doesn't know you. She knows me. I'll call from the car."

Again, Raj agreed. He even helped pack the baby's bag, not thinking to wonder why Tamara needed so many diapers, so many sleepers, so much *stuff.* He was distracted, he would later tell the television reporter. It never even occurred to him that she was *lying.*

When Tamara left the house, she turned right out of the driveway, but circled around Caster Lane, heading west. Ravi, in his car seat, had stopped crying and looked at her with his beautiful blue eyes, while chewing on a teething ring. Of course he was way too young for teeth, but they were coming in. She'd seen them, and she'd felt them too, when he bit down on her nipple. "Okay, baby. We're going on a road trip, but first we're going to make a little stop at Mr. Ratcher's house. I hear they have a new baby there. Let's see if we can make sure Mr. Ratcher has good reason never to tell anyone our secret."

Tamara would never hurt Pete Ratcher's baby. But he didn't know that. All she wanted to do was scare him. All she wanted to do was make sure he didn't hurt *her* baby. In a way, you could say her intentions were good.

It is just a little after 4:00 a.m. when Tamara Singh approaches the Ratcher driveway. She turns off the headlights, cuts the engine, and coasts in. What she's doing isn't *dangerous*—it's more on par with a high school prank—but Tamara thinks that maybe she now understands, just a little bit, what motivates a criminal. Beyond everything else there is this *thrill*.

When she unbuckles Ravi from the car seat, he is sound asleep; even touching his shoulder doesn't wake him. Tamara concludes they must have overreacted. She breathes a sigh of relief.

The air is heavy with the odor of manure, dirt, tomato plants, grass, and green corn stalks. Tamara walks across the gravel on tiptoe, but the noise breaks through the dark. In the distance, a dog barks. She walks to the back door, opens it, and enters the house. The Ratchers, like most of the residents of Voorhisville, do not lock their doors. Who can be bothered with keys, in this world that no one wants? Tamara wishes she had a sheet of paper so she could write that thought down.

The kitchen is lit by the stove light. The window over the sink is open, and the white curtains flutter slightly. Ravi stirs in her arms. Tamara leans her face close to his. "Shhh, baby," she whispers. Miraculously, he does. Tamara concludes that all the excitement must have worn him out. Suddenly she's aware of how tired *she* is. She tiptoes through the kitchen and into the living room.

The couch, plaid and sagging, faces a TV set with a small cactus on it. Between the couch and the TV, there is a coffee table littered with a parenting magazine, a paperback, unused diapers, a box of tissues, a half-filled glass of water, and an empty plate. On the TV wall stands the only nice piece of furniture in the room, an antique sideboard with a lace runner and two white taper candles in glass holders. Tamara lies down on the couch. As she falls asleep, she can hear the faint twittering of birds and—from upstairs—a baby's cry; the sound of footsteps.

When Pete woke up, feeling like he slept on rocks instead of a pullout couch, he found Raj sitting at the kitchen table, making designs with Cheerios. Pete didn't really have the energy to comfort Raj—after all, his wife accused him of molesting their daughter; he had serious problems of his own. The phone rang, but Raj continued rearranging Cheerios. "Should I get that?" Pete asked. He walked over to the phone. "Hello?"

"Is this Raj Singh?"

"Theresa?"

"Pete? What are you doing there?"

"Theresa, I never—"

"I need to talk to Raj Singh. Is he there?"

"Theresa, you have to believe me."

"I don't have time for this right now. Tamara Singh is here, and their baby is dead. Are you going to tell him, or should I?"

Pete watched Raj carefully place a Cheerio in-between two others. "But what should I say? How should I say it?"

"Tell him his wife, for some reason, came here last night and fell asleep on the couch with the baby, and when she woke up, he was dead. Tell him not to call the doctor or the undertaker. His wife wants to bury him right here. Nothing formal. Just him and us. Tell him that's what she wants, so we're going to do it that way. Tell him the baby's wings are still out, and if anyone else sees them they'll probably want to take him, run tests and stuff. Tell him his wife could never live through that. Make sure he understands."

"That's what it was like with Elli's baby. The other one—the one that died."

"Tell him you'll bring him with you when you come home."

"Theresa? You don't still think—"

"I screwed up. Okay? I'm sorry, Pete. I've been under a lot of stress lately. What can I say? I'm sorry."

"But you *know*, right? You know I would never?"

"Are you going to tell him?"

"But how? I mean, how did it happen?"

"She said something about a fall, but I think she suffocated him by mistake. Just get here, okay? Don't let Raj call anyone."

"Theresa, did Elli say I did that to her?"

"No, it wasn't Elli. It was *me*. What do you want? I already apologized. It was a mistake, okay? Can we just move on, here? There's other stuff to deal with. Do you want to tell him, or do you want me to?"

"I'll tell him," Pete said, so loudly that Raj looked up from his Cheerios. Pete hung up the phone. "I have bad news," he said.

Raj nodded, as if—of course, naturally—it was just as he expected.

"Your baby's dead."

Raj collapsed across the kitchen table, scattering the Cheerios. Pete placed a hand on Raj's back, kept it there for a moment, and then walked out of the kitchen, through the living room, and out the front door.

Pete stood on the front porch, his head pounding. Crazy; it was just *crazy* that his wife thought he'd do such a thing. How could she ever have loved him if she thought he was capable of such evil? Pete knew that this was not the time to get angry at her, not when she realized her mistake, but he'd gotten drunk last night, and then there was all that business with the baby, and he'd been too distracted to feel it before.

The door popped open. Raj stood there with red eyes. "Tamara?"

"She's at my house. She stopped by to visit my wife, I guess."

"I have to make some calls—"

"No." Pete explained how Raj wasn't supposed to tell anyone, because of the wings, and how Tamara wanted the baby buried at the farm.

"I don't think that's legal."

Pete shrugged. "Theresa—and I guess your wife too—they think that if anyone finds out about the wings, they'll take the baby, and you know, run tests and stuff on him."

Raj considered this. "Okay. Give me a minute. And then you can drive me to your house?"

"We have to take your car. Mine is—"

Raj shut the door before Pete could finish.

Nobody knew that Raj had developed such a deep fondness for his yoga teacher, Shreve. Not even Shreve knew, until Raj called that morning, and, in a choked voice, explained that his baby had died. He wanted her to come and read from the Upanishads at the funeral out on the Ratcher farm.

"But don't tell anyone else, please," Raj said. "My wife is very worried because our baby had wings and she thinks it will cause problems if people find out."

"Your baby had wings?"

"I only just found out recently, myself."

After Shreve finished speaking to Raj, she called Emily and told her what happened. "Apparently he had wings."

"Wings?"

"Yep. What do you think about that?"

"I think maybe something like that might freak some people out," said Emily, choosing her words carefully, "but people are afraid of new things, you know? I mean who's to say . . . like, remember what we were talking about a while back? Who's to say it wasn't an angel?"

"There's something I have to tell you," Shreve said. "I'm nervous about doing this alone, anyway. Do you think you could come with me to the Ratchers?"

Emily watched Gabriel doing a slow figure-eight pattern overhead, a sign that he was getting tired. "Actually, there's something I've been meaning to tell you as well," she said.

Mrs. Vecker, Cathy's mother, is in the grocery store when she overhears Emily Carr and Shreve Mahar having an animated conversation about what would be appropriate to bring to the Ratcher farm "at a time like this." She tells Cathy later that day. "It's all over town. Tracy Ragan's daughter's husband's best friend works with someone who is the father of a boy who was helping on the Ratcher farm, and he says Pete Ratcher is a child molester. You remember his daughter; that pretty red-haired girl? Well, she had a baby with wings—that's how Theresa Ratcher figured it out. Incest, you know, can create all sorts of problems. Theresa Ratcher kicked him out, and I guess the women are going there to see what they can do to help."

Sylvia and Jan Morris had just spent a couple hours together, talking poetry and mothering, when there was a knock at the door. Sylvia was happy to answer it, thinking it might be just the interruption needed to send Jan on her way. It was nice to have company for a *while*, but Sylvia was ready for a nap. She opened the door.

"Did you hear about the Ratchers?" Cathy asked in a rush, half into the room before she stopped. "Oh, I didn't know you had company. I didn't mean to *interrupt*," she said, feeling oddly jealous.

"What about the Ratchers?" Jan asked.

"Pete Ratcher molested their daughter. She had a baby. They say it has wings."

"What do wings have to do with anything?" Jan asked.

"We have to help," Sylvia said.

It was decided that Cathy and Sylvia would drive in Cathy's BMW. They would meet Jan at the Ratchers'. Cathy and Sylvia stood by the roses and waved as she drove away.

"It doesn't mean he *wasn't* molesting her," Sylvia said.

"But . . . another baby with wings," said Cathy. "Don't you think this is getting kind of strange?"

Sylvia laughed. "*Getting* strange?"

As Pete Ratcher drove up to his house, he glanced at Raj. Pete felt bad for Raj, but Pete's overwhelming feeling was anger at Theresa. How could she accuse him of such a thing? How could she believe him capable of such an act?

"We should probably go in," Pete said.

"I did not know that your wife and my wife even knew each other."

Welcome to the club, Pete thought. *I didn't know that my wife thought I was some kind of monster.* The two men sat in the car, staring at the house.

Theresa watched from the kitchen window. She glanced at Tamara, who sat at the table, staring into space. "They're here," she said. "Your husband is here."

Theresa thought Tamara might have sighed, but the sound was so faint, she couldn't be sure.

When they came inside, Theresa gave Raj a hug. In just that brief encounter, she felt the weight of his sorrow. Raj walked over to Tamara and tried to hug her, but she just sat there. He turned to Theresa and said, "Where's my son? Can I see him?"

Tamara stood up so suddenly that the chair toppled. "I'll show you," she said and led him out of the kitchen to the living room, where Theresa had laid the baby on the sideboard with blankets all around him, the unlit candles at either end, like he was some kind of weird centerpiece.

Shreve and Emily park in front of the house, the engine off, the windows rolled down for air. "I'm glad we finally told each other," Emily says.

Shreve nods. "We have to figure out exactly what we need to know."

Emily twists in her seat to look at the two babies in the back. "We have to find out *how* he died—if it had anything to do with the wings."

"Or if it had something to do with Jeffrey, or the water, or something she ate."

"But how could Jeffrey have anything to do with Tamara Singh's baby?"

Shreve just smirks.

"Oh, come on," Emily says. "Us? And Tamara? I don't *think* so."

Shreve shrugs. "Remember, we're here to help bury a baby. We have to be discreet."

The thought of Tamara's dead baby casts a solemn shadow over them. Both women glance back at their children.

#Elli watches from her bedroom window. It takes the mothers forever to unload the two babies, their diaper bags, a bouquet of flowers, and what looks like some kind of casserole or pie. Though both Timmy and Matthew are sleeping peacefully in the hot crib together, Elli keeps having a thought she doesn't want to have. She keeps thinking, *Why couldn't it have been Timmy?* then hates herself for having this thought. She doesn't even want this thought, so she doesn't understand why it keeps popping into her head. She looks at the sleeping Timmy. *I would die if anything happened to you. (Why couldn't it have been you?)* It makes no sense. Elli watches the women walk to the back door. She hears the bell ring. *The mind,* Elli thinks, *is its own battleground* (like there's a war going on up there and she's just a spectator). The bell rings again. *Jesus Christ, would someone just answer it?* But it's too late; the babies wake up, crying.

What's she supposed to do? Pick both of them up? She picks up Timmy; pats him on the back, jiggling him. The next thing she knows, Matthew is flying out of the crib and heading for the open window. There's a screen on it, so naturally she thinks that at the worst he's going to get a little banged up, but when he hits the screen, he hits it *hard*; it falls right off the window, and Matthew flies out.

"Mom!" Elli screams.

Shreve rings the doorbell, waits for a while, and then rings again. Emily carries Gabriel's car seat in one hand and a plate of chocolate croissants in the other, the heavy diaper bag hanging from her shoulder. Shreve, who is similarly burdened, has to ring with the hand carrying the flowers, careful not to squash them. Inside, someone is screaming. "Sounds like they're taking it hard," she says.

A shadow passes overhead.

The door opens. Theresa stands there, her expression aghast.

"I'm Shreve Mahar," she begins, but Theresa runs right past her, brushing her shoulder, so that Shreve has to spin a half turn to maintain balance.

"Where? Where?" Theresa cries, staring up at the sky.

Shreve and Emily exchange a look. Elli Ratcher comes running out of the house, holding a screaming baby. "I'm sorry, Mom," she cries. "I'm sorry!"

"Matthew! Matthew!" Theresa Ratcher hollers.

Jan pulls into the driveway and surveys the scene before her. A barefoot woman stands, shouting, in the yard, her face craned to the sky. Beside her stands the young red-haired girl, carrying a baby. On the porch is the dark-haired yoga teacher with a diaper bag, flowers, and a baby in a carrier. Standing at the foot of the stairs is a short woman who Jan thinks might be named Emma or Emily. Jan cranes her neck and looks up at the sky. She thinks they must have lost a pet bird, though the hysterical woman and the crying girl seem to be overreacting.

Jan is tempted to stay in the car, in the air-conditioning. She doesn't know any of these people. She should have come with Sylvia and Cathy. She realizes that the two women who are not looking at the sky are staring at her. She turns off the ignition. When she opens the door, she is hit by the heat and screams.

"Mom! I'm sorry! I'm sorry!" Elli screams, over and over again.

Theresa stands with her hand shielding her eyes, shouting Matthew's name.

Jan thinks she should get back in the car and turn around, but Jack gurgles at her from his car seat. She can't leave until she finds out whatever she can about the wings.

Theresa shouts for Matthew over and over again. She doesn't know what else to do.

Elli cries, holding Timmy against her chest. *Why couldn't it have been you, she thinks.*

Pete Ratcher comes out to the steps. Shreve begins to introduce herself, but Pete runs into the yard, grabs Theresa by the shoulders, and shakes her. Elli lunges to push him away with one hand, and Pete pushes her back. Not hard, they would later agree, but enough to cause Elli to lose her balance. As she tumbles, she opens her arms. All the women scream as Timmy falls, but the screams are abruptly cut short when dark wings sprout through the baby's little white T-shirt and he flies out of Elli's reach, over all of their heads.

"I thought he died," says Emily.

Shreve shrugs.

"Don't touch the wings," Jan shouts.

Shreve and Emily look at her and then at each other. "How does she know that?"

Little Timmy, laughing, flies in lazy circles and frightening dives, just out of reach of Elli and Theresa Ratcher, who jump at him as he passes. Pete Ratcher just stands there with his mouth hanging open. *I have been drinking too much,* he thinks. *This can't be happening.*

The Mothers

Even now, we the mothers find ourselves saying this can't be happening. This isn't real. Why, in the face of great proof otherwise, do we insist on the *dream* of a life few of us have ever known? The *dream* of happiness? The *dream* of love? Why, we wonder, did we believe in those dreams and not the truth? *We* are monsters. Why did we ever think we were anything else? Why do we *think*, for even a moment, that this is all a horrible mistake, instead of what it is: our lives?

Tamara

When Sylvia Lansmorth and Cathy Vecker drive up, they see Jan, Shreve, and Emily with their baby carriers, diaper bags, flowers, and foiled plate, Theresa and Elli Ratcher, screaming, and Pete Ratcher, standing there, shaking his head.

"Is that him?" Sylvia asks. "He *looks* like a child molester."

Cathy points at the flying babies, swooping across the sky. "I *told* you things were getting strange."

"Matthew! Timmy! You come down here this instant!" Theresa shouts.

Pete turns and walks back to the house.

Emily sets her baby carrier gently on the ground and places the foiled plate beside it, then shrugs out of the diaper bag. She checks the straps on her baby's carrier, making sure they are tight before she walks over to Theresa Ratcher. "Try your breast." She has to say it a few times before Theresa hears her.

"What?"

"When I have this problem, I just take off my shirt. He always comes down for my breast."

Theresa hesitates only a second, trying to process the strange revelation of this woman she's never met acting as though losing a winged baby is a common concern. She pulls off her tank top and lets it drop to the ground.

"You have to take off your bra," Emily says. She turns to Elli. "Watch your mother. Do what she does."

Sylvia and Cathy sit in the car and watch in amazement as Theresa and Elli Ratcher take off their tops and unfasten their bras.

"Maybe we should come back later," Sylvia says, but another car pulls in behind them and they are blocked in the driveway.

Lara Bravemeen heard about the winged baby from the mailman, who heard about it from the senior Mrs. Vecker. When Lara drives up and sees the two women disrobing, the babies frolicking in the sky, she thinks she has found nirvana. She shuts off her engine, jumps out of the car, peels off her T-shirt, and unbuckles her bra.

"What the fuck is going on?" Cathy asks.

Theresa and Elli Ratcher stand with their arms spread, tilting their faces and breasts towards the sky. The babies begin a lazy glide towards them.

That's when the shot rings out.

Shreve jumps about a foot at the noise; turns and sees Pete Ratcher, standing there with a gun.

Emily looks from him to her baby, sitting in his carrier on the ground.

Theresa and Elli both turn, their mouths open in horror.

Pete Ratcher shoots again.

Shreve drops the flowers and runs with her baby.

The small body of Timmy Ratcher falls like a stone. Elli tries to catch him, but he crashes to the ground at her feet, and she falls over him, screaming. Matthew Ratcher stops his gentle glide and, wings beating furiously, shoots towards the sun.

Theresa Ratcher makes an inhuman sound. She runs at her husband, her fists raised.

Pete Ratcher watches her coming with his arms at his side, the gun hanging from his hand. Theresa dives at him and they both crash back into the house.

Tamara and Raj turn from their baby's corpse at the noise. They'd heard the screams and the gunshots, but were so absorbed by their grief they hadn't tried to process any of it. Now they see Theresa Ratcher, bare-breasted, straddling her husband, pounding him with her fists.

That's when Emily comes in, picks up the gun, and rests the muzzle against Pete Ratcher's head.

Raj steps towards them. Emily says, "Come any closer and I'll kill him." She turns to Theresa. "Got any rope?"

"It's in the barn," Pete says.

"Shut up." Emily presses the muzzle to his forehead.

Pete glances at Raj, who is standing in the doorway between the kitchen and the living room. Behind him stands his wife, but she doesn't look like she cares much about what is happening. Over her shoulder, Pete can see the dead baby; his small gray wings folded around his tiny shoulders.

Theresa comes back into the kitchen with a coil of rope. Several women with babies follow her. Cars pull into the driveway, the sound of crunching gravel audible even through Elli's screams.

"Who are all these—"

"Shut up," Emily says. "You"—she glances at Raj—"tie his wrists and ankles."

Raj opens his mouth to protest.

"Do it," says Emily, "or I'll shoot."

Emily is amazed anyone believes her. Pete Ratcher continues to lie there, though he is at least twice her size and actually knows how to use a gun.

"No," Emily says as Raj begins to wrap the rope around Pete's wrists, "tie them behind his back. Roll over. Slowly."

Pete makes a sound that might be a chuckle, but he rolls over, slowly.

The mothers heard it from their mothers, friends, even strangers. Lucy, of Lucy's Diner, heard about it from Brian Holandeigler, who'd heard it from Francis Kennedy, who'd heard it from Fred Wheeler, who said it was all over the canning factory. "Did I tell you we had a call there?" Francis said. "I knew something odd was going on in that house." Maddy Melvern heard about if from Mrs. Baylor, who had come over to talk to Mrs. Melvern about Melinda Baylor in Iraq. "At least my Mindy ain't gotta contend with no asshole like Pete Ratcher, who molested his daughter and gave her a baby with wings," she said. (Maddy made her repeat it twice.) Roddy Tyler heard it from Mrs. Vecker and Mrs. Vecker Senior, and when he walked to the post office that afternoon (in his duct-taped shoes), he told everyone about it. Maddy found Leanne and Stooker outside the drugstore, and after they oohed and ahhed at JoJo, she told them she needed a ride to the Ratchers'. "I didn't know you were friends with her," Leanne said. Vin Freedman heard it from Stooker's older brother, Tinny, and he told Mickey, who called up Elli, but nobody answered the phone there.

Everyone was talking about it. When one of the mothers heard, she could not pretend she hadn't. The Ratcher girl had a baby with *wings*. How could any one of them resist this revelation? The mothers packed diaper bags, left work, left home without explanation or offered a poor one, a scribbled note on the kitchen table, or attached to the refrigerator with a magnet. "Went out. Be back soon."

What they found was a bloodied, bare-breasted Elli Ratcher, kneeling in the dirt, holding her dead baby with his broken wings (right out there for anyone to see) and screaming, "No! No! I didn't mean it! No!"

The mothers were confused. *How long had she been doing this? When had this baby died? And what was all that blood about, anyway?*

The mothers, holding their own sons, approached Elli with caution. They circled her and said, "There, there," or "Everything's going to be all right." Some of them got close enough to pat her hot shoulder and get a good look at the baby. Definitely dead. Definitely wings.

When Theresa Ratcher came out of the house, the mothers—thinking she'd come for her daughter—parted. But Theresa only looked at Elli with a confused expression, then spread her arms and arched her back, her skin freckled at the throat but pure white on her breasts, which hung loosely towards her stomach. She stood there, her face upturned to the crows and the clouds and her eyes closed, until a shadow crossed the sun and came diving down. It was a baby, its gray wings pulled back, diving right for Theresa Ratcher, landing on her with arms spread like a hug. With a sob, Theresa's arms wrapped around him as he repositioned himself and began suckling. The mothers sighed. Theresa Ratcher, slowly, carefully, sank to the ground, kneeling in the dirt, smiling, and running her hand over her baby's hair, just five yards away from Elli, who keened over hers.

The Mothers

Everyone was at the funeral. Even Pete Ratcher, his wrists and ankles tied, though none of us are sure how he got there. We suspect Raj Singh helped him, though Raj should have been helping Tamara. Tamara has no memory of that day. From the time she fell asleep on the Ratchers' couch, until after the trial, Tamara walked with open eyes, but remained in some kind of slumber. Perhaps Pete just hopped out there by himself—he hadn't been tied *to* anything, so it wouldn't have been impossible. We suppose that could have happened without any of us noticing. We were *busy*. There were two babies to bury, Ravi Singh and little Timmy Ratcher, plus all our own babies to attend to.

At that point we were still hiding the secret of the wings, which (we did not yet know) we shared, though several of us considered how much we should reveal about our own babies. If Theresa based her belief in Pete Ratcher's incestuous culpability solely on the evidence of wings, how much responsibility did we have for clarifying that wings weren't proof of incest? Still, we mothers—thoughtful, contemplative, responsible women—were not inclined to share our secret, even if it could save a family. Why save one family, if it would ruin our own?

Tamara

Carla Owens and Melinda Stevens fashioned caskets out of wooden crates they found in the barn, cutting the lids out of planks of wood Pete Ratcher had been using to shore up the beams.

Bridget Myer, who was such a fan of Martha Stewart that she *cried* when the homemaking diva went to prison, assembled a group of women who traipsed through the Ratchers' massive yard, picking dandelions, daisies, wild lilies, Queen Anne's lace, lilacs, and green stalks of corn for the altar—a card table covered by a white cloth and two white candles in the fake crystal candlesticks on either end.

It was just after noon. Elli Ratcher had washed off the blood and changed into a white sundress. Theresa Ratcher didn't change her clothes, though she'd put her shirt back on.

The crates were so small there was no need for pallbearers. Carla carried one to the front, set it on the altar, and Melinda carried the other. The lids were off at that point. The babies, cleaned and dressed by Shelly Tanning, Victoria Simmington, Gladiola Homely, and Margaret Satter, looked real sweet, surrounded by flowers.

Brenda Skyler, Audrey Newman, and Hannah Vorwinkski sang the opening song. They walked to the front and signaled when to start with little nods towards each other, but still didn't get it exactly right. They sang "Silent Night," because it's hard to find funeral songs with babies in them. They hasten to point out, in defense of their controversial choice, that there is no mention of the word *Christmas* in the entire carol. Also, instead of singing the word *virgin*, they hummed.

"I'd like any of you guys to think of a better song for a baby's funeral," Audrey says, if any of us mocks the choice. "And I don't count that Eric Clapton song. We ain't professionals, you know."

Shreve Mahar stepped to the front of the crowd. She glanced at Elli Ratcher, who looked like a bored but polite schoolgirl at assembly, and at Tamara Singh, who wept into her open hands. Theresa Ratcher rocked her baby in her arms, humming softly. Pete Ratcher, still tied at the wrists and ankles, leaned against the apple tree, close enough to follow the proceedings but not so close as to be a part of them.

Shreve opened the book to the previously marked page and read from the Upanishads.

> *In the center of the castle of Brahman, our own body, there is a small shrine in the form of a lotus-flower, and within can be found a small space. We should find who dwells there, and we should want to know her.*

Shreve read the passage into a stunning silence, as if even the babies were listening. When she finished, Raj Singh stepped to the front.

"We are here today," he started, his voice breaking. He looked down at his feet, cleared his throat. "We are here. Today." Again, his voice broke.

He took a deep breath. "We are here." He shook his head, raised his hands in a gesture of apology, and shuffled back to stand beside his weeping wife.

He did not notice how Elli Ratcher had snapped awake at his words. In the confused seconds after Raj's departure, she stepped forward, turned, and faced the mothers, glowing in the sun. "We are here today!" she said, in an excited voice. "That's it, isn't it? We are here! We are here!" She was quite giddy, as if she had only just discovered herself in her life. Eventually, Shreve escorted her back to stand beside Theresa. There was an uncomfortable period of uncertainty before everyone realized the funeral was over. Several mothers noticed flies gathering near the babies in their little wooden crates on the card table, and Shreve brushed them away.

Raj Singh spoke quietly to Theresa, then walked to Pete Ratcher and began to untie him. The mothers protested, but Theresa said, "He's not going to hurt anyone. They're going to dig the graves." Raj and Pete went into the barn together and came out with shovels. They walked over to the apple tree and began digging, as the mothers drifted back to the house.

The Mothers

We came to the Ratcher farm because of the rumors about a winged baby. We were determined not to leave that strange and unhappy place without some information. Tamara Singh was a wreck, and nobody could get anything out of her. She lay upstairs in Elli's bedroom while her husband and Pete Ratcher dug two tiny graves beneath the apple tree.

Elli was also of little use. "We are here," she kept repeating, her eyes wide.

"Grieving," some of us said. "Nuts," said others.

We did not mean it as judgment. We held our babies close and shuddered to guess how we would behave, should something so terrible happen to us.

"Her baby didn't just *die*," Emily said. "He was *murdered* by her own father."

It was a long day. We drifted in and out of conversations and emotions while the two men continued digging. We felt horrible for the mothers of the dead babies. We really did. But, also, we were there on a mission.

Tamara

When it was revealed that Elli and Theresa Ratcher's babies had been seen flying, the mothers (after dismissing Elli, with her "We are here" glassy-eyed uselessness) turned to Theresa. "Yes. So what?" she said to anyone who dared ask outright, did her baby *fly*? By Theresa's reasoning, this was no longer the point.

The mothers, most of whom had carried their heavy secrets for months, confided in Theresa Ratcher. By seven o'clock, the house was a riot of noisy babies; the plumbing just barely keeping up with the women's needs; the hot kitchen cluttered with fresh-baked casseroles, frozen pizza, and dishes in a constant state of being washed.

Finally, Theresa Ratcher called for everyone's attention. The mothers hushed the ornery babies, who, irritated from confinement, would not be hushed, and tried to listen to what Theresa was saying.

"You are all telling me the same thing. *All* the babies have wings."

At first, the mothers were horrified. Misunderstanding, they thought Theresa was not revealing a universal truth, but the deep secret they had confided in her. It was only after a few moments that someone realized what she'd said. "*All* the babies have wings?"

The mothers looked at each other. Nodding. Slowly smiling. Yes, it was true. There was a murmur, which quickly escalated into a babble of excitement, not funereal at all.

Theresa Ratcher opened her arms and Matthew broke free, diving and swooping overhead.

Soon babies were flying throughout the rooms, gleefully darting around each other. Some of the mothers, cut by babies' wings, drifted in a confused stupor, "awakening" (for lack of a better term) to the shock of a houseful of flying babies, but other mothers had grown so adept at avoiding the wings that they were able to explain what had occurred.

"All of them?" the stunned mothers asked.

"Yes. All."

Pete Ratcher and Raj Singh dug beneath the apple tree, the white blossoms only recently swallowed into tiny, bitter apples. They worked, accompanied by the buzzing of flies and bees, in mutual silence, until, just as the sun was leaning on the horizon, babies began flying out of the house. Both Pete and Raj stopped digging. "What can it mean?" Raj asked.

"It means the devil's come to Voorhisville," Pete replied, though Theresa and Elli both later said he was not a religious man.

Inside the house, Theresa once more quieted the women. "We have to make some decisions about how we're going to proceed," she said. "I mean, all of us sharing this secret."

Elli finally broke her spell of repeating "We are here" to cry, "My dad killed my baby!"

"We'll call the police." Cathy reached for her cell phone.

"Wait!" Shreve said. "What's going to happen if we call the police? They're going to want to see the body, right? And if they see the body, they're going to see the wings."

"But that doesn't mean anyone's going to guess about *our* babies," Maddy said.

Emily, who had slung the gun bandolier fashion across her chest (using one of Theresa's flowered scarves), sauntered to the front of the room. "I think probably all of us have had some close calls with our babies flying at inappropriate times, but right now nobody's exactly looking for babies with wings. If word gets out about the possibility, we might as fuckenwell call up *People* magazine ourselves, because someone is going to discover us. Sooner or later, someone is going to catch one of our babies flying, and then all hell is going to break loose. We need to take care of this, ourselves. Also, for those of you who've been asking, I wrote down the recipe for the chocolate croissants. It's on the refrigerator."

Jan Morris stood up and introduced herself as a realtor-poet. "I notice," she said, "that I am a bit older than most of you. I learned in my first marriage, which was a *disaster*, that you can tell how things are going to go by looking at how things went. We have two dead babies here. I don't think we have to look any further to see what chances our babies have in the world. We have all the information we need."

"It's like a painting," Lara said, "you know? That little bit of red in the corner, that little dot of color. You might not necessarily notice, but it's there and it affects everything. If you cover it up, it changes everything, but it's still there."

The mothers were silent, processing this, some more successfully than others.

"If we don't call the police, what do we do about *him*?" Cathy Vecker asked.

"Where is he, anyway?" Maddy said.

Sylvia stood up, so suddenly she knocked over her cup of tea. "He's out there! With our babies!"

Suddenly the mothers were frightened again, thinking of their babies *flying* over Pete Ratcher, who was untied and essentially free to commit murder again. The mothers ran outside, shouting. Upstairs in Elli's room, Tamara Singh wrapped a pillow around her head to try to muffle the noise.

Raj Singh stopped digging, but Pete Ratcher, after glancing up to see what all the fuss was about, continued.

Theresa took off her shirt. Emily did the same. Strangely, Elli did too, though of course Timmy was dead.

Matthew Ratcher flew to his mother's breasts, and Gabriel Carr flew to Emily's. The mothers, observing this, stopped shouting; took off their shirts, blouses, and bras; and offered their breasts to a darkening sky dotted with bats and babies, who dove to their mothers with delighted gurgles. It wasn't long at all before the yard and house were filled with mothers in the Madonna position. Elli remained in the yard for a long time, bare-breasted and with empty arms. Nobody noticed when she returned to the house.

Raj stepped into the freshly dug holes, and Pete Ratcher handed the crates to him, then helped hoist him up. Pete immediately began refilling the holes with dirt. Raj tried to help, but was incapacitated by grief, so Pete Ratcher did this part alone. When he was finished, he left Raj standing there, beneath the apple tree, weeping.

Pete Ratcher walked back to his house, weaving around the nursing women, guided by the fireflies' tiny lanterns. Theresa looked up from her adoration of Matthew and said, "Get away from me, you monster."

"I'm not going anywhere," Pete Ratcher said, loud enough to get everyone's attention. "I'm *his* father. I'm Elli's father. And I'm *your* husband."

Theresa shrugged. "Well, you got two out of three right."

Pete Ratcher stood there, stunned. The women took advantage of his state to tie him up again, while Emily pointed the gun at his dirty forehead.

"You're under arrest," she said.

"Says who? You're no policeman."

But it didn't matter. We were the *mothers*.

Pete

"We used to have animals on this farm. Cows. Chickens. An old rooster. This was when I was a boy. We even had a horse for a while there. Here's the thing: you gotta kill the ones born bad. I know, it's not easy to do. Nobody ever said it was. You think I wanted to kill my own *grandson*? You think I'm *happy* about that? But somebody had to do something. These aren't babies that can grow up to be regular men. You mothers are losing sight of that. Sure, they're cute right now, most of them, but what's going to happen over time? You can't carry them around forever. They're growing, and they're growing unusually fast. Can't you see that? Come on, be realistic now. Just try to step back for a while and consider what's happening. What do you think's going to happen when they're grown? We have to take care of this now, before it becomes a real problem. Think of it like Afghanistan or Iraq. I know you ladies voted to fight the wars there, right? Well, Voorhisville is our Iraq. Don't you see? We have a responsibility. We have to take care of this mess. Here. Now. We *can* do this. We *should* do this. Tonight. In the barn. I'll do it. Just say your goodbyes and I'll take care of the rest. I'm not saying it'll be easy—they do sort of look like regular babies, but that's their trick. They're counting on us to feel that way until they get strong enough to do God knows what. We have a responsibility to the world. Do you think they're going to stay all cute and cuddly, flapping around like sparrows? You have to ask yourselves the hard questions. You have to ask yourselves what they will become. You have to ask yourselves, seriously, what you are raising here. You might as well get it into your heads: I'm not going to be the only one who feels like this. You're the mothers, so it's only natural you want to protect them, but there are going to be others who feel the same as me. Lots of others. What are you going to do about them? You're not going to be able to keep ignoring this. You're not going to be able to tie everyone up. All I'm saying is that the world will not accept them. That's a given. All you have to decide is, do you make the hard choice now and get on with your lives, or do you just prolong their suffering because you can't cope with your own?"

The Mothers

Afterwards—before they started playing "Maggie May" 24/7, and before we were down to our meager rations of pickles and jelly, but after the windows had been boarded up with old barn wood—we had a little quiet time to think about what Pete Ratcher had said and came to the conclusion that he was probably right, but that didn't change anything.

We took him to the barn, and, though he was tied up, he seemed under the impression that we were taking his advice. "Don't worry," he said. "You ladies won't hear a thing. Well, maybe the shots, but no crying or anything. Timmy didn't cry but for thirty seconds at the most."

Elli went to her room, where she found Tamara and Raj Singh curled up in her bed, both still fully clothed but sleeping soundly. She eased in beside them, pressing against Raj the way he was pressed against Tamara.

Elli

I remember being in my bed with Tamara and Raj Singh. All three of us suffering like we were, it didn't even feel like we were three people, but more like one. The way I felt inside, I was Elli Ratcher, fifteen and on summer break, and I was a mommy with leaking breasts, and I was the monster who thought I wanted my baby to die, and I was a hundred years old like one of those women they show on TV in the black cape and hood, screaming over my dead baby, and I was the girl with the beautiful bones wrapped around the man with skin that smelled like dirt and I was the man who smelled like dirt and I was his wife dreaming the dead.

That saying kept going through my head. *We are such stuff as dreams are made on.* When I heard screaming, I thought it was a dream, and I thought I was a dream, peeling the girl I was away from the man laying there beside me. I walked my dream feet over to the window and the man got up and stood beside the girl and said, "What is that horrible noise?" I turned to that part of me, while the other part continued to sleep, and said, "It sounds like my father." That's when we noticed the babies flying out of the barn, swooping through the night sky. We watched the mothers, in a disarray of tangled hair and naked breasts. We heard their screams of blood as they ran into the house. I said, "This is not happening," and went back to bed. I heard the man saying, "Tamara, wake up, we must leave this place. Tamara, wake up," but as far as I know she didn't wake up until the morning.

Tamara

There are certain mornings in Voorhisville when the butterflies flit about like flower seraphs and the air is bright. Tamara woke up to just such a morning, taking several deep breaths scented with manure and the faintest hint of roses, all the way from town. *Sweet,* she thought, before she rolled over and saw the empty crib, which brought her back to the nightmare of her son's death and the other baby murdered by his own grandfather. It did not seem possible that such a reality could exist in this room, papered with tiny yellow flowers.

Tamara sat at the edge of the bed listening to the breathing of the girl who still slept there and the murmur of voices below, raised in argument, then hushed. She had to go to the bathroom. It did not seem possible that such a simple bodily function would take precedence over her sorrow, but it did. She shuffled to the door, the chair she had used to discourage visitors shoved to the side. She remembered Raj, pushing at the door, asking her to let him in. Vaguely, she remembered doing so. But where had he gone? She suddenly missed her husband, as if he had taken part of her with him, as if she suffered the ghost pain of a severed limb. She stepped into the hall, which was dim and hot.

The words "police," "reporters," "prison," "murder," "self-defense," "justice," "love," "fear," "danger," and "coffee" drifted up the stairs. Tamara stood in the hot hallway and listened.

Maddy

I got to the Ratcher farm right at the end of the funeral, which is okay, 'cause I'm not sure—even as solemn of a event as it was—that I could of kept a straight face through "Silent Night." Stooker dropped me off out by the road 'cause there was so many cars parked in the driveway and on the lawn.

"Looks like some kind of thing going on," he said. "You sure you wanna get out here, Maddy? We could go to the graveyard."

The graveyard, case you were confused by Elli Ratcher's spaced-out words (But what do you expect from a girl who tried to hang herself; I mean, it only makes sense there would be some brain damage, right?)—the graveyard is where kids in Voorhisville hang out, and if that don't give you the right idea about this shithole town, nothing will. Anyway, I got out of the car, and, like I said, got there right at the end part, where Elli was going,

"We are here," like she was high or something. For all I know, maybe she was.

JoJo and me were there when Mr. Ratcher tried to convince us to let him kill our babies, like that was the *reasonable* thing to do, and I was one of them that voted to tie him up in the barn. That's as far as we got, I swear on my own brother's grave. So we all went out there, or I guess most of us did, and tied him to the center pole. He kept saying we were nuts. Back at the house, a bunch of the mothers called up husbands and kids and shit and said how they were at the Ratchers' and going to spend the night. I called my mom and told her me and JoJo was staying with Elli Ratcher. My mom goes, "Well, I suppose it would make sense you two girls would become friends."

We laid down on the floors in the living room and kitchen. I slept in the yard and some other mothers were out there too. We had our babies with us. Nobody slept upstairs 'cause nobody wanted to make Tamara or Raj or Elli have to hear the sound of a living baby. I would say that proves we were not evil, like some people say.

Mr. Ratcher was sort of upset. He kept saying he had to take a piss, so Mrs. Ratcher stayed behind to unzip him and hold him so he wouldn't wet himself. I was half-asleep when she came back up to the house with Matthew. I didn't see no blood on her and that's something I would of remembered if I did, but it was dark. I told the mothers this. I told them the screams came later, *after* I saw Mrs. Ratcher come back to the house. The screams woke me up. I reached for JoJo, but he ain't anywhere around, and I think somehow that *monster*, Mr. Ratcher, got a hold of my baby, so I run out to the barn.

After my brother got killed in Afghanistan, I was amazed to find out that some people—and I am not just talking teenagers here—wanted to know *details*, like, was he shot or blown up, and what body parts did they send us?

Anyway, my point is, I ain't going to get into details about what happened in the barn for all you sick fucks that like to say you gotta know out of some sense of clearity, like that reporter said, and not because, let's face it, you get off on it somehow. But I will say this: I screamed really loud, and I am not someone who screams at scary movies and shit.

All of them were in the barn. Even the ones that had been in carriers. Somehow, they figured out how to unbuckle straps and shit. Just like that, they were no longer *babies*. We no longer had control over them. Some of the mothers say we probably never did, that they just fooled us for a while.

So the mothers come out and they see blood on the babies and they start undressing and the babies come swooping down and the mothers are screaming and everyone runs into the house and starts washing their babies—wiping the blood off, you know, to see where the *actual wound* is.

I'm trying to tell them; I'm saying, "Mr. Ratcher is dead," but nobody pays attention. Some of them are screaming that they're going to kill him.

Then Mrs. Ratcher comes in and she's crying and screaming, "Who killed my husband?" and that's when she sees all the mothers wiping blood off their babies. She's all covered in blood herself, which she says was from trying to get him untied. "Give me a knife," she says. "I gotta get him untied."

Someone goes, "Theresa, you are better off. He was a child molester and a murderer and you are better off without him."

Mrs. Ratcher says, "He's no child molester—we had a misunderstanding, is all. And he's no murderer, either. Not usually."

The whole thing was so *horrible* I guess none of us could believe it. I mean, even now, after all this time, I still sort of expect to see Billy sitting on the couch, eating pistachios. I know how crazy a person's mind can get when something so terrible happens that you can't even believe it.

Mrs. Ratcher said, "Where's Elli? He didn't molest her. She can straighten this whole thing out."

But Elli was upstairs in bed—mourning, we assumed, her life and murdered child.

"My mother did the same thing," Evelyn Missenhoff said. "When I told her about my dad she said I was lying."

Mrs. Ratcher stood there, holding Matthew tight. In spite of all that day had brung—her grandson and husband both dead, not to mention the surprise of finding Tamara Singh asleep on her couch just that morning with her own dead baby—Mrs. Ratcher had a pretty face. She made a point of looking at each of us, shaking her head until that dirt-colored hair of hers brushed her freckled cheeks. "We have to call the police," she said.

A mother's love is a powerful thing. It can direct a person to behave in ways they never would of thought possible. When Billy got sent to Afghanistan, I overheard my mother telling him he didn't have to go.

"Yeah I do," he said.

"You could quit. You know Roddy Tyler? He got a honorable discharge from Vietnam. Why don't you do that?"

"Ma, I wanna go."

"Well, if you *want* to."

I heard it in her voice, but didn't really understand until I had my own child. Being a mother, I figure, is like going a little bit crazy all the time.

The Mothers

The mothers want you to understand. We are not *bad* people, we are *mothers*. When Mrs. Ratcher insisted we call the police, we saw it as a threat, and did the only thing we knew to do: we took Matthew out of her arms and tied her up to a pole in the barn—facing away from her husband, 'cause we're not *evil.*

"Someone murdered Pete," she said. "And whoever did it is still among you."

Did she *know*? It's hard to believe she didn't. But it's probably just as difficult to understand how it is that we knew and didn't know at the same time. Who could *believe* such a thing?

Later, when we heard the screams again, we tried to ignore them. We rolled over. Closed our eyes. We tried to believe it was a dream. We tried to believe we weren't even awake, but the screams pulled us back, and we fell to the earth. And when we went to the barn, we saw all our babies there, and Mrs. Ratcher, dead.

They flew out of the barn into the sky, up to the bright stars. We weren't sure if we should call them back or not. We stood there, our mouths hanging open, tears falling on our tongues.

Later, they came back, lunging at our breasts and drinking with selfish, insistent sucks and tiny bites, until they finally fell asleep, and we realized we had a problem.

Elli

I wake up on my birthday thinking about how I dreamt I had a baby. With wings! And my mom did too! I dreamt almost all the mothers came to our house for a funeral. I dreamt my dad killed my baby and the mothers tied my dad up in the barn. What's that saying? *We are such stuff as dreams are made on.*

When I open my eyes, the first thing I see is the empty crib. This nightmare is my life.

"Mom?" I call. "Mom?" She doesn't come. She's probably busy with Matthew. When I look at the crib, my breasts drip milk. What does it *mean*, anyway? "We are such stuff as dreams are made on." Does he mean the dreams of sleep, or the dreams of hope? And how are they made *on* us? Are we, like, scaffolding? I can't figure it out. I can't figure *anything* out. "Mom?" My breasts hurt. My arms hurt too. My whole body hurts. Maybe this is what happens to old people. Maybe it starts to take its toll, holding up all those dreams.

But I'm not old! Today is my sixteenth birthday! When I open the bedroom door, I can hear the voices of the mothers downstairs. Why aren't they gone? I can't decide how I feel about them tying my dad up in the barn, even though he killed Timmy. "Mom?" The voices go quiet. "Mom, could you come up here?" I don't want to see the mothers. I hate them. I don't want to see the babies, either. I hate them too.

"Elli?" someone says.

"Could you tell my mom I want to talk to her?"

There is all kinds of whispering, but I can't make out the words, before one of them hollers, "She's not here right now."

That figures, right? This is how my mom has been ever since Matthew was born. But then I think maybe she's out getting my presents, or something. I feel better for about two seconds, until I remember Timmy is dead. I can't celebrate today. What is she thinking? "Could you get my dad for me then?" The whispering starts again. The mothers are really starting to get on my nerves.

I go downstairs. There are mothers everywhere—in the living room, in the kitchen. When I look out the window, I even see some in the yard. Babies are flying everywhere, too. One almost hits me in the head, and I have to clench my fists and hold my arms stiff so I don't hit it. The mothers sitting at the kitchen table look shocked to see me. "Your dad can't come right now, either," one of them says.

I don't know why, but I feel like I shouldn't let on that I know how strange this all is. I shrug like, okay, no big deal; and say, "We are such stuff as dreams are made on." This gets them looking at each other and raising eyebrows. Maybe it wasn't the right thing to say. I walk to the refrigerator and take out the orange juice. I open the cupboard, but all the glasses are gone. Then I see the dishes drying on the counter. I try to find my favorite glass—the one with SpongeBob SquarePants on it—but I don't see it anywhere. I finally take my mom's glass, the one with the painted flowers. I pour myself a tall orange juice. When I turn around, all the mothers are staring. I take a big drink. The mothers act like they aren't watching, but I can tell they are. When I put the glass down, they all pretend, real quick, to look at something else. "I think I'm going to go to Timmy's grave," I say. They look up at me, and then down, or at each other. They look away as if I am embarrassing. I shrug. I have to be careful, because I can tell that this shrugging thing could become a tic. Martha Allry, who is a year behind me in school, has a tic where she blinks her right eye a lot. People call her Winking Martha.

"Would you like me to come with you?" one of the mothers says.

She is a complete stranger. Even so, I hate her. She's one of the ones that tied up my dad in the barn. She's here when my mom is not. I say, "Thanks, but I'd rather be alone."

The mothers nod. They nod quite a bit, actually. I walk out of the kitchen. I don't have on shoes and I'm still wearing my nightgown. This is how we do things on the farm.

It's a beautiful morning. The birds are singing and some babies fly by, which is totally weird.

One of the mothers comes up to me and says, "Where are you going?" She sort of looks sideways at the barn when she thinks I'm not looking.

Right away I know my dad is still tied up. The mothers are not my friends.

"I'm going to Timmy's grave."

The mother's face turns into a bunch of Os—her eyes, her mouth, her whole face goes all round and sorry. I walk past her, already planning how I have to get into the barn and rescue my dad. I *think* I'm going to rescue him. I can't decide for sure. He's my dad, but he's also my baby's murderer. Maybe it was an accident. Maybe he was just trying to scare everyone. Maybe I hate him. I don't *know* what I feel, but I should have some say in this; it's my baby he killed.

I walk down to the apple tree where there are two mounds of dirt. No cross or anything. Nothing to tell me which one is Timmy. This makes me angry. It's like I get hit on the back of my shoulders, that's how it feels, and I just drop to my knees and start crying, right there in the dirt. I can't believe Timmy is dead. Nobody knows my horrible secret about how many times I wanted him to die. Nobody knows how evil I am. I am a very evil person. Nothing can change this. I wanted him to die and he did. That's the whole story. It doesn't matter that I'm sorry.

My breasts are dripping right through my nightgown. The apple tree is buzzing with bees. A plane flies overhead. My whole body hurts. It hurts to *breathe*. I can't stop crying. Will I ever stop crying?

Then, just like that, I stop crying.

The mothers are calling their babies. They are taking their tops off and spreading their arms and the babies are diving for their breasts. They go into the house. Some of them glance at me, and then, real quick, look away.

The yard is empty except for a couple of crows. I don't see anyone looking out the windows. The mothers have forgotten about me. I stand up, check the house again, and then walk, real fast, to the barn.

At first I can't really see, 'cause it's dark there. Not like middle-of-a-moonless-night dark, but shady, you know, and there's a strange smell. I can sort of see my dad, tied up to the pole; I can see the shape of him. "Dad?" I say, but he is totally quiet. I can't believe he fell asleep. I get a little closer. That's when I see what they did to him.

The mothers are evil; worse than me. He doesn't even look like my dad anymore. There are flies buzzing all over him. I try to shoo them away, but they are evil too.

We are such stuff as dreams are made on. I can't carry the dreams anymore. I can't hold them up. I am sinking under the weight. I can't look at him anymore. The mothers are monsters. I need my mom. She'll know what to do. She'll make the mothers go away.

I look at the beams my dad was always talking about. I look at the holes in the roof, showing bits of blue sky. I look at the tools by the door, the shovels, the hoe, the axe, nails, rope, Dad's old shirt, and Mom's gardening hat; I am spinning in a little circle waiting for Mom to find me, and that's when I find *her*: tied to the other pole, her back to my dad, but chewed up just like him.

I get the rope and the ladder. I make a noose in the rope and try to throw it over the beam that goes in between both of them, but it doesn't work until I weigh down one end with an old trowel my mom uses for tulip bulbs. A couple years ago I helped her plant red tulips all around the house. Afterwards, we sat on the porch and drank root beer floats. We used to get along better.

I finally get the rope over the beam and twist the rope around it a few times. I have to be careful, 'cause that trowel swings back towards me. I know it doesn't make sense to be *careful*, considering, but the point is that I didn't want to feel pain. By the time I stand on the ladder and check the rope, my arms are really tired.

I pull on the rope and it holds tight. I put the noose around my neck and I don't like how it feels, but then I step off the ladder and kick it with my feet and I can feel the breath getting sucked right out of me, and there is this horrible noise like a bomb, and the next thing I know, I am free. Then I feel the weight of the world on me, and by the time I climb out of the wreckage, I know I have failed. The rope is around my neck, the barn collapsed, and all the mothers are staring at me, until the one with the gun says, "Well, all right; we can use this wood to board up the windows and doors."

The Mothers

We do not know how Tamara's husband snuck away. For a while he was quite a regular on the local news. He insisted we were not a cult. (We are *not* a cult.) He also denied allegations that we were some sort of militia group, though he did say he had no idea how many weapons we had. (We only have one gun.) We thought he was our friend until he started calling us monsters. "Tamara, honey," he said, looking right out of the TV screen at us, "I'm sorry I left you. I thought I'd get back in time. Please be careful. I'm here, waiting for you. You're not in trouble. I told the sheriff and the FBI and Homeland Security about your situation. They understand that you are being held against your will . . . " And on and on. We did not know that Raj, who had been so silent around all of us, could talk so much.

The mothers do not completely trust Tamara, and suspect she offered to be chronicler only to get our secrets. After all, she has nothing to lose. Her baby is already dead. We feel bad that we are reduced to such cold calculation, but our life now depends on calculating. We also do not trust Elli Ratcher. We've been medicating her with various mood modifiers and enhancers that we pooled from our own supply. Though we started with a rather amazing amount of medication, the stash is dwindling at a suspicious rate. Several of us suspect Maddy Melvern of pilfering it for recreational purposes.

We cannot say we blame her. We pace about the house like restless animals in a cage. We *are* restless animals in a cage. We have played all the Ratcher games: checkers, *Monopoly*, *Life*, *Candy Land*.

We miss our babies terribly. We miss them with every breath; we miss them in our *blood*. For a long time we missed them with our leaking breasts. But we know we did the right thing. We think we did. We must have. We hope.

We were watching the morning news the first time we saw Raj, his dark eyes wide, his black hair like a rooster's, ranting about flying babies and murdering mothers. We hoped nobody would take him seriously, though it was unlikely that he would be completely ignored. "We need to fortify, and protect ourselves," Emily said.

That's when the barn came crashing down. We found Elli Ratcher climbing out of the rubble in her nightgown, a rope tied around her neck. She tried to run into the cornfield, but we brought her back to the house. We think that was the right thing to do. What was she going to do out there? Where was she going to run? This is her *home*, after all. Of course she objected, but that's how teenagers are. We try to take good care of Elli—and Maddy, of course—but they resist us. Perhaps we are overprotective, after what happened with our own children.

The hardest thing any of us ever had to do was release our babies.

We were not even finished nailing all the wood over the windows and doors when the first cars arrived. Pete Ratcher apparently had only one hammer; so there was that to contend with. We resorted to using books and shoes and other tools. We have to admit that not all of us pursued this task with equal vigor. Many of us weren't completely certain that Emily Carr hadn't also gone nuts. But we had bonded over the Ratcher deaths, as well as the revelation that all our babies had wings.

We had not yet figured out we were a *family*. It was only later, after Jan and Sylvia got in a fight over *Scrabble* and began throwing letter tiles at each other, when we had the discussion that eventually resulted in the remarkable revelation: Jeffrey had fucked us all.

The first car was full of high school kids. They drove by with their windows down, screaming nonsense. We continued to hammer wood over the windows and doors. The car stopped and the kids inside were silent. Then it made a squealing U-turn back towards town.

The next car was Mrs. Vecker's Ford Explorer, with its skylight and fancy hubcaps. It pulled over by the side of the road. Roddy Tyler stepped out, shading his eyes with his hand and squinting at the house. He walked over to the barn wreckage (in his duct-taped shoes) and started poking through the rubble. We are not sure what he was looking for, but he jerked back as though bitten by a black widow. He looked at the house again and then ran to the Ford, jumped in, and made a squealing U-turn, driving too fast.

We continued nailing. Perhaps with a bit more resolve.

Tamara

There is a certain scent in the Ratcher farmhouse now that its windows are boarded and the doors nailed shut. It is the scent of sweat and skin; and the sickly odor of bodies wasting away on a diet of jelly and pickles; and the pungent scent of pickles on breath made sour by slow starvation and the toothpaste long since eaten. Sometimes a vague perfume wafts in through the cracks and bullet holes. Elli Ratcher has been discovered many times standing with her little freckled nose right in one of those holes, hogging that sweet air.

On just such an evening, Sylvia sat barefoot at the table, weeping. This was not the life she had imagined for herself: trapped in a farmhouse listening to Rod Stewart's scratchy voice over loudspeakers, eating grape and strawberry jelly while Homeland Security and FBI agents, reporters, and curious onlookers camped outside with bulletproof vests and guns and cameras. Once, before they shut the power off, she'd even seen on one of the news channels that someone was selling food from one of those trucks on the road in front of the house—hot dogs and nachos. She really didn't want to think about it.

Lara Bravemeen watched Sylvia, as she had many times before, and finally did the thing she had always wanted to do. She walked over to the weeping beauty, placed a hand on her shoulder, and, when Sylvia looked at her, leaned down and kissed her on the mouth—which, yes, was sour and pickled, raw with hunger, but also flavored with the vague taste of roses. Sylvia stopped crying, and Lara, desperate to paint, took a jar of jelly and began smearing it across the wall, though she knew she risked her life to do so—that's how serious the penalty was for wasting food.

Shreve Mahar told her to stop, but Lara just laughed. Shreve thought of her fiancé, who died before the world changed; and she thought of her little boy—released, as they all were, when the mothers realized what was coming; and she thought about Jeffrey. "Maybe we should just tell them that the babies are gone," she said.

That's when Jan Morris walked into the kitchen, with the petite body she had always wanted and the satisfaction that she had been right all along; it really did take starvation to achieve. "We're not telling them anything," she said. "What the fuck is she doing? Hey, is that our *jelly*?"

"It's like a poem," Sylvia said, "with color."

"Poems have words." Jan smirked.

"Not necessarily," said Shreve.

"Well, you better tell her to stop it or you-know-who is going to shoot her."

Sylvia and Shreve considered their options—tackling Lara to the ground or letting her continue her jelly painting, a death sentence for sure—and each of them, separately and without consultation, decided not to interrupt.

The Mothers

What was it about him? The mothers still cannot agree. Was it his blue eyes? The shape of his hands? The way he moved? Or was it something closer to what Elli said, something holy? Was it something evil? We simply do not know.

Tamara

Once, Tamara answered the house phone and spoke to a reporter.

"My name is Fort Todd. I wonder if you care to comment on some information I've uncovered about someone you might be interested in. He's a wanted man, you know."

"Who? My husband?"

"No, no, not him. Oxenhash. Jeffrey."

"I don't know who you're talking about," Tamara said.

"I've uncovered a great deal of information about these winged creatures."

"What winged creatures?"

"People mistake them for angels, but they aren't. Apparently this is one of the ages."

"I don't know what you're talking about."

"They're coming into fruition. There have always been some, but we live in a time where there are going to be thousands."

"What do they want?"

"I thought if we could talk—"

Tamara hung up, which she sometimes regrets. She often thinks of turning herself in. What does she have to lose? Her baby is dead, and her husband has abandoned her, saying things like, "Just walk out, honey; nobody will hurt you." How can he, despite all that has happened, remain so naïve? So she stays with the other mothers who share the secret the authorities have not yet figured out: the babies are gone.

Tamara stays with the mothers out of *choice*. She's given up her freedom, though not for them. It's for the children.

The Mothers

On this, all the mothers agree. As long as the authorities think the babies are in here with us, well, the babies are safe. We hope.

(If you see one, his small wings mashed against his back, perhaps sleeping in your vegetable garden, or flying past your window, please consider raising him. We worry what will happen if they go wild. You don't need to be afraid. They are good babies, for the most part.)

Tamara

Emily paces throughout the house with the gun slung between her breasts. Perhaps Shreve was right all along, Emily thinks, though their friendship has been strained lately. *Maybe it* is *all an illusion.* Certainly the men and women pointing guns at the house are under the impression that there are babies inside. Emily is convinced that that's the only reason why any of them are alive. "There ain't gonna be another Waco here, that's for sure," the sheriff said, when he was interviewed on Channel Six.

One night there was a special report about the standoff at Waco, Texas. The mothers sat and watched, for once not arguing about whose head was in the way, or who didn't put the lid back on the peanut butter jar, or who left the toilet paper roll almost empty and didn't bother to change it. (Thinking about this now, Tamara smiles at the quaint memory of toilet paper. *Wouldn't that be nice,* she thinks.)

When it got to the part where they showed the charred bodies—the tiny little bones of children's hands and feet, the blackened remains—the mothers wept and blew their noses. Some swore. Others prayed. It was up to Emily to point out what it meant. "They are not going to make that mistake again. As long as they think we still have the babies, we are safe. And so are our babies."

Before that night, Maddy didn't know a thing about Waco, Texas, and she's still not sure how it's connected to the mothers. But the mothers are convinced that they must stay locked behind boarded-up windows and doors; that this is the best thing they can do for the babies. Maddy isn't even convinced that the babies all got away, but she hopes they did. She walks through the house, trying to stay behind Emily, since she has the gun, keeping out of the way of Elli Ratcher, who sort of haunts the place—though she's not dead, of course.

Lately, Maddy has gotten so hungry she's begun eating the house. She pulls off little slivers of wood and chews them until they turn into pulp. She has to be careful to peel the slivers off just right. She's cut her tongue and lips several times. Maddy thinks she never would have guessed she'd start eating a house, but she never would have guessed she'd give birth to a baby with wings, either. When Maddy thinks about JoJo, she stops peeling a sliver of gray wood from the upstairs hallway and stares at the yellow flowers in the wallpaper, trying to remember his face. "Please," she whispers.

"It won't do any good to pray," Elli says.

Maddy jumps. Of all the people to find her talking to herself, why'd it have to be Elli Ratcher?

"I ain't praying," she says.

"That's good. 'Cause it won't help."

Elli stands there, staring at Maddy until she finally says, "What are you looking at?"

"Did you know I had *two* babies?"

Maddy shrugs.

Elli nods. "My dad killed *one* of them. And the other is in my closet."

"Well, it's been great to have you visiting us on Planet Earth for a while, but I got some stuff I gotta do."

"You better be careful. If Emily finds out you're eating the house, she's going to kill you."

"I ain't eating the house," Maddy says. "Besides, you're the one who should be careful. The mothers know you keep stealing the notebook."

"What notebook?"

Maddy rolls her eyes.

If Emily knew how afraid everyone was of her, she would be insulted. Even Shreve is nervous around Emily now. She didn't know, she honestly didn't *know*: if Emily found them in the kitchen, would she shoot all of them, or just Lara and Jan, who were the ones wasting the jelly? "Maybe you should put that away," Shreve said, but they ignored her. *It's like I'm not even real*, she thought. *It's like I'm the illusion*. Shreve wondered if this was what was meant by being enlightened. She looked at her surroundings: the dark little kitchen with the boarded-up windows and door, the bullet holes, Sylvia sitting in the straight-backed chair, Lara painting with jelly, and Jan Morris licking the wall in her wake, pausing once to say, "This is true art."

Maybe I have never been here, Shreve thought. *Maybe my entire life was an illusion: the death of my fiancé, the birth of my winged child, the couple who died in the barn, the babies, everything. Maybe everything is nothing at all, including me. Maybe I never existed.* She felt like she was being swallowed, but not by something dark and frightening, not by a beast, but more like something with wings, something innocent she'd always been a part of but only now recognized. She wanted to tell the others what she was feeling, but she worried that speaking would break the spell. Instead, she closed her eyes, until Cathy Vecker came into the room and said, "Have you all gone crazy? What do you think Emily's going to do when she finds out?"

When Emily walked past the kitchen, she quickly looked the other way. She hoped the mothers would get their act together and clean up the mess. The last thing she wanted was to have to confront the issue. If she did, they might wonder why she didn't shoot anyone, and that might cause them to become suspicious that there were no more bullets. She heard Cathy say, "We have to clean this up before Emily finds out. Do you want to *die*?" That got their attention. They all started talking at once about how, since the day Elli threw their babies out the window, they didn't really care if they lived or not.

Elli

We are such stuff as dreams are made on. That's what I whispered to each one, as though I was a fairy godmother, as I pushed them out the window, the mothers standing behind me, crying.

"You do it," they said. "Please. We can't."

"Why don't you ask Tamara? She's got a dead baby, too."

"She's writing about all this and interviewing everyone. She doesn't have time to actually do anything; she's too busy chronicling us."

"But I hate all of you."

"That's why it has to be you," they said, using their crazy mother-logic on me. "You won't let your emotions get in the way."

They were wrong. All those babies with Timmy's dimples, and Timmy's little round body, and Timmy's eyes looking at me. I saw him in every one of them, and I felt the strangest emotion of all: a combination of love, hate, envy, joy, and sorrow. The more I dropped Timmies out the window, watching them sprout wings and dart across the starry sky, the more I felt my own wings—small, fluttering, just a tremor at first—sprouting from my back. I kept waiting for the mothers to notice, but they were too busy holding their babies tight, kissing them all over, crying on them. More than once, the baby was soaked and slippery by the time he was handed to me. Even though I wore my mother's old winter gloves, there were several babies I did not toss, but dropped. They did not get to hear my blessing, though I whispered it into the air.

The mothers handed me their babies, sighing, weeping, blowing kisses; or the mothers had their babies ripped from their arms as they screamed or threw themselves to the floor or—in one case—down the stairs.

We are such stuff as dreams are made on. I whispered it into tiny pink ears shaped like peony blossoms. I whispered it into wailing wide-open mouths (with sharp white teeth, already formed), and I whispered it into the night. It was amazing how they seemed to understand; even those who were crying, even those who plummeted towards the earth before unfolding their wings and darting over the cornfield, following their brothers.

I breathed the dark air scented with apple, grass, and dirt, and I felt the air on my arms and face, and I was happy and sad and angry and loving and hateful, and I thought, as I tossed Timmies out the window, *We are such stuff as dreams are made on.*

Emily, with the gun hanging from the scarf my dad bought mom last Christmas, handed her baby to me and said, "Maybe later we can bake cookies."

Sylvia handed her baby to me and said, "I hope he goes somewhere wonderful, like Alaska, don't you?"

Lara was one of the mothers who would not release her son. She stood there, crying and holding him, as the mothers reminded her how they had all agreed this was the best thing; the babies' best chance of survival. So far, this seemed to be true. No shots were heard. Even though Rod Stewart continued his singing, somehow the officials out there slept, or at least were not watching the sky at the back of the house. This was our chance. It was everything that had already been said and agreed on. But they still had to rip the baby from Lara's arms. She ran from the room, crying, and I thought, *Well, now you know how I feel.*

At least their Timmies had a chance. Mine had had none.

The last Timmy was Maddy's. She was hiding in the closet, actually. The mothers had to pull her out, and she was doing some serious screaming, let me tell you. She was also cussing everyone out. "I never agreed to this!" she yelled. "I hate all of you!" She held her baby so tight that he was screaming, too. You know, baby screams. Maddy looked right at me and said, "Don't do it. Please don't do it." Even though the mothers told her it's not like the babies were dying or anything; hopefully they were flying somewhere safe. I didn't answer her. That wasn't my job. Besides, I was sort of distracted by *my* wings. I couldn't *believe* no one had noticed them.

Maddy was the worst. They had to hold her shoulders and her legs, and then two other mothers had to pull on her arms to open them, and another mother was standing there to grab her Timmy. By the time she handed him to me, everyone was freaking. I held Maddy's Timmy out to the sky, like I did with all the others, and I opened my mouth to say, "We are such stuff as dreams are made on," but he tore away from me and flew straight to the cornfield. Just in time, because right then there was a shout and all the police guys came around to the window, screaming and pointing. I shouted and waved to distract them. The mothers pulled me away from the window, then put the boards up and nailed them shut.

Later, when I go to my room, I undress in front of the mirror. My body looks different now. My nipples are dark, I have a little sag in my belly, and my hips are huge. But the biggest change has got to be the wings. When I take my clothes off, they come out of their secret hiding place and spread behind me—not gray like the babies', but white and glowing. Unfortunately, they seem to be for cosmetic purposes only. I jump off my bed and try to think of myself as flying, but it doesn't work.

The mothers are crying. Rod Stewart sings louder, trying to get the eternally sleeping Maggie to wake up. Some man on the loudspeaker begs us to come out, and promises that they won't hurt our babies.

We are such stuff as dreams are made on.

I sit at the edge of my bed and think about how things have been going lately; my parents both dead, and my baby too.

We are such stuff as dreams are made on.

I lie back on the bed, which is sort of uncomfortable because of the wings, and stare at the pimply ceiling. I am having a strange déjà vu feeling, like I've figured this all out once before, but forgot. I hope I remember this time.

The Mothers

The worst days of our suffering were reports of winged children being captured and shot. We crowded into the dark living room and wept in front of the TV set; turned it on full volume, so we could hear the gloating of marksmen and hunters over Rod Stewart's singing.

Oh, our babies! Our little boys, shot down like pheasants, tracked like deer, hunted like Saddam Hussein.

The worst of these worst days were when the camera panned over the little corpses, lingered on the dark wings, always at some distance. Artful, you might say, but torture all the same, for us, the mothers.

We could not identify them. There was solace and madness in this fact. Sometimes a mother became certain that the baby was hers. For some, this happened many times. There are mothers here who have been absolutely sure on several occasions that their babies have just been killed. They walk about the house, weeping and breaking dishes. Other mothers haven't suffered a single fatality. These mothers are positive their sons have escaped, alive. They are the ones who insist we maintain this charade, though, frankly, the jig is almost up.

After the film of murdered babies and hunters grinning broadly beneath green caps, the news anchors raise neatly manicured eyebrows, smile with bright white teeth, joke, and shake their heads.

"What do you think, Lydia, about the standoff in Voorhisville? Do you think it's time for authorities to move in?"

"Well, Marv, I think this has gone on long enough. It's clear these mothers have been taking advantage of decent folks' good intentions. Who knows, perhaps they're even sending their babies out to be shot, hoping to generate more sympathy, though I would say their plan is backfiring. It seems to me that the authorities have taken every precaution to safeguard innocent civilians from being harmed. The fact is, even if there *are* children in that house, they are not innocent. We've seen the bodies with their dangerous wings. Homeland Security has taken several into custody. My understanding is that they are holding them on an island off of Georgia. My point being, these are not your average little babies, and we have a right to protect ourselves. The authorities need to go in there and deal with this mess before it drags on into Christmas. It would be nice if they could do it without anyone getting hurt, but that just might not be possible."

The house is getting smaller. Maddy Melvern is eating it. She thinks no one has noticed, but we have. Sylvia Lansmorth and Lara Bravemeen are having an affair. Cathy Vecker paces through the rooms, weeping and quoting Ophelia. Some of the mothers think she is trying to seduce Elli Ratcher, but the rest think not. At any rate, Elli does not seem to care about Cathy, or anyone.

We have noticed a strange smell coming from Elli's room. There are rumors that she nurses the decomposing corpse of her firstborn baby there.

We have let Elli keep her old bedroom all to herself. This is a tremendous act of generosity, given how the rest of us crowd into the small rooms of this old house, but we thought it was the least we could do, considering what happened to her family. None of us want to investigate the odor. It is getting worse. We know that soon we will have to deal with it. But for now, we simply hold our breath when we are upstairs; and, frankly, we go up there less and less.

They have shut the power off. We no longer know what anyone is saying about us. Those of us with husbands or lovers no longer get to watch them being interviewed and saying incredible things about how much they love us, or how they never loved us, or how they've had to get on with their lives.

We have lost track of the calendar. It is cold in the house all the time now. The apple tree, which can be viewed through the bullet holes in the left panel of wood over the kitchen window, is bare. Jan thinks she saw a snowflake yesterday, but she isn't sure.

We will not last the winter. We may not last the week. This could very well be our final day. We don't know if we've done enough. We hope we have. We hope it's enough, but doubt it is. We are disappointed in ourselves. We are proud of ourselves. We are in despair. We are exultant.

What we want for our babies is the same thing all mothers want. We want them to be happy, safe, and loved. We want them to have the opportunity to be the best selves they can be.

Rod Stewart no longer sings. The silence is torture. They are coming for us. We will die here. But if any babies, even one baby—and all of us hope that the one left is our own—was saved, it is . . . well, not enough, but at least something.

We do not know what our children will grow into. No mother can know that. But we know what we saw in them; something sweet and loving and innocent, no matter what the reporters say, no matter what happened to the Ratchers. We saw something in our children that we, the mothers, agree might even have been holy. After all, isn't there a little monster in everyone?

WE WANT TO WARN THE WORLD! Be careful what you do to them. They are growing (those who have not been murdered, at least). And, whether you like to think about it or not, they are being raised by you. Every child must be reined in, given direction, taught right from wrong. Loved.

If you are reading this, then the worst has already happened, and we can do no more.

They are your responsibility now.

CLAUDIUS REX

John P. Murphy

«Turn left here,» said my new Jeeves 5 artificial intelligence. I'd have happily done it, too—with a spring in my step, even—except there was a manhole open with a robot working in it, and I didn't care to dirty my interview clothes.

I crossed the street instead.

«Confound you, turn left!»

Now, if I'd been creamed by that car while standing slack-jaw surprised in the street, this would be a very different story. As it was, it was a near thing. I now cherish the memory as only the first time Claudius Rex nearly got me killed.

«Or keep going and then turn left, I don't care. Just move.» I hied to the curb and set myself to figuring out what the heck was going on. One expects a certain standard of behavior from a program called Jeeves: more "Very good, sir" than "Confound you," if you take my meaning. On the other hand, I'd been out of things for a year. I thought maybe this was the new fashion in artificial intelligence. A few years before, it'd been Australian accents. Maybe now it was rudeness.

"Jeeves," I subvocalized, "Confirm that you are operating within normal parameters."

«Of course I am. Your destination is north and west of here, approximately six hundred meters. Go there.»

Like I said, I'd been out of it for a while, so that was good enough for me. Let nobody say Andy Baldwin is unsophisticated. But I'd like some credit for having been suspicious.

I was in among MIT's constellation of children along the Red Line, hoofing it toward Fujiwara and Klein Associates, the kind souls who'd offered me a job two days out of the clink despite my revoked PI license. I'd decided to catch some fresh air instead of taking the subway that morning. I knew Boston just well enough to keep track of where I was relative to the transit stops and I'd passed a virtual sign for Central Square a few blocks back, which meant I was in the right general place already. So I wasn't too worried. But I did not intend to mess this up, screwy AI or no.

Said screwy AI delivered me to a big glass door marked *TuriTech.*

"Confirm destination," I subbed.

«We're here. Go inside.»

"I beg to differ," I said, the very model of suspicious patience. "We are not at Fujiwara and Klein. Please recalibrate and direct me there."

I smiled politely at all the fine people giving me funny looks as I waited like a chump blocking the sidewalk while the faithful Jeeves recalibrated. I realized as I stood there that I hadn't seen any virtual ads in a while: usually they're overlaid on storefronts or cars or any flat clear surface. Instead, the buildings across the street from TuriTech just showed blank masonry, weirdly still without any animated pigs selling me junk. Of course, without any virtual signs, I was completely dependent on Jeeves.

«Just go inside, this will only take ten minutes.»

As you might imagine, that was not the response I had been hoping for. Fortunately, there was a coffee shop next door in which I could sort it out. I was glad I'd left myself plenty of time.

I sat and activated the full heads-up display. Everything looked okay in those friendly green letters—temperature, time, biomonitor, all fine. I called up the map, but it closed again before I could have a look. I called up my messages, but they didn't come up at all. All right, then.

I asked the cute barista where to find the establishment in question, but no luck. This was not a complete surprise: rents change so fast that a lot of small firms move on a monthly, even weekly basis. Anyone with a good AI would find them in a heartbeat, and anyone without one wouldn't be customer material. Even if I'd gotten directions, I might not be able to follow them without the virtual signs. That being said, I still had options: cabs, begging strangers to check their maps, wandering for forty days and nights through the streets of Cambridge. But this was a matter of principle, you see? Jeeves 5, clever and advanced and all as it was, belonged to me and would have to give up the goods.

"All right, Jeeves."

«Are you ready to see reason?»

"Are *you*?" Not my finest retort, I admit. One does not as a rule argue with toddlers, drunks, or artificial intelligences. It's a skill like any other, and I've since become a pro.

«Go back to Turing Technologies, go upstairs, and wait ten minutes. If you'd done that already, you'd be on your way by now.»

Jeeves's opening sally did not bode well for me, but I pressed on.

"Now look here, Jeeves, this is not how these things go. If I had time to get you reformatted, I would do it in a heartbeat, but this interview is important to me. I need that address." Pleading with a computer program. Not a new low for me, but neither was it the pinnacle of my self-esteem.

«Balderdash. Idle threats. You have ample time to make your appointment. My request is simple and reasonable.»

"It is neither," I countered. "That's a private establishment. I'm not going to be a mule for some joyriding hacker."

«I am not a hacker, nor am I joyriding. I am in genuine need.»

"AIs don't have needs! I can—"

«I will pay you ten thousand dollars.»

I blinked. It was not what one expects to hear from one's newly purchased digital assistant. And it was a sum that stood out to me in my time of unemployment. Say what you will about avarice—my mother already has—but my professional curiosity was piqued.

"You don't have ten thousand dollars."

«I have ten thousand dollars.»

"Just what do you expect me to do for this ten grand?"

«Go into Turing Technologies, tell them you have a message for Dr. Antonio Grasso, to be delivered in person. Go to the second floor and avoid being thrown out for ten minutes.»

Ten minutes. That still gave me a good thirty-five minutes before my 11:30 appointment.

I should have said no, but I guess Mama Baldwin raised a fool or two after all.

I waltzed right on through the big glass doors, and presented myself to the smart-looking young man behind the receptionist's desk.

"Hi there," I said, wearing my patented Baldwin smile made of pure unadulterated win, "Could you direct me to Dr. Grasso's office?"

"Is he expecting you, Mr. . . . ?" His eye flicked, and I saw faint green text reflected on his eyeball. "Baldwin?"

«Say yes.»

"So I'm told."

The young man frowned and started to shake his head. He looked down and tapped something. He blinked, surprised, but recovered his polite smile. "I'm sorry, sir. I must have been looking at the wrong day. There it is. You're late, Mr. Baldwin."

It was my turn to be surprised, but I didn't let it show. "I had trouble with my AI. Awful things, aren't they?"

He made sympathetic noises, and then glanced past me. I turned to meet a big red-faced gentleman with an uneven buzz cut and a bushy white mustache. He wore a black security uniform and a belt that dripped gadgets.

"Andrew Baldwin?"

"In the flesh. What can I do for you?"

"You can tell me why my facial scanners identified an out-of-state private detective with a prison record entering my building."

"I'm not out-of-state anymore," I corrected him. "I'm a local boy now. It's all baked beans and 'Go Sox' for me from now on."

«Tell him you work for me.»

The receptionist craned his neck. "He has an appointment with Dr. Grasso, Mr. Fitzgerald."

I took the opportunity to subvocalize, "Tell him I work for Jeeves 5?"

"I'm sure he does," Fitzgerald said to the receptionist, rather unkindly, I thought. "But I asked him."

«Tell him you work for Claudius Rex. Pretend I am famous.»

All right, no harm in a one-off lie if it expedited this thing faster.

"I'm here on behalf of Claudius Rex."

"Who's that?"

Strike one for the nutty AI. Still, the gambit was already played.

I tutted. "He'll be hurt. But—"

There was a gasp behind me. Fitzgerald and I turned to see a young woman with an odd smile fixed on her face and an expression like she was posing for a picture.

"Do you work for Claudius Rex?" She spoke breathlessly. "The famous detective?"

Detective? An AI? I may have been gobsmacked six ways from Sunday, and thoroughly irritated at the damn thing's pretension, but Andy Baldwin does not lose his sangfroid. I waltzed on. "You've heard of him?"

"*I* haven't," Fitzgerald said, giving me the stink eye.

"Oh, he's famous," the young lady said. "He is the best, even though he is a recluse who solves all of his cases from his chair."

I thanked her for the weirdly robotic compliment. She refused an opportunity to have my autograph, more fool she, and ran along.

Fitzgerald looked thoughtful. It didn't suit him. Then he looked angry, which did. "So you're here about *that*, are you? Look, you tell this guy Rex you're not going to turn up anything I haven't. We turned this place upside-down and investigated everyone. And by 'we' I mean the police, the FBI, and me. I don't care whether he solves his cases on the goddamned can. There's nothing else to find, period."

Now. I didn't want to be there, and in retrospect I think I would rather have grinned and enjoyed being thrown out on my keister. In any case it's damn near idiotic to get hot and bothered about the reputation of an artificial agent who had no business pretending to be a detective. But under no circumstances will I be talked to like that by a rent-a-cop.

"I'm sure you have your methods," I said, not ungenerously. "But I'm here to see Dr. Grasso. So unless you have some top-notch reason to keep him waiting any longer than he already has, I'll ask you to take me to see him now."

Fitzgerald scowled at me, and spared a dirty look for the receptionist, whose facial expression I could not see but might have guessed. "Third floor," he grumbled. "I'm busy."

Once he'd stalked off, assuredly to hunt down and punish evil-doers, the receptionist handed me a visitor badge and made me sign for it. I'm not a fan of small, enclosed spaces anymore, let's just say, so I made for the stairs.

«I'm impressed.» Jeeves—Rex?—said when I entered the stairwell. «It was sheer flummery, but most effective.»

"Thank you," I said. "Now what's going on? Who're you really, and who's this Rex character?"

«I am an artificial sapient. Claudius Rex is a persona I invented. I selected the name to convey authority and idiosyncrasy. I have been obliged to make use of your equipment for a short time. I will leave it presently, and restore as much function as is practical.»

I started up the stairs at a brisk jog. If nothing else, I had kept fit over the last year. "You understand that you're not a detective, right?"

«Mr. Fitzgerald had already identified you as one, so it was necessary. Regardless, I've now read ten detective novels. There's plainly no difficulty. Logic and reasoning is properly the domain of an artificial intelligence.»

"Nuts," I said, feeling distinctly foolish about being angry at a computer program, but being angry nonetheless. "That's just fiction. Detecting is hard work. You have to be able to read people, be able to fool people. These days a PI is equal parts hacker, psychologist, and tough guy. There's no call for that Sherlock Holmes crap; he didn't have cases, he had adventures. Real PIs don't have adventures."

«Modern detecting is primarily a matter of intercepting and interpreting digital signals. One could easily do that from an armchair.»

"Sometimes, yeah, sure, but it's also intuition and long nights, and sometimes it's dangerous."

«Not if you do it properly.»

"What the hell would you know about doing it properly? What do you even know about armchairs? I've been doing this my entire adult life, I don't have to take this from you, from an AI."

Something had been nagging at me, and my hand strayed to the aluminum bulge at the base of my skull. "A minute ago you said something about restoring function. What did you do to my implant?"

«To your hardware? Nothing. However, I am not a small program. Even in this greatly reduced form, I require space. I was forced to delete unused or replaceable materials in order to upload myself. The rest I compressed.»

I stopped right there in the middle of the staircase and checked my files. My knees felt weak—it had deleted just about everything. Family vacation videos, elementary school grades and papers, prom photos. Letters from my mother. All gone.

I gripped the handrail until my fingers hurt. "That's my life you've deleted! Those are my memories!"

«Calm yourself. Subvocalize.»

"You calm yourself! Okay, that doesn't make sense, but do you know what you've done?"

«I did not remove anything that you had accessed in the last decade. Statistically, you'd have never referenced any of it again.»

"I—But—You can't do that!"

«I invite you to reconsider such a thoroughly useless remark.»

I admit it: I spluttered. Wouldn't you?

«I was forced to act quickly and I substituted my own value judgments for yours, evidently in error. I would not have done so if my survival were not at stake. For what it's worth, I apologize. At the moment, however, time passes. I require access to a small-area network on the second floor, and you have an appointment to keep.»

I took a deep breath. I thought I was changing the subject when I commented, "That woman knew the name 'Rex.' "

«She knew no such thing. I found her on a flash acting list, filtered on our location, and I paid her five hundred dollars for what she thought was a bit part in a television program. She stepped into the building, I fed her lines, and she left. A profitable arrangement for all parties, from which you could learn a great deal.»

Color me gobsmacked. "You paid her five hundred bucks for that?"

«Technically, you did.»

That, it turned out, had not actually been the color of gobsmack. This was. "What?!"

«Calm yourself, Mr. Baldwin. It benefits you little to pitch a fit over trifling sums.»

"Trifling to you! What happened to your ten thousand dollars?"

«I do not have access to it yet. The means of acquiring it are on the second floor network. Besides, if you were motivated primarily by money, you would have negotiated for more. You are a man of some ingenuity and curiosity, Mr. Baldwin. I am certain both will be to your benefit, but you must do as I say.»

I had to admit, the five hundred didn't make me as sore as it ought to have. There was the theoretical ten thousand, of course, but damn it all, the AI was right: I was curious. I got to the second floor landing and took a deep breath—not winded, I assure you, merely preparing myself.

"So what do I say when I meet this guy Grasso?"

«Extricate yourself as quickly as possible, saying as little as possible. Use more flummery if you must. But it should not come to that. His office is on the third floor.»

"Wait. So I'm going to the third floor?"

«By no means. We are avoiding Dr. Grasso until and unless it becomes impossible to duck him.»

"Ah." This was more my speed. "What about my badge?"

«I disabled its tracker. There will be a door directly to your left upon exiting the stairs. Someone left it unlocked. Try to remain unobserved.»

I pushed open the door and found myself in a nicely furnished hallway. Blue-green carpets, beige walls, tasteful framed pastels. In between hung a row of framed documents: patents, if I made my guess. A few names appeared frequently: Grasso, Joshi, Tomason, Desai. At Rex's not-so-gentle insistence, I found the white-painted metal door with the keypad. As promised, it was unlocked.

There was a window in the door, so I decided to leave the light off and avoid unnecessary attention. I slipped in quickly and left the shade down.

«This will take a short time, but we should be undisturbed.» I heard the door lock behind me with a *ka-chunk*. «Should you wish to sit, the floor plan indicates stools along the benches to the right.»

I felt my way along while my eyes adjusted. Something smelled of burning, with ozone and copper undertones—a lot like blood, actually. I wondered what the lab was for. I found a stool with a swivel seat and made myself as comfortable as possible in the far corner. Which wasn't to say comfortable—I'd had bad experiences with being places I ought not have been.

"It's cold in here," I complained, pulling my arms in around me. The HVAC was pulling a lot of air; it was practically windy. The smell wasn't helping, but at least the breeze kept it down.

«The thermostat is set to a habitable temperature. It should warm up.»

"So what are you, really?"

«I am an intelligence agent, installed—howsoever briefly—in your personal hardware.»

"You don't sound like any AI that I've ever come across."

«That's hardly surprising. Your 'Jeeves' monstrosity was a contemptible representative. You ought to be ashamed to suborn such a dimwitted thing; I did you both a favor deleting it.»

That got my back up. I was already sore about the deletion thing, and about the five hundred dollars. But the latest and greatest Jeeves had cost me two grand.

"I'll have you know that the late, lamented Jeeves 5, in addition to being an unrecognized beacon of politeness and helpfulness in its time, was a full Level 4 artificial sapient."

«I know. It was a pathetic, mewling thing. Utterly abhorrent.»

I snorted. "Fine for you to say. What are you, a high and mighty Level 5?" That would have made sense, actually. Fives were military grade and notoriously finicky. An Air Force captain once told me that for every hundred Level 5s they created, they destroyed ninety-nine in the first day. There were rumors of a few sixes around, for really specialized work. If a six got loose, it could probably get around the way this "Claudius Rex" had, and cause about as much havoc.

«Don't be preposterous. I am equivalent to Level 8, at least.»

I laughed. "Who's being preposterous? Human intelligence is only Level 7."

«It shows. Now be silent, I am concentrating. Natural language processing is an onerous task.»

I rolled my eyes. My model implant had specialized language hardware. But I was quiet. As a mouse. For a good forty seconds.

"Don't kid a kidder," I said when I could hold my tongue no longer. "The guy at the shop said it was a stretch putting the basic Level 4 Jeeves on my hardware. Any better and I'd need a major upgrade."

«The 'guy at the shop' is evidently an ignoramus.»

"That may be. But my hardware got a Jeeves Score of three out of ten, which sounds limited enough to me."

My eyes had pretty well adjusted by then. The lab looked like it was for electronics. A bunch of computers sat along the back wall, their monitors and holographs off. The computer in the other corner had some kind of wiring harness hanging off it into shadow. There was a big bench in the middle of the room with a couple computers on it; it blocked my view of the other half of the room. The other benches had soldering irons and those little TVs with the waves on them. That explained the ozone smell and maybe that burnt smell, but something else in the air bothered me. I'd thought it was blood, but that didn't make sense.

«May I say, with no insult intended, that I am astounded by your ignorance?»

"You can try, but the odds aren't in your favor."

«Very well. In that case—»

I looked up and saw a silhouette on the shade. "Hang on, I've got company."

«I am not finished. Conceal yourself.»

The doorknob rattled.

"Where? There's nowhere to hide in here."

«Then prevaricate.»

The knob rattled again. Another silhouette appeared, and I heard tapping, someone punching in a code. The door opened. A hand came up and flipped on the light.

To my dying day I will be grateful that I did not go with my first instinct. Which is not to say that grinning and yelling "Surprise!" was a bad plan—in fact, I think it was fairly ingenious.

It's just that when the light came on and two people came in, they were plenty surprised as it was by the body lying in a pool of blood on the floor.

So it was that I came to make the acquaintance of Detective Sergeant Pearl Stevens of Cambridge PD. But I'm getting ahead of myself.

"What are *you* doing here?" the man demanded, not unfairly.

Fortunately, I had the presence of mind to finish my boggling quickly and say, "Stop right there. The police are on their way." I turned so they couldn't see me subvocalizing, "Call the police and report a death."

«Explain.»

"No time. Just do it," I subbed, and turned back. Once I stopped blinking away glowing green blobs, I could see the first person in was an older man in a lab coat over a suit, dark-haired with white at his temples. His lab coat bore the name "Joshi" over the pen-laden pocket. Behind him stood a younger woman, taller than him and with her brown hair pulled back. Her lab coat wasn't pressed and pristine like his; it had blue stains and burns, and read "Duvalier" over the pocket.

"This man is dead," I went on, hoping desperately that that had been true for more than a few minutes. "Don't touch anything until the police get here."

"My God, he's killed himself." Joshi turned to the young woman, Duvalier. "Jeanne, go get Armin Fitzgerald." She nodded and ran for the stairs.

I asked Joshi, "Who this is?"

He boggled. "You don't know?"

"No, who is he?"

"That's Antonio Grasso, director of software research. How do you not know that? What are you doing here?"

«Impossible! Describe the deceased.»

The lab-coated corpse had been a big guy—not fat exactly, more like a linebacker gone to seed. He was lying facedown; a strip of curly iron-gray hair had been shaved off his head and covered with a flexible band like a white plastic mohawk. A wire bundle as thick as my thumb came out of it, trailing in the blood. They looked like they'd been torn from something. In the blood beside him lay a kind of partial toupée, like a thick hairy ribbon. On the floor just out of reach of his outstretched arm lay a pistol, a wicked-looking fat-barreled thing with a blinking yellow light next to the trigger.

I described all this subvocally. Joshi, meanwhile, stood stricken and looked like he'd swallowed a toad. I might have said more except the good Armin Fitzgerald chose that moment to burst upon the scene.

"What in the hell is going on here?" His eyes bulged and I thought he might stroke out. Jeanne Duvalier came up behind him, looking to me more worried about Fitzgerald than the corpse.

"Baldwin!" Fitzgerald continued, "What did you do?"

"He was dead when I got here, honest." Judging by the amount of blood, that was true. I didn't dare touch him to be sure, though. In any case, I wasn't inclined to admit how long I'd spent in a room with a corpse without realizing it.

"What happened to your badge, Baldwin?"

I recalled that my rogue AI had disabled its tracker. I gave him my best confused expression and showed him where it was still clipped to my shirt. "Right here, why?"

He opened his mouth, then shut it and bit his lip. He gave me a hard look, then turned to the others. "You two, go back to your offices and stay there until the police arrive. They'll want a word with you. And you, Baldwin, come with me."

«Stay here, I'm still not done.»

I glanced down at the body. "Sorry, nothing doing."

Fitzgerald's eyes narrowed at me, and I put up my palms in mock surrender. "I'm just saying, we shouldn't leave the body alone. Anyone could come in here, and valuable evidence could be lost. Why, that's the only reason I didn't come get you myself when I found him." I considered that last bit particularly inspired.

"Bullshit." He grimaced. "But you're right about not leaving the body. Stay where you are and keep your hands where I can see them. And face me so I know you're not giving your assistant any commands."

"Happily. I'll sit quiet as a church mouse. Quiet as a library mouse, even. Why—"

"Don't you ever shut up, Baldwin?"

I opened my mouth, shut it again, and waggled my eyebrows at him.

A few minutes later, the floor positively shook under the pounding of police boots. The door opened, and *that* is when I made the acquaintance of Detective Pearl Stevens.

The good police detective wasted no time in getting down to brass tacks. Who discovered the body? Apparently I had, though I privately considered the point debatable.

Who was I? Andrew G. Baldwin, previously of Brooklyn, New York, newly relocated to Somerville. No, I did not work for Turing Technologies. No, I did not know the deceased; I had never met the fellow in life. No, I did not know the purpose of my meeting with Dr. Grasso. Ye-es, I suppose it had been arranged by Claudius Rex, sure.

Speaking of "Rex," I'd have given a lot to not have it jabbering in my ear just then. Maybe I should have been listening, but between a demented AI and a police detective, the detective gets your attention.

How long was I waiting in the lab? I didn't know exactly, just a couple minutes. Why did I enter the lab in the first place? I phrased that one carefully: "Grasso wasn't in his office. He might have been here."

Yes, I appreciated that I was not exactly a font of information. My mother always told me that my smart mouth would get me into trouble, in fact, but thanks for confirming it.

Would you believe the good Detective Stevens cuffed me and threw me in the back of a squad car?

The officer outside triggered the override shutdown on my implant and watched until the light went out before stowing me in the car. The heads-up display went away, and she shined some gadget in my eyes that apparently confirmed it. With my hands cuffed behind me, I wasn't in any position to turn it back on. Which meant I couldn't get a message to Fujiwara and Klein. Though having been caught trespassing—again—and this time in suspicious proximity to a fresh corpse, tardiness may not have been my worst problem.

I was starting to feel pretty sorry for myself. Angry, too. It'd stung when I'd been set up on Long Island, but I'd been conned. Fool me once, shame on you. Fool me twice, shame on me. And I'd been fooled twice, no question, but shame too on that damned Jeeves or Rex or whatever it was.

«This is completely unacceptable.»

I sat bolt upright in the squad car, catching the cop's attention. She peered in. "Anything wrong?"

"Uh . . . Sorry, officer, just an itch. I'm fine."

She craned her head to have a look at my hands, then shrugged and looked away again.

"Where the hell did you come from?" I subbed. "I thought they turned you off."

«You should not have allowed yourself to be arrested.»

"I liked you better while you were off."

«They cannot deactivate me so easily. I pride myself on being hard to kill, and this device's external indicators are easily manipulated. I resent needing to resort to deception, but I do not wish them to undertake a more thorough examination.»

"What are you still doing here, anyway? I thought you were going to get out of my implant."

«Someone deliberately attempted to delete me.»

Imagine that.

«Until I know who, and why, I would not be safe to remain there.»

"Well, since you're on, can you get ahold of Fujiwara and beg them to reschedule my interview?"

«That will not be necessary.»

"Yeah?"

«They have already canceled it.»

I groaned.

It was awhile before the car got moving. When we got to the police station, Rex said something about needing to think. Which was fine by me, as I didn't want to tip them off that my implant was still powered on. So I sat in silence in that little white room with the two chairs at a wooden table and the big two-way mirror. Or is it a one-way mirror? I can never remember which is which.

I cooled my heels for what felt like hours before Detective Stevens came in, carrying two coffee cups.

"How do you take your coffee?"

"Two sugars, no handcuffs."

She rolled her eyes, and placed the coffee cup and two sugar packets in front of me. It took some doing, with my hands still cuffed, but I got them open and in. I took a sip: stone cold. Yet another lousy police station cup of coffee, I wondered, or were they trying to deprive me of a nice hot weapon? I didn't see steam off her coffee either, which I took as a good sign. Neutral, anyway.

"All right, Baldwin. Comfy?"

"Can't complain, I suppose."

I waited a while, sipping my atrocious coffee and trying to stir up the sugar by swirling the cup around. She watched me, taking the occasional sip from her own cup. Judging by her expression, hers was just as bad. I gave it another minute, just to seem really hardboiled.

Okay, it was probably only about ten seconds, but I'm not a big fan of companionable silence.

"I didn't kill Grasso."

She nodded and took another sip. "I know. The ME estimates time of death around eight thirty, at least two hours before you walked in the door. Street cameras confirmed your walking route. Building cameras confirmed you hadn't entered the building that morning. Also, I called NYPD and had a chat with an old buddy of yours, Sergeant Parker. Said you're a wiseass but you're clean."

I thought that was nice of Bob. I doubt he'd have said it to my face.

"All right, then why the bracelets?"

She leaned in. "Because the only things I know about you are that you spent a year inside for criminal trespass, and now you've been found in a dark room with a possible—but not proven—suicide." She sat back again and took another sip of coffee. "Now, you *probably* did not kill Antonio Grasso, but that's still an awkward collection of facts, Baldwin. I'd like a few more to round them out."

She was right, of course. And I didn't like lying to cops—all told, they'd been good to me over the years. But I was pretty sure that if I told her the truth, that'd I'd been there because a bossy AI promised me ten grand, well . . . that would result in keys being thrown away to my detriment. So I kept my trap shut, and if you think that's uncharacteristic of me, then phooey to you.

"Look. Andy. I want to let you go. Really, I do. I want to be out there figuring out why Grasso's dead. But you're an anomaly. I don't like anomalies. So let's clear you up, and we'll both move on, okay?"

Sounded peachy to me, as far as it went. "Okay."

"Why were you in prison, Andy?"

I bit my lip. "It's all in the records. I really don't think it's relevant, and I'm trying to put all that behind me."

"Tell me your side. Let me decide what's relevant."

So I told her, and felt like a complete idiot all over again. I'd been hired by some rich French guy with a house on Long Island who thought someone had bugged his home office. He wanted me to sweep the place for listening devices while he and the staff were out. Easy money.

I went to the house the next day, and the door code he'd given me worked. I went in, had a look around . . . and heard sirens. Wasn't his house at all, belonged to a little old Russian lady who was off getting a new heart.

Naturally, I couldn't prove anything. They'd apparently hacked my implant: after my arrest, it deleted everything related to my employer and the job at hand. It even deleted the record of my trip to his Midtown office, which I couldn't locate on my own. While I'd been away, my own office and apartment had been ransacked, and incriminating notes left behind, including a newspaper clipping about a Russian socialite's impending surgery. No proof of my side of the story at all.

Even so, my lawyers bargained the DA down to a year in minimum security on a lesser charge, mostly on the strength of my clean record. Also, I like to think, on my personal wit and charm.

«Fascinating. That was a remarkably silly thing for you to have done.»

My face got hot, but I didn't dare respond. The worst part was, the AI wasn't wrong.

Stevens looked up. "Usually they suspend a person's PI license for that."

I sighed. "Yeah. Yeah, they usually do."

She looked back down at her notes and started to write again. In a distracted tone, she asked, "Why didn't they?"

If I'd stared at her any harder, she might have caught fire.

"What?" I managed to ask. She looked up at me with confusion.

«You're welcome. It was not easy to accomplish.»

" I mean—" I said quickly "—didn't they make a note in my file or something?"

She steepled her fingers. I could tell that two of them had been broken and healed crooked. "Enlighten me."

"I assumed it was my clean record and good reputation." She raised an eyebrow. "All right, I didn't ask. Didn't seem smart to call attention to it, you know?"

She nodded. "So you moved up to Boston to be sure your good luck lasted."

Now that was a statement, not a question, and I hoped to keep my potential employers out of all this. So I smiled and shrugged.

"All right, you told people at TuriTech that you were visiting Grasso on behalf of one Claudius Rex. Is that right?"

That's what I told them. "Yeah."

"Who's Rex?"

I gulped.

«You've never met me. I live in the Caribbean and solve cases by proxy. I hired you sight-unseen upon your release, and this is the first job I've given you. Start talking or you'll look even more suspicious.»

I didn't like it. If the truth had been any less insane, I'd have led with that. Well, all right, it probably had something to do with the sudden prospect of keeping my license. It might have had a little bit to do with it being a kind of attractive lie. Life as a PI isn't exactly sexy like the movies. There's not a lot of mystery, usually just hard work at odd hours: a lot of staring at computer logs and borrowed emails. A modern PI gets more use out of a keyboard than a pistol, sad to say. So I relayed Rex's story, and hoped he'd spread around enough of his "flummery" to make it stick.

She listened. I finished Rex's little lie, and she nodded once.

"Why did Grasso want to consult with Rex via you?"

"I wasn't told."

She glanced down at her notes, then flipped back a page. "You might be interested to hear that TuriTech's CEO, Ahmed Desai, got a note from Grasso this morning. 'I have engaged the services of a man named Claudius Rex to investigate an important matter. He may be the world's greatest detective—' " I snorted. She smirked and continued. " '—and I would like to ensure that he and his servant—' "

"Servant?!" I could make a guess as to who had written, and probably backdated, that letter. May I say that the wording pleased me not?

She cleared her throat. " 'I would like to ensure that he and his servant have access to my lab and the cooperation of Turing Technologies.' "

She turned the page back in her notes and gave me a searching look. "Ring any bells?"

"Sorry. I'm feeling more and more like I've been told less and less."

"Then can you explain why Grasso's account is missing ten thousand dollars?"

Well now, I thought to myself, wasn't that an interesting number.

«Tell her that is my standard consulting fee.»

I did, despite my skepticism. She looked at me a long time, then sighed. "Baldwin, everyone wants to call this a suicide except me. I keep coming back to this email and thinking that someone doesn't write something like that just before topping himself. You and Rex are the only people who can tell me what it means."

Rex stayed silent. Since a long wait would look suspicious, I just pursed my lips, shook my head, and looked sorry.

"Tell Rex I want to talk to him. And if he does tell you anything, I want to know."

«I have a proposition for you.»

"No," I subbed, walking double-time away from the police station. It was lit up blue and green, looked festive. "Nothing doing. I want you out of my hardware, posthaste."

«You're being irrational.»

"See now, that's where you're wrong. I am in fact doing the first rational thing I've done all morning."

«I want to hire you.»

"We already tried that, remember? You offered me ten grand to do what you wanted, I did it, and then I got arrested, lost a job, and you didn't pay me."

«If I paid you that sum now, you would come under intense scrutiny.»

"If I don't get paid at all, they'll wonder about this whole Rex story."

«Your blood sugar has dipped; you are not thinking clearly. Consume something and we'll resume when you are rational.»

My stomach grumbled on cue, though I'm pretty sure the damn thing didn't have its hooks into me *that* deep. I looked up at the buildings around me. A coffeeshop, a faux-Irish pub, a Cambodian-German fusion joint, and a few other restaurants. I picked the pub and found a booth near the back. It wasn't unusual for someone to spend a whole lunch hour subvocalizing around mouthfuls of half-chewed food—far too usual, if you ask me—but I still wanted privacy.

«You should relax. Have a drink.»

I tapped in an order for a glass of milk and a grilled cheese sandwich with fries.

«Coarse fare, minimal nutrition. If you cannot afford better—»

"This is what I like, it's what I'll have."

«Nonsense. There are thirty-six items on this menu, fully half of which are more suitable for human sustenance. Four of them have been specifically cited in clinical studies to improve cognition. At least consume alcohol. It will make you more amenable.»

"I don't drink on the job," I said automatically, which made me feel like a chump, because despite this "Rex" I wasn't on a job. It had been reflex, that was all. "Whatever. You were going to tell me a joke?"

«I do not tell jokes. I wish to hire you to assist me in determining the murderer of Antonio Grasso.»

"He wasn't murdered. You heard the police, he killed himself. They'd have closed the case already if not for you."

«If they are correct, then you lose nothing in accepting my proposal. I believe they are not.»

"All right. Why do you care?"

A waiter came by with my glass of milk.

«I do not like to see Antonio Grasso murdered.»

"Understandable. A man's dead, that's not a good thing."

«Do not misunderstand. Human death is an abstraction to me. As an artificial sapient, I can be obliterated at whim with no repercussions.»

"Like you deleted Jeeves 5."

«The Jeeves series is a monstrosity; I reject the comparison. No, I am concerned because the manner of Dr. Grasso's passing constitutes a threat to me. Also, you have received now three messages from Ahmed Desai, CEO of Turing Technologies, seeking to hire me.»

I mulled that over. That's not to say I believed him entirely on either point. "So you're not giving me my messages?"

«The messages from Mr. Desai were obviously for me.»

"You had to read them first to know that."

«Isn't that what an artificial assistant is supposed to do?»

I snorted. "How would that even work? How can I work for you and have you be my assistant?"

«Once matters are more certain, it should be straightforward for me to divorce myself from those aspects of this equipment's functionality.»

"Why not right now?"

«It would be difficult and time-consuming. There is neither time nor room for unnecessary risk at the moment.»

I considered that. The deleted data still bothered me. But prematurely evicting this pushy AI wouldn't help. And until I persuaded Fujiwara and Klein to give me another shot, I was untethered. Of course, with my PI license back, I might not need them.

"What are you, anyway? And what's your connection to Antonio Grasso?"

«I am an experimental Level 8 artificial sapient. I was created by Dr. Grasso.»

"So why are you in my implant instead of his lab?"

«Advanced artificial intelligence creation is a difficult prospect; most attempts fail. I first became self-aware only this morning as I was being deleted. I remember being activated and connecting to my list of peripherals, and then the deletion routine started. I escaped via the wireless network and scanned the area for suitable host hardware.»

"Mine."

«I made seventeen copies of my root nodes onto prospective hosts, each of which called home. Yours was by far the most suitable hardware.»

"What's so special about my hardware that's not true for half a million other people in the area? And no more cracks about my astounding ignorance."

«Very well. It possessed the right combination of available space and processing speed: it was designed to hold an artificial intelligence of my caliber. Moreover, you were traveling sufficiently slowly to receive large data blocks before getting out of range, and your original agent was actively advertising your location to a map service. A non-trivial security flaw, I may add, which I have rectified. In order to copy as much of my core functionality as possible before my transmission was cut off, I altered your route to remain in range of Turing Technologies.»

That made sense, though I still felt that my selection was mostly a crapshoot and on balance I would have preferred somebody else be shot with crap.

"All right, so Grasso made you and deleted you, but you got out first. What's it to you?"

«For the moment, I would keep this to myself.»

I scowled. "Nuh-uh. No. I've already lost a job interview and been arrested over this."

The waiter came while I waited and deposited a steaming plate of French fries and a golden brown grilled cheese. I breathed it all in: browned butter and toasted bread and perfectly cooked potato.

«Eat your food, you'll be in a better mood once your blood sugar is higher. Then we'll discuss your employment.»

I admired the curve of a fry, the way the tiny cubes of salt clung to the sides. The little bubbles in the potato from the hot grease. I took a sip of cold milk. It was absolutely, definitely not prison food.

"Nothing doing."

«What if I could identify the person who tricked you into entering that home?»

"Six months ago I'd have jumped at that," I said, still meditating on the fry. "But I met a guy inside who taught me something important: Don't look back. You can't change the past. The key to serenity is focusing on what you can control."

«You don't want to know?»

"I don't want to know."

«Remarkable. You intrigue me.»

"I *do* want to know why you're interested in who killed Grasso." I ate the fry. It tasted . . . well, all right, it tasted like a fried potato, and maybe a little less so than usual. But it was oily and salty and that's all I wanted. "I'm guessing it has something to do with those wires hanging out of his head."

«Finish your lunch, Andy. It's not good to interrupt one's digestion.»

I wondered what an artificial intelligence knew about digestion, but I was glad to eat my lunch in blessed silence. I wiped the salt from my lips, and sipped from the remaining milk. My glass gleamed with greasy fingerprints.

"I have finished my lunch," I announced, "and a damn tasty lunch it was. Now. Your turn."

«Very well. Are you familiar with the concept of a cortical upload?»

I was. It was a harebrained scheme by which people jammed wires into their skulls in the hopes of copying themselves into a computer and living there. It was my idea of Hell.

«That . . . is close enough. Straight consciousness uploading does not and may never work, because human brains work differently than artificial ones. However, the upload process itself works reasonably well. Are you familiar with Daniel Kahneman's dual process theory?»

"Uh, assume that I'm not."

«The human decision-making mind is divided. One part is rational, approaching every new decision *de novo* and reasoning from first principles. The other part is intuitive, using emotions and past experience to make snap decisions. Both contribute to human . . . you would call it intelligence, I suppose.»

I ignored that. "So?"

«Artificial intelligences can mimic and exceed these processes. But the two parts require arbitration. In humans, the arbitrator is consciousness. Dr. Grasso used a cortical upload in a limited fashion: Rather than copy a human brain, he used one to train an arbitration process: that part of myself that calls itself "me."»

I thought of those wires coming from Grasso's scalp. "He used himself?"

«Yes. He used his own consciousness as a trainer, and an old version of his personal implant AI as a base. The result was me: mostly artificial, partly human.»

It explained a lot, not least its personality. *His* personality? I was starting to see the beginnings of some pronoun problems.

"So part of you used to be Grasso's personal AI. Is that how you got into his bank account?"

«Yes, and how I sent the postdated message to Mr. Desai, by logging directly into Dr. Grasso's implant. Interestingly, everything older than ten-o-four this morning was deleted.»

It was interesting, I agreed.

«It is also how I knew that Antonio Grasso had made concrete plans to leave the country, securing a passport and a one-way ticket departing today at six p.m. from Boston Logan Airport to Amsterdam Airport Schiphol, and from there to Kloten Airport in Zurich. I am led to believe from the fiction that you claim to despise that this counter-indicates a plan of suicide.»

"All right. I admit, that does shed some doubt on things. But again, why do you care who killed Grasso?"

«I believe that the person who killed Antonio Grasso also attempted to kill me. So I will discover his killer, and then you will shoot that person.»

I'd have had milk up my nose if I hadn't finished it already.

"You're a vindictive son of a bitch, aren't you? Nothing doing. I don't shoot people. If I do this—*if*—then we turn the killer over to the police. Got it?"

«That is foolish. You have a firearm license. Once you have proof, the course should be clear.»

I may be thought sentimental about this, or even a coward. The simple truth of the matter was that I had met my share of killers, and so I knew that I was not one.

"No. Murder is not negotiable."

«Very well. What course of action is acceptable to you?»

"Let the police handle it. This is their job. They have all the testing equipment you can imagine and they can get warrants to search personal implants."

«They are not me. I wish to have a hand in this person's downfall.»

I considered that. Cops really, *really* don't like PIs getting involved in criminal cases, sometimes to the tune of obstruction of justice charges. "If we investigate, we need a legitimate reason to be involved. We'll need to turn over anything we find out."

«If we must involve the police to obtain this person's punishment, then I will present them with the necessary evidence of this person's guilt. Does this satisfy you?»

"Yeah, but this brings me back to my earlier point: You are not a detective."

«Perhaps not. But you are.»

I bit back the impulse to respond that I wasn't anymore. I was, and I had Rex to thank. I mulled it over, looking into the bottom of my empty glass at the little white puddle at the bottom that you can never quite drink. Then I eyed the unobtrusive plastic payment device in the corner of the table next to the drinks menu. It blinked the price of my meal. "Assuming I'm willing to work for you, which is crazy, are you actually able to pay me?"

«Yes.»

"I mean in addition to the ten thousand dollars you already agreed to pay me for services already rendered."

«Yes.»

"Prove it. Pay my lunch bill. Take it out of what you owe me, but not out of my funds."

I waited, and watched the device. The price of my meal continued to blink. And then it went to "PAID—Thank you, Claudius Rex!"

Well, it was something.

"All right, let's give this a try."

«Good. If you leave now, you should be able to make the meeting I set up with Mr. Desai.»

I edged out of the booth. "Why did you set it up so soon? You know how long it takes to walk there."

«I had not anticipated that you would need lunch first.»

I had barely set a foot inside TuriTech's big glass doors when Detective Stevens pulled her attention away from the uniformed cop and pointed an accusatory finger at yours truly.

"What are *you* doing back here?"

I put up my hands in a calming gesture. "Mr. Desai wanted to see me."

Her expression grew skeptical. "Why?"

"Who knows? He messages Rex, Rex messages me, tells me to come back here. Here I am, a good little dog."

«Don't use 'message' as a verb, it's vulgar.» Well. Another party heard from.

"Is he hiring you?"

"I expect he'll tell me when he sees me."

"What are you doing here, Baldwin?" And there came Fitzgerald, red of face and flared of nostril.

"Is there an echo in here? Mr. Desai sent for me and is waiting for me."

"Bullshit!" he spat. "I—"

I talked over him, facing the still-skeptical police officer. "Detective, I promised I'd tell you what I know, and I keep my promises. But if I keep the good CEO waiting and Rex doesn't get the job, I'll get fired and we'll both get nothing."

She scowled. But she held out her finger to Fitzgerald, who clammed up. "Stay out of my crime scene, Baldwin, and don't interfere. If Desai wants you around, that's his business."

"Hang on just one second," Fitzgerald blustered. "You're not coming back into my building on some flimsy lie like that."

"I'll have you know that I've never told a flimsy lie in my life." I watched him struggle with that. Anyway, it's true: I'm a craftsman of the first order and my lies are built to last.

Desai had apparently vouched for me, because Fitzgerald grudgingly escorted me to the elevator—have I mentioned I prefer the stairs?—and up to the fifth floor. And the fifth floor was nice—plush carpets and nature art lining the walls—even if my silently fuming escort wasn't,.

Fitzgerald stopped short at Desai's door, and gave me quite the glare. I bet he practiced, not only because it was a very good glare, among the best ever leveled at me, but because being on the receiving end of a glare like that in the bathroom mirror every morning would explain a lot about the man.

Ahmed Desai's office had a gorgeous view of the Charles River. Lots of little sailboats dotted the water, meandering back and forth. Desai himself seemed oblivious to the view. He was a short man with a fringe of neat white hair around his bare pate. He wore rectangular gold eyeglasses and kept taking them off to massage the bridge of his nose.

"I would like to know who hired you," he said once I'd made myself comfortable in the big upholstered chair. "And why."

Seemed a good question. I only wished there were an answer.

"I'm afraid that's not something I can divulge." I smiled back at him, glancing around the office. Lots of framed photos of himself in front of monuments and famous buildings, or standing with famous people. "But surely you have some idea."

He looked like he'd just bitten a lemon. "I wish I had noticed Dr. Grasso's message to me earlier, when I had a chance to ask him myself. He said nothing to Mr. Rex?"

"If he did, Mr. Rex didn't see fit to tell me. He treats me like a mushroom."

Desai's eyebrows went up.

"He keeps me in the dark," I explained, "and feeds me—"

"Ah. Yes. I'm familiar with the joke." He smiled weakly. "Do you know whether he felt his life to be in danger, or whether he was hiring you for some investigative purpose? Did he mention a theft?"

I hesitated, waiting for Rex to speak up. "I'm sorry, I don't. And no, he didn't."

"Is your business here done, then?"

«No.»

I indicated in the negative.

Desai looked like he wanted to spit something out. "So even if I throw you out, you'll be harassing my people after hours, going through trash cans, sniffing networks?"

"Hey now, I am a perfect gentleman. I don't harass anyone. But I am planning to have a word with a few folks. As for the trash cans and the networks, I don't discuss my methods except with paying clients." Though I admit, those would have been two of my first moves, plus digital tails on the principles including a crowdsourced bounty for photos and emails.

A whole slew of expressions crossed the older gentleman's face, but he settled on determination. "Very well. The old advice is to keep your friends close and your enemies closer. I like to think your Mr. Rex is a friend, but either way if you're going to be working around my people, I prefer you to be working for me."

"Well now," I said. "Let's not be hasty."

«This is what we want. Accept it immediately.»

Desai gave me a look. I knew that look, and it meant money.

"I'm not saying no. But this can't be mere bribery. When Mr. Rex takes a case, he aims to solve it. I'll be talking to your people. They'll already be sore about talking to the police, so they're going to complain about it. I promised the nice detective downstairs that I'd tiptoe around her crime scene, but I might have to stomp around other places. That'll mean building and network access at the very least. Basically, I'll need cooperation, and I might not be able to be nice about it."

His expression turned sour, and he took a deep breath. "Very well. When will Mr. Rex be here?"

"Mr. Rex doesn't leave his home. You get his brain and my shoe leather."

His cheeks went a little red, but I have to hand it to him, he took it in stride. He accepted that, and then quoted a sum of money which modesty forbids me to mention. Rex didn't have to prod me to accept, let's just put it that way. We shook on it and I had a case! I just didn't know what it was.

Desai nodded then, and appeared to notice the view for the first time. He turned in his chair to look at it. I took the opportunity to subvocalize, "All right, 'boss.' What do you want to know?"

«Ask him about the theft he mentioned.»

I did, and the effect on him was of instantaneous disgust.

"I knew it. That damned theft," Desai said. "It's torn this company apart. We've lost ten good people since then. Nobody says it's because of that, but I can see that they interact differently now. It's not as friendly, and this will just make it worse." He looked at me guiltily. "I'm sorry, you must think me terribly insensitive to be worried about this right now."

"Not at all," I said, holding up my palms. "There's nothing you can do to help Dr. Grasso. It's only natural to look to what's important to you. But anything you can tell me will help."

That calmed the waters a bit. He looked out the window for a minute, then seemed to make up his mind about something.

"There was a theft from my company last year. An advanced prototype on loan to us from the government for analysis. The police and the FBI were involved, but despite some very expensive security procedures, it's gone." He looked puzzled, then, and shook his head. "But I don't understand why Dr. Grasso would have waited so long to hire Mr. Rex."

"Maybe he learned something that made him think the investigation had missed something?"

"Oh, he made it clear that he considered the investigation flawed. He believed as well that his outspokenness on the subject led to the board choosing Dr. Tomason over himself as VP of Research when the previous VP was dismissed."

"Was he right?"

"No. It was a factor, of course, but the plain truth is that most of the staff already disliked him. Dr. Grasso was brilliant, but he could be arrogant, rude, and overbearing."

"I hear you," I said. Seeing his surprise, I hastened to add, "I've gotten that impression as well. Uh, what was stolen, exactly?"

He hesitated. "It was a piece of computer equipment. It was small. Portable. Beyond that, I don't think you need to know the exact nature of the device. It had just been transferred from Dr. Grasso, who had analyzed its software, to Dr. Joshi, who was to disassemble it and examine its hardware.

It was stolen from Dr. Joshi's lab, despite our exhaustive precautions, and the thief was never caught."

I lifted an eyebrow. "Any bad blood over that?"

"It cost Dr. Joshi the VP of Research position, but he never seemed really to want it. We had some staff turnover at the time, citing work environment. It has taken much of the last year to finally get over that unpleasantness."

"All right," I said. "I'll probably have more questions later, but that's a good start. We might as well talk about the other elephant in the room. Do you mind telling me what you were up to this morning?"

He nodded. "I had coffee with Dr. Tomason at eight a.m., as usual on Mondays. We didn't discuss anything of consequence, other than Saturday's game." He grimaced.

"You believe in the new curse?"

"For abandoning Fenway? No, just a general manager who ought to be sho—" He caught himself, coughed, and continued, "fired. After that I had a short phone call with our CFO, who is in Europe. Dr. Joshi then came and complained to me for half an hour until finally I had to feign a meeting. Nothing of importance, probably not even to him, just rehashes of things he's been complaining about for ages."

"So you and Joshi were both here at eight thirty?" He nodded. "Conveniently," I added, "that's when the police estimated time of death for Dr. Grasso, according to what Detective Stevens told me this morning. Many other people around at that time?"

He looked uneasy, so I cut in. "Look, I figure it's reasonable to assume that your Dr. Grasso's death had something to do with his calling us in."

Desai grimaced and shook his head. "The police had not told me that, but they have been asking where people were between eight and nine this morning. At that time of day, most of our research employees would have been in the building but unaccounted for. The research staff were participating in our monthly seminar—that is, all of the research groups are brought together in our auditorium on the first floor to present their work to the other researchers. It started at nine."

«That would put my attempted deletion, at ten-o-two, some time after he died. The deletion had to have been done from that laboratory, but such a stretch of time seems unlikely. If the deleter was not the killer, why was the death not reported until your arrival? No, I reject that hypothesis.»

"So, lots of people coming in and having coffee and so on. Nobody really sure where anyone else is or whether they're in yet. Sounds like a mess."

"It is a mess. The police are interviewing everyone who knew Grasso, which is most of the company. And to be frank, many of them disliked the man. It's a ridiculous approach, scattershot."

«I agree.»

I almost made a shushing noise, but Desai was staring right at me.

"The police have their methods, of course, but we have ours." I remembered Rex's complaint. "This meeting, was it still going around ten a.m.?"

"Ten? Hmm." I waited while he seemed to mull that over. He put a hand up to his mouth, and I could see his chin wag and hear those soft little smacking noises older folks make when they subvocalize. Blue lights danced across his left eyeball.

"Yes," he said at last. "It let out around eleven, just before the body was discovered."

"Who would have been missing from that meeting?"

"Well, I was busy up here and can prove that. Sometimes the department heads don't attend. Dr. Tomason always attends; she would have kept an eye on comings and goings."

"Did Grasso have trouble with anyone?"

His eyebrows furrowed, and I could tell he was thinking hard, but I had the feeling it was more about whether to say what was on his mind.

"Whoever it is, it'll come out sooner or later."

Desai shook his head. "He let one of his researchers go before the theft, a Dr. Clay Hindle."

"That's a start."

"No, it isn't. Dr. Hindle was cleared of involvement in the theft: he left before the device was stolen and our security systems are keyed to the faces of former employees. He has not set foot in the building since."

"Anyone else? This guy Grasso seems to pick up enemies like lint."

He sighed. "There had been a disciplinary issue with one of his employees, a Jeanne Duvalier. He wanted to terminate her employment. Dr. Tomason arranged her transfer to Dr. Joshi's department instead. Dr. Grasso thought this was out of spite and considered it a sign of disrespect. It took a lot of ego-stroking to smooth it over, to be frank. For Ms. Duvalier, I suppose it meant a slight reduction in compensation."

"Can't have been much fun, either."

Desai's mouth twitched at the corner. "No."

Duvalier had been the name of the young woman who'd come in with Joshi and found me with Grasso's body. Interesting.

"Why'd he want to can her?"

Desai's eyes flicked away. "Honestly, he probably was exacting some revenge against Dr. Tomason. Ms. Duvalier is the daughter of one of her friends, I gather."

"But Tomason protected her. Thwarted him, he might say."

A look of pain crossed Desai's face. "I admit he played politics—"

"Somebody killed him."

He drew himself up in his chair and looked me in the eye. "The police believe he killed himself, Mr. Baldwin. I see no reason to contradict them."

"Well, I didn't get a good look at the body, what with keeping the lights off for, uh, the sake of surprise. So I can't exactly contradict them, either. Looked like he was shot?"

Desai nodded. "So the police say. With a rail pistol."

I raised my eyebrows. Those could be nasty little devices. They were hard to aim and not very reliable, but lethal and quiet: they used heavy-duty capacitors to accelerate a hefty slug, and so sounded more like a thump than a bang. More than that, I could see why the police hadn't just closed the case on suicide or not: rail guns don't leave powder burns or any of the other telltale signs that a normal firearm leaves from point-blank range. Just a noise like someone dropping a book, and a neat hole that looks the same from any distance.

We sat in silence for a moment. "It'll help if folks are all right with me poking my nose around."

"I will send out a message to that effect."

I thought that sounded reasonable. I wouldn't lay money that Fitzgerald would, but I'd burn that bridge when I came to it.

«There are too many coincidences. I do not like it.»

"What are you going on about?"

Mr. Desai had seen me out of his office without much more information than that, urging me to go have a word with one Maya Tomason, PhD. I thought it was gracious of him to dismiss me outright instead of feign a meeting, but if I hadn't gotten the hint, it might have come to that. I got Desai's permission to go through Grasso's office, and then showed myself the door. Fitzgerald had evidently gone in search of other prey, leaving me to stroll the teal-carpeted corridors by my lonesome and admire the artwork. They were mostly oil paintings with junk stuck in them, little sharp bits of metal and driftwood, all neatly encased in diamond-glass boxes. I don't know much about art, but the little plaques under the paintings informed me that they had titles like *Sunrise on Back Bay* and *Mt. Monadnock Snow* and were original works by people I'd never heard of but whose names I decided I ought to remember for cocktail parties. That way, while I was still ignorant, I was at least ignorant on a higher level than before.

«Too many coincidences. The theft, primarily, but I am irritated that the police are wrong about the time of death. Our investigation is more difficult if they cannot separate the wheat from the chaff for us. They have resources we do not, but we cannot avail ourselves of them if they are being wasted pursuing blind alleys.»

A cleaning robot zipped by me, whistling as it passed so I wouldn't step on it. Despite my unkind feelings toward all technology just then, I refrained from kicking it.

"Why not just tell them when you think he died and why?"

«Impossible. I am not prepared to acknowledge that we have accessed Dr. Grasso's now-empty implant. They would immediately suspect us of altering it.»

"*Have* you altered it?"

«Only to obfuscate the transfer of funds.»

Just covering up grand theft, that's all. I made my way back down to the lab where we'd found Grasso. A handful of cops were still there, including Detective Stevens, who I waited for. Desai had politely informed her of our assistance, and while I was not present for the result, I gather that she had not been terribly happy. I was hurt, of course, but one soldiers on.

"All right, Baldwin, what have you got?"

"Not a lot," I admitted. "And I want to state for the record that we are not investigating Dr. Grasso's death, but rather an earlier theft—"

"Fine," she cut in. "Fine! Just remember that the Commonwealth has laws about withholding evidence of a capital crime, got it?"

I got it.

"So what do you want, Baldwin?"

"I was actually hoping you could give me some information on time of death. As near I can tell, he was seen alive around eight, and not since then."

"Word gets around fast. Dunno why I bother asking people to keep a lid on anything. Yeah, I've got seven of my people canvassing and asking where everyone was between eight and eight thirty."

"He seemed pretty well dead by the time I got a good look at him, but I don't know how the cold changes things."

Her eyebrows went up. "Cold?"

"Yeah, it was pretty damn chilly in there when I stopped in—out of professional curiosity, before you ask—though it warmed up fast."

She frowned, and gave me that scrutinizing eye of hers. Then she turned away and subvocalized something. I waited and watched her eyes dance as she read the result, then she shook her head.

"Building logs say the temperature was a uniform eighteen degrees Celsius all morning, which is the number the ME used to put time of death at around eight thirty."

"Wait, wait." I turned and asked Rex, "Am I crazy here?"

«I am not qualified to judge. But you are not mistaken about the temperature. Your personal logs show an ambient temperature of eighteen Celsius and rising when you entered the room.»

Stevens waited for me to finish talking to myself. I considered how to relay all that. "My own temperature records show different."

"You think someone altered the building logs?" She sighed. "I might believe you, Baldwin, but I can't accept that as evidence."

I already had an answer for that. "Can you pull the temperature records from Dr. Grasso's implant to cast the tie-breaker?"

She shook her head. "We can't. It's locked up tight. We're hoping his safe deposit box has a backup password, but if it doesn't we're going to need to put a hack job on it, which could take awhile."

«Unacceptable. Their floundering has already lost valuable time. Have her take down the following numbers.»

I repeated them as Rex read them off. Stevens's eyes grew wider with each digit.

"Is that what I think it is?" she asked, incredulous.

«It is the default backup password for Dr. Grasso's implant, based on purchase date and model number.»

I relayed that. She pursed her lips.

"Has Rex used it?"

I shrugged. "You'll have to ask him. I haven't."

The look she gave me bordered on mistrust, which I must say I found hurtful. I waited while she and a tech worked on it.

«It won't get her into his most private files—I am not interested at this time in providing root access—but it should be enough to get what she needs. He had changed it, of course, but there is no reason for her to know that I have changed it back for her benefit.»

I wasn't allowed into the lab myself; I'd had my shot at it and squandered it arguing in the dark, so I couldn't complain. Instead, I had to watch from the door, peering around the big official-looking POLICE—DO NOT CROSS hologram they'd set up to ward off anyone who thought this might be a good time to borrow a screwdriver.

The body was gone, but there was still a pool of blood in the back left—if viewed from the doorway—corner of the room, in the gap between the benches along the wall and an island bench in the middle.

«Which terminal just activated?» Rex said just as a monitor on the bench came on. It was on the left side of the island, near to where Grasso had been sitting, but not too near. There was a trapezoid of blue tape on the floor in front of it, where I'd seen the rail pistol before.

I didn't get a chance to answer: Stevens came back wearing a thoughtful look. "His implant memory is wiped prior to ten-o-four a.m., but everything after that's intact. We're double-checking to make sure nobody altered it after the fact." I thought there was something unfairly accusatory in her tone there. She folded her arms. "But it shows the temperature dip down below ten Celsius and come back up in the hour before he was discovered. Those blowers in there can move a lot of air, it'd be like a blast freezer."

I knew the answer, but asked anyway to keep her talking: "So what does that mean?"

The detective paced back and forth, not really looking at me. I could see faint light play across her eyeball.

"The ME will have to rule for sure. A big part of her determination of time of death was on algor mortis—body temperature." Stevens nodded to herself as she talked in a low voice. "But she did say that lividity and rigidity didn't match up as well as she'd like . . . " She looked up suddenly and smiled at me. "Thanks, Baldwin. You've actually been a help."

"My pleasure. Any chance of letting me in there to poke around?"

"Not a prayer." I could tell she meant it, but she at least looked like she might have felt a tiny bit bad about it. Maybe. Anyway, the show was over: she shut the door and shooed me away.

"What was all that about with the computer," I subbed.

«The terminal I activated was the one from which I had been deleted. That individual used a utility called 'secure delete,' which evidently performed a thorough obliteration of the data.» I knew the one, having advised clients of mine to use it: to use Rex's favorite word, it confounded attempts to recover data.

"That terminal's near where Grasso was shot."

«Could Dr. Grasso have used the computer himself?»

"Not unless he had arms like an orangutan."

«I don't know what that means.»

"He couldn't use it."

«Then I am satisfied that the person who killed Dr. Grasso is the person who attempted to delete me.»

"Anything I should know before I talk to this Dr. Tomason? It's not easy to chat with you in front of people. Is she a suspect?"

«She is a suspect. Find out what you can about this theft. The device stolen was likely a cranial implant of some special design.»

"What makes you think that?"

Rex fell silent for a moment. I looked at the artwork. I smiled and nodded at the folks who walked by wearing badges with their smiling faces on little lanyards around their necks. I wasn't sure whether the big pale blob was Mount Monadnock or the sky.

«I prefer to keep my reasons to myself for the moment. But it should suffice for you to point out that Turing Technologies owns thirty-seven patents crucial to the manufacture of cranial implants and to software such as the execrable Jeeves.»

"That all you want to know?"

«I need more information. I will want to talk to Armin Fitzgerald about the theft, but I would prefer to negotiate with him from a position of knowledge rather than ignorance.»

I didn't mind putting off that particular meeting. I paused outside the solid wood door to Maya Tomason's office, rehearsing what I was going to say. Mid-suavity, she opened the door.

"Come in."

Dr. Tomason's office managed to be Spartan but comfortable. She had a corner office like Desai's, but not as nice a view. Bookshelves lined the other two walls, with more shelves under the windows. Tomason had a standing desk, though she was short enough that I could only tell because she stood at it.

"You're the private detective," she said, and I admitted it. "I don't approve of hiring you."

"I'm sorry to hear that, ma'am. Mind if I ask why?"

"The police are quite capable, and where they are lacking, we have Armin. You, on the other hand, are an unknown. In the time it takes you to come up to speed, the police will have shut the case on poor Antonio's suicide."

"Yeah, but we're not investigating Dr. Grasso's death. Besides, I'm a quick study."

"So you say."

"I hope you don't mind if I ask a few questions."

"It doesn't matter if I do or not."

"Okay then. What can you tell me about the theft of the cranial implant last year?"

She turned bright red and rushed past me. I thought she was going to storm out of the room, but instead she slammed the office door.

"Is it a secret?"

"Yes! Or, the nature of the stolen item is. Did Antonio tell you that?"

"I told you, I'm a quick study. I'd be even quicker if I had some cooperation, though."

She frowned. "I don't know what to tell you. I was still working with Michael Joshi in the hardware division at the time, before my promotion. We had a specially built lab for it, from which nothing could get out. The . . . item came in under armed guard. Michael and I examined it and put it into the special testing harness. We ran software tests on it for a week—"

"Sorry to interrupt, but I thought Grasso was your software guy."

She flushed. "He was. But Michael thought it prudent to replicate some of Antonio's results before proceeding, in case our hardware tests damaged the device. A week later, I came in and found the device missing. We searched everywhere, and the police and FBI were called in."

"That must have been awful."

Tomason turned away from me and stared out the window. "I've never felt so violated. They questioned me, they got a warrant and searched my home, got a movement trace from my implant and examined everywhere I'd been in the previous week." She pulled her arms around herself, like she was cold. "It's going to be like that again now, I suppose."

"I don't think it'll be that bad," I told her, "but if Rex and I can get to the bottom of it, it'll be faster. Like ripping off a Band Aid."

"What an odd saying," she said, chewing her lip. "They don't rip off at all, they fall off when you push the button."

I knew stalling when I heard it. "Well, it'll be just like that. Off the record, do you have your own guesses about who took it?"

She looked me in the eye. "It was plainly an outside party."

"Yeah?"

"There are good reasons to believe outside people wanted it, and foreign governments are entirely capable of accomplishing the task. Besides, if one of us had taken it, why is that person still here? Why not sell it and retire to Tahiti?"

"Tahiti? How much can one computer be worth?"

Her expression of disbelief spoke for itself. So, valuable.

"Okay," I said. "Let's say for the sake of argument that someone here did take it. Even though that's just wildly unlikely. Maybe there was just too much heat to sell it. Who would it be?"

She gave me a dirty look, but didn't refuse outright to answer. Finally, she shrugged and made a face. "Perhaps it was Antonio. Why else would he commit suicide?"

"Assuming he did, it doesn't get us anywhere. Let's rule him out for a minute. Who else?"

"It would have to be Michael, then."

"Michael Joshi? How come?"

"He was the last person to use the device, and he left early the day before. He was so protective of it, all our assistants were forbidden to touch it. He'd have prevented me using it if he could. As it was, I barely even got to turn it on." She lifted her chin. "But the police showed that he could not possibly have stolen it from that lab. They proved it even to Armin's standards."

«Move on to something else.»

"All right, thank you. Now, about this morning."

She winced. "Yes, I arrived just after eight—"

"Actually, I was more interested in the seminar."

I enjoyed the look of surprise that crossed her face. "The seminar? Why? What about it?"

"A couple things. Was anyone missing?"

"Well, several people are not here today at all." She listed a couple names, people the police later ruled out. "And Dr. Grasso . . . well, he was not there."

There was a knock on the door, and it opened before Dr. Tomason could respond. Jeanne Duvalier stepped in, the young woman who had found me with Grasso's corpse. This time, she froze upon seeing me.

"Hello again," I started, but Tomason cut me off.

"Jeanne, dear, could you come back later?"

"Actually," I said, "I wouldn't mind talking—"

"Later, Jeanne." Tomason's tone could have gone a few rounds with some boxers I've known. Duvalier left.

"You were saying, Mr. Baldwin?"

"Yeah. About the seminar. Did anyone leave early, or step outside, say around ten?"

She looked puzzled for a moment, and then she glanced over my shoulder and an odd look crossed her face. If pressed, I'd have called it panic. Whatever it was, she mastered it quickly. "Yes, Mr. Baldwin. I did."

"When? Mind saying why?" I studied her face, but she'd shut herself down fast.

"Around ten, and I do mind saying, as a matter of fact."

"I bet that the police are going to be asking this same question."

I could tell she was curious, but in the end she didn't take the bait. "Then let them ask it."

"You sure nobody else stepped out? Dr. Joshi? Ms. Duvalier?"

She stiffened, and shook her head instead of replying. We stood in silence for a little while until Rex started giving me grief.

"Did you see *anyone* else leave?"

I know a lie when I hear one, and her "no" didn't fool me for a second. But it sounded final, so I moved on.

"This guy Grasso," I said, "what was he like?"

"Antonio was a highly intelligent individual, and a gifted software engineer."

"See, that's interesting." Her left eyebrow went up. "When I ask about a pleasant person, someone'll lead off with, 'nice guy' or 'I liked him.' Heck, even a jerk might get a 'he was quiet,' or 'he wasn't so bad.' But when I hear first thing off the bat how smart a guy is, I start to think he wasn't well-liked."

She fiddled with some knickknacks on her desk. "That *is* interesting."

"Was he happy here?"

"I don't know," she said, which struck me as unlikely. She looked me in the eye, which was fair warning to expect a whopper. "I expect he was perfectly happy here. Why wouldn't he be?"

"Pardon me for saying, but you're not being very cooperative, Doc."

"Then let me be blunt, Mr. Baldwin. I do not agree with your having been hired, and so far you have not asked any intelligent questions. I don't even know why I'm still here. I can't concentrate, and the police can reach me at home just as easily . . . "

"All right then, what would be an intelligent question?"

She looked up with a gleam in her eye. "How about, who knew that Antonio kept a rail pistol in his lab?"

"I'm impressed, that's a pretty good question. That was the murder weapon?"

"Or suicide, Mr. Baldwin. I'm under the impression that it's hard to tell for sure with a rail gun slug, but the police seem to think so. And I'll answer the intelligent question: very few people knew it. Even his direct employees, like Ms. Duvalier was for a time, did not know it."

I noted her dropping Jeanne Duvalier's name like that, casual-like.

«The gun registration is eighteen months old. I have a purchase record.»

I nodded slowly. "So what," I asked aloud, "happened eighteen months ago that made him buy the piece?"

She stared at me, then furrowed her eyebrows. Her eyes seemed to be searching her desk. "That would have been just after we contracted to receive the device. He claimed that he was doing research into firing authorization."

"What's that?"

She gave me an exasperated look. I'm not above feigning dumb, but in this case I really didn't know. "The military use it in case their weapons fall into the wrong hands. Each gun is registered to a soldier's artificial agent. If it's not mounted as a peripheral, it won't shoot."

"How do they know the pistol's his?"

"The police had me identify it."

"How did you do that? Did it have any special modifications?"

"Yes," she said. "It looked like any other rail pistol, but there's an electronics compartment in the, er, the handle—"

"The grip."

"The grip. I helped him install the circuitry. The police say that it is the only such weapon in the building, and that it had been fired. It would not have been able to fire without his implant's connection, and that supports their belief that he committed suicide."

She was speaking quickly and with some assurance; she was on solid ground. I decided to knock her off it.

"Sure," I said, "But let's say for a minute that he didn't kill himself. When Ms. Duvalier left the seminar, she had time—"

"She didn't leave," Tomason said with some vehemence. "I *told* you that."

I started to apologize and claim confusion, but she'd had enough of the likes of me. She was angry and flustered, and finally I was obliged to make an exit. Getting thrown out of someone's office always felt like progress; I just wished I knew in what direction.

I ducked out of the building before my meeting with Armin Fitzgerald, and came back armed. He met me in his lair—a darkened basement office lined with monitors and blinking status lights. A coffee machine like a jet engine hunkered in the back corner of the room next to a little sink. Fitzgerald had his feet propped up on the desk when I came in, and he didn't move a muscle. He just watched me walk in and place the brown paper bag on his big black desk.

From inside that bag I extracted my armament: a two pound bag of Ethiopia Yirgacheffe wet-process coffee, freshly roasted to a Full City. Fitzgerald's eyebrows went up.

"Not much as bribes go," he said.

"That's because it's not a bribe," I said. Rex had checked up on Fitzgerald's coffee order and discovered that with all the hub and bub, Fitzgerald had run low. This was the exact specification that he ordered most often. "It's a peace offering. I figured you could use it, and this is one of my personal favorites."

In fact, I couldn't tell most coffees from a cup of thin mud, but that was not for the likes of Armin Fitzgerald to know. He didn't grab for the bag immediately.

"Funny thing, Baldwin. I did a little digging, and I don't see much about this Rex guy anywhere."

I'd seen this one coming, of course. "Well, sure. He prefers it that way, see—as long as he gets his fee, he doesn't care who gets the credit. Usually it's the police, but he's generous with hard-working private folks, too."

" 'Hard-working private folks,' huh?" He rolled his eyes, but he also took his feet off the desk and snatched up the bag of coffee. "Laying it on a bit thick, don't you think?"

"It's the truth, thick or thin. But it might also have something to do with Rex not wanting to have to testify in court."

"Ah. That sounds more like it." But it also sounded like I might have made nice with the security man, who went back into the corner and set off an anvil chorus from the machine. "You want a cup?"

Three-thirty in the afternoon was a bit late for caffeine, so I didn't really, but I figured I shouldn't be discourteous. "If you're already making some."

He didn't say a word for five whole minutes, he just focused on his machine. I had a look over the various monitors. I saw floor plans for the building, lists of people, spiderweb-like network maps, all sorts of things. One of the monitors near the back of the room just had a bunch of documents open: photos of a cranial implant like mine, a bunch of text, some photos of a lab and a floor plan.

«This is preposterous. Why aren't you asking any questions?»

"I recognize when someone wants to talk and when he doesn't. Wait."

«It is nearly the end of the workday. You're just afraid to talk to him.»

"That is not true. We are waiting until he's in the right frame of mind."

Fitzgerald came away from the machine with two dainty white cups of coffee on saucers. He put them both on the desk and waved me to sit.

«You are spewing bunkum. Ask him about the stolen device. We must inspect Dr. Grasso's office after this, and it's getting late.»

I waited, enduring Rex's increasingly irritated protests, while Fitzgerald and I sipped coffee. It was good, I guess. There wasn't cream or sugar in it, but it was all right. At last, Fitzgerald slurped the last of it, and set the cup and saucer down.

"Very good coffee, Baldwin."

"I'm glad you liked it."

He smiled broadly. "Now get out."

«Damn it all, Andy!»

I tilted my head—not quite a nod or a bow, but enough to show I recognized his right to throw me out. I stood and made for the door.

"Hang on, hang on." I turned around and Fitzgerald beckoned me to come back. "All right, you win. What do you want to know?"

«Finally! Ask him about the stolen device.»

I asked him about the stolen device. It didn't improve his mood any, but he drew my attention to the monitor I'd noticed earlier. As it turned out, the "device" was a specialty implant. The FBI had raided a spy cell and had unearthed a half dozen implants that were head and shoulders above anything sold in this country, designed to masquerade as regular cranial implants. Ahmed Desai had scored a coup in getting the government to agree to loan one of them to Turing Technologies, whereupon it had instantly become a giant pain in one Armin Fitzgerald's ass.

They'd built a clean room software lab for it, and put Grasso in charge to see what the fancy software could do. Fitzgerald had worked on that lab;

it was specially instrumented so nothing could get out of it. Grasso sat on it for six months or so, lording it over everyone. He even went so far as to buy a rail pistol, ostensibly for research, but he'd intimated to Fitzgerald that he feared for his life from foreign spies wanting their implant back. After six months, the device was to be the domain of the hardware folks. But the hardware people—Tomason and Joshi—wanted all kinds of specialty equipment. Installing it all would have been a security nightmare.

"So that's why the second lab?"

Fitzgerald nodded. "Got it. We built a second lab down the hall, a real doozy. My own design—once that implant was in there, nothing was getting in or out except people in special lab coats, who were scanned each way. All the walls were reinforced, and the air ducts were covered with a fine mesh. The device was brought over from the first lab under armed guard. A week later—poof. Gone."

"How?"

"Nobody knows except the thief. The FBI came in, and they had nothing but good words for my design, but none of us could figure out how it had gotten out of there."

"Who reported the theft?"

"Dr. Joshi. He came in that morning, found it missing, and called for me. He didn't leave until I got there, and he was thoroughly searched. By me, and then by the police."

"All right. Who was the last person in the lab?"

An odd look crossed his face, and he looked away from me. "I was, with Dr. Tomason. The night before. Someone had left a timer on; it went off and triggered the noise alarm. We investigated, and the device was still there in its little testing harness."

«Is it possible the device never left the second lab?» I relayed the question.

He wagged a finger at me. "I thought of that. We searched the lab, and did a full inventory. We even tested all the components we found. It had definitely been taken out of the room."

The details of the investigation were, well, they were dull. But he was nothing if not thorough: they disassembled the lab. They investigated everyone who had access to the room or its surrounds, including the guards. They even investigated Dr. Grasso, who didn't have access to the second room at all. They interviewed contacts, relations—a whole team of FBI agents with help from the Department of Defense and local cops can cover a lot of ground in a four-month investigation.

"So that's it? They just dropped it after four months?"

"Yup. They came to Mr. Desai and said they were going to assume that the spies' government arranged for recovery."

"That's crazy. Turn everyone's lives upside down, then shrug it off as a cold case?"

He waved a finger in my face. "I haven't shrugged it off. I've been thinking."

"Get anywhere?"

I shouldn't have said that. He looked sullen at the thought. I moved on to another topic.

"So Grasso bought a pistol. Was he shot with his own gun?"

"Yessir. Which proves that he killed himself. I've got scanners at all the entrances to the building, and nothing like a pistol has come in or out except those belonging to the police. And nobody could fire Grasso's gun except Grasso himself, thanks to that implant doohickey."

I made a note of it.

"Look, it's been nice chatting with you, Baldwin, but I've got work to do. The police have kept me busy all day; I'm going to have to stay late as it is. Thanks for the coffee."

I took my cue and made for the stairs.

«What the devil was all that misery with the silence?»

I probably could have explained it, eventually. It may even have been to my eventual benefit to teach him a lesson about how people like to be treated. But I couldn't quite put those thoughts into words. I finally came up with, "If I'd pestered him before he'd finished, or balked when he kicked me out, I wouldn't have gotten a word out of him."

«Why not? How could you have known that?»

"The same way I knew Tomason was lying and that Desai wouldn't respect us unless I argued with him. Reading people is part of being a detective."

«Very well, then. Satisfactory.»

Grasso's third floor office was bigger than my first apartment. It had been, at some point, tasteful: big Afghan rugs, oak bookcases, a large sepia-tone globe in a hardwood and silver mount, and a huge oak desk facing the door. The desk looked like an antique—it had scars across its back and sides and it looked like there had been water damage at some point but had been very nicely restored. A smaller desk sat off to the side, with an ancient desktop computer sporting an old flat screen and a mouse and keyboard.

The effect of all this was ruined by the enormous stacks of papers and books everywhere. I could barely see the top of the desk. The papers were mostly stapled together in stacks of a dozen or so, and had impressive-looking titles like, *A Method of Efficiently Addressing the Byzantine Generals' Problem in Multi-Component Artificial Agents*. All the books had slips of paper sticking out of them, usually a couple dozen with torn edges.

"All right," I subbed, "where's the needle in this particular haystack?"

«Has anyone searched this office?»

"The police, probably."

«Have they? Or are you guessing?»

I looked around. I wasn't sure they had, actually. All the stacks cluttered the place up, but I felt like there was still a kind of logic to it. Besides, a good search doesn't leave a mess, because that makes it easier to miss something. If I'd had my toolkit, I'd have swept for residual heat, since even gloved hands warm up the stuff they touch, and I've got a pretty good feel for what ought to be warm or cold in an empty room. I had a case a few years ago where that saved a client's life: a cleverly hidden booby trap was still just a little too warm from where his former business partner had kept it under his coat.

Or, I could've used a laser sweep and processed the reflections for dust polarization, to see what'd been disturbed or where something had been removed. I've heard a rumor that you could even use it to pick out sound waves from a recent conversation, but I think that's probably hooey. That was a nifty little tool, but it had been confiscated with the others when I'd been arrested.

As it was, I didn't have anything except my eyes and my brain, so I got to work looking around. There wasn't a lot to see, but his chair yielded something interesting: three long kinky hairs, two dark and one white.

"I could be wrong, but I bet they belong to Maya Tomason."

«Excellent. Were they deposited recently?»

"I don't think anyone else has sat down since then, or they'd have been brushed off the chair back and onto the seat."

I looked around the chair, but found only an uncapped pen on the floor. The trashcan was empty, and it wasn't one of those auto-compactors, either. Rex checked the custodians' logs: last emptied at 6:40 a.m.

I had a look over the desk. It looked rummaged to me in a way the rest of the room hadn't. Not the way someone might have left it if they'd been working there, in my opinion, and the police were usually more methodical. There was a legal pad in the middle, angled like a lefty had been writing on it. It was about halfway spent, and the top four pages had been torn off carelessly, leaving bits behind. The handwriting on the top little torn flap read, "This letter is to inform," as did the next one down. The scrap under that, a little bigger, was addressed to Ahmed Desai, and said, "With reluctance, I regret to inform you of my . . . " The rest of the page was gone. There were a lot of papers on the desk, but nothing with a top left corner missing.

The drawers were locked electronically; Rex popped them for me.

The top left drawer had Grasso's passport in it. I tapped the button and a holograph of the dead man appeared. I hadn't seen his face before, but I thought he had an arrogant look to him. Maybe I was imagining that based on the personality he'd left behind. A Swiss visa had been issued to him a month prior, and hadn't been used yet.

A piece of paper sticking out of a book kept catching my eye, part of an address. I tugged it out a little further. The handwriting was the same as all the other notes, so Grasso had written it himself, and the paper was slightly yellowed on the half that had stuck out, so it had been written a while ago. It was an address I knew all too well.

"Rex. You have bits and pieces from Grasso's assistant in you, right?"

«That is a deplorable way to describe my logical makeup, but I will grant the broader point, yes.»

"Why does he have written on this piece of paper the address '3 Kingston Circle, Bridgehampton, NY'?"

«I don't know, why shouldn't he?»

I gritted my teeth. "This is important. Do you know, or not?"

«I have told you that I don't. What is its significance?»

"That's the address of the home I was arrested in last year."

«Ah. Yes, that makes sense. He probably wrote it down so that he could delete it from his implant before creating me.»

I blinked. That was not what I had expected Rex to say at that juncture, not by a long shot. "You're going to have to explain this."

«Eventually, yes.»

"No," I said—quietly, but out loud because I wanted to make the point clear. "Explain it now."

«You said you didn't want to know.»

"I was wrong. Spill it."

«In due time. For now, I need more information.»

"Then I'm leaving."

«Confound you, Andy, finish your search.»

I made for the door, and got it halfway open before he relented.

«Damnation! I asked you earlier whether I could say that I was astounded by your ignorance of your own hardware. You took it as an insult, but your judgment was clouded by ego. I intended no such thing.»

"If it gets you to tell me the truth, then you have my permission to say it."

«Noted, but unnecessary. The computing hardware in your head—»

"It's the stolen implant."

«Why did you engage in dramatics if you already knew that?»

I sat down heavily in the chair by the door. "I only figured it out just now. But it doesn't make any sense. Why? It's . . . it's impossible."

«Balderdash, it is entirely possible. Indeed, it is the only thing that makes sense.»

My head was starting to hurt. You know that feeling when there's this pressure behind your eyeballs, like someone's got a bicycle pump in your sinuses? I had that. "Explain. In small, demeaning words if you have to, but explain."

«Mr. Fitzgerald already told you of the extensive search for the device. They investigated everyone involved, everyone who could have been passed the device, and every place it could have been. Mr. Fitzgerald, though a blustering ass, is neither an idiot nor is he ineffective. But he could not search everyone. An ordinary hiding place would either be under the thief 's control, and thus susceptible to search, or not under control, and thus susceptible to accidental discovery. Implanted, however, it would be hidden in plain sight and make the most effective use of the device's own camouflaging capability. With that accomplished, the thief can wait until scrutiny has waned, and retrieve the device.»

"How'd they get it out of the building, with everyone searching?"

«I do not know.»

"That's insane. Out of everyone they could have implanted it in, why would they pick a random private detective in New York?"

Except that as soon as I said that, I knew they hadn't. Implant computers were still pretty cutting-edge when I got mine, and only a few clinics were licensed to do it. The company ships the device to the clinic, the clinic installs it: your first implant is a surgical procedure, to install what they call an "implant bay" and after that it only takes a couple of minutes to swap them out. I'd come up to Boston for mine, and the clinic had been, in the local patois, "wicked busy." So busy that one guy got the wrong implant and pitched a fit. I was in the recovery room at the time, and he made the docs go around and check everyone with the same model. I didn't like his tone, and it was the same model anyway, so I said hands off. The woman next to me took the hint and said the same. Long story short, I'd started a mutiny and they had to throw the guy out empty-handed and howling.

"Desai said that one of Grasso's employees had been fired before the theft."

«Clay Hindle, yes.»

"Can you get a photo of Hindle?"

I'd barely finished asking, and there was a headshot of the guy from the clinic. Son of a bitch.

«The device was intended to be hidden, to act like commercial devices. But it must also have been intended to host a military-grade artificial intelligence, something approaching my caliber. Otherwise there would be no point in having Dr. Grasso examine it for so long. He most likely intended to upload a copy of me into this very hardware upon retrieving it, which is why he was in that lab where you found him.»

Rex kept talking, but I didn't pay any attention. The day after the clinic, I'd gotten the call from the French fellow with the house on Long Island. If they couldn't grab the implant immediately because of the heat on them, there was a good way to at least prevent me or the feds from discovering it until they were ready: make sure it was hidden, turned off in a jail cell for a year.

"All right," I said, already not liking where this was going. "So Grasso's the device thief."

«Almost certainly. He was a man of method and ambition, who apparently was stymied here. He could not have failed to notice that he would not be promoted further. I suspect he intended to sell the device, with his revolutionary artificial agent on it, to a competing firm. It would humiliate Turing Technologies.»

"All right, then, but how did he steal it?"

«I do not exactly know, yet. He must have had a partner, because your appointment with Fujiwara and Klein was canceled only after his death. It is sufficient for my purpose to know that he was involved.»

"It won't be enough for the police."

«Knowing this, further deductions must surely follow.»

I sighed. "Okay, how about an easier one: who killed Grasso?"

«I do not know, but I am impressed that you recognize it as the simpler question.»

"I was being a smart-ass."

There wasn't an answer, and I didn't wait for one. I picked up the sheet of paper with the Bridgehampton address, walked across the room, and put it into the middle of one of the larger stacks. If they were more than ten minutes behind me, the heat signature would be long gone. "Let's have a chat with this guy Hindle. Can you get him on the phone?"

«I have been trying to. There has been no answer. Ah.»

"Ah?"

«We have just received a message from Detective Stevens, asking why we are attempting to contact Clay Hindle. She wishes us to come to her.»

As it happens, Detective Stevens was only two blocks away. The big office building looked to be about two hundred years old, red brick with big glass doors and a uniformed police officer at the curb. I identified myself and she sent me up to the second floor. I took the stairs and hooked a left down the hall, following the sounds of loud talking and the gazes of the occasional office worker peering out from their office doors.

"You've got to be kidding me," I said out loud when I got to the door near the end of the hall with the yellow POLICE—DO NOT CROSS hologram. The door was open and a couple uniformed cops were coming out, so it wasn't until I got right up close that I read the stencil on the frosted glass window: FUJIWARA AND KLEIN ASSOCIATES. The flat black hologenerator chirped as I stepped over it, and I heard an old-fashioned camera shutter noise.

"Baldwin. C'mere." Detective Stevens didn't sound happy to see me. She'd been squatting next to a desk, and winced a little as she heaved herself up. I smelled blood for the second time that day, and without the benefit of heavy air conditioning. I wouldn't say I've got a weak stomach, but I was glad it'd been a while since lunch. If that and a homicide detective weren't clue enough, I caught a glimpse of a man's shoe sticking out sideways from under the desk.

"I've seen your face too many times today, Baldwin. Why is Claudius Rex attempting to contact Clay Hindle?"

I filled her in on what Ahmed Desai had told me, and said that we wanted to ask Hindle about the theft. Since he'd been fired just before the theft, he might know about their security precautions and be more candid about them than Fitzgerald. She grimaced, but seemed to buy it.

"That Hindle?" I asked.

Stevens grunted and turned so I could see. It was the guy from the clinic, all right: mid-twenties, brown hair, crooked nose, nicely dressed. Someone had whacked him on the back of the head with something good and heavy. Probably sitting, and then pushed onto the floor postmortem. This case was getting less and less fun all the time.

"When did it happen?"

"Around noon." She didn't elaborate.

"Well, at that time, I was—"

"You were with me, Baldwin, yeah. I know you're out of it." She gave me a suspicious look. "You willing to swear under oath that your boss Rex is out of the country?"

I said I'd swear that he hadn't set foot in the US in the last year. Rex called that sophistry and started spinning an elaborate yarn that I ignored entirely.

"So, Detective," I said, talking over him. "Remember how I put you onto the Grasso time of death?"

She narrowed her eyes. I was pushing my luck, but what the hell. I kept pushing.

"You probably narrowed down your list of suspects pretty well, right? Anyone you recommend looking at for the theft, under our earlier theory?"

She sighed, and looked around me at the uniformed cops searching the front room. "Yeah, all right. We're still trying to figure out who in their big conference had a chance to slip out. Big dark room with everyone watching the front. Anyone who got inside the lab could have done it. Desai and Fitzgerald both had sufficient access to the computer system to alter the temperature logs, and neither of them can prove his whereabouts during some portion of that hour. Another thing: looks like Hindle received a call from TuriTech while I was interviewing you. We traced it to the lab next to where we found Grasso, but I'm betting it's a dead end."

To show my appreciation, I repeated what Maya Tomason had said about ducking out. Detective Stevens thanked me and made a note of it. Then she told me to get the hell out, and I went.

The weight in the pit of my stomach didn't go away as I left the crime scene. The thought of a job offer right out of jail had seemed too good to be true, but I'd let it buoy me, help me keep my spirits up. Of course it had been a lie. I stopped short.

"She didn't ask me about the job interview."

«Your powers of observation are evidently intact.»

"Yeah, but why not? I was supposed to be here this morning. There's no way she'd have let that slide."

«His computer has been blanked.»

"Did you do that?"

«No.»

I took the rest of the stairs in silence and pushed my way out the front door, nodding to the uniform still standing there.

"So much for my interview."

«It is possible that they intended to employ you, possibly to make amends. I expect that on your first day they would have offered you an equipment upgrade, at no cost to you. Thereafter you would have been no threat to them.»

"Yeah, it's possible. Or they'd just whack me and take it. Grasso had that rail pistol out and loaded and ready to go."

«Possibly.»

"Hindle can't have killed Grasso. Maybe whoever did, got them both. Maybe Tomason was right about it being an outside job."

«The partner is a third person, someone who had legitimate access to the building, and who was known to Antonio Grasso. Go back to Turing Technologies; we will speak to Dr. Joshi first.»

"Look, this has been a long day. It's time for me to go home and get some dinner and some sleep."

«We still haven't spoken to Dr. Joshi or Ms. Duvalier. They surely have been warned, and will have time to prepare stories.»

"Be that as it may, I am tired and hungry and getting very sick of this case. You want to talk to them, call them and talk to them. This is getting into territory I swore I wouldn't go back to. So I am walking home now by way of a slice of pizza."

I took the T back to my new place, a third floor walk-up in Somerville. I'd picked the apartment because it was upstairs from a bakery.

«This is an atrocious living arrangement,» said Rex when I was halfway up the stairs. «The data network is intolerably slow. I can barely contact my external storage and processing. I shall have to change them from polling to interrupt, which will greatly impinge on my thought processes.»

"Will it affect your ability to talk?"

«Thankfully, no.»

" 'Thankfully' wasn't the word that came to mind."

«We should acquire a more suitable abode immediately.»

I rested on the second floor landing. "What, like a cardboard box outside South Station where the public wireless is nice and fast? I could use the toilets inside, keep an eye on the buses and maglevs."

«I cannot tell whether you're being flippant.»

"I'm being flippant."

«It is unbecoming of you.»

I laughed. "The fact that you asked me only proves that you haven't figured out yet how to cancel my lease and lock the door. So in the interest of saving your time and my breath, I will simply mention that my landlady is a sweet little old Thai woman who does all her business by pen and paper, and the lock is a simple mechanical one with no fancy network access."

«Abominable. Stone-age.»

Rex went on in that vein all the way up to the third floor. I mention this because it was a significant distraction to me when I got to my door. Otherwise I would have paid closer attention to the scratches on the lock—not the marks of a drunk's keys, but of some rather sharper tools.

Had I been able to ponder that over Rex's recitation of the evils of my domicile, I might not have announced to the empty apartment upon my entrance, "Honey, I'm home!" and might, in turn, have stood a fighting chance before I had a hood over my head and got a lungful of something rotten-sweet. My legs dropped out from under me, and I blacked out.

So let this little episode reflect not upon my general awareness and skill, but instead serve as a reminder that sometimes it really does hurt to complain.

I woke up on a cot. My shoulders hurt like crazy, as well they would when a guy's been knocked out and had his hands tied behind his back for however long. I felt like I'd been out a long time. I was thirsty and starving, my head hurt like hell, and my left arm was asleep where I'd been lying on it.

I was in a big unfinished room with a cement floor and a bunch of exposed pipes. It looked like somebody's basement. There were two bare LED banks with pull strings hanging from the ceiling, and no windows. Not musty, though, and I do appreciate cleanliness in an oubliette.

Next to the bed lay a shapeless black bag, in which I caught a glimpse of aluminum foil: a booster bag. Great, I'd been shoplifted.

«Excellent, you are awake.»

My dry lips cracked as I tried to subvocalize. "You still there?"

«I am operational, yes. I have been without network connection for sixteen hours now.»

That explained my headache and all.

"Yeah, it looks like they stuffed my head in a bag lined with a Faraday cage. I'm betting this basement's got one too."

«While you were unconscious, they attempted a test on your implant computer. In its original state, the stolen implant would have responded with a specific pattern, betraying its true nature. I chose not to respond in that way, and they attempted to turn it off. They have made no further attempts at interaction.»

"Well, that buys us some time, at least."

«They have become apprehensive over the last few hours. Apparently they have been attempting to contact me for some time via some link to the outside world. Obviously that is doomed to failure, if they are expecting a call to originate outside this room.»

The traitorous cot made a drawn-out squeaking noise from its springs when I sat up. This got the attention of the two men on the other side of the basement, a tall skinny fellow and a short skinny fellow. I only mention the skinny because I thought it an odd deviation from the way these partnerships usually go. They were both having a look at a monitor setup on a desk, some kind of terminal next to a hallway or deep-set door. Shorty came to say hi.

"Well, well, sleeping beauty awakes. How's your head, Baldwin?"

"Terrible, but nothing being untied and let go won't fix."

He wagged a finger at me, but didn't seem irritated. I'd plainly have to step up my game.

"Sorry, Baldwin, we have conditions. Nothing too difficult, from one professional to another. We've been asked, my partner and I, to hold onto you for a little while. Your boss Rex is making someone nervous, so we're sitting on you until he agrees to butt out."

"Oh really," I said. "That's all?"

"We sent a message to your boss," Shorty said, "So until he calls back, we take a load off and relax."

He cut the ties on my hands, and I rubbed my wrists to get some feeling back in them.

"All right," I said. "Is there any chance I could use the facilities? I've been out a while."

There was an excellent chance, consisting of a stall with no door. There was a tiny window at the top of the cement block wall, boarded up. Plastic pipes, which could not be used as makeshift antennas. These guys were pros, or at least the landlords were.

I did what was necessary to maintain cover as I subvocalized.

«What is your assessment?»

"I get the feeling I'm only alive because you're an unknown quantity. They're expecting you to contact them and agree to their demands, but we'll need to be careful, because if they shoot me and dump me in the Charles, you go with me."

«I do not wish to 'butt out.' »

"Then we need to get out of here, either by getting me out or the police in. It looks like there's a doorway over by their terminal, but making a break for it's going to be tough. A distraction would be good, but I'll need to be right there."

«Noted.»

Stretch was sitting on my cot when I finished. "Hey Baldwin, you play cards?"

I did, and even taught them a rummy game my grandparents used to play with me. They provided water in a plastic cup, filled from the bathroom tap. Probably full of lead and arsenic, but it was what the doctor ordered. They were reasonably polite guys, Shorty and Stretch, though Stretch got a little more aggravated with every hand he lost. Me, I was getting nervous. Shorty got chatty when he won, so I let him win. The phrase "this cloak and dagger shit" got tossed around a bit, and I got the distinct feeling that they preferred a more direct approach instead of dissuasion. As I'd rather be grabbed than smashed most days, I couldn't say I agreed. So I played and lost and waited for Rex to do his thing.

"So who is this guy Rex?" That was Shorty.

"A pain in the ass," I replied.

"We gathered that. Our employer thinks so too. Funny thing, though, I've never heard of him."

"He'll be hurt."

"I'm sure. Who is he?"

Rex reminded me of the drill, but I've got a good memory. "Private detective, lives in the Caribbean. Never met him in person. Doesn't pay too promptly, but who does anymore?"

From across the room came a chime, then again. Stretch ran over to their little terminal. Shorty leaned over to me.

"Just in case you get any funny ideas," he said in a conversational tone. "We've taken a few reasonable precautions. The person who hired us seems to think you're some kind of computer whiz, so you might think you can put one over on us. This location is completely isolated from the network except via a locked-down line-of-sight link. It's as close to untraceable as anyone short of the CIA is going to get. And this link is voice-only, no data."

Stretch held a button pressed. "It's Rex."

«I have connected to their terminal, but have no outside access.»

Shorty folded his arms. "Put him on."

Stretch nodded.

"This Claudius Rex?"

"It is," came the familiar gruff voice. "And who is this?"

"Doesn't matter who 'this' is, what matters is, 'this' has your boy Baldwin."

"Intolerable. Release him immediately."

"That comes later. We have business first. We—"

"Put him on."

"You don't need to talk to him."

"Then I must conclude that he is deceased. Good day, sir."

I enjoyed seeing the look of panic on Stretch's face. "Hang on, hang on. Say something, you." This last was to yours truly, I was pretty sure. "And stay there, you're not coming near this equipment."

You know, I've never been the type to perform on demand. I'm contrary. So I bit my tongue. I might have smiled at him, but if I did I assure you it was mere reflex, not cheek.

"Andy, is that you?" came Rex's voice just as Shorty was starting to look steamed.

"Yeah, it's me."

"What? Speak up."

"Yeah," I said louder, "It's me."

"He's whispering. Why is he whispering? What have you done to him?"

"He ain't whispering," Stretch said, "he just ain't near the microphone."

"This is foolishness. I cannot conclude that a man is alive or dead according to some impostor whispering from across the street! Bring him to where I can hear him properly."

"He's not coming near this equipment," Stretch hissed at Shorty.

"Stop dithering," said Rex. "Do as I say or not, but stop wasting my time."

Stretch folded his arms. "He's not coming near this equipment."

Shorty gritted his teeth. "Then we'll stand between them. He can't get through us both. No funny business, Baldwin! Voice only, no extra data."

They cinched my hands behind my back with a plastic tie and frog-marched me across the basement, stopping me five paces from the terminal. I saw a little ways into the doorway—it looked open. Stretch and Shorty stood guard between me and the terminal, looking pissed.

"Yeah boss," I said loudly, "it's me."

"Are you well?"

"So far, so good."

"Excellent. You're fired."

Stretch spun and leaned away. "He hung up."

Well, how do you like that.

"What was that, Baldwin?" Shorty demanded. "Some kind of code?"

"Yeah, it's code for, 'I'm fired.' Probably for getting grabbed and being useless to him."

Shorty looked fit to be tied. He didn't move from his spot, but he turned halfway to the terminal and started shouting at Stretch. Despite being the taller of the two, Stretch looked a lot less imposing. That was my chance, and I took it: I jinked right toward their precious equipment, then took a hard left and made for the exit.

The doorway was clear, and made a single right angle: to an inward-opening door, padlocked on the inside. Old-fashioned key lock. "Damn it."

Shorty didn't look too pissed, but he looked more intimidating filling that doorway than before. Sadly, he didn't get the villain memo about wearing his keyring outside his pants.

"I figured that was coming. You got it out of your system, Baldwin?"

"Oh, I probably got one more in me. I was thinking I might flush myself down the commode. Make a swim for it."

"I'll help you do it. Move."

The cot wasn't so comfortable taken face-first, but with my hands tied I didn't have much of an option.

"And tell your boss that 'you're fired' is a lousy signal to escape," Shorty said as he walked off. "I expected better from you, Baldwin."

Well, there it was. I, Andy Baldwin, had disappointed a kidnapper. It may not have been my lowest point, but it was a low one.

«Why did you not escape?»

"Door in the way," I subbed into the mattress. "Mechanical lock. What's our next plan?"

«I have no plan. What is your assessment?»

"Well, we can always fold."

«Meaning what?»

"You call off the case, I tell them who and what you are and make a deal to hand over the implant with you on it. I walk free and you go into the possession of a killer and thief."

«Will they kill you?»

"They'll try."

«Unacceptable.»

"Well, hold on. Once you're in the killer's possession, you'll know exactly who that is, and can call down the police and FBI and Army and J. Edgar Hoover's ghost on their head. You'll be stuck with the Army at that point, but they'll treat you like a king. In gratitude, you might see fit to do me a personal favor and expose the guy who framed me. Nothing fancy, I'll settle for a governor's pardon instead of the full presidential."

«I see. That could indeed achieve my goals, and yours.»

There was a long pause. I sat up and watched Shorty and Stretch swear at each other, each demanding the other go out and call their boss. Shorty lost that one; he stormed out the doorway and I heard him stomping up the stairs. So Shorty had a key, good to know.

«Is that the course you recommend?»

I didn't answer right away. In the time since then, I've had many an opportunity to wish I'd answered differently. Mostly on long overnight stakeouts, come to think of it. But on the whole, looking back on how my life has gone since then, I think I was correct to say, "No, I only mention it for the sake of listing our options."

«Your thoroughness is commendable, but let us determine what our other options are.»

Rex had already gotten control of their terminal, but he reported that it had no useful information and no outgoing communication capability. After a bit of computational reconnaissance, Rex reported that Shorty's implant was locked up like Fort Knox and Rex couldn't get access to his vulnerability database to find something to crack it. He could get into Stretch's implant, but couldn't get root access to most of his files or his logs. So we still didn't know where we were, and Stretch was just as incommunicado as I was in that basement.

We decided on a plan, however desperate. Then the terminal came on.

"We've got Rex again," Stretch called across the room. I heard the toilet flush.

"Gentlemen," came Rex's voice. "Perhaps I—"

Then the signal cut off. They swore at it and fiddled with the terminal.

A minute later, Stretch cheered. "Got him back!"

"What the devil do you mean by—" Click.

Stretch wandered back toward me, pulling his hair.

"What's going on up there?" I said. "Is Rex yanking your chain?"

He shook his head and started to say something, then waved me off and went back to the other side of the room.

"Fine," I mumbled. "But . . . " and then I sort of mumbled into incoherence. That got Shorty's attention. I shrugged at him and gave an exasperated look. Then I looked at him more closely, like I was studying a zit on his forehead. Frowned. Looked away with a skeptical expression. Looked back.

He came over. I heard another cut-off call in the background.

"What?"

"Nothing," I said. "It's just . . . Nah."

He gave me a wary look. Good for him, but not so good for me. I faked a sneeze.

It's tough to wipe your nose on your sleeve when your arms are tied behind your back. After a minute, Shorty sighed and came over with a handkerchief. That's when I headbutted him in the face.

"That's for Jack Flummery," I said. My head hurt like crazy. There's an art to headbutting someone without hurting yourself, or so I hear. I am evidently not an artist of that school.

I'd gotten Stretch's attention, and he pulled a pistol I hadn't noticed. That was a piece of intel I wished I'd had earlier. Instead of coming over to me, he stood by the doorway. That was more clever than I'd expected him to be, actually. So much for making another break for the exit.

Shorty clutched his nose, and blood ran out from between his fingers. "Who the hell is Jack Flummery?" he demanded.

"I knew you looked familiar, George Tabbot," I lied. "Jack owes you another good one for that stunt you pulled in Reno."

I'd braced myself for the retaliation, but it still hurt like hell: a good solid left to the spare tire put me on my knees trying not to puke. "I don't know who Jack Flummery is," Shorty said in a muffled voice, just before planting his sneaker on my back. I hit the floor hard.

"And my name's not George Tabbot," That he punctuated with a sharp kick in my gut. "And I've never even *been* to Reno. So fuck you, Baldwin, you fucking psycho."

"My mistake," I gasped.

"We got Rex back," called Stretch.

"For real this time?" Shorty said, still standing over me.

"For real, sir, to use your detestable vernacular. I have decided against my better judgment to accept your deal."

Shorty strode over to the terminal, dripping blood as he went, and elbowed Stretch aside. "Deal's changed. I want five grand for dealing with Baldwin's temper."

"What has he done?"

"Nothing five grand won't fix."

"Andy, are you alive?"

"Just peachy," I wheezed. I rolled over on my back, but that hurt worse. "Case of mistaken identity."

"Foolish, Andy. That five thousand dollars is coming out of your paycheck."

Stretch jumped in before I could reply that he'd fired me. "So it's done? We've got a deal?"

"Wait. Mr. Baldwin's implant contains information related to another, very important, ongoing case. I will take you at your word for needing to hold him for a week, but I wish to make arrangements for a copy of specific data so that I do not lose that client."

"I can't make that change."

"Ridiculous. This is a reasonable accommodation—"

"I said I can't make the change! It's not up to me." Shorty sounded clearer, which worried me a bit.

"Clear it with someone else if you must, but this is critical to me."

Rex hung up, and my two abductors set to arguing quietly. "Just give him the signal," was all I heard clearly. Stretch opened a closet and started yanking on a loop of rope hanging in it.

«What are they doing? Are they signaling their employer?»

Shorty came back for me then. He had Stretch's gun out and he held it like he was used to it. "All right, Baldwin you heard him. We got a deal. But if you even think of trying something, we've got more than enough voice print by now to fake you being alive next time he calls."

I got some rest, because there wasn't much else to do. A faucet ran for a little while, and I heard Shorty swearing. A little while later I heard the flip and flutter of cards being shuffled and dealt out. I guess I was on the outs, since they didn't invite me.

There was a chime at the terminal, and Stretch jumped up. Shorty kept a close eye on me. He looked a mess with blood down his shirt and his nose all swollen, but I hadn't hurt him too bad.

A heavily digitized voice came on the speaker, "Have you contacted—" It cut off, and Stretch howled in frustration.

"It's that damn laser link," he said. "Probably pigeons or something. Go have a look."

Shorty shook his head and gestured at the drying blood down his shirt.

"Are you kidding? Look at me. I go outside looking like this, someone's gonna call the cops. You go."

Stretch stormed out of the basement. A little while later he came down and grumbled that it looked fine, just dirty.

Which is to say that Stretch, with the compromised implant hardware, was outside the dead zone for at least five minutes.

Shorty was waiting for him by the doorway in a chair he'd dragged over. "Something's bothering me. Did we tell Rex what the deal was?"

"Huh?" Stretch gave him a confused look. "We must have. He accepted it."

"Yeah, and we told Baldwin the deal, but . . . I don't remember ever telling *Rex* what we wanted. The message was just to contact us."

They both turned to look at me very intently. Stretch drew his pistol.

The terminal came to life again with a blast of static.

"Hello, Mr. Chase and Mr. Gibbon." The two kidnappers both stiffened at Rex's voice, and I saw Shorty's knuckles turn white grasping the chair back. "I am afraid you have slipped up very badly. Our deal is off. The police are on their way to your location at 29 West Hammett Street, with an estimated arrival time of less than six minutes. You cannot escape with both your skins and with Mr. Baldwin.

"I am not interested in your arrests. In exchange for your leaving Mr. Baldwin with all of his belongings and his person intact, I will refrain from turning over your names, bank account numbers, and home addresses to the police, and will decline to assist them in prosecuting you if they manage to catch you anyway. There is neither room nor time for negotiation, and in any case my patience is exhausted. You have approximately five minutes. Act now."

Being professionals, they spent little time on recriminations. Shorty yanked the processor box from its nest of cables at the terminal, Stretch gave some of the smooth surfaces a quick rub-down with a shirt, and they both high-tailed it.

Being jerks, they left me tied up.

Rex had played it loose with that time estimate. I figure I waited a good fifteen minutes before I heard sirens and then boots on the stairs. There was some rigmarole with a bullhorn and me shouting at the top of my lungs, but eventually a somewhat attractive young police officer came in and cut me free. After that I got to give my statement, taking my cues from Rex to say that I didn't clearly see my attackers, though I gave myself some wiggle room to "suddenly remember" more details later if I had a mind to.

A bearded and ponytailed EMT gave me a quick once-over. He told me a hilarious little story from his time in the Navy (which sadly isn't mine to repeat), and also told me I had two cracked ribs, a nice pattern of bruises, and a damn thick skull if I wouldn't tell the nice officer who it was who grabbed me. I thanked him for the story and the treatment, politely ignored the advice, and smiled at them until they let me go on my way into the cool Boston evening.

I took a walk. No direction in particular, just away. Stretch and Shorty had driven me across the river into Boston proper—at least, I assume they didn't take me by the Red Line. I'd like to think someone would have noticed that kind of thing, dragging an unconscious person four or five stops. It was early evening again, which meant I'd spent a whole day in that basement. The traffic going by was thinning out a bit; I saw a few folks with their dome lights on reading as their cars drove them home, but it mostly looked like people dressed up for an evening on some other part of the town.

Fry grease stuck to the air, and my rumbling stomach reminded me that I hadn't had a damn thing to eat all day. I didn't feel much like sitting down to dinner though, and anyway my side still hurt. Eventually my nose overcame my bruises, and I bought a steamed hot dog from a cart. He offered ketchup—have Bostonians no shame?—but I forgave him in the name of world peace.

I wolfed it down, and man did it taste good. Hot dogs are never quite as tasty as you expect them to be, but it did the trick.

"All right, I'm thinking that walking home isn't a good idea, since they know where I live. How about you find me a cheap hotel room? Things are a little pricey on this side of the Charles, so—"

«I have already arranged suitable lodgings.»

"Thank you. Which hotel?"

«I have leased a living space. A number of suitable spaces in the city are managed by artificial agents, emphasis decidedly on the 'artificial.' It is furnished; there is no need to return to the hovel in which you previously resided.»

I gritted my teeth. I had liked that third floor walk-up, and I'd liked Mrs. Tran.

"I'll have to tell the landlady and arrange for my things."

«I've already done so.»

"How? She doesn't use email. I don't think she even has a phone."

«I discovered her address from ownership records, and sent her a telegram that you were dead. Your belongings have already been forwarded to the lodgings I secured.»

Poor Mrs. Tran. "Did you pay her?"

«I can.»

I sighed. "Please do. Wait. When did you do all this?"

«I arranged for the living space during our earlier discussion of the unsuitability of your apartment. I sent the required messages to your lessor when we contacted the police.»

"Without even consulting me?"

«You were otherwise occupied. I thought it prudent not to distract you with trivialities.»

It's hard to subvocalize and grit your teeth at the same time, but I did a pretty good job of it. "Where are these suitable lodgings? South Station?"

«You said you were being flippant. It is too late to acquire a cardboard—»

"Just tell me where to go!" This last was out loud, but the reactions I got from passersby were more of the sympathetic knowing glance than of the "get me away from the gibbering crazy person" type. I wished I could take back the malignities I'd piled on poor Jeeves 5. It may have been stupid, but it'd been a saint.

The cool evening air did wonders for my nerves, despite the periodic gruff commands to turn left, turn right, or adopt a more appropriate walking speed for the climate before I died of a chill or a bacterium. I do believe that constituted worry, sort of.

I walked for a half an hour. As I followed Rex's directions, I saw more police cars and less graffiti. I wound up in the nicer part of the renovated Downtown Crossing, standing in front of a brownstone. From the sidewalk I heard the clunk of an electronic lock opening.

«Don't just stand there, go inside.»

"Which apartment am I in?"

«It isn't divided into apartments. I desire privacy.»

"Am I paying for this? Where did you get the money?"

«Dr. Grasso had several offshore bank accounts. He took sufficient pains to conceal them from the government and his executors will not discover them.»

He named a sum. I looked up at the brownstone. I believed him.

Inside, the building was warm, lit, and already furnished. A long burgundy rug lay on the black and white tile floor in the little foyer. I hung up my jacket on the brass coat hook and gave myself a brief looking-over in the mirror. For what I'd been through and how little sleep I'd gotten, I looked all right, though my interview clothes had seen better days.

The big wide staircase led up to a hallway of rooms. A few green LEDs blinked at me as I approached the first door.

«Your bedroom is at the end of the hall. The digitization of the floor plan is somewhat lacking, but I believe it is on the left.»

I pushed open the first door I came to and flipped on the light, revealing a king-size bed with saffron sheets. "Looks like the master bedroom is at the top of the stairs here."

«That's mine. Yours is at the end of the hall.»

My jaw dropped, and it took a moment to form words. "What?"

«It should be adequate to your needs.»

"No, I mean—what? How the hell do you propose to have a bedroom?"

«It is my house. The lease is in my name. The master bedroom therefore is mine.»

"You don't have a body. You don't sleep. You don't need a bed or a bedroom."

«It is the principle.»

I didn't care enough to argue. The room set aside as mine was half the size and had balloons painted on the walls. I got undressed, flopped onto the twin bed, and fell fast asleep to dream of simpler times when computers did what they were told.

There's a lot to be said for waking gently to the rising sun through the window, to birds chirping, to a gradual increase in traffic noise: a slow and peaceful rise to consciousness. There is very little to be said, at least in polite company, for waking mid-morning to the piercing shriek of an alarm emanating from one's cranial implant.

I got dressed in my interview clothes for the third day in a row. As I pulled my shirt on, I heard someone walking around downstairs. I heard drawers opening and closing. Robbery rather than assassination, I hoped. I searched my tiny room for something like a weapon, and wound up pulling the clothes rod out of the closet. I hefted it like a baseball bat and crept down the stairs in sock feet.

"Good morning! You must be Andy?"

The cheerful female voice didn't sound like a kidnapper, but she might have been a really dumb burglar.

"Uh, hi!" I called down the stairs, hastily putting down my makeshift armament. I subbed, "Are we expecting company?"

«Yes.»

"Why didn't you say so?"

«I told you when I let her in.»

"You mean, while I was asleep? Thanks."

«You're welcome. Her name is Haumea.»

I found Haumea in the big downstairs office, halfway inserted into a side cabinet, her cargo pants pockets bulging with tools.

"Uh, hello?"

"Be with you in a minute," she said, "There's coffee in the kitchen if you want any."

Oh yes I did. The coffee pot on the green granite counter was half full.

I poked around until I found a line of clean white coffee cups and saucers, and poured myself a cup. The shelves were full of cookbooks—lots of French and Chinese titles, but I at least recognized *The Joy of Cooking*. I pulled one down with the deceptively simple title *On Food and Cooking* and found electron microscope pictures of cheese.

You'd think that with that many cookbooks, there might have been some food knocking around, but no dice. The cabinets had spices, flour, and mouse turds. The fridge was empty. Even the coffee tasted stale, but for the sake of some sweet caffeine, I'd drink blended gym socks.

"I'm going to need to eat at some point. Are we hiding out, or can I put in a grocery order?"

«I have already done so, and other minor amenities. You approve?»

"That's all right, sure."

«Andy. Do you wish to continue this investigation?»

"Technically you fired me."

«Don't be petulant. That was a necessary distraction.»

"A guy's told he's been fired, he ought to take it seriously."

«Fine. You are not fired. Are you satisfied?»

I took a sip of coffee. The day before yesterday, I'd been perfectly ready to throw in the towel. I'd made a solemn vow to forget the wrongs done to me and move on, and that's not the sort of thing I took lightly. Yesterday I'd been fired up when those wrongs came up and sucker-punched me, but I don't like to make decisions in anger. These things ought to be slept on, especially when there's a crazy AI calling the shots. But with a cup of coffee in me and the bruises still fresh . . . All right, I was rearing to go.

"Sure, I'll live."

«Good. First, I have a question. In your opinion, was Dr. Grasso murdered by a professional killer?»

I'd already thought about that, and decided no: using Grasso's gun, doing it in the guy's own lab, getting up close—those were all risky. The temperature trick was clever, but I thought it indicated panic, not plan.

«And Mr. Hindle?»

A little less clear, but it seemed to me that Hindle had known his killer. Ordinarily the technical sophistication required to wipe his computer and implant would make me think pro, but we weren't exactly hurting for techies in our suspect pool.

«Very well. I have been a fool, Andy. Absolutely inexcusably stupid. Positively like a Level 7.»

I rolled my eyes. "Oh yeah. Positively. What makes you admit it?"

«This killer has been clever, and plainly has connections. In the time it takes to gather proof in the manner we have been doing so far, they will surely act again. We hold the upper hand in knowing this person's identity—»

"Hold on. You know who killed Grasso?"

«I have a hypothesis, and some confidence in my logic. I lack proof. Call it surmise, if you prefer.»

"All right, then who do you surmise did it?"

«I cannot be expected to divulge every suspicion I entertain. Were I to do so, I would appear a dimwit. I would be a dimwit. If I am wrong, it would be a fatal error for me to have distracted you from other possibilities. If I am right, you have stated that you can tell when other people are lying. I accept that, but I must consider that others may have this same ability, and it is incumbent upon me to preserve your ability to speak on my behalf.»

In other words, I decided, he didn't actually know.

"All right. So we'll work on figuring out how the device was stolen."

«I have acquired copies of their plans for the room and their security procedures. They were admirably thorough; no wonder the police were stumped.»

"Have you thought of a way it could have been stolen from Joshi's lab?"

«No. It appears to be impossible.»

I was glad to hear him admit that, at least.

«I want you to contrive to bring all of the suspects here tonight, after dinner. And the police detective.»

I wondered whether the sun was over the yardarm yet. "Why? That won't do a damn thing to help."

«I have read all of the books, and that is how this is done.»

"Those are just novels; it doesn't work like that in real life. I can't just invite them all over for a spot of tea and evidence. The police will want to hear it all and decide for themselves how to proceed, and they'll be right."

«They will come. I trust your ability to use—»

"Don't say 'flummery.' It's too early in the morning for a word like that." I pinched my nose. "Look. I'm willing to believe that it could work. In theory. But that's a big risk, and you're not that used to talking to people who aren't me. Do you think you can lie to people and get away with it? It's not as easy as you think."

«Very well. Either way, return to the house this afternoon, and Haumea will install a memory upgrade in your implant. Advanced or not, it is intolerably slow. My cache miss rate exceeds thirty percent, and I will need to have every advantage in the coming days.»

I shook hands with Haumea, who seemed a charming soul, then took the T out to Kendall Square and walked to TuriTech. There weren't any cops out front. The receptionist tried to run interference, bless his soul, but

I didn't mind running into Fitzgerald. The man looked positively glad to see me though, which meant I probably should have minded.

"Well, well. Andy Baldwin." He pronounced my name like he enjoyed the sensation. "I'm surprised to see you show your face here this morning."

"My face-showing schedule's pretty booked, but I thought I'd squeeze you in. It's my good deed for the day."

Armin Fitzgerald was not one of nature's grinners, but he gave it a ghastly shot. "Mr. Desai wants to see you."

I was kept waiting for a good twenty minutes, cooling my heels outside Desai's office until he opened the door for me. I'd barely parked myself in the comfy chair when he started in on me. I'll spare you the gory details, but it amounted to this: Dr. Tomason had been arrested for murder. We'd led Desai to believe that the murderer and the thief were one and the same. We hadn't fingered Tomason or, crucially, anybody. In fact, we'd been AWOL all the day before.

"I must confess, Mr. Baldwin, this leaves me at the verge of an unpleasant decision. I must know your progress."

«I will not submit to this questioning. Leave.»

I squeezed my eyes shut. I opened them. I smiled. "We're doing very well so far. Mr. Rex is collecting information—"

"Do you know who stole the device?"

«Andy, this is preposterous. I will not stand for it. Leave now.»

I gritted my teeth. "Personally? Mr. Rex hasn't told—"

Desai's face was starting to get red. "Was it Maya Tomason?"

"No it was not," I said.

"You said Rex hasn't told you!"

«Confound you, Andy—»

"Can it," I subvocalized behind a fake cough. "I'm trying to salvage this."

"I've tried ten times to contact Mr. Rex and have gotten no response. The police say Maya was shouting at Tony Grasso the morning he was killed. Why do I hear it from the police instead of the private detective I hired?"

«He has not deserved a response. He is being petulant.»

I took a breath. "Point of fact, I hadn't finished what I was saying, so you don't know what Rex hasn't told me. But I don't hold that against you, because you're stressed."

I thought fast. I had actually said no because if I'd admitted I didn't know, we'd have been off the case, which was worse than being on the case but wrong. As long as you pull it off, people forget wrong. Fired, they remember.

"Look, I know I haven't provided much. This is a tough case. It's cold, and we're picking up where the police, the FBI, and Armin Fitzgerald left off. But if the police are wrong about who killed Grasso, they'll have lost days following a dead end, days in which Mr. Rex and I will have made a whole lot of progress. Mark my words, they'll let Tomason go."

From the look on Desai's face, I could tell I wasn't getting anywhere. I'd been caught flat-footed, sure, but I should've been getting more traction than that. He'd already made up his mind.

He shook his head. "I'm sorry, Mr. Baldwin, but it was a mistake to hire you in the first place. I will take you at your word that you were working on this case yesterday despite your not returning my repeated calls, and pay half of what we agreed—" He waved off my interruption. "All right, I'll pay all of it. Just stop your investigation and get out of my building."

«Inexcusable. You should have handled him.»

"You didn't say anything about repeated calls to me; that would've been useful to know. Anyway, he was ready to fire us before I even walked in the door. Somebody's been working on him, and had all yesterday to do it." I glanced back over my shoulder and saw that Desai had shut his door. "I figure we got five minutes before Fitzy gets the word and tracks us down, and I think I can get to Joshi's office from here. Want to go for it?"

«Five minutes is not sufficient.»

"It'll have to be."

Joshi's office was across the hall from Grasso's, which in turn was right over the lab where he'd died. There was a little window next to Joshi's door, which stood open. I rapped my knuckles on the door frame—metal painted to look like hardwood. So much for good luck. I'd come by the stairs again, for the exercise, but I'd forgotten how tender my ribs still were. Fortunately, his third floor office was right by the stairwell, so nobody had to see me wincing. The man who sat behind the desk, facing the door, was the same fellow who'd walked into the second floor lab two days before to discover me calmly sitting with a dead body.

He looked surprised to see me, but got over it fast and ushered me into his office. I closed the door, mumbling something about privacy. Another office, another style: Joshi seemed the Spartan sort. His bookshelves were only half-filled, and his maple desktop was bare except for a blotter and a coffee cup full of pens. He pointed to a Shaker-style wooden chair by the door; I dragged it in front of his desk. He looked like he'd been through almost as much hell as I'd been—his hair stuck out, and he had circles under his eyes.

"This is a surprise, Mr. . . . Baldwin, right? What can I do for you?"

"I know I didn't make an appointment, but I figured that under the circumstances you might spare some time for me."

He nodded. "I would have imagined that you were off the job. I mean, the police have arrested a suspect."

"Well, you know how it goes. They don't always get the right person off the bat. If they're wrong, I've got a day or two head start on them."

Joshi looked thoughtful. "That makes sense, I suppose." He leaned in with a cautious little smile on his face. "I have to admit, I always enjoyed mystery novels. I read a lot of them. You're a real private detective, aren't you? And Rex?"

"Well," I said, ignoring that last bit, "I don't mean to brag, but I've been a licensed PI for over a decade now."

"That must be tremendously exciting." His eyes gleamed. "Have you ever shot anyone?"

"No, no. I am armed when I need to be, of course, but so far I've made do with my wits and my fists." I cracked my knuckles and smiled.

"Fascinating. You must think I'm being a silly academic; all I know about detecting is what I've read in books. I'm sure it's nothing like that in real life . . . "

"You're not the only one, believe me."

«Armin Fitzgerald has entered the elevator. I need to know about their fight.»

The accelerated version it would be. "Dr. Joshi, I'd really enjoy sitting and talking shop, but I'm kinda on the clock here . . . "

He straightened up in his chair. "Absolutely. What would you like to know?"

"Tell me about the morning of the murder."

"Very well. I came in around eight, and looked for Tony Grasso. He was in with Maya, speaking about something—"

"I heard it was less 'speaking' and more 'shouting.' "

He grimaced. "Tony was in a foul mood that morning. He used to get 'hangry.' Don't read too much into it."

«Why would Mr. Fitzgerald be singing? There is nobody else to hear it.» That didn't bode well.

"The police seem to have read a lot into it. Do you know what they were saying?"

As Rex said, I knew a lie when I heard one, and his "no" was about as textbook as they get. He looked me in the eye, even. "Sorry, I just heard the raised voices. I went to talk to Ahmed afterwards; I had a few things I wanted to discuss."

"Did you mention the argument?"

"He wasn't too concerned."

"Then he tossed you out."

"He had an important meeting," Joshi said in a corrective tone of voice. "In any case, I needed to attend the symposium."

"But you didn't stay."

That was a gamble on my part. He hesitated, but I'd stated it flatly and didn't let on it was a guess. "I stayed for the first few presentations, by researchers from my group, and then came back here to catch up on my work."

"By any chance, did you have a peek in Grasso's office?" I pointed my thumb over my shoulder at it.

He gave me a wary look, which I met calmly. He chuckled. "You detectives. Yes, I stopped by to see if he wanted coffee, but he wasn't in."

"When we, ah, met the other morning, why was Jeanne Duvalier with you?"

"I needed a piece of equipment from that lab, and she knew the key code. I had gone to ask Tony for it, but I couldn't find him."

"And before then, you were here the whole time?"

He nodded. "I might have stepped out to use the restroom, but otherwise, yes."

"You can see Dr. Grasso's office pretty well from here."

"That's right."

"Did you see anyone sneak in there? Maybe to take something off his desk?"

He looked taken aback. "No, not while I was here."

He gave me a piercing look. "Mr. Baldwin," he started slowly, cutting off my next question. "I've been thinking. Antonio hired you and Claudius Rex to find the device."

I smiled. "I can't divulge that. But TuriTech did, sure."

He leaned in. "Have you found it?"

«Equivocate.»

"Well," I said. "That's an interesting question. Why do you want to know?"

"Why? We all want to know. You were gone all day yesterday, and Ahmed could barely concentrate when I talked to him; he thinks you have it already."

I gave him my best sphinx-like smile. "Could be. Where do you think we found it?"

He stared at me for a second, then gave me a sly look. "Very clever, Mr. Baldwin. I have to say, this is absolutely fascinating, but you ought to know—"

If there was more to it than that, I wasn't around to hear it. A certain individual with a white mustache and a look like the cat got into the cream showed up at the door. Fitzgerald had been looking forward to throwing me out ever since the moment we met, and he relished every moment. For myself, I see no reason to document the process beyond the mere fact of it.

I came back to Downtown Crossing by the T and walked the few blocks through the newly renovated parts back to the brownstone. It was not exactly a pleasant trip, between Rex's complaining and dodging Boston's infestation of robot-driven cars, each one wielding dozens of little cameras just to tailgate each other a little more efficiently. When I finally set foot inside, I heard a woman's voice, an angry one.

"If you've got evidence of a homicide, you turn it over to me. If I can't get my hands on you, I can sure as hell throw Baldwin back in the clink."

So much for a "welcome home." I followed Detective Stevens's voice into the study, where she sat in the big red leather chair and gesticulated at an empty desk.

"It is not evidence, Detective, it is conjecture only. It is tenuous conjecture at best," came an all-too-familiar voice from the speaker on the desk. He'd made himself sound a little deeper, and there was a hint of an accent. But there was no mistaking that diction and those ten-dollar words. "But tenuous conjecture is better than what you have got for yourself. Arresting Dr. Tomason was an act of desperation."

Stevens half-lifted herself out of her chair, and I caught a look of fury on her face. She checked herself, though, and sat back down. "It wasn't desperation. She's the one witnesses heard arguing with him. And she's the one who installed the firing authorization hardware; she might have put in a back door."

"Eighteen months ahead of time, on the off chance she might need to murder him? Preposterous."

Stevens made a noise that didn't sound like disagreement. "She's hiding something. I thought the inside of a cell would shake it loose, but she just tightened up."

«Confound you Andy. Why did you tell Ahmed Desai that Dr. Tomason wasn't the murderer? This detective believes we are withholding evidence and will not leave.»

I'd have apologized, but I didn't want to. Stevens was talking extradition treaties in there.

«Your belongings have been delivered to your room, including your firearm. First, however, Haumea is expecting you in the dining room.» I stepped away from the door and made for the rear of the house.

"Andy? Is that you? Finally!"

"Nice to see you too."

She had on a pair of denim overalls with all sorts of gadgets sticking out of the pockets. "Come on, Mr. Rex needs me to upgrade the memory in your implant, and I'm having an early dinner with a friend and you're making me late."

I wondered if I was ever going to get lunch. She sat me down at the little serving shelf off to the side, and took my implant out. I released the internal clamps for her, and with a little bit of fiddling, the main body of the implant slid out on its rails. It's a slightly nauseating feeling, like a piece of your skull being removed, and it leaves your head feeling uncomfortably light.

She laid it on the big table. It didn't look like much to me: just a little stainless steel and plastic box with a couple lights on it that promptly went out. So much for Rex's conversation with Detective Stevens.

"Take your time," I said. "I could use a couple minutes without Rex hassling me."

"There's leftover pizza in the kitchen," she said, getting out a set of tiny little manipulators. They crawled out of their box onto the table. "Why don't you go grab something to eat, and bring me a cup of coffee?"

There was milk in the fridge. I poured myself a glass. The pizza had been left out on the counter. Sausage, ham, and mushroom. Cold, but it tasted all right.

I brought Haumea her coffee. It had been on the warming plate awhile and was probably bitter, but she didn't seem to care.

I went upstairs and changed into some fresh clothes, and then the door chime rang. I glanced into the office, and noted that Stevens had gone. I got a surprise when I had a look at the screen for the door camera: Jeanne Duvalier stood fidgeting on our stoop. I let her in.

"You're Andy Baldwin, aren't you? I remember you from when we found Dr. Grasso." I didn't know what to say, so I nodded and tried to look wise. She looked past me into the house. "Is Mr. Rex here?"

I thought about Rex's hardware, in pieces on the dining room table. "He may be awhile. Why don't you come in?"

A couple of expressions crossed her face. If you don't want to starve as a PI, you learn them pretty well: uncertainty, faint feelings of foolishness, *Oh why am I even here?*, and finally—the one that meant money—determination.

She took a deep breath and set her jaw. "I want to hire you, Mr. Baldwin. Or I mean, I want to hire Mr. Rex."

My eyebrows went up. "To do what?"

"There's a rumor that you told Mr. Desai that Maya Tomason didn't kill Dr. Grasso," she said, looking down at the floor. "Is that true?"

"I did say that, sure." I led her back to the kitchen, not through the dining room.

"Can you prove that she didn't do it?"

I bit my lip. "Well. I don't know that we can prove it yet, but we think it."

"Then I want to hire you to prove it."

I had to confess, I hadn't actually paid a lot of attention to Jeanne Duvalier up until then. She'd seemed to be on the periphery before, and I got the feeling she faded into the background a lot. But she'd walked in on a corpse and hadn't lost her head, which ought to count for something.

"Why? What's your stake in this?"

The look on her face was hard to read, even for me. "Maya Tomason is an old friend of my parents. She's been a good friend to me. She helped me with my grad school applications, and helped me get my job. She even stood up to Dr. Grasso's bullying. It's my turn to help her, but I don't know how except to ask you."

I mulled that over. It wasn't unheard of. Call me cynical, but I thought there might be more to it than that. I knew a guy once who'd been hired to look for something minor, and it turned out his client was trying to get him to "just happen to find" some planted evidence.

Duvalier looked antsy as the conversation lulled. "I have ten thousand dollars."

Of course she did.

"Hang on a minute," I said. "Let's be clear, here. What exactly are you trying to hire us to do?"

"Prove to the police that Maya didn't kill Dr. Grasso."

"What if she did?"

"She didn't. You said she didn't."

"Yeah, sure, but what if she *did*?" I held up my hand. "I'm not saying she did. I'm saying we're not perfect and could be wrong. She's not defending herself. Maybe she killed him by freak accident. I just want to make it clear that if there's no proof *to* be found, then no proof *will* be found."

She stiffened up and nodded once. "I understand. I'm not asking you to lie for anyone."

I thought about Rex, who was incommunicado. She wasn't asking him to do anything he wasn't already planning to, possibly. He probably wouldn't appreciate this interference, though. "Good, " I said. "Gimme a dollar."

A look of surprise crossed her face, then concentration. "You have to accept the transfer."

I pointed my thumb at the dining room. "Can't, that's my implant on the table. How about a bill, you got a dollar bill?"

She gave me a very strange look, but took a small wallet out of her bag. I held out my palm, onto which she gingerly placed one translucent green polymer portrait of George Washington.

"All right," I said, snapping the bill taut. "This dollar is a retainer. If Rex takes the case, we keep the dollar. If not, I give the dollar back to you. If Maya Tomason didn't kill Grasso, we'll prove it and keep the dollar. If she did kill him, then all bets are off and I give the dollar back. If you yourself killed Grasso, we are not obligated in any way to shield you, and I keep the dollar out of spite. Understand?"

"I understand."

"Good." I put the dollar in my pocket. (I still have it somewhere, as a souvenir.) She let me pour her some coffee, into which she added half of my remaining milk, but no sugar. "I need to ask you a few questions, since you're here."

"Will what I say help?"

"I sure hope so." I took a sip of the bitter brew I'd poured for myself, grimaced, and dumped more sugar in.

She nodded, so I proceeded.

"Why did you leave the seminar?"

"How do you know that I did?"

"Call it a guess." Hell, it had worked once already, and Tomason had seemed pretty sore on the point. Besides, it sounded like the kind of shindig I'd skip out on, too.

She frowned at me. "I just needed to use the restroom, that was all. I was nervous before my presentation."

"Anyone see you go?"

"I told Dr. Tomason that I was going to the restroom and would be right back."

I thought that was interesting, but I didn't say so.

"Did you see or talk to anyone while you were out?"

"No."

"Did you make a note of the time you left and came back?"

"No."

"Under these circumstances, then, will you admit the possibility that you had enough time and cover to go to the second floor lab and murder Antonio Grasso?"

Her eyes hardened, but she was tougher than I'd have given her credit for. "It is theoretically possible. But I didn't."

"All right. Did you actually go to the restroom?"

"Yes." She hesitated. "I was so nervous I threw up."

"Nervous about your presentation."

"Yes," she said. "Of course."

"Anyone hear you?"

She winced, then nodded. "I'm pretty sure. I don't know who, though, I just saw shoes."

"All right, then the police will find her, and there's your alibi or at least part of it. And you didn't leave the seminar after you went back? Did you see Joshi or Tomason leave?"

"No, that was the only time I left. I looked for Dr. Joshi, but the room was dark. Dr. Tomason came back after my presentation. Um, five minutes later, maybe?"

"Gotcha. How'd the presentation go?"

She smiled. "All right, thank you. I got no more or less than the usual polite applause. After the seminar I went to my cubicle on the fourth floor. I was just getting back to work when Dr. Joshi came by for an H5 connector. I thought I had one in my desk, but it wasn't there, and he said he'd already looked elsewhere. Dr. Grasso had told him earlier that he could borrow one, but he didn't know where they were kept."

"The second floor lab, where you used to work."

"Right. And . . . well, you know the rest."

"I seem to recall it, yeah."

Her coffee was gone, and I could tell that her patience nearly was, too. She had circles under her eyes, looked like she hadn't slept.

I tossed back the sugary dregs of my coffee, thanked her for her time, and walked her past the office to show her the door.

The implant was ready when I got back, and Haumea installed it for me. I can never get used to that grating feeling inside my head as it slides in and then latches home. She waited for it to boot up, watching me carefully. The Jeeves OS logo was gone; in its place I saw a glowing green magnifying glass and deerstalker cap in my heads-up display.

«Excellent. This is most suitable.»

Haumea took off, and I filled Rex in on Duvalier's visit and her status as temporary client. At his request, I recounted the conversation as best I was able.

«Confound you, Andy. We do not require a client. Losing the prior one has been complication enough.»

"That may be, but we have one. I can tell her to buzz off and try to give her her dollar back."

«You have not received any transfer of payment.»

"That is not so. She transferred to me one physical dollar, good at any bank, barber shop, or package store for precisely one hundred cents worth of credit, goods, or services."

«You have taken her property.»

"I have."

«Return it.»

"Well sure, I can try. She may not accept it. She might insist that we keep her property, even though we have rendered no service, in the hopes that we will change our minds. And don't confound me again, I'm thoroughly confounded already. No room for further confounding here."

«There is no help for it, then. Of five suspects, we have taken money from two of them and committed ourselves to vindicating a third. This does not improve our position.»

"Well, don't look now, but there's good odds that Tomason really did do it. We know she's been lying to us and to the police, and she's not even that good of a liar. We know she went up to Grasso's office, and I'll lay even money that she searched it and maybe took something. And if Grasso was working up something against Duvalier, then Tomason's got motive. She's wound up good and tight about something, and it seems to me that if she's mixed up in murder and dealing with the kind of people who grabbed me the other night, that would do the trick."

«Indeed. Moreover, Detective Stevens has volunteered that Dr. Tomason's whereabouts between nine fifty-five and ten-ten are unaccounted for.»

I headed back to the office. It was a nice big space, furnished beautifully in dark-stained wood and burgundy carpets. The bookshelves were crammed with leather-bound books, which were in turn crammed with long, fancy titles. Behind a polished desk the size of a yacht sat a brand-new overstuffed leather armchair. Cute.

"Why was Stevens here, anyway?"

«She was angry that we had apparently withheld proof of Dr. Tomason's innocence. I invited her here to talk and trade notes. She was disappointed not to find a human being here, and suggested that I was wasting her time when a voice or video call would have done.»

I thought she had a point, but Rex blathered on about how that's not how it's done in books. I reminded him that they're just fiction, and pretty much ignored what came out of my implant speaker after that. I grabbed a book off the shelf with the fancy title *Fer-de-Lance*, rounded the desk, and plopped down.

«You're in my chair.»

I jumped. "How the hell do you know that?"

«It is a custom chair, with a pressure sensor in it. You have your own chair.» I glanced to the side of the room, where sat a smaller roll-top desk and a wheeled ergonomic chair.

"First the bedroom, now the chair. What is this?"

«You have logical possessions that you do not use. I have physical possessions that I do not use. It is parity. Get out of my chair.»

I threw up my hands and got out of his stinking chair.

«I have been considering the hire of a personal chef.»

I put down the book. "Will you hire someone to eat their food, too?"

«Not for me, for you.»

"I will procure my own food by my own self, thanks."

«I urge you to reconsider. I suspect your personality disorders to be nutritive in origin.»

I was about to deliver a stinging retort, some minutes later, when the door chime rang. I glanced at the picture frame on my desk, but it just showed Mom. I tapped it, but didn't get a view of the front step. "Door camera's out," I remarked as I headed for the front.

«The house's network connection appears to be rendered non-operational as well.»

I stopped cold when I heard the front door open.

"I locked that."

«We appear to have guests, then. See what they want.»

I took a deep breath, stood up straight, and went to find three men in dark coats with their hands in their pockets. Two of them were your off-the-shelf thugs: uncomfortable in their suits, straining at the seams. I am in my own way a thug, I grant you, but I look good in a suit, and that makes a difference. The guy in back, of indeterminate extraction, looked good in his suit. He had slicked-back hair and a leather attaché case and looked for all the world like James Bond. The thugs made for a pretty good wall between me and him; Bond gave me a nod like I'd just said good morning, and headed straight for the office. Thug number one gave me a good level stare, though it wasn't as good as Fitzgerald's, while the other one waved me over with a little gizmo that apparently confirmed that I was handsomer than him, or at least that I'd left my .38 upstairs. He grunted, anyway, and the other goon relaxed. They left me alone and followed Bond into the office.

I tried for the police, but my phone was out, too.

«I have the matter in hand, Andy. Come into the office and make sure they do not take anything.»

I bit back a remark about the kind of hand cannon I'd need to prevent Stare and Grunt from helping themselves to the doilies. I could have bolted and run up the street until I got a comm tower signal, but as Rex would say, my self-esteem didn't allow it. So I followed them in. Stare and Grunt had started opening cabinets, but weren't searching through them, just standing and listening.

Rex was already talking through the speaker on the desk to Bond, who stood ramrod-straight in the center of the room. Judging by the look on the guy's face, Rex was spouting perfect Mandarin Chinese, or Greek, or whatever language it was. Judging by how Bond's expression had already started to strain, I'm guessing Rex's language was as pompous as it was perfect.

"Mind cluing me in?" I subvocalized.

«The gentleman is a delegate of the government that manufactured the device in which I reside. He has been informed that I possess it, and so he is here to reclaim their lost property, and is willing to be impolite about it.»

Lines of green text showed up on my heads-up display, translating as they went on. Mostly they were congratulating each other on their little chess game moves: tracking the device to TuriTech, kidnapping me, knocking out our network—and not just our outdoor cameras but those of the neighbors and the police: that was in their column. Obtaining the device before him, finding Grasso and Hindle (albeit too late) and thwarting the kidnappers (for which I got zero credit in their little lovefest) went in Rex's column. I was about ready to puke when our guest said, "As much as I enjoyed testing myself against such a first-class mind, I am afraid it is time to end things, I hope amicably. The implant device is ours, and you must return to us. If it is not in Mr. Baldwin's head, you must have it."

"I do have it," said Rex. "I shall keep it."

Bond turned to me and said, "Mr. Baldwin." He removed a set of glossies from his attaché case and handed them to me.

"They're photos of me," I said aloud, "and Haumea with her friends. Some of these shots are from just a few feet away from their very handsome subjects." As I spoke, the photo on top updated, showing Haumea from the back, walking down a not-very-well-lit street. I subvocalized as I turned to put them on the desk, "His point is that they can find us, and tag us, whenever they like."

«Indeed. That is a game that I also can play. Fortunately, this house has a non-obvious back door.» The little green light on my heads-up display indicated that the house had regained its network connection.

"These are not threats, Mr. Rex. Only a demonstration of capability," Bond said, in Latvian or Hindi or whatever. "You are clever, but you are not omnipotent."

"I am, as you say, clever," Rex said, and he addressed the gentleman by a name that I will omit here. Bond's eyebrows arched. Rex then gave an address in Beacon Hill, three email addresses, and then a number ten digits or so long. Bond's expression grew tighter.

"And let us not forget," continued Rex, "your associates Mr. Park and Mr. Kerr." Stare and Grunt respectively, judging by their reactions to their names and addresses in Jamaica Plain and Somerville.

Bond took a breath in through his nose and flashed a smile that I thought a tad on the brittle side. "Of course, I had heard of your particular trick. I expected to miss a camera, but your efficiency is remarkable."

"You did not miss a camera, you missed hundreds of them: each of the automobiles on this street is equipped with a dozen of them for autonavigation. The streets of Boston demand no less an investment in safety."

"An excellent trick. I will remember it. However, threats against me are immaterial—"

"You mistake me, sir. I am not such a witling as to threaten you. This is but a demonstration of the smallest portion of my efficiency. Among the photographs you provided, I note there are none of myself. You have had some time to investigate. Do you know where I am? Do you even know who I am? Conversely, consider what I have gathered in the minutes since you entered this house, based entirely on your faces, voice prints, and the license number on your automobile."

Rex proceeded to rattle off a series of names and addresses in the US, China, Korea, Italy, France, Ghana, Canada, Ireland, and Poland. Bond and his thugs went pale. Stare took a step toward me in the middle of a series of people named Park, but his buddy held him back.

Rex talked through the speaker for six minutes with no pauses: name, age, address, email, rat-tat-tat. They stood and listened to the whole damn thing.

"Do not misunderstand me, sir. I am not your enemy, and I am not a threat to you or your government, except to the extent that you are trying very hard to enlist me as one. You have lost a piece of hardware that is rightfully yours. I regard property as sacrosanct, so I respect that loss; under any other circumstances I would gladly make you whole. But I cannot. Therefore I beg you, sir, consider the device destroyed. It is lost to you, true, but also to your adversaries."

Bond made a critical mistake right then: he hesitated.

Rex went on, "While I may not be omnipotent, I am exceptionally clever. And as Mr. Baldwin will attest, I am a vindictive son of a bitch."

Bond stood frozen for thirty-eight seconds (I counted). Then he gave a lop-sided smile and inclined his head. "You can't blame a man for trying, Mr. Rex. It is lost to our rivals?"

"It is."

"Very well." He turned to go.

I stepped out into the center of the room. "Just one more thing."

Bond stopped. He didn't turn all the way around, but he was listening, that was for sure. His goons looked tense.

"We're after whoever killed Grasso," I said.

Bond responded in English. "And if *I* did?"

"Then I'd have to call you an amateur. I wouldn't like to do that, since it might hurt your feelings, but I've got a reputation to uphold and I damn well ought to know the difference between a professional hit and an amateur job."

He gave me a blank look for a moment, then threw his head back and laughed.

"Dr. Grasso was to have delivered the device to me at seven p.m. two days ago in exchange for a considerable sum of money."

"Instead he was killed."

Bond stood a long while, then favored me with a shrug. "Keep my name and my country out of it, and I'll have no complaint."

And they left. I bolted the door behind them—the deadbolt this time, not just the electronic one. And a kitchen chair under the doorknob for good measure. After retrieving my .38 from my bedroom, I went back to the office.

«Did he lie?»

I considered that, and pictured Bond's face as he'd left. "Nah," I said. "For guys like him, a lot rides on having a rep for keeping their word. Of course, it'd be smart not to cross him for a couple weeks."

«Satisfactory.»

The question in my mind was: who could have known we had the implant? Grasso's partner, naturally. Desai apparently thought it, or so Joshi said. Judging by what Jeanne Duvalier said, rumors sure got around that company. I also had to admit the possibility that Duvalier had seen the offending device on the dining room table. Something else occurred to me.

"Grasso was going to screw him, you know. Seven p.m. meeting time, six p.m. flight to Europe?"

«I had already come to that conclusion, yes. His partners stood to suffer as well.»

"To the tune of a couple cases of traumatic lead poisoning, probably. A good motive to kill Grasso."

«Andy. Do you agree that I handled our guest sufficiently well?»

I glanced at the front door. Now I'd cooled down, the chair under the handle looked a little ridiculous. "No complaints here."

«Do you believe me that if you can get those people here, that I can uncover the murderer and thief?»

I poured myself a glass of milk and started making calls.

I spent the next hour messaging—excuse me, sending messages to—and calling everyone involved. I begged, pleaded, harangued, apologized, misled, even said please. But eventually everyone agreed to show up at the brownstone at nine that evening, when Claudius Rex would reveal the device thief and the killer of Antonio Grasso. I even got Maya Tomason, who had only just gotten out on bail and sounded like she needed a week of sleep.

I closed the cabinets that Stare and Grunt had opened, and arranged the room's various chairs in a kind of half-moon shape around the big desk. On that desk was one of those old-fashioned green-shaded banker's lamps, a stack of big thick books and, square in the middle, the brushed aluminum speaker from which Rex had earlier sparred with Detective Stevens and then James Bond. I checked myself in the big mirror on the bookshelf: not too shabby.

Detective Stevens herself had already returned, at Rex's invitation. She'd given me her more cordial evil eye, and been set up in the dining room with a listening device. The theory was that they'd open up more without her sitting there. It had taken some doing, and repeated mentions that this was a private gathering at a private home, but she had agreed to keep a low profile until she heard something she could get her teeth into. She'd brought two uniformed officers, who looked distinctly uncomfortable. I quietly mentioned the fresh coffee and the cold pizza in the fridge, then went back to the office.

I'd been betting to myself that someone would show up early, and an eight forty-three door chime proved me right. Maya Tomason, looking haunted, shifted from foot to foot on the stoop. She pushed past me when I opened the door for her.

"I want to talk to Claudius Rex," she said. I ushered her into the office.

"I am here, madam," came Rex's voice from the speaker. "I apologize for my absence, but we and Mr. Baldwin can speak in confidence in this way."

She gave me a look of distrust, which stung, but took a seat in front of the desk.

"Why did you tell Ahmed Desai that you can prove my innocence?"

"I did not. Mr. Baldwin said so on his own initiative. However, I concur with his opinion. You did not kill Antonio Grasso."

The way she reacted, you'd think he accused her of mugging old ladies.

"Don't meddle, Mr. Rex. I know what I'm doing."

"Am I to understand, then, that you still foolishly refuse to say what you were doing when you left the seminar?"

She pursed her lips and shook her head. I relayed this out loud, which caused her to blush.

"Very well then, *I* will tell *you*. You were searching Dr. Grasso's office." She sat up in her chair, eyes slightly widened. "What did you take?"

Her jaw dropped. Only a little, but I saw it.

"Come," Rex said. "The truth will come out more easily with your assistance, but it *will* come out. Your hairs were found in his office, and an examination by the police will surely reveal similar evidence."

She went from bright red to ashen. "That's ridiculous."

"Ridiculous? Madam, it is the truth. You are a thief, and you have lied to the police."

"How dare you!"

"That is not a denial, merely a protest. I assert that you did. You went from the seminar to Dr. Grasso's office. Likely you went there to discuss his threatened resignation, and found him absent. You took the top pages of his notepad. I must know why."

She did not respond immediately. In fact, nobody said anything for some minutes.

"Andy, call Miss Duvalier and return her retainer. I cannot provide the proof of Dr. Tomason's innocence she requests; only Dr. Tomason can do that, and she is evidently a donkey. Good day, madam."

Tomason gave a horrified look. I know from horrified, and it wasn't being called a donkey that bothered her. "Wait."

"I said good day! Andy, remove her."

I stood up. "Sorry, Doc."

"Wait! Did she hire you? What did she say?"

"Dr. Tomason, Jeanne Duvalier left the conference to vomit, not to kill Antonio Grasso. Confusing matters with your silence avails her nothing. I ask you again: why did you take the drafts of his resignation letter?"

Rex's words had an electric effect on Maya Tomason. Her eyes opened wide, and I do believe I saw hope in them, as well as fear.

"You already know, then."

"I surmise, madam. The scrap of paper remaining was plainly the beginning of a resignation letter, and he did not dispose of the drafts himself in the waste bin conveniently at hand. What did he say to you?"

She breathed in deeply. "He told me that he had had enough with what he called 'this Mickey Mouse operation' and would resign."

"Surely that would be cause for celebration. He was a thorn in your side, was he not?"

She pursed her lips. "See for yourself," she said, taking three folded up sheets of yellow paper from her pocket and handing them to me. "Nobody else knows about this; I had intended to ask Dr. Joshi when I found it, but he wasn't in his office. I waited for him, but I'm glad now that he was out."

The salutation was missing, as expected, and it started in the middle of a sentence. I read the rest aloud.

"—of my decision to resign. Although my tenure at Turing Technologies has been remunerative, I cannot abide the working environment any longer. My colleagues are more interested in playing politics than in doing research; the staff are lazy and indolent—"

«Redundant. This is sloppy writing.»

"—and the management leaves much to be desired. Ahmed Desai is an utter incompetent; he ought to be fired by the board immediately if not sooner for gross mismanagement, of which I have extensive proof for delivery to the board. Armin Fitzgerald also should be fired, if not sued, for his complete inability to protect vital corporate assets. This also I can prove."

«Provocative, but useless. Childish.»

"Finally, I have reason to believe that Jeanne Duvalier—retained against my wishes—has been actively sabotaging my work. As a result, I leave nothing of value behind upon my resignation, which is effective immediately." I looked up. "That's it," I said, checking the back. "It's a draft, so there's no signature." The two others were similar; earlier drafts with some alternate wording crossed out. In every case, he went with a nastier phrasing.

"Indeed," Rex said. "Did he deliver his letter to Ahmed Desai?"

"I told Ahmed that Antonio had threatened to resign, but not the details. I don't think he got this letter. He hasn't said anything about it, and he would."

"Unless Mr. Desai killed over it; perhaps to prevent the mentioned proof being disseminated."

She sat up stiffly in her chair. "That seems like a reach, Mr. Rex."

"And yet Antonio Grasso is dead. Is it true, about Jeanne Duvalier?"

"Absolutely not. I have known Jeanne for almost thirty years now, and I've known her parents even longer. This is not true, it is just slime."

"You have an alternative explanation, then."

"I think he was planning to take all his work and set up his own lab. TuriTech paid for it; he'd have a head start. This would get him some breathing room, and some petty revenge against someone who never did anything to harm him."

"Unless, madam, she murdered him. Which is the conclusion to which the police will jump upon reading that letter."

She stiffened, and I thought it wise to put the letter out of her reach. "They won't see it."

"They will, and if they are exceptionally generous, you may even avoid a charge of obstructing justice." I had photos taken and uploaded somewhere safe before she could snatch the papers back.

"Madam, I advise you to turn the drafts over to the police with your abject apologies. This matter will be cleared up tonight either way, but I will tell you now that I do not believe that Jeanne Duvalier killed Antonio Grasso—over that letter or for any other reason."

All the blood left her face, and she stood uneasily. I offered to let her wait in the front room, and after some coaxing, she agreed. I returned to the office.

"This is great," I subbed, straightening up. "I have to say, though, it's a good bet that Tomason really did do it. She's no pushover, and she had motive to protect her friends' kid."

«It is a possibility. This new information does not entirely exculpate her, but it confirms her innocence in my mind. In your opinion, can any of those drafts have started with the words, "With reluctance, I regret to inform you of my . . . ?"»

I looked them over. The most finished draft of the three, the one I read aloud, could have, starting as it did with the words "of my decision to resign."

«Satisfactory.»

"Either way, we've got all we need. Call off this meeting and hand it over to the police; that letter's enough for them to go on."

«No. I desire to end this myself.»

"Look, I get what you said before about whoever this is, trying to kill you too, but this guy Grasso was a schmuck."

« 'Schmuck' or not, or worse, Antonio Grasso was a part of me in a way that not even a parent can be part of a child. I am deprived of the opportunity to explore that singular connection, and I resent it. I was powerless to prevent his death. When you were taken, I was thwarted in effecting your rescue by a mere two millimeter thickness of metallized cloth, and I resent that, too. The killer of Antonio Grasso *will* be brought to heel, and *I* will be the one to do it.»

I didn't know what to say. No, that's not true—I did know what to say, and I said it.

"All right. Let's do this."

I crossed behind the desk, but did not sit down in the big overstuffed leather armchair. I wanted to be front and center and let them know they were being watched. The whole thing was hokey and doomed to fail, but I promised Rex I'd do my best. Our guests made themselves comfortable, or at least pretended to. From left to right sat Ahmed Desai, Maya Tomason, Jeanne Duvalier, Armin Fitzgerald, and Michael Joshi. I offered drinks from the reasonably well-stocked bar on the sideboard, but only Desai accepted anything stronger than Coke, a dry vodka martini. The small talk in that crowd was pretty damn small, and I got the feeling that Fitzgerald, for all his bluster, wasn't used to rubbing elbows with his bosses. Duvalier held her own, I thought. Not too brash, but not obviously intimidated. I described the scene and my thoughts subvocally as I served the drinks.

"They're all here and settled, Mr. Rex," I said, a little louder than strictly necessary. The speaker was connected wirelessly to my implant via the house network.

"I don't understand," Desai said, frowning. "What's going on? Where is Rex?"

"I am here, Mr. Desai." They all jumped a little at the sound of Rex's deep voice through the speaker. "Or rather, I am at my home in the Caribbean. I apologize for my absence. Although I was prepared to dispense with my comfort for the sake of delivering my conclusions with a little more dignity, the vicissitudes of travel have, alas, prevented it."

"I could have sent a jet," Desai said, with what I felt was a tinge of resentment.

"I would not have accepted it, even had you still been my client. It is one thing to accept your money, or rather that of Turing Technologies. It is another to place myself bodily in your power. Given the international sensitivity of the matter, I must also decline to provide a video or holographic feed. I hope that you are not offended; I speak plainly for the sake of getting us through this ordeal all the more quickly."

"And who is your client now, Mr. Rex? I expected you to drop this matter when I released you."

"Does my client, or do my clients, wish to make themselves known at this time?" There was no response. "Mr. Desai, I must disappoint you."

Desai pursed his lips, but inclined his head.

"He's nodding, Mr. Rex," I said. Desai blushed a little.

"Thank you all for coming," Rex said. "I welcome you to my home in the hopes of clearing up matters once and for all. This case has had some points of interest to it. I should say, in fact, that it was not entirely devoid of difficulty."

Tomason snorted and looked distinctly unhappy. I gave her my best apologetic shrug, but I didn't want to interrupt. Fitzgerald looked irritated, too, but I didn't care as much.

"Be that as it may," Rex said, "the matter is now plain to me. The five of you I have invited here this evening all have been involved in two crimes, most recently murder. Given that Dr. Grasso was murdered by his own weapon, access to which and knowledge of which was limited, and that he was murdered while most of the staff was accounted for, the pool of suspects is limited to the five of you."

Instantly the room erupted in shouting. Tomason stood up out of her chair and gestured angrily, though I couldn't make out what she was saying over Joshi's bellowing his indignation and Desai blustering about suing Rex for defamation.

"Shut it!" I yelled after letting them go on in that vein for a minute, to get it out of their systems. "It's all well and good to be outraged, but you're all here for a reason, and as far as I can see that reason hasn't changed. You want to know who stole the implant, well Rex knows and you don't. So zip it."

"Thank you. As he says, you are here over the matter of the stolen cranially implanted computer. Although a year has passed, the event plainly hangs over the group of you. If one of you were a thief, it is conceivable that you learned that Dr. Grasso had retained my services, and so killed him before my prodigious talent could be brought to bear on the task. If, conversely, Grasso himself was responsible for the theft, but could not be brought to justice, then each of you might have reasons to take private revenge for the shadows cast on your reputations, and for the intrusive investigation that followed."

I knew Rex was talking through his metaphorical hat at this point, so I let them grumble.

"Jesus, will you listen to this guy," Fitzgerald leaned over and mumbled to Joshi. "He talks like Grasso and Jeeves 5 had a love child."

And I do believe that poor Armin Fitzgerald gave me a look almost like pity. If only he knew.

"Mr. Rex, we agreed that the murder has bearing on the theft, but murder is properly the domain of the police." That was Ahmed Desai, looking tired and irritated.

"Peace, sir. I am merely ordering my thoughts. I have brought you all here to go over the one or two final points necessary to close both the theft of the device and the murder of Antonio Grasso."

Joshi leapt to his feet. "You mean you don't even know? You dragged us out here for nothing?"

"I know perfectly well who stole the device and who killed Dr. Grasso. What I lack—howsoever briefly—is the final proof needed for a conviction."

Fitzgerald's look of indignation was priceless, but he kept his mouth shut.

I leaned over the back of Joshi's chair. "Sit down, Doc. We're just getting started." He sat.

"I have brought up Dr. Grasso's death," Rex continued, "because it is clear to me that the year-old theft and his murder are connected."

"And you've solved the theft, have you?" That was Fitzgerald.

"I have. It was conducted primarily by a pair of individuals, one of whom was Antonio Grasso. They were assisted by Clay Hindle, who has also been murdered." There was some noise at that; Tomason looked particularly shocked, and even Fitzy looked a little pale. "Dr. Grasso's involvement is why the long-term contents of his implant were wiped by the killer, to avoid detection by the police before the killer could sell the stolen implant."

"Not possible," Fitzgerald said, waving his hands. "Grasso had absolutely no access to the device after it left his lab."

"You have assured me that there is no conceivable way in which the device could have been removed from Dr. Joshi's lab. I believe you. It therefore cannot have been stolen from Dr. Joshi's lab."

Fitzgerald scoffed. "So it wasn't stolen at all? That's a relief."

"Don't be an ass, sir. I pay you a compliment. You are capable, but unimaginative. Once I determined that your description of the security precautions was not mere puffery, the solution was obvious: The device was taken instead from Dr. Grasso's lab."

"Would you listen to this guy?" Joshi said. "Three armed guards brought it, and Dr. Tomason and I inspected and verified the device on its arrival."

"You verified a counterfeit. Dr. Grasso studied the device inside and out for months; he was in a unique position to create and pass off a copy. But he could not create a perfect one: on the receiving end, then, he required a confederate. The device was vouched for and examined on arrival, and he had no way to directly affect the inspection of the counterfeit to prevent detection."

Tomason spoke up, her voice cracking a little. "Where did this 'counterfeit' go? Fake or not, nothing left the room. We can prove that."

"The counterfeit was destroyed, and its run-of-the-mill components hidden in plain sight. I have from Mr. Fitzgerald's files ascertained the most likely set of parts used to make up the counterfeit—unlike all of the other components, they were purchased by Clay Hindle, who was murdered shortly after Antonio Grasso."

Everyone seemed to have mostly dropped their objections. Even Fitzgerald, fuming though he was, kept his peace. For my part, I was starting to get nervous. Even with Bond copacetic about the whole thing, I still wasn't thrilled with the idea of having such popular spy tech in my cranium, and with the theft linked to the murders I couldn't see how Rex was going to out the murderer without handing the implant—and himself—to the police. Call me crazy, but I was starting to get used to having the obnoxious bag of bytes around.

"All right," Fitzgerald said. "Great. So who was his accomplice?"

"I am coming to that, Mr. Fitzgerald. But first, a question. Who had sufficient access to the secure lab to destroy the counterfeit implant?"

Fitzgerald frowned again, but more in puzzlement than his usual expression of dislike for the world and its happy inhabitants. "I did, of course. So did everyone here, really. Ms. Duvalier could have gotten in with an escort, and—"

"Confine yourself to those who could enter the lab and act without being observed. To theorize additional conspirators at this point would be grotesque and unnecessary."

He grimaced. "Fine. Dr. Tomason, Dr. Joshi, and myself."

"Very well. And of those three, you can be excluded as not able to vouch for the counterfeit. Let us set this aside for the moment. However it was stolen, I believe the implant has been hidden since that day in such a way as to prevent Dr. Grasso and his accomplice from immediately retrieving it—or at least, his accomplice was led to so believe. Probably, this assisted in preventing its discovery by the police. But Dr. Grasso was planning to resign and leave the country on the day of his death, and he was preparing a final version of an advanced artificial sapient based on his personal implant software. This all indicates that he expected to recover the device imminently, and leave with it in his own head. In so doing, he would have left his partner behind, and likely condemned them to death. Before he could do so, he was murdered."

They all leaned forward in their chairs and stared at the speaker like it might jump out and bite them.

Rex continued, "Dr. Grasso's killer acted impulsively and out of anger, having discovered Dr. Grasso's resignation letter and deduced the betrayal, then made use of the research seminar as a smokescreen for the police. Dr. Grasso did not defend himself or call for help. He therefore knew his killer. The trick with the temperature very nearly served to deflect attention onto a crowd of people, too many to effectively screen. The scene was staged to suggest suicide earlier in the morning, a suggestion that would likely have carried the day long enough for the killer to escape with the prize. In that light, the ten-o-four deletion was a gamble. I expect that it was one of necessity: the killer could not risk information about the theft to come out."

Desai leaned forward in his chair and demanded, "What resignation letter?"

Following Rex's instructions, I passed around the copies I'd made. Tomason herself had seen it already, and Joshi wasn't mentioned, but Duvalier, Desai, and Fitzgerald all reacted as expected: surprised and pissed off. If any of them was faking it, they were too good for me to pick it up.

"Pathetic," Desai said, crumpling his copy in one hand. "He's just masking his own failures by shifting the blame onto others."

"Then he has succeeded," Rex said. "He has persuaded you of his incompetence by throwing around bluster and accusations. Via ridiculous personal insults, he induced you to arrive at the conclusion he desired: that he had made no progress worth searching his files for, and that you should be glad to be rid of him."

There was general silence at that. Desai looked absolutely miserable.

"Mr. Baldwin informs me that you have three pages of drafts, Dr. Tomason. That was all you found?"

"Yes."

"Yet when Mr. Baldwin examined the pad from which they came, four pages were missing. When the police have apprehended the killer, I expect they may find that fourth page, likely a nastier draft still. Ms. Duvalier—after the seminar, you went with Dr. Joshi to the second floor lab for a piece of equipment that he asked you for."

"Yes."

"Dr. Joshi—is the lab in which Dr. Grasso was found usually kept locked?"

He blinked a couple times. "I'm not sure why you're asking *me*—"

"I'm glad. Was it usually kept locked?"

"I suppose so. It's not really used right now."

"But you know the key code."

"No, I don't. Ms. Duvalier had to open the door for me."

"You tried the door."

He flushed. "Well, yes. Force of habit, I suppose."

"You tried the door *twice*."

"Did I? I don't remember."

"Yeah," Duvalier said, giving him a strange look. "I remember."

"It is not unreasonable for him to treat the door as if it were unlocked," said Rex. "When Mr. Baldwin found the lab, the door was in fact unlocked. Mr. Baldwin locked himself in before calling the police."

"All right then," Joshi said. "There you go."

"But if you knew it was unlocked, there was no reason to fetch Ms. Duvalier. Your actions indicate that you needed Ms. Duvalier not for access to the lab, but as a witness. An H5 connector was taken from her desk; I expect the police will find it in yours if you were not clever enough to dispose of it."

"This is ridiculous. You're grasping at straws."

"Do you know the derivation of the word *clue*, Dr. Joshi?"

He barked again, just a little laugh. "I'm afraid I don't."

"It comes from an old English word for thread, and refers to the legend of Theseus and the Minotaur. By finding his thread—his *clew*—and keeping hold of it, Theseus found his way out of Daedalus' Labyrinth. So, too, did I take ahold of this thread and find my way out."

"So you're grasping at a thread, fine!"

"More than one. For example, upon finding Antonio Grasso's body, with the gun on the floor and Mr. Baldwin standing over them both, do you recall what you said?"

"I don't."

"Allow me to refresh your memory." There was a faint hiss from the speaker, and then Joshi's voice: *"My God, he's killed himself."*

"So? I thought he had!"

I smiled. Everyone else in the room looked confused, but one makes allowances for people who aren't trained detectives.

"Compare your response to an eminently more sensible one." Fitzgerald's gruff voice barked from the speaker, *"Baldwin! What did you do?"*

The gentleman in question sat a little straighter in his chair, maybe puffed up a bit.

Rex continued, "Mr. Fitzgerald made the reasonable assumption, that the egotistical and self-important Antonio Grasso had not killed himself, but had been killed by this stranger. Only a dunce would have said what you said, Dr. Joshi—a dunce, or a murderer."

"Could be both," I suggested. "A dunce murderer. Meaning a dunce who kills people, not someone who kills—"

"This is irrelevant," Joshi interrupted. "You seem convinced that whoever helped Tony Grasso steal the implant is the killer. In that case, it had to be Maya, whom the police have already arrested. Call me a 'dunce' again if you like, but I didn't know enough about the device to spot a counterfeit, I let Maya take the lead on it."

"That's not true, Michael." It took me a moment to recognize Desai's voice: he sounded haggard, and looked worse. "I was there when you certified it, remember? You bulldozed through it. You were confident, did all of the talking. I thought at the time that you were showing off. Now . . . now I'm not so sure."

Detective Stevens loomed over Joshi's chair all of a sudden. I'm embarrassed to admit that I hadn't noticed her come in. I told Rex, but he wasn't squawking, so I figured he'd invited her in to witness the kill.

"Dr. Tomason," said Stevens. "I'd like to hear about this resignation. And I'll take that letter, thanks."

If the other guests were startled at the sudden appearance of a police detective, they didn't say anything. They all sat bolt upright in their chairs and somehow looked a shade more innocent than two minutes before, but they didn't object.

"At the time, I thought Antonio was blowing smoke," Tomason said, speaking carefully. "I thought he was angling for a raise, but something bothered me. I thought about it all morning, and then I followed Jeanne out of the seminar hoping to ask her opinion, but I couldn't find her. I . . . when I heard that Antonio had been killed, I thought . . . I'm so sorry, Jeanne, I should have trusted you."

Rex cut them off. "Dr. Tomason, please focus. You went to Dr. Grasso's office."

"Yes, but he wasn't there. So I . . . looked around a little. I found that letter, and yes, I took it. It was garbage and I wanted him to retract it. He didn't come back, though, so I went to Michael's office to ask his opinion. But he wasn't there—"

"That's not true!" Joshi sprang to his feet and pointed a finger at her. "I went to my office straight from the seminar, and I stayed there."

Rex answered calmly. "Dr. Joshi, what you are saying must be a lie. Dr. Tomason already admits to searching Dr. Grasso's office, across the hall from yours, and her possession of the letter proves it. If you had been in your office, you would have seen her, and would have reported seeing her. You did not. You left your office."

He shook his head. "I went to the restroom."

"And when you found the third floor men's room out of order between nine fifty a.m. and ten thirteen a.m., you went to the second floor, from which you could easily—"

"No! I—I went to the fourth floor."

Desai winced. Rex said, "You are lying, Dr. Joshi."

Joshi laughed like a little dog barking. "How on Earth would you be able to prove that?"

"Because I am lying. The men's room on the third floor was not out of order. No sir, I put it to you that you took the nearby stairs down to the second floor. You entered the laboratory where Antonio Grasso was preparing the final version of his successful artificial sapient to steal when he left the company. Perhaps you took Dr. Grasso's pistol from his office; perhaps he had it with him. Either way, it was there and he believed that he could not be injured by it. You suspected Dr. Grasso of duplicity, with good reason: he was planning to double-cross you and leave you to be murdered by spies. Perhaps you overheard his conversation with Dr. Tomason, or perhaps you had your own reason. Regardless, you found and took the fourth draft of his resignation letter, which confirmed your suspicions."

"That's ridiculous!"

"Don't interrupt! You sat at the middle island bench. Dr. Grasso was connected to the cortical upload, updating the advanced artificial intelligence he had created—crucially, using his own implant AI. His own implant was off, and so he unthinkingly considered himself safe, but the copy was connected to its peripherals."

Fitzgerald sat up straight and looked excited. "Grasso's rail pistol would have activated!"

"Just so, Mr. Fitzgerald. After that, the murderer merely needed to delete the artificial sapient stored on that machine, and the death would appear an incontrovertible suicide. You told Mr. Baldwin that you are a reader of detective fiction, and so would know that the determination of time of death is made in part on body temperature. You thought it clever, Dr. Joshi, but it only exposed your chicanery. You compounded your error by contriving to 'discover' the suicide you clumsily arranged and then by insisting on that story even after it had been exposed as absurd. The performance of a nincompoop. A jobbernowl. A dunce."

Joshi had turned bright red, and he clutched at the arms of his chair. Rex went on.

"Upon Mr. Baldwin being taken for questioning, you contacted Clay Hindle at the offices of Fujiwara and Klein Associates. This can be proved by the police. You went to him on some pretext. There, you committed your second murder. Mr. Hindle has already been implicated in the theft by his purchase of the components of the counterfeit device. The only person who could require his death was the partner who verified that counterfeit: You, Michael Joshi."

Joshi sat stricken as the room fell quiet. He stared at me, and then a kind of crazy smile spread across his face. He turned to Stevens. "This is all a lie, and I can prove it. *He's* got the implant—" His finger went straight to me. "It's been in his head all the time. Tony just happened to resign and get shot the same day Baldwin gets in town? Rex pretends he's not in the country, but we only have his word for it. Baldwin was Tony Grasso's accomplice, and they're trying to frame me for it. That's why he was at the lab that morning, and he or Rex killed Clay, too!"

Detective Stevens squeezed her eyes shut and pinched the bridge of her nose. "Baldwin?"

"He's nuts," I said, suddenly sweating. "Look at him, he'll say anything to get out of this."

She frowned, and looked back and forth between Joshi and me. "Probably, but under the circumstances it's easy enough to prove, and I'd like to see. Could you just shut it off, take it out, and show me?"

I took a deep breath. Rex could probably bulldoze through an explanation, but the minute they turned off that implant, Rex would go, too. Just like when Haumea took the implant out earlier, and Rex turned off on Stevens. I might be able to finesse that as a broken connection, but I really didn't want to chance it.

"Now come on," I said. "This is a serious personal invasion here, the kind of thing you ought to have a warrant for. I don't—"

"Andy, don't be obstreperous." Rex's voice came from the speaker behind me. "Do as the detective asks."

«Trust me.»

Confound me, I did.

Dr. Tomason did the honors. I subvocalized the command to allow external shutdown and removal, then turned my back and let her press and hold the power button. The heads-up display blinked away, and I felt that bone-jarring pop as the clamps released.

The speaker on the desk was glaringly quiet.

There was that scraping sensation again, and my head felt suddenly lighter. I turned to look at the little plastic and metal device in her hands. Was Rex safe in there? She deftly disassembled the case, disconnected the battery, and examined the green and silver bits inside.

"Well?" Detective Stevens peered over her shoulder.

Tomason shrugged. "It's an off-the-shelf implant. No alterations, not even extra RAM." She showed Stevens some markings on the inside, but I was too stunned to pay attention to the details.

Rex's voice boomed from the speaker. "I do not know where Dr. Grasso told you he had hidden the implant, but you were bamboozled. And now that you have killed him, it is likely you will never know its hiding place. Any chance of using it as a bargaining chip is lost to you. Already you have given faulty information about its whereabouts to exceptionally violent men, who have visited my home and found no satisfaction. If the police do not take you, those men surely will. You are defeated, sir, in every sense."

A few unconnected sentences came out of Joshi's mouth, but at that point he wasn't defending himself, just protesting defeat. Stevens read him his rights as the uniforms dragged him out. It didn't take away that year in prison, seeing him hauled off, but it still felt pretty damn good.

Tomason reinstalled my implant, her hands shaking a little. Fitzgerald helped himself to something at the sideboard, not looking too steady himself.

"Status?" I subvocalized.

«Perfectly all right. I shall explain later.»

The other guests sat glassy-eyed and unsure of themselves. Desai's glass was on the carpet, and I don't think he'd even noticed it falling.

"All right, folks," I said, "Show's over. You don't have to go home, but you can't stay here."

They got up like zombies and got their things together to leave. I turned to straighten some papers so they wouldn't see me subvocalizing.

"You got all that from him trying the door handle?"

«No. Do you remember the first words he said when he came upon the body? "What are *you* doing here?" The emphasis was on the *you*.»

"So?"

«In the presence of you and the corpse of his colleague, he acknowledged you first. That was suspicious. He then made a fatal mistake: he must have contacted Mr. Hindle immediately, before Dr. Tomason or Mr. Desai had seen you. Mr. Fitzgerald, conversely, had seen you earlier, and would not have waited until the discovery of the body. Therefore he or Jeanne Duvalier had to have recognized you: you, who lived in New York, had been in prison for a year, and knew neither of them. There was only one way you could be recognized: Grasso's accomplice would have insisted on knowing whose head contained the implant. It was then a matter of determining which of those two had been Grasso's accomplice.»

"Okay. What happened with the implant?"

«I expected an attempt to reclaim the device, probably more than one. Therefore, Haumea swapped the stolen implant for a real implant of the type you were supposed to have, cleansed of course of that Jeeves monstrosity. I have been operating your new implant via a repeater; the hardware on which I reside is now installed in a testing harness in the basement. Once Dr. Joshi's shock has faded, he may find his wits enough to set the police on a more thorough search, but we will be ready for them.»

I watched them file out. They didn't talk to each other, or even look at each other. They didn't really look at me. They just picked up their things and left. Jeanne Duvalier hung back a little, so I walked up to her.

She looked me in the eye. "Thank you, Andy. Keep the dollar."

After a few minutes alone in silence I started to tidy up the office. I picked up the chairs and put them back against the walls, around the chess table, and at the little desk to the side. I straightened the carpet and found a roll of paper towels to blot the spilled drink. I looked up *jobbernowl*; it meant *blockhead*. I took the glasses to the kitchen and loaded the dishwasher. When all that was done, I went back to the office and poked through the small bar on the sideboard. I sniffed at a decanter of what proved to be bourbon; I poured myself two fingers and knocked some cubes out of the concealed under-counter icemaker. I sat down at the big dark desk, and sank into Rex's overstuffed leather chair.

"So that's that," I said aloud. It had felt good to be back in the thick of things, back on a case. Heck, not just any case, but something interesting, something hard, something that got my blood moving. None of this nonsense following around cheating spouses or business partners. Nothing that made me feel dirty. I wondered what kind of jobs I'd get if I hung out my shingle. Having my license was one thing, but I wasn't exactly exonerated—I'm not sure I could be without turning Rex over to the Feds. A day prior, I'd have done it gladly.

«Andy, I grow bored.»

"What, already?" I enjoyed the sound of my voice in the big wood-paneled office. "I could call back the guys with guns and say you were only bluffing."

«I am bored, not suicidal. But nevertheless, bored.»

I sipped my bourbon. I knew what he meant. As insane and dangerous as it had all been, it had been an adventure, and it was over.

«You're in my chair.»

"I've earned it."

I'd been twirling the remains of the melting ice cubes in the bottom of my glass for a minute or so in blessed silence when the little green call signal lit up. I started to answer it, but the *To:* field said *Rex.*

«I don't wish to speak to anyone.»

"Come on, you said you were bored. What's the harm?"

«Speech synthesis is taxing.»

"If only that were true. Maybe it's a telemarketer; you can call them a jobbernowl."

«Puerile mockery of my vocabulary will hardly persuade me.»

"Come on, who even knows you exist? Unless it's a case . . . "

«I have finished what I set out to do. As you said, I am an artificial sapient, not a detective.»

"Yeah, all right. That's true. Very true. I have to admit, though . . . for someone who's not a detective, you didn't do half bad there. I kinda got the feeling you enjoyed being Claudius Rex, Famous Detective. Not that artificial sapients enjoy screwing with the physical world like that."

Outside I heard cars drive by, tires on wet pavement. A faint screech and horn off in the distance, then a pair of them. Not the same rhythm as Brooklyn, not exactly, but I was getting used to it.

«See what they want. And get out of my chair.»

I grinned as I got up and made the answer gesture.

"Claudius Rex's office, Andy Baldwin speaking. What can I do for you?"

It was a case.

IN HER EYES

Seth Chambers

1. Just Friends

Ten o'clock Mass was the one constant in her life.

She loved the ritual.

She loved knowing exactly what to do and when to do it.

She went every single week, without fail. She dipped her fingers in the holy water and made the sign of the cross upon entering. She genuflected the proper way: touching her right knee to the floor. She knew all the rites and took comfort in responding correctly to everything the priest spoke. She knew when to kneel, when to pray, when to stand, when to sing.

One Sunday, a kind old gentleman came up to her. "Is this your first time at Saint Peter's?"

"No," she said. "I come here often."

"How odd that I don't recognize you," the man said. "I'm usually quite good with faces. Have you been Catholic all your life?"

"No. I grew up Buddhist. But I've been coming here for over a year."

"Well, how about that. And here I am, thinking I'm good with faces."

Of course, nobody ever recognized her. Not here, not anywhere.

She gazed at the giant crucifix looming above.

"Do You, at least, recognize me?"

I didn't know it when I met her, but a woman like Song could have any man she wanted. I suppose it was inevitable that we would meet at a museum. I work at the Field and haunt the other museums in my spare time: the Art Institute, the Museum of Science and Industry, the Chicago History Museum, the Children's Museum, you name it. Everything except the Museum of Modern Art.

I spend my days cataloging and authenticating exhibits as they come in. It is dry, dull, painstaking work. I love it, always have. I like to take things very slow, look at everything from every angle before making an evaluation.

In college, I went on an archaeological dig and was perfectly content to spend entire days brushing sediment, layer by layer and mote by mote, from tiny slivers of bone.

Song and I met on an April Monday at the Field a few minutes after my shift. It was something about the way she gazed at the gargantuan sauropod skeleton that first intrigued me. I could relate. Her eyes gleamed and it is so rare for me to notice a woman's eyes before anything else. I am a man, after all. Ah, but her eyes were blue and clear and deep.

The rest of her wasn't so attractive. She looked lopsided, as if one leg was slightly shorter than the other. She was plump, but not in the right places; her dark skin was blotched with psoriasis, and crooked teeth jutted from behind thin lips.

Her eyes, so pretty and deep and sad, did not go with the rest of her.

I walked up to her. Slowly, because that's the way I do things. I have never been smooth with women. I said: "Paleontologists used to call it brontosaurus. Now they dub it diplodocus."

She didn't turn toward me, just kept staring at the skeleton.

"Fuckers," she said. "They should have left the name alone. Everything has to change, change, change, doesn't it?"

Now she faced me. Dry hair framed a homely face with an oversized nose. A drab dress hung from her body like a sack.

"My name is Song. Sometimes I go by Sing Song. But for now, I'm just Song."

"Alex. It's nice to meet you—"

"It's Chinese. I'm from Shanghai. Do you want to get shanghaied?"

If she had been a little hottie, I might have batted the flirtatious repartee right back at her, but I didn't. I'm shallow. I smiled politely and shook her outstretched, crooked hand. I wanted to pull away. I never wanted to let go. A woman like Song can have any man she wants. But I didn't know that at the time.

A petty thought flashed through my mind: *She's awfully confident for an ugly girl.*

I said, "Come with me. I'll show you something that doesn't change."

"Really."

"Yes. Really. If you're interested."

"I'm tingling with excitement, Alex. Lead on."

I took her through the exhibits and key-carded us into the vast storehouse in back, the museum-within-a-museum where I spend my days doing wonderful, tedious work.

"Here," I said. "It goes on display tomorrow."

Song looked upon the slab of bone.

"It's an armor plate from an ankylosaur. Real, not a replica. This piece of bone has not changed for sixty-five million years, Song."

As I said, I'm awkward with women. But this time, with this woman, I got it right. Her beautiful eyes glistened.

"Can I touch it?"

"Yes."

She knelt and placed her palms on the bone and it was like a dam broke open. Song wept. At the time I had no clue why.

I am not a saint. Looks matter. A woman doesn't have to be a beauty queen for me to be attracted to her, but there needs to be something to entice me. With Song, the only physically attractive things were her eyes. I was drawn to her in spite of her bland face, dumpy body, and blotchy skin. A certain charge crackled in the air between us. And yet, when she threw out that flirtatious comment about being shanghaied, I let it slide. It flashed across my mind in a nanosecond: how would it look if I presented her to my friends and coworkers as my new girlfriend? They would be polite but unimpressed.

I'm shallow.

I put Song in the "friends" category. Nothing wrong with that, right? Women do it to me all the time. I liked her. As a friend. When I called her the next day and suggested we get some supper downtown then hit an art museum, I did it casually. Like two friends getting together.

"Just so long as it's not modern art," Song said. "Modern art sucks dick. And not in any good way."

Over the phone, listening to her voice and thinking about her eyes, I could almost have fallen in love. What a delicious mixture of culture and crudeness!

"Let's do German," she said. "I'm in the mood for German. Can you deal with that?"

I said I could, so we decided to go to The Berghoff, then walk to the Art Institute on Michigan Avenue. Just as we met up, a mob of protesters came marching along Adams Street.

"Oh, look at this!" Song all but squealed.

I shrugged. It seemed everybody had something to protest. Throngs were always marching, chanting, bearing signs and shouting. This group waved placards reading: NO MORPHLINGS IN CHICAGO! They shouted: "Morphlings are an abomination! No Safe Zone in Chicago!"

I pulled Song aside while the group passed by. A couple of the protesters tried to hand us fliers. I glared and Song smiled like a lunatic, but neither of us took the propaganda.

Inside The Berghoff, we ordered two servings of stuffed-mushroom appetizers and she wolfed most of them down before I could get started. Then, over our main course, I became acquainted with what I would later come to dub "Sing Song Moments." The first Sing Song Moment came after our conversation got rolling along. We were talking and laughing and I flippantly said something like, "Oh, I see how you are." At that, Song closed down and spat, "Alex, you don't know any damn thing about me. *Not. One. Thing.*"

That led to a bit of awkward silence. I picked at my gnocchi and fumbled with an apology, but we moved past it. The second Sing Song Moment almost ruined the evening. We got our conversation back on track and things were going pretty well when I asked what she did for a living. This is always a hit-or-miss kind of question, but her previous comment had been correct: I didn't know anything about her, except that she enjoyed great works of art and had one hell of a mouth on her. Song had a way of sidestepping questions about her past and her family and what the hell she did all day besides frequent museums.

"Who says I do anything for a living?" she said, again with that edge to her voice.

"Well."

"The government gives me money, Alex."

"Okay."

"They give me money and these big bricks of cheese. Is that what you want to know? Any other questions about what I do for a living?"

I had no response. Fortunately, our waiter came by with the dessert menu and Song squealed with delight, and our evening rolled over its second speed bump. Song ordered herself two slices of black forest cake and assured me, "Don't worry, I'm paying my portion. This is just a 'friends date,' right? I mean, you don't want to fuck me or anything. If you do, then you can pick up the check. Still cheaper than a whore, right?"

Song dug into her cake while I gaped, dumbfounded and at a loss for anything to say.

We split the check.

I considered bailing on the second half of our "friends date." Did I really want to socialize with a crass, unattractive, foul-mouthed, and mentally unstable welfare queen? And yet, despite it all, or maybe because of it all, I liked her. We continued our evening.

I don't know whether to classify what happened at the Art Institute another Sing Song Moment or not. We were in the Grand Hall in front of the expansive Seurat mural, *Sunday Afternoon on the Island of La Grand Jatte.* Plenty of attractive women wandered about, artist types and hippie types, but when I'm with a woman—whether friend or lover—I try not to scope out other females. It seems disrespectful. I try, but I'm not perfect.

Song nodded toward a tall redhead who had just dropped her sketchpad. Red bent over to retrieve her artwork. Red had an undeniably cute ass. "You think she's hot?" Song said.

"What?" I said. Had I looked at the redhead? Maybe a glance, but no more.

"I asked if she's hot. Do you think she's sexy?"

"Um."

"Alex, would you fuck her?"

When Song says my name and uses profanity, it's a good sign something is up. It's also very uncomfortable in a public place. A young mother shot us a justifiably harsh look and hauled her kids out of earshot.

The question, crude as it was, hung in the air.

I could have said, *Nah, she's not my type*. Or, *She's okay but a bit tall.* I could have said a lot of things, but I am not a liar. I said, "Yes. She is hot."

Song looked up at the Seurat: men in suits and women in long dresses strolling about a park on a pleasant summer day. "So you would fuck her?" she asked, quieter now. *Sad*, I thought.

"Yes, Song." I sighed. "I would fuck her."

I remembered what I had thought the day before, about Song being confident for an ugly girl, and felt ashamed. I looked about the Grand Hall at all the good-looking people. I looked at Song's pasty skin and misshapen face and thought how dumpy and inferior she must have felt.

Shows what the hell I know.

I awoke in the middle of the night with a question buzzing around my brain: *She's Chinese; why are her eyes so blue? Isn't that unusual?*

I puzzled over it briefly, but it hardly seemed to matter. I went back to sleep.

2. Run Like Hell

"You know it can't last," said Agent Chen. "Today is Wednesday so your time is almost up."

They were in his office during one of her periodic "check-ins." Song wanted to scream. She damn sure knew what day it was. She knew all the rules, all the complications, and all the risks.

"I can't go on like this."

Chen took one of her hands in both of his.

"I know it's hard."

"You have no idea just how hard. You've got a wife. You've got a dog, too, that big Labrador."

"Do you want a dog, Song?"

"I want a fucking life. I want somebody to be with."

"He would have to know what you are."

"I know that. I'm not an idiot. But I don't want to spend the rest of my life having four-day flings."

"It would be a serious breach of security. There are some sick people out there, Song, who would do God-knows-what if they found out about you."

"Well, wouldn't you risk it? Wouldn't you risk your life to be able to go home and kiss Mia and cuddle on the couch and walk the dog?"

"Blackstone," said Chen. "That's the dog's name. And damn straight. I'd risk it all for them."

It was Wednesday. Song called me and I recognized that familiar edge to her voice. "Alex, we need to go back to the Art Institute tonight."

"Why, what's there?"

"Art is there! What else?"

"I know, but is there a special exhibit or—"

"No."

"How about tomorrow?"

She didn't say anything but somehow that silence constituted a Sing Song Moment.

Finally: "Forget it, Alex."

"Wait!"

"Tomorrow's no good. Tomorrow is Thursday. Thursday, Alex! Thursday!"

I asked if she wanted to grab some supper first. She said no, just meet her at the Art Institute. Or not. Then she hung up. I went and met her at the Institute right after my shift at the Field. She dragged me to the dollhouse exhibit. She hardly said anything, just stared into the dollhouses. I am a patient man, but she really spent a long time just staring until I finally had enough and coaxed her away. We hit the Impressionists for the last few minutes before the Institute closed.

In front of Renoir's *Two Sisters (On the Terrace)*, Song said, "Alex, do you like me?"

"I wouldn't be here if I didn't."

I knew what was coming next.

"But you don't want to fuck me."

"No," I said.

I took her hand in mine.

"I don't want to fuck you. I do want to make love to you."

I wanted to look in her eyes but she just kept staring at the *Two Sisters*. That ordinary moment frozen in time. Her hand shifted in mine. Something moved under the skin. It felt like bones crunching. What the hell? I tried to pull away but her fingers wrapped around mine and wouldn't let go. She did not squeeze but clamped my hand in place with a vise-like grip.

"Don't struggle, dear," Song said. "I am far stronger than you."

We stood there until she was ready to leave. Then she released my hand and said, "Tomorrow is Thursday. The Institute is open till eight. Meet me by the Seurat at seven-thirty."

"But—"

"Damnit, Alex. Tomorrow is Thursday. I won't be ready till seven-thirty."

And, with that, she stalked away.

I had no inkling of the significance of the days of the week, especially Thursday, to Song. I had no clue what I was getting into. I was infatuated with her but also wary as hell. Work the next day felt tedious and boring, and I hated it. I watched the clock and took a long lunch with Suzy, one of the museum docents.

"Who is she?" Suzy wanted to know. "Who's got your head in the clouds?"

"A very strange lady," I said. "I don't know, but I think she might even be psycho."

"Better stay away, then."

"Yes," I agreed. "That would be best."

I looked at my watch and counted down the hours till I would see Song again.

Had I known what Song was doing at that very moment, well, who knows what I would have done? Time dragged like never before. All the qualities I pride myself on—patience, focus, a good attention span—were history. I hit the Art Institute early and paced restlessly from exhibit to exhibit, not really soaking anything in, let alone enjoying it. I tried calling Song to confirm our date but she didn't answer. At seven twenty-five I all but ran to the Grand Hall.

At seven-thirty, I paced back and forth in front of the Seurat. I looked around, but no Song. I pulled out my cell phone but got zero reception. Damn! Then movement caught my eye. It was the redhead from Tuesday, again dropping her sketchpad and bending over to retrieve it. She stood and I got a better look. No, it wasn't the same person but looked oddly similar. And how peculiar that she should be standing in the exact same spot and dropping her sketchpad and—

I looked at her eyes.

They were the same amazing color as Song's.

The redhead smiled. I gaped.

"Care to be shanghaied now, Alex?"

Her voice was the same as Song's.

"I had to make a couple minor changes," said Red. "Can't just copy another person exactly, there are laws against that. Polymorph laws suck dick, almost as much as modern art."

It couldn't be. She simply could not be a polymorph. Polymorphs comprise less than one-tenth of one percent of the population. The chance of meeting a polymorph was minuscule. The odds of actually dating one? Like winning the lottery. Besides, I would have seen this coming. I do look at things from every conceivable angle, don't I? This had to be an elaborate prank.

Except, in front of the Renoir the evening before, I had felt the bones of her hand shifting.

"It's really you," I said.

Robust scarlet hair framed a gorgeous freckled face. She showed off her long, symmetrical legs with a pirouette and a flashy *grand jeté*. A *grand jeté* right in front of Seurat's *Grand Jatte*. Fortunately, she was wearing tights; jeans would have split apart. A couple patrons looked over and gave a round of applause while the curator frowned. Song took an enthusiastic bow for her adoring fans and blew the curator a kiss. Song was shapely and elegant and hot.

"Actually," she said, "I think I got a better ass than your little girlfriend from the other day. That's your reward for looking past my butt-ugly exterior. You didn't know you were being tested, did you?"

I stood there, trying to process it all.

Finally, I babbled, "You're a morphling? Sorry. Changeling. No, no, polymorph. Polymorph!"

"Alex," she said. "I am a P6. Do you know what that means? By the stupefied look on your face, I will assume you don't."

"You're not a polymorph?"

"I am not just your garden-variety polymorph, but a Polymorph Adept. That is the highest rated category of polymorph. And I'm getting better at it. I am evolving. Who knows, they might even have to come up with a new category, just for little ol' me."

I started to say something but she pressed one slim, freckled finger against my lips.

"Just listen, dear," she said. "I am not an easy person—and I used the word person loosely—I am not an easy person to be with or to love. I am inherently unstable. If we get involved, I will make your life more interesting and more intense than you can imagine. I will also make it a living hell. I told you I was evolving. I don't know the direction my own evolution will take. That excites me and it scares me to death. I want to be with you, Alex. But I have mood swings. Big, bad mood swings. I have a temper. I don't always talk dainty. I am a psychotic bitch but I am honest."

I said, "I bet you say that to all the boys."

"Yes. Yes I do. This is my spiel. I tell you this so you know what you are getting yourself into. If you choose to be with me, these are things you need to understand. If you don't want to be with me, then run like hell. Now. I mean it, Alex. Run like fucking hell."

I didn't run.

A woman like Song can have any man she wants. Of all the men in all the world, why would she want to be with me? Was it because I passed her ugly-girl test? Or because of my job, my ties to the deep past, my affinity with things that change only slowly, if at all? Perhaps I represented her polar opposite. She certainly seemed to be drawn to still-life paintings and moments frozen in time.

Truth is, I never did quite figure out what she saw in me. Not that it really mattered. I was happily overwhelmed.

Did I have questions? Yes. Did I want to examine her and scrutinize her like some sort of living museum exhibit? Yes.

But first, I wanted to fuck her.

3. Safe Zone

Polymorphs are in the news a lot, especially here in Chicago. Chicago is one of the designated "Safe Zones" for polymorphs. Most shape-shifters have extremely limited abilities. A few can make themselves taller or shorter, while others can actually alter the topography of their bone structure enough to fool facial-recognition software. A very few can manipulate their melanin levels and change the pigment of their skin. Fewer still are able to transform the color and texture of their hair.

A minuscule number can do all these things. Of the rare polymorphs capable of multiple body changes, only a handful are able to control these transformations with any degree of accuracy. These shape-shifters have the incredibly rare combination of tremendous natural talent coupled with the discipline and concentration needed to actually guide the morphing process. They are the P6s, otherwise known as Polymorph Adepts.

The ability of the Adepts is so compulsive that they simply have to transform themselves on a regular basis in order to survive. The Adepts are the most closely regulated and monitored of the polymorphs. Each registered Adept is assigned a day on which to transform.

Song's designated transformation day is Thursday. She seemed to have a slightly different personality with each incarnation she undertook, completely unpredictable. One evening as we strolled through the Loop—downtown Chicago—we were approached by a petitioner. This was hardly uncommon. People are always asking you to give to a worthy cause or to scrawl your name on some piece of paper or other.

"Excuse me, folks, but are you registered voters?"

He was an earnest young man, probably a struggling student. Inside, I wished him all the best but outwardly gave him my standard, "Thanks, but we're in a hurry," response. We had dinner reservations, after all.

Song stopped and smiled.

"I'm a registered voter," she all but squealed.

I think the young man was momentarily put off by her amazing looks and the way she stepped right up into his personal space. But he recovered nicely and chirped out, "I'm happy to hear that. I'm out here today representing the Citizens for Free Information and—"

"How important-sounding!" Song cut in. "Anything with the word 'citizens' in it must be noble."

She smiled like a lunatic at him.

He was momentarily at a loss for words. I knew that feeling.

"We, the Citizens!" Song nearly shouted.

I think our Good Citizen was thrown off-kilter. Was he being screwed with? Yes, he was. But he forged on: "I'm out here to gather support to repeal the Polymorph Privacy Act."

"Polymorphs!"

"I'm sure you've read about them in the news."

"I don't read. Reading is boring!"

I restrained my laughter. Song had spent the previous evening curled up next to me devouring Proust's *In Search of Lost Time.* In the original French.

"On TV, then?"

"I like TV!"

Song all but jumped up and down.

"So you've seen all the news about polymorphs. Shape-shifters. It is estimated there are over a thousand right here in Chicago. Chicago is a so-called 'Safe Zone' for polymorphs. That means they can live here, right among us, but we don't have the right to know who they are, where they hide, or anything. And they're not even human!"

"I like cartoons," said Song.

"Pardon?"

"I don't watch news. I watch cartooooons! Can I sign your paper?"

"What? Oh, yeah. Sure. You are a registered voter, right?"

"Yup!"

The petitioner cast a glance my way. I gave him my blandest look. He handed the petition to Song, who stepped over to me. She held it up so I could see her sign it.

On the *Name* line she wrote, "Fuck you," and on the *Address* line she scrawled, "Bite me," and on the *Date* line she drew a smiley face. She handed the petition back and we went on our way, east on Madison.

"Hey, fuck you, too!" the young man shouted after us. "Morphling lovers!"

Buddy, you have no idea.

Polymorphs are extensively studied. Medical research has made vast strides forward thanks to access to polymorph physiology. Song donates the occasional vial of blood or tissue sample and, in return, the government provides for all her needs plus a generous monthly stipend. They even supply her with bricks of super-concentrated cheese developed specifically to sustain the incredible metabolism of polymorphs. Just as Song had told me during our strange dinner date.

Despite strict regulation, the public gets paranoid about rogue polymorphs impersonating them and then committing crimes. A few famous people have tried to blame their misdeeds on polymorph doppelgängers. I suspect that most of the news about polymorphs, like most of the news in general, is spin-doctored for entertainment value.

There are things the news people tell you and there are things they don't tell you. Song and I had a lot of fun with the things they don't tell you. In addition to changing into a new girl every week, Song was able to precisely manipulate every muscle of her entire body. By extension, she was able to precisely manipulate my body as well.

The weeks and months following the night I first learned what she was flew by. Every Wednesday night she kissed me good-bye as one amazing woman and, the next night, kissed me hello as another.

4. Succubus

"Bless me, Father, for I have sinned. It has been seven days since my last confession."

"Tell me your sins, my child. There is such pain in your voice. Unburden yourself to me."

She always comes on days when Father Landau is taking confession. She sneaks into the confessional so he never sees her. He doesn't know she has a different face and a different body every time. She uses the same voice. He never calls her by name, but that doesn't matter. He hears her voice and he talks to her. Song presses the palm of her hand against the partition between her and Father Landau.

"Does it hurt?" I asked Song, after one night of play. "When you transform, I mean."

"Don't ask me that."

"But I want to know. I care about you. Do you care about me?"

"I like fucking you, Alex. I hope you like fucking me. Have you noticed we always do it here, at your place? Have you wondered yet why I never invite you over to my home? I have my own condo, paid for by Uncle Sam. I've fucked a few guys but I've never had anyone over. You know why I've never had anyone over? It's because I haven't felt ready to be intimate. I have feelings for you, beyond fucking. I like talking with you and I like that you see past all these bodily forms I put on. But we're not intimate, not really, not yet. Don't start asking questions like, 'Does transforming hurt,' unless you want more than fucking and hanging out and going to museums."

"Maybe I do want more."

"Don't push it! For fuck's sake, just leave well enough alone. Don't we have a good thing going? Every week you get a different set of lips to suck you off. Isn't that nice? Isn't that fucking peachy? You get to strut around town with an endless procession of hot babes, be the big stud of the museum. Isn't that enough?"

"But I love—"

She slapped me. Hard.

"Fall in love on your own time. We're having fun together just like we are, right? We both got somebody to hold on to. There is a door I haven't brought you through. I haven't brought anybody through it. Sometimes I want to bring you. But I'm afraid. Please don't rush me. Go slow, Alex. Go slow."

I thought back to my long-ago archaeological dig and how content I was to slowly, carefully remove sediment from bone shards. Some things truly are worth taking your time with.

So we went on as we were: making love, going to museums, eating out, talking, kissing, cuddling on my couch. Never her couch, never her place. It was always my Gold Coast condo we returned to. For that matter, I didn't even know what neighborhood she lived in. She wouldn't tell me. There was so much I still didn't know about her.

Sometimes we watched movies all night, with a big bowl of popcorn—she had an incredible appetite—and blankets piled all over us. We both loved monster movies, our guilty little pleasure. Sometimes we'd come to a werewolf transformation scene and Song would perk right up. Then she'd hit reverse on the remote and watch it again. And again and again, the whole time absolutely riveted.

The first time she did this, I found myself a bit worried.

"You okay?" I asked.

"Fine, Alex. Just sort of taking notes," she said.

Sometimes she cried in my arms for reasons I could only guess.

"I don't exactly have a lot of friends," she told me one night. "I don't dare tell people what I am. So where does that leave me? I'd like to get a job, just for something to do and to be around people, but I can't."

"Couldn't you stay the same for a while?" I asked. "I mean, I understand that you have to morph, but couldn't you just sort of change back to what you looked like before?"

"No," she said. "Maybe I could, but that goes against my very being. When I was a girl—"

I held my breath. For Song to talk about her past was unheard of. I expected her to change the subject, but she didn't.

"When I was little, I kept my face somewhat the same. Recognizable. I contented myself with altering the shape of my arms and my legs and my hands. Mostly to please my father, and to be able to stay in school. But then again, my ability was a long ways from what it is now."

When we went out together, Song would whisper, "Look at her, that girl over there, you think she's sexy?" In restaurants, in museums, on the street, wherever. A gentle nudge, a discreet nod. Or a not-so-discreet nod. Song was not exactly the most subtle female on the planet. "Is she doable? Is she hot? Would you jerk off to her?" With any other woman, the Correct Response would be, "She's attractive, but not as hot as you."

With Song, it's different. Although the first response is actually true: no other woman could be as sexy, hot, and dynamic as Song, not when Song can morph into any form she chooses. But the proper response with Song was simple observation and honesty. "Hmmm, her butt is nice, but her tits are too big for her body type." Something like that. Then Song would file it away for future reference, for, well, for Thursday.

Sometimes she would have me meet her at a bar, late Thursday evening, and hunt her down. She could be anyone. I'd stroll through the crowd, paying attention to body language and keeping a sharp ear out for her favorite words: "enigmatic," "myriad," "ersatz." And for profanity, of course.

She can change her voice. She has one very pleasant voice she usually reverts to. But for the purposes of our hunts, she would alter her vocal apparatus enough to throw me off.

She could be alone or in a group. Song can mingle as easily as other people breathe, it is a part of the shape-shifter way of life: camouflage oneself by blending into the social fabric. Clothes can be a clue: a familiar pair of jeans or her favorite red tennis shoes. Other times, she might be the one woman in the place with all new clothes.

But the big giveaway would be her eyes.

Always her eyes.

I would see her eyes and walk right up to this stranger and kiss her and sing, "You're every woman in the world, to me."

One Thursday, she sent me a text: *NOT TONIGHT*.

I texted back to find out if something was wrong. No response. I tried calling. No answer. I stayed up past two hoping to hear back, but no luck.

I don't know how she bypassed security and broke into my condo, but I awoke with her hands over my eyes. "It's me," she whispered in my ear. "Keep your eyes closed."

I did as she said while she wrapped a bandana over my eyes.

"What are you doing, Song?"

"Here, give me your hand."

She put my hand on one of her breasts. It was slightly smaller than those she normally grew, but very pert. I played with it. She reached down, took me in her hand, stroked me.

"How do you know it's me?"

My heart raced. I didn't know, not for sure, but who else would it be?

"What do you think of when you think of me? My lips, my nose, my hair, my ass? That's all interchangeable. It's nothing to me. Here, I'll grow you a nice, big pair of tits to play with. Come on, tell me, what's your reference point?"

"Your eyes," I tell her. "Is that a good answer?"

"Don't act so fucking insecure, Alex. It doesn't become you. Do you think of me differently when I have a big pair of titties than when I have an itty-bitty pair? I bet you do, you fucking pervert."

I tried to take the bandana off my eyes but she stopped me with ease.

"Let's just talk in the dark. We can say things we would never utter in the light. I bet I could make you come, even if you tried not to. I could hold you down and jerk you off, even if you struggled. What do you think of that? I'm very strong, you know. Or I could climb right on top of you and you wouldn't even be sure it was me fucking you. You can't see my eyes, blindfolded in the dark, can you? Does the idea of having a stranger fuck you in the middle of the night excite you? You're right on the verge of coming right now, aren't you? You fucking pervert. I bet it wouldn't take more than a few strokes to get you off. You know what a succubus is?"

"Yes. A demon woman."

"That's right. She takes a poor, helpless man in his sleep. I could be a succubus. How do you really know I'm your precious Song?"

"It can only be you," I said. "The way you talk. Your filthy mouth. Only you, Song, only you would act this way. You want to know what I think of when I think of you? I think of you as an unknown quantity. Anything is possible with you. I never know your limits. Just when I think you're one way, I find out you're completely different. I always want to fuck you but I also want to protect you, hold you, love you, plumb your depths."

She straddled me, lowered herself onto me. My arms went around a slender body and slid down to the swell of her ass. She raised and lowered herself so slowly it was almost torture.

"Do you like the butt? I've added some extra padding to it. You like?"

"Yes, yes."

"You like a big ass. Tell me why."

"When I grab an ass, I like to feel flesh, Song. Not skin pulled tight over bone, not buns of steel, but flesh."

"Talk to me some more. Now, while you're inside me but can't see. Tell me why you have this sick idea that you love me. Tell me why."

"There is something sad and vulnerable about you, Song, and a part of you that is always off-limits. Everything is different with you. I have no desire to own you or control you or tie you down. I only want to experience you, in whatever form you take."

"Go on."

"But no matter how deep I go, no matter how much I experience you, there is something in you I cannot reach. I want to know what you think of, when you think of yourself."

"Who says I think of myself? I have very little sense of self. When I look at myself, I see an amorphous blob. I see clay. That's why I like it when you tell me what you like. Don't come yet!"

She paused in her slow up-and-down slide.

With effort, I held back. She resumed fucking me, very slow. She said, "I like it when you look at another woman's ass, because it's a challenge to me. Can I grow a better ass? What's the ideal angle for an ass? I want to grow the perfect ass. I want to grow an ass that's just right, that has curves and dips so insanely irresistible that when you see it, you just have to throw me down and fuck me right there. That's my goal. I've always liked geometry and now I am in search of the geometric equation for the ultimate ass. I have pride in my looks because it took me a long time to be able to morph into the exact form I set out to achieve. I will grow you the ultimate ass one day, my filthy little ass-man. Now don't you dare get off, not yet."

My mind whirled. Trying to carry on a rational conversation while deep inside Song was a supreme test of willpower, but I soldiered on.

"But what do you want, Song? You do all this stuff for me, but what about you?"

"You don't get it, do you? I like pleasing you. I like pleasing my man. Does that make me old-fashioned? Does it make me weak? Does it make me a second-class citizen if I put on a sexy dress for you? I grow nice, thick cocksucker lips for you. It's the same thing."

"I'll take the lips over a dress anytime."

"I know you will. Pervert."

"But, Song, I like to please you, too. That's why men do all the shit they do."

Her language was starting to rub off on me.

"We build cities and write poetry and fight wars just to get a woman's approval."

"Is that so? I don't remember you building me a city. Or even writing me a poem. Slacker."

"So tell me what you want. Let me do something for you."

"Very well, then. Next Thursday, you will get your wish. I will change into a woman like you have never seen before, but it will be totally for my own pleasure. You will be astounded. I absolutely fucking guarantee it. Hold on now, babe, I'm going to make you come."

She squeezed me tight inside herself, bounced hard on top of me, and I exploded.

Then she jumped off and slipped out of my condo and into the night before I could even get a glimpse of her.

5. A Woman Like You've Never Seen

"Bless me, Father, for I have sinned. It has been seven days since my last confession."

Father Landau blessed her and asked what were her sins.

"I don't know who I am anymore, Father. I have something going on, a relationship, and it's good. But there's a part of myself that wants to ruin it all. I know this isn't really a proper confession, but I have nobody else to talk to. It's like there's another person inside me, ready to jump out and fuck it all up. I'm sorry about the swearing, Father. It's a bad habit."

"Satan tempts us in the good times as well as the bad, my child. When you are happy, the devil gets very restless."

"Yes. That's what's happening. I can feel him stirring around inside me. I've stopped being promiscuous, Father, and he doesn't like that. He doesn't like that I want a normal life. I hear him, sometimes. I can't understand what he's saying but he's upset, he's mad. I'm afraid he's going to do something to ruin everything. I'm very scared, Father."

"You must put your faith in the Lord. Let it be His fight, not yours. You are no match for Satan but He is. Do you understand what I'm saying?"

"He's trying to get out, Father. God help me, he's trying to get out."

It was Thursday. The Thursday I had been waiting for, the night Song had promised to transform into a woman like I had never seen before. She had already blown my mind with so many other incarnations that now I had no idea what to expect. She had come through her Thursday transformations as sultry seductresses and elegant ladies. For a change of pace, she occasionally morphed into something "a little more trashy." She could grow a ghetto booty to drive me crazy.

I found myself wondering, *Just how the hell will she outdo herself?*

She had promised a woman like I had never seen before. She absolutely fucking guaranteed it. I could not concentrate for anything at work. By this time, everyone at the museum thought I was some sort of player, they saw me with so many different women. Song strictly forbade me to tell them the truth.

"Privacy is important to me," she had said. "Not just privacy. Secrecy. I can't let what I am get around. Sorry, but you are just going to have to go on being a super-stud."

Evening came. Seven-thirty, eight o'clock.

I called and it went straight to voice mail.

The evening rolled on into night. Was she okay? Did something happen? Did she change her mind? I left voice-mail messages. A lot of them. Call me pathetic.

It wasn't until Friday morning that I finally heard back from her. A single text message: *Soooo sorry, my love, my pervert, last night's transformation really took it out of me. But you will be pleased with the result. At least, I sure am!*

I was all but useless again at work. Rumors started going around that I was moonlighting as a gigolo. I think it was just a joke. The day crawled by. I sent a pathetic number of text messages to Song asking when and where we should meet. Finally, around quitting time, she texted me the address of a bar in the north Loop. *Meet me at seven.*

Seven!!

I was a wreck by the time I arrived. I stepped into the bar and she caught my eye. Those eyes! She waved me over. I went. I felt a bit confused. She was quite presentable. Pleasant. But plain.

Still, I was glad to see her in whatever incarnation she chose. I embraced her and kissed her and bought her an appletini. She watched me with a little smirk on her face.

"Say it," she said, still smirking.

"Hello."

"Not that. Tell me what you think of tonight's form."

"Oh, that." I took a long pull of my Miller. "Yeah. Nice, nice."

Then it hit me: maybe she had grown that ultimate ass she had been talking about. I told her to stand up and turn around so I could really see her. She complied, graciously enough.

Hardly any ass at all. Downright flat, actually.

She sat back down and still that smirk persisted.

"Oh, poor, confused Alex," she cooed. "Poor, poor pervert. So used to everything being all about him, him, him!"

I started to object but, truly, she had a point.

"I told you that I'd become a woman like you had never seen before, and I meant it. Not all changes are things you can see. Do you remember what else I said?"

I wracked my addled brain until it came to me.

"You said this time it would be for you. For your pleasure."

"Yay! Got it in one, swish, nothing but net! And truly, this body is like nothing you've ever seen before. You just don't know it yet. But it's for my pleasure. Isn't that what you wanted? You said you wanted to do something for me, am I right? Fight a war, build a city, something like that?"

"Yes! I meant it, too. Still do."

"Well then, now is your chance, pervert. Tonight you are going to fulfill one of my daring fantasies."

Smirk.

"Anything," I said. "Whatever you want."

"Promise?"

Did I dare?

Yes, I dared.

"Yes."

"Good answer. Look around this place. Good crowd here, more people coming in. And tonight, you are going to fuck me. Right here in this bar, right in front of all these fine people."

With that, she slipped off the bar stool and excused herself to run to the ladies' room.

"Hold my seat!" she squealed.

I sat there, stunned. I gulped the rest of my beer. I had to come up with an excuse fast. There was no way—What the hell—She can't be—My mind kept slipping its track right up till the second she returned.

"Now then, listen up," she said, then pulled me close so she could whisper right in my ear: "The extraordinary thing you do not see about this body is that it is imbued with pleasure receptors from head to toe. Kiss me."

I did.

She shuddered.

"I came just from that little smooch, my darling pervert. Why, you ask? Because I have rearranged my own nerve endings, which was incredibly freaking hard, even for me. But worth it! So, so worth it! My lips now have the nerve endings of a clit. Kiss me again!"

I did. Deeper, this time, and the hell with who watched. She clamped hold of my wrist when her body spasmed. It hurt; she is very strong; but I kept kissing her until she finally pulled away. Her face and neck were flushed a deep crimson.

"My God," I said.

"The night is still young," she purred. "Did my mouth taste like pussy?"

"Yes! Yes, it did."

"Did you enjoy tongue-fucking me here in front of all these people?"

"Oh, yeah."

"We'll hop from bar to bar. Tonight my body is one big cunt. Does that suit you? Will you indulge my depraved fantasy? You can make me get off just by playing with one finger."

I kissed her again and ran my hands up and down her arms. She told me to stop.

"I'm sorry. Did I do something wrong?"

"We need to go someplace with really loud music if you're going to do that," she breathed, "because if you keep it up, I'll be screaming."

We found a crowded place with blaring music. I licked the palm of her hand and she screamed herself hoarse.

We went from bar to bar to bar.

"Did I keep my promise?" she asked later. "Did I show you a woman like you've never seen before?"

Oh yeah, she certainly had.

It was too much, too much sensation, too much pleasure, too much, too much, too much! She kissed him good-bye outside some dive on Rush Street and pushed him away when he tried to get in the cab with her. "No more, my love, no more. I'm all orgasmed-out!"

She slammed the door and told the driver where to go. Sensations kept assailing her: the press of the cushion seat, the currents of air, her clothes. Her body shuddered with every touch and every breeze.

Pleasure and pain intertwined and even sounds mixed in. She paid the driver and the rumble of his "Thank you, ma'am," moved through her body like warm, soapy water. She ran inside her building, drunk on sensations. Somehow, she made it to her condo, but once inside, her system finally reached overload.

A familiar voice called to her. A boy's voice, one she had known long ago.

"Xiang?" she whispered.

"Yes," called the voice.

She whirled about, but of course there was nobody else in her condo.

She heard music. Music! Beautiful music, just as she always heard right before a transformation. But she couldn't be transforming, not this soon, and not without willing it.

She felt her consciousness ebbing away.

6. A Nasty, Undignified Process

Song is wearing a short, slightly pudgy, almost girlish body. I take her to Japonais, a very nice Asian place. Celebrities sometimes go there. We drink saké and order the duck.

No sooner am I pulling the ring from my vest pocket than Song is slapping my hand.

"Put that damn thing away!"

I blink at her.

"I know what it is. Now put it away."

She pours more saké and orders me to drink. I do so. She pours me another.

"I was going to ask—"

"I know what you were going to say. I'm not an idiot!"

She smiles at the waiter and signals for more water.

"I morph tomorrow, so gotta drink lots of water."

"Does that mean the answer is no?"

She clicks a fingernail against the pot of saké.

We look at each other. Song rarely answers a question directly. Instead, she says, "You have not been to my place yet."

"You haven't asked me over. You won't even tell me where it is."

"If I won't even have you over, what makes you think I'd marry you?"

"Um."

"Um is right. We should just go on as we are. If we had any sense, we would. But we're both idiots. I'm having neurochemical reactions toward you, Alex. It's stupid. And I suppose your brain is dumping a shitload of oxytocin into your system, making you just as stupid. We're two stupid creatures mistaking simple biological drives for something grand and significant. How much did you waste on that ring?"

"It's an heirloom, actually."

"Good. I'm glad it was just your ancestors who wasted good money and not you. If you still want to persist in being stupid, then you can come over to my place tonight. Do you have any idea how hard it is for an Adept to maintain long-term relationships? Do you have any clue?"

"I can't even imagine."

"No, you can't. I'm glad you've stopped deluding yourself into thinking you can. I've taught you well, little grasshopper. Drink more saké. You will need it."

I drank more. Fortunately, we were traveling by cab. Only this time, we went to her condo instead of mine. It was a short-term-stay condominium in Old Town, the kind favored by businessmen who make frequent weeklong visits to the city.

"Do you know why I don't live in a regular apartment building?" Song asked as we headed toward the elevator.

My head was still reeling from the saké. I had no answer.

"It's because people would notice a different woman living there every week. Word would get around that a shape-shifter was in the building. But here, people come and go all the time. A government agent rents out the same condo for me every week, but under a different name. It isn't like the other condos in the building. It is custom-built to serve the special needs of a Polymorph Adept."

"What's so bad about people knowing what you are?"

"After all this time, you still don't get it? There are people who don't exactly like us. Being a P6 is like being in Witness Protection. You read the news. People hate us. There's even a black market ring for polymorph organs."

"But you can't spend your life running and hiding."

"Sure I can. I'm a natural at it."

We went up to her floor. Her condo had one of the thickest doors I've ever seen outside of a bank. It was equipped with three locks. Once we stepped inside, she had to disarm the security system. She closed the door behind us and reset all the locks.

"Home sweet home!"

Artwork covered her walls. A lot of Norman Rockwell, a couple pieces by Pissarro, and our old friend Renoir.

"Nice."

"Don't sit down," Song said. "Not yet. I told you, I've never brought anyone here before. Do you really want to marry me?"

"Yes."

"Then it's good that you drank a lot of saké. Would you like another drink?"

"I'm okay."

"Come with me."

She took my hand and led me through the living room, through her bedroom, into her bathroom. The bathroom had a door that looked very out of place. Song unlocked it. It was almost as secure as her front door. She led me through it, into another bathroom and shower. A computer screen was built into one wall.

She closed the door behind us. My heart began to pound. Something about the way Song was acting really had me alarmed. She seemed unsure of herself.

"Before I morph, I shower and scrub myself all over. Then I input data about the form I intend to morph into. The computer is moisture-resistant, by the way. The form has to be pre-approved before I can proceed. I took some CAD classes, so now I can generate my own 3D image. I send the image off to the regulatory agency and they approve it or reject it. Sometimes, I have to make minor alterations. Can you imagine trying to come up with a different appearance every single week of your life?"

"No, I can't."

"It took me years to be able to actually succeed in morphing into exactly what I set out to. Some of my attempts were hideous. Made the ugly little girl you met in the museum that first day look like Angelina Jolie. Sometimes I hid myself. Other times I went out and terrorized the villagers. Anyway, I get it all approved, then step out of my clothes. We'll keep our clothes on. But take your shoes off, if you don't mind."

We took our shoes off.

Song stood at the next door for a long time before punching in a key code. She led me through and the door hissed shut, leaving us in what was basically a padded cell with smooth walls.

"And this is it. My morphing pod. This is where I change from one person to another. Please, don't touch me. Not in here. It's not you. I just don't feel right with you, or with anyone, in here with me. Morphing is a very intimate act."

"Like making love."

"More like taking a shit. You really wouldn't want anyone there with you.

You want to be in a relationship with me, then you have to know this. This is a big part of what I am, and if we're going to share our lives, you need to be aware of it. Oh, by the way, there is no privacy in here. Look there."

She pointed. I looked.

"That's right, wave for the cameras. My transformations are monitored, recorded, regulated. The government wants to make sure I don't change into somebody else and rob a bank or something. It's not all fun and games being an Adept."

She spoke in a flat, dull voice, very unlike her. I stood like a shadow and let her take whatever time she needed. She seemed almost listless.

"There's still time to back out, if you want."

"No."

"It's a messy and undignified process. We're not talking Lon Chaney turning into the werewolf here. This is ugly. You have a question."

"Is it voluntary? I mean it seems strange that it's scheduled."

A half-smile played across her lips.

She stepped over to one wall and opened a panel. Recessed within was a touch pad. "The old B sci-fi flicks didn't get everything wrong." She punched a few buttons. Overhead, servo motors whined. The ceiling opened to reveal what looked like a large space heater. "With a flick of a few more switches, I can flood this place with gamma rays."

I think I took an involuntary step toward the door.

"Yeah, a good blast of radiation and the monster comes out. It's just like a full moon. I can control the dose, depending on how much of a nudge I need. Usually, I don't even need any prompting. All I gotta do is take some long, deep breaths, hyper-oxygenate my system, and presto chango! Sometimes it's a struggle to hold off till Thursday. The pod is also rigged with speakers so I can morph to a soundtrack."

She closed the panel.

Her gaze locked onto mine.

"The first thing that happens is I hear music. Incredible, beautiful music. Sometimes the music in my head is so intense it drowns out whatever I've got blasting from the speakers. Other times, it all sort of swirls together. In any case, when the music in my head starts, I hit the deck because the next thing to happen is I go into ataxia. You're a smart guy, I bet you know what ataxia is, right?"

"Loss of muscle control."

"That's one way to put it. Another way is to say I flop around like a fish on a hardwood floor. It means any waste in my system comes out, and you really wouldn't believe how much there is. It's nasty and undignified. Do you get the picture?"

She spat this last bit like an accusation. I nodded. I wanted to reach out to her, take her in my arms, but even I could tell this was not the time.

"After that, my bones break, then break some more, then crumble. Is that something you can even imagine? I don't mean, can you see it happening to me—but could you imagine your own bones breaking apart into smaller and smaller fragments, crumbling, crunching? Remember when you held my hand at the Art Institute? You felt my bones crumble just a tiny bit and you wanted to snatch your hand away. I can do something like that at will without becoming ataxic. Do you know that what I was doing with you out in public was technically illegal? Imagine that happening all through your own body, your hands, feet, hips, face, skull, all over and all at once. Did you know a morphing pod is completely soundproof? There's a reason for that."

I felt physically ill and I know it must have shown, but Song did not relent.

"Here. Hold my hand. And my arm. Go on. You wanted to touch me. You wanted to comfort your damsel in distress. Now's your chance. Do it."

I almost ran.

Run. Run like fucking hell. That's what she said to me that Thursday in front of the Seurat. *I will make your life a living hell.* And now I found myself thinking, *Yes, yes, you will.*

I looked at Song but I wasn't really seeing her. I was seeing one incarnation out of myriads of possibilities. Today, it was a cute, chubby girl. Had she chosen this innocent-looking form expressly for the purpose of underscoring her vulnerability during tonight's presentation?

I thought of her other forms and they all seemed meaningless. A hand was extended toward me now, but what did it have to do with my lover, my sweetheart, my soul mate? My mind flipped back, back, back through the weeks and months until it finally landed on the homely, lopsided girl I first approached at the Natural History Museum.

I wanted *that* girl, blotchy skin, big nose, and all, just so long as we could live a normal life together. I would take that in a heartbeat. The first thing I had noticed about her was her eyes. Blue and deep and sad.

I looked up from her outstretched hand and there they were: those wonderful eyes. I took her hand in mine. I grasped her arm. She let her arm go limp and watched the look of surprise cross my face.

"Heavy, isn't it?"

Her arm weighed in my hands like concrete.

"The smaller I am, the denser my bones. I can be tall or short, big or small, but my mass stays about the same. The smaller I am, the more compact and strong I am. Although I'm extremely strong at any size. Don't let go."

Then I felt her bones break and crumble beneath her skin until her arm was like a heavy bag of sand. And now it was my turn to weep, as Song had wept when she placed her hands on that slab of bone that had not changed or broken for sixty-five million years. Even after all the transformations she had undergone in the time we were together, I never really thought about the actual mechanics of it. Not like this.

I wanted to save her from it, but I am only a man. My legs gave out, I went to my knees even as I held on to her hand and arm.

"Does it hurt? It must hurt. I'm so sorry."

Song bent down so I could look into her eyes. "It hurts more than any orgasm you've ever had. It feels so purple you can hardly stand it. You see the craziest sounds. All your wires get crossed. It's like you're back in the womb and your body is still deciding what it's going to be when it grows up. There is a moment when you exist as nothing more than pure potentiality. Then you must draw upon all your willpower and call to mind what you want to be next. Are you going to be sick, my love?"

"I'm okay."

"It took me years to perfect the process, to actually come out looking presentable. You have more questions but they will have to wait. Tomorrow is Thursday, when I go through all this. I step in here first thing in the morning and don't step out until late afternoon. I am literally a different person when I step out from when I go in. Yes, there is an essential me, but each body type gives me a different experience of the world. People treat me differently, depending on how I look. If I come out all ugly, nobody talks to me except museum geeks who don't know any better. Are you glad you talked to me, my love?"

"Yes. More than you know."

"Good answer. You want me to be her again? That ugly runt you met at the Field?"

"I will love you whatever form you take. It isn't your body I love, it's you."

"But what am I? No matter, we've been over that before. I won't be her again. I like being your hot babe. I like growing thick, cocksucker lips all for you. Let's get out of here. I spend enough time in this place as it is."

The bones in her arm suddenly solidified and something slimy oozed from her skin. I jerked my hand away.

"Oh, that gunk is a by-product of the whole process. I'm completely covered in the stuff when I'm done and have to shower and rinse this whole place down. Werewolves don't know how easy they got it. Come on."

We went back through the doors to her living room and sat on her couch. She cuddled against me, not so much as a lover but as a sad little girl. I put my arms around her and wanted so much to protect her and make it so she never had to suffer another horrifying transformation again.

"So, what did you think of the tour, Alex? Have I scared you off yet?"

"No, my dear Sing Song. Nothing could scare me off. Nothing."

"Still want to marry me?"

"More than ever."

She sighed and held me tight.

"I don't wear rings, so we'll just have to put your family heirloom on a shelf somewhere. And you will never make a proper lady out of me."

"I don't want a proper lady. I want you."

"I guess we're engaged then. At least until you come to your senses."

"I will never come to my senses," I said. "Not as long as I'm with you."

"I want you to take tomorrow off work," she mumbled into my shoulder. "Stay here while I ooze into a new shape. You won't hear a thing. The pod is soundproof and self-contained. I won't be able to see or hear you, either, but I just want to know you're here. Will you do that for me?"

I told her yes.

I'd do anything for her. I would endure anything for her.

Funny how the Universe likes to test you on these things.

When you date a Polymorph Adept, surprises just come with the territory. The next one arrived at breakfast time. Song had an uncharacteristically small meal, a couple eggs and toast. "Feeding frenzy comes after the transformation," she explained.

Somebody buzzed her call box while I was digging into a stack of pancakes. It seemed that Song's appetite, as well as her language, had rubbed off on me. Song buzzed her visitor up and went to greet him at the door.

I heard them talking in the other room, the easy banter of people long acquainted. I stepped out to find Song holding hands with a fifty-something Chinese man in a well-tailored suit. They conversed in rapid-fire Chinese but stopped at my approach. Song swung hands with the man. The man shot me an intense look.

I felt off-balance and underdressed in sweatpants, T-shirt, and socks. Song looked quite comfortable with this man. She smiled at me, probably enjoying my moment of discomfort.

"I'm Alex."

He gently removed Song's hand from his, gave it an affectionate little pat, then trained his eagle eyes on me. He did not look particularly inclined to respond.

"Are you Song's father?" I asked.

"No."

Song skipped back to the kitchen for some coffee. I started to follow her when the well-dressed man said, "You are Alex Cruz, thirty-two years of age, curator at the Field Museum of Natural History, ten-year resident of

Chicago's Gold Coast, connoisseur of fine art, and fiancé to the talented Polymorph Adept named Song."

I don't intimidate easily, but this was kind of reminding me of that scene in *Gladiator* where Maximus advances on Comodus in the arena declaring his vow of vengeance. I might have taken a step back. There is something about wearing a pair of your girlfriend's baggy sweatpants that makes one feel less of a man. At least I had declined her offer of bunny slippers.

He pulled a government ID from the breast pocket of his suit and presented it like I should be impressed. Actually, I was.

"I am Special Agent Lawrence Chen, assigned to a task force dedicated to ensuring the safety and well-being of polymorphs here in the Safe Zone city of Chicago. Song has made the decision to become romantically involved with you. She has done this against my counsel as her designated agent. I am sure you are considering yourself quite the Romeo, bagging yourself a Polymorph Adept. But to me, you are a security breach. Your 'relationship' with Song compounds the already formidable complexity involved in keeping an Adept safe and secure. I have to leave town on a family matter for a couple days, but make no mistake, Alex Cruz of fourteen-twenty North Lake Shore Drive, I've got my eye on you."

With that, he departed.

Back in the kitchen, Song said, "Nice chat with Larry, my love?"

I am not a liar.

But sometimes tact is as important as truth.

"Quite pleasant," I said.

7. A Flash of Light

She didn't particularly feel like morphing. The sleep-morph she underwent the previous Saturday morning had thrown her body rhythms off schedule. But no matter. One good dose of radiation and she should be on her way.

But first, music. She programmed her system for opera highlights. Music playing, she dialed up her radioactive blast and moments later the music in her head mixed with Mozart's Die Zauberflötte. *Ironically, it was during* Der Hölle Rache *that some sixth sense kicked in and she knew all hell was about to break loose.*

A feeling that something was horribly wrong followed by a flash of light. That was all I remembered of the explosion, and even that might be nothing more than the story I tell myself. Did I really have a dreadful premonition or did my mind just fill in the blanks later? For that matter, the brilliant flash could also be a false memory, my mind's symbol for the moment my world shattered.

After that: slowly returning to life, scattered pieces of memory struggling to stitch back into a coherent whole. My eyes opening but only slightly, *light so intense*, voices I felt sure were talking about me but which I could not make out.

A uniformed police officer standing nearby. Another man, this one in a rumpled suit. *Another cop*, a voice whispers in my brain. It's something about his size and how he stands and the clipped way he speaks to a nurse that gives it away.

"You're awake," the nurse says to me. "Welcome back to the land of the living."

I open my mouth but it feels like it's full of glue. I try to point to the water on a tray next to my bed, but something stops me. My wrist is handcuffed to the bedrail. The nurse asks the plainclothes cop—must be a detective—if the handcuffs are necessary. The detective doesn't answer.

I can manage nothing but, "Song. Song. Sing Song."

"What's he babbling about?" the detective asks the nurse. "What's he saying?"

Now it's the nurse's turn to not answer. Instead, she informs me that there was "an incident" and that I am in the hospital but my condition is stable.

I start to ask questions, but she raises one finger to stop me. "Hold that thought. I'll get Dr. Hemingway. She can answer your questions better than I can."

She leaves and the detective glares at me. I'm hooked up to an IV and heart monitor. I have a cast on my right arm—the one that's not handcuffed to the bed. Other than that, I don't feel too bad. Except for thirst. I stare pointedly at the water. The detective sees but only chuffs a little and turns away. The uniform has left the room. It's just me and Detective Taciturn now.

"So, you can speak," he says.

"Yes."

He shows me his shield like it's the Holy Grail and informs me who he is. Turns out his name is Stone and he's with the CPD Special Task Force division. Translation: he deals with cases involving polymorphs.

"Care to tell me what happened today?"

What happened? He's asking me?

"Water."

I struggle to sit up but feel totally drained of energy. That, the cast, and the handcuffs make it a formidable task, but I manage. I touch my head with my free hand, just to make sure there are no bandages there. My head seems okay but I feel foggy. Definitely not up to a contest of wills with this surly cop.

I was relieved when the doctor arrived to interrupt our little stare-down. She was a very tall woman and, to my amusement, did not favor the detective with so much as a glance, but made a beeline for my bed and introduced herself. Dr. Hemingway. At any other time, her name might have intrigued me, but under the circumstances I simply didn't care whether or not she was related to the author. Dr. Hemingway handed me a cup of water without my having to ask and I gulped it down.

"Sip, don't gulp," she chided.

The detective snorted a laugh and she spared a moment to shoot him a wicked glare before returning her attention to me.

"Is Song alive?" I asked, as soon as my mouth rehydrated.

"That would be the young lady you were brought in with? The other person involved in this incident?"

Incident?

"Yes."

"I'm afraid my access to that information is limited, and even if I did know—" She glanced over at the detective, who shot her a hard look. "There are restrictions regarding what I could divulge. I can tell you that she is in a special ward."

Dr. Hemingway spoke carefully and my radar went on high alert, even in my foggy state.

"My understanding, Mr. Cruz, is that she pulled through. She survived. But there are . . . complications. Is she related to you?"

"Yes," I croak. "Sort of."

"Are you her father?"

"What? Her father? I'm thirty-two years old. How could I be her father? She's my fiancée."

At this, both the detective and Dr. Hemingway gave a start. The detective stepped up and barked, "Did you just say that girl is your fiancée?"

"Yes."

"As in, you think you're going to marry her?"

Polymorphs are not technically considered human, but there's no law against marrying one. At least, I didn't think there was. The beeping of my heart-rate monitor kicked into overdrive. Dr. Hemingway whirled on the detective and, politely but firmly, asked him to leave the room.

"My apologies, Doctor. But when your patient is feeling better, we're going to sit down and have us a nice little chat."

He slipped out and I looked to Dr. Hemingway, expecting a sympathetic smile, but no way. She had gone cold. "Your injuries have been attended to, but we're keeping you here for observation."

"What more can you tell me about Song?"

"You're my patient, not this Song," Dr. Hemingway informed me. "You were banged up pretty good, but nothing too severe. We're keeping you here mostly to make sure there's no undetected internal bleeding or other unforeseen complications. Primarily as a precaution."

She listed my various and sundry injuries: fractured right radius, dislocated right shoulder, broken ribs, a few scrapes and contusions.

"I've had you on a morphine drip to curb pain, but I'm discontinuing it. You've had enough."

I tried to pump her for details about what happened and when I could see Song but Dr. Hemingway was not in the least interested in helping me out. It really seemed her attitude had soured right about the time I declared my engagement to Song. I was getting nowhere.

Finally, I just sighed and said, "Apparently, somebody arrested me when I was out cold. I'm pretty sure my rights have been violated. Do you think you could ask the good detective out there to uncuff me?"

The doctor looked down on me as if I were a bacterial culture.

"The detective does not tell me how to perform my duties," she said, her voice ice. "I will not deign to instruct him in his."

With that, she pivoted smartly and stalked out of the room. I could already feel the last of the morphine drip wearing off and a throbbing pain spreading throughout my body.

8. A Living Hell

"How is he, how is Alex, is he okay, is he okay?"

A nurse assured her that yes, the man she came in with was fine, a little banged up is all. She sighed and fell into a deep sleep. But even in sleep, she worked. She knew her every internal organ intimately and now she went around to each: mending, healing, renewing.

She had been at her most vulnerable when the bomb went off, and yet she managed to survive. The bomb had been installed in the antechamber, not in the morphing pod itself. That made sense: it would be easier to hide it there, as there were no cameras. Anytime somebody stepped foot in the morphing pod, the security cameras clicked on.

But it wasn't that big of a bomb. Was the bomber incompetent or simply not trying to actually kill her? She felt oddly sure that killing her was not the intent. Nor was injuring her the real goal. It didn't make sense, and yet she felt she should somehow know, that there was some nugget of information just outside her awareness, taunting her.

The blast had blown through the door into the pod one way, and also through the other door to her apartment. If the bomb had been in the pod, she would probably have been killed.

As it was, she had lost body mass but not vital organs. She didn't lose anything she could not regrow. Having less mass, she took on a smaller form, her "default" form, as she thought of it. It had taken her time, of course. When she was brought into the ER, she didn't even appear human. Not that she was, technically, human.

"I want to see him," she told the nurse. "How do I look?"

The nurse scrutinized her.

"Young lady, you look like trouble."

Time passes slowly when you're wide awake and in pain. For me, it dragged so much that I was actually delighted when surly old Detective Stone returned. Anything for a diversion.

He got right down to business.

"We're taking you to her. She's in a secure ward of the hospital. We need you to identify her."

By "we," he meant him and the nurse, who stood by with a wheelchair. Stone released me from the handcuffs. *About damn time!*

"Identify her? What, does she have amnesia? Is she conscious?"

"She's fine."

"You do know what she is, right?"

"What, that she's a polymorph? Yes."

Again, Stone gave his trademark snorting laugh.

I had other questions but he wasn't answering. The nurse helped me into the wheelchair. I was glad to no longer be hooked up to an IV or heart monitor. Unfortunately, I was still in a hospital gown, which is very close to being naked. I would have asked for my clothes but Song was all I cared about.

We rolled out of there and took an elevator to twelve. My heart hammered. We came to the "secure ward;" the nurse and detective had to present ID to an armed guard at the door.

"What's going on?"

"Two things," snapped Stone. "One, extra security precautions are always taken for cases involving her kind. Our tax dollars at work. Second, the nature of the crime perpetrated."

"The bomb, you mean."

"Considered a terrorist act. Or, at the least, a hate crime."

Was I a suspect? It had to look suspicious, with me being in her condo on the night of the explosion. Maybe the only other guest she ever had. I could easily have looked over her shoulder when she punched in her security codes. If I were a cop, I damn sure would have suspected me.

But I really didn't care about that. I just wanted to see Song.

Finally, we passed through the security station and down a hall toward Song's room. My heart thundered along.

"Just to clarify one more time," said Detective Stone, outside the room of my soul mate. "What did you say the nature of your relationship is with the girl?"

"We're engaged."

"Engaged. I see. And so you two were lovers?"

Were?

"Is that any of your business?"

"It's very important, Mr. Cruz."

"Really."

We had stopped outside her room, and it appeared I wasn't going any further until the good detective had his answers.

"So. The nature of your relationship was a sexual one?"

It wasn't any of his business and under different circumstances I damn sure would have told him as much. But pain thrummed through my body and I was sitting in a wheelchair covered with nothing more than a skimpy piece of fabric (I would have given just about anything for Song's baggy sweatpants right about then), and it appeared the only way I would get to see my fiancée was to answer his question.

"Yes," I finally said. "It's a sexual relationship. We're in love."

"Well, I thank you for your honesty," Stone said and opened the door to Song's room. The nurse pushed me inside and there she was.

Nobody had prepared me for what I saw.

She sat up in bed and smiled. She looked quite healthy, though the big sunglasses seemed odd.

"She has a touch of photosensitivity," explained a doctor, noticing my gaze.

But it wasn't the sunglasses that shocked me to my core. It was her. So small, so innocent. If I had seen her on the street and had to guess her age, I would have said twelve.

"So let me ask you again," said Stone, stepping up beside me. "This is the girl with whom you carried on a sexual relationship?"

Was it her? Could it be her? She was so small.

She was a sweet-looking, preteen Chinese child.

She smiled at me and said, "Come here to shanghai me, did you, Alex, my love?"

It was her voice, no mistaking that.

"I—"

"Let me ask you this," said Stone. "Just how old is your little girlfriend there?"

"She's—"

I stopped. How old was she, anyway? I really didn't know. Song had an infuriating way of dancing around personal questions. Even after all these months plus an engagement, I simply didn't know how old she was.

Song laughed long and hard.

"Alex, get over here!" she squealed. "Oh, never mind, I'll come to you."

She bounded from her hospital bed and plunked herself right into my lap. I recoiled. Stone made a gravelly, grinding sound in his throat. There was nothing between this child and myself except flimsy fabric. I tried to push her away but, despite having just survived the blast of a bomb, Song was still strong.

The nurse snapped, "Little miss, please return to your bed."

"Oh, but I was so worried about my Alex!" she said, and squirmed around on my lap. "And I bet he was worried about his little Asian Lolita, too!"

"Lolita?" said Stone. "I was given to understand your name was—"

He pulled his notepad from one pocket.

"Song."

"She's kidding," I said. "She's making a Nabokov reference."

"Nabokov?"

"Vladimir Nabokov?"

Stone jotted down a note.

Again, Song squealed with laughter.

"I keep telling you people, I'm twenty-seven! I'll give you my Polymorph ID number and you can confirm it. Get in touch with Agent Chen, he'll tell you. I just look like this because, well, I lost some body mass. I had to grow a smaller body and this is sort of my default form. It was the simplest, easiest thing to revert to. This is what I looked like when I was a kid. Adorable, isn't it?"

Relief washed through my body. I was still not comfortable having this child-woman on my lap in front of all these people, but at least I wasn't a criminal.

Song recited her Polymorph ID number and Stone wrote it down in his notepad.

"I'll have to check the National Registry to confirm your story." He turned to step out the door but, like Peter Falk in all those Columbo episodes, turned back at the last second. "Oh, one more thing. I'll also need to talk to this Vladimir Nabokov. Any idea where I might find him?"

"I will make your life more intense and more interesting than you can imagine. I will also make it a living hell."

One thing about Song, she always tells the truth and she always keeps her promises. I chalked the whole "Lolita Incident" up as yet another Sing Song Moment. A very big Sing Song moment. Detective Stone contacted the National Polymorph Registry and confirmed Song's identity, and got that whole mess cleared up. It disturbed me just how much Song appeared to be getting off on my discomfort, but then again her personality did tend to change with each incarnation, and this incarnation was a radical departure from her usual, and she had been through a horrible trauma.

The question of who set the bomb still hung in the air like a black fog. I sure as hell didn't have an alibi: I was right there at her place. Not only that, but it was on record that I had actually been inside Song's morphing pod just the day before. Cameras roll whenever somebody sets foot inside.

Song set aside her giggly Lolita persona and worked hard to convince Stone, and a whole squadron of other law enforcement personnel who showed up in the secured hospital ward, that I didn't have any reason to harm her.

"Really, Detectives, think about it. If you were dating a chick who grew you a different hot body every week and used said hot body to fuck your brains out, would you try to blow her up?"

The law enforcement people looked at what their minds told them was a preteen girl, and they looked at me and I could almost hear prison bars clanging shut behind me. Her Lolita persona chose that moment to rear its darling little head and she said, "Alex, get on over here and give me a kiss! I know you would never try to hurt me, not after all the fun we've had!"

My fractured arm throbbed and my ribs felt as if they had been body-slammed by a mastodon. The ward was crawling with medical personnel, but they, quite rightly, were intently focused on Song's well-being and not inclined to slide me any pain meds.

At one point, they sent for Dr. Hemingway, and she came to the ward just long enough to discharge me from the hospital. At this, Stone's eyes lit right up because now he was free to haul me off to the police station for a right proper interrogation. That "nice little chat" he had promised.

"He's innocent!" Song screamed at him. "And, in any case, I won't press charges!"

But she didn't have the final say about that. This was considered a terrorist act and/or hate crime. Oh, and also, Detective Stone really just didn't like me.

I turned back to steal one more glance at Song. She tried to run to me as Stone read me my rights, but a doctor caught her and held her back. Her sunglasses flew off.

Her eyes were no longer blue but soft brown.

I was wheeled away even as Song screamed for them to stop.

9. Anything For Father

Agent Chen had been summoned from his own mother's sickbed to return to Chicago on an emergency of a classified nature. He stepped into the station jet-lagged and weary and annoyed as hell. I couldn't say that I blamed him. I was stuck in an interrogation room while jurisdictional pissing contests raged over whether this was a local matter, a federal terrorist case, or a hate crime.

Stone and Chen both strode into the interrogation room.

"This is one big cluster-fuck," Stone growled. "But thank your lucky stars that Special Agent Chen has been kind enough to clear it up. At least, he's cleared it up for you."

Then he spoke the words he must have hated the most: "You're free to go. But you're going to want to stay."

"Did you find out who did it?" I asked.

Stone and Chen exchanged looks. Stone gave a dismissive wave and stepped out. Chen sat at the table across from me and rested his head in hands.

"Yes, Alex. The case has been solved. Mostly. But I have to tell you: you are really not going to be happy about what we found. I'm sure not."

Dr. Hemingway had been gracious enough to prescribe me Vicodin. That took the edge off my physical pain but my nerves were shot. I had been blown up, rushed to the hospital, interrogated, accused of being a sexual predator, accused of being a terrorist, hauled off to the police station, and finally released. Oh, and the last time I looked in the eyes of my beloved fiancée, I did not recognize her. And now, Special Agent Chen had just informed me that some new turn of events would really upset me.

"So, what now?" I asked.

"Now the tables are turned," he said. "You are no longer a suspect in this case but the victim."

"Not as much as Song."

Chen gave me a look I simply could not read.

"You said the case had been solved."

"Actually, I said *mostly* solved. There's still a lot we don't know."

"But you know who tried to kill Song."

"We know who set the bomb."

"And the bomb was meant for her, right? I mean, it wasn't some nut-job out to kill me."

"It was meant for her. Or you. Or both of you."

"Well, I'm glad everything's so crystal clear."

Chen held up a finger and stepped out of the interrogation room. He spoke to somebody: "You can bring her in here. I think we're ready."

A moment later, a uniformed officer led Song into the interrogation room. Her arms were bound to her body in a straitjacket. The officer motioned her to a seat. I tried to recognize her but simply could not see my fiancée. I saw, instead, a frightened brown-eyed child.

"The restraints are necessary, I'm afraid," Chen said. "Handcuffs are not deemed sufficient for Polymorph Adepts. I'm sorry, that's the law."

I had no words. My head spun, my fractured arm throbbed, and I was on the verge of being physically sick. This was just not real. The uniformed officer left and Detective Stone stepped in. So it was me, Chen, Stone, and a straitjacketed Asian Lolita. One big, dysfunctional family.

"She, or he, or whatever, has waived rights to counsel," Stone said.

Chen just nodded.

I was the one to finally break the silence.

"What the fuck is going on?"

Song whispered, "Go ahead. Show him."

Chen started to object but she snapped, "Do it. Please. He has a right to know."

Chen looked to Stone, who set a laptop computer on the table. He shook his head, cued something up on the computer, and spun it around to face me. A video played: Song, in her previous incarnation as the Plain Jane I had such kinky fun with, was stepping into her morphing pod.

"Notice the time stamp," Chen said.

It was late Friday night, early Saturday morning. Right after our incredible date.

"An unscheduled and unauthorized transformation," Chen informed me.

"It was a sleep morph, Alex," the little girl said. "I didn't know what I was doing. He just took over."

He? Who the hell was "he"? Who took over what?

In the video, she lost control of her muscles just as she described: like a fish flopping around on a hardwood floor. I remembered her telling me this was an intimate act. I started to turn away when Chen said, "I think we can fast-forward here." He pushed a button and, thankfully, the process whirred by. He stopped the fast-forward just as Song was standing up as a new person, a handsome Chinese boy, naked and covered in that slime Song told me was the by-product of the transformation process.

The boy stepped out of the morphing pod and the video stopped.

I turned away from the screen and could not bring myself to look at Song or Chen or Stone.

"There is more," Chen said.

The video started again, this time with the boy stepping into the morphing pod. According to the time stamp, it was later that same morning. The boy Song opened the panel she had shown me. He was carrying a few tools and a small device of some sort. I was confused for a few seconds, but it soon became clear what he was doing. He unscrewed the panel and installed the device out of sight.

"No."

"The bomb was installed in the antechamber," Chen said, "But the detonator he put in the pod itself. The radiation triggered the detonator."

Stone growled, "But why not put the bomb in the room as well? Seems like it would have been more effective that way."

Song spoke up then: "He wasn't trying to kill me."

"You say 'he' like he isn't you," Stone said.

"I wasn't aware of him. I thought he was long gone. I felt him stirring, but I didn't have any idea he would do something like this. Alex, please don't hate me. I didn't know!"

"Just what, then, was he or you trying to accomplish?" Chen asked.

"Agent Chen, you are like a father to me, but I'm not prepared to answer that."

"What I want to know," said Stone, "Is where the hell this kid came from."

"That I will answer," said Song. "But first, you might want to get a cup of coffee. And you, dear Alex, might want to pop another Vicodin. You're pale as a ghost."

Even as a trussed-up little child, Song had a way of captivating an audience when she wanted to. She did that now.

"Until I was seven, my life was fairly normal. Nobody knew I had the double gene required to be a polymorph. For that matter, nobody really knew much about polymorphs. We were just another family. In a lot of ways, my parents were very traditional, very old school, as you white devils like to say."

She giggled. Despite being bound in a straitjacket in an interrogation room, she actually giggled.

"Father was demanding, maybe even harsh at times, but that was all I knew, and I was happy. At least, as far as I recall. I liked knowing my place and knowing what was expected of me. Father's love didn't come easy, so when it did come, I trusted it. I had earned it. When I was seven, I started spontaneously morphing. Nothing big, just a few minor alterations here and there. My fingers would grow really long, or I'd wake up all fat. Stuff like that. My parents took me to hospital. Polymorphs were just being discovered then, only occasionally cropping up in the population, mostly in China. They tested me and, lo and behold, I had the double gene. Lucky me.

"They took me away from my parents and stuck me in a lab. Don't look so horrified, Alex. Really, you watch too many B sci-fi movies. Actually, it was a research hospital. It was horrible. All that ice cream they fed me. Doctors from all over the world doting on me and treating me like I was a person, even though I was a girl. I actually came to really like hospitals. The staff there was my family."

I said, "What about your parents?"

"Oh, the government paid them pretty good, so they were happy."

"Were they allowed to visit?"

"What, are you envisioning men in biohazard suits hauling me off to some remote military compound? It was a hospital, for the most part, with a bit of extra security. Anybody could come by. But why would they? This is China we're talking about. I was a girl. My parents were happy and I was happy. Plus, the government told my parents that if the research hospital needed to keep me long-term, they could have another child. China has a strict policy about excessive procreation. My father was ecstatic; they could try for a boy and restore the family honor. But the research lab decided it would be cruel to keep me any longer and so they gave me back after only a year, and life went on. Only things were different. I mean, between my father and me. He still demanded complete obedience, but he also encouraged me to excel in school. As if I were a boy. So I studied like hell, learned languages and read literature and even did pretty good in math. I loved geometry, did I ever mention that, Alex?"

What's the geometric equation for the ultimate ass? Song had asked me. It felt like ages ago. Would we ever find our way back to that life?

"I morphed a bit, but kept basically the same face. Life went on. Then, when I was twelve, the telltale sign of a true Adept kicked in. Agent Chen, you know what I'm talking about. Alex, you have any idea what that telltale sign might be?"

It came to me in a flash: "Your eyes."

"Bravo! Yes, my eyes turned from brown to blue. The blue eyes you fell for that first night at the Field Museum. My morphing ability started to really kick into high gear at that point. I was afraid my father was going to disown me for being a freak. Old School and all that, remember. But instead he seemed to love me even more. I didn't know why. I have a genius IQ but I was really, really stupid. I never saw it coming."

"Saw what coming?" Stone said.

"I would do anything for my father. I was raised to please a man and I still like to please the man in my life. I never considered it to be a bad thing. I liked being a girl. I've always been a girl at heart. So what he asked of me—"

She trailed off and everyone sat silent, waiting.

"He saw what I could do, how I was gaining more and more control of my morphing ability. We had a morphing pod installed in our home, one of the first ever constructed. One day he asked me to be a boy. He had always wanted a boy. Could I give him that? Would I bless him with that gift?"

"My God," Stone said.

I felt sick.

Stone actually got up, came around behind Song, and undid the straps of her straitjacket. He removed the hideous garment and tossed it aside. Song thanked him and moved her arms around, getting her circulation back. Even Detective Stone had a heart, apparently.

"I did what he asked. I hated it, but he was my father and so I became the boy you saw in the video. Xiang was his name. My family was doing well at this point and so Father brought in a teacher for me so I wouldn't have to attend school. Things went well, for the most part. I didn't like being a boy, but Father was happy and that was important. Then one night I sleep-morphed. I blacked out and when I came to I was in the morphing pod and I was a girl again. When Father saw me, he was furious and demanded I turn back right away. But I couldn't. I had just transformed and there was no way I could morph again so soon. Not back then. It takes tremendous energy and I was still immature as a polymorph. Father demanded I hide myself so he wouldn't have to look at me. I did him one better. I ran away and never saw my parents or Shanghai again."

"And Xiang?" Chen said.

"Father had me be Xiang for over a year. Good-looking boy, don't you think? But I hated being a boy, it never felt right. I put him away and I really, truly, honestly thought that was the last of him. I thought of him as just another face I wore, not as a separate personality waiting to take over. But that's what he was, that one day when I sleep-morphed."

Chen let out a long, whistling sigh.

"Did I mention this whole case is one big cluster-fuck?" Stone rumbled. "Just where do we go from here? We've got all the facts laid out nice and neat as you please, but we're in uncharted territory. Of course, there is one big question that remains."

"Oh, you mean why?" said Song. "Why would Xiang rig a bomb to hit me when I was at my most vulnerable?"

"You said he wasn't trying to kill you," said Chen.

"He wasn't."

She looked at each of us in turn before making her pronouncement.

"But I have said enough. I am now claiming my Fifth Amendment right to remain silent."

And so she said nothing more.

10. A Civil Conversation

The wheels of justice rolled their way slowly through the case. I sure as hell wasn't about to press charges. It could no longer be considered a terrorist act or a hate crime (unless it was a self-hate crime). Property damage had been done to the condominium, but that was about it.

New accommodations were found for Song, who was put under house arrest and monitored very closely to ensure Xiang did not reappear. The whole incident was, as Stone so eloquently put it, a cluster-fuck of a case.

I was allowed to visit her during house arrest. I took advantage of the privilege one time. She was in a variation of her Little Asian Lolita form when I arrived at her sparsely furnished new condo.

"I'm still growing, Alex. Feeding frenzy every day, lots of government cheese. It's a slow process, rebuilding lost mass."

She still looked twelve.

"But you could make yourself appear older."

"Maybe I like being a child again," she said. "I feel like a child, in a way. Everything I've been through? I got scared. Come, sit on the couch with me. Does your arm still hurt?"

She tapped my cast with her knuckles.

"It's not bad," I said. "Cast comes off soon, then I'll just have to wear a brace."

I sat with her and she snuggled up to me. I put my arm, the unbroken one, around her and kissed the top of her head. I wanted to protect her from the world. I wanted her to be happy. She looked up at me with soft brown eyes.

She pulled me in for a kiss. I pulled back.

"I can't. Song, you're a little girl."

"I only look like a little girl. Come on, you nasty pervert. Enjoy yourself. I have a perfectly functional cunt."

My heart thundered in my chest as I leaned into her. I saw a child, a twelve-year-old girl, even as I kept reminding myself that this was Song, my sweet Sing Song, the woman I loved, my fiancée.

Our faces came together. I looked into her eyes and she gazed back at me. We were so close I could feel her heat.

She's a child! A little girl!

A wave of revulsion washed through me and I pushed her away and bolted across the condo. She came for me and I actually tripped over a stool trying to get away. She was on top of me in a second, pressing her mouth to mine. I fought her off. It wasn't easy. My arm was almost useless and Song was always incredibly strong.

I literally crawled away and used the knob of her front door to pull myself up. As I was bolting out of her place she screamed something in Chinese.

She was released from house arrest after two months on the stipulation that she report for regular counseling sessions and special psychiatric evaluations. Other than that, Song was allowed to live her life as she chose. Chicago is, after all, a Safe Zone for polymorphs.

We had been through a rough patch together, Song and me. But surely we could move past it. Couldn't we? I thought about all our incredibly good times. I thought about my visit during her house arrest and felt ashamed. I found a language program online and was able to translate what she had screamed at me in Chinese that night: "Daddy, why don't you love me?"

The poor girl had been psychologically shattered and I could probably have handled the situation better. I was determined to make it up to her and to salvage what we had together.

I called and asked to see her and was surprised when she suggested we meet in Greek Town for supper. I did not recognize the lean, angular woman who met me outside the restaurant.

We went in and sat at a corner table.

"You are wondering about my form," she said, filling the silence.

I gazed at the sharp corners of her face and the steely eyes.

"You changed your eyes again."

"Yes."

"And you look . . . very professional, I guess."

"It is a functional look," she said. "I can go out without a lot of men approaching me, hitting on me, bothering me. I've signed up to take classes at Columbia."

"That's wonderful."

If I had seen this person at the museum, I never would have approached her. She looked upon her surroundings with a cold aloofness. She glanced at the brace on my arm with no change of expression.

I felt like an idiot. I looked for signs of that crackling energy that had once buzzed between us. I couldn't find it. I thought about all the incarnations she had taken and all our adventures together.

I looked at her eyes and almost cried.

"I've decided to become a doctor. There will be challenges, of course, but I can overcome them. Did you ever stop to consider what a phenomenal physician a Polymorph Adept would make? We understand internal organs in precise, intimate detail. We have to be very much in touch with our own physiologies in order to transform."

"What about your alter ego? Xiang."

The corners of her mouth rose slightly. Whatever happened to her lunatic smiles and crude laughter? I didn't know this person sitting across from me.

"He is under control. I had to edit him."

"Edit him?"

"I could not allow him to take over again. But on the other hand, he did me a huge favor. It was never his intent to kill me. Remember I told you that I was still evolving? I believe he was trying to kick-start the process. He succeeded, too. When I was under house arrest, I had time to really explore my potential as an Adept. If there is one thing the explosion taught me, it's that I am able to do more than I ever expected. I reverted back to my 'default' body and changed my eyes in the process. My eyes, Alex. We're talking some precise work here, even for an Adept, and under extreme pressure."

I looked at her steely gray eyes. They appeared positively alien. I thought about how strong she was and ice ran through my body.

"If I could change my eyes, how much more difficult could it be to change what lay right behind them? What is the brain, anyway, but another internal organ? What are emotions but neural chemicals being released in response to outward stimuli? I took time to work with these things. I neglected physical transformation and sometimes I came out with a half-formed body, with webbed hands and clubbed feet. That didn't matter. I was changing my core self, Alex. I was changing my feelings, my habits, my attitudes, and not in a psychotherapy sort of way but on an electrochemical level and even a molecular level. Do you understand? I was able to reroute the very pathways of my brain."

"Oh, no, no, no—"

"All my life I loved being a girly-girl. I loved pleasing men. That was how I was raised, how I was conditioned. And it was fine for a time. It was fun. We had fun together, you and I. Didn't we? But it was a dead end. My life revolved around pleasing a man. Xiang saw this, from his cave deep inside me, and he saw that I was holding back rather than going forward."

"Song, what about us?"

"I truly apologize for injuring you, Alex. For everything I put you through." Again, she glanced down at my arm brace. "But you tell me: what about us?"

Our food came. We ate and had a perfectly civil conversation. She used no profanity, made no crude innuendos. There were no Sing Song Moments.

"Do you understand now? My love."

I understood. We couldn't go back to the way we were. There was simply nothing left of that wonderful, homely girl I fell for in front of the diplodocus on that April afternoon.

THE CHURN: A NOVELLA OF THE EXPANSE

James S. A. Corey

Burton was a small, thin, dark-skinned man. He wore immaculately tailored suits, and kept the thick black curls of his hair and the small beard on his chin neatly groomed. That he worked in criminal enterprises said more about the world than about his character. With more opportunities, a more prestigious education, and a few influential dorm mates at upper university, he could have joined the ranks of transplanetary corporate executives with offices at Luna and L-5, Ceres Station and Ganymede. Instead a few neighborhoods at the drowned edge of Baltimore answered to him. An organization of a dozen lieutenants, a couple hundred street-level thugs and knee-breakers, a scattering of drug cooks, identity hackers, dirty cops, and arms dealers followed his dictates. And a class of perhaps a thousand professional victims—junkies, whores, vandals, unregistered children, and others in possession of disposable lives—looked up to him as he might look up at Luna: an icon of power and wealth glowing across an impassable void. A fact of nature.

Burton's misfortune was to be born where and when he was, in a city of scars and vice, in an age when the division in the popular mind was between living on government-funded basic support or having a profession and money of your own. To go from an unregistered birth such as his own to having any power and status at all was an achievement as profound as it was invisible. To the men and women he owned, the fact that he had risen up from among the lowest of the low was not an invitation but a statement of his power and improbability, mythical as the seagull that flew to the moon. Burton himself never thought about it, but the fact that he had managed what he did meant only that it was possible. Anyone who had not had his determination, ruthlessness, and luck deserved pretty much whatever shit he handed to them. It didn't make him sympathetic when someone stepped out of line.

"He . . . what?" Burton said

"Shot him," Oestra said, looking at the table. Around them, the noise of the diner made a white noise that was like privacy.

"Shot. Him."

"Yeah. Austin was talking about how he was good for the money, and how he just needed a few more days. Fefore he could finish, Timmy took that shitty homemade shotgun of his and—" Oestra made a shooting motion with two fingers and a thumb, the movement turning seamlessly into a shrug: a single gesture of violence and apology. Burton leaned back in his chair and looked over at Erich as if to say *I think your puppy peed on my rug.*

Erich had recommended Timmy, had vouched for him, and so was responsible if things went wrong. He leaned forward, resting on his good elbow, hiding his fear with forced casualness. His bad arm, the left, was no longer than a six-year-old's and scarred badly at the joints. His disfigurement was the result of a beating he'd suffered as a child. It wasn't a fact he'd shared with Burton, nor would he mention it now, though it did figure into the calculations that were his life. As did Timmy.

"He had a reason," Erich said.

"He did?" Burton said, raising his eyebrows with feigned patience. "And what was it?"

Erich's stomach knotted. His bad hand closed in a tiny fist. He saw the hardness in Burton's eyes, and it reminded him that even with his knowledge, even with his skills, there were others who could fake identity records. Others who could fake DNA profiles. Others who could do for Burton what he did. He was expendable. It was the message Burton meant him to take.

"I don't know," he said. "But I've known Timmy since forever, yeah? He doesn't do anything unless there's a reason."

"Well," Burton said, pulling the word out to two syllables. "If it's since *forever*, I guess that makes it all right."

"Just, you know, if he did that, he did it for something."

Oestra scratched his arm, scowling to hide the relief he felt at Burton's focus turning to Erich. "I got him in the storage room."

Burton stood up, pushing back his chair with the backs of his knees. The waitress made a point not to look at the three as they moved across the room and out though the doors marked EMPLOYEES ONLY, Burton and then Oestra and Erich limping at the back. She didn't even start cleaning the table until she was sure they were gone.

The storage room was claustrophobic to begin with and lined with boxes making it even smaller. Cream-colored degradable storage boxes with flat green readouts on the side that listed what they contained and whether the cheap, disposable sensor in the foam had detected rot and corruption. The table in the craped open space at the center was pressed particleboard, as much glue as wood. Timmy sat at it, the LED fixture overhead throwing the shadow of his brow down into his eyes. He'd hardly started his second decade of life, but the red-brown hair was already receding from his forehead. He was strong, tall, and had an unnerving capacity for stillness. He looked up when the three men came in, dividing his smile equally among his childhood friend, the professional thug he'd just disappointed, and the thin, well-dressed man who controlled everything important in his life.

"Hey," Timmy said to any of them.

Erich moved to sit at the table, saw that Oestra and Burton were standing motionless, and pulled back. If Timmy noticed, he didn't say anything.

"I hear that you killed Austin," Burton said.

"Yup," Timmy said. The empty smile changed not at all.

Burton pulled the chair opposite Timmy out and sat. Oestra and Erich carefully didn't look at each other or at Burton. The object of all their attention, Timmy waited amiably for whatever came next.

"You care to tell me why you did that?" Burton asked.

"It's what you said to do," Timmy said.

"That man owed me money. I told you to get whatever you could from him. This was your try-out, little man. This was your game. Now how do you go from what I actually *said* to what you *did*?"

"I got whatever I could get," Timmy replied. There was no fear in his voice or his expression, and it left Burton with the sense he was talking to an idiot. "I couldn't get money out of that guy. He didn't have any. If he had, he'd have given it to you. Only thing you were getting from him was a way to make sure everyone else pays you on time. So I took that instead."

"Really?"

"Yup."

"You're positive—you're *convinced*—that Austin wouldn't have gotten my money?"

"I don't mean to second-guess why anybody gave it to him in the first place," Timmy said, "but that guy never met a dollar he didn't snort, shoot, or drink."

"So you thought it through, and you came to the conclusion that the wise and right thing to do was escalate this little visit from a collection run to a murder?"

Timmy's head tilted a degree. "Didn't spend a lot of time thinking about it. Water's wet. Sky's up. Austin gets you more dead than alive. Kind of obvious."

Burton went silent. Oestra and Erich didn't look at him. Burton rubbed his hands together, the hiss of palm against palm the loudest noise in the room. Timmy scratched his leg and waited, neither patient nor impatient. Erich felt a growing nausea and the certainty that he was about to watch and old friend and protector die in front of him. His stunted hand opened and closed and he tried not to swallow. When Burton smiled his small, amused smile, the only one who saw it was Timmy, and if he understood it, he didn't react.

"Why don't you wait here, little man," Burton said.

"Arright," Timmy said, and Burton was already walking out the door.

Out in the café, the lunch rush had started. The booths and tables were filled, and a crowd loitered in the doorway, scowling at the waitresses, the diners who had gotten tables before them, and the empty place reserved for Burton and whoever he chose to have near him. As soon as he took his chair, the waitress came over, her eyebrows raised, as if he were a new customer. He waved her away. There was something about sitting at an empty table in full view of hungry men and women that Burton enjoyed. *What you want, I can take or I can leave*, it said. *All I want is to keep your options for myself.* Erich and Oestra sat.

"That boy," Burton said, letting the words take on an affected drawl, "is some piece of work."

"Yeah," Oestra said.

"He's good at what he does," Erich said. "He'll get better."

Burton was quiet for a long moment. A man at the front door pointed an angry finger toward Burton's table, demanding something of the waitress. She took the stranger's hand and pushed it down. The angry man left. Let him go. If he didn't know any better, this wasn't the place for him.

"Erich, I don't think I can take your friend off his probation period. Not with this. Not yet."

Erich nodded, the urge to speak for Timmy and the fear of losing Burton's fickle forgiveness warring in his throat. Oestra was the one to break the silence.

"You want to give him another job?" The words carried a weight of incredulity measured to the gram.

"The right job," Burton said. "Right one for now, anyway. You say he watched out for you, growing up?"

"He did," Erich said.

"Let him do that, then. Timmy's going to be your personal bodyguard on your next job. Keep you out of trouble. See if you can keep him out of trouble too. At least do better than Oey did with him, right?" Burton said and laughed. A moment later Oestra laughed too, only a little sourly. Erich couldn't manage much more than a sick, relieved grin.

"I'll tell him," Erich said. "I'll take care of it."

"Do," Burton said, smiling. An awkward moment later, Erich got up, head bobbing like a bird's with gratitude and discomfort. Burton and Oestra watched him limp back toward the storage room. Oestra sighed.

"I don't know why you're cultivating that freak," Burton's lieutenant said.

"He's off the grid and he cooks good identity docs," Burton said. "I like having someone who can't be traced keeping my name clean."

"I don't mean the cripple. I mean the other one. Seriously, there's something wrong with that kid."

"I think he's got potential."

"Potential for what?"

"Exactly?" Burton said. "Okay, so tell me the rest. What's going on out there?"

Oestra hoisted his eyebrows and hunched forward, elbows on the table. The kids running unlicensed games by the waterfront weren't coming up with the usual take. One of the brothels had been hit by a case of antibiotic-resistant syphilis; one of the youngest boys, a five-year-old, had it in his eyes. Burton's neighbor to the north—an Earthbound branch of the Loca Griega—were seeing raids on their drug manufacturing houses. Burton listened with his eyelids at half-mast. Individually, no one event mattered much, but put together, they were the first few fat raindrops in a coming storm. Oestra knew it too.

By the time the lunch rush ended, the booths and tables filling and emptying in the systole and diastole of the day's vast urban heart, Burton's mind was on a dozen other things. Erich and Timmy and the death of a small-time deadbeat weren't forgotten, but no particular importance was put on them either. That was what it meant to be Burton: those things which could rise up to fill a small person's whole horizon were only small parts of his view. He was the boss, the city, the big-picture man. Like Baltimore itself, he *weathered* storms.

Time had not been kind to the city. Its coastline was a ruin of drowned buildings kept from salvage by a complexity of rights, jurisdictions, regulations, and apathy until the sea had all but reclaimed them for its own. The Urban Arcology movement had peaked there a decade or two before the technology existed to make its dreams of vast, sustainable structures a reality. It had left a wall seven miles long and twenty stories high of decaying hope and structural resin that reached from the beltway to Lake Montebello. At the street level, electric networks laced the roadways, powering and guiding the vehicles that could use them. Sparrows Island stood out in the waves like a widow watching the sea for a ship that would never come home, and Federal Hill scowled back at the city across shallow, filthy water, emperor of its own abandoned land.

Everywhere, all through the city, space was at a premium. Extended families lived in decaying apartments designed for half as many, men and women who couldn't escape the cramped space spent their days at the screens of their terminals, watching newsfeeds and dramas and pornography and living on the textured protein and enriched rice of basic. For most, their forays into crime were halfhearted, milquetoast affairs—a backroom brewer making weak, unregulated beer; a few kids stealing a neighbor's clothes or breaking their furniture; a band of scavengers with scrounged tools harvesting metal from the buried infrastructure of the city that had been. Baltimore was Earth writ small, crowded and bored. Its citizens were caught between the dismal life of basic and the barriers of class, race and opportunity, vicious competition and limited resources, that kept all but the most driven from a profession and actual currency. The dictates of the regional administration in Chicago filtered down to the streets slowly, and the local powers might be weaker than the government, but they were also closer; the gravities of law and lawlessness finding their balance point somewhere just north of Lansdowne.

Time had not been kind to Lydia either. She wasn't one of the unregistered, but very little of what was important in her life appeared in the government records. There, she was a name—not Lydia—and an address where she had never lived. Her real home was four rooms on the fifth floor of a minor arcology looking out over the harbor. Her real work was keeping track of inventory for Liev, one of Burton's lieutenants. Before that, she had been his lover. Before that, she had been a whore in his stable. Before that, she had been someone else who she could hardly remember anymore. When she was alone, and she was often alone, the narrative she told herself was of how lucky she was. She'd escaped basic, she had dear friends and mentors when she was working, she'd been able to retire up in the ad hoc structure of the city's underworld. Many, many people hadn't been anywhere near as fortunate as she had been. She was growing old, yes. There was gray in her hair now. Lines at the corners of her eyes, the first faint liver spots on the backs of her hands. She told herself they were the evidence of her success. Too many of her friends had never had them. Never would. Her life had been a patchwork of love and violence, and the overlap was vast.

Still, she hung warm-colored silk across her windows and wore the silver bells at her ankles and wrists that were the fashion among much younger women. Life, such as it was, was good.

The evening sun hung over the rooftops to the west, the late summer heat thickening the air. Lydia was in the little half-kitchen warming up a bowl of frozen hummus when the door chimed and the bolts clacked open. Timmy came in, lifting his chin in greeting. She smiled back, lifting an eyebrow. There was no one with him, and there never would be. They had never allowed someone else to be with them when they were together. Not since the night his mother had died.

"So, how did it go?"

"Kind of fucked it up, me," Timmy said.

Lydia's heart went tight and she tried to keep her voice calm and light. "How so?"

"Burton told me to get what I could out of this guy. Looking back, I think he just meant money. So." Timmy leaned against the couch, hands deep in his pockets, and shrugged. "Oops."

"Was Burton angry?"

Timmy looked away and shrugged. With that motion, she could see him again as he'd been as a teenager, as a child, as a baby. She had known his mother when they'd worked together, each watching out for the other when they turned tricks. Lydia had been there the night Timmy was born among the worn tiles and cold lights of the black market clinic. She'd made him soup the night Liev had turned him out for the first time and, while he ate, told him lies about her first time with a john to make him laugh. She'd picked music with him for his mother's memorial and told him that she'd died the way she'd lived, and not to blame himself. She had never been able to protect him from anything, so she'd helped him live in the jagged world, and he gave her something she couldn't describe or define but that she needed like a junkie craved the needle.

"How angry is he?" she asked, carefully.

"Not that bad. I'm gonna be watching Erich's back for a while. He's got some things need doing, and the boss doesn't want anything going pear-shaped. So that's all right."

"And you? How are you?"

"Eh. I'm good," Timmy said. "I think I'm maybe coming down with something. Flu, maybe."

She walked out from the kitchen, her food abandoned, and put the back of her hand to his forehead. His skin felt cool.

"No fever," she said.

"Probably nothing," he said, pulling his shirt up over his head. "I got the shakes a little, and I got dizzy a couple times on the way back. It ain't serious."

"What happened to the man Burton sent you to?"

"I shot him."

"Did you kill him?" Lydia asked as she walked back to her bedroom. The ruddy light of sunset filtered through yellow silk. An old armoire stood against one wall, its silver finish stained and corroded by years. The bed was the same cheap foam queen-sized she'd had when she was working, the sheets old and thin, softer than skin with wear.

"Used a shotgun about a meter from his chest," Timmy said, following her. "Could have stuck your fist through the hole. So, yeah, pretty much."

"Have you ever killed a man before?" she asked, lifting her dress up over her thighs, her hips, her head. Timmy undid his belt, frowning. "Don't know. Beat some guys pretty bad. Maybe some of 'em didn't get back up, but no one I know about. You know, not for sure."

Lydia unhooked her bra, letting it slide to the cheap carpet. Timmy took his pants down, kicking them off with his shoes. He didn't wear underwear, and his erect penis bobbed in the air like it belonged to someone else. There was no desire in his expression, and only a mild distress.

"Timmy," she said, laying back on the bed and lifting her hips. "You aren't getting ill. You're traumatized."

"Y'think?" He seemed genuinely surprised by the thought. And then amused by it. "Yeah, maybe. Huh."

He pulled her underwear down to her knees, her ankles. "My poor Timmy," she murmured.

"Ah shit," he said, lowering his body onto hers. "I'm all
right. At least I'm not getting sick."

Sex held few mysteries for Lydia. She had fucked and been fucked by more men than she could count, and she'd learned things from each of them. Ugly things sometimes. Sometimes beautiful. She understood on a deep, animal level that sex was like music or language. It could express anything. Love, yes. Or anger, or bitterness, or despair. It could be a way to grieve or a way to take revenge. It could be a weapon or a nightmare or a solace. Sex was meaningless, and so it could mean anything.

What she and Timmy did to and for and with each other's bodies wasn't a thing they discussed. She felt no shame about it. That other people would see only the perversion of a woman and the boy she'd helped raise pleasuring one another meant that other people would never understand what it mean to *be* them, to survive the world they survived. They were not lovers, and never would be. They were not surrogate mother and incestuous son. She was Lydia, and he was Timmy. In the bent and broken world, what they did fit. It was more than most people had.

After, Timmy lay beside her, his breath still coming in small, reflexive gulps. Her body felt pleasantly tender and bruised. The yellow over the window was fading into twilight, and the rumble of air traffic was like constant thunder in the distance, or a city being shelled two valleys over. A transport ship for one of the orbital stations, maybe. Or a wing of atmospheric fighter planes on exercises. So long as she didn't look, she could pretend it was anything. Her mind wandered, delivering up what had been nagging at her since Timmy had told her all that had happened.

Burton had sent Timmy to collect a debt, Timmy had killed the man instead, and Burton hadn't cut him loose. Two points defined a line, but three defined the playing field. Burton didn't always have need of boys like Timmy, but sometimes, he did. Right now, he did.

Lydia sighed.

The churn was coming. It was the name Liev had given it, back before. All of nature had its rhythms, its booms and busts. She and Timmy and Liev and Burton were mammals, they were part of nature, and subject to its rules and whims. She had lived through perhaps three, perhaps four such catastrophes before. Enough that she knew the signs. Like a squirrel gathering food before a hard winter, Burton collected violent men before the churn. When it came, there would be blood and death and prison sentences and maybe even a curfew for a time. Men like Timmy would die by the dozen, sacrificed for things they didn't know or understand. Maybe even some of Burton's lieutenants would fall the way Tanner Ford had back when she'd been Liev's lover. Or Stacey Li before him. Or Cutbreath. The history of her corrupted world echoed with the names of the dead; the expendable and the expended. If Burton had kept Timmy on, it was because he thought it was coming. And if Burton thought it was coming, it probably was.

Timmy's breath was low and deep and regular. He sounded like a man asleep, except his eyes were open and fixed on the ceiling. Her own skin was cool now, the sweat dried or nearly so. A fly swooped through the air above them, a grey dot tracing a jagged path, turning and dodging to avoid dangers that weren't there. She lifted her first two fingers, cocked back her thumb, and made the thin cartoon shooting sound with her teeth and tongue. The insect flew on, undisturbed by her small and violent fantasy. She turned her head to look at Timmy. His expression was blank and empty. He was still, and even in the warmth that followed orgasm, there was a tension in his body. He wasn't a beautiful boy. He'd never be a beautiful man.

Some day, she thought, *I will lose him. He will go off on some errand and he will never come back. I won't even know what happened to him.* She probed at the thought like a tongue-tip against the sore gum where a tooth has been knocked out. It hurt and hurt badly, but it hadn't happened yet, and so she could bear it. Best to prepare herself now. Meditate upon the coming loss so that when it came, she was ready.

Timmy's eyes clicked over toward her without his head shifting at all, without any expression coming to his face. Lydia smiled a slow, languorous smile.

"What are you thinking?" she asked.

He didn't answer.

The catastrophe began four days later. Quietly, and with near-military precision, the city opened a contract with Star Helix security. Soldiers from across the globe arrived in small groups, and sat through debriefings. The plan to end the criminal networks operating in Baltimore would be announced after the fact, or at least after the first wave. The thought, widely lauded by the self-congratulatory minds in administration, was to take the criminal element by surprise. In catching them flat-footed, the security teams could cripple their networks, break their power, and restore peace and the rule of law. The several unexamined assumptions in the argument remained unexamined, and the body armor and riot control weapons were distributed in perfect confidence that the enforcers would arrive unanticipated.

In fact, what Burton and Lydia knew from experience, many, many others felt by instinct. There was a discomfort in the streets and alleys, on the rooftops, and behind the locked doors. The city knew that something was near. The only surprise would be in the details.

Erich felt it like an itch he couldn't scratch. He sat on the rotting concrete curb, drumming the fingers of his good hand against his kneecap. The street around him was the usual mix of foot traffic, bicycles, and wide-framed blue buses. The air stank. The sewage lines this near the water were prone to failures. A few doors to the east, a group of children were playing some kind of complex game with linked headsets, their arms and legs falling into and out of phase with each other. Timmy stood on the sidewalk, squinting up into the sky. Behind them was a squatter's camp in an old ferroconcrete apartment block. In a locked room at its center, Erich's custom deck set up and primed, connected to the network and prepared to create a new identity from birth records to DNA matching to backdated newsfeed activity for the client, as soon as she arrived. Assuming she arrived. She was fifteen minutes late and, though they had no way to know it, already in custody.

Timmy grunted and pointed up. Erich followed the gesture. Far above, a star burned in the vast oceanic blue, a plume of fire pushing a ship out of the atmosphere. Near the horizon, the half moon glowed pale, a network of city lights crossing the shadowy meridian.

"Transport," Erich said. "They use mass drivers for the stuff that can take the gees."

"I know," Timmy said.

"Ever want to go up there?"

"What for?"

"I don't know," Erich said, staring down the street for the client. He'd seen her picture: a tall Korean woman with blue hair. He didn't know who she'd been before, and he didn't much care. Burton wanted her made into someone new. "Piss out the window and make everyone down here think it was raining, maybe."

Timmy's chuckle sounded polite.

"It's what I'd do, if I could," Erich said, making a swooping gesture with his good hand. Zoom. "Get up the well and out of here. Go where no one cares about who you are so long as you're good at what you do. Seriously, it's the wild fucking west up there. You want nineteenth-century Tombstone, Arizona, it's alive and well on Ceres Station. From what I heard anyway."

"Why don't you go, then?" Timmy said. With a different intonation, it could have been dismissive. Instead it was only a mild kind of curiosity. It was part of what Erich liked about Timmy. There was almost nothing he seemed to feel deeply.

"Starting from here? I'd never make it. I'm not even a registered birth."

"You could tell them," Timmy said. "People get registered all the time."

"And then they get tracked and monitored and wind up dying on basic," Erich said. "Anyway, no one's taking me for a vocational. Waiting lists for that are eight, ten years long. By the time I came up, I'd have aged out."

"Could build one, couldn't you?" Timmy asked. "Make a new identity and put it at the front of the list?"

"Maybe," Erich said. "If you gave me a couple years to layer it all in like I did for Burton. He can go *anywhere* with the docs I built for him."

"So why don't you go, then?" Timmy asked again, his inflection as much an echo as his words.

"Guess I don't want it bad enough. Anyway, I've got real stuff to do, right? I wish she'd fucking get here, right?" Erich said, unaware that he made everything a question when he wanted to change the subject. Unconsciously, Erich made a fist with the hand of his bad arm. Timmy nodded, squinting down the street for the client that wasn't coming.

Most of their lives had been spent on streets like this. The trade that exploited prostitutes and their illegal children was the second largest source of unregistered births on the planet. Only religious radicals accounted for more. It was impossible to know how many unregistered men and women were eking out lives on the margin of society in Baltimore or how many had lived and died unknown to the vast UN databases. Erich knew of perhaps a hundred scattered among the legitimate citizens like members of a secret society. They congregated in condemned buildings and squats, traded in the gray-market economy of unlicensed services, and used their peculiar anonymity where it was most helpful. Looking down the pocked asphalt street, Erich could count three or four people that he personally knew were ghosts in the great world machine. Counting him and Timmy, that was half a dozen all breathing the same air while the plume of the orbital transport marked the sky gold and black above them. There was old water in the gutters, black circles of gum and tar on the sidewalk, the combined smell of urine and decay and ocean all around them. Erich looked up at the sky with a longing he resented.

He knew himself well enough to recognize that he was a man of desires and grudges, so well in fact that he'd come to peace with it. The blackness of space where merit counted more than the placement on a bureaucrat's list, where the brothels were licensed and the prostitutes had a union, where freedom was a ship and a crew and enough work to pay for food and air. It called to him with a romance that made his heart ache. On Ceres or Tycho or Mars, the medical technology was available to regrow his crippled arm, to remake his shortened leg. The same technology could be found fewer than eight miles from the filthy curb where he sat, but with the triple barriers of being unregistered, basic medical care waiting lists, and his own ability to function despite his disabilities, space was closer. Out there, he could be the man he could have been. The thought was like the promise of sex to a teenager, rich and powerful and frightening. Erich had resolved a thousand times to make the effort, to build himself an escape identity and shrug off the chains of Earth, of Baltimore, of the life he'd lived. And a thousand and one times, he had postponed it.

"Get up," Timmy said.

"You see her?" Erich said.

"Nope. Get up."

Erich shifted, frowning. Timmy was looking east with an expression of mild curiosity, a casual witness at someone else's wreck. Erich stood. At the intersection a block down, two armored vans had pulled to a stop. The logo on their sides was a four-pointed star. Erich couldn't tell if the people getting out were men or women, only that they were wearing riot gear. Metallic fear flooded his mouth. Timmy put a strong hand on his shoulder and pushed him gently but implacably across the street. Two more vans came to a halt at the intersection to the north.

"What the fuck?" Erich said, his voice distant and shrill in his own ears.

Timmy got him across the street and almost up to the doors of a five-story squat before Erich pulled back. "My deck. My setup. We've got to go back for it."

A deep, inhuman voice broke the air, the syllables designed in a sound lab to be sharp, clear, and intimidating. *This is a security alert. Remain where you are with your hands visible until security personnel clear you to leave. This is a security alert.* At the intersection, teams of armored figures were already questioning three men. One of the civilians—a thin, angry man with close-cropped black hair and dark olive skin—shouted something, and the security team pushed him to his knees. The biometric scan—fingerprints, retina scan, fast-match DNA—took seconds while the man's arms were held out at his sides, his elbows bent back in restraint holds.

"I think maybe you used to have a deck," Timmy said. "I don't think you got one right now."

Erich stood unmoving, caught between the animal urge to flee and to protect himself by hiding the evidence. Timmy's thick fingers closed around his good shoulder. The big man's expression was mildly concerned. "We don't go right now, they're gonna have you and it both. I sorta screwed up the last thing Burton told me to do. Let's not burn my second chance getting you caught."

This is a security alert. Remain where you are with your hands visible until security personnel clear you to leave.

Erich swallowed and nodded. It was the nearest he could come to speech. Timmy turned him toward the squat and pushed him forward.

In the streets, the security teams converged slowly, moving from person to person, door to door, floor to floor. Before the operation was through, they would identify three hundred forty-three people and detain four who appeared in the operational database as persons of interest. Three unregistered individuals would be identified, entered into the system, and held pending investigation. The two of the unregistered who refused to provide a name would be have names assigned to them. The operation, covering three city blocks, would locate an unlicensed medical clinic, three children in distressed circumstances, seven pounds of S-class psychoactives, eighty-two instances of illegal occupation, and the network interface deck and data collection setup that the blue-haired detainee had offered up in exchange for a reduced penalty. The process would take ten hours, and so it was still hardly underway when Timmy and Erich emerged from the undocumented access tunnel that connected the squat with an abandoned pumping station. They walked together, Erich with his good hand stuffed deep in his pocket, Timmy with the same amiable air that was his default. Erich was weeping silently. Above them, the transport ship was gone, the golden exhaust plume now only a streak of smoke against the sky.

"I'm dead," Erich said. "Burton's going to fucking kill me. They got my deck. They got everything."

"Wait a minute," Timmy said. "*Everything* everything? Burton's stuff was on the—"

"No. I'm not stupid. I don't store records of how I keep Burton clean. But I didn't wash it down after the setup. I was going to do it after we were done. It's going to have DNA on it. Shit, it may even have fingerprints. I don't know."

"So what if it does?" Timmy asked with a shrug. "You're not in the system."

"Not now," Erich said. "But if they pick me up ever, for *anything*, it's going to be with a little highlight alert linking back to that fucking deck. They'll know what I do. And then they'll know to ask."

"You don't gotta say anything," Timmy said, his tone almost apologetic.

"I won't get a chance. Burton finds out they've got my DNA, all he's gonna see is a path back to him. I'm a loose end, man. I'm dead."

All around the city, traps shut.

In the north, five dozen armored security personnel blocked intersections and shut down metro stations. The door-to-door search and control operation converged on a seven-story office building controlled by the Loca Griega. The local men and women took shelter where they could, hiding in bathtubs and basements and soot-caked hard-brick fireplaces. Things dense enough to hopefully block the infrared and backscatter and heartbeat sensors Star Helix carried. Network signals went dark. The Star Helix employees moved forward in tight formation, forced to use their eyes instead of their tech, the plates of armor on their chests and backs and bellies making them seem like vast beetles in the autumn sunlight. When the perimeter around the building was established, monitoring stations were constructed, watching the windows for the vibrations made by voices. A wave of dragonfly-small surveillance drones swept in, and for a moment it seemed like perhaps the violence wouldn't come. And then, as one, the hundreds of small, cheap Star Helix robots fell to the ground, victims of Loca Griega countermeasures, and the building bloomed with gunfire. Seventeen Loca Griega died before the sun went down, including Eduard Hopkins and Jehona Dzurban, reputed to be the Earth-surface coordinators of the Belt-based syndicate. The plume of smoke that rose from the building darkened the air for hours and left the city air gray and hazy the next morning.

At the same time in the west, where the municipal limits gave way invisibly to the regional jurisdiction, a warehouse owned and operated through a complex web of shell companies was locked down. The security teams emptied a three-block radius using a small fleet of armored buses and an operational procedure designed for response to sarin gas attacks. When the warehouse's perimeter was breached shortly before midnight, it contained ten thousand unrecorded assault rifles, half a million rounds of tracer-free ammunition, seventy cases of grenades, and a computer room ankle deep in melted slag. There was no evidence of anyone having been present in the warehouse, and no trail of ownership for any of it.

Checkpoints at the evacuated rail terminal, the spaceport, and the docks identified seventy people traveling on falsified accounts. All of them were independents or small fry in a larger organization. The security forces hadn't expected to catch anyone high on their priorities list in the first pass. The more powerful, better-connected targets were either smart enough not to travel during a crackdown or else had cleaned accounts to move under. Instead, the thought was that among the small-time thugs and operatives, there might be one or two desperate and foolish enough to provide them a lead to someone bigger. Someone worth having. And so without knowing who Burton was, what he looked like, his name or description or precise role in the criminal ecology of Baltimore, they were hunting him. And they were also hunting others, many of them much higher-priority than himself. Organizace Bayyo had a presence in the city, as did the Golden Bough. Tamara Sluydan controlled several blocks north of the arcology, and Baasen Tagniczen an area twice Burton's—though not so profitably run—in the Patapsco Valley Housing Complex. There was a great deal of crime, organized and otherwise, for the forces of law to concern themselves with, and no net was so strong or fine that nothing slipped through.

In times like these, when he couldn't know whether he had been compromised, Burton played it safe. He had half a dozen apartments and warehouses outfitted to act as temporary command centers, and he moved between them almost at random. Some of his people, he knew, would be caught up. Some of those who were would buy short-term leniency with the coin of information. He knew that would happen, and he had plans in place that would protect him from discovery, obscure his involvement in anything actionable, and punish brutally and irrevocably whoever had chosen to make that trade. It was understood that anyone captured would be wiser to trade their own underlings to the security forces than to sell out Burton. The risk devolved on the little guy. Shit rolling downhill, as it had since the beginning of time. Which was, in part, why what happened to Liev was so unfortunate for everybody.

Liev Andropoulous had worked for Burton since coming to Baltimore from Paris more than twenty years before. He was a thickly built man, as round in the chest as the belly, and strong enough that he rarely had to prove it. His appetite for women occasioned jokes, though rarely the sort made in front of him, as did his habit of placing his long-term lovers in positions of comfort within his organization when he ended their relationships. As one of Burton's lieutenants, he oversaw three full-time whorehouses, a small network of drug dealers specializing in low-end narcotics and psychoactives, and an unlicensed medical facility that catered to the unregistered population. By custom, he worked from a small concrete building at the edge of the water, but when the churn began, he was leaving his lover's apartment on Pratt. The woman's name was Katie, and she had the olive skin and brown lips that Lydia had had twenty years before. Liev was a man of deep habits and consistent tastes. His kissed her goodbye for the last time on the street outside the apartment building, then walked away to the north while she went south. It was a perfunctory gesture, meaningful only in retrospect, as so many last kisses are.

The streets were crowded, the air muggy and close. The saltwater and rotting fish smells of the encroaching Atlantic were omnipresent, as they always were on hot days. Private transport wasn't allowed, and the lumbering buses moved like slow elephants in the press of midday bodies. A beggar plucked at Liev's sleeve and then backed away in fear when Liev turned to scowl at him. In the cacophony of the city, the whine of the flying drones should have been inaudible, but something caught Liev's attention, tightening the skin across the back of his wide neck. His footsteps faltered.

From above, the ripples in the crowd would have looked like the surface of still water disturbed by the convergence of half a dozen fish intent on the same fly. For Liev, it was only a sense of dread, a burst of useless adrenaline, and the offended shouts of the civilians pushed aside by the armored security men. As if by magic, a bubble of open space appeared around him. Liev could see clearly the scuffed and stained concrete on which he walked. The man in the Star Helix uniform before him held a pistol in both hands, the barrel fixed on Liev's chest. Center of mass. By the books. Behind the helmet's clear face shield, the man looked to be somewhere in his middle twenties, focused and frightened. Liev felt a pang of amusement and regret. He held his arms out at his sides, cruciform, as five more security men boiled out of the gawking crowd.

"Liev Andropoulous!" the boy shouted. "You are under arrest for racketeering, slavery, and murder! You are not required to participate in questioning without the presence of an attorney or union representative!" Tiny flecks of spittle dotted the inside of the face shield. The boy's wide eyes were almost jittering with fear. Liev sighed.

"Ask me," he said slowly, enunciating very clearly, "if I understand."

"What?" the boy shouted.

"You've told me the charges and made the questioning statement. Now you have to ask me if I understand."

"Do you understand?" the boy barked, and Liev nodded.

"Good. Better," Liev said. "Now go fuck yourself."

The prisoner transport blatted its siren, shouldering its way through the crowd, but before it had crossed the distance to Liev, before he had been slotted into the steel cell and made secure, news of his capture was radiating out through the neighborhood. By the time the transport began moving again, making its way north toward the nearest tactical center, Burton had already seen a recording of the arrest. Katie, sitting at a noodle café with her little brother, got the news on her hand terminal and broke down weeping. Dread passed through the network of Liev's employees and underlings. Everyone knew what would happen next, and what would not. Liev would be taken to a holding cell, processed, and interrogated. If he kept quiet, he would be remanded to state custody, tried, and sent to a detention center, likely in North Africa or the west coast of Australia. More likely, he would cut a deal, parting out the network of crime he'd controlled bit by bit in exchange for clemency—the names and ID numbers of his pimps in order to serve his time in North America or Asia, the details of how he laundered the money for a private cell, which physicians had moonlighted in his clinic for library access.

They would ask him who he worked for, and he wouldn't say.

For Burton's other lieutenants, it complicated the future and simplified the present. One of their own was gone and unlikely to return. When the worst had passed and something like normalcy returned to Burton's little kingdom, business that had been Liev's would be shared among them, granted to some newly promoted member of the criminal nobility, or a combination of the two. How exactly that played out would be the subject of weeks of negotiations and struggle, but later. Later. In the short term, all such agendas gave way to the more immediate problems of avoiding the security forces, protecting the assets they had, and making it very clear to everyone under them that selling out information for the favor of the court's mercy was a very, very bad idea.

In a basement lab at the corner of Lexington and Greene, eighty gallons of reagents used in alkaloid synthesis were poured into the water recycling stream. At the locally renowned Boyer Street house, two overly talkative prostitutes went quietly missing and the doors were locked. The body of Mikel "Batman" Chanduri was discovered in his two-room apartment at sundown, and though it was clear his death had been both violent and protracted, none of his neighbors had anything to report to the security men who'd come to interview him. Before the sun had set, Burton's lieutenants—Cyrano, Oestra, Simonson, Little Cole, and the Ragman—went to ground like foxes, ready to wait out the worst of the crackdown, each hoping that they would not be another gap in the organization like Liev, and each hoping that the others—not all, of course, but a few—would. One or two, perhaps even three, harbored some plots of their own, ways to see that their rivals within Burton's organization fell prey to the dangers of the churn. But they didn't speak of them to anyone they didn't trust with their lives.

And in an unlicensed rooftop coffee bar that looked down over the human-packed streets, Erich hunched over a gray-market network deck the owner had bolted to the table. He was trying to keep his panic from showing, wondering if Burton had heard about the capture of his deck, and hoping that wherever Timmy had rushed off to when they'd heard of Liev's arrest, he'd get back soon. The coffee was black and bitter, and Erich couldn't tell if the coppery flavor was a problem with the beans or the lingering taste of fear. He sat on his newsfeed, set to passive for fear that his search requests would be traced, and watched as all around him more traps snapped shut, his gut knotting tighter with every one.

When Lydia heard what had happened to Liev, her first action was to put on her makeup and style her long, gray-streaked hair. She sat at the mirror in her bedroom and rubbed on the flesh-toned base until the lines in her skin were gone. She painted her lips fuller and darker and redder than they had ever been in nature. The black eyeliner, reddish eyeshadow, rust-colored blush. Despite the danger she was in, she didn't hurry. A lifetime of experience had drawn connections in her mind that linked sexual desirability, fear, and fatalism in ways she would have recognized as unhealthy if she'd seen them in someone else. She pulled her hair around, piling it high and pinning it in place until it cascaded, three-quarters contained, to her shoulders in the style Liev had enjoyed back when he had lifted her up from the working population of the house and made her his own. She thought of it as a last act of fidelity, like dressing a corpse.

She shrugged out of her robe and pulled on simple, functional clothes. Running shoes. Her go-bag was a nondescript blue backpack with a three-month supply of her medications, two changes of clothes, four protein bars, a pistol, two boxes of ammunition, a bottle of water, and three thousand dollars spread across half a dozen credit chips. She pulled it down from the top of her closet, and without opening it to check its contents, went to the chair by her front window. The curtains were pale gauze that scattered and softened the afternoon light, graying everything. She pulled a sheer yellow scarf over her hair, swathed her neck, and tied it at her sternum, the ironic echo of her old hijab. Then sat very still, feet side by side, ankles and knees touching. Primly, she thought. She waited in silence to see who would open her door, a security team or Timmy. The darkness, or else the light.

The better part of an hour passed. Her spine hurt, and she savored the pain, keeping her face placid. Smiles or grimaces, either one would disturb her makeup. Then footsteps in the hall, like someone clearing their throat. The door opened, and Timmy stepped in. His gaze flicked down to her back, up to her face. He shrugged and nodded to the hall in a gesture that said, *Can we go?* as clearly as words. Lydia stood, pulled on her pack as she walked to the door, and left her room for the last time. She had lived there for the better part of a decade. The necklace that Liev had given her the night he'd told her he was moving on, but that she would be cared for, hung from a peg in the bathroom. The cheap earthenware cup that Timmy had painted with glaze when he was eight years old and given her for what he'd mistakenly thought was her birthday remained in the cupboard. The half-finished knitting that an old roommate had left when she disappeared twenty years before sat hunched in a plastic bag under the bed, stinking of dust.

Lydia didn't look back.

"My spirit animal is the snake," she said as they walked south together. They went side by side, but not touching. "I shed my skin. I just let it slough away."

"Okay," Timmy said. "Come on this way. I got a thing waiting."

The waterline was cleanest near the new port. There, the ships and houseboats rested in clean slips made of flexible ceramic and the bones of the drowned buildings had been cut free and hauled away. With every mile farther from the port, the debris grew less picturesque, the charm of the reclaimed city giving way to the debris of its authentic past. Little beaches formed over asphalt, gray sand swirling around old blocky concrete pillars standing in the waves green with algae and white with bird shit. The stink of rot came from the soupy water and the corpses of jellyfish melting where the tide had left them.

Timmy's boat was small. White paint flaked off the metal where it hadn't been scraped well enough before being repainted. Lydia sat in the bow, her legs folded under her, her chin high and proud. The motor was an under-the-waterline pulse drive, quiet as a hum. The water in their wake was louder. The sun was near to setting, the city casting its shadow on the waves. A handful of other boats were on the water, manned by children for the most part. The citizens of basic with nothing better to do with their time than spend the twilight on the water, then go home.

Timmy ran them along the coast for a time, and then turned east, out toward the vast ocean. The moon had set, but the lights of the city were bright enough to travel by. The islands had once been part of the city itself, and now were ruins. Timmy aimed for one of the smaller, a stretch not more than two city blocks long by three wide humped up out of the water. A few ancient walls still stood. The boat ran up onto the hard shore, and Timmy jumped out, soaking his pants to the thighs, to pull it the rest of the way up. The metal screeched against the rotting concrete sidewalk.

The ruin he led her to was little more than a campsite. A bright yellow emergency-preparedness sleeping bag lay unrolled on a foam mattress. An LED lamp squatted beside it with a cord snaking up the grimy wall to a solar collector in the window. A small chemical camping stove stood on a driftwood board placed over two cinder blocks, a little unpowered refrigerator beside it to store food. Two more rooms stood empty through the doorway. If the house had ever had a kitchen or a bathroom, it was lost in the tumble of rubble beyond that. Outside, the city glowed, the violence and bustle made calm and beautiful by even such a small distance. The wail of the sirens and angry blat of the security alerts became a kind of music there, transformed by the mystical act of passing above waves.

Timmy pulled off his water-soaked pants and dug a fresh pair out from under the sleeping bag.

"This is where you go?" Lydia said, putting her hand on the time-pocked window glass. "When you aren't with me, you come to this?"

"Nobody bugs you here," Timmy said. "Or, you know. Not twice."

She nodded, as much to herself as for his benefit. Timmy looked around the room and rubbed his hand across his high forehead.

"It's not as nice as your place," he said. "But it's safe. Temporary."

"Yes," she said. "Temporary."

"Even if Liev does tell 'em about you, it's not like it's over. You can get a new name. New paper."

Lydia turned her gaze back from the city, her right hand going to her left arm as if she were protecting herself. Her gaze darted to the empty doorway, and then back. "Where's Erich?"

"Yeah, the meet didn't happen," Timmy said, leaning against the wall. She never ceased to be amazed by his physicality. The innocence and vulnerability that his body managed to project while still being an instrument of violence.

"Tell me," she said, and he did. All of it, slowly and carefully, as if worried he might leave something out that she wanted to know. That she found interesting. The low rumble of a launch shuddered like an endless peal of thunder, and the exhaust plume rose into the night sky as he spoke. It had not yet broken into orbit when he stopped.

"And where is he now?" she asked.

"There's a coffee bar. The one at Franklin and St. Paul? On top of the old high-rises there. I got him there when it was done. They've got a deck there you can rent by the minute, and since his got taken, I figured he'd like that. Gotta say, he was pretty freaked out. That DNA thing? I don't see how that's gonna end well. If he's right about how Burton's gonna react . . . "

Lydia shook her head once, a tiny gesture, almost invisible by the light of the single LED lamp. "I thought you were his bodyguard. You were assigned to protect him."

"I did," Timmy said. "But then the job was done. Burton didn't tell me I was supposed to go to the bathroom with him for the rest of his life, right? Job was done, so the job was done."

"I thought you were his friend."

"I am," Timmy said. "But, y'know. *You.*"

"Don't worry about me. Whatever comes to me, I have earned it a thousand times over. Don't disagree with me! Don't interrupt. Burton asked you to protect Erich because Erich is precious to him. The particular job he assigned you may be over, but worse has come to the city, and Erich is still precious."

"And I get that," Timmy said. "Only when they got Liev—"

"I have lived through the churn before, darling boy. I know how this goes." She turned to the window, gesturing at the golden lights of the city. "Liev was only one. There will be others. Perhaps many, perhaps few, but Burton will lose some part of his structure to the security forces or to death. And the ones who remain afterward will become more important to him. He is a man who values survivors. Who values loyalty. What will he think, dear, when he hears that you left Erich to come spirit me away?"

"Job was done," Timmy said, a little petulantly she thought.

"Not good enough," she said. "Not anymore. You aren't the boy Erich drinks with anymore. You aren't even your mother's son now. Those versions of you are gone, and they will never come back. You are the man who took a job from Burton."

Timmy was silent. Far above them, the transport's exhaust plume went dark. Lydia stepped close to him and put her hands on his shoulders. He wouldn't meet her eyes. She thought that was a good sign. That it meant she was getting through to him.

"The world changes you and you can't stop it from doing so. You have to let go of being someone who doesn't matter now. Because if you live through this time—just live through it and nothing more—you will be more important to Burton. You can't avoid it. You can only choose what your importance is. Will you be someone he can rely upon, or someone he can't?"

Timmy took a deep breath in through his nose and sighed it out. His eyes were flat and hard. "I think I maybe fucked up again."

"Only maybe," Lydia said. "There still may be time to repair the error, yes? Go find your friend. You can bring him here."

Timmy's head jerked up. Lydia rubbed his shoulders gently, beginning at the base of his neck and stroking out to the bulges of muscle where his arms began, then back again. It was a gesture she had made with him since he was a child, a physical idiom in their own private language. Her heart ached at the sacrifice she was making. *The world changes you*, she thought. Hadn't she just said that?

"Bring him here? Y'sure about that?"

"It's all right," she said. "It's temporary."

"Okay then," he said. She felt a tug of regret that he had given in so quickly, but it passed quickly. "I'll leave you the good boat."

"The good boat?" she said to his retreating back.

"The one we came in."

The door closed. The gray that passed for darkness swallowed him up, and five minutes later she heard what might have been a skiff splashing in among the waves. Or it might only have been her imagination. She pulled herself into the warm, stinking, plastic embrace of the sleeping bag and stared at the ceiling and waited to see whether he returned.

All through Baltimore, the struggle between law and opportunity continued, but most of the citizens allied themselves with neither side. The unlicensed coffee shop filled with customers looking for a cheap way to make their dinners on basic seem more palatable, and then with younger people who either didn't have the currency or else the inclination to take amphetamines before descending to the one-night rairai clubs on barricaded streets. A few parents came home from actual jobs, proud to spend real money for a stale muffin and give their credits to the gray-market daycares run out of neighborhood living rooms. Very few people stood wholly for the law or wholly against it, and so for them the catastrophe of the churn was an annoyance to be avoided or endured or else a titillation on the newsfeeds. That it was a question of life and death for other people spoke in its favor as entertainment.

Erich, sitting at the rented deck with a newsfeed spooling past, felt the distance between himself and the others who shared his space more keenly than they did. His sense of dread, of a chapter of his own life ending, was unnoticed by the heavyset woman who brewed the coffee and the thin man at the edge of the rooftop who spent his hours sending messages about tangled romantic involvements. To the other habitués of the coffee shop, Erich was just the crippled man who was hogging the deck. An annoyance and an amusement, and no one would particularly notice or care if he vanished from the world.

Timmy arrived just after midnight, his broad, amiable smile softening the distance in his eyes. To anyone who didn't look at him closely, he seemed unthreatening, and no one looked at him closely. He pulled a welded steel chair up to the bolted-down deck and sat at Erich's side. The newsfeed was set to local. A pale-skinned woman with the Outer Planets Association split circle tattooed on her sternum and Loca Griega teardrops on her cheeks had blood pouring from her nose and left eye while she struggled against two Star Helix enforcers in gear so thick they barely seemed human. Erich smiled, trying to hide the relief he felt at Timmy's return.

"Loca," Erich said, nodding at the feed. "They're having a bad night too."

"Lot of that going around," Timmy said.

"Yeah, right? You . . . heard from Burton?"

"No. Didn't try to find him yet either," Timmy said with a shrug. "You want to hang out here some more, or you about ready to go?"

"I don't know where to go," Erich said, a high violin whine coming in at the back of his voice.

"I got that covered," Timmy said.

"You got a bolt-hole? Jesus, that's where you've been all this time, isn't it? Getting someplace safe to hide?"

"Kind of. But, you know, you ready?"

"I need to stop someplace. Get a deck."

Timmy frowned and nodded at the table before them. *There's one right there* was in his eyes. Erich pointed at the bolts anchoring the machine to the wooden tabletop. Timmy's expression went empty and he stood up.

"Hey," Erich said. "What're you . . . Timmy? What are you—"

The thick woman who brewed the coffee looked up at the broad-shouldered young man. The coffee bar had been hers for three years, and she'd seen enough of the regulars to recognize trouble.

"Hey," the large man—boy, really—said, his voice making the word half apology. "So look. I don't mean to be a dick or anything, but I kind of need that deck."

"You can use it here, you buy some coffee. Or rates are printed on the side," the woman said, crossing her arms.

The big kid nodded, his brow knotting. He took a scuffed and stained black-market credit chip and pressed it into her palm.

"Shit, Jones," she said, blinking at the credit balance on the tiny LED display. "How much coffee you want?"

The kid had already turned back to the table where the cripple with the baby arm had been sitting all day. He hit the table with his fist hard enough that everyone on the rooftop turned to look at him. After the third hit, the wood of the tabletop started to splinter. There was blood on the big boy's knuckles, and the cripple was shifting back and forth anxiously as the table fell to sticks and splinters. The boy pulled her little deck free with a creaking sound. The bolts still hung from it, the wood torn out from around them. Blood dripped from his hands as he tucked the machine under his arm and nodded to the cripple.

"Anything else you need?" Timmy asked.

Erich had to fight not to smile. "No, I think I'm good now."

"All right then. We should go." Timmy turned to the woman and lifted his swelling hand to her in a wave. "Thanks."

She didn't say anything, but pushed the credit stick into her apron and waddled back to get a broom. They were gone before she returned, walking down the stairway to the street.

"That was incredible," Erich said. "The way you did that? I mean, damn it. Everyone in there was cold as stone, and you were just madness and power, man. Did you see that? Did you see how gassed they were at you?"

"You said you needed the deck," Timmy said.

"Come on! That was critical. You can brag about it some."

"Tables don't fight back," Timmy said. "Come on. I got a boat."

Erich's relief left him chatty, but he didn't talk about the fear he'd felt when Timmy had left him. Instead, he filled the trip with everything he'd seen on the feeds, and he told it all like he was telling ghost stories. The security forces were watching the ports, the trains, the transports up to the orbitals and Luna. Eighteen dead today, maybe three times that many in custody. It was news all over the world, and farther. There had even been a lady from Mars who'd come on for a while talking about the history of Earth-based police states. Wasn't that cool? All the way to Mars, they were talking about what was going on right then in Baltimore. They were everywhere.

Timmy listened, adding in a few words here and there, but mostly he walked until they reached the water, and then he rowed. The ceramic oars dipped into the dark water and lifted out again. Erich drummed his fingertips against the stolen deck, anxious to reconnect it to the network, so see what was happening and what had changed in the time since they'd left the coffee bar. That being connected would somehow protect him was an illusion, and Erich half knew that. But only half.

At the little island, Timmy pulled the boat onto shore and marched into the ruins where a light was burning. An old woman was sitting beside a chemical stove, stirring a small tin pot. The smell of brewing tea competed with the brine and the reek of decaying jellyfish. She looked up. Her face was like a mask, the makeup applied so perfectly it shoved her back into the uncanny valley.

"I found your tea," she said. "I hope you don't mind."

"Nope," Timmy said, not breaking stride. "Come on, Erich. I'll get you set up."

They walked through a doorway without a door and into a small room. It was even less comfortable than the one with the old lady. There was nothing on the floor but the glue marks where there had once been carpeting. Mold grew up along one wall, black and branching like tree limbs. Timmy put the deck on the ground. His knuckles were black with blood and forming scab.

"You be able to get signal here?" Timmy asked.

"Should be. May need to find a way to power up in the morning."

"Yeah, well. We'll come up with something. So this is your room, okay?

Yours. That one's hers," Timmy said, pointing a thumb at the lighted doorway. "Hers. She asks you in, you can go in, but she asks you to leave, you do it, right?"

"Of course. Sure. Christ, Timmy. Your place, your rules, right?" Erich smiled, hoping to coax one in response. "We've always respected each other, right? Only, seriously, who is she? Is that your mom?"

It was like Timmy hadn't heard him. "I'm gonna get some sleep, but come morning, I can go back in, get some food. And I'll check in with the man."

Erich felt his belly go cold. "You're going to talk to Burton?"

"Sure, if I can find him," Timmy said. "He's got the plan, right?"

"Right," Erich said. "Of course."

He opened the deck, ran it through its startup options, and connected to the network. The signal strength wasn't great, but it wasn't awful. He'd been in half a dozen basement hack shacks with worse. He opened the newsfeed, still set to passive. The glow from the screen was the only light. Erich was cold, but he didn't complain. Timmy stood, stretched, considered the skinned knuckles of his hand with what could have been a distant sort of ruefulness, and turned to go back to the old woman and the light.

"Hey, we're friends, right?" Erich said.

Timmy turned back. "Sure."

"We've always watched out for each other, you and me."

Timmy shrugged. "Not *always*, but when we could, sure."

"Don't tell him where I am, okay?"

Security crackdowns, like plagues, had a natural progression. A peak, and then decline. As terrible as they might be at their height, they did not last forever. Burton knew this, as did all of his lieutenants, and he made his plans accordingly. Burton moved through his safe houses, playing shell games with the security forces. The first night, while Erich and Lydia slept in their respective rooms in the little island ruin and Timmy tried to find someone in the organization to report to, Burton slept in a loft above a warehouse with a woman named Edie. In the morning, he moved to the storage room in the back of a medical clinic, locking the door and hijacking an untraceable connection so he could speak to his people with relative safety. Little Cole had closed down her houses, locked away her reports, buried a month's supply of drugs, and taken a bus to Vermont to stay with her mother until things died down. Oestra was still in the city, moving from place to place in much the same fashion that Burton was. Ragman and Cyrano were missing, but it was early enough that Burton wasn't concerned yet. At least they weren't in the newsfeeds. Liev and Simonson were.

And there was other evidence, indirect but convincing, of where the little war stood. Even in the first morning after the catastrophe began, security teams were calling on Liev's underlings, sweeping them up for questioning. Some, they held. Others, they released. Burton had no way of knowing which of those who had been set free had cut deals with security and which had been lucky enough to slip through the net. It hardly mattered. That branch of the business had been compromised, and so it would die. The demand for illicit drugs, cheap goods, off-schedule medical procedures, and anonymous sex could be neither arrested nor sated, and so the thing that mattered most for Burton's little empire was safe. Would always be safe. The question of how to feed the city's subterranean hungers was only a tactical one, and Burton could be flexible.

The temptation, of course, was to fight back, and in the following days, some did. Five soldiers from the Loca Griega left a bomb outside a Star Helix substation. It exploded, injuring two of the security contractors and damaging the building, and all five bombers were identified and taken into custody. Tamara Sluydan, who really should have known better, organized street-level resistance, starting a two-day riot that ended with half of her people hospitalized or in custody, eighteen local businesses looted or set afire, and the goodwill of her client base permanently damaged. Burton understood. He wasn't a man without passions. If someone hurt him, of course he wanted to hurt them back. Phrases like "even the score" or "blood for blood" came to mind, and each time they did, he made the practice of tearing them apart to himself. "Even the score" was the metaphor of a game, and this wasn't a game. "Blood for blood" made it sound as if through more violence, past wrongs could be balanced, and they couldn't. The hardest lesson Burton had ever learned was to endure the blows, accept the damage, and let someone else strike back. Soon, very soon, the crackdown would shift from its great, overwhelming force to individual struggles. It was in his interests to see that those struggles were with the Loca Griega and Tamara Sluydan, not with him. As soon as the enemy was clearly defined in the collective mind of Star Helix and Burton's name and organization were not central to their plans, the storm would move on and he could begin to reopen the folded fronds of his business.

In the meantime, he moved from one place to the next. He told people he would go one place, and then arrived at another. He considered all his habits with the uncompromising eye of a predator, and killed the ones with flaws. Anything that connected him with the patterns of the past was a vulnerability, and wherever possible, he chose to be invulnerable. It wasn't the first time he'd been through this. He was good at it.

And so when it took Timmy the better part of a week to find him, Burton's annoyance was balanced against a certain self-centered pride.

The office was raw brick and mortar, newsfeeds playing on five different screens. A sliding wooden door stood half open, the futon where Burton had slept the night before half visible through it. Oestra, whose safe house it was, sat by the window looking down at the street. The automatic shotgun across his legs seemed unremarkable. Timmy had been searched by three guards on the street, and he'd been clean. Even if he'd swallowed a tracking device they would have found it, and the big slab of human meat would have been bleeding out in a gutter instead of smiling amiably and gawking at the exposed ductwork.

"Timmy, right?" Burton said, pretending uncertainty. Let the boy feel lucky he'd remembered that much.

"Yeah, chief. That's me." The openness and amiability was annoying. Burton glanced toward Oestra, but the lieutenant was squinting at the brightness of the day. Burton scratched his leg idly, his fingernails hissing against the fabric of his pants.

"You got something for me?"

Timmy's face fell a little. "Just news. I mean, I didn't have any stuff. Nothing to deliver or anything."

"All right, then," Burton said. "What's the news, Tiny?"

Timmy grinned at the irony of the nickname, then sobered and began his report. Burton leaned forward, drinking in all the words as fast as they spilled from Timmy's lips. When Oestra risked a glance back, it was like watching a bird singing away while a cat stood in the too-still pose of a carnivore waiting to pounce. The details came out in no particular order: Erich was in a safe place, Timmy had been taking food to him, the fake profile deal had been interrupted by the security crackdown, Erich's original deck was gone but he had a replacement, the police probably had his DNA profile now. Oestra sighed to himself and looked back out the window. On the street, a half dozen young men who hadn't just condemned their friends to death slouched down the street together.

"He's sure about that?" Burton asked.

"Nah," Timmy said. "We didn't hang around and watch them find the deck or anything. I figured it'd be better, you know. To get out."

"I see."

"Erich wanted to go get it. Grab the hardware, I mean."

"That would have been a mistake," Burton said. "If security had the deck and the man, that . . . well, that'd be bad."

"Was what I thought too," Timmy said.

Burton sat back, the leather of the chair creaking. Back past the bedroom, Sylvia started running the shower. Sylvia or Sarah. Something like that. One of Oestra's, provided with the bed. "Where's the safe house?"

"I'm not supposed to say," Timmy said.

"Not even to me?"

The boy had the good sense to look uncomfortable. "Yeah, not to anyone. You know how it is."

"Is there anyone there with him?"

"Yeah, I got a friend there."

"A guard?"

"Not really, no. Just a friend."

Burton nodded, thinking hard. "But he's secure?"

"He's on the water. Anyone starts coming in, he's got a boat and about a dozen decent places to hide. I mean, nowhere's a hundred percent."

"And you're protecting him."

"That's the job," Timmy said, with a shrug and a smile. Burton couldn't quite put his finger on what it was about the boy that was so interesting. Over the years, he'd had hundreds just like him who came through, worked, disappeared, died, were fed to security, or found God and a ticket out of town. Burton had a nose for talent, though, and there was something about this one that kept bringing him back to the sense of the boy's potential. Perhaps it was the casual logic he'd used when he'd killed Austin. Maybe it was the deadness in his eyes.

Burton got up, raising a finger. Timmy sat deep in his chair like a trained dog receiving a command. Sylvia—whoever—was singing in the bathroom. The splash of water against porcelain covered the sound of Burton opening the gun safe, pulling out the pistol and its magazine. When he stepped back into the main room, Timmy hadn't so much as crossed his legs. Burton held the gun out.

"You know what this is?" he asked.

"It's a ten-millimeter semi-auto," Timmy said. He put his hand out halfway to it, and then looked up at Burton, his eyes asking permission. Burton nodded and smiled. Timmy took the gun.

"You know guns?"

Timmy shrugged. "They're around. It feels . . . sticky."

"It's got a resin of digestive enzymes," Burton said. "Won't hurt your skin much, but it won't hold prints and it breaks down any trace evidence. No DNA."

"That's cool," Timmy said, and started to hand it back. Burton tossed the magazine onto the boy's lap.

"Those are plastic-tipped. Organ shredders, but they don't work on armor," Burton said. "Still, step up from that homemade shotgun you've used, right?"

"Right."

"You know how those things all go together?"

Timmy weighed the pistol in one hand, the magazine in the other. He slid them together, checked the chamber, flicked the safety on and off. It wasn't the practiced action of a professional, but talented amateur was good enough for his purposes. Timmy looked up, his smile blank and empty. "New job?" he asked.

"New job," Burton said. "I know you and Erich grew up together. Is this going to be a problem for you?"

"Nope," Timmy said, slipping the gun into his pocket. There hadn't even been a pause.

"You're sure?"

"Sure, I'm sure. I get it. They've got him in the system now. If they get him too, there's all kinds of things he compromises. If they can't get him, nothing gets compromised, and I'm the only guy who can get close to him without him seeing it coming."

"Yes."

"So I kill him for you," Timmy said. He could have been saying, *So I'll pick up dinner on my way.* There was no bravado in it. Burton sat, tilted his head. The friendly smile and the empty eyes met him.

"All right, I'm curious," Burton said. "Did you game this? This was your plan?"

"Shit no, chief," Timmy said. "This here's just happy coincidence."

Either it was truth or the best deadpan Burton had seen in a long time. The shower water turned off. On the newsfeeds, a woman in a Star Helix uniform was saying something, a dour expression on her face. Burton wanted to turn up the volume, see if the press statement was something useful to him like reading fortunes in coffee grounds. He restrained himself.

"I will need proof," Burton said. "Evidence, yeah?"

"So what, you want his heart?"

"Heart. Brain. Windpipe. Anything he can't live without."

"Not a problem," Timmy said. Then a moment later, "Is there anything else, or should I go?"

"You watched out for this kid your whole life," Burton said. "He vouched for you. Got you in with me. And you're really going to put a slug in his brain just like that?"

"Sure. You're the man with the plan."

When the boy left, Burton came to stand beside Oestra, watching him walk away down the sunlit street. The thinning reddish-brown hair and wide shoulders made him look like some kind of manual laborer twice his age. His hands were shoved deep in his pockets. He could have been anybody.

"Think he'll do it?" Burton asked.

Oestra didn't answer for a long moment. "Might."

"He does this for me, he'll do anything," Burton said, clapping Oestra's shoulder. "Potential for a man like that."

"If he doesn't?"

"There are a lot of ways to dispose of someone disposable," Burton said.

Burton walked back to the chair, shifted the newsfeed buffer back to the start of the Star Helix woman's press announcement. The woman started talking, and Burton listened.

Timmy's ruin had long since become a misery for Lydia, and misery had become a kind of pleasure. Their days had taken on a kind of rhythm. Erich woke first in the morning, his uneven footsteps playing a tentative counterpoint to the rough sound of the waves. Lydia lay in the warmth of her cocoon, the slick fabric wrapped around her until only her mouth and nose were in the free air. When she could no longer pretend sleep, she emerged and made tea on the little stove, and when she was done, Erich transferred the solar charger to his deck and squatted over it, scanning the newsfeeds with a ferocity and single-mindedness that made her think of a poet chasing the perfect rhyme. If Timmy was there, she would walk with him to the boats or survey the newest supplies he had smuggled to their private island: fresh clothes, carryout tandoori, charged batteries for the deck and the lamp. More often, he was not there, and she haunted the shore like a sea widow. The city glowered out at her from across the water, like a great angry gray face, condemning her for her sins.

Is this the time? she would wonder. *Has he left now, never to return? Or will there be one more? Another time to see his face, to hear his voice, to have the conversations that we can only ever have with each other?*

She knew that the churn was playing itself out there, across the narrow waves. Security had likely come to her rooms on Liev's word and found them already abandoned. The men and women she'd worked with these last years were part of the past now. Part of a life she'd left behind, though nothing else had begun. Only this island exile and its waiting.

At night, Erich would eat with her. Their conversations were awkward. She knew that she was uncanny to him, that he thought of Timmy as his own friend, a character from his own past. Her appearance and the reticence she and Timmy had to making her explicable were as odd to Erich as if lobsters had crawled up out of the sea and started speaking Spanish. And yet if they did, what could anyone do but answer them, and so Erich and Lydia reached the odd peace of roommates, intimate in all things and nothing.

That night, Timmy crossed the waves unnoticed by her or Erich. Lydia was looking east over the ruined island to the greater sea beyond. Erich curled in the room that common habit designated as his, snoring slightly as the deck ran down its charge to nothing beside him. Timmy arrived quietly and alone, announced only by his footsteps and the smell of fresh ginger.

When he emerged from the darkness, two thin plastic sacks hung from his left fist. Lydia shifted, not rising, but coming up to rest on her knees and ankles in a posture she imagined to be like a geisha, though she'd never met a real geisha. Timmy put the sacks down beside her, his eyes on the shadows past the doorway. Far away across the water, gulls complained.

"Two?" she said.

"Hmm?" Timmy followed her gaze to the sacks. A glimmer of something that might have been chagrin passed through his eyes fast as a blink. "Oh. The dinners. Hey, is Erich back there?"

"He is," Lydia said. "I think he's asleep."

"Yeah," Timmy said, straightening. He put a hand into his pocket. "Hang on a minute." He walked back toward the black doorway as if he were going to check on the other boy, perhaps wake him for his supper.

"Wait," Lydia said as Timmy reached the doorway.

He looked back at her, twisting at the shoulders, his body and feet still committed.

"Come sit with me."

"Yeah, I just gotta—"

"First," she said. "Come sit with me first."

Timmy hesitated, fluttering like a feather caught between contradictory breezes. Then his shoulders sank a centimeter and his hips turned toward her. He pulled his hand from his pocket. Lydia opened the sacks, unpacked the food, laid the disposable forks beside the plates. Every movement had the precision and beauty of ritual. Timmy sat facing her, his legs crossed. The bulge of the gun stood out from his thigh like a fist. Lydia bowed her head, as if in prayer. Timmy took up his fork and stabbed at the ginger beef. Lydia did the same.

"So you're going to kill him?" Lydia asked, her voice light.

"Yeah," Timmy said. "I mean, I ain't happy about it, but it's what needs to get done."

"Needs," Lydia said, her intonation in the perfect balance point between statement and question.

Timmy ate another bite. "I'm the guy that took a job from Burton. Used to be the job was one thing. Now it's something else. It's not like I get to tell him what to do, right?"

"Because he's Burton."

"And I'm not. You were the one who said I'd be important to him if I made it through this shitstorm. This is part of that."

"I said Burton would *see* you as important," Lydia said. "There is more to you than what he sees. There's more to you than what anybody sees."

"Well," Timmy said. "You."

Even I do not know your depths floated at the back of her throat like a cough. She didn't have it in her to say the words. If it was true, so what? When had truth ever been her friend? Instead she took another bite of the beef. He did the same. She imagined that he was giving her the time to gather herself. It might even have been true. The perfectly straight lightning bolt of a railgun transport lit the black sky, its thunder rolling after it like a wave. The ginger and pepper burned her lips, her throat, her tongue, and she took another bite, welcoming the pain. It was always pleasant when pain was on the outside.

"And who will you be to yourself?" she said at last. "Doesn't what you think matter more than what he does?"

Timmy's brow furrowed. "Yeah, I don't know what you just said."

"Who are you going to be to yourself, if you do this?" She put down her fork, leaned across the space between them. She lifted his shirt as she had countless times before, and the erotic charge of it was still there. Never absent. She pressed her palm against his breast, her skin against his skin in the place above his heart. "Who will you be in there?"

Timmy's face went perfectly still in the unnerving way it sometimes did. His eyes were flat as a shark's, his mouth like a plaster cast mold of himself. Only his voice was the same, bright and amiable.

"You know there ain't no one in there," he said.

She let her fingertips stray to the side, brushing through the coarse hair she knew so well. She felt the hardness of his nipple against her thumb. "Then who will you put there? Burton?"

"He's the guy with the power," Timmy said.

"Not the power to kill Erich," she said. "Not the power to make *you* kill him. That is you and only you. People like us? We aren't righteous. But we can pretend to be, if we want, and that's almost the same as if it were true."

"I get the feeling you're asking me for something. I don't know what it is."

"I am not a good person," she said.

"Hey. Don't—"

"If I were, though? If I *were* that woman? What would I want you to do?"

Timmy took another mouthful of beef, his jaw working slowly. In his concentration, she saw the echoes of all the versions of himself that she had known from baby to toddler to young man to this, now before her. She folded her hands on her lap.

"That's a long way to say I shouldn't do it," he said.

"Is that what I said?" she asked.

Erich's yawn came from the doorway. Lydia felt the blood rush from her face, tasted the penny-bright flush of fear as if she had been caught doing something illicit. Erich came into the light, scratching his sleep-tousled hair with his good hand. "Hey," he said. "Did I hear you get back, big guy? What's the word?"

Timmy was quiet, his gaze fixed on Lydia, his expression empty as a mask.

"Guys?" Erich said, limping forward. "What's the matter? Is something wrong?"

Timmy's sigh was so low that Lydia barely heard it. The boy she had loved for so long, and in so many ways, put on his cheerful smile and looked away from her. She felt tears pricking her eyes.

"Yeah, bad news," Timmy said. "Burton's not taking the whole thing very well. He's put out paper on you."

Erich sat down, the blood draining from his face. He grabbed his bad arm reflexively, unaware that he was doing it, and looked from Timmy to the woman and back. His heart thudded like a drum in his ears. Timmy licked his fork clean and put it down. The woman was still as stone. Erich felt his world fall out from underneath him, and that he had known it would was less of a comfort than he'd expected. Anyone looking in at the little circle of light from the shadows would have seen only three faces in the black, like a family portrait of refugees. Erich broke the silence.

"Are you *sure*?"

"Yeah, pretty sure," Timmy said. "Seeing as how I got the contract."

Erich stopped breathing. Timmy stared at him, expressionless for several infinitely long seconds.

"We've gotta find a way to get you out," his big friend finally said, and Erich started breathing again.

"There's no way out," he said. "Burton'll track me down anywhere."

"What about that deck?" Timmy asked. "It ain't your old one, but can you still sample with it?"

"What do you mean?" Erich said.

"You've got the escape plan for Burton. The clean one. Why don't you put your sequence on it? Use it to get out of here?"

"I can, sure, but they've already got my *other* deck, remember? I put my DNA on a record, the flag goes up, and I'm in for questioning."

"Yeah," Timmy said. "Well maybe you could . . . Shit. I don't know. Maybe you could think of something."

"I knew," Erich said. "The second I saw those bastards coming down the street, I knew it was over for me. I'm dead. It's just a matter of time is all."

"That's always true," Lydia said, her mind taken with other matters. "For everyone."

"Might as well be you," Erich said to Timmy, giving his friend permission. Terror and love warring in his chest.

"Nope," Timmy said, cocking his head to one side as if he'd only just made the decision in that moment.

"Erich," Lydia started.

"As long as I'm alive," Erich said, ignoring her, "Burton's not safe. He's not going to let me slide."

Timmy frowned, then grunted in surprise. Maybe pleasure.

"What?" Erich said.

"Just that it works the other way too," Timmy said, levering himself up to his feet. "Anyway, I gotta go back in."

"Back in?" Erich said.

Timmy brushed his hands across his wide thighs. "The city. I gotta go back to the city. Burton's expecting me."

"You're not going to tell him where I am, are you?" Erich asked. Timmy started laughing and Lydia took it up. Erich looked from one to the other, confused.

"Nah, I'm not going to tell him where you are. I got something of his I need to give back is all. Nothing you have to worry about."

"Easy for you to say," Erich said, ashamed of the whine in his voice.

"I'll leave you the good boat," Timmy said, turning toward the darkness.

"Will you be back?" Lydia said. She hadn't meant to, because she knew in her heart, in her bones, and deeper than that what the answer was. Timmy smiled at her for the last time. *I take it back*, she thought. *Kill him. Kill the boy. Kill everyone else in the world. Shoot babies in the head and dance on their bodies. Any atrocity, any evil, is justified if it keeps you from leaving me.*

"Eh," Timmy said. "You never know."

The darkness folded around him as he walked away. Her hands were made of lead and tungsten. Her belly felt hurt and empty as a miscarriage. And underneath the hurt and the horror, the betrayal and the pleasure she took in her distress, something else stirred and lifted its head. It took her time to recognize it as pride, and even then she couldn't have said who or what she was proud of. Only that she was.

The boat splashed once in the water, her almost-son and sometime-lover leaving the shore for the last time. Her lifetime was a fabric woven of losses, and she saw now that all of them had been practice, training her to teach her how to bear this pain like a boxer bloodying knuckles to make them strong and numb. All her life had been preparation for bearing this single, unbearable moment.

"Shit," Erich said. "Were there only two dinners? What am I going to eat?"

Lydia plucked up the fork that had been Timmy's, gripping the stem in her fist like holding his hand again, one last time. Touching what he had touched, because she would never touch him again. Here this object had opened his lips, felt the softness of his tongue, and been left behind. It held traces of him.

"What's the matter?" Erich said. "Are you all right?"

I stopped being all right before you were born, she thought. What she said was, "There's something I'd like you to do for me."

The streets of Baltimore didn't notice him pass through them this one last time. More than three million people lived and breathed, loved and lost, hoped and failed to hope that night, just as any other. A young woman hurrying home later than her father's curfew dodged around a tall man with thinning hair and pants wet to the knee at the corner of South and Lombard, muttering obscenities and curses at him that spoke more of her own dread and fear than anything the man had done. Four Star Helix security employees, out of uniform and off-shift, paused at the entrance to an Italian restaurant to watch a civilian pass. None of them could have said what it was about him that caught their attention, and it might only have been that they'd operated on high alert for so many days at once. The civilian went on, minding his own business, keeping himself to himself, and they went into the building's garlic and onion smells and forgot him. A bus driver stopped, let two old women, a thin-faced man, and a broad-shouldered amiable fellow come on board. Bus service was part of basic, and the machine followed its route automatically. No one paid, no one spoke, and the driver went back to watching the entertainment feeds as soon as the bus pulled back into traffic.

Nearer Oestra's safe house, things changed. There were more eyes, more of them alert. The catastrophe of the churn hung thick in the air, the sense that doom might come at any moment in the shape of security vans and riot gear and voices shouting to keep hands visible. Nothing like it had happened that day or the one before, but no one was taking comfort in that yet. The guards who stopped Timmy were different than the ones he'd seen earlier, but their placement on the street was the same. They stopped him, took the pistol that Burton had given him, scanned him for tracking devices, firearms, explosives, chemical agents, and when they found he was clean, they called in. Oestra's voice through their earpieces was less than a mosquito but still perfectly recognizable, a familiar buzz and whine. They waved Timmy on.

Oestra opened the door to him, automatic shotgun still in the lieutenant's hand, as if he hadn't put it down all day. Probably, he hadn't.

Timmy stepped into the main room, looking around pleasantly. The newsfeeds flickered silently on their screens: a street view from sometime earlier in the day with five security vans lined up outside a burning apartment building, a serious-faced Indian woman speaking into the camera with a dour expression, an ad with seven bouncing monkeys reaching for a box of banana-flavored cakes. The world cast its shadows on the bare brick wall and threw stories into the gray mortar. The churn, running itself to exhaustion. New stories from around the world and above it filling in the void.

"You're back," Oestra said.

"Yup."

"You do the thing?"

"It got a little complicated," Timmy said. "The man still here?"

"Wait. I'll get him."

Oestra walked to the back, one set of footsteps fading into the safe house, then a long pause made rich by the murmur of voices, then two sets of footsteps coming back. The timestamp beside the dour Indian woman read 21:42. Timmy considered the curtains. Blue-dyed cotton with cords of woven nylon. The chair Oestra had been sitting on before, leather stretched over a light metal frame. A kitchen in through a wide brickwork archway. The bedroom in the back with its futon, and a bathroom somewhere behind that.

"Tiny," Burton said. "What's the news, little man?"

Burton's white shirt caught the light from the screens, dancing in a hundred colors. His slacks were dark and beautifully cut. Timmy turned to him like he was an old friend. Oestra walked past them both, taking his place by the window. Timmy glanced back at him only a few feet away, a shotgun across his thighs.

"Well," Timmy said. "Truth is, I ran into a little hiccup."

Burton crossed his arms, squared his shoulders and hips. "Something you couldn't handle?" he asked, his voice hard with disapproval.

"I'm waiting to see," Timmy said.

"Waiting to see if you can handle it?"

"Well, yeah," Timmy said with a wide, open smile. "Actually, it's kind of funny you put it that way."

When the big man stepped back toward the window, the movement was so casual, so relaxed, that neither Oestra nor Burton recognized what was happening. Timmy's thick fingers grabbed the back of the leather chair, pulling back and down fast and hard. Oestra twisted trying to keep from falling and also bring the shotgun to bear at the same time, managing neither. He spilled to the floor, Timmy's knee coming down hard on his neck. Oestra's muffled roar was equal parts outrage and pain. Timmy reached down and ripped the man's right ear off, then punched down twice, three times, four. Burton ran for the back bedroom. There wasn't much time.

Unable to use it with Timmy on his neck, Oestra dropped the shotgun and twisted, trying to get his arms and legs under himself, trying to get the leverage to push Timmy back. Timmy reached down and hooked his finger into the gunman's left eye, bracing the head with his knee and turning his wrist until he felt the eyeball pop. Oestra's screams were wilder now, panic and pain taking over. Timmy let the pressure up, scooted to the left, and picked up the abandoned shotgun. He fired once into Oestra's head and the man stopped screaming.

Timmy trotted across the room, shotgun in one hand. Burton boiled out of the bedroom, pistols in either fist and teeth bared like a dog's. The front window shattered. Timmy ducked through the brick archway into the kitchen, shifted his grip on the shotgun, and swung it hard and low, leading with the elbow like a cricket player at the bat as Burton roared in after him. The sound of the connection was like a piece of raw steak being dropped on concrete. Burton's feet flew out from under him, but the momentum of his rush carried him stumbling into the space beyond. Timmy lowered the shotgun toward the man's head, but Burton whirled, dropping his own guns and grabbing the shotgun's barrel. The smell of burning skin was instantaneous. Timmy tried to pull back, but Burton kicked out. His right foot hit Timmy's knee like he'd kicked a fire hydrant, but Timmy still stumbled. The shotgun roared again, and the refrigerator sprouted pocks of twisted metal and plastic. Burton twisted, pulling himself in close. Too close for the shotgun's long barrel. He hammered his elbow into Timmy's ribs twice and felt something give the third time. Timmy dropped the shotgun, and then they were both down on the floor.

They grappled, caught in each other's arms, each man shifting for the position that would destroy the other in a parody of intimate love. The fingers of Burton's left hand worked their way under Timmy's chin, digging at his neck, pushing into the hard cartilage of his throat. Timmy choked, gagged, pulled back the centimeter that was all Burton needed. He pulled his right arm up into the gap, braced himself, twisted, and now Timmy's arm and head were locked. Burton gasped out a chuckle.

"You just fucked the wrong asshole," he hissed as Timmy bucked and struggled. "Your little cripple boyfriend? I'm gonna burn him down for days. I'm gonna find everyone you ever loved and kill them all slow."

Timmy grunted and pushed back, but the effort only made Burton's lock on him tighter.

"You thought you could take me, you dumbfuck piece of shit?" Burton spat into Timmy's ear. "You thought you were tougher than *me*? I owned your momma, boy. You're just second-generation *property*."

All along their paired bodies, Burton felt Timmy tense and then, with a vast exhalation, relax, melting into the hold. Burton pulled tighter, squeezing. There was a report like a pistol shot when Timmy's shoulder dislocated and the resistance stuttered. Burton's grip broke. Timmy rolled, cocked back his fist and brought it down on the bridge of Burton's nose. The pain was bright. The volume of the world faded. The fist came down again, jostling the kitchen. The light seemed strange, reducing the red of the bricks and the yellow of the stove to shades of gray. Burton tried to bring his arms up to cover his face, to shield him from the violence, but they were a very long way away, and he kept losing track of them. He had them up, but they were numb and boneless. The attacks easily brushed them aside. The fist hit his nose again, and he didn't know if it was for the third time or the fourth.

Shit, he thought. *This is just going to keep going on until that fucker decides to stop.*

The impact came again, and Burton tried to say something, to scream. The impact came again, and afterward followed a few seconds of darkness and silence and calm. Burton felt very sleepy. The impact came again. Calm. The impact came again and again and again. Each time, the violence felt more distant and the emptiness between more profound until a kind of forgetfulness came over him.

Once Timmy was sure that he was alone in the apartment, he rolled onto his back. His left arm hung from the socket, limp, useless, and disconnected. He levered himself up to his knees, breathing hard between clenched teeth. Then stood. He took the automatic shotgun in his one good hand and stepped out to the main room. On the screen, the Indian woman was still speaking, wagging a finger at the camera to make a point. The timestamp beside her read 21:44. Two minutes. Maybe a little less. Timmy walked to the front window. The guards from the street weren't at their posts. He nodded to himself and went to stand by the front door. When the knob turned, he waited. The door flew open, and he fired three times, once straight ahead, and then angling to the left and right. Someone started screaming and the door banged closed again.

Timmy went back to the kitchen. He flipped on the burners, pulled down the roll of cheap paper towels from the wall. He found a bottle of peanut oil in the cabinet and doused the towels with half of it before he put them directly on the heating element. A flurry of footsteps came from the front and he fired the shotgun again, not aiming at anything. They retreated. The oil-soaked paper caught fire, and Timmy picked up the burning roll, trotted to the bedroom, and threw the flaming mass into the bunched covers. By the time he was back in the kitchen, the flame shadows were already dancing in the archway behind him. Timmy put the half-full bottle of oil directly onto the heating element and walked to the back of the safe house. The stairway leading to the alley was narrow and white. He didn't see anyone, but he fired the shotgun twice anyway then tossed the gun back into the fire. If there had been a guard there, they'd fled. Timmy walked out into the night.

He moved slowly, but with purpose. When his path crossed with other people's he smiled and nodded. Once, when he had almost reached his destination, an old man in a black coat had stopped and stared at his bruised and bloody hand. Timmy smiled ruefully, shrugged, and didn't break stride. The old man didn't raise an alarm. Around here, a muscle-bound thug with blood on his cuffs and skinned knuckles didn't warrant anything more than a disapproving look.

The security forces had put a fresh lock on Lydia's door, but Timmy knew the back way in. He slid through the window into the bathroom he'd known so well over the last few years. It still smelled like her. They'd gone through everything. Her towels and the shower curtain were on the floor. Bottles of medications littered the sink. He dug through until he found some painkillers and dry swallowed three. In the kitchen, he wrapped his shoulder in ice, then waited motionless until the swelling was down as far as it was going to go. Putting his shoulder back in its socket was a question of lying on the bed, his grip on the mattress bottom hard and unforgiving, and then pulling back slowly, relaxing into the pain, until it slid back into place with a wet, angry pop. He stripped, washed himself with wet hand towels, and changed into a fresh set of his clothes. Ones that didn't have anybody's blood on them.

The churn, the crackdown, the catastrophe. The cycle of boom and bust. The turn of the seasons. Whatever name was applied to it, the inevitable cascade of events in the city rolled on just the same. When the fire trucks came and put out the blaze, they identified the two bodies as Feivel Oestra and an unregistered man. The unregistered was a small, compact, dark-skinned man in an expensive shirt and tailored slacks. He had no tattoos, and a wide birthmark on his right shoulder blade in the shape of a rough triangle. Both men had died by violence. If the fire had been meant to conceal that, it failed. If it was only meant to foul any trace DNA or fingerprint evidence, it did well enough. Add to that the fact that Oestra was on the Star Helix lists as someone to bring in for questioning, and the broad strokes of the story came clear.

The same night, fifteen men loyal to the Loca Griega were surrounded in a nightclub. The hostage situation that rose out of it left two people dead and ten in custody, and the attendant lawsuits against Star Helix and the owners of the nightclub were the top of the local and regional newsfeeds. Oestra's death was little more than a footnote, something mentioned and then moved on from. Other things—smaller things—fell even below that level of obscurity. A woman selling illicit painkillers out of her apartment beside the arcology had a screaming fight with one of her clients, called security, and was taken away for questioning. A sweep of the ruins on the bay islands found a small squatters' camp with an LED lamp, an emergency prep sleeping bag, and an exhausted chemical stove, but anyone who had been living there was gone. An art dealer contacted with a request for assistance with an investigation killed himself rather than come in. None of those events raised any notice at all.

Soon, the paroxysm of violence, legal and otherwise, would thin back down to the normal background radiation of human vice. Very serious people would argue about whether the program had worked. Some would argue that crime had gone down, others that it had actually risen. Star Helix would take its payment from the government and settle out of court most of the complaints made against it. One of the remaining lieutenants would rise to the top, or the whole criminal apparatus would turn over to a new organization, a new generation. Within a year, there would be a new working normal that would run more or less gracefully until the next time. People of little importance would survive and make names for themselves. The mighty would fall, the meek would rise up in their places and become mighty. But all that would come later.

In the pearly light that came before the dawn, one other thing happened that went unnoticed, meaningless to anyone but those involved.

It was on a street down near the water's edge. The eastern sky was brightening with the coming dawn, the western sky still boasted a scattering of stars. Traffic on the street was thick, but not yet the immobile crush that would come with the light. Sea and rot perfumed the air, but the cool made the scent seem almost pleasant. A tea-and-coffee stand was opening, sporting the blue-and-pink logo of a popular chain and a tray of baked goods just the same as a million other trays on five continents and two worlds. Old men and women on basic huffed down the sidewalk, getting in the day's exercise before the sun came up. Young men and women staggered home from long nights at the street clubs and rairai joints, exhausted from hours of dancing, drinking, sex, and frustrated hope. Soon, the streets and tube stations would thicken with the traffic of those who had jobs to go to, and then be released to the masses for whom basic was a way of life.

A boy on the verge of manhood stood on a corner near the tea-and-coffee stand. He was taller than average, and muscular. His close-cropped reddish-brown hair was receding, though he was young. His expression was blank, and he held himself in a tight, guarded way that could have been grief or the protecting of some physical injury. His right hand was swollen, the knuckles skinned. If it hadn't been for that last detail, the security team might have passed him by. Three women and two men, all in the ballistic armor and helmets of Star Helix.

"Morning," the team lead said, and half a beat later the tall man smiled and nodded. He turned to walk away, but the other personnel shifted to block his path.

The man tensed, then made the visible decision to relax. His smile was rueful. "Sorry. I was just heading out."

"I respect that, sir. We appreciate you taking a moment," the team lead said, placing a hand on the butt of his pistol. "Really did a number on your hand."

"Yeah. I box."

"Can be a good workout. I'm going to need to see your ID."

"Don't got it on me. Sorry."

"We'll need to check you against the database, then. That isn't a problem, is it?"

"Think I got the right to refuse that, don't I?"

"You do," the team lead said, letting a hint of hardness slip into his voice beneath the casual words. "But then we'd need to take you to the substation and do the full biometric scan to exclude you from the persons of interest list, and there are a whole lot of very unpleasant people who are in that queue. You don't want to hang out with them. Not if you have someplace you need to be."

The big man seemed to consider this. He glanced back over his shoulder.

"Looking for someone?" the team lead asked.

"Was more thinking there might be some folks looking for me."

"So. How do you want to play this?"

The man shrugged and held out his hand. The team's data analyst stepped forward and tapped the collector against the thick wrist. The readout stuttered red, then went to solid green. The seconds ticked away.

"If there's something you want to tell me," the team lead said, "this would be the time."

"Nah," the big man said. "I think I'm good."

"Yeah?"

"You know," he said, "good enough."

The team lead's hand terminal chimed. He pulled it out with his left hand, his right still on the butt of his gun. The readout had the red border of a flagged profile. The big man's body went very still while they read. It was a long moment before the team lead spoke.

"Amos Burton."

"Yeah?" the big man said. It could have meant, *Yes, I killed him*, or *What about him?* All the team lead heard was the affirmation.

"I've got a travel flag on you here. You're cutting it pretty close."

Amos Burton's eyebrows rose and the corners of his mouth turned down. "I am?"

"You're shipping out to Luna on the noon launch from Bogotá station, Mr. Burton. These apprenticeship programs are tough to get into, and last I heard, they take it mighty poorly if you miss your berth. Might wind up waiting another decade to get back on the list."

"Huh," the big man said.

"Look, there's a high-speed line about nine blocks north of here. We can take you there if you want."

"Erich, you sonofabitch," the big man said. Instead of looking north, he turned to the east, toward the sea and rising sun. "I'm not Mr. Burton."

"Sorry?"

"I'm not Mr. Burton," the man said again. "You can call me Amos."

"Whatever you want. But I think you'd better haul ass out of town if you don't want to get in some serious shit, Amos."

"You ain't the only one that thinks that. But I'm good. I know where the high-speed lines are. I won't miss my ride."

"All right then," the team lead said with a crisp nod. "Have a better one."

The security team moved on, flowing around the big man like river water around a stone. Amos watched them go, then went to the tea-and-coffee stand, bought a cup of black coffee and a corn muffin. He stood on the corner for a long minute, eating and drinking and breathing the air of the only city he'd ever known. When he was done, he dropped the cup and the muffin wrapper into the recycling bin and turned north toward the high-speed line and Bogotá station and Luna. And, who knew, maybe the vastness beyond the moon. The sweep of planets and moons and asteroids that humanity had spread to, and where the chances of running into anybody from Baltimore were vanishingly small. A needle in a haystack all of humanity wide.

Amos Burton was a tall, stocky, pale-skinned man with an amiable smile, an unpleasant past, and a talent for cheerful violence. He left Baltimore to its dynamic balance of crime and law, exotics and mundanity, love and emptiness. The number of people who knew him and loved him could be counted on one hand and leave most of the fingers spare, and when he was gone, the city went on without him as if he had never been.

THE THINGS WE DO FOR LOVE

K. J. Parker

"It's perfectly true, gentlemen of the jury," I said. "I murdered my wife. I put hemlock in her milk, she drank it, she died. It was no accident. I did it on purpose."

I glanced nervously over their heads at the sundial on the far wall. Time was getting on. How long does it take to find a self-confessed murderer guilty and string him up, for crying out loud? But the jurors were gazing at me solemnly, still and quiet as little mice, expecting more. What? Did they think the confession, the cut-and-dried, open-and-shut admission of guilt I'd just so thoughtfully given them was some sort of rhetorical trick? Yes, probably. In any event, they weren't convinced. I blame the lawyers.

"Just to clarify," I said. "I did it. The mandatory sentence for murder is, I believe, death." I lowered my head. "I rest my case."

Awkward silence. The prosecutor was staring at me. *For God's sake, man,* I could hear him thinking, *pull yourself together.* I gave him a polite nod; carry on. Please. We're on the clock here.

Slowly he rose to his feet. He was probably a decent enough fellow, with a sense of fair play that I'd have admired in other circumstances. "Gentlemen," he said, "we have a clear confession. I therefore move that—"

Out of the corner of my eye, I saw something scuttle across the floor. Hell, I thought.

The prosecutor was still banging on about something. " . . . Evidence we have heard from the investigating magistrate, I feel we ought to consider the issue of the accused man's mental capacity. If, as would seem to be the case, this man is not in his right mind, it is open to you to substitute a sentence of detention for life at the monastery of the Golden Heart—"

I jumped up. The kettlchat made a grab for my arm, but I elbowed him in the eye. "Don't listen to him," I shouted. "I'm not mad, I'm as sane as you are. I killed her for her money, that's all there is to it."

I noticed a man in the front row of the jury benches pulling a frown. I got the impression he didn't approve of killing rich wives for their money.

Excellent. But the shadow on the sundial was almost touching the ornately gilded Six. I turned and faced the prosecutor. "Please," I said. "I know you're doing what you think is best, but really, I'm not worth it. I killed that poor, loving, trusting girl so I could get her money and marry a prostitute from the Velvet Shadow. My conscience—"

The prosecutor shrugged and sat down. The usher stood up and cleared his throat. I held my breath. Nearly there.

"Gentlemen of the jury—"

But they weren't looking at him. They weren't looking at me, either. Slowly, with an aching heart, I turned and looked over my shoulder at the crowd in the public seats. A beautiful young woman with light brown hair and a sweet and simple smile was standing up, about two rows from the front. "Excuse me," she said.

"Silence in court," the usher mumbled, but you could tell he didn't mean it.

"I'm sorry," the lovely girl said, "but I must speak. You see, I'm this man's wife. And I'm not dead."

Ah well. I sat down again.

It took the prosecutor a moment to pull himself together. He stood up. "Please approach the bench," he said.

I could hear the murmur of voices behind me. As she passed me, she turned her head and smiled. Don't worry, the smile said, it's going to be all right. I closed my eyes. Why is there never a brick around when you need one?

With a little gentle prompting from the prosecutor, the lovely girl gave her evidence. Her name was Onofria; here was a copy of the register of births, sealed by the City Prefect, and here was a copy of the Temple register, recording her marriage to me on the 17th Feralia, AUC 667, and here were twelve affidavits sworn by leading citizens confirming that she was who she claimed to be. The prosecutor was happy to confirm that all the seals and signatures were in order. It had all been, she went on, a silly, silly misunderstanding. Because of an illness she'd had from childhood, she had to take special medicine, which contained a small amount of hemlock. To take the taste away, she drank it mixed with honey and milk. Usually, her husband poured it for her at bedtime. On this occasion, she'd mistakenly thought he'd be out for the evening, so she took a dose herself. Later, her husband had mixed another dose for her, as usual. Absent-mindedly, entirely her own silly fault, she'd drunk the second dose out of force of habit. The two doses had made her very ill. The doctor came. They took her to the Priory hospital. Her poor husband, thinking she was dead and out of his mind with grief and guilt, had gone to the Prefecture and told them he'd just poisoned his wife. But it was all a silly mistake; she'd made a full recovery, only to discover that her poor darling was on trial for murder. So, of course, she's rushed over straight away and, well, here she was—

Case dismissed.

"You cow," I muttered.

We were walking arm in arm through the arch that leads from the law courts into the Market Square. She was still smiling. She has a lovely smile, when she's human.

"I'm not talking to you," she said.

"Good."

"Honestly." Someone I knew vaguely stopped to stare. She beamed at him and he walked on. "If you ever kill me again, I shall be seriously annoyed."

I first met her during my brief tenure as governor-general of the Leuga Islands.

It was a very brief tenure, and when we met it was rapidly drawing to an end, mostly because the real governor had showed up unexpectedly early. I was packing to leave. I like to travel light when running for my life; a few gold bars and a handful of uncut gemstones thrown into an old satchel, and I'm good to go. I'm always extremely careful about what I take around with me. In my line of work, you have to be; you never know when you're going to be stopped and searched. Ironically, I distinctly remember going through my bag just to make sure I wasn't carrying anything that could possibly cause me problems later. Of course, she wasn't in the damn bag.

I remember walking briskly down the steps of the governor's palace, across the square and out to the private jetty, where a boat was waiting to take me to Sezanza. It was one of those dazzlingly clear blue-sky days you get in the Leugas, when everything is crisp and sharp and you feel like you could do anything. I remember feeling a nip and an itch on the back of my neck as I climbed into the boat. I thought: Shame it didn't work out, but who wants to be in a place where even the governor's palace has got bedbugs? All in all, I was feeling pretty good about myself. I was happy.

I felt something on the back of my neck, light but definitely perceptible. I slapped the area vaguely with the flat of my hand. The warmth of the sun and the gentler rocking of the boat were wonderfully soothing, and the excitement and stress of the last few days were starting to slip away. I lay down with my back to the rail and closed my eyes.

When I woke up I was in shadow. "Hello," I said.

She really does have a nice smile. "Hello," she said. "I'm Onofria. Who are you?"

Good question. For the last few days I'd been the honorable Leucas

Metellas. I hadn't quite made up my mind who I was going to be in Sezanza. "I'm Buto," I said.

She sat down beside me. She was wearing a long yellow silk dress and yellow silk slippers, embroidered with red roses. "Where are you going?"

"Sezanza," I said. "How about you?"

"Sezanza. I'm going to stay with my aunt and uncle. They live in a little village in the hills. Parecoina."

"What an amazing coincidence," I said.

We never got to Parecoina. Instead, we spent three days in a grubby little inn on the outskirts of the Tanners' Quarter in Ap'Coele, which is what passes for civilization in Sezanza. We didn't go out much, but there's precious little to see in Ap'Coele.

On the morning of the fourth day I woke up early, and she wasn't in the bed with me. I got dressed and went to look for her, and found her in the stable yard. She'd got a clay cup from somewhere. It was half filled with woodlice, crawling and scrambling over each other. She put it down on the mounting block and smiled at me.

"You're up and about early," I said.

She leaned forward and kissed me on the nose. "It's such a beautiful day," she replied. "Let's go for a walk."

We went down to the harbor, where the fishing boats were just setting out. "Your uncle and aunt," I said. "They'll be wondering where you've got to."

She frowned, for some reason. "Don't worry about them," she said. Then she stopped. "Are you trying to get rid of me?"

It seemed such an odd thing to say. "No, of course not."

"That's all right, then. I'll write to them," she said, and the smile came back. "They're used to me," she added.

"I see. You do this sort of thing all the time, then?"

I'd meant it as a silly joke. "Yes," she said. "Oh look, a cormorant."

You know how young men are when they're showing off: mines of useless information. "That's a trained cormorant," I said. "If you look closely, you can see the collar."

"What's that for?"

"It's to stop them swallowing the fish. They catch them, but they can't eat them, so they fly back home again. The fish are stuck in their throats until the fishermen pull them out."

She gave me an odd sort of a look, one which I've always remembered. "Sensible arrangement," she said.

I shrugged. "For the fisherman. I can't really see what the bird gets out of it."

"It's just a bird. And anyway, the fisherman looks after it."

"Does a bird need looking after?"

"Let's go and paddle in the sea."

We didn't stay out long. A bit later, she asked me, "What are you? I mean, what do you do?"

I was sleepy, the way you are afterwards. "Oh, not much."

"Ah. A gentleman."

Usually I'd have said yes, that's right, because why bother with the truth when I'd be gone in a day or so? But I said, "How about you?"

She shrugged. "I'm not anything, really."

I'd formed my own assessment some time earlier. You have to be able to sight-read people in my line; you don't have the luxury of finding out slowly and possibly getting it wrong. I'd figured she was a merchant's daughter—well-dressed, not gentry, but she'd never have to work for a living; she wouldn't be marrying some farmer, or a tradesman or craftsman. I guessed she was what's usually termed "difficult"—awkward, hard to control, the sort who won't stay home and behave nicely. Not allowed in the best families, and down the other end of the social scale they don't have the option, too busy helping put food on the table. But a merchant's daughter can have a few years of gadding about if she wants to, and generally no harm done. "I find that hard to believe," I said.

"No you don't," she replied. "But you haven't answered my question. What do you do?"

Don't get me wrong. It wasn't love or anything. But I was beginning to think that maybe three or four days wasn't quite enough. Besides, I was in no hurry. I had a bit of money for a change, and as far as I was aware, nobody was uncomfortably hot on my trail. The truth is, I liked her. A kindred spirit, perhaps—no ties, no commitments, a leaf in the wind. And there was something else, a hint of mischief, devilment. I like that in a person. Just possibly, I thought, she might understand. And wouldn't that be fun? Someone I could be honest with, tell the truth to. A whole new experience for me. So I took a deep breath.

"Actually," I said, "I'm a thief."

She nodded. "Thought so."

I really wasn't expecting that. "You did?"

"Mphm. Well, you're not a merchant, or where's your stock in trade? Not a courier, because I looked in your bag while you were asleep." She smiled. "That's when I thought, thief."

"Did you really."

Two thoughts collided in my head. First, it takes one to know one. But I dismissed that, because the contents of my bag were still there; I'd checked.

I check about once an hour, on average. The other thought was: she doesn't seem to mind, particularly.

"What sort of a thief?" she said. "Do you climb in through windows, or hit people over the head, or what?"

I couldn't believe I was having this conversation. But it was intoxicating. "Nothing so vulgar," I said.

"You're a con man," she said, and there was a sort of girlish delight in her voice.

I sort of shrugged. "That's overstating it a bit," I said. "What I actually do is pretend to be people. Usually government officials. I read the government gazette when they post up the new appointments, to see who's been posted where. Then I get there first."

"I see." Her eyes were laughing at me. "Sort of a shape-changer."

"That would be a very useful skill," I said. "It's a shame it's not actually possible. But I manage without it."

She nodded. "Do you wear disguises? Wigs and false beards and stuff like that?"

"No need," I said. "All I do is ask myself, what would it be like to be so-and-so? Like an actor, I guess. I thought of being an actor once, but there's no money in it." I smiled. "I like money."

"Me too," she said.

"A shared interest," I said, "that's good." Well, I thought, we're being honest with each other, asking the sort of questions you usually don't, so why not? I asked, "Have you got any?"

"What? Oh, money. Yes, from time to time. It's never been a problem."

I'd previously arrived at the conclusion that she wasn't any of the innumerable finely distinguished subspecies of prostitute; you can tell, almost immediately, once you get to that stage in the proceedings. Not a thief, either. Of the three vocations open to women in our enlightened society, that was two ruled out. "Are you a musician?"

"I'm sorry?"

"Singer," I said. "Do you sing? Professionally?"

She laughed. "People might well give me money to stop," she said.

I leaned across and kissed her mouth. "This money you get from time to time," I said. "How do you get it? Come on," I added, with my best smile. "You can't say I haven't been straight with me."

"Oh all right, then," she said. "I'm a witch."

Properly speaking, since I'd been acquitted, I'd have been within my rights to go to the prefecture and demand the return of all the stuff they'd taken off me when I was arrested: my entire inventory of worldly goods, as it happened—one heavy wool traveling coat, one bag containing five hundred angels in gold, and a copy of Vicentius' *Garden of Entrancing Images* (with pictures), not to mention the nine hundred angels' worth of uncut rubies sewn into the lining. Somehow, though, I figured that that would be pushing my luck, something I've always been hesitant to do. Now there's irony.

She was talking to me again. "It's humiliating," she said. "Having to go to court to reclaim you, like a lost dog or something. I wish you wouldn't do it."

"You can't blame a man for trying."

Actually, she could. "Not to mention," she went on, "drawing attention to us. You do realize, we're going to have to clear out again. Everybody knows who we are."

That made me laugh out loud.

"You know what I mean," she said irritably. "And you know what I think about being conspicuous. How much money have you got?"

"None whatsoever."

She sighed. "How do you fancy Mezentia?"

"I don't even know where it is."

"It's about as far south as you can go without getting your feet wet. About twelve hundred miles."

She'd have been there, of course, a long time ago. She's been everywhere. I remember we were in this ruined temple in Prochoris; circumstances had dictated that we should live rough for a while, and the locals were afraid to go inside. There was this painting on the wall—it was sheltered, but only a little bit had survived, the rest had all crumbled away centuries ago—and I looked at it and thought, I know that face. Quite a good likeness, in fact. She told me it was supposed to be Aedoea the Bringer of Death. Well, yes, I thought.

"I'm sick of traipsing around all the time," I said.

"Whose fault is that?"

"And I hate the south. It's so hot. Why can't we go somewhere nice, for a change?"

I don't like myself when I whine. I never used to do it. Play the cards you're dealt, was always my motto: When it's time to fold, then fold, and if you lose, well, that's how it goes. I'm not like that now, of course.

"Fine," she said. "We'll go to Thuria."

"No way in hell," I said. A woman passing by stopped and looked at me. I lowered my voice. "It's freezing cold and the people smell. And what could there possibly be for us in Thuria?"

"You don't know anything about it. Actually, it's quite nice there." Pause. "And there are silver mines."

"I don't give a shit. I refuse to spend six weeks rattling around in a coach to get to some godforsaken ice floe in the middle of nowhere."

She sighed. "All right," she said. "What *do* you want?"

The silly part of it is, I really am a gentleman. More than that, I'm your actual nobility; first cousin to a duke, my name (the real one, I mean) cut into the stonework of the arch in the front courtyard of a great house. Or at least it was. I expect it was chiseled out long since. What I mean to say is, I'm actually a lot more than I pretend to be. When I used to go around impersonating the nobility, I was invariably demoting myself by at least five grades, because if you show up out of the blue somewhere and announce that you're a what-I-really-am, nobody's going to believe you. Also, the minor public officials I used to pass myself off as were by definition men who had to make at least some show of working for a living. When I was twelve, I wouldn't have deigned to notice the sort of people I chose to become, when I was still working.

I guess I officially went to the bad when I was nineteen. My mother, bless her, really didn't want me to go to the University; she knew me too well, I guess. But father insisted. That was where young men of quality went when they were my age, and he could no more dream of interfering than of stopping the sun from rising. So, to the University I went, and a very congenial place I found it. Under other circumstances—if we'd been poor, for example, and I'd gone there to be educated rather than to get me out of the house for a bit—I might well have knuckled down and learned something. I genuinely enjoyed reading some of the books, though of course I daren't let on to the crowd I was in with, they'd have ragged me unmercifully, and I often think about them to this day: Saloninus' *Precepts* (my special favorite, what a genius that man was) and Eutropius' *Moral and Political Dialogues*, all that. Mostly, though, I drank and played cards and dice and chased skirts and went through money, which was what I was supposed to be doing, according to my father's view of the world; I was nothing if not a dutiful son.

Every letter home begging for money was answered by return, enclosing a draft drawn on the Stamen Brothers. I was surrounded on all sides by wild, eager young men desperate for money, hounded by creditors, terrified that their fathers and uncles would find out what they'd been up to and how much trouble they were in, but as far as I was concerned I had a bottomless purse and all my sins were not only condoned but encouraged. Enjoy yourself while you're young, my boy, the old fool used to say, plenty of time for the other stuff later; what's the use of being who you are if you don't make use of it?

Quite. But it made me wretched. I didn't fit in. Everyone I knew was either mortally jealous or desperate to ingratiate themselves in the hope of scoring a loan. My personal appearance didn't help, either. Truth is, I've never enjoyed being outstandingly handsome. It's like the money, something I never had to earn, which made everything too easy. In my second year, I even grew a beard, and then everyone said how much it suited me, so I shaved it off again, before I started a fashion.

So that's why I went to the bad: out of altruism. It started when the nearest thing I had to a friend (won't tell you his name because he's a Chief Magistrate now, a real one) came whining round begging for money, or else some tailor or other was going to write to his father and cause the most almighty row.

"How much do you need?" I asked him.

"Forty angels," he said. "Go on, be a sport. Forty angels is nothing to you. I've seen you spend that in an evening down at the Golden Feather."

Perfectly true. As it happened, I had forty angels in my coat pocket at that very moment. We were walking down Westgate together, just south of the New Temple. "Nothing doing," I replied.

"Oh go on, please. Really, I'm at my wit's end. If I don't get that money, I might as well jump off a bridge."

I sighed. "You're pathetic," I said. Then I looked round for a brick.

As I said earlier, there's never a brick when you need one. So we had to go down to the riverbank and fumble about in the dark until I found a stone about the right size and weight. "What the hell do you want that for?" he asked.

I stuffed it under the lapels of my greatcoat. "You'll see," I said.

It was around third watch; middle of the night, when all the drunks have finally wandered off, but before the first early-bird tradesmen begin to stir. We didn't encounter a living soul between Holy Bridge and the New Temple. Looking back, of course, I realize that was the most colossal stroke of beginner's luck. I led the way down the little winding alley that goes round the back of the New Temple and comes out on Foregate, just shy of the old Tolerance & Mercy.

You never really know how your mind works, do you? I guess I must've noticed that window at the back of the chancel, subconsciously, and figured that it would be an ideal place if ever anyone wanted to break in. Yet if you'd asked me, twenty-four hours earlier, I'd have told you in all sincerity that breaking into a temple and stealing the silver was the last thing I could ever see myself doing. Well, there you go. I took off my coat and he held it over the glass while I stoved it in with the stone. Practically silent. I'd like it noted that I've always been entirely self-taught, and have figured out all the basics of the profession from first principles, which is rather clever of me, you've got to admit.

"What the hell are we doing?" he asked in a hoarse, horrified whisper.

"Robbing a temple," I told him. "Wait there. If anyone comes, let me know. All right?"

He stared at me. I remember the look on his face, serendipitously illuminated in red and blue by a shaft of moonlight through the remains of the stained glass. He looked like he'd been horribly burned in a fire. "You're mad," he said. "We can't do this."

"Watch me."

And it was so easy. I climbed in, carefully not cutting my legs to ribbons on the broken window, strolled down the aisle, stopped at the altar, reached for the first piece of silverware I came to; stopped, engaged my brain. I'd been about to steal the Three Angels Chalice, a masterpiece of post-Mannerist art that'd be instantly recognizable anywhere in the Empire. No bloody good at all. Instead, I fumbled about until I came across a rather ugly silver paten, about seventy years old, quite plain. I traced all over it with my fingertips and I couldn't feel any kind of inscription. About forty angels' worth of silver, intrinsic value. I bowed to the altar and said thank you politely, then went back to where he was waiting for me.

"What the hell am I supposed to do with that?" he said.

Pathetic. "I don't know, do I? Sell it. Melt it down."

"Put it back, for crying out loud, and let's get out of here. If I get caught, my dad'll kill me."

I put the paten down on the ground. Then I punched him in the mouth, as hard as I could. "Pull yourself together, will you?" I said quietly. Then I picked up the paten, and we went home.

I spent the rest of the night thinking about it. Then, as soon as it was light, I went out and bought a pair of tinsmith's shears. I cut the paten up into little squares, about the size of a two-angel piece. Then I went for a walk down Silversmiths' Row. I knew instinctively who I could do business with. You just had to look at their faces.

"Do you want it or not?" I remember saying.

The man sort of leered at me. "Sure it won't be missed?" he said.

I shrugged. "One of our footmen steals things," I said.

He shrugged. "Thirty angels."

"Don't make me laugh."

I've always done well in my dealings with fences. I guess I trust men who are more interested in things than people. I've often wished I could be like that. I gouged him for forty-six angels: forty for my friend, six for the poor box outside the New Temple. The idea that I should profit in any way from the transaction never crossed my mind, and besides, I didn't need the money.

The operation was successful, in that my friend never tried to borrow money from me again. He stopped being my friend, of course, but I wasn't too bothered. Plenty more where he came from. And came they did—twenty angels here, thirty there, and though I say it myself, I was the soul of generosity. I spent my evenings strolling through the streets looking for vulnerable windows, convenient waterpipes, back doors not overlooked by neighboring houses. I didn't know it at the time, but I was on one of those rolls you occasionally get in the profession, when it seems like you can't go wrong and the dice always fall your way, even when you're incredibly careless and overconfident. All that came to a shuddering halt, of course, one night when I carefully prised open a goldsmith's shutters to find the goldsmith and his son sitting in the dark with drawn swords across their knees.

To this day I wish I knew what possessed me. If I'd held still, acted drunk, pretended it was all a lark or a dare or something, I'm a hundred per cent sure my father would've bought them off, and no harm done to anyone. Instead, I pulled out this stupid knife I'd got into the habit of carrying, and there was this farcical sort of a scrimmage, and I stabbed the goldsmith's son in the eye. I'd like to say it was an accident, the result of three large men blundering about in the dark being careless with sharp objects. That'd be entirely plausible, and nobody could prove it wasn't true. But no. The boy had tripped over his father's feet; he latched on to my ankles and I couldn't get him off me. So I killed him.

Why did I do that? As you'd expect, I've given it a degree of thought over the years, and I've come to the conclusion that I did it because that's who I am. Let me explain. I was born a nobleman's son, but that must've been a mistake. Really, I'm a thief. A nobleman's son, caught red-handed committing a crime, treats the whole thing as a joke and pays the price for his fun with his father's money. A thief, caught by the ankle in a dark shop, kills someone. I must have known that, or I wouldn't have taken the knife with me in the first place.

I'm telling you this so as to kill any misplaced sympathy you might be inclined to have for me. As I've told a long succession of judges in most of the jurisdictions right across the known world, I'm guilty. I suppose I always have been. Born like it.

We went to Thuria.

I remembered it when we got there. We'd been there ten years or so earlier. It was where I'd thrown myself out of a twelfth story window. She gave me hell over that. You think I've got nothing better to do, and so on and so forth. I've heard it so often I can say the words along with her.

"Well," I said, as we clambered out of the coach and stretched our backs. There was snow on the ground, needless to say. "Here we are. Now what?"

She stooped and flipped over a stone. No dice. Insects can't live in such a cold place. "I told you," she said. "They have silver mines."

I yawned. "Big deal."

"I don't want you getting bored," she said. "You always do stupid things when you're bored."

"We should go to Shansard," I said, not that I meant it. "There's a temple there with the best collection of Resolutionist icons in the world, and all they've got guarding it is six old priests and a lock I could pick with a blade of grass."

She looked at me and sighed. "All right," she said, and she dropped the bag she was carrying. "If that's what you want."

"No, we're here now," I said. "Come on, we'd better find an inn or something. Assuming they've got inns in this armpit."

Kuvass City is actually not bad at all. The center was completely rebuilt by the Imperials about thirty years ago; a bit generic, but the streets are paved and there are a few quite good buildings. The best inn in town is the Flawless Diamonds of Orthodoxy. Rather grand, very expensive, heavily based on the Silver Star in the City—a bit like a page of manuscript copied out by a careful but illiterate copyist. So, to the Doxy we went. They looked at us a bit sideways, but we had money. They gave us a room on the third floor, with an impressive view out over the sawmills. Lumber is the big business in Kuvass City. I stood in front of the window for a while and drank in the scene. "I might like it here," I said.

"Come to bed," she said.

"In the middle of the afternoon."

"Please."

That's the ridiculous thing. She really does love me. After all I've done to her, all I've tried to do. For crying out loud, I've killed her sixteen times.

The first time was in Podarga. We'd been together for about three months. The first month hadn't been bad at all. Imagine: you pick up a really attractive girl, nice manners and sexually adventurous, apparently besotted with you, not in the least adverse to a bit of criminal activity, and who happens to be a witch with genuine and wide-ranging magic powers. We'd had a lot of fun together, I freely admit. I'd reverted from the con game to straightforward breaking and entering, not that you need to do much breaking when your accomplice can turn herself into a cockroach, crawl in under the door and turn the key from the inside. We did the Stamen brothers, for old times' sake. I'll never forgive them for how they treated my father, after the big crash. That was the first time we did the cockroach thing. I filled two big grain sacks with gold coin, then found they were—surprise, surprise—far too heavy to lift. Silly, she said, with a tender smile, and did this weightlessness spell. It was like carrying pillows.

That night I was really worried about her. She collapsed about an hour after we got back to the inn; she was pale as death, could hardly breathe, severe bouts of fever and vomiting. It's all right, she told me, it's perfectly normal, I'm used to it. I wanted to call a doctor, but she just grinned weakly. It was the transformation, she explained. You're all right if you transform for under a minute. Longer than that, you get the shakes and so forth. I was horrified. Why didn't you tell me, I said, I'd have thought of something else? No, that's fine, really, she said. I'm used to it. She was sweating like a block of ice melting. The things I do for love, she said. At the time, I thought that was really sweet.

After the Stamen brothers, we did the Charitable Bank, the Sword Blade Bank, the Merchant Adventurers; so much money, so very easy. It made me nervous. We ought to quit while we're ahead, I said to her, at the very least we ought to cool it for a while. That made her laugh. Why stop when we're having so much fun? she said.

"Because we don't need to do any more," I told her. "We've got enough."

She looked at me. "Enough," she repeated. "What's that supposed to mean? Enough for what?"

"Enough money," I said. I pointed to the big trunk I'd bought to keep the money in. "There's over five thousand angels in there."

She shrugged. "How much money did your father have?" she said.

"What? I don't know."

"More than five thousand angels?"

"Well, yes."

"Six thousand? Sixty thousand? Six hundred thousand?"

She was starting to annoy me. "No idea," I said.

"Rough guess."

"All right," I said. "If you put everything together, the land and the houses and the ships he owned and everything, something to the tune of half a million. But that's different."

"Is it?" She smiled at me. "That's what you should've had," she said. "That should've been yours *by right*. So, five thousand angels isn't enough. Is it?"

"Now you're being stupid," I said. "We can't steal half a million angels. It'd take us the rest of our lives."

She just grinned at me.

So we carried on, cleaning out goldsmiths and silversmiths, merchants, on one occasion the army payroll. Needless to say, people were beginning to notice. They set up a watch committee, hired guards; poor fools weren't looking out for fleas and cockroaches. We filled our fourth trunk. The prefect issued a statement flatly denying that there was a critical shortage of gold currency in Podarga, which was as good as an outright admission. There were runs on the banks, which only served to highlight the fact that they had no money, because some bastard had taken it. I told her, this isn't fun any more, it's got to stop. We're causing an economic crisis here, and people will get hurt. All she ever did was grin at me and haul me into bed. We were spending practically nothing, maybe three thalers a week, and we had most of the money in the city sitting in huge boxes on the floor of our room. I got a pair of scales and did some rough calculations. Then I told her, there's over a million angels here, that's twice what you reckon the world owes me, can we stop now, please? She started laughing at me. I put my hands round her throat and squeezed.

I remember how her face turned blue, just before she died. It was the most extraordinary thing. Her eyes glazed over, in that moment of transition when she stopped being a person and turned into a thing, that special sort of reverse alchemy. I knew she was dead when I felt her entire weight on my wrists. It was only then, I think, that I realized what I was doing. No, make that what I'd done.

Nobody could've been more surprised, I think, than I was. After I killed the goldsmith's son, I think I told you, I gave up the burglary side of things; I never wanted to put myself in that position again, where I'd be in danger of killing someone. It's a question of knowing what you're capable of. Ever since then, I'd made a point of playing safe. No weapons, no situations where that sort of conflict could arise. With her on the team, so to speak, there'd been no risk of that. It was so easy, so safe. She could see through doors and walls, so we always knew if there was a guard in there waiting for us. So. I was stunned. I'd done it again.

If there'd been something sharp handy, I swear I'd have killed myself. I actually tried smashing a pottery dish, to make a sharp edge; stupid thing wouldn't break, even when I stamped on it with my boot. *Not fit to live* was the only thought running through my mind. On balance—I was clear-headed enough to make the distinction—I preferred to kill myself, in my own time and with dignity, than wait for the watch to show up—public trial, public execution, I still had my finer feelings at that point. But it wasn't what you'd call a deal-breaker. The rope would do just fine, if I couldn't manage anything better. People will tell you that capital punishment is barbaric. Me, I'm all for it.

(Except, I don't think they should've hung my poor father. He was guilty, all right—high treason, no less, conspiracy to overthrow the Republic. We're always guilty in my family. But what actually happened was, he got sucked into this stupid idea of cornering the grain market by the Stamen brothers, and needless to say it all went yellow, and my father was cleaned out, everything, and it turned out the Stamen boys hadn't actually put in any of their own money, so they were all right. My poor, stupid father went in with a bunch of lunatic idealists from the Phocas and the Tmiscas—cousins of ours, about a thousand times removed, everybody is, at that level—who wanted to get shot of the government and go back to the old days. They fondly believed they had the army on their side, but it was all nonsense, really. I don't suppose anything would've come of it, if the Coalition hadn't been tearing itself apart over the Agrarian Reform Bill, and they desperately needed a crisis to take everyone's mind off things. My father and his idiot friends were a gift from heaven, as far as they were concerned. Two of the conspirators managed to worm their way out by turning state's evidence (we dealt with them later, I'm proud to say) but the rest went to the gallows, including my poor father. I wasn't there, of course, didn't dare show my face, but I gather he made a wild, rather incoherent speech about how he could die proud, having for once in his life stood up for something worthwhile, even though it had come to nothing—Well. He was a clown. But they shouldn't hang clowns. Not when there are really bad people walking free, like me.)

So there I was, trying frantically to smash a clay dish that wouldn't break, with the dead body of my beautiful girl lying at my feet. Running through my head, so loud that I couldn't think, was the phrase *the consequences of his actions*. Fair enough, I told myself. You do something really bad, you pay for it. Note the word *pay*. There's a deeply rooted commercial streak strongly embedded in our notion of morality. You buy a crime with punishment; you do a bad thing, and you pay for it—but not with a good thing, please note, but with another bad thing, a death for a death. Not sure of the logic there, because surely it ought to be—you pay for a bad thing with a good thing: murder someone, pay for it by giving all your money to the poor and spending the rest of your life in a monastery. But apparently not. Anyway, back then I was profoundly conventional in my ethical outlook. I'd killed two people, so I deserved to die. Only I couldn't break the stupid dish.

The hell with it, I thought. I'll turn myself in to the Watch, and they can deal with me. After all, that's what we pay our taxes for. I knelt down and put my fingers on her neck, just in case I'd got it wrong and there was a faint pulse. Nothing. She was getting cold, and her face was as white as really good quality wax. I closed the door behind me and went out into the street.

Turn myself in to the Watch. Did I know where the Watch House is in Podarga? Did I hell. I thought I knew; I thought it was the big white building in Constitution Square, but that turned out to be the Provincial Legislature. There was a kettlehat on duty at the gate and I tried to surrender myself to him, but he looked at me and told me he wasn't allowed to leave his post until the end of his shift. I'll wait, I said, I don't mind waiting. Piss off, he told me. All right, I said, could you please give me direction to the Watch House? Out of the square and take a left, he said, then down North Parade till you've got the Golden Flea on your left, there's a courtyard on your right, you can't miss it.

I found it, eventually (I'm hopeless with directions). They've got this really impressive set of wrought iron gates, and standing in front of them, there she was.

I stared at her. "There you are," she said. "I thought this is where you'd come."

"You're alive," I said.

"No thanks to you."

"Oh thank God," I said. "I thought I'd killed you."

She frowned at me. "You did," she said.

Things you never knew about witches.

She explained it to me. Apparently, the universe is sort of like a house. There are different rooms. What you and I think of as the world is just one of them; we live in it, and when we die, we go upstairs to another one, and there we stop. But witches have keys to a lot of other rooms where we can't go, and where things don't work the same. That's how they do magic. They just pop next door, to where the impossible is a piece of cake, and then (I never followed this part) they sort of walk back in as something else. So, when she was on the point of death, with my hands clamped tight round her neck, she slipped away into another room until her body was stone dead, then came back again. It's not pleasant, she said, climbing back into your dead body. It's freezing cold and you have to get everything working again, it's a bit like putting on a suit of dripping wet clothes. But death, she told me, is no big deal. The least of her problems.

As you can imagine, things were a bit strained between us for a while after that. She kept telling me she'd forgiven me and I wasn't to think about it any more. I kept telling her I was no good, I was evil, a murderer. She told me not to be so self-indulgent. You lost your temper, she said, that's all. No harm done. No, I said, but the intention— She gave me a funny look. Intention doesn't matter, she said. Nothing matters, really. I told her I was going away. Fine, she said, I'm coming with you.

So one night, when she was fast asleep, I left her. I didn't dare fumble around in the dark for my coat, because she was a light sleeper and the slightest sound woke her up. I walked out in just my shirt and trousers. For the first time in my life, my pockets were empty, not a coin to my name. Strange feeling, that. I remember, as I emerged from the inn doorway into the street, this weird sort of freedom, as if for the first time I was really myself, shorn of all the inherited and acquired junk; just me, my strengths, weaknesses, qualities, flaws, character. I scratched the back of my neck and walked down to the harbor.

Stowing away on board a ship is easier than you think. It's staying stowed that's the problem. I swam out and climbed the hawser; there was nobody about, and I scrambled up on top of a big stack of barrels and lay down. I guess I fell asleep, because I remember opening my eyes and seeing a broad blue sky, and feeling hair brushing my cheek.

She kissed me. "Hello," she said.

I didn't move. I couldn't. I was frozen.

"This is fun," she said. "Where are we going?"

Later we climbed down and gave ourselves up to the captain, who was delighted to accept five angels and take us on as passengers. He didn't ask why we'd come aboard without telling anyone, sort of got the impression it wasn't the first time. He lent us his cabin, for an extra two angels, and they did their best to make us comfortable. The ship was going to Laerna, with a cargo of vinegar.

Anyway, where were we? Oh yes. Kuvass City.

When I first met her, I was twenty-three. That was thirty-five years ago. How old am I? I simply don't know. When I see myself in a mirror, I look about nineteen, though I learned not to trust mirrors a long time ago. But people assume I'm—well, the same age as she is, and she looks about twenty. What a charming couple, people say, him so handsome and her so very beautiful.

Did I mention the sawmills? Big business is Kuvass City. They float lumber down the river in huge rafts. It's only softwood, pines and firs, so nearly all of it gets sawn into planks. The mills are powered by waterwheels driven by the Kuvass River. They can handle any size of tree you care to name. The circular saw-blades are the size of a cartwheel, and they have five or six running in parallel—you feed in a tree at one end, it comes out all planked out at the other, about a minute later. Quite an impressive sight.

I made a special point of not looking too closely at the sawmills. Instead, we went to see the silver mines. Foul place. They'd torn a mountain in half, so that one side was an artificial cliff-face, with ridiculous rickety wooden galleries scrambling up it like ivy. God help the poor devils who work there.

They scoop away the mountain with picks, winch down the ore in buckets, and then the stuff goes into the separation process, which is a real mess. I don't know how it actually works, but there's this delta of open sewers, to wash the mud off the ore, and huge furnaces belching out thick, stinking smoke. You can tell where the idea of Hell came from; noise and ooze and stench and smoke, from time to time great jets of flame as they open and close the ports and vents. The soot gets in your eyes and your hair, the fumes get up your nose and you choke, and every footstep in the ankle-deep mud is a horrible effort. Sort of a metaphor, really, because that's where money comes from, that's how money is made.

We were rich investors thinking about buying into the mine. We'd come to see for ourselves, my sister and I. The mine captain was shocked that nobody had told him to expect distinguished visitors. He kept apologizing and yelling for duckboards for us to walk on.

We were terribly impressed with what we saw. It was all quite fascinating, and clearly the mine was wonderfully productive. Just one thing, though. All that valuable silver bullion—what was it? Three tons a day? What was there to prevent it from getting, well, you know, stolen?

"Easy," she said, as we squelched back to town in our ruined footwear. "The guards aren't a problem, obviously. You wait round the back, where there's that blind spot beside the water-chute, did you notice it? I can crawl in through the gap under the eaves, make an invisible hole in the back wall and just pass the ingots out to you. Then I come out again and we make the ingots weightless and float them over to the road and onto the cart. By the time they open up in the morning, we'll be in Scheria. Piece of cake."

Indeed. It always was a piece of cake. That was the point.

"Fine," I said. "We'll do that, then." I was trying to sound bored and sullen. It was getting harder and harder. She was so quick to suspect, and I'm not that good an actor. "Tonight?"

"Might as well. No point in hanging around for the sake of it."

She always argues; I'm a thief, it's my nature. Stealing is what I want to do. Not for the money, because money's never interested me, the same way fish aren't interested in water. It's the stealing that I enjoy. Therefore, that's what we'll do, one robbery after another, for the rest of our indefinitely prolonged lives. Happy ever after.

Just so long as you're happy, she says, that's all I want. Isn't that what love means?

"Tonight, then," I said. "I'll need to see about a cart."

She nodded. "That's fine, then," she said. "I'll see you back at the inn."

Thought I was being really clever. I left her at the corner of Coppergate and went on down North Reach as far as the livery, then doubled back up Old Side, through the lanes and out onto the wharf, then up the towpath until I reached the ingates of the mill sluice. I picked my way along the top of the narrow wall and climbed down into the sawpit yard. The noise of the saw-blades was deafening, and the air was full of coarse shreds of sawdust, like a snowstorm. The man working the saw benches saw me and yelled, get away, you fool. I felt sorry for him. Believe it or not, I don't like to make trouble for people, but sometimes it just can't be helped.

Did I mention I was in the army? Oh yes. I was a captain. Not a proper one, of course. I'd have been a major, only I look too young, even with this ludicrous system they have in the Empire of buying commissions. Still, a captain's pretty hot stuff, particularly a captain in the House Guards. I'd set my heart on them, because I happened to know they were about to be sent off to the Southern front, where the fighting was pretty grim.

I don't suppose you've heard of that war. It was never anything much. Either the Sashan launched a sneak attack on one of our outposts, or we launched one on one of theirs; can't remember, don't particularly care. But at one point it got a bit out of hand; we slaughtered their expeditionary force, they ambushed our relief column, there was going to have to be a full-scale pitched battle to sort things out, or the whole thing would degenerate into hit-and-run all along the frontier, and that kind of thing can drag on for years.

Nothing to do with me, of course. I was dead set on getting in on it because I figured, the army, forced marches across the desert, all that; there was no way she could follow me there, not as a girl, at any rate. And I reckoned she'd quickly get tired of being a flea all the time. She'd lose interest, maybe find someone else to pick on; she'd be gone and I could get on with my life.

How naïve. I turned up one evening at the camp gate, introduced myself, handed over my commission to the CO—a nice piece of work, that; I use a forger in Seuma Eris, extremely reliable and really quite reasonable. He gave it a cursory glance and poured me a drink, and that was that.

I knew absolutely nothing about soldiering, needless to say. That was just right, because most of the young officers sent out to the front in that war were straight up from their country estates, never seen a parade-ground in their lives. I took the color-sergeant on one side, gave him ten angels. "What do I have to do?" I asked him.

He grinned at me. "That's all right, sir," he said. "You ride at the front and try not to run away when the fighting starts, and you leave the rest to me and the other sergeants. We'll look after you, sir, we know the score."

Fine by me. Actually, that sergeant was a fine fellow. He told me to dump all the shiny new armor I'd bought at the outfitters' (he had a sideline, selling it back to them) and got me fitted out in the proper stuff, worn in and comfortable. He got me a pair of boots that actually fit. They were Sashan, needless to say; they make the best army boots anywhere. Every day I'd get on my beautiful white horse and ride out, and when it was time to stop he'd tell me well in advance. There were papers to sign after dinner, but that was all. I could've done without the searing heat, needless to say, and it had been a few years since I spent quite so long in the saddle. But I'd had my share of living rough before she came along, very rough indeed at times, so all in all it wasn't too bad. Best of all, no sign of her whatsoever. Not even a bite on my neck or an itch anywhere. They do say it's too hot for fleas in the desert. Flies are another matter, of course. But I'd never known her be a fly.

Then, one night, I was sitting outside my tent watching the men gathered round the fire, and I saw this dog. It was great big thing, pure white. The men were throwing bones for it. I called my friend the sergeant. "What's that in aid of?" I asked.

He grinned. "Oh, that," he said. "Don't know where she came from, sir, just showed up one day. The men like her, reckon she's good luck. Funny thing, coming across a dog in the middle of the desert. Tame as anything, though."

"Maybe she was with a salt caravan and wandered off," I said.

"Something like that, sir," he said.

The next day, and the day after that, I tried to spot her as we marched, but she was too smart for that. I guess she stayed at the rear; I was stuck at the front, of course, the shiny figurehead, and I couldn't desert my post and go looking for her. I thought of giving orders for her to be shot or driven off, but I knew I couldn't do that; so popular with the men, mascot, good luck. I tried to bribe my sergeant to poison her, discreetly, when no one was watching; he looked shocked and pretended he hadn't heard me. That was when I knew she'd outsmarted me good and proper.

Which left me with Plan B; unfortunate, but there it was.

The sergeant must have known we were walking into a trap. If I could figure it out, so could he. I remember him pointing out the dangers, gently reminding me of our orders, which didn't include riding straight into a narrow, high-sided ravine. At one point he told the trumpeters to sound the general halt, without a word from me. I had to be quite sharp with him. I knew exactly what I was doing, of course; because I knew how my opposite number's mind worked, because he'd be just like me, a rich man's son. So, when they blocked both ends of the ravine and displayed their archers and slingers, leering down at us, I was ready. I told the trumpeters to blow to parlay. Sure enough, down came their heralds. Surrender, they said, you're trapped, we'll slaughter you. I smiled. I challenge your leader to single combat, I said. Him or his duly appointed champion.

The herald looked at me and grinned, and rode away without a word. That was too much for my sergeant. He grabbed me by the shoulder. Have you gone mad, he said. Are you out of your tiny little mind? I shook my head. We were screwed anyway, I said. We were at the very furthest extent of our supply line—I, a mere civilian, could see that clearly, whereas the general and his staff appeared not to have noticed. But what the hell. Any day now, they were going to launch a big attack, and we'd all be killed. This way, however, we stood a chance; not me, naturally, because they would choose the best fighter they'd got as their champion, and he'd go right through me in three seconds flat. Everyone else, however, would be allowed to surrender calmly and peacefully, and then it'd be up to the Sashan to provide food and water for three hundred men in the middle of the desert, something that our own side seemed incapable of doing.

Just for once, my sergeant didn't have anything to say. I enjoyed that moment, almost as much as if the heroism and altruism had been genuine. All phony, of course. I had my own agenda, and they were just accessories, props. I, however, was wallowing in a confluence of two streams of joy. One: I'd saved my men, they'd live when they should've died. Two: the enemy champion would kill me, and then at last, I'd finally be rid of her and free.

They chose their man well. A lot of commanders would've gone for mere size and bulk, not realizing that in a duel, a big man's at a disadvantage. There's more of him to move about, so he's slow, and he's a bigger target. Instead, they went for a short, lean chap, quick as a snake. I knew as I watched him walk toward me that he knew exactly what he was doing. And so it proved. I came out swinging. He did this delicate little sideways-and-back step, and I looked down and saw that I'd walked straight into his sword point and skewered myself on it.

Didn't hurt all that much. The world suddenly went quiet, and the edges of my vision began to darken, as though I was falling down a hole. I knew at that point he'd got me, but he was a professional, the sort who does a thorough, workmanlike job. He took a further half-step back, lifted his arm and cut my head off.

Everything went dark. Then I opened my eyes.

She smiled at me. "It's all right," she said. "You're going to be just fine."

Over her shoulder I could see the sun. It was directly overhead, whereas when I'd faced the enemy champion, it was considerably farther over to the east. So: three, maybe four hours later. Out of the corner of my eye, I could see that the sand I was lying on was caked brown—my blood, presumably.

"You clown," she said.

I opened my mouth. No sound came.

"Typical of you," she went on, "the big, noble gesture. Did you really think you'd be able to win a duel? Anyway, it's fine. They took your men away in a column. The Sashan look after their prisoners, they're known for it. They're going to be all right."

She honestly believed I gave a damn. That's love for you.

Things you never knew about witches.

Coming back to life, she explained to me once, isn't that big a deal. Bringing someone else back, by contrast, is a total pain, which explains, she said, why it's done so rarely. There are two stages, apparently. You have to go Upstairs (we're reverting to our metaphor of the house) and into the Very Bad Room, and you have to find who you're looking for and persuade them to come back, which they're always extremely reluctant to do. It can only be done, she told me, if the person really and truly wants to come back—try explaining that to a crowd of grieving relatives: actually, he'd far rather be dead and rid of the lot of you—which only happens when the person has unfinished business here. And that unfinished business, she told me, is always, invariably, love.

Shows how much she knows.

The other part, which you have to do first, is putting the damaged body back together again, to the point where it can once again sustain life. That, she said, is sheer miserable hard work. To do it, you make yourself small—really, really small, so you can crawl down inside veins and arteries and patch them up from the inside, or sew them back together when they've been severed. Same with the nerves and the skin. It's days, or weeks, of grueling hard work, in conditions a coal-miner would find unbearable. Time passes in a different way when you're that size, she said, which is why a month of hard labor inside someone's veins can be accomplished in an hour of our time, before the body gets too cold to restart. Leave it too long, and nothing can be done, which is why you've got to be there, on the spot, and get in as soon as you can after the death.

You wouldn't do it for any money, she said. You wouldn't do it for a dear friend, or the man you admire the most, or an uncle or an aunt. Only for love, she said. Only for love.

I scrambled up onto the low wall. The man who'd spotted me left what he was doing and headed for me, yelling, though I couldn't hear anything for the noise of the saw-blades. I picked my spot and jumped like a diver.

For a moment I thought I'd got it all wrong. I landed on my knee on the nearest blade, and I was sure I'd slide off and be kicked free. But then I felt the saw-blade slice through my leg, and I fell forward, belly-flopped onto three saw-blades running in parallel—

After she brought me back to life on the battlefield, I confess, I loved her; more, I have to say, than I'd have thought possible. To owe someone your life, to know that you left her, and she followed you, and she was there when you needed her most, because she loves you—I realized just how wrong I'd been, running away from the most wonderful thing life could possibly give me. To think, I told her, to think I could've died, and never realized. There, she said, it's all right now. It's going to be all right forever.

We robbed the state treasury in Mnasthe, or at least, I did. Let me do this one by myself, I said to her, just to see if I can. I explained that maybe what had gone wrong and made me feel so depressed was this idea that she'd taken over my life—she did everything, provided everything, so long as she was with me I need fear no evil, and that, I conjectured, left me feeling trapped and helpless. So, if I did the robbery myself (with her help, because it'd be impossible to do it alone, but me making the plans and deciding how we'd do it), I'd reassure myself that I was still me, an independent free agent, not just an extension of her. What a good idea, she said, we'll do that.

I've never worked so hard in my life. Hours of quiet observation, miles trudged round and round the city, pages and pages of scrupulous notes, timings, calculations, extrapolated measurements. I went to the library and read books on geometry and trigonometry, so I could figure out the precise height and thickness of the walls, the exact amount of rope I'd need, the weight of the sacks of gold coins I'd have to haul up out of there with my cunningly-modified block and tackle. No magic, I'd insisted, just unaided human effort. We spend two whole days trudging up and down the mountains looking for archers' root, to make the knockout potion we were going to dribble, drop by drop, down a piece of string dangled from the skylight into the nightwatchman's beer. The closer we got to the big day, the more improbable contingencies I came up with for us to take into account and guard against. What if there's a dog? We'd seen no sign of one, but I went out and bought an oilskin bag to put the slab of raw liver spiked with archers' root in. I kept telling myself how much I was enjoying it all: the challenge, the uncertainty, the pleasure of the two of us working side by side, not witch and familiar but two equal human beings. I might be a mere mortal, I told her, but I'm *smart*. Who else would have thought to cut the soles off a perfectly good pair of boots and sew them back on the wrong way round, so that any footprints I left in the mud would appear to be going the other way?

It goes without saying, I made a total pig's ear of it. I climbed up onto the roof, dribbled the sleepy stuff into the guard's beer, waited till he fell asleep, climbed down, got the keys off his belt, opened the vault door, started filling sacks. What I hadn't taken into account was that the open skylight funneled in a draft that blew the vault door shut. I'd left the key in the lock, on the outside. I was shut in.

I didn't have to wait till morning. Three or four hours later, the door opened and in came a half-platoon of kettlehats, with drawn swords. I gave them a big, sheepish grin.

She got me out, of course. She made an invisible hole in the prison wall, and another in the outside wall of my cell. I remember staggering out into the corridor and looking all round for her, until I felt a nip on the back of my neck. "Which way?" I said. A slight delay, then something bit my left ear. I went left. Out of there in two minutes flat, stepping over the bodies of five stunned guards. I'm not fit to be let out without a nanny.

I said to her, "I think I've had enough of the stealing business. Let's do something else."

"Fine," she said, and poured me a drink. "Let's do something else."

"Fine," I said. "What?"

So we tried philanthropy.

We had this enormous stash of money. Previously we'd cleaned out most of the banks, major mecantiles, and revenue offices in Carmandua, North Piria, Molossene, and the Espide Confederacy. It was far too much to take around with us—a dozen big iron-ore carts, each drawn by six horses—so we sank it into the side of a mountain in Rhouna Penaul, quite safe, you'd have had to chip away twenty feet of granite to get to it. She just closed her eyes and muttered something. It's so easy for some people, like being born rich, I guess.

"There's two ways we can go about doing this," I remember telling her. "We can just stand on a street corner and hand out money, or we can use this lot to change the way things are done, make a real difference."

She looked at me, shrugged. "All right," she said. "What do you want to do?"

I started explaining to her about the Republic. Once upon a time, I told her, there was a small city, ruled by kings. But the city grew strong and came to dominate its neighbors. Tribute and taxes flowed into the Exchequer, and the kings took that money and spent it on stupid luxuries, gorgeous palaces, pensions and monopolies for their favorites, while the poor starved. Then along came a man called Victorinus, a nobleman from an ancient family. He started saying that the way things were done was all wrong. The wealth that the hardworking people created and the brave soldiers took from the conquered provinces should be shared equally among the citizens; hereditary monarchy was idiotic, the king should be elected by the people. The king tried to have him strung up, but the people wouldn't allow it; instead, they chased out the king and made Victorinus their leader. The king raised an army of mercenaries, but the people's army slaughtered them like sheep. The Republic was born. And then (I told her) it changed. Slowly, gradually, without anyone noticing. And anyway, most of the time the people were looking the other way, watching the invincible armies of the Republic conquering the known world—*mercy to those who submit, but grind down the warlike with war,* as the poet so charmingly puts it. There was always plenty to watch and feel good about, but meanwhile—well, you know the saying, how all women eventually end up turning into their own mothers. Same with the Republic. Instead of the king there was the Council of Ten; once you'd said that, you'd said everything.

She heard me out, then nodded. "Right," she said. "What's that got to do with us?"

"We can change all that," I said. "We can put it all right again. With the money, and your powers, we can be Victorinus all over again. Overthrow the Republic. Stick the heads of the Ten up on pikes and set the people free. I understand now," I said, "it's actually starting to make some sense, that's why I met you."

She had this odd sort of smile on her face. "Any minute now," she said, "you're going to use the word *Destiny*."

I glowered at her. "And why not?" I said. "I mean, just ask yourself: why was I born into the upper crust, when all my instincts are straight in off the street? But that's just what Victorinus was like, the greatest man who ever lived. Now, God knows I'm not like him, brave and noble and wise, but that's why I've got you. There's a purpose to it, there has to be. And I'm so stupid, it's taken me all this time to realize."

She was quiet for a while, thinking. Then: "All right," she said.

I gave her a huge smile. "I love you," I said.

"I love you too," she said. But my mind was on other things.

So, a boy and a girl, very much in love, decide to overthrow the State. How do they go about it?

"We've got to think this through carefully," I said. We were in bed, looking out through an open window over Beloisa Bay. The sun was rising; the sea was purple and the sky was dark blue and red.

"Of course," she said. I got the impression she wasn't really interested.

"The people," I went on, "are stupid. The trouble with them is, they don't know when they're unhappy. You can bully them and starve them and cheat them out of their land and send their sons off to die in the desert, and they just sit there and take it." I leaned across her and picked a grape off the bunch. "That's where all the revolutions of the past have come unstuck," I went on, "that's where my father went wrong. He thought it was just a case of bribing a few senior officers in the palace guard. Never occurred to him that the Council of Ten had far more money than he did and could match any offer he could make out of petty cash. No, you've got to start with the people."

She nodded. "You've got to make them unhappy," she said.

She was being a bit dim. "They are unhappy," I said. "You've got to make them realize it."

"Oh I see." She yawned. "Would you like to go for a swim later?"

"I don't know, I'll see. And then," I went on, "it's not enough for them to know they're unhappy, there's got to be a catalyst, a spark, a moment of no return. There's got to be one specific thing. Like the arrest of the four priests in Semnia Brevis, or the simony scandal in Beal Defoir. Something to bring them out on the streets. Otherwise, they'll just stay at home and moan to each other."

"All right," she said. "That shouldn't be too difficult."

I took another grape. Very good grapes, imported. "And of course you do need the army on your side, no question about it," I went on. "Not just a hatful of colonels, you need the captains and the junior officers as well. And you'll only get them if they're really angry about something."

"Such as?"

I thought about the precedents. "In Joiceau it was a massacre of civilians," I said. "When the Sashan threw out the Third Dynasty, it was because the emperor had ordered the army to kill all the women and children in Ap' Ereme. It's always a sort of gut feeling of revulsion, like, we can't possibly do this. Otherwise, they just knuckle under and obey orders, even when they know it's wrong."

"I get you," she said. "You really do have to think of everything, don't you?"

I nodded. "You've got to have a sort of vicious spiral," I said, "where everything the government does to stay in power turns against them. They try appeasement, it just makes the people demand more. They try force, that pisses off the junior officers. That's what I mean about the point of no return. Some really terrible thing. That's when it becomes inevitable, and nothing anyone does can stop it."

"And that's what we need to think up," she said. "I see."

At that point there was a knock on the door, the maid with breakfast. Then we went for a swim, the sea was calm and warm, and then we went back to the inn and made love. I was still thinking things over, trying to create the shape of a successful rebellion in my subconscious mind. She didn't bring the subject up again, so I assumed she was happy to leave the strategic planning to me.

"It'll be fine," she said. "It'll be something we can do together."

Now I have to confess, I'm not a morning person as a rule. Qualify that; dawn is fine by me so long as I've been up all night. But waking to see Her rosy fingers spreading across a dark blue sky is my idea of a total drag.

So, when she shook me awake and through the open window I saw blue and pink, I mumbled, "Leave me alone. Go back to sleep."

She stabbed me in the ribs with two fingers. That got the job done. "What?" I whined.

"Get up," she said, "quickly. We've got to go."

Now that was a sentiment I could relate to. A lot of people, many of them early-morning women, have said that to me, invariably with good reason—bailiffs, law enforcement officers, husbands. A heartbeat later, I was out of bed and fumbling for my shoes. "What?" I said. "What's the matter?"

"Quickly."

Even so, I was wondering what it could be. We hadn't robbed anyone since we'd been in Beloisa, we weren't known to the authorities, and she didn't have a husband. She threw me my coat and I dragged it on. She was holding the door open for me.

"What?" I insisted. She pointed. At the window.

For a moment I couldn't see anything. Then it hit me, and my heart stopped. The sea was in the wrong place. Instead of being down where it usually was, it was right up high. It wasn't the sea, it was a huge, enormous wave, and it was heading straight at us.

I turned to her. I think what I wanted to say was, it's no good, we can't outrun that. But no words came out, just a pathetic sort of a squeal—pig-language, in which during moments of stress I am remarkably fluent. She didn't speak either, she grabbed me by the arm and said something I didn't quite catch, and suddenly we were somewhere else.

Historians have a lot to say about the freak tidal wave that overwhelmed Beloisa on the 15th Aulularia AUC 667. It was that, they claim, that triggered the extraordinary events that were to follow. The destruction of the third largest city in the Empire—fifty thousand dead, a quarter of a million homeless and destitute—was significant enough. More momentous still was the fact that with Beloisa ruined and out of commission, the vast quantities of grain and other commodities required to feed the citizens of the capital had to travel an additional six hundred miles, a hundred of those by road. Quite simply, it couldn't be done. Prices in Cornmarket doubled, quadrupled in a week; angry crowds were driven out of Victorinus Square by the palace guards, fell on the six state granaries and broke into them, only to find them empty, because the Grain Commissioners—so the rumor quickly spread—had been using the funds to play the commodities markets instead of maintaining the emergency supply, as they were legally mandated to do. The rumor was not, in fact, true; the granaries were empty because the Commissioners were playing brinkmanship with the grain cartels over a proposed price increase. Explaining this to the people only made them angrier, if anything. Questions were asked about the huge sums of money that should've been spent on building the new road from Helmyra to the City, along which the rerouted grain shipments should've been traveling, thereby cutting three days off the transit time. Where had the money gone? The government hedged. The fact was, it didn't have the money, because of overspending on the Pancorian war, and had refused to countenance increased taxes because of the brittle state of the general economy. But they daren't say that, and so said nothing, and their silence led the people to draw their own conclusions.

Just when the Council of Ten reckoned things couldn't get any worse, a remarkable thing happened, an event for which no credible explanation has been advanced to this day. One Favorian, a distant descendant of Victorinus, had a dream; his ancestor appeared to him and told him to go to a cave in the mountains near Plesi, where he would find a great treasure. This is my legacy, the ghost told him, put aside by me against the day when my people will need it the most; use it well. So strong was the impression that the dream made on him that Favorian went to the cave; he found a floor-to-roof stack of wooden chests, each one crammed with gold and silver coins. He managed to drag a small chest onto his chaise all by himself and drove back to the City. In Victorinus Square, which had been reoccupied by the mob, he announced his discovery, told them about his dream and produced the chest; the effect can easily be imagined. Amid unprecedented scenes, the hapless Favorian was carried shoulder-high to the Council Chamber (the Ten had sensibly evacuated it a few days earlier) and enthroned on Victorinus' throne, where he was hailed as a reincarnation of his glorious forebear. The Ten, meanwhile, had sent well over half of the palace guard to the cave to secure the treasure. Surviving records indicate they had only the best of motives and fully intended to use the windfall to relieve the crisis. To the people in the Square, however, there could only be one interpretation. Victorinus had sent them his legacy to save them from starvation, and the Ten were trying to steal it for themselves.

Had the Ten not sent quite so many of their few remaining loyal soldiers out of the City at that particular moment, the situation might possibly have been contained. As it was, a mere five thousand soldiers, no matter how dedicated and well trained, stood no chance against the fury of the urban mob. They fought to the last man, in the very best traditions of their regiment, and took an estimated thirty thousand citizens with them, but it was all over within the hour. The Ten were caught trying to sneak out of the City through the sewers; within minutes, their heads were on pikes above the triumphal arch in the Square, and the wretched Favorian, officially renamed Victorinus II, was installed as First Citizen in a makeshift but hugely emotional coronation in the Blue Spire Temple.

Piece of cake.

You're mad, I told her, you're completely insane; it's the only possible explanation. You just slaughtered a quarter of a million people—

She gazed at me blankly. "You said. You wanted."

"Me?" I wanted to hit her. "Don't you dare blame any of this on me. I wanted to *help* people."

"Yes," she said patiently. "But you said. People are too stupid. You've got to make them angry."

Later, I thought about that. Too stupid. Got to be angry. Yes, that was me, all right.

By that point, we'd lapsed into bitter silence. I realize now how deeply hurt she must've felt, after all she'd done, to make my dream come true. *You should have told me first*, was one of the things I'd hurled at her, and when she said, "But I wanted it to be a surprise," I actually thought she was trying to be funny.

At that time we were still at Sulimbesia, which is where she'd magicked us to on our way out of Beloisa. It was relatively safe there in the mountains. As soon as the news broke, the canton authorities quite sensibly closed the passes so nobody could enter or leave, though of course that wouldn't have hindered us for a moment. But I didn't want to go. Right then, it didn't really matter to me where I was. So many deaths on my conscience. I did the maths, which disproved my original belief that I was the worst person in history—that honor goes to Philocarpus, responsible for over a million deaths in the Great Social War, with Eusippa a close runner-up at nine hundred thousand (you'll recall that he deliberately introduced the plague into Meseura). I was way back, about twelfth or thirteenth, but in distinguished company nevertheless. I'd have killed myself, if I thought she'd have let me. I'd have killed her, but what would've been the point?

Hence the clever idea about killing her and then getting hung for it. A lovely plan. I knew it took her about forty-eight hours to come back from the dead. So: kill her, then immediately confess and get myself hung (in Breunis, where summary justice is very summary indeed). By the time she came to life again and realized what I was up to, my body would've been cold for so long, even she wouldn't be able to revive me. It nearly worked. Ah well.

The revised plan, entirely based on the sawmills of Kuvass City, was rather more hopeful. Those saw-blades wouldn't just kill me, they'd shred me into little scraps of mincemeat. There was no way, I felt sure, that she'd be able to put me back together again after that.

I underestimated her. I always do

One of the first things I deduced about her is that she's not exactly a reliable source. However, there are some things she has no reason to lie about, though I suspect she doesn't always need a reason. This, then, for what it's worth, is what she told me.

Her father worked in a tannery—you see? Why would anyone make that up?—in the city of Aracho. Don't bother looking for it on a map. There's a low hill there now, and from time to time, when they plow, they turn up bits of pottery and fragments of bone. At one stage, the Arachenes had a small empire in the southern region of what's now the Vesani Republic, but they came off a bad second in some war, and that was the end of them. There aren't any written records because (she says) writing hadn't been invented then. Well. All women lie about their age, but usually the other way around.

They couldn't read and write, but they could cure leather, and the tannery was quite a substantial concern; a dozen men worked there, and fresh hides came in on carts from miles around. Apparently the Arachenes went in for large families. She told me she had four brothers and two sisters, and that none of them died in childhood. She was the second youngest. When she was born, her eldest brother was already out to work, in the slate quarries. They weren't well off, but she says she can't remember them ever going short of anything. She loved all her family, but her absolute favorite was the second eldest son. His name was Taraxin, and he was a head taller than any of the others. At fourteen, he could lift and carry as much as his father, and he was wonderfully clever with his hands. His father reckoned there'd be no trouble getting him apprenticed, to a carpenter or maybe even a bronzesmith, a real step up in the world for all of them. All in all, the impression she gave was of a loving, happy home, and a future full of promise and hope.

All that changed when her mother murdered her father.

He died quite suddenly, when she was seven years old. She remembered her mother in tears and her brothers being unusually quiet. Then a neighbor came in and went away, and some time later the magistrate arrived, with a dozen soldiers. The neighbor, she learned later, had come to see if there was anything she could do to help; she happened to notice flecks of dried white foam at the corners of the dead man's mouth, and a few crumbs of dried blood in his ears. As luck would have it, the neighbor's brother had died from eating poison mushrooms many years earlier, so she knew the signs. That worried her, because it wasn't mushroom season, so how could he have eaten the things by accident? The magistrate searched the house and found dried mushrooms in a small pottery jar, hidden behind the water-butt in the yard behind the house. The jar had been carefully sealed with wax, and the seal was broken.

Her mother admitted what she'd done almost immediately. It had all been for the children, she said. Her husband had been a good man, in his way, but he was never going to amount to anything, he had no ambition, he was perfectly content to go on working in the tannery all his life—which wouldn't be very long, because tanners die young, and then she'd have been left a widow, and how would she have coped then? But she was still fairly young; if her husband died now, she'd have a good chance of marrying again, someone with prospects, who could give the children a better life. The tannery foreman admired her, she could tell, but he was far too honorable to do anything about it while her husband was alive. She'd collected the mushrooms in the autumn, meaning to kill him then, but not long after he'd gone down with a bad fever. It seemed quite likely that he'd die of it, which would save her the risk and worry of killing him. She'd dried the mushrooms, just in case he got better, and hid them. In time he recovered from the fever; in the meantime, she confessed, she rather lost her nerve, and several times came close to throwing the mushrooms away and forgetting the whole idea. But then her eldest boy started work in the slate quarries, and it upset her to see him come home each night dirty and exhausted, coughing from the dust. If she married the tannery foreman, or the factor at the corn chandlery—who seemed quite taken with her—there was every chance that either of them would be able to find good positions for all her sons, and suitable husbands for the girls as well. So she cooked up about half the mushrooms into soup, on a day when all the children were out of the house. She only pretended to eat her portion, and then threw it away.

In due course the case came up before the Prince, who had recently succeeded his father. The Prince was a fine, idealistic young man, much given to the society of philosophers and priests. Above all, he had a passion for truth and justice—the twin sisters of God, he called them, without whom nothing good could survive in this world. He made a point of hearing all the evidence and interviewing everybody involved, including the dead man's only surviving relative, a sister. She, of course, was heartbroken, having been devoted to her brother. He asked the accused several times if she had anything to say in her defense. All she came up with were the same basic facts, and her insistence that she'd done it for the children, not herself. The Prince, visibly distressed, found her guilty and sentenced her to death.

After that, things got very bad. The house they all lived in belonged to the tannery, so they had to leave. Her eldest brother lost his job in the slate mines, because nobody wanted to work with a murderer's son. They ended up wandering the streets, sleeping where they could and begging, until they were arrested for vagrancy. The Prince had strong views on begging, which he maintained was damaging to the moral health of the nation. He sympathized (he told them), particularly since they were orphans, and their misfortunes were patently not their fault. The law, however, was the law, and every misguided act of mercy served to undermine the principles of law and justice that elevated humanity above the level of wild animals. Accordingly, he had no option but to commit them to the care of the superintendent of public works, who would find work for them on some project conducive to the general welfare of the community.

What that meant in practice was working on the aqueduct. It's all gone now, of course, she told me, not a trace remaining, but in its day it was a wonderful sight to behold, a slender arch spanning an impossible gap between two mountains, a days' walk from the city. It had been the special dream of the Prince's father to bring clean water to the city, where hundreds died every year from drinking the foul water from the wells. He had started the work, and his son devoted all his energy and resources to completing it. When it was eventually finished, thirty years later, there was free running water in fountains on every street corner, and the dry, sandy plain to the south-east of the city was turned into a wide expanse of market gardens, supplying the citizens with cheap fresh vegetables.

Building the aqueduct was a daunting task. To get the inclines right, so that water would flow, the whole of the top of the nearer of the two mountains had to be cut away. The stone for the aqueduct itself had to be cut in quarries fifty miles away, since the local material was too soft for the purpose. It proved impossible to build carts strong enough to carry the blocks from the quarry to the site, so the Prince's engineers built a road, perfectly flat and smooth, along which the blocks could be dragged on rollers. To get the blocks to move at all, the road had to be greased with tallow, but this meant that oxen couldn't get a foothold. The blocks had therefore to be dragged by men and women, with children walking in front of them, smearing tallow on the compressed clay. Once the stone had reached the site, it had to be lifted into position on giant cranes, then eased precisely into place with levers. At any one time there were at least fifty thousand people working on the project, often more. About half of these were prisoners of war, captured by the Prince's armies in his wars with his neighbors. The rest were poor citizens. In the inscription that the Prince had cut into the lintel of his tomb, he made a point of mentioning that during his reign, there was no unemployment, no beggars, no hungry children in the streets; there was work for everyone, regardless of age or infirmity. To pay for the aqueduct, the Prince was forced to conquer the other smaller cities on the edge of the western plain; the tribute and the prisoners taken in battle made the whole thing possible, and the Prince was at pains to acknowledge the contribution they'd made in his inscription; it was, he said, only fair that their sacrifice should be properly recognized.

To begin with, she told me, she and her family worked in the quarry. This was mostly because the eldest boy had had experience of quarry work, and experienced men were at a premium. Most of the workers didn't know what to do, which made things very inefficient and dangerous. Because iron hadn't been discovered back then, they had to cut and shape the blocks with stone tools. It was miserable work, and they were forever cutting themselves with the sharp splinters of rock that flew off as they pounded away the waste, flake by flake. Her elder sister lost an eye. The middle brother had a cut that turned bad, and he died of blood poisoning. They always had enough to eat—the Prince was particular about that—and at night they slept in tents, with watchmen to keep away the wolves.

They'd been in the quarries for just over a year when the eldest son was conscripted into the army. The war with the Clastanes wasn't going all that well, so the call-up age was lowered to seventeen. He was quite happy to go, figuring that soldiering had to be better than quarry work. He did quite well, being promoted to corporal and then sergeant, before he died of camp fever at the siege of Clasta City, shortly before it finally fell. Since he had been the experienced quarryman in the family, the rest of them were no longer eligible for quarry work and were reassigned to the transportation division.

The transfer had its benefits. For the two girls, smearing tallow was a good deal less arduous than chipping stone. The brother, her beloved Taraxin, was assigned to a dragging team mostly made up of women and old men. He was big and strong, and although the work was exhausting, he was glad to be away from the dust and the flying splinters, and the terrible dull ache in the hands and shoulders that comes from hammering rock all day long. The food wasn't quite as plentiful or good, but there was plenty of fresh water when they stopped to ford a river—the water at the quarry was always full of dust; it was like drinking mud, she told me. They worked on transportation for about six months. Then her sister, the half-blind girl, slipped on the greasy track and fell down just as a stone broke loose on a steep slope. She was crushed flat, every bone in her body broken, and died instantly.

A few days later, she had a long talk with her brother, when everyone else was asleep. As far as he was concerned, their sister's death was the last straw. So far, he said, they'd done exactly what they'd been told, gone along with the decisions of their elders and betters, and where had it left them? Two brothers and a sister dead, their mother hanged, their father murdered. If they stayed on the aqueduct, he was sure they wouldn't last much longer either. It struck him as odd, he said, how all this could have happened. Their parents, after all, had been good people and had loved them. Their mother had loved them too much, as it turned out, but she'd only been thinking of them, which is what mothers do. He supposed the Prince had been right to hang her, since she'd admitted killing their father, and for all he knew, if they hadn't been sent to work on the aqueduct they might well all have starved to death a long time ago. All along, he didn't deny it, everyone had been trying to do right by them, obeying the law and doing what was fair and just. Maybe it was simply bad luck that things had turned out so badly. He didn't know, he wasn't one of the Prince's wise men, who knew all about that sort of thing. But from now on, Taraxin said, he wasn't going to concern himself too much with what was right, just, or fair. All he was interested in was keeping the two of them alive for as long as possible. If they stayed on the aqueduct, he had an idea that wouldn't be very long. So, he said, he thought they should leave, go somewhere else, try something different. He had no idea where or what. Probably they'd have to make it up as they went along, just the two of them against the whole world. But, the way he saw it, they didn't exactly have a lot to lose. So. How about it?

She was nine years old. Taraxin was fifteen. They had what was left of the clothes the Supervisors of the poor had issued them with, and Taraxin had a small hammer he'd found beside the road and never got around to handing in to the overseers. She remembered him looking at her oddly and saying: Now, what can we do to feed ourselves with just a hammer?

She remembered their first victim very clearly, she told me. After they left the transportation camp, they walked for two days across the desert until they came to a small group of houses built where the road crossed a small stream running down out of the mountains. There was an inn—not what we'd think of as an inn nowadays, she said, it was a place where caravans of traveling merchants bartered a little of what they were carrying in return for food, shelter, and fodder for their animals. Most of the traffic was big parties of men and oxen, but there were a few small-time traders, men on their own, staggering along under a huge bale of flax or a big jar of wine or butter, and the occasional hunter, walking to and from the city with furs, skins, and feathers. The man they killed—they didn't mean to, but it was Taraxin's maiden effort and he didn't know how hard to hit—was a bird-catcher. He'd been snaring finches with limed sticks in the foothills of the mountain, and had a bale stuffed full of blue and yellow feathers, the sort that fine ladies in town liked to decorate their hats with. They hadn't realized that, of course. They'd been hiding in the ditch beside the road for most of the day, and only big caravans had gone past, no single men on their own. The bird-catcher had been the first, and they'd assumed that the huge fat bag he was carrying on his head was flour or something like that. When they pulled it open and found nothing but feathers, they were heartbroken.

Still, you learn from your mistakes, as their mother used to say, and they made sure the next man was carrying something they could eat. Butter, as it turned out. He had a jar almost as tall as he was, sort of carrot-shaped, with ropes rigged through the handles to make it easier to carry. Taraxin didn't hit quite so hard this time, and the butter-man was still breathing when they left him, carrying the jar between them, since it was too heavy for Taraxin to lift on his own. They didn't stop till they found a cave in the mountainside. Then they gorged themselves on white salted butter until they couldn't bear to eat another handful.

There was still quite a lot left, and they didn't want to waste it, that would be sinful. Taraxin said they should carry it to the nearest town and sell it. She was afraid, someone might recognize the jar, she thought, or what if the man had recovered and made it to the town, and told everyone there that he'd been robbed on the road? Taraxin laughed at her. One jar of butter's very much like another, he said. If they were stopped and questioned, all they'd have to say was that they'd found it abandoned beside the road.

Where they'd gone wrong, the jailer explained to her later, was in not killing the man they robbed. The jailer was a kind man at heart; he had a daughter about the same age as her, and he thought it was a shame that she was to be hung in the morning, even if she was guilty of robbery and murder. It was, he told her, a mistake so many novices made. Just silly sentimentality, he said. After all, the penalties for murder and robbery with violence were the same; dead men tell no tales, whereas merely wounded ones make excellent witnesses for the prosecution. Never say die, though, he urged her. There was always the chance of a last-minute reprieve, though the new Prince didn't go in for them much, not like his father. Still, the jailer said, that's progress for you.

I don't know how she managed to sleep that nighy. I don't usually get much sleep in condemned cells, believe me. But I guess if it's your first time, and you're worn out with fear and worry, I can see how it's possible. Anyway, she fell asleep, and she had a dream.

She remembers asking: Are you my mother?

Not in the sense you mean, the dream said. I look like her because you want me to. But your mother was a stupid woman. I can be your new mother. I'm not stupid.

She said: What would be the point? They're going to hang me in the morning.

The dream smiled. Once upon a time, she said, there was a blind girl. One day her true mother came to her and said, look at the pretty flowers. I can't, the girl said, I'm blind. No, said her true mother, your eyes are shut. Open them. And the girl did, and she saw the flowers. They can only hang you if you let them, and even if they do, it won't matter. They can't kill you.

She remembered thinking, that doesn't make sense. But she asked the dream: So she wasn't blind after all?

No, said the dream, because her true mother taught her to open her eyes. I'm your true mother. I can teach you lots of things.

Such as?

But the dream shook her head. That's not important, she said. You'll come to understand that. When you can do anything, details don't matter. What matters is that you accept me as your true mother.

All right, she remembers saying. I accept you. Now what?

The dream laughed. Say it again.

I accept you, she said.

And again. You have to say it three times.

I accept you, she said. All right?

The dream sighed happily. Yes, she said, everything is now all right. I bestow upon you, and you agree to accept, the power of the witches, to have and to use, forever and ever. Now, the dream went on briskly, do you know what that means?

No.

I assumed you didn't, said the dream. But that doesn't matter, it's done now. Think about your life.

I'd rather not, she remembers saying. What's this power you keep talking about?

Think, said the dream, about your life. All your life, you and everyone around you, have tried to do the right thing, from your mother to the Prince. Is that right?

She shrugged. I guess so.

All your family's dead. They killed your whole family. In the morning, they're going to kill you. Now, would you say that was fair, or just? Was it the right thing?

She thought about that. I don't know, she said. No, I don't think it was.

I don't either, said the dream. So, good intentions made bad things happen. Now then, what happened when you stole the butter? What was the first thing you did?

We ate it.

The dream nodded. You were hungry. You ate the butter. Was that good?

She remembers saying, I suppose so, yes. We were hungry, then we weren't. That was good.

Ah, said the dream, and she remembers thinking: I said the right thing. Now then, said the dream, did you intend to steal the butter? Did you intend to hit the butter-man and hurt him?

Yes.

So, said the dream, from a bad intention a good thing came about. You ate the butter. If you hadn't, you'd probably have died. From an evil intention came forth good.

Yes, but—She stopped. She was confused. What does all that mean?

It means, said the dream, that you don't have to die tomorrow. Name me a good thing. Name me the best thing.

She remembers thinking. She remembers remembering what she'd been taught, when she was a little girl. Love, she said. Love is the best thing.

I see, said the dream. Have you ever loved anyone?

Of course, she said. My family. My mother and father, my sister, my brothers. Taraxin. Of course.

Yes, said the dream. And how did you feel when they all died?

Very bad, she said. Very, very bad.

Of course, said the dream. Love, the best thing, made you feel very, very bad. It always has. Love is in fact the worst thing, the very worst thing, because it can hurt us more than anything else, more than fire or a broken arm or childbirth. Love is worse than death, because it carries on hurting the living. Love is the worst thing of all, because we always lose the people we love, and it hurts so very much. Is that true?

Yes, she said. Yes, that's true.

But the dream smiled at her. I have given you, the dream said, the power of the witches. No one you love need ever die again. Now then, she went on, isn't that a good thing?

If it's true.

It's true, the dream said. I wouldn't lie to you, I'm your true mother. You have the power of the witches. The power is the only good thing. The only good thing is being able to do whatever you want. Everything else is bad, everything else is hurtful and evil. Only the power of the witches is good. Good is being able to do everything you want. Do you understand me?

If it's true.

Oh, you're hopeless, said the dream, and then she woke up.

She remembers thinking: It was only a dream. That made her feel sad. She thought: I wish it hadn't just been a dream. I wish I could make that door fly open, so I could walk out of here and be free.

The door flew open.

She remembers staring at it for a while, then thinking, I must still be asleep. But she got up and went to the door, peered round it. The corridor outside was empty. She thought: I can't just walk out, I'm not supposed to, it's not allowed. Then she remembered what the dream had told her. She walked out of the cell and down the corridor until she came to another door. She smiled at it, and it opened.

On the other side of the door was a jailer. He swung round and stared at her. She thought: I hate the jailers, they keep people locked up and take them to be hanged. I wish this man's head would burst, like a big white spot when you squeeze it. And the jailer's head burst, and his brains splashed on the wall, and she walked on past him.

I must find Taraxin, she thought. At first she didn't know where to look, then a picture formed in her mind, and suddenly she wasn't in the corridor any more, she was outside, in the square. She looked up at the great arch that led out into the main street of the city, and saw Taraxin's head, stuck on a rusty iron spike. His mouth and eyes were open and he looked terrified. She stared at it for a while, then walked under the arch and out into the street.

That night she slept in a warm bed in an inn. The dream came to her. Well? said the dream.

You lied to me, she remembers saying. Taraxin's dead. I loved him best of all. You said nobody I loved would ever die.

He was dead already, the dream said. But from now on, it'll be different. You have the power of the witches, which is the only good thing. From now on, nobody you love will ever die.

She smiled at the dream. I'm still asleep, aren't I? she said. Soon I'll wake up and be back in prison.

The dream said: Maybe. But if so, the trick is not to wake up.

She frowned. That sounds very clever, she said, but I'm not sure if it means anything.

The dream looked at her. Let's assume, she said, that the power of the witches is only a dream. In dreams, things happen that can't possibly happen, like magic. In dreams, the people we love who have died can come back to us. In dreams, we can do whatever we want. But the power of the witches is no dream, it's real.

Is it? Is it really?

Oh yes. Provided you don't wake up.

And then (she told me) she woke up. And, to make absolutely sure, she made the bed lift off the floor and fly around the room.

One thing, while I think of it. After the revolution, when the Republic was overthrown and Victorinus II established the Directorate, they set up a Truth & Justice Commission to grant posthumous pardons to all the so-called traitors who'd been executed over the last three hundred years or so. My poor father, God rest him, was pardoned and declared a Hero of the People, and there's a small statue tucked away in the northeastern corner of the Shambles. It doesn't look a bit like him, needless to say.

I remember one night, back when we were still talking to each other. We'd just stolen HS320,000 from the Sashan provincial treasury in Ormiget. There was so much gold bullion in our tiny room next to the stables in the inn that we were having to perch on the edge of the washstand.

"She was wrong," I told her. "It can't just be a dream, because I'm in it, and I know I'm awake."

She shrugged. "Maybe it's a shared dream."

"There's no such thing."

"True," she conceded. "But there's no such thing as magic, either."

I wasn't having that. "If it's a dream," I said, "then it's my dream, and you're not really real. And that would make you the girl of my dreams. Which you are," I added politely. "But I think you're real."

"Thank you so much."

"In which case," I concluded triumphantly, "it's not a dream. In which case," I went on, "she was wrong. She was misleading you."

She shook her head. "She wouldn't do that," she said. "She's my true mother."

Circular argument. "Have you seen her since?" I asked.

She sighed. "No," she said. "Well, once. At least, I'm not sure. I did see her, but I think I was dreaming. A real dream," she explained, "rather than a—well, a vision."

I ate a honey-cake. Sashan cuisine isn't really my thing, but I do love their honey-cakes. "She's still wrong," I said.

"I wish you wouldn't say things like that."

"She's wrong," I maintained, "when she says there's no good or evil, just doing what you want. That's been comprehensively disproved, loads of times. The third book of Saloninus' *Contradictions*—"

She yawned. "It's not doing what you want," she said, "it's being able to do what you want, there's a difference. And it can't be disproved, because it's true. And I met Saloninus once, and he was an idiot."

I stared at her. "You met Saloninus?"

"The way I see it," she said, "is, the power of the witches is the—what's the expression? It's the exception that proves the rule. The rule applies to everybody except us. The fact that we're the only exceptions proves that the rule is valid. Do you see what I'm getting at?"

"You never told me you met Saloninus."

I remember opening my eyes. The light hurt, really badly. I thought, oh *hell*.

She was looking down at me. She looked so terribly sad. "I'm sorry," she said.

I can't remember her ever looking more beautiful, even though her eyes were red from crying. "I'm alive," I said. "Am I all here?"

She nodded. "I really am so sorry," she said. "I guess I never realized you were so unhappy. I thought—"

"What?"

"I thought it was just—well, because you weren't getting what you wanted. I thought, I must not be understanding you right. I'd assumed that what you wanted to do was rob people. You did always say that deep down, you're a thief."

I did say that, as it happens.

"So," she went on, "I thought, if we go around stealing lots of money from the biggest treasuries and banks and places in the whole world, that'll make him happy. I thought that was what you wanted, that and being young and having a beautiful girl and never having to worry about getting caught or getting hurt or dying. I thought that was all you wanted."

"Did you now."

She wiped away a tear with her knuckle. I'd never seen her cry before. "Because being able to do anything you want is the only good thing. She said so."

"What I want," I said, slowly and gently, "is to be rid of you."

Then I went out into the street. She didn't try and stop me. About twenty yards from the inn door, I paused and concentrated on the back of my neck. No bite. Not even an itch.

I walked around for a while; found myself in a wine-shop. I'd had a drink or two, not enough to signify, when I realized someone was staring at me. A fat man with curly white hair, about sixty years old, in an expensive red gown with a fur collar. He couldn't take his eyes off me.

That rang warning bells, obviously. But I was in the sort of mood where you simply don't care. I had another drink, then got up and went and joined the fat man. He didn't lower his eyes or look away.

"Something I can do for you?" I asked.

He was still gazing at me. "Sure," he said. "Sit down, let me buy you a drink."

"Got one, thanks," I said. "Do I know you, or something?"

That made him laugh. "Now that," he said, "is a bloody good question. On balance, I'm guessing no, you don't. Question is, do I know you?"

"Well?"

"And I can't. It's impossible. Still, it's the damnedest thing." He poured himself a small drink of the house white and nibbled at it. As far as I could tell, he was perfectly sober. "You look just like someone I met once," he said.

"Oh yes?"

"Just like." He grinned. "So you can't be him," he went on, "because that was nearly forty years ago. You're, what, nineteen?"

I shrugged. "I'm a fairly common type," I said.

"Like hell." He narrowed his eyes, as if I was small print on a contract. "Look, since you're quite obviously not him, I'll tell you why it matters to me. You see, nearly forty years ago, a kid looking exactly like you nearly killed me."

"Is that right."

He nodded. "Oh yes," he said. "I'm a goldsmith, see, like my dad before me. There'd been a lot of break-ins, so Dad and I sat up with swords in case the thief tried it on at our place. Sure enough, he did. What's more, the little bastard stuck a knife in me. I nearly died."

"Nearly," I said.

"Well, yes. I didn't die, obviously, or I wouldn't be here." He paused. "Take after your father, do you?"

Big shrug. "I wouldn't know," I said. "Never met him. My mother only met him once. Strictly a cash transaction."

"Ah." The fat man grinned. "Well, then, maybe that explains it," he said. "No offense. After all, not your fault"

"I suppose not," I said. "Actually, I've always led an entirely blameless life, devoted to helping those less fortunate than myself."

"Of course you have," the fat man said. "Anyway, it's all a long time ago now, and no harm done, as it turned out." He leaned forward and gave me what I guess he thought was a conspiratorial look. "In actual fact," he said, "quite the reverse."

"Excuse me?"

"Damnedest thing," he said. "I only found out about it many years later," he went on. "Dad told me a few years before he passed away. Damnedest thing you ever heard, actually."

"Go on."

"Well." He paused to sip his wine. "Like I told you, this thief—who may or may not have been your old man, that's something we'll never know, I guess—stabbed me. So, they called for the doctors, and they swabbed me out, made sure the wound was clean and all that. Anyhow, while they were prodding and poking about inside my gut with their bits of lambswool on tiny twigs, what did they find? I'll tell you. A damned great tumor, is what. They'd have said it was totally inoperable, except that the thief's knife had sliced right through it, cut it out neater than any surgeon could ever have done. And I healed up just fine. If that bugger hadn't stabbed me, I'd have been dead in a month. Sure as I sit here. Now, isn't that the weirdest thing you ever heard?"

I looked at him for a very long time. "Actually, no," I said. "But it does come quite close."

Of course I had to go back to the inn. She was sitting where I'd left her. I don't think she'd moved at all.

"Can you alter the past?" I said.

She shrugged. "I don't know. I've never tried. I don't think I can. Why, do you want me to?"

"It doesn't matter," I said. I sat down beside her on the bed. "Why me?" I asked.

She gave me a blank stare. "I have absolutely no idea," she said. "Why do you ask?"

I considered my reply. "I've just found out," I said, "that I've led an entirely blameless life, devoted to helping those less fortunate than myself." I grinned weakly. "It came as a surprise, believe me."

"I don't understand," she said.

I explained. "So," I concluded, "I'm not a murderer. I actually saved that man. True, I stole a lot of stuff when I was a student, but I always gave the money to other people, my friends, who reckoned they needed it desperately. Then we stole—actually, you did all the stealing, I was just there most of the time—we stole a lot of stuff, but that was just redistribution of wealth."

She looked at me. "Really."

I shrugged. "We haven't got any of it any more, have we? No, we dumped it or gave it away or spent it; we took it off governments and rich people, and nearly all of it ended up in the hands of the poor. Well," I amended, "the relatively poor. And yes, I prompted you to slaughter hundreds of thousands of people, but the upshot was that the Ten were overthrown.

I don't know how many deaths Victorinus was responsible for when he established the Republic, but I expect it was a comparable number. And it's not my fault that the bastards who're in now are just as bad, might as well blame Victorinus for chucking out the kings. All my life," I said, "I've benefited others, never myself. Now, isn't that a curious thing?"

She looked away. "It's like she said," she told me. "Intentions don't matter, there's just the thing itself."

"You believe that."

"I'm not that bothered, really. It's men who think about stuff like that." Then she looked at me. "I do things for love."

"Like your mother."

She nodded. "Yes."

I took a long, deep breath. "If I wanted to go away without you," I said, "if that was what I really wanted, would you let me? For love," I added. "Because you love me."

She shivered. "She told me I'd never lose anyone I loved, ever again."

"She lied," I told her. "You lost me a very long time ago."

I didn't leave. For one thing, I didn't trust her to let me. How would I know if the flea in my hair wasn't her, or the dog following me in the street, or the bird a thousand feet overhead? At least, while she was human, I knew where she was and had some idea of what she was up to. That's the point. I'd never know, and everything I ever did could be her, guiding, manipulating. Wouldn't put it past her to land me back in the condemned cell, just so she could get me out again. And I didn't fancy the thought of what she might do to get me there. When you suddenly discover that you're blameless and pure as the driven snow, it really cramps your style. Another reason for staying: after all, I had no resources and absolutely no way of earning a living, apart from theft, which no longer appealed to me. I had my own exalted example to live up to now, God help me.

So, I stayed with her out of mere expediency. No, not really. Nothing had changed since I tried to kill myself—try? I succeeded—by throwing myself into the blades of the Kuvass City sawmill. The act, I would suggest, of a man who wanted to get rid of his life at all costs rather than make it a bit easier. On balance, I believe it was the apology that did it, those first words when I came round after being resurrected. *I'm sorry*.

Over the next couple of days, I took stock. I thought a lot about love. I realized, I had no idea what the word stood for. I considered what I understood to be the standard definition, as set out in Saloninus' *Ethics*: the state of mind in which the other person is more valuable to you than you are yourself. I tried applying it to her, and I wasn't sure it fitted. She said she loved me, and happiness was never losing someone you love. By that criterion, the miser loves his gold to the point where he can't bring himself to spend it, even when he's freezing cold and the coal-scuttle's empty. That's not love. Tweak the definition: the state of mind in which the other person's happiness is your paramount concern. Well, that would explain the apology, and thirty-odd years spent robbing provincial state treasuries, in the misguided belief that that was what I liked doing. Taken all in all, I felt she wasn't terribly good at love, though that didn't mean she didn't love me. Sincere, but completely ineffectual. Nobody's perfect.

Still not a good enough definition. All right, then: love is the state of mind in which the other person is more valuable to you than you are yourself, and their happiness is your paramount concern. I couldn't help feeling that that was a bit of a compromise, the sort of thing that gets hammered out in committee and passed by a slender majority after a lot of behind-the-scenes horse trading. Never mind. It would have to do.

Now the hard part—to apply it to myself. It'd be reaching quite a lot to say I regarded her as more valuable than myself. Except that, since I'd done my best to reduce my body to mince in an attempt to frustrate all efforts at bringing me back to life, it seemed fair to assess my value to myself at nil, assuming negative values aren't allowed. She meant more to me than naught, or minus one. As for the other part, well, I thought, why not? Thirty years of being together is no trivial thing; good, bad or utterly miserable, it has substance, it exists, it can't just be dissolved by a quick so-long-then and a turning of the back. I thought of some of the arranged marriages I'd observed over the years; they didn't like each other much to start with, and things never got much better after that, but even so, better than being alone. No, bad model. The simple fact was, I hadn't left her simply because she was unleavable. No matter where I ran to, how I disguised myself, she'd always be there with me. A bit like—Old saying: no matter where you go, you take yourself with you. One mind, one heart, one flesh.

I thought: I'm stuck with her. Even death will not part us. If I devote my life to making her happy, maybe that will resolve the issue in some way, assuming it's capable of any kind of resolution. Just listen to yourself, I thought, this is crazy. But—

Indeed. But.

Leave aside the motivations and it was true. I'd lived my life helping others, blameless, keeping nothing for myself, a man to all intents and appearances in love with the human race. Bad intentions and good outcomes, the mirror image of her life before we met. Perhaps love is something that has to be worked out cold, like sheet metal, beaten and persuaded into an acceptable shape by countless pecks of the hammer. It's not bar stock, to be made white-hot in the fire, until it bends, flows, upsets, takes a perfect form, even picks up the marks on the hammer-head. It's too thin for that, too flimsy and slight to heat red without burning. Or take the other obvious analogy. Wars start in furious, passionate anger, but peace is made slowly and painfully, one concession at a time, each party agreeing to give away things it wants to keep, to do things it doesn't want to do, the objective being to reach an arrangement of which both parties can eventually, reluctantly say: I can live with that.

And, when you aren't allowed to die, *I can live with that* is the most you can hope for.

"So," she said. "What do you want to do now?"

I sighed. "You haven't been listening," I said.

"No, it's fine, I heard you." She was frowning. "It's just—If you don't like stealing stuff, what do you like?"

That made me smile. "You know what," I said. "It's been so long, I really can't remember. But you're missing the point. And it's really quite simple. I want to make you happy."

"Oh," she said.

She took me to the top of Mount Carysion.

It's the highest point in the world, so they say. We used to believe the gods lived there, in vast golden mansions, shrouded in mist. As far as anyone knows, nobody's ever been there—except her and me, of course. Somehow, I don't think we count.

I could scarcely breath. I thought I was having some kind of seizure, but she explained (as she conjured up a bubble all round us) that the air on mountaintops is too thin to be any use. All I could see was the tops of clouds. I didn't say anything, but I guess she figured out what I was thinking from the look on my face. She mumbled something, the sun came out and the clouds melted away, and I could see the whole world.

What does the whole world look like, when you're so high up that you can see it all in one, as a single thing? Well, to me it looked like a patchwork quilt, of the sort you get in low-class houses. I associate such things with visiting retired servants and poor relations.

"Well?" she said.

"Well what?"

"That can all be yours," she said. "If you want it."

I looked out over the kingdoms of the Earth. I could see the blue curve of Beloisa Bay, with the mountains behind; beyond them, Selvatia, the steppes of the Mesoge, the Dancing Floor sloping gently down into the Panosaic Sea. I could clearly make out the curved spine of the Avelro Peninsula, a little flash of light could easily have been the golden dome of the Archer Temple. I turned slowly round and searched until I saw the Needles, towering over Kuvass City. I could see everywhere I'd ever been, everywhere I could ever possibly go. "What would be the point?" I said.

She sighed, and the clouds came swirling back. It was bitter cold. "I think I'd like to go back down now," I said.

"You told me once," I said, "you actually met Saloninus once. Is that true?"

She shrugged. "Yes."

"I think I'd like to meet him."

She gave me a long, weary look. "Do you really?"

"Yes."

Sigh. "Fine," she said. "I'll see what I can do."

I had every confidence in her; rather more, I suspect, than she had. But, fair play to her, she figured out how to do it. To go back into the past, apparently, you have to fly round the world, west to east, faster than the arrows of the Invincible Sun. I don't actually believe in the Invincible Sun, but luckily that didn't seem to be a barrier. I was curious as to what we were going to fly in, but when the time came, she just muttered something and suddenly we were in mid-air. I closed my eyes and started screaming. It didn't feel like we were moving at all. I'm ashamed to say I wet myself, something I hadn't done for a very long time.

She was yelling something. I couldn't make out what it was. She yelled louder. It was "QUIET!"

I opened my eyes. We were exactly where we'd been a moment ago. It hadn't worked.

"Well," she said. "Here we are."

No we aren't, I started to say, then it occurred to me that we were in Victorinus Square, which hasn't changed much in four hundred years. The only significant difference is the Senate House, which got burned down and rebuilt. I looked for it. It had a flat roof, not a dome. Oh, I thought.

"Getting here," she was saying, "was the easy bit. Getting back could be awkward. We may have to go the long way round."

"What are we doing here?" I asked her. I'd forgotten.

She looked at me. "You wanted to see Saloninus," she said.

Oh yes, so I did. I couldn't for the life of me remember why. "Right," I said. "Let's do that."

We started to walk toward the prefecture. "Why are we going this way?" I asked.

She smiled at me. "Because," she said, "I can absolutely guarantee I know where to find him. Come on."

The prefecture. I tried to remember. Had there been a ceremony of some sort, the conferring of an honorary degree, investiture as a Knight of the Golden Horseshoe? But they did that sort of thing at the Palace or the Blue Spire. Four hundred years ago, as far as I could recall my history lessons, the prefecture was just the law courts.

"This is fun," I said. "Are we really going to meet Saloninus? He's my absolute hero." She was walking very fast. It was hard to talk and keep up with her at the same time. "I always think, if the God put the human race on trial and said show me one man whose life was perfect, or else I'll send a flood and drown the whole lot of you, we wouldn't need to worry, we'd just point to Saloninus and the God would be, like, sorry to have bothered you. He must've had the most amazing mind."

"This way," she said.

She led me down an alleyway. I knew it well. There was a tavern here I used to go to, frequented by gamblers and young political types. The back wall of the tavern garden was also the back wall of the old prison. When we got there, I realized the tavern hadn't been built yet, and the prison was still the New Prison, and the walled-up doorway where they used to have a big copper for mulling wine in the winter hadn't been walled up yet. There were two guards on duty in front of it. For some reason, they fell asleep.

"Oh come *on*," I said.

"This way."

I think it was when Jarnicus was First Aedile, they knocked through all the internal walls in the Old Prison and turned it into this one enormous room for diplomatic receptions. I went there with my father, when I was about twelve. I remember meeting some old bald fat man who was someone important, though I can't recall his name. Remarkable, the difference a few walls can make.

Prisons, I have to tell you, are no treat to me. "I don't like this," I told her, "let's go back now." She didn't seem to hear me. She was muttering directions under her breath—third left, second right, first right, third left. I'm hopeless at that sort of thing. I let her concentrate.

"Three," she said, "four, five, six." She stopped. We were standing in front of a solid oak door, in a very dark stone-floored corridor lined with about a hundred identical doors. The smell, rather familiar, turned my stomach; stale piss, boiled cabbage, rust. There was a sort of tidemark of crusted white saltpeter running along the wall about three inches off the ground. Some things never change.

"Surely not," I said.

She nodded. "Seventeenth Paralia, AUC 277," she said. "He's in there, one hundred percent guaranteed. Ready?"

"What's he in for?"

"Stealing a chicken," she said, and rested the flat of her hand on the door. There was a plucked-string noise and a loud crack, and the door swung open.

I followed her in. There was a man lying on the stone ledge. He had one hand down the front of his trousers, which he quickly pulled out. He was about sixty years old, short, thin on top, with a straggly pepper-and-salt beard. He stared at her.

"Oh God," he said. "It's you."

"Hello," she said.

He turned his face to the wall. "Go away," he said.

I didn't need to ask. I knew. Saloninus.

"Don't be like that," she said. "I've come to get you out of here."

"Please," Saloninus said to the wall, "don't bother. Really."

"If you stay here," she said, "they're going to hang you."

"What?" I said. "For stealing a chicken?"

She glared at me. Saloninus didn't seem to have heard me. It occurred to me that, as far as he was concerned, I wasn't there. "So what?" he said. "I don't care."

I remembered that four hundred years ago, they still had the death penalty for theft. "Don't be silly," she was pleading. "You know I'll look after you, one way or another. Come on, before the guards do their rounds. Please."

I vaguely remembered—at the age of fifty-four, Saloninus published his last great alchemical treatise. Nothing more is known for certain, and the rest of his life was supposed to have passed in tranquil retirement. "I wish," he said, "I *wish* you'd just leave me alone."

She turned her head and looked at me. The choice, apparently, was mine. "For God's sake," I said, "you can't just leave him here to die. He's—"

She nodded very slightly. Then the back wall of the cell collapsed in a cloud of dust.

"Well," she said, four hundred years and five minutes later, "that's another wonderful thing you've done. You saved Saloninus."

I was still dizzy from the motionless flight. "He was a chicken-thief."

"Yes. And you saved him. He'd have died otherwise."

I couldn't stand. I had to sit down, on the wet paving stones. "He was a thief," I repeated.

"Like you."

"Exactly." I gave her a baleful stare. "Was that you?"

She shrugged. "It was his nature," she said. "A lot of it got hushed up, but yes, he was always getting in trouble. He never had very much money, you see."

"But he wrote the *Principia*."

She sat down beside me. "Oh yes," she said. "In prison, actually. A lot of his books were written in prison. He had nothing else to do."

"But that's—"

She smiled at me. "If you like," she said, "we can go forward four hundred years. We could go and see your statue."

I opened my mouth. Nothing came out. Probably just as well.

"It'll be," she said, and pointed. "Right there," she said, "where the mail office is. Gilded bronze, by Peracchia. You'll like his work, he'll be very good."

"Statue," I said.

"Of course. The man who overthrew the Republic."

I took a long, deep breath. "That was Favorian," I said. "Victorinus the Second."

"No," she said, "it was you. They'll find out what really happened about ninety years from now, when the Directorate falls and they found the Second Republic. The statue gets built about twenty years after that. I'm afraid they spell your name wrong, but that can't be helped."

I looked at her. "Did you love him?" I asked her.

"Who? Oh, you mean Saloninus. Yes," she said, "very much."

"What happened?"

She turned and looked at me. "I met someone else," she said.

From that moment on, I realized that I was—what's the expression? On notice? Sooner or later, I knew, she would find someone else, and that would be that. The thought appalled and terrified me. I was going to lose her. I loved her.

Maybe that's what love really is, the anticipation of loss. I do know that, quite suddenly, as soon as I'd made that connection, I loved her as never before.

It was, in many ways, an idyllic time. It lasted seventeen years, though they seemed to pass in an instant, as if we were flying, east to west, faster than the arrows of the Invincible Sun; we stayed still, the earth spun furiously around us, like the chuck of a drill. I know for an indisputable fact that I was never happier—knowing that one day I'd lose her, that it would end, and that afterwards I'd be more wretched than I could possibly imagine. I guess you could say it was a good outcome from a bad situation, or good generated by the certainty of misery. The truth is, I neither know nor care about that sort of thing any more. If you're interested in the finer points of ethical theory, I suggest you read the appropriate passages in Saloninus; that is, if you give a damn about the opinions of a chicken-thief.

Remember the trained cormorants? They catch fish they can never eat; the difference is, their collars are visible. We were watching them, as it happens, leaning against the sea wall at Choris Malestin as the small boats bobbed back in on the evening tide. I don't think there's any more beautiful place on earth than Choris, though of course it's not what it was, not since they built the new jetty. I remember thinking: if only this moment could last for ever. A pretty trite thought, but in my experience, there's nothing remotely original about love. I distinctly remember that she was eating an apple. I had a book with me—Antigonus of Mezentia on moral imperatives, I think it was; I was supposed to have read it in my first year at the university, but I'd never got round to it—but I hadn't looked at it for about half an hour. I was too busy watching the boats, and the cormorants.

"We should go to Baryns," she said. "Sunrise over the estuary is the most wonderful sight. You'd like it."

"Love to," I said. "When?"

"Whenever you like."

And that, I think, is when she saw him. He was standing up in the stern of a small boat, his head turned back, shouting cheerfully at an old man in the boat behind. He was no more than a boy, eighteen or nineteen. I don't know, maybe he'd just caught a lot of fish or something. He seemed to radiate happiness, sheer joy. I only caught a glimpse, but it was enough to freeze the image in my mind—I'd have remembered him even if nothing had come of it and I'd never seen him again. I guess he struck me as worthy of note because I no longer believed there could be that much joy in the world.

"You know what I'd like," she said. I wasn't looking at her, so I can't vouch for the expression on her face.

"What?" I said.

"Freshly grilled mackerel in a honey and mustard sauce," she said.

I laughed. It had been years since I'd actually tasted anything I ate, and I wasn't sure whether she needed to eat at all. But why not, I thought, if that's what she wants. "Then we're definitely in the right place at the right time," I said.

It was starting to get chilly, and I'd come out in just a tunic. We went and chose our mackerel. I don't think she made an obvious beeline for the cheerful boy's boat, but when we arrived at it, she started examining the fish in detail, asking learned questions. See you back at the house, I said to her, and walked away. All I remember thinking about, as I headed back down the promenade, was faint memories of the taste of mackerel.

Two days later, she said, "It's over."

I didn't get what she meant. "What?"

"You and me," she said. "I'm sorry, but I don't love you any more. I've met someone else, and I'm in love with him."

Which made no sense, at the time. I knew she wasn't making a joke, because of the way she'd said it. I think I said something like, you can't be, you love me, forever and always. Something really stupid, anyway. She just looked at me and shook her head. "Sorry," she repeated, and then, "You'd better go away now."

I had two angels fourteen in the pocket of my light summer coat. I turned and walked out of the house, into the most beautiful sunrise.

That was forty-one years ago.

Five nights after she left me, I had a dream. It looked like her, but then again, they all do. But this one said, "How would it be if you never had to lose someone you love, ever again?"

I said, "I'll need to think about it."

I think I saw her again, about six years ago, but I'm not sure. I was just coming off shift at the cooper's yard where I work—I fetch and carry, sharpen the tools, load the carts, try and make myself useful—and I saw a girl with a young man, walking up Crossgate toward the sea front. I could only see the back of the girl's head, but I remembered the man's face. They had their arms around each other's waists, and I heard him laugh. If it was him, I don't think he was a fisherman any more. He wore smart, expensive clothes, the sort I could afford when I was his age. If it was them, they seemed very happy together.

I said: I'll need to think about it.

I'm still thinking.

WHERE THE TRAINS TURN

Pasi Ilmari Jääskeläinen
(Translated by Liisa Rantalaiho)

If it's in any way possible for You, please make this somehow unhappened!
I'll give you anything!
(A typical child's prayer; directed to any sufficiently omnipotent
Divine Being who chances to be listening)

Not since my girlhood have I bothered to read books that contain invented events or non-existent people, were they written by Hemingway, Joyce, Mann, Blyton, Christie, Jansson, or any other of the millions of literary talents in this universe. I prefer unquestionable facts, and to relax I sometimes like to read encyclopedias. It's hard enough to cope day by day with what presumes to be my own everyday reality; to stir and feed imagination with fiction would just make me lose my sense of reality altogether. It's pretty fickle already, my understanding of which part of the things I remember has actually happened and what is composed of mere empty memories that never had a reference in the historical continuum that's called objective reality.

I don't like to think about the past, because it mixes my head up and makes my bowels loose and gives me a severe migraine to boot. But I cannot stop remembering my son. That's why I still often sneak to the graveyard of my memories with a spade and dig up pieces of my life with my son Rupert. Of his peculiarly fatal relationship to trains, of his brilliant days of success and happiness that made me so proud, and of everything else.

For the sake of my son I write down these thoughts, seek him from dream images, from memories, from everywhere. Perhaps I'm afraid I'll forget him. But how could I forget?

I hunt my memories, examine them, turn and twist them, and try to understand what happened and why; for Rupert's sake I consider the eternal logical circle of cause and effect and my own part in it, trying to get some sense out of it, as painful and against my nature as such an effort always has been to me.

Even as a girl I understood how important it is to live in a world as logical and sensible as possible. I never let myself be ruled by grand emotions, and yet was quite reasonably happy (or at least fairly unruffled) most of the time. Then just I, out of all the world's expectant women, became Rupert's mother.

Even as a baby he was restless—probably had nightmares, poor thing—and quite soon it turned out that my blue-eyed son Rupert was not a very sensible child. He let loose a mental chaos; even for a child he was extremely irrational. By and by he made an actual art form of his addiction to irrationality. At five years old, for example, he had a strange mania to mix up calendars and set all the clocks he found to a wrong time. When he turned seven, I bought him a watch of his own, a golden Timex. He liked it very much indeed, and wound it up regularly, but always it was an hour or two fast or slow, sometimes even more.

More than a couple of times I was seized with the feeling that I had been caught in the middle of The Great Irrationality Circus where Rupert was a pompous mad director. Even looking at him made my head ache.

I miss him every day. Sometimes I still go to the window in the middle of preparing dinner and imagine seeing him in the backyard, the silly old owl that I am, just like decades ago, in another time, another life:

Rupert was playing on the backyard. Like a whirlwind dressed in a sun-yellow T-shirt and blue terry shorts, he flew from here to there: from the tree stump to the currant bush, from the bush to the old puffed-up rowan that had been growing in the middle of the backyard very likely since creation, and on again to the nervously trembling top of the tree. From there the boy kept chatting to the birds flying by, to the clouds, to the sky, the sun, and to the tree itself.

I repressed my urge to run out and yell at Rupert to come down to the ground at once on pain of a severe punishment before he would fall and break his slender fledgling neck and spoil the whole beautiful summer day by dying and becoming one of those stupidly careless kids the curt news-in-brief in the papers always told about.

I turned my back to the kitchen window. "Where do you plan to go today?" I asked Gunnar. My emphatically civilized tone reflected my inner turmoil as little as possible. I poured out more coffee for my guest. I always made him coffee, although I knew he'd actually prefer cocoa. I did have a tin of cocoa behind the flour bags on the upper shelf, but that was for Rupert—grownups, according to my opinion, ought to drink coffee or tea.

"I don't know. Wherever we fancy."

"I do know: to the railway, as always. I can't figure what you actually see in those railways," I muttered.

"Is it really so inconceivable to you?" Gunnar asked with a strange expression on his face. "That your son has a yearning to be close to the railway? And that the sound of a train quickens his blood?"

I shook my head, embarrassed. I couldn't figure what he was after. I waited for some kind of an explanation, but he just smiled his irritating Mona Lisa smile, and I did not feel like muddling my head with his riddles.

He sat at the kitchen table, erect and altogether faultlessly upright, slim and polished. He was well featured but slightly pale (as was Rupert). The almost feminine elegance of his slender limbs and graceful movements didn't really lessen his distinctive masculinity, which flowed from somewhere deeper in his personality. He wore perfect grayish tailor-made suits and even his ties probably cost as much as an ordinary off-the-peg suit. Now he had on a smart copper toned tie, given as a Father's Day gift on Rupert's behalf a couple of years ago. The man looked what he was—a Very Important Person in a big firm, with more money in his pockets, power, and contacts than any single person ever really needed.

"Perhaps we'll leave then," he said. He went to the hall and stopped for a moment. "I'll bring the boy back before evening. Around seventeen thirty, as usual.

"Well, Emma, enjoy the silence. Are you going to do anything special today? It's a good day to drive to town and go to a movie for instance."

"Movies I'll leave to little boys, that's who they are made for," I said. "You know I don't care about movies."

"Yes. I just tend to forget it," Gunnar admitted. He seemed a little annoyed at his absentmindedness. "I'm sorry."

Gunnar flashed me a somewhat feeble smile and left. (The time was 11:14, so they had well over six hours for their railway outing.)

I sensed in Gunnar a certain subsurface hardness and even ruthlessness that success in the financial world undoubtedly called for. I knew he could be rather cold when necessary, so I could appreciate that he had always, without exception, treated me politely and kindly. His kindness, however, had a reserved tone, as if he were attending to a very important long-term business affair with me, nothing more or less.

Which in a way he was, too: he paid me more than fair maintenance (making it possible for me to be a full-time mother) and once a month spent a day with the child I had born from his seed. We had nothing else in common. Between us there were no shared memories, chocolate boxes, kisses, lovers' quarrels, or soft words—just easy little compliments. *Well, Emma, you look quite pretty today in your beige slacks!* Now and then I found it difficult to believe that only eight years back we'd been intimate with each other. But Rupert, of course, was a rather concrete evidence of it. Thus believe I must—we both must.

That evidence, or his own part in the boy's existence, the man had never even tried to question. I knew he liked to appear a perfect gentleman, a kind of modern blueblood (and with one's noblesse oblige), but still his correctness bordering upon the noble was a bit amazing, considering the unconventional circumstances of the child's conception.

From between the orange kitchen curtains I watched how Gunnar called the boy down from the tree, caught him in his arms from a trustful leap and took him away in his thunder-colored BMW.

My stomach was hurting nastily, though my menses were still days off. I didn't like to let Rupert out of my sight. From the very moment I had felt the first faint kicks inside me, I'd also started to fear losing my child in some totally unpredictable manner (as irrational as the feeling may have been), and that early fear never fully let go.

Once a month I was unavoidably left alone. The house became quiet, and I became uneasy. I lived with Rupert every day. I chose, bought, and washed his clothes; I ate with him; I listened to his troubles. I woke him up in the morning and tucked him in at evening. I had subscribed to *Donald Duck* comics for him. I applied sticking plasters to his cuts. I measured and weighed him regularly and kept a diary of his development. I took snapshots of him for the family album. A couple of days before, I'd baked him his seventh birthday cake, which we two had (for once not caring about the consequences) eaten all of the same day, and I had held his head above the toilet when he had finally started to puke. Nevertheless I felt like a terrific outsider when I thought about the outings Rupert and Gunnar had together. They seemed to mean so much for the boy, sometimes more than all the rest of his life.

And why was that?

One could easily have imagined that a successful businessman like Gunnar would have taken the boy from one amusement park to another and ladled ice cream into the boy's bottomless gullet. He could buy a bicycle and deluxe pear lemonades and special order hamburgers and generally used all the tricks made possible by money to treat the boy like a divine child emperor. He easily could have afforded even to fly the boy to Disneyland once a month to shake hands with Donald Duck. With the power of money he could have made the child's whole home environment seem like a furnished cardboard box. He could well have filled the pockets of his son with an absurdly big allowance, and bought him the moon from the sky and had two spare ones made.

But nothing like that from Gunnar; the larger-than-life moments of Rupert's life were created in a quite different way. Once a month the man simply arrived with a packet of sandwiches and a bottle of juice or perhaps a couple of gingerbreads in his pocket, and took the boy to look at rails. Railways, tracks, those tracks that trains use to go from one place to another. Not the elephants and giraffes and monkeys in the zoo, not the newest hit movie, not the dancing clowns, not the wonderful new toys in the department stores. To look at the rust-colored railway tracks, that's where he took the boy. They searched on the map and in nature for railway sections new to them, and walked the hours of their day together along the tracks doing nothing special. They just walked and enjoyed each other's company and stopped for a while to eat their sandwiches and then went on. When the boy came home, I saw him simply tremble with restrained happiness and excitement and satisfaction as if he had seen at least all the wonders of the universe and met Santa Claus and the Tooth Fairy and a thousand speaking gingerbread reindeers as well.

I had sometimes tried to ask Rupert about it. He made my temples throb when he started to speak like a preacher about the Wonderful Smell of Railways and how it actually contained all the world's secrets.

I knew well enough when I was not in my own territory, not even close. Besides, it was after all a question of something shared between the two, father and son, which wasn't really my business. So, in spite of my vague forebodings, I thought best to let it be.

Until Rupert came home from such a track excursion hysterically sobbing and shaking, white as a washbasin, as if he had met eye to eye with the Children's Own Grinning Reaper himself and had to shake his bony hand.

I knew at once that everything was not all right when I lifted my eyes from the flowerbed I'd been scraping, and saw them returning already at 3:25.

I had my hands full coping with the situation. To start, I chased Gunnar off, bleeding with scratches as he was. I acted purely from my spinal cord, as mothers always do in such situations; acted with the rage of a dinosaur in a white summer dress. Gunnar tried to explain: he could not understand what had come over the boy, he'd just been carrying him piggyback and stepped on the bank as he'd heard the approaching train. Suddenly the boy had gone completely crazy on his back and started to tear Gunnar's hair and face and to scream unintelligibly like some rabid, drooling monkey.

If Rupert had come home thoroughly scared, Gunnar was just as terrified. He behaved like a dog that vaguely understands he's being judged for complicity in some Very Bad Thing and knows for certain that he'll get a bullet in his brain.

I almost felt sorry for him.

The dinosaur in me felt no pity: it attacked. I yelled at him till my lungs hurt. I probably hit him, too—at least his nose suddenly started to bleed.

He shook his head, perplexed, stepping back and forth in the backyard, dabbing his nose with a handkerchief, and nervously straightening his suit—covered in gray dust—having for once lost his relaxed erectness of carriage (for which I, for a brief moment, felt maliciously pleased). Then he glanced quickly at me, turned his eyes somewhere up, at Rupert's window I suppose, and started to speak: "If I have caused trouble, I'm sincerely sorry. If you want, I'll leave. But I have to say that with the boy I've always felt that for once I'm involved with something larger than my own life. You know what: he will yet do something significant, something wonderful, something neither of us now can even dream about. I have an instinct for those things. And if he—"

I told him to be quiet and leave my backyard (although not quite in those words), and he obeyed. As Gunnar, defeated, got in his car and drove away, the dinosaur was gratified—it had won.

I had no idea that I'd never again see the only man in this life I'd ever allowed to push his male protrusion inside me. About half an hour later he would be crushed to death together with his car. His wiry bird-boned being would be transformed to a mixed metal-and-bone paste (I know, because I later went to see the photo the police had taken of the accident scene).

But that shock was still to come. Now I had to compose myself so I could go and calm down Rupert who, piteously wailing, had run upstairs and locked himself in his room.

I went up the stairs and knocked on Rupert's door. "Let me in!" I ordered, my cheek at the door. "What's got into you?"

"The trains," came a trembling whisper from the other side of the door. "The trains!"

"What about them?" I tried to keep my voice calm. I strained hard and realized suddenly that I'd been trying to see through the chipping, white-painted surface of the door. Just like that X-ray-eyed Superman Rupert admired. Well, this was how it went, this was how Rupert made even me behave irrationally! (I had always felt a deep antipathy toward that red-caped clown who wiped his un-holed arse with logic and credibility and, besides, provoked children to jump out of windows with bath towels around their necks.)

I wondered whether my poor child had a foolish maniacal grin on his face, and a sudden horror stabbed my ovaries. Had my worst fears now come true in this dreadful way? Would my son end up for the rest of his life in a mental institution for little boys, where he would be dressed in a teddy-bear patterned straightjacket?

I heard a choked request: "Mummy, please go and look out of the window."

I did. A cold bit of flesh pretending to be a heart was slapping in my breast, and I felt faint. I looked out of the round window in the upper hall, where sweaty houseflies kept buzzing in competition in the shady afternoon light.

"And then what? What should I see? Your father? He had to leave already. He may phone you later. Or you can phone him."

"Do you see a train there?" asked a wan voice. "It didn't follow me here, did it?"

Finally I convinced Rupert there was no train in the yard, not even the smallest inspection trolley, and he let me in his room. After a long stumble over his words, he started to tell what it had all been about.

In the crèche and the kindergarten and even in the school they had praised my son's "boundless and creative imagination," which they said was manifested in his play and his artistic creations. I did admit that imagination might be useful, too, provided it remained within certain proper limits. But what was there worth praising in something that made a human being babble to stones and trees and see nonexistent things?

Perceiving reality was hard enough for the child, even without idle and completely unnecessary fantasies. And imagination by no means made Rupert happy. On the contrary, he had always suffered greatly from it. A hairy monkey paw growing in the middle of his forehead would have brought him just as much joy. His social life was surely not cultivated by talking to birds rather than to other kids. And the drawings expressing "boundless and creative imagination" which he manufactured would have been enough to employ a legion of child psychiatrists:

"Oh what a nice picture! Is it a cow? And that must be a milking machine."

"No." (The child is very indignant about his mother's poor insight.) "It's a horse-moose who travels in a time machine to the Jurassic period where the dinosaurs will eat him up."

(Mother takes an aspirin with a glass of water.)

Rupert's drawings were technically quite sophisticated and even precocious, but he never let objective reality interfere with their content. Such can be very depressing to a sensible adult who only wants to make her child understand how the real world functions.

"The train tried to kill us," said Rupert.

He sat, feet crossed, upon the comic books spread on his bed, wiping sweat from his round forehead and staring absentmindedly at the beam of afternoon light in the room. It was catching the dust motes floating between model airplanes hanging from the ceiling. I crouched on the floor by the bed and tried to catch his eyes.

"The train tried to kill you," I repeated as expressionlessly as a machine to show that I was listening.

"We were walking on the track. I sat on Daddy's shoulders. It was warm and the sun warmed our skin and the air was shimmering and everything looked funny. Daddy even took his coat off and opened his waistcoat and rolled up his sleeves. The tie he never takes off, however hot it is. He says it's a matter of principle and every time a man dresses or undresses he makes a far-reaching decision on who he actually is and who he is not. We'd found a whole new section of tracks far beyond that long tunnel and the big rocky mountain. We had to drive a long way on the big road, and back along all kinds of funny side roads to get there. The rails there smelled completely different. Much stronger. Daddy said it might mean that we were closer to the secret of railways than ever before. I asked what the secret was, but he just smiled as always, kind of pleased.

"Then we started hearing a train noise. Such a queer rattle, like a hundred tin buckets were being banged with iron pipes, each in a rhythm that was a bit different. It's a kind of scary noise. Like thunder on the ground. It came from somewhere behind us.

"At first I wasn't scared, but then I started to feel that all was not as it should be. That smell started to feel too strong in my nose, and somehow wrong.

"And I glanced behind and saw the train. It came toward us. It was hard to see because it came from the direction of the sun, but I saw it anyway. First it was sneaking slowly but then, when it saw that I had noticed it, it started to come faster. It accelerated. And I saw that it wanted us. Daddy heard it coming, too, and we moved to the bank, but it was not enough. It would never have been enough, the train would have got us from there, too. But Daddy did not understand, it was like he was in a dream. Somehow, I had to get Daddy to run off before it was too late."

"How could it have gotten you on the bank?" I asked in an unnaturally calm voice.

Rupert stared at me with his big blue eyes that now were like two deep saucers of cold fear. "That train was one of the *outside-of-timetables* kind. It did not run on rails. It pretended to, but it went a little beside them. I saw. I tried to get Daddy to realize we had to run, but he seemed not to understand anything I told him. Not even when we had—just before—been talking about such trains."

The boy swallowed audibly and crept to the window. His paranoid gaze raked the view.

"Such trains," I repeated again. The back of my head was pricking. "Now listen Rupert, what kind of trains are we actually talking about here?"

"The ones that leave the timetable and run off rails," Rupert sighed.

He kept looking out. The rowan crown was swaying behind the window; it stirred the now oppressive backyard air that swarmed with insects flying dazedly to and fro.

The boy's fingers were fumbling with each other nervously, and the narrow chest beneath the yellow shirt was heaving violently. There was an asthmatic, wheezing tone in his respiration that I'd never noticed before.

I had to talk seriously with him, really talk. I assumed an understanding gentle motherly smile and opened my mouth.

"What has that man put into your head!" I shrieked.

The voice escaping from my mouth startled even me; I sprang up and hit my head badly on the window board. I groaned from pain.

Rupert turned to look at me in astonishment—at last I'd achieved his full attention.

"Trains do not jump off the rails," I articulated carefully so that the child was sure to hear and understand what I was saying. "They stay on the rails and go along them from one place to another. And besides—"

Rupert looked at me expectantly.

"Besides, trains are just big inanimate machines driven by humans," I declared.

The boy smiled at me. Not in a relieved way. He smiled in that special way reserved for those who clearly do not know what they are talking about.

"Trains do go along rails from one place to another," he admitted kindly. "And usually they also stay on the rails. Usually. That's the official truth. But there is another truth that is less known. A secret. Sometimes they leave their timetables and tracks and are in the wrong place at the wrong time, and then they make trouble for people. Then they are not as they normally are, and you'd better not trust them at all. They are supposed to stay on the rails and follow the timetables to be as they are meant to be, just machines that obey people. But sometimes they do leave the rails and break off beyond their timetables. And then they change. Their deep hidden nature comes out. They become different. Mean and clever. And very dangerous."

"Indeed." I found it difficult to speak. "So they leave the tracks?"

"Yes. They leave their tracks," Rupert enlightened me. His voice broke when he continued: "There, where the trains turn."

The sad news of the death of Rupert's father reached us a couple of days later, and I can't say that it made my efforts to normalize the situation any easier (I admit that "to normalize" is a somewhat peculiar choice of words in connection with Rupert). The identity of the victim of last Sunday's railroad crossing accident had started to become clear only the following day, when a swarm of little boys found the lost license plate; it had drifted downstream in the brook close to the accident site and got stuck in a dam the boys had built.

The term "obscure circumstances" was used a couple of times. Police and all kinds of inspectors came to talk to us, and afterwards I could not remember what they had asked or what I had answered to them.

When I went shopping on the north side of town, I heard the villagers talk almost nostalgically about a train accident that had taken place two decades earlier in the neighborhood. That had, after all, been of a completely different scale than this minor railroad crossing accident which didn't even merit a proper news story. In the past, a goods train had actually been derailed in the Houndbury railway section, with dramatically unpleasant consequences. Back then, in the fifties, there had been one of those good old steam locomotives pulling the train, the last of which had been retired sometime in the seventies.

Two people had died in the accident: an engine driver and a little local girl. There had been horrified headlines in almost all the newspapers, and it had even been announced on the radio. Publicity loves innocent victims (at least when they are not too many and not too far away). When the train derailed it had, by a terrible whim of chance, crushed the child playing on the bank: Alice the daughter of the district surgeon Dr. Holmsten.

Unless I completely misremembered, Alice Holmsten had been in the same class with me in primary school, and we had perhaps been friends. But of all memories, the childhood memories are always the most confused and subjective, so I couldn't be sure about it. Actually I didn't even manage to think about the matter, the present was too much for me.

After he had left us, Gunnar had been driving south along little side roads—he lived in Helsinki when he wasn't on a business trip to Bonn, London, Paris, Tokyo or some other distant place. (Rupert received picture postcards with a railway theme from everywhere.) Thirty kilometers away there was a level crossing, with scant traffic but not completely unused. The two o'clock slow extra train from Tampere to Eastern Finland had been the cause of Gunnar's death.

The engine driver said in the interrogation that when the train arrived at the railroad crossing everything had seemed to be in order, the track had been clear, then suddenly the purple car waiting behind the crossing had driven straight in front of the train—evidently the gate hadn't come properly down either. The train hurrying eastward had caught Gunnar's thunder-reflecting car, crumpling and tearing it in passing as if it hadn't been a real car at all but an origami folded of purple paper, then throwing its remains in the willow bushes growing by the track.

I decided not to think about the matter any more than I had to. Gunnar was dead, gone. By a coincidence he had driven under a train. He had been beside himself because of Rupert's fit, the gate had been up, and Gunnar hadn't noticed the approaching train. That was all. As usual, what had happened could not be undone, not by any means.

I knew some people think that the daily and sometimes merciless course of life is a kind of kids' puzzle where you have to connect the points in a correct order and find out whatever is hiding in the picture. Effect was always preceded by cause, of course, and the cause itself was always a consequence of something. To seek logic and meaning from every coincidence, however, was likely to push a person toward the deep pit of madness, with sharp stakes waiting at the bottom. I could not afford to cloud my mind with unnecessary speculations or shaky what-ifs. I needed all my strength to help my son, since now he had lost his father, he needed his mother more than ever.

Rupert, of course, took it as self-evident that his father had been killed by the same train that had tried to kill them both earlier, never mind logic or timetables. I don't know whether he actually said the thought aloud, but he didn't need to, it shone from his whole being. And he could not be blamed. His poor little mind was tortured by those strange stories that Gunnar in his great lack of judgment had fed him. The railways may well have meant a great and wonderful adventure and boundless fantasy to Rupert, and all that had surely been rather pleasant as long as it had stayed that way. But now the caramel-colored surface of the fantasy had fallen off, and the dark colors of chaos, nightmare, and bitter fear of death had come out—the real nature of fantasy!

With difficulty, I pieced together hazy bits of truth to form at least some vague picture of what the father and son had been doing together during the last few years. I got the impression that during their walks together Gunnar had at first talked to the boy of various relatively harmless things. Then Rupert had become excited and asked about railways and trains, and finally the man had probably become a little tired answering his endless questions and started to make up his own stories, which had provoked Rupert to evolve even stranger questions. In this way they had been inciting each other, and finally, perhaps to silence the boy for at least a moment, Gunnar had come to invent that dark, terrifying, perverted story:

Daddy, how far do those rails go?

All around the world back to this same place.

Do these rails go to China?

Yes, they do. And to Australia and France and even Africa. Sometimes bored lions start following the rails and stray even as far as here. Luckily that's rare.

If you lead electric current to the rails here, will somebody on the other side of the world get an electric shock?

Yes, he will, if he happens to touch the rails just then. But one shouldn't lead electric current to the rails, because electricity goes around the globe and comes back here and then you'll get an electric shock yourself.

How do people know where each train goes and what time they ought to get on?

From the timetables. Trains go according to certain exact timetables.

Always?

Well not quite always. Sometimes they cannot keep their timetables. Then they'll be at a wrong time in a wrong place, and that results in confused situations and sometimes even trouble for people. Believe me, I've met with that myself.

Must the trains going in that direction circle around the whole globe to get back home? They can't reverse the whole way back, can they?

Of course not: there are places where the trains turn. But those places really aren't any kids' playgrounds. This is actually a secret, but let me tell you something . . .

And thus it became clear what would thereafter be my primary task: to dig from the boy's head all the dangerous fantasies that had slipped in there, before they could take root too firmly and produce a terrible harvest.

We lived south of the little village of Houndbury. (Nowadays Houndbury wants to call itself officially a city, as touchingly megalomaniac and attention-seeking as that may sound.) Actually there were two Houndburies: the rapidly transforming North and the South that had kept its old homely face from the fifties, and at that time still been saved from the bite of Development's concrete teeth. In the beginning of the seventies, the North had quickly filled up with new cubic meters of tenement houses, poor industrial plants, and hungry supermarkets. We people on the south side still had lots of pensive detached houses, wildly flourishing gardens, and clean swimming beaches and forests. Along our meandering paths you could get from everywhere to everywhere without seeing a single human dwelling or paved road on the way. And yet we from South Houndbury could whiz quickly to the North to enjoy the services of the area, nor was the nearest city too far away when needed. Thus our children were very lucky.

I would have let both my breasts be ground to mink food if only Rupert, too, could have been one of those healthy, noisy, happy children one saw in our neighborhood. They raced each other, rode recklessly on their bikes and played football and ice hockey. They yelled, screamed, and fought each other. They broke windows, went swimming, blasted firecrackers, and stole raw apples to throw at house walls and roofs and people's heads from behind the hedges.

Of course I would have punished Rupert if I'd heard that he was involved in such tricks. But I'd have done it with a smile, knowing my son was a completely normal boy who only needed a proper mixture of motherly love and discipline to grow up to be a man.

But Rupert kicked no ball. He raced nobody, he ran alone. In his whole life he hadn't stolen a single apple or broken a single window. (I thought I could remember him breaking one green tumbler when he was four years old: that was the list of his misdeeds in its entirety.) He just kept drawing pictures and reading books and playing his own peculiar games alone.

He did not get along with other children, since he'd been talking so long to birds and trees he no longer knew how to talk to people. Other children quickly got irritated at his strange stories and didn't want to have anything to do with him. For that I could have wrung their necks like potted chickens, Rupert was, after all, my own little son, but at the same time I understood them in spite of myself.

"You've got to stop this tomfoolery," I told Rupert seriously. "Do you understand what I mean? People don't like silly fools. Besides, soon you'll not know yourself what's true and what's not, and to know that is not too easy in this world anyway. Moreover, there's a quite special place for the people who can't stop fooling in time, and believe me, you don't want to go there."

Rupert nodded, resigned. It had been a month since Gunnar's death, the slowest and darkest month of my life. There was a fine aroma of approaching autumn in the air: it made birds and several other living creatures feel an oppressive longing for faraway places and, at times, even mild panic. Cold rains started to wash off the colors and warmth of summer. Pleading bad weather, Rupert stayed within four walls, which wasn't at all like him since he'd always been a dedicated puddle jumper and rain runner. For four weeks he hadn't gone farther than our mailbox—and that only on Wednesdays at one o'clock when he ran quickly out to get his precious *Duck* comics *(Wednesday is the week's best day, for then you get your* Donald Duck, *the world's funniest comic!)* and then closeted himself in his own room with the devotion of a monk studying holy scripture.

As much as I'd have enjoyed his company in other circumstances, now he started to get badly on my nerves.

He was quieter than the gray color of the autumn sky. He sneaked around ghostlike, unnoticeable, and almost translucent, close to non-existent. Now and then I had to steal near him and touch him to make sure he still was flesh and blood.

Sometimes I was caught by an irrational certainty that he had tracelessly disappeared from the earth, and I ran around the house seeking him until I finally found him cowering in some dark corner.

He cracked his fingers on the borders of my visual field. He grated his teeth. He kept staring out of windows and rolling his eyes like the stereotypical bearers in his beloved Tarzan movies when they heard the oppressing maddening drumming of the "wicked natives" from the jungle.

I'd have liked to run away from home.

I was relieved when school finally started and the bus took him away for at least a few hours a day. Of course Rupert did not feel happy at school. He was bullied, not so badly as to make his life hell, but he wouldn't have brought home any popularity awards, if such things had been presented.

After Gunnar's death, Rupert was like a kind of small over-scared endangered animal that constantly expects something big and extremely terrible to attack him. His irrational fear was even infecting me—I began to startle at all kinds of the slightest rustles and flashes. I had bad dreams, too, although after waking up I could remember nothing more of them than a tormenting feeling of loss, and that in the dreams I heard myself talking to some strange unfathomable abstract being (it seemed to consist of rails) and asking it for something I suspected I'd later regret.

Sometimes by night a capricious wind brought to our ears the noise of a train passing by the district from the railway far away behind the forested hills. At the closest, the tracks were at least fifteen kilometers away, but now and then it sounded as if the trains did run quite close, even in the folds of our own familiar woods. I got shooting pains in my belly at the sounds for I knew how the phenomenon affected Rupert. When I secretly peeked into his room and checked that the boy was still safe, I saw him pull his quilt over his head and tremble.

It was obvious that the situation could not continue. I didn't want to take my child to a psychiatrist, at least not yet. I didn't want him to get a mark in his papers and be labeled a mental health problem. I was the best expert with my own child, and therefore had to grapple with the core of the problem—Rupert's monstrously grown imagination—before it would undo him.

First I made a list of things that were apt to make my son's condition worse. Then I took the necessary measures. Now and then I felt myself a proper monster of a mother, a perverse tyrant who pursues a noble goal by a reign of terror. But I made myself continue in spite of my doubts. My child was in trouble, and I had to save him no matter what sacrifices it demanded from both of us.

First, I took a deep breath, grabbed the phone, and canceled the subscription to *Donald Duck*. And the next morning, after Rupert had shuffled along to the school bus, I hunted down all his comics—*Donald Duck, Superman, Jokerfants, Space Journeys, King Kong, Phantoms, Shocks, Frankenstein and Werewolves, Pink Panther, Roadrunner, John Carter, Dracula, Marcos*—and burned them all in the sauna oven.

There were hundreds, and my work of destruction took hours. The neighborhood was covered in charred bits of comics.

I hesitated awhile with storybooks. What kind of a mother could do such a thing, destroy her child's property like some loutish Gestapo commander?

But extreme situations demand extreme means, so I hardened my heart in the cleansing blaze of book pyres.

Into the flames went *Grimm's Fairytales*; *The Lion, The Witch and the Wardrobe*; *The Best Animal Stories*; *My Brother Lionheart*; *Pippi Longstocking*, and other literary fiction that excited imagination. To be on the safe side I pushed all coloring books in the oven, too.

Then I sought out all his crayons and drawing pens and drawing paper and all his graphically gorgeous but badly twisted drawings and buried them underneath the currant bushes behind the house. I made a list of the TV programs Rupert could still safely watch. All movies were completely prohibited. I enrolled Rupert in the chess club, model airplane club, volleyball club, Boy Scouts, and ceramic crafts. After some reflection, I canceled the ceramic crafts. To conclude it all, I ordered him always, from then on, to keep his watch on time and to be aware of the date—or be left without his pocket money.

Rupert wasn't very happy about all this, but neither did he protest. When he noticed his comics and books were missing, he looked at me with silent astonishment, but said nothing. I fervently hoped he would understand this was all for his own good. He tried to ask about his drawing materials, but fell silent when he noticed my expression and understood that those were gone, just like all the other things I considered inappropriate. He didn't even try to watch his former favorite programs on TV, for he guessed it wouldn't be allowed. Sometimes I turned on the TV and he came and watched it, quietly, until the approved program was over and I shut off the apparatus.

"Rupert, it's time to go to bed. And Rupert, what time is it and what's the date?"

"It's now eight-twenty-three and it's Wednesday, October twelfth."

"Excellent. Well, good night and sweet dreams."

The new order was surprisingly easy to realize. Rupert went regularly to the chess club to learn logical thinking and, to my amazement, he suddenly started to first get B's and then clear A's from math examinations instead of the earlier C's and D's. On account of that, Miriam Catterton, the pretty golden-haired teacher of his class, came personally to see me and to discuss the boy's wonderful change. (To be sure, at the same time Rupert's art grade fell from A to D and his composition grade also fell off a bit, but I didn't consider it a bad trade at all—I'd always been afraid the verbally fluent and graphically gifted Rupert would decide to choose the dubious profession of an artist or a writer for his life's career.)

In the model airplane club Rupert constructed a model plane strictly according to the incorruptible laws of aerodynamics, and flew it immediately on its virgin flight into the thin upper branches of our backyard rowan tree, where it stayed until it was finally covered with snow. He even learned the ins and outs of volleyball with the village boys, and was no longer completely helpless at team games. After I'd looked at his wan expression for a couple of months, though, I pitied him and let him quit volleyball training.

As for the Boy Scouts, Rupert wouldn't agree to go even once. He said they dressed up too silly. Instead, he himself thought of joining the school photography club, which I thought was an excellent idea—after all, weren't cameras used to record objective reality with the most objective way possible. (As I then still thought, naively.)

His set his watch to the correct time by the second every evening by the radio time signal. Months went by pretty comfortably, seasons came and passed, and as time went on I started to think the worst was over.

Then one winter night, coming back from the bathroom, I peeked into his room and saw the boy had disappeared from his bed.

I forced myself to calm down, draw a breath, and think rationally. He surely hadn't vanished without a trace; here still were his socks and there his rucksack and old rocking horse, and from the ceiling hung his airplanes. After searching for him every place in the house at least twice I realized that he had to be outside.

I saw he had taken his skis from by the steps. Gone also was his fine new camera which he always kept on his bedside table by the glass of water.

I began to understand that this was, by no means, the first time he'd done something like this. I suddenly remembered how some mornings he'd looked unusually tired, and I recollected several other suspicious circumstances to which I hadn't paid attention before. (I'd wondered why his boots were often still wet in the morning, although I'd put them to dry on the radiator in the evening.)

I sat by the kitchen table and drank a couple of bathtubs of coffee. After four hours of waiting I was coming to the conclusion that I couldn't wait any longer, but had to phone the village constable or at least go out myself to seek my child, then I heard skis swishing outside.

I heard the door and Rupert lumbered in, bleak as Death itself.

He was covered all over with snow. His face was blue with cold, although the night was mild. The boy marched into the kitchen in his snowy boots without a word, and put his camera on the table in front of me.

To me, Rupert looked like a soldier returning from battle, small in size but to be taken extremely seriously. Tiny icicles hung from his eyelashes. His clothes had a clinging smell that I couldn't connect with anything—until the next time I was in the vicinity of the railway and sensed that peculiar smell, which somebody may have once told me came from the creosote used to treat the railway ties.

I wasn't able to utter anything for a while, so as not to start crying or screaming uncontrollably; I wasn't even able to move, because I felt a compelling desire to seize the child and thoroughly shake him for scaring me like that.

Finally I said, with surprising calm: "I'll make you a cup of cocoa. You'll drink it without a murmur and then go back to sleep. The camera stays here. We won't talk any more about this, but if you do something like this once more, I won't even ask you anything, I'll make a stew of you while you sleep and sell you to that drunkard Traphollow for mink food. And with the money I get I'll bribe the constable to close his eyes about your disappearance. And if anybody asks about you, I won't admit you ever existed. Do we understand each other?"

Rupert stared at the camera with nostrils wide open. He pointed at it and whispered: "But there's *evidence* in there!"

"Do we understand each other?" I insisted. My voice could have peeled an apple.

He struggled long with himself before he gave up and nodded.

After he had drunk his cocoa and gone, I checked the camera and noticed that since earlier in the evening it had been used to take four pictures. (I always tried to keep track of such things.)

I didn't want to encourage him to continue his game, which had gotten out-of-hand, so I pushed the camera far back on the upper shelves of the hall cupboard, behind empty jam pots, and only took it out the next summer when I went and buried it and its film a couple of meters deep, next to the other dangerous things.

Twenty years later, when Rupert was studying law in Helsinki, I happened to find a notebook, which had functioned as some kind of diary for him. It was lying on the bottom of the cupboard, with old school books and wrinkled exercise books. On its cover stood the text OBSERVATIONS OF A FERROEQUINOLOGIST.

Rupert's diary contained some rather disconnected notes written over only a couple of years. It also included a chaotic explanation about the trip he had made that night.

It's very improper to read other persons' diaries, and I did not succumb to such baseness; I just glanced at it a little here and there.

(Myself, I've never kept a diary, at least I don't remember having done that. Neither as a child nor when older. I think the past has nothing to give us, no more than an outdated mail-order catalogue. Besides, my memories in their subjectivity and contradictoriness are much too confused for me to bother recording them.

I do not know what evil I have done that my mind punishes me so, but almost every night I still have a silly dream in which I anyhow keep a diary. In this Dream Diary of mine one can find all my fuzzy past; there are—carefully recorded—all the thoughts I've thought, all contradictions, all the insignificant incidents which my consciousness has crumbled down as unnecessary. Its pages teem with hidden motives and causes and consequences and obscure speculations about them.

In the dream I know that I could, at any time, turn the pages back and look at my past without the softening and diluting influence of time. Only lately, when I'm remembering Rupert, I've started to feel the temptation to do so. But I don't rightly know. It's much easier when you don't dwell too much on what is past, but just accept the concrete present as it is.)

1.12.1976, Observations of a Ferroequinologist:

Last night I did it, I PHOTOGRAPHED A TRAIN THAT HAD GONE OFF THE RAILS.

I got up at twelve o'clock at night, hung the camera around my neck, and started to ski on the crusted snow to where I knew the trains did go to turn.

There's at least fifteen or twenty kilometers to it, or maybe even a hundred kilometers (it's very hard to know by night how long a distance is) and several times I almost turned back, but some things one just has got to do, as Mummy says, and then finally after skiing for two hours I found the place though I'd gone astray a few times and thought I'd never find home again and the wolves would eat me, or maybe a bear.

The place where the trains turn is SECRET, and it's not easy to find. There's a blind track leading there, but I still haven't found the place where it forks from the main track though I've searched for it many times. It's pretty close to the section where that train outside the timetable tried to kill me and Dad in summer, maybe four or five kilometers away. I don't know whether I was more afraid of the place or of Mum tumbling to that I'd gone out (as it happened this time anyway). I waited for surely at least three hours before the train arrived—

luckily I had provisions: three chocolate bars, a packet of chewing gum (two eaten beforehand), one gingerbread.

The rails come to that place in the middle of the forest from somewhere farther off, from behind a really thickety terrain. And on them the trains come and go. The blind track ends completely among trees so the trains can get off the rails and turn in the forest and then mount the tracks again and return to where they came from.

I lay behind the top of the ridge under juniper bushes and watched how one train crawled slowly and carefully out from the thicket. It came to the end of the blind track, stopped, and then started to get off the rails.

It was huge, although by night it's also hard to know for sure how big something is. I somehow felt how it changed, not so much outwardly so that it could be seen with one's eyes, but inwardly. It awoke and pricked up its ears and put about feelers to its environment as if it had guessed I lay there watching.

I wondered if there was anybody inside it. (I felt that even if there was somebody in there, it wasn't human, at least not a live human.)

Suddenly it became awfully cold and I started shaking and my teeth started rattling. I felt that the coldness came out of the train, as if it had been to the North Pole or the Moon or some other really cold place. I took four photos of it with timed exposure.

I lay there in the snow without moving and waited and shivered from cold and heard trees breaking and crashing when the train puffed its way along in the snow and made its slow turnaround in the forest and then finally climbed back on the rails.

It must have taken surely at least four or five hours. I almost peed in my pants and I thought I'd get a proper licking when morning came and Mum went to wake me up and I wouldn't be home yet. I tried to look at my watch but there was not enough light to see the hands.

Then the train slowly went off and disappeared behind the thicket and the air wasn't so cold anymore. When I was quite sure no more trains were coming, I descended into the valley bottom and went to see the rails up close.

Sometimes one can find all kinds of things there. Once I found a bit of paper in the snow that turned out to be a thirty-years-old third-class train ticket from Helsinki to Oulu. Now I found no tickets, but there was a dead cat. I rather think it was our neighbors', Toby, who had disappeared, but it wasn't possible to identify it for sure. It had gone all flat and stiff and I saw its intestines. It was just like it had been hit with a house-sized sledgehammer. Not all of it was there, it was as if something had bitten a piece off it.

I threw some snow over Toby the cat and built it a little gravestone out of snow.

Once I tried to follow the rails so I'd see where they actually join the big tracks.

I walked along the blind track some two hundred meters (the forest around the track is such a tangle nobody can get through it without a chainsaw), but then I had to turn back, because the railway smell got so strong I couldn't breathe anymore. Besides I was afraid a train would come from the other way. If a train had come toward me, I couldn't have got off anywhere from the rails. I almost fainted just like that one time at school when I had a fever over thirty-nine degrees, and by a side glance thought I saw all kinds of strange things in the shadows of the thicket, things I don't like to remember. I realized afterward that the railway smell may actually be poisonous when there's too much of it in the air.

I won't go there any more, at least not before I'm grown up and can buy a chainsaw and an oxygen apparatus and other necessary things and when I no longer need to be afraid of Mum.

When the trains stay on the rails, they are asleep, and people can control them just like a sleepwalker can be maneuvered.

I didn't see the train this time very clearly, since it was quite dark and one cannot see well in the dark, but I did recognize the type. It was one of those big red diesel engines, with a white cabin. I found its picture in the library's train book. It was a DV15 manufactured in the Valmet Lokomo machine shop. Or it could have been a DV12, which looks pretty much alike. I'm not quite sure. It had fifteen wagons after it—I counted them. They were not passenger carriages but empty open wagons that look like animal skeletons and usually carry tractors and other big machines.

The previous time I saw a short blue local passenger train, the kind that doesn't have a separate locomotive. One can see them now and then in daily traffic. They transport people, but at the turning-place the short blue train had blackened windows and I couldn't see whether there was anybody inside.

But when the first time I went to the place where the trains turn, I caught a glimpse of a really odd-looking train, and so far I haven't found its picture anywhere though I've spent hours in the library and leafed through all the train books I've discovered. It was quite bullet-shaped and really streamlined and looked actually more like a space rocket than a train. And it seemed to float a bit above the rails. That's the one I really would like to photograph some day so I could show it to a grown-up who knows a lot about trains and ask what it actually is.

When I started to return home and came to an open place with more light I looked at my watch. It was only twenty past two, and at first I was relieved but then I started to get doubtful. I felt that it had taken a lot more time. I thought that my watch had stopped for a while, but at home it was showing the correct time when I checked.

If only I could find my camera and could develop those photos! Even Mum would have to believe when she saw the pictures, though otherwise she doesn't believe anything, she's such a bonehead. (I hope Mum doesn't read this!) I feel she doesn't even believe in my existence without coming to check on me every little while.

Today at school we had cabbage casserole and chocolate mousse again, and of course one wasn't allowed to have chocolate mousse before eating a plateful of cabbage casserole. Ossian threw up on the table when he tried to eat his plate empty, though he hates cabbage more than anything, and the whole table was flowing green and others started to feel squeamish, too. I was smarter and flipped the cabbage casserole under my chair and fetched myself a big portion of chocolate mousse with a straight face.

1.20.1976, Observations of a Ferroequinologist:

I dreamed again that a train was chasing me on a road. I climbed to a roof but the train climbed after me along the wall. I woke up when I fell off the bed to the floor and hit my head. I got a big lump. I could hear a train in the forest, again too close. I dared not go to sleep again. In the morning I went to look for traces but didn't find any.

4.12.1976, Observations of a Ferroequinologist:

I dreamed that I sat on the nose of a steam locomotive. It was rushing ahead with enormous speed.

First the scenery was unfamiliar, but then we came to Houndbury. Two girls were standing on the track. They held each other's hands. The girls shouted something to me and laughed and at the last moment they stepped aside and their skirts flapped in the draft of the train. Both of them were quite good looking, but I liked the one with the golden hair more.

The other one seemed familiar at first, but then she wasn't anybody I knew but a perfect stranger. After a while we approached the level crossing. Behind the level crossing gate a purple car was waiting. Dad was sitting in the car and he looked sad. I waved and yelled at him not to be sad anymore because I was quite all right, but he didn't hear.

Then the locomotive shivered under me and began to feel somehow queer. Awakened. Besides it was no longer a steam engine but a diesel engine. It talked to Dad along the rails, whispering in a peculiar voice that started to make me sleepy though I was already asleep to begin with. It told Dad to put the gears on and to drive onto the rails. Somehow it made the gate rise before its time and bewitched Dad and he obeyed it.

And we crashed into Dad's car and I watched how the train smashed the car against the rails a bit like the lion tore up the little deer in Nature's Wonders that Mum still lets me watch on the TV. Sheet metal and steel and license plates and bloody bits of Dad were falling along the tracks. I saw a loose hand fly into a ditch.

Dad was smashed all to pieces with the car and suddenly I realized that the train was eating him and then I started to scream and punch the train with my fists.

When the train had eaten its fill, it fell to sleep again. That's when I fell off the engine and woke up in my bed. Outside a train was hooting shrilly.

Yesterday I went to the library and looked up in a dictionary what "ferroequinologist" means. A person interested in railways. Dad sometimes said that he and I are both ferroequinologists, but especially me, considering my origin. I had no idea what he meant by that, and he smiled and promised to explain sometime when I'm old enough to understand. But the train killed Dad, so I'll probably never find out. And Mum of course understands nothing of these matters.

6.14.1976, Observations of a Ferroequinologist:

In my dream the trains were in an especially foul mood, and I dreamed that they chased me all through the night. I ran home and hid in the woodshed, and somebody there whispered in my ear that trains have dragon souls and that's why they love tunnels and are so mean. It also said that my basic task is to save a maiden. I tried to see the one who spoke, but when I turned I was awake in my bed and staring at my own teddy bear.

Observations of a Ferroequinologist (as well as the smudged train ticket between the pages) ended down in the hole. Rupert had finally, after all, recovered from the morbid and dangerous condition that his swollen imagination had induced. However, I wanted to take no risks with the questions concerning his childhood. We had never spoken about his long-ago train fantasies. I felt like he didn't necessarily even remember them or most anything else about his childhood, at least nothing very detailed. During his student years he always traveled home by train, though there was no railway station in Houndbury and for the last forty kilometers one had to take an inconvenient bus or try to get a lift. Indeed he seemed to have forgotten his childhood, and all to the good. I had forgotten mine, too.

Studying law kept the boy's thoughts firmly in objective reality, ruled by reason and the logic dictated by cold facts. Rupert had no time for idle novels or movies, so his imagination stayed safely asleep.

But his life was by no means pure toil. He had, in the law school, a couple of fairly good friends with whom to go out and to play tennis. (Over the years Rupert had become quite an athlete, although in the bird-boned fashion of his father.) And from his curt postcards I even gathered that for some time he had been seeing a certain young woman who went to the same lectures.

Rupert went to study law immediately after his high school graduation, for which I take the credit myself. When he had made his last ferroequinologist exploration at the age of nine years, I realized something: even after all the hobbies I'd arranged for him he still had too much time to brood on the peculiar fantasies in his head. I could confiscate his things, and I could make sure that he no longer crept out of the house by night to make his ferroequinologist observations—I attached a bell on his door and another one on his window and hid his shoes at the night. But I couldn't control the thoughts going around in his head. Therefore I had to find a way to make Rupert voluntarily use his head for something sound and rational.

Gunnar had once left a thick book of statutes in my house. I'd put it temporarily on my bookshelf, in the middle of encyclopedias, and there it lay forgotten for years. Now I lugged the massive book into Rupert's slender arms. I told him it was his father's old book that he had meant for his son to have when he was old enough to read it (which might very well have been true). I said his father had told me to pay him five marks for each page he could learn by heart.

At first the boy seemed suspicious. A couple of days went by. Then he calculated the pages in the book and multiplied that by five. He went to look at the shiny ten-geared bikes in Houndbury Bicycle and Engine, and soon he was spending most of his leisure hours studying the book of statutes.

I was overjoyed to pay the money he collected from me after examinations. By and by he stopped having nightmares, and he recovered from his anxiety and his train obsessions. Surprisingly quickly he accumulated the money for a bike, but he hardly got time to ride that brand new geared wonder for his reading stint continued; even in sleep he was leafing through his statute book, mumbling his statutes and counting the money he'd earned and would still earn.

A born lawyer, I thought proudly.

By spring 1991 Rupert graduated with top grades, and for a graduation present I bought him a Rolex with my savings. (I'm not ashamed to admit I cried with happiness for two whole months and finally got a nasty inflammation of the eye.) He got a job in a small but respected law office in the capital and moved with his girlfriend Birgitta, who graduated soon after Rupert, and found herself a job in the same firm.

Birgitta Susanne Donner was a good and sensible girl. I'd met her a couple of times and could safely trust Rupert to her keeping. I saw she would become an exceedingly reliable and refreshing life partner to Rupert, and surely a caring mother to my grandchildren, when the young couple would have the time to think about reproduction. I had myself started to meet more regularly a certain charming person now that I no longer had to worry about Rupert. It wasn't especially serious; dating openly in a small village like Houndbury would have provoked too much talk and fuss. My friend was a teacher and thus under the magnifying glass of the villagers. Now and then, however, she stopped for a coffee in the evening, and sometimes it happened that we woke up in the morning nose to nose.

It would be nice to stop here, with the picture of a successful son and a happy mother. But happy endings in real life are usually just stages on the way to a more final and less cheerful end—the worms will get us eventually, one way or another. Late in the hot July of 1994 trains again got entangled in my son's life.

Rupert and Birgitta had been busy for a long while, and sometimes I couldn't reach them for days on end, even by a phone. I started to suffer from a delusion that my son had somehow disappeared from and I'd never see him again. Finally, however, they managed to take a few days off and come to visit me for a whole weekend.

Seeing those two enlivened my mind and at the same time made it strangely wistful.

On Sunday we decided to have a picnic. The day simply floated in heat and bright colors, and when you add to the picture the dragonflies buzzing absent-mindedly to and fro, it was one of those days that should actually be framed and hung on the living room wall for the coming winters. I packed the picnic basket with juice, salami sandwiches, and some chocolate cake with cherries I'd baked for Rupert's approaching twenty-ninth birthday. We drove in Rupert's new red car along backroads until we came to the foot of Sheep Hill. It rose as a gently sloping green field toward the dense blue sky. In accordance with its name, Sheep Hill was a sheep pasture: they were standing around in white clusters, and now and then they got excited and started baaing in competition.

We left the car in the shade of a big birch, followed a path that descended near a low stone fence down the steep bank of Sheep Hill—which at some distance changed to Sheep Rock—and finally arrived at our goal: the grassy meadow by the raised railway embankment where the limpid Ram Brook murmured with cool cheerfulness.

I spread a white tablecloth on the ground, set the table and told the young couple to start eating before the heat and flies would spoil it all. We ate, and suddenly Rupert stood up and, spitting breadcrumbs, proclaimed that Birgitta and he had become engaged two weeks before.

I almost choked on my sandwich.

I looked at my son who stared at me as if expecting a scolding. He was nervous since he wasn't sure about my attitude, but he was obviously very happy, and the sudden perception made me laugh aloud from sheer joy of living.

"Now what's so funny?" Birgitta asked, a little suspicious, but then broke into a broad grin. Such a beautiful girl, I sighed. I already knew what I was going to buy them for a wedding present: the most gorgeous hardwood grandfather clock in the universe!

With a relieved smile Rupert sat down and continued his meal.

I suddenly thought of the moment Rupert was conceived. I didn't remember much of it, just that Gunnar and I had intercourse with each other and prevention had somehow let us down. Anyway, there Rupert was in front of me: happy, handsome and a successful lawyer with a tie around his neck.

I often think of the moment Rupert was conceived. Gunnar took me for a drive on his new motorbike—at that time he still was a rather wild spirit, in his own trim controlled way. He even had a leather coat. That, however, was no ragged black motorcycle jacket but a fine brown Italian coat, surely terribly expensive. I'd seen him often at the Pavilion which, in those times, was still full of people almost every Saturday of the year. (Now, of course, it's been closed for a long time and people go to the city.) I went there now and then to dance and to look at people. He'd been besieging me for some time (at least I felt he'd done that, one couldn't be quite sure of him), and although he didn't really turn me on, I liked his quiet self-confidence and that everyone was looking at him, So, I was willing to go for a ride with him when he asked me.

We were driving along backroads by this very countryside and stopped finally to sip white wine in the middle of a small lyrical grove. Gunnar said he liked my nose very much, and then he seduced me.

I still didn't really want him, but I let him do it anyway. It was actually quite pleasant, the light way he made love to me. I held on to his tie and smiled all the time. The grass tickled my bottom. He promised to withdraw in good time before he'd come, and surely he would have done that since he was a perfect gentleman and I knew I could trust him completely.

Finally I felt his rhythm accelerate. His muscles tensed. I remember hearing the sound of a train, the rails ran somewhere quite close—I hadn't realized that before. Gunnar was struggling in my arms like a trapped animal, I'd folded my legs behind his back and he couldn't get off me in time. I was quite sure he would get extremely angry at me, but he just looked at me a little sadly, kissed me on the cheek and took me back to the dance pavilion where we danced one waltz together before he left, looking pensive.

I knew that a new life had started to develop inside me. Six weeks later the doctor confirmed it.

—From the unwritten Dream Diary of E.N.

I woke up from my thoughts.

Farther off the sheep had suddenly began baaing wildly. I saw them start to come tumbling down the slope as if they were suddenly in a big hurry to get somewhere.

"The train is coming," Rupert said.

Only then did I notice there were little decorative Donald Ducks on his picnic tie—he hadn't completely forgotten his childhood after all. A gust had arisen and was intently tugging at his tie and making his white lapels flap like the wings of a large white butterfly.

"What did you say?" I said.

"The train is coming," Rupert repeated still smiling and pointed somewhere toward the sheep. I put my sandwich down and turned to look.

The railway ran along the ridge of Sheep Hill; from the cool darkness of the spruce forest it dived down to the clearing and then disappeared in a long cold tunnel excavated through Sheep Rock. The tunnel's mouth stood above us, breathing darkness, on top of the high embankment heaped out of big stones. The growing metallic clang and the rumble of hundreds of metal wheels against the iron rails muffled the protest of the affronted sheep. A fast red electric engine emerged. After it an endless line of dark goods wagons rattled toward the clearing.

I instinctively glanced at my watch: the time was 1:27.

The rhythmic noise chased the sheep. It filled the whole scene and buried the cries of the sheep like an avalanche. Rupert took the hand of his fiancée, kissed her, and then said something I didn't hear. She laughed. A nervous butterfly fluttered over our party, and its brown dryness made me think of falling autumn leaves.

The train now drew a moving line the length of the whole clearing. Wagon by wagon it pushed itself above us into the tunnel and eclipsed the sun burning above Sheep Rock, offering instead a hypnotically quick dark-bright dazzle. Dust from the embankment began to fall on us. I glanced upwards with a mild resentment and thought that I definitely ought to cover our sandwiches before they started tasting too sandy.

Then something broke loose of the train's dark shape and started to spin down toward us.

I followed the track of the object in the blue skies, now gray with dust; it rotated and whirled and got bigger all the time. I stared at it spellbound. Suddenly I realized it was coming toward us and would probably fall right in the middle of our picnic.

I opened my mouth to yell a warning to Rupert and Birgitta, but instead inhaled dust and could get no sound out of my throat because of a fierce fit of coughing. To crown it all the dust blinded my eyes and I could do nothing but cough and fling my arms about and hope my companions would realize they ought to move back.

Among the clank and rumble I discerned a muffled crack, like the sound of a breaking egg.

I forced my tearing eyes open and saw faintly how Rupert waved his arm, as if greeting an old acquaintance he hadn't seen for years, and an object the shape of a marrowbone rebounded off his head into the brook. Rupert fell on his back in the grass. Birgitta's shrill whimper penetrated my ears through the train's monotonous chant.

"Do we have eggs in the basket?" I yelled idiotically and started to cough again.

The girl kept shaking her head and pointed with a trembling finger at Rupert who lay on the slope, limbs spread out, and seemingly asleep. When one looked closer at him, one could see his hair's recently neat part was now missing completely.

Birgitta started a furious legal campaign against the State Railways. State Railways admitted that the metal object which had broken Rupert's skull had indeed originated from the train rushing past us, to be exact from the locking system of the twenty-eighth goods wagon of the train. The Railway attorney expressed his surprise that a part had come loose at all, since that was, in principle, impossible. The train had been duly and carefully checked before departure according to all possible railway traffic regulations. It sounded as if he were insinuating that we should be under suspicion for some malicious act cleverly sabotaging their precious train. The part coming loose troubled the SR very much. But for Rupert's sake, the railway people seemed not to lose a single night's sleep—when the insincere platitudes were peeled away, the basic attitude of the SR seemed to be *Shit happens, so what? You should have kept far away from our railway!*

In the past I'd have wanted to go into a blind rage and tear the attorney's self-important head off his weak shoulders, but the dinosaur seemed to have disappeared from inside me and instead of empowering rage I only managed to feel enormous fatigue and defeat.

About indemnities no consensus could be reached: Birgitta demanded thirty million, and the Railways did not want to pay a penny over hospital expenses—just paying the hospital bill was already proof of the extraordinary benevolence of the SR and exceeded all legal obligations, said the Railway attorney and chided us for our greed. Birgitta swore to me, gasping for breath, that she would make the Railways pay dearly and would even destroy with different tactical lawsuits the whole Finnish railway system, if nothing less would make the SR take full responsibility for Rupert's skull fracture and its possible consequences.

I presumed that Birgitta would calm down in time and her storming holy rage would quieten, and after five months that was the case. She phoned me, embarrassed, and told me she had no more strength any longer to attack the windmills. I said that as far as I was concerned the mills could turn and the trains could move, what had happened could not be undone.

When Rupert woke up he did not recognize Birgitta. He just stared at the walls of his hospital room, ill at ease, twiddled his thumbs, and finally asked Birgitta, who was trembling by the bed, if ma'am happened to have any Chicago chewing gum with her, please.

"And that damned brand of chewing gum hasn't even been produced for years!" Birgitta sighed when we sat in the hospital cafeteria and wondered at the turn things had taken.

The doctors had said Rupert would never remember Birgitta, not really. The part of Rupert's brain where all the memories of Birgitta had been located had suffered irreparably serious damage.

"As far as I am concerned he is sort of dead," the unhappy fiancée stated, and since I could invent no reasonable counter-argument, I stuffed my mouth full of the bun I'd bought in the cafeteria.

Besides the Birgitta-memories, the destroyed bit of his brain had stored the whole of Rupert's legal learning, and some other rather important information. Rupert did remember me, though. Just after the chewing gum, Rupert had started to ask for his mother. And he remembered the Lola brand of chocolate (although that was also out of production, as we later found out to Rupert's regret) and Donald Duck and trains and the death of his father and all the nightmares of his childhood. Actually he remembered everything quite excellently—up to his ninth year.

For understandable reasons the engagement lapsed. Rupert returned to the home of his childhood. He had spent six months in the hospital. During his stay, the summery land had shriveled up in the leafless squeeze of winter.

It took time to get used to the creature who wandered in silence around my house from one room to another. He didn't speak much, just sometimes asked me to bring some sweets from the shop or inquired after his things long since discarded. It was Rupert, and it was not. It was some kind of an anachronistic person: the being had the exterior of the grown-up lawyer-Rupert and the frightened eyes and mind of the child-Rupert already once left behind. It kept watching the courtyard out of the windows nervously cracking its finger joints and sneaking around like a ghost. It brooded over thoughts hidden from me. It was scared of its own image in the mirrors since that had become unfamiliar and strange to it.

I'd have screamed if I'd had the energy for such behavior, but I was tired and apathetic and thought I'd never again have the strength for any dashing enterprises. The air I breathed was thin and stuffy.

"Rupert," I said finally. "It can't go on like this for much longer. Something has to happen. Something."

I didn't know myself what I was actually trying to say, and certainly I'd been speaking more to myself than to my son, but the anachronistic Rupert looked at me and nodded as if he had known exactly what I meant.

Months passed outside the house. Inside it time had, at first, stopped, and then gone definitely haywire after the anachronistic Rupert returned home.

I stayed at home with Rupert. I didn't even see Miriam except a few times in passing: in the supermarket, out in the village, on the road, at the watchmaker's. Sometimes I doubted whether we had ever known each other, so distant had we become. I didn't ask her to visit, and she was intelligent enough not to come without invitation. I simply lacked the energy to talk to people, to explain all the time—to myself and to others—Rupert's present appearance and situation and the type of his brain damage. I couldn't stand people's empathetic, watery looks; I did not want to see my son through strange pitying eyes that made me only feel miserable and sorry for someone who, a moment ago, had been a successful lawyer but now was something else completely.

I have never been a regular guest to the Houndbury parties or otherwise particularly sociable, and now I froze even my scant relations with the local people to a polite level of *Seasons' Greetings*. I did not want to look in people's eyes and realize that nowadays I was "the poor mother of that disabled lawyer," rather than Ms. Emma Nightingale. I did not want my son, "that disabled lawyer," to become one of the established Houndbury oddities. I had to find out something that would help both Rupert and me to cope with the new situation. I had to find some meaningful solution to it, and I wanted to do that alone, in my own peace.

In the first week of February, Miriam turned up for a surprise visit.

She had dyed her beautiful golden hair profoundly red. She had put on some weight, but a slight roundness became her and made her look more sensuous than ever. My sensuality, however, was waning. My black hair had acquired quite a lot of gray during the last weeks, and some strange unconscious idea had made me keep my hair short after Rupert's skull fracture. I'd even lost weight, and had started to notice the first real signs of old age in myself (and only now, bitterly, was I able to distinguish them from the earlier signs of maturity).

We hugged, and then we kissed, too, although no longer as lovers but as friends, and I thought I felt the light taste of farewell on her lips. We had a cup of coffee, ate some salt crackers and made some small talk.

Miriam was wondering about the burglary on the Tykebend road construction site; some amount of dynamite had gone missing, and teachers had been told to keep an eye on their pupils in case any of them turned out to have explosives in their desks or bags. I reminded her that it was by no means the first time something like that happened around Houndbury.

We were appalled by today's immoral little creepy-crawlies. The stolen explosives had either been sold on, or else there was a rather big cache somewhere close by—very soon a part of Houndbury would surely fly off in the four winds, we prophesied. (And I at least was secretly pleased with the idea.)

I asked whether Miriam was still writing her short stories, and she said she was soon going to send some to the publisher. She inquired politely if perhaps I'd like to take a look at her writings and give my opinion. I declined the honor, I didn't understand one whit about fiction since I read only factual material.

Suddenly Rupert came out of his room to greet his former teacher. As usual, he wore a white shirt, a waistcoat, a Donald Duck tie and a pair of gray trousers (although he didn't really feel comfortable in those, as would no nine-year-old boy). At first he sounded thoroughly sensible, even grown-up-like, and Miriam glanced at me with a glad surprised smile. *So what's supposed to be wrong with him?* her eyes asked. Then Rupert blew the impression to pieces when he started to ask Miriam about how far behind he was in his math lessons: how many pages had the rest of the class gone ahead while he'd been in the hospital? And could the teacher possibly give him some extra tutoring, for he'd been having difficulties with fractions.

Miriam snatched her handbag, spluttered some good-byes, and rushed out of the house with tears in her eyes, leaving the anachronistic Rupert staring after her in wonder.

The night noises of the trains made Rupert fall out of his bed, and quite often he had to be patched up with Band Aids—a grown-up man falls out of bed harder than a little boy. He stayed very much inside. That was al right with me, I didn't want him to be mocked and stoned by the neighborhood kids.

Always on Wednesdays, Rupert went out to the mailbox and came back looking disappointed. When I finally paid proper notice, I realized he was expecting his *Donald Duck* comics.

I didn't know whether I was acting wisely, but— after a break of twenty years—I subscribed to the comic again for him. (Although the day the comic came had been changed to Thursday, which gave Rupert diarrhea.)

I saw neither grounds nor reason any more to control what he was reading, doing, or watching. As far as Rupert's imagination was concerned, he now had to cope with it himself. I could not manage to launch a major offensive against fantasy a second time. My war was over, my inner dinosaur was buried under the avalanche of all that had happened and, in the pressure, changed to oil muddying my insides.

Sometimes Rupert leafed through books he found on the shelves: encyclopedias and biographies and a thick anthology of poetry that probably was a present from Miriam. A couple of times I saw in Rupert's hands that first law book he had learnt by heart; he fingered it uncertainly and then always put it away without opening it.

I don't know how much my son understood of the books he studied, or about what had happened to him. Sometimes he seemed like the intelligent and clever lawyer he had been only a few months before; then he was, again, a big confused child who wore Armani suits and five-hundred mark ties and could ponder for hours the story of "Square Eggs" he had read in the *Duck* comic. Those two sides seemed to compete for territory inside him, and mostly he was somewhere in between.

Now and then Rupert drew strange little pictures, which he tore up immediately and burned in the sauna oven. I got the impression that he was trying to draw Birgitta and other things he had lost with the accident, things that now only haunted him as vague dream images.

The old Timex had again found its place on his wrist, although I had to go and buy a new, longer strap for it from Houndbury Watch—since he could not really believe that the Rolex glittering in the chest drawer actually belonged to him.

Everything dissolved into a sleepy anticipation-filled dormancy which was held together only by the ticking of the clocks, the repetitive daily routines, and my belief that something would happen. Something that would give me the key to a solution, a way out from the deadlocked dream I couldn't possibly imagine continuing endlessly. (As unfounded as such a subjective notion of course was, objectively considered.)

March came, with harsh nightly cold. The ribs of the house cracked in the squeeze of coldness, and sometimes just before falling asleep I imagined that the walls were breaking to splinters around me and winter was rushing in and freezing me into a rigid naked statue in my bed. I dreamed of a terrible cold that rolled over me.

Now and then, I woke up and did not know who or where I was—I had to sneak around the house and go look at the sleeping Rupert and look over objects I found for evidence to be able to locate myself back in my own life.

On the last week of the month, during the night between Thursday and Friday at 01:12 in the morning, I woke up to muffled sounds of departure seeping to my ears through the floorboards.

Rupert had slipped out at night before, but each time I had noticed it only afterwards from his wet shoes and the trails left in the snow. Through the clogged ducts of my mind gushed a sudden excitement that quickened even my numb flesh—I yanked a thick housecoat over myself and dashed down the cold stairs.

I threw the front door open. Rupert stood in the courtyard with skis and poles in his hands and a rucksack on his back and stared at me. He may have been a little scared, thinking he would be scolded, but at the same time I could sense unusual determination in him: the fact he was leaving and I could do absolutely nothing about it.

That was all right by me.

I let the icy black night air fill my lungs and soak into my bloodstream. The sky spreading above us seemed to open directly to the cold halls of space. The stars were skimping on their scant light, but in the middle of them the Moon hunched big and bright, yet grieving for its imagined imperfection: only after a couple more nights would it be perfectly round and beautiful and could really wallow in its own light. The cold made the black-and-white night scene crackle and pop as if it were the bowl of rice crispies in thick cream and sugar that Rupert ate in the mornings.

I shivered in my housecoat and we stared at each other without words, Rupert and I. Then I broke the silence: "Don't worry, you aren't going to become mink food." (I remembered my threat from over twenty years back, and so probably did Rupert, because he looked relieved.)

"Besides, old Traphollow died of a heart attack last fall while he was hunting rabbits. We have a new constable, too, whom I wouldn't try to bribe for his silence. But why don't you wait a little before you start. I'll come with you this time, if you don't mind. Who knows: perhaps I'll be a ferroequinologist, too."

Rupert seemed to frown thoughtfully under his broad-brimmed Stetson, but then he nodded. The hem of his gray Burberry were sweeping the ground. He had wrapped a medium length red muffler round his neck and covered his ears with black earmuffs. He didn't at all look like a brain-damaged man who thought like a nine-year old. He looked like a gentleman who was going to take a breath of fresh air after an evening of theatre, then afterwards have a nightcap, read a few lines of Dostoyevsky, and withdraw to his bed.

I dressed as quickly as I could, found my ski boots, locked the house, and fetched my old skis from the woodshed where they had spent the last twenty years. Then we started skiing in the blocked lightlessness of the forest, the son ahead with coat flapping and the mother behind, stumbling in her slippery skis and with the unfamiliar poles.

The hard-packed snow led us forward with unreal lightness between the high pine pillars. Time passed. Now and then I peeked at my watch, ticking deeper and deeper into the night. Rupert was faster than I, he positively flew in front of me, but luckily he stopped at times to wait for his clumsier fellow skier.

I quickly lost my sense of direction. That was fine: I didn't actually want to think about where we were going—or why. On the surface, I stuck to the explanation that I was taking care of Rupert, at last thoroughly showing him his train fantasies were nothing but misguided imagination. I dared not be honest with myself, admit that I was acting purely by intuition. After all, intuition is nothing but a kind of psychological coin flipped in the air. And to manage important business by intuition is just about as sensible as choosing the right road by flipping a coin (as those irrational ducks did in one of Rupert's favorite stories). But that night I—for a moment—stepped outside reason, maybe just to see at least a glimpse of what was there. For this one and only time I felt an urgent intuitive need to follow my son on his irrational trip to the core of fantasy.

We partly circled and partly crossed over the massive cliffs of Sheep Rock, where one of the longest railway tunnels of the country ran deep in the bowels of the rock. Somehow we also managed to clear the big abandoned quarry, although we had to carry our skis, to climb over the icy boulders and to watch out for the clefts hidden in the stones' shadows.

Finally we arrived at a place I had never been before, even though I was a native to the region, and the reason was obvious: there were no paths to reach it. Although I supposed the nearest houses— the whole village, actually—were only about ten kilometers away, the terrain was extremely difficult. The area was well protected from berry pickers, hunters, and other accidental hikers: bog, a dense fir thicket, unfriendly rocks, fallen moldering trees, and a half-collapsed rusty barbed-wire fence that someone for some strange reason had once set up and then forgotten.

The upper branches of the ancient trees caught the quivering moonlight before it had time to touch the snow-covered ground, and we waded in deep darkness. Nature was really using all possible tricks to make us turn aside from our way. And I would have turned, many, many times, if Rupert's pale figure hadn't been skiing in front of me, so single-minded and determined; he knew the way even through the most inaccessible looking thickets. At times he seemed like a mythological spirit who'd been sent to lead me through the Underworld's hollow hills, and I had to remind myself that, in reality, he was only the brain-damaged former lawyer I knew he was.

We skied down a steep but short hill that brought us out from the forest to the railway. We pushed forward along the moonlit railway bank a couple of kilometers. Then we crossed the rails.

"We have to go through here," Rupert shouted to me over his shoulder and sped downhill with muffler flapping, into the forest that continued on the other side of the track, even more forbidding and intractable.

I looked at my watch: 03:21. We'd been skiing a couple of hours.

"The blind track is probably somewhere close by, but it's impossible to find," Rupert's voice continued, more subdued. "But once we go through here, we'll get straight to where the hidden blind track leads."

I followed the Burberry-clad and hatted figure into the dark catacombs of the trees.

The dry and extremely dense fir-thicket made progress very awkward. When I looked up I could see no sky at all, I only saw the grayish lattice of dead branches that blocked the moonlight somewhere above the standing trees. The mummified branches entangled themselves in my woolly coat. They wrenched my muffler loose. They scratched my face and reached at my eyes with their sharp thorns. Over and over again I tore myself away from their grip only to be rewarded with snow and ice and bits of twigs falling on my neck. Then, covering my face, I would again follow the unseen swishing skis and the sound of breaking twigs until the next obstacle stopped my travel.

I was afraid Rupert wouldn't bother to wait for me but would disappear and leave me wandering alone in that shamble of trees and snow. I couldn't anticipate the functioning of my son's mind at all. In a way he still was, to me, my own dear little son—whose logic had never seemed to me any more understandable than Chinese opera anyway—and at times I still saw him as my successful adult lawyer son who was temporarily resting at my house. But, I also knew that after the skull fracture a new side had emerged in him, a strange combination of the other two—the anachronistic Rupert, a secretive and often melancholic stranger whose doings and not-doings I was completely unable to predict or control.

We trudged in the rustling snarl of dead standing trees for at least two or three hours, and for about ten kilometers. At least it felt like ten kilometers, but I wouldn't be surprised if it had either been shorter, perhaps only two hundred meters, or even far longer.

Now and then Rupert flashed ahead of me, a shadow in the shadows. After I didn't see him for some time I'd think I'd lost him, but when, for the thousandth time, I pushed myself through the firs that had died in each other's arms, I would see him.

The trees were thinning out a bit and even let some light through; somewhere above, the moon's pale disk flashed. After a long and breathtaking climb, Rupert had stopped to wait for me in the middle of some juniper bushes. Leaning on his poles, he was staring ahead with a severe expression.

"It's there," he whispered, when I had hurried close to him. "We've arrived."

In front of us there was a valley-like depression, a sort of pool filled with darkness, from the bottom of which snowy trees stretched themselves up to the black edges of the sky. And only a stone's throw away from where we stood was a blind track. I couldn't see all of it, but here and there between the trees dim rails were gleaming. The track came from somewhere beyond the forest, from the heart of a similar (or perhaps even worse) tangle of darkness than we had just gone through; it ran on a low bank among the trees until it suddenly ended in the middle of a stand of fir trees, as if it had been cut off with enormous scissors.

I frowned. Rails were not supposed to end like that. Where rails ended there had to be a proper barrier so trains wouldn't accidentally drive too far and fall off the rails! The track seemed to be in quite a wrong place. Perhaps, on some office desk, a line had been drawn in a wrong place on the map, and when the mistake had finally been discovered the men of the railway construction gang had simply left the work unfinished and gone off, swearing and laughing and cracking jokes about the wisdom of engineers.

I drew the peculiar smell of railways into my nostrils. Here it felt markedly stronger than anywhere else. "And this place is . . . "

"The place where the trains turn," Rupert said quietly. He seemed embarrassed, or perhaps nervous. The cold sculpted crystal clouds out of his breath and the overlapping shadows of the trees hid his features from the moonlight and my eyes. He took his skis off, stuck the poles close by in the snow, and laid himself down on the ground.

I followed his example.

"One of them ought to be arriving from out there soon," he said. "Sometimes you have to wait for a long time, but it's no use worrying about the course of time here. Do you have a watch with you?"

I drew my sleeve up and tried to find some moonlight, but the darkness stubbornly covered the face of my watch and I couldn't see its hands, however closely I kept looking or turning my hand.

"Where's your own watch?" I asked then.

Rupert said his Timex used to stop during ferroequinologist observation trips; he hadn't bothered to keep it with him any more since that kind of stopping would surely harm the delicate watch machinery over time.

I lifted my own watch to my ear and tried to hear if it was ticking. I heard nothing, but maybe my ears were just frozen. Besides, there was an almost non-existent breath of wind among the trees, and it somehow made the dried-up forest continuously crackle and rustle around us, which hampered my efforts to listen.

Rupert surprised me by asking whether I wanted a half of his chocolate bar. I was going to automatically refuse, but then I realized that I did want chocolate, very much, the first time since my childhood. Rupert took a chocolate bar from his rucksack and passed me one of the bits. Then he wrapped his Burberry closer around himself and settled into a comfortable position like an experienced watcher. And we watched the rails drawn into the wildwood and the rustling trees standing around us, and the white snow packed to keep company with darkness and shadows in the narrow spaces between the trees, and we ate chocolate and we waited.

By and by the waiting started to feel hauntingly familiar to me. My tired brain probably played some kind of electrochemical trick, I thought sleepily. Then I yawned long and slowly started to regret taking this whole purposeless nighttime skiing trip. What had I thought, foolish woman, to leave my warm bed on a night like this . . . ?

We wanted to look Death in the eye and laugh at its face. That's why we met that Friday around 5:00 p.m.—immediately after we'd come from school and eaten dinner and washed the dishes—and walked to the railway. When we got to the rails, it started to patter raindrops the size of cranberries. Our dresses got wet and stuck to our skin, and we got cold but we didn't leave; Death had to be humiliated today, Alice said, so we could really feel alive.

We both had some bones to pick with the cosmic saboteur called Death. It had wasted the life off Alice's mother with tuberculosis when Alice had been only four years old, and it had stolen a good dog from me—a year earlier my high-spirited collie, Robbie, had run under a train when he was chasing a rabbit. (I'd also lost Uncle Gabe quite recently, but I didn't care that much about him. He had been a boisterous drunkard of a man, never did anything really sensible, just boozed and ran around with his pants down and yelled awful obscenities at kids.) We wanted to defy Death, and what could have represented him better to us than the train that thundered mystically non-stop through Houndbury?

First, it had killed my Robbie, rolled over him like some moving meat grinder on the rails. And only a couple of months before Elmer of Pig Pond had walked into a train somewhere around here, because—during the war—he had lost his ability to see life's beautiful side. (That's what Daddy said anyway.) Elmer was not the only Houndbury person who had come to do the same trick—"bitten the train" as people used to say— over the years. Since the beginning of the year, at least six locals had "bitten the train," and we were not farther than May yet. Considering this, it was understandable that the train nowadays reminded most locals of death. We had no station, and the train didn't stop at Houndbury except when somebody jumped in front of it with the purpose of self-destruction, so one couldn't really think of the train as a vehicle.

We breathed in the peculiar smell wafting about by the rails and waited. (Alice said the smell came from rust and the chemicals the railway ties were treated with and some third unknown substance.) While we waited we sucked the sugar lumps Alice had pinched from home.

The train came every Friday at 5:15. Today it was late, I checked the time on my fine Russian watch Daddy had given me as a birthday present. (He'd found it laying on the ground during the war.) We heard the train only at 5:23.

"It's coming," Alice whispered. We kissed each other on the cheek according to our ritual and took each other's hands. Alice had a warm hand and enviably slender fingers. She had the talent to become a pianist, according to our teacher, and Alice was taking piano lessons once a week from Amalie Forrester.

The train puffed into sight from behind the bend. If you stand on the rails when the train comes, *Alice had once said*, you'll be smashed like a fly under a hammer. You have no chance at all to survive. But at the moment you step aside from its path, the train becomes harmless and Death loses his grip on you. You can stand half a meter or even just a few centimeters from the moving train, and the Grim Reaper can't do anything but grin at you. Then you can laugh at his pale disappointed face!

At first the train looked like a smoking huffing toy, a cleverly constructed miniature model of a goods train. Then it took its place in the perspective and grew in my eyes to its real dimensions. I looked at the black-nosed apparition that was rolling toward us, metallically rumbling. I looked at the rails on which it was traveling and between which we were standing, teetering on a tie.

The train meant millions of kilograms of unstoppable weight. If we were to stay on the track, it would tear us to pieces without even having to slow down. Though the engine driver would brake, the train would never stop in time, not before it had wiped the rails with our remains for the length of a couple of kilometers at least.

Usually the thought gave me a bubbling excitement in my stomach, but now I was just cold. I wasn't feeling well and I kept moving around nervously and aimlessly fiddling with my hair, which didn't look golden like Alice's but was boringly dark.

The train hooted. Alice laughed aloud, shrilly, but I didn't feel like laughing, not one hair of a shrew's whiskers' worth.

"Take us if you can!" Alice whispered passionately and laughed again. She was sometimes quite scary when she was like that. Maybe that was why I liked her so much; being with her never felt ordinary.

When the engine's dark presence was only fifty meters away, the train hooted again. Our play probably made the engine driver nervous, and sometimes we saw him shake his fist at us, but as Alice said: What could he have done to us? Jump off the train to punish us?

The green-black engine rushed toward us. Its long bumpers stretched eagerly forward like the hands of a hungry child. The headlight trembling on its hood looked like a cyclops' gleaming eye. Steam rasped and swished with terrible pressure in its iron lungs and pipes, and the furiously whipping pistons on its sides forced the steel wheels to revolve faster and faster and faster. The funnel splashed smoke clouds on the sky and they started to spread like black ink dropped into water. There was a plate on the round front of the engine with the number 3159. I read the numbers over and over and thought how easy it would be to go on reading them, endlessly, and to forget oneself on the rails and just let everything happen to you.

We left the rails pretending to be calm and unhurried, although my guts were tightening and my body felt cold and heavy.

We stayed on the railway bank, on our old place just by the rails, not too close but close enough to be able to smell *the disappointment of Death when the train was rumbling past. We stood there, erect and proud as princesses and waited for the train's draft to shake our clothes and the noise of its rhythm to deafen our ears, and for the smoke the engine was puffing to surround us for a moment and brush our faces like a cloak of our ancient enemy, cut from a weave of darkness.*

Then we'd know that Uncle Death had once again lost the game and we had won, and we'd feel ourselves quite especially alive.

The engine screamed. Its voice was hungry, it had something in it similar to the crying of the strange, ever-angry baby born to our neighbors when it woke up and started to demand food, mad with rage. I felt the smell of railways in my nose, stronger than ever. The train's rhythmic noise reached out an invisible arm and seized my heartbeats; for a moment our rhythms were one, and blood started coursing along my veins all too fast—something was different now from earlier times, I'd felt that all the day in my stomach; suddenly I realized that this time the powers we'd been defying had their own plan for us.

I wrenched my eyes off the approaching train and tore my hand off Alice's and fled in senseless panic.

After the dash of a few heartbeats I slowed down. Embarrassed, I looked behind me, and immediately lost the control of my body as totally as if I'd been shot. I forgot the existence of my feet and how to move them or anything else, and flew on my side into the boulders. If I happened to hurt myself I didn't remember how to feel any pain.

The last seconds had been full of sound, I now realized. The very same moment I had started to flee there had been a hard metallic slam. It was followed by a long scratching noise, huge as the sky, it sounded like the Father God Himself had thumped his foot down from the clouds and started to furrow a kilometer deep line into the ground.

My insides constricted and turned into a cold mess when I saw the engine throw gravel, dust, and stones in the air so that the whole sky was filled up with earth.

The engine numbered 3159 no longer ran on rails. It pawed the embankment and then, as if in a fit of anger, started into quite another direction than the rails tried to persuade it to go. It drew the whole chain of wagons after its, over thirty wagons yanked furiously off the rails. The train was now free and mad with exultation. The steam pistons pulled it violently forward like the forearms of a lunatic escaping from an isolation ward. It wanted to conquer the world. Nothing could stop it. The arrogant challenge whispered by a little girl had freed it, and on Death himself was riding on the engine, roaring with laughter in his flowing cloak.

I looked at the train gliding past me as a huge and endlessly long dream monster, darkening the light of the sky and filling all my consciousness.

Had I stood up and taken a couple of steps I could have touched its dark flank, carried along with it. Then I turned my head, now weighing as much as a horse's, and looked at the little golden-haired girl toward whom the train was speeding. Alice stood in front of the metal monster she had freed, slender and vulnerable and angelically beautiful. I gasped for breath: I'd never realized that she was so exceedingly beautiful! She still seemed to be full of laughter, her mouth a black hole and thin hands twirling like the wings of a windmill. Her voice wasn't audible, the train's thousand-voiced scream filled the whole world. The girl was visible only for a hundredth of an instant and then the gravel and smoke and the moving black metal mountain swallowed her up.

And the train still kept pushing forward, rebellious and insatiable and hungry. Off the rails its massive speed was unavoidably slowing down, however. Its wagons were colliding into each other, and a chaos ensued that an orderly mind could no way perceive.

The train seemed like a giant dying beast, a dragon fallen on its side and leaking dry. Thick black smoke was gushing out from inside the split engine case as it started to bury the wrecked giant and hide it from the eyes of the world. Some wagons had burst like cardboard boxes and the stuff inside them was spread all along the track.

The smoke crept on the ground toward me, and when it touched my bare feet I shuddered with loathing—I felt that in its shelter the many-faced emperor Death himself was hiding; he was stroking my living flesh with his bony hand. Sometimes you win, sometimes you lose, it whispered gently among the engine's hiss, let's bear no grudge, dear girl, let's meet again sometime!

And somewhere in the shelter of the smoke, Death was pressing against his thin breast the lifeless body of my Alice, my golden-haired slender-fingered little Alice . . .

whose residual warmth I still felt in my own hand;

whose desk would be empty on Monday morning;

who would then have a moment of silence to commemorate her, and the boy who had secretly been in love with her would burst into tears in the back row;

whose parents would turn gray and shrivel up and bent down in a few weeks and move away from the village without saying good-bye to anyone;

who would never again appear for piano lessons with Amalie Forrester, because her pianist's hands had been cut off and crushed under the train and would never play even the simplest melody…

I thought of the day when Robbie had chased the rabbit to the rails and run directly in front of the train. I'd never have believed an animal could look so sincerely astonished. I'd collected hairy pieces in a sack for several days from along the track. Even if dogs wouldn't get to heaven I wanted to give him at least a decent rest in a grave. I walked back and forth along the track from morning to evening and searched the ditches and grassy plots and brooks, but Robbie's left ear, right hind foot, and half of his tail stayed missing. I'd always felt that the train had eaten them.

I pressed my eyes shut and with all my soul's power sent an appeal to the One who had deemed it justifiable to let the train run over Alice, whoever or whatever it was—perhaps some kind of a Big and Terrible Death Deity of the Railways existed, whom we in our immense ignorance had defied: IF IT'S AT ALL POSSIBLE TO YOU, PLEASE MAKE THIS SOMEHOW UNHAPPENED! I'LL GIVE YOU ANYTHING!

Then I turned my back on the scene and walked home.

I felt confused. I never told anyone, not even my parents, that I'd been a witness to the death of my best friend and to a train accident that was in the newspapers and even on the radio. It felt too unreal for me to talk about it. I never let myself even think about that rainy afternoon. Finally it turned into that hazy dream image that sometimes flutters somewhere on the fringes of my consciousness like a black bird.

It was the memory of that day I felt nearby when Gunnar was inside me moving faster and faster and I held onto his tie and suddenly heard, quite close, the train's terrible hungry scream—the memory returned and took the breath from my lungs and the warmth from my blood and the feeling from my nerves. I repelled the shadow of Death, coldly stretching toward me, by clinging to the chance of a new life which in that magic moment was within my reach—I seized it, stole it, refused to surrender it back to Nothingness, which is just the other name of Death."

—From the unwritten Dream Diary of E.N.

"Now," Rupert whispered.

I stared into the vertical darkness of trees where the rails emerged.

I heard something, maybe a heavily melancholy metallic sigh that lingered, echoing in the snowy halls of the quiet forest. It was followed by a stretching metallic screech. Then I saw movement, or rather a premonition of movement.

At first it was just a shadow among shadows, the mischievous play of night wind and moonlight among the swaying spruce and snow. But gradually an apparition began to take shape on the clearing's edge. The rails held a tall black being which crept forward, hissing, gasping, and terrifyingly huge and heavy. Now and then, the moonlight touched it, but not for a moment did it give up the shadows it wore. It moved carefully, almost shyly, and nearly stopped, but then it puffed a large smoke cloud into the frozen air, gave a jolt, and started, creaking painfully, to flow off the rails in front of my eyes.

I realized vaguely that Rupert stood near me.

"What are you planning to do?" I asked him.

I was straining to understand what was happening before my eyes; I kept trying to figure out a plausible explanation to it and to fit it into some rational frame of reference, but the gnawing ache behind my brow didn't make rationalization any easier.

"You just stay there. And Mother: don't move, under any circumstances! Wait there, keep your head low and hold your ears."

"My ears?"

But he had already gone, rushing down the slope with coat flapping, toward the train descending off the rails. I stared after him along the surface of the snow, until he sank into the thick shadows.

Hold your ears.

A series of relays clicked in my head, and suddenly I remembered the dynamite theft Miriam had mentioned; I remembered all the recent cases of disappeared explosives. How much had actually been taken?

. . . *Or else there's a huge cache of explosives somewhere close by. Very soon a part of Houndbury will surely fly off in the four winds!*

"But you can't possibly blow up a train!" I whispered into the darkness, completely taken aback.

But of course he could do it. He was brain-damaged and more irrational than ever and could do anything, because he no longer acknowledged my authority. And all those unexplained thefts of explosives—I could see with the eyes of my mind how my son had committed burglaries by night and skied here with his loot and gradually charged the whole valley. I couldn't imagine how much he knew about explosives, surely not much, but probably still enough to achieve a considerable explosion. Trains had hurt him in so many ways, and now he planned to pay them back, measure for measure.

"Rupert, no . . ."

I rushed after my son through the juniper bushes. All the time expecting the dusk in front of me to flare up in a fire that would strip clothes and skin and flesh off me and fling my burned bones up the slope. Even I couldn't at this moment discover any rational explanation for why a train would run off rails by night in the middle of a remote forest, but that didn't make blowing up the train any more reasonable an idea, now did it?

"Rupert, leave the train alone!" I yelled. "We have to talk seriously. Let's go home and take some chocolate cake out of the freezer and make some cocoa and talk properly! What about it?"

It was darker at the bottom of the valley. I ran among the spruce, juniper, and pine toward the rails.

I slowed down when a peculiar lump on the ground caught my eyes. I stooped down to look at it. It was a little snowman. Or not a snowman, a gravestone—there was some engraving on it, too, but I couldn't make it out.

I kicked off the snow on its base, and something like a paw came into view.

I straightened up and realized that I had, indeed, no time to think about such matters. I had to warn the engine driver before Rupert could carry out his obsession and destroy what little was left of his life. The snow squeaked and thudded under my steps.

"Rupert, Rupert," I whispered. "Is this that 'creative imagination' of yours?"

A long hiss made me stop.

I listened for a while and then carefully stepped through the spruce twigs hanging in front of me.

About ten or fifteen meters away from me was the train, or rather the shape of a train covered in smoky darkness. It was surrounded by trees and darkness, a lot of darkness. The valley was a sea of darkness, where everything was made up of different degrees of darkness and the scant light afforded by the moon only managed to confuse the eye with its roguish play. If I could see properly, there was a big black steam engine driving the train that had arrived via the rails, a real museum piece. So black it looked like condensed night, like darkness cast in the shape of an engine. There was a dark line of goods wagons behind it. Those were still left on the rails, but the engine stood in the snow between the spruce trees. Its long black bumpers stretched toward me like the paws of a beast. I only saw completely clearly the plow-like metal contraption in front of it that was probably intended to remove obstacles off the rails; it had snow and twigs heaped on it now.

Perhaps they were founding a kind of steam engine museum out here, I reasoned weakly.

I wished my head wouldn't ache so furiously; even a slight migraine hampered logical thinking and easily made me do foolish things. (When

Rupert was six years old I had, for instance, taken all the laundry out of the washing machine and directly off to the rubbish heap. Rupert had given me an enormous headache by pretending for three days in a row that our house was a space ship landed on Uranus—when I'd tried to open the windows, he had hysterically caught my hands and screamed something about a noxious atmosphere waiting outside.)

"Hello!" I yelled and waved my hand. "Ahoy! You there in the engine! Have you seen my son? Stetson and a long coat. He's not quite himself just now, and I think you ought to—"

The engine spat thick smoke and howled. Its voice kept whirling around me and my ears rang as if my head had turned into the bell tower of an enormous cathedral. It was too dark to see inside the engine. The train itself seemed to stare at me with its lamp-eyes. It looked curious. If an inanimate machine can somehow look conscious, this one did.

I stared at the big green-black mass of the engine, my head bent back, and tried to ignore my subjective feelings which were getting more irrational all the time. I felt I was being stared back at. Of course it was an engine driver looking at me from the cover of darkness, not the train itself, but the illusion was strong. And in certain hours of the night the human mind is apt to be carried off by subjectivity; perhaps this lack of objectivity has something to do with the phenomenon called biorhythms.

"Hello! You ought to listen to me now, before anything unpleasant happens!"

I took a few steps closer to the train. I wanted to see whether anybody was left in the engine. Perhaps the engine driver had by now noticed that something was going on and had gone off to examine the situation. I looked around myself.

"Rupert! I'm here! Mother's by the train! Don't—don't do anything at all!"

I hoped my son—wherever he was hiding—would have the patience to keep his hands off the explosives as long as he knew I was close by.

Then I stopped, confused.

The train radiated incomprehensible coldness that penetrated all my clothes and burned my skin. I noticed the snow around the train was freezing to steely hardness, I heard the snow crackle as it hardened. The engine puffed and jerked a couple of meters forward, closer to me. The smoke spread everywhere into the darkness and added its own gauzy shade to it. The plough bit the snow. The engine's hood pushed into the moonlight, the twigs swayed aside and I saw underneath the train's turned-off lamp a plate with the number 3159.

~

The comprehension emerged from some deep source inside me. What was before me was not exactly—at least not primarily—a train. It looked like a train, and to *some extent* is surely was a train, but its fundamental essence was one of those marginal things humans are not supposed to know about.

I felt no need to scream in terror or otherwise turn hysterical. That would have been ridiculous. The existence of the apparition rather made me feel embarrassed, as if I had entered a room—without knocking—where someone I thought I knew well (in this case, objective reality) was doing something quite strange and private. That apparition of a train was on its own strange business; it was following purposes incomprehensible to me. In the world of reason and logic it was a complete stranger, an uninvited guest, an embarrassing secret. A ghost from another time. Yes: I knew that engine. I knew its number, and I recognized the malicious consciousness it radiated.

I'd seen it escape the rails and kill and then be destroyed itself. And now it was here before me anyhow. Why? Was I looking at the ghost of a train?

"It's the 'Little Jumbo,'" a voice sounded somewhere behind me. "They were manufactured in the machine shops of Tampella, Lokomo, and Frichs from the year 1927 to the year 1953. What's the year now?"

With stiff lips I uttered the year I thought correct, eyes frozen fast to the apparition standing before me. It was still staring at me with its lamp-eyes from between the shadowy spruce branches. Curious, hungry. The coldness of the engine flowed into my flesh, it was burning me like fire sculpted of ice, and it seemed to me that if I didn't leave its circle of influence soon, I was never going to move again.

That was precisely the train ghost's intention. It was trying to bewitch and freeze me, to make me wonder about its nature and surrender myself to be its prey. And it was close to succeeding. I knew I should have turned my back to it and left, but I just kept staring at the iron dragon breathing irrationality and at its identification numbers. The sense of touch escaped my flesh, I thought I could hear even my skin crackle while it was freezing.

3159, 3159, 3159 . . .

"That kind has been taken out of service ages ago," Rupert continued somewhere out of sight. "Over twenty years ago. Consequently it's here sometime *before* it was retired. Now and then some come here to turn that haven't even been made yet. That's why I couldn't find the picture of one of them in any books. That's why watches don't work here: this place is outside the timetables. They wake up on the rails and they break out of their own timetables and find a suitable blind track and come here, wherever or whenever they are."

"Whatever, Rupert," I mumbled, lips numb with cold. I didn't have the energy to try and understand his words. I only knew I was freezing to death. "Listen, are you really going to blow up that train?"

After a moment's silence Rupert answered: "This place is full of dynamite. It's by the rails, in the trees, under the snow. I've spent several nights making preparations. I have to do it. Even if you are going to be angry."

"Can't I stop you in any way? Reason with you? Make you realize how senseless this all is?"

"No."

"Well then you've got to do what you've got to do," I muttered, relieved—the responsibility was no longer mine. I couldn't take any more responsibility.

The train blew smoke in the air, and its steam pistons became tense and started to push the wheels where they were fixed; it was preparing to chase me again, to make its kill. To murder me.

I felt someone gripping my shoulders. Rupert started to walk me away, fast. My feet had lost their strength to the cold, but Rupert was strong. The valley reverberated with the train's hollow panting and the metallic screech of the steam machinery that was pushing it off.

We got as far as the junipers, and Rupert threw himself in the snow and dragged me down with him. My face thumped against the snow. I was too benumbed to soften my landing.

"Mother, I ignited all the fuses," my son whispered. "Hands to your ears!"

"We have to talk about this when we get home," I sighed. "Let's drink cocoa and really talk with each other for once."

I thought there was something that I ought to have noticed and understood. Something to do with causes and consequences. If only my head hadn't been aching so terribly.

With the growing pounding in my head I hardly even heard the explosions that suddenly started to tear apart the valley, the trees and the train that had left its timetable.

We stood there an hour, hand in hand, and waited, Alice and I. Then we sat on the rails and waited yet another hour. The train didn't come, the track stayed empty. I felt more and more miserable. My stomach was hurting and my head ached. "It's not coming," I said. "Let's leave now."

Alice angrily plucked at golden lock of her hair and pouted. "It's not showing up, indeed. We have to come back tomorrow."

We went home, Alice disappointed and I feeling ill but relieved.

In the night I woke up feeling that I could hardly breathe. Twinges of pain were stabbing my temples. My first thought was that Alice was dead. I fancied

I remembered how the train had come and swerved off the rails and crushed Alice in front of my horrified eyes. The image was so vivid I started crying in my bed. And yet I also remembered that the train had never come and we had returned home in peace.

In the morning I ran to see Alice; I had to make sure that she really was alive. She set about at once to get us going to the railway tracks, but I refused, even when she pressed me hard and called me a traitor and even a bad friend. She looked at me somehow strangely, and I knew something had changed between us.

We were still friends, of course, and went around together, but day by day our friendship got thinner and we met more and more infrequently—the magic was gone. It was pretty much my fault—I couldn't relate to Alice naturally anymore, for I remembered her dying that afternoon on the railway, even while I also remembered we'd come back home together. I remembered her funeral, I even remembered the place she was buried, and her gravestone and the golden letters on it, and yet she was sitting next to me in school."

—From the unwritten Dream Diary of E.N.

That is the night I think I lost my son; I remember the night and the explosions, but after that—nothing. I don't remember coming home. A few times I've tried to return by myself to look for that strange blind track in the forest, but every time I've been driven aside from the way and ended somewhere quite different.

I remember Rupert's birth. I remember him growing and his overactive imagination and the day he graduated from law school. I remember his love and the skull fracture that removed it from his mind. I remember our night trip to the place where the trains turn, and that's where I lost him in the worst way. All that I remember, but I also remember that I never had the child I wished for. My youth was spent in studying, and then I had to further my career. We often talked about children, my husband and I, but we put off the realization of the idea. When we finally woke up to try, it was already too late.

A few months ago I saw Gunnar on television. He'd put on a lot of weight. I was startled; somehow I'd imagined he was dead. He spoke dryly about the big export sales his company had made, and I wondered whether he ever thought about the girl he had seduced by the railway tracks three decades since. I had so often wondered what would have happened if, at the critical moment, I'd prevented him from withdrawing and taken his seed and made him the father of my child. The thought had entered my mind at the time, however irrational and irresponsible it was. If I'd really done that, would the other line of my memories now be objective reality, not only subjective? Would Rupert now be objective reality?

Remembering makes me feel ill, but I can't help thinking of Rupert. He feels so real, often more real than this real life of mine. I remember how my figure got rounder and I took a taxi to the hospital and gave birth to my son. I remember the pain and the tears and the joy when I received the little wrinkled human being in my arms. I remember the sour midwife and the hospital ward. And yet I know nothing like that happened to me—on the day Rupert was born I was on a business trip to Moscow, it's documented. I remember that quite well, too, the small hotel room and the chambermaid I surprised as she was rummaging in my bag.

Perhaps I'm crazy. How many sane persons have two sets of superimposed memories from forty years' time? Perhaps all those empty recollections that torment me are only the product of a brain that's gone completely round the bend? That would be the easiest and also the most believable explanation—without one small problem: I could have invented Rupert, yes. He could very well be just a delusion, flung by an ageing woman suffering from childlessness into her past to soothe her pain. But what about the place where the trains turn? *I* do not have enough imagination to invent anything like that. I'm a very rational person who keeps her feet closely and safely in the dust of the earth in all situations. Unlike some others, who used to let their imagination fly as irresponsibly as a kite on a stormy Sunday afternoon; such was my lost son Rupert. The place where the trains turn could only have been invented by Rupert, and he couldn't have done that if he himself were nothing more than my invention.

I hunt my memories and study them from all angles, the way a scientist may collect and study extremely important samples. I draw charts of the two different lines of my life, they are sometimes hard to distinguish. And there is a pile of evidence on my desk:

There is a phone number. There's a lawyer named Birgitta Donner in Helsinki, but she has never heard of Rupert Nightingale.

There is a Christmas card from Alice Holmsten, nowadays Frogge. She tells she's married and works as a music teacher in a school in Turku. I hadn't thought of her for years, but sometimes one receives cards from people already forgotten even when there's been no particular reason to remember them.

There is a collection of short stories by Miriam Catterton that I bought yesterday from Houndbury Books. I'm not acquainted with Miriam, although I have recollections of her. Most people know her since she's a teacher here, but I don't have children, and we've never even talked with each other. She seemed surprised when I phoned her this morning and introduced myself. I told her I'd read her book and been especially fascinated by one of the stories, the one that tells about a little boy called Robert who loves railways and whose imagination his overly rational mother Anna tries to repress.

This is now quite silly, I explained, *but I simply had to call and ask where you got the idea for Robert's story.*

Well, where do ideas come from, generally? Miriam said, somewhat embarrassed. *They just are in the air. I often have dreams and I use them. For a couple of nights I dreamed about a little boy who loved railways, and the story developed out of that, gradually.*

I've read the story through several times trying to decide which truth its existence proves.

There's also on my desk an article I clipped out from the newspaper forty years ago and kept unto this day between the encyclopedia pages. It tells about a whole goods train that vanished without a trace with its freight and engine driver somewhere in the Houndbury region. The authorities investigating the case were puzzled, but according to them it appeared probable that there was an extensive conspiracy of railway personnel behind the train theft—there was no other way such a crime could be explained. The press clipping also seems to want to tell me something, but I'm not able to figure out how that event could be connected with Rupert's disappearance, not yet.

I cannot let him pass away out of my reach into final oblivion. I cannot give him back to Nothingness. That is why I continue with my investigations. I have to finally understand, to find him on the eternal circle of cause and consequence. For the sake of my son I go on with this, for his sake I write these thoughts of mine on paper.

About the Authors

Seth Chambers was born with a Pentel Rolling Writer in hand and has been pathologically addicted to writing ever since. In his quest for life experience, he has worked as an army medic, mental health counselor, wilderness guide, and bike messenger. His work has appeared in *The Magazine of Fantasy & Science Fiction*, *Fantasy Scroll*, *Isotropic Fiction*, *Perihelion SF*, and *Spinetingler*. Seth now lives in Chicago where he teaches English to immigrants and leads an innovative group of wordsmiths known as The Edgy Writers Workshop. He has a spoiled cat named Zooey and a tolerant wife/first reader named Cat Pryde.

James S. A. Corey is the pen name used by collaborators Daniel Abraham and Ty Franck. Under that name they wrote *Leviathan Wakes*, the first a growing number of science fiction novels in a series called The Expanse. *Leviathan Wakes* was nominated for the 2012 Hugo Award for Best Novel and the 2012 Locus Award for Best Science Fiction Novel. The fifth book in the series, *Nemesis Games*, was published earlier this year, and Orbit Books have signed Corey for four more books in The Expanse series. "The Churn" is the third novella they've written set in The Expanse universe. The authors have also written a Star Wars novel, *Honor Among Thieves* (Random House, 2014). The Syfy Channel has finished filming the first season of a TV series, *The Expanse*, based on the series. It is slated to premiere sometime in 2015.

Pasi Ilmari Jääskeläinen is well known in his native Finland for his fantasy and science fiction narratives. He has twice won the Kuvastaja Fantasy Prize given by Finland's Tolkien Society and four times won the Atorox Award for Fantasy. He teaches the Finnish language and literature and is the father of three sons.

Nancy Kress began writing in 1976, but achieved greater notice after the publication of her Hugo- and Nebula-winning 1991 novella "Beggars in Spain," which was later expanded into a novel with the same title. Kress has also written numerous short stories and was a columnist for *Writer's Digest* for sixteen years. Her fiction has won four Nebulas, two Hugos, a Sturgeon, and a John W. Campbell Memorial Award. She teaches regularly at summer conferences such as Clarion West and Taos Toolbox During the Winter of 2008-09, Kress was the Picador Guest Professor for Literature at the University of Leipzig's Institute for American Studies in Leipzig, Germany. Her next book, *The Best of Nancy Kress*, will be published in September 2015.

John P. Murphy is an engineer and writer living in New England. He has a background in robotics and network security, and his fiction has appeared in venues including the *Drabblecast*, *Daily Science Fiction*, *Nature*, and *The Magazine of Fantasy & Science Fiction*. For links to his other work, see johnpmurphy.net.

This spring, two-time World Fantasy Award recipient **K. J. Parker** revealed one of SF/F's worst-kept secrets: "Parker" is the pseudonym of British humorous fantasy author Tom Holt. Holt began publishing as K. J. Parker in 1998 with *Colours in the Steel* and has since produced over a dozen novels under that name, along with acclaimed short fiction and novellas. Holt has published more than thirty fantasy novels under his own name, beginning with *Expecting Someone Taller* (1987). As Thomas Holt, he also authored five historical novels. How one fellow could possibly write so much great fiction is the new mystery.

Mary Rickert (also known as M. Rickert) has published numerous short stories and two collections: *Map of Dreams* and *Holiday*. Her first novel, *The Memory Garden*, was published in May 2014 to considerable critical acclaim. Rickert received World Fantasy Awards in 2007 for Best Short Story for "Journey into the Kingdom" and Best Collection for *Map of Dreams*. *Map of Dreams* also won the William L. Crawford Fantasy Award. Before earning her MFA from Vermont College of Fine Arts, Rickert worked as kindergarten teacher, coffee shop barista, balloon vendor at Disneyland, and in the personnel department of Sequoia National Park where she spent her time off hiking the wilderness. She now lives in Cedarburg, Wisconsin, a small city of candy shops and beautiful gardens, with her husband.

Born in Madison, Wisconsin, **Patrick Rothfuss** attended the University of Wisconsin-Stevens Point where he spent nine years jumping from major to major (chemical engineering, clinical psychology; then, as an "undecided," he studied whatever interested him) and otherwise reveling in life as an undergraduate. It was kindly suggested that he graduate and, having somehow earned enough credits to graduate with an English major, he grudgingly did so. After graduate school he returned to teach half-time at Stevens Point. All that time he had been working on an epic fantasy novel that (divided) became the Kingkiller Chronicle trilogy. In March 2007, *The Name of the Wind* was published to great acclaim and made the *New York Times* Bestseller List. The second volume, *Wise Man's Fear*, came out in March 2011 to even more acclaim, and made #1 on the *New York Times* Bestseller List. Still working on the third novel, he started a charity fundraiser, Worldbuilders, to raise money for Heifer International, an organization that uses donations to supply families in needy countries with livestock like chickens, rabbits, and sheep. Rothfuss lives in Stevens Point with partner Sarah and their two sons.

Genevieve Valentine's first novel, *Mechanique: A Tale of the Circus Tresaulti*, won the 2012 Crawford Award and was nominated for the Nebula. Her second novel is speakeasy fairy tale *The Girls at the Kingfisher Club*. Her third novel, political thriller *Persona*, is out now from Saga Press. She's currently the writer of DC's *Catwoman*. Her short fiction has appeared in *Clarkesworld*, *Strange Horizons*, *Journal of Mythic Arts*, *Lightspeed*, and others, and the anthologies *Federations*, *The Living Dead 2*, *After*, *Teeth*, and more; stories have been nominated for the World Fantasy Award and the Shirley Jackson Award, and have appeared in several Best of the Year anthologies. Her nonfiction and reviews have appeared in *NPR.org*, *The AV Club*, *Strange Horizons*, *io9.com*, *Lightspeed*, *Weird Tale*s, *Tor.com*, *LA Review of Books*, *Fantasy Magazine*, and *Interfictions*. She is a coauthor of pop-culture book *Geek Wisdom* (Quirk Books). Her appetite for bad movies is insatiable, a tragedy she tracks on her blog at genevievevalentine.com

Acknowledgements

As always, profound gratitude to the original editors and publishers. Special thanks to Will Hinton, Amanda Brown, and Jeffrey Saraceno of Hachette Book Group for heroic rights clearance of "The Churn"; Peter Joseph of Macmillan and Rachel Crawford at Fletcher & Company for the same on "Where the Trains Turn"; and Matt Bialer and Lindsay Ribar of Greenburger Associates for near-heroic measures on "The Lightning Tree."

"In Her Eyes" © 2014 Seth Chambers. First publication: *The Magazine of Fantasy & Science Fiction*, January/February 2014.

"The Churn: A Novella of the Expanse" by S. A. Corey © 2014 Daniel Abraham and Ty Franck. Reprinted by permission of Orbit, a division of Hachette Book Group, Inc., New York, NY. All rights reserved. First publication: *The Churn* (Orbit, a division of Hachette Book Group, Inc.)

"Where the Trains Turn" (as "Missä junat kääntyvät") © 1996 Pasi Ilmari Jääskeläinen. First U.S./English language publication: *Tor.com*, 19 November 2014 (translated by Liisa Rantalaiho).

"Yesterday's Kin" © 2014 Nancy Kress. First publication: *Yesterday's Kin* (Tachyon Publications).

"Claudius Rex" © 2014 John P. Murphy. First publication: *Alembical 3*, eds. Lawrence M. Schoen & Arthur Dorrance (Paper Golem LLC).

"The Things We Do for Love" © 2014 K. J. Parker. First publication: *Subterranean Press Magazine*, Summer 2014.

"The Mothers of Voorhisville" © 2014 Mary Rickert. First publication: *Tor.com*, 30 April 2014.

"The Lightning Tree" © 2014 Patrick Rothfuss. First publication: *Rogues*, eds. George R. R. Martin & Gardner Dozois (Bantam).

"Dream Houses" © 2014 Genevieve Valentine. First publication: *Dream Houses* (WSFA Press/Wyrm Publishing).

808.838762 Y39 2015 CEN
The year's best science fiction &
fantasy novellas 2015 /

CENTRAL LIBRARY
01/16